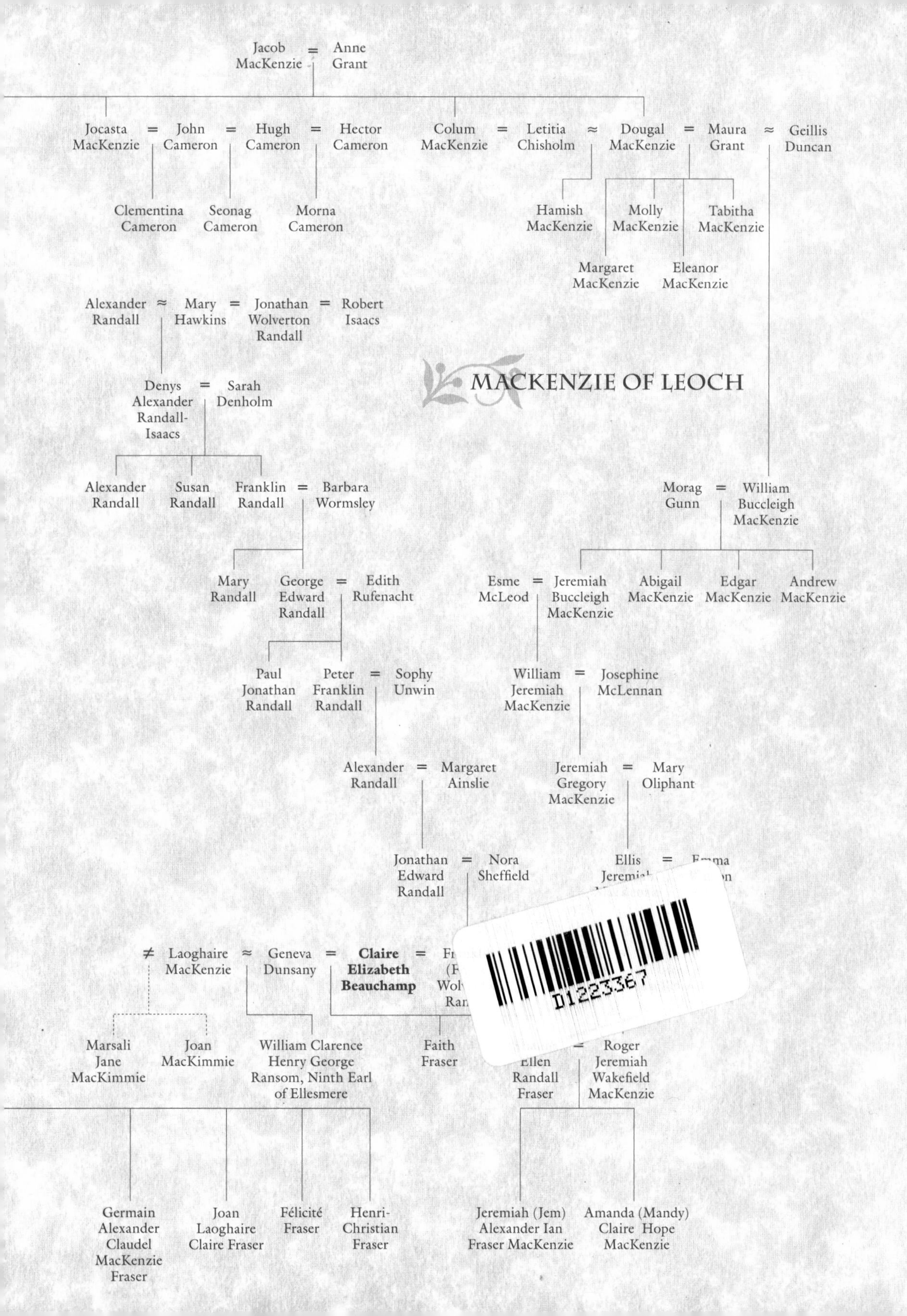
MACKENZIE OF LEOCH
Jacob MacKenzie = Anne Grant
Jocasta MacKenzie = John Cameron = Hugh Cameron = Hector Cameron
Colum MacKenzie = Letitia Chisholm ≈ Dougal MacKenzie = Maura Grant ≈ Geillis Duncan
Clementina Cameron
Seonag Cameron
Morna Cameron
Hamish MacKenzie
Molly MacKenzie
Tabitha MacKenzie
Margaret MacKenzie
Eleanor MacKenzie
Alexander Randall ≈ Mary Hawkins = Jonathan Wolverton Randall = Robert Isaacs
Denys Alexander Randall-Isaacs = Sarah Denholm
Alexander Randall
Susan Randall
Franklin Randall = Barbara Wormsley
Mary Randall
George Edward Randall = Edith Rufenacht
Paul Jonathan Randall
Peter Franklin Randall = Sophy Unwin
Alexander Randall = Margaret Ainslie
Jonathan Edward Randall = Nora Sheffield
Morag Gunn = William Buccleigh MacKenzie
Esme McLeod = Jeremiah Buccleigh MacKenzie
Abigail MacKenzie
Edgar MacKenzie
Andrew MacKenzie
William Jeremiah MacKenzie = Josephine McLennan
Jeremiah Gregory MacKenzie = Mary Oliphant
Ellis
≠ Laoghaire MacKenzie ≈ Geneva Dunsany = Claire Elizabeth Beauchamp
Marsali Jane MacKimmie
Joan MacKimmie
William Clarence Henry George Ransom, Ninth Earl of Ellesmere
Faith Fraser
Ellen Randall Fraser = Roger Jeremiah Wakefield MacKenzie
Germain Alexander Claudel MacKenzie Fraser
Joan Laoghaire Claire Fraser
Félicité Fraser
Henri-Christian Fraser
Jeremiah (Jem) Alexander Ian Fraser MacKenzie
Amanda (Mandy) Claire Hope MacKenzie

BY DIANA GABALDON

(in chronological order)

OUTLANDER

DRAGONFLY IN AMBER

VOYAGER

DRUMS OF AUTUMN

THE FIERY CROSS

A BREATH OF SNOW AND ASHES

AN ECHO IN THE BONE

WRITTEN IN MY OWN HEART'S BLOOD

THE OUTLANDISH COMPANION (nonfiction)

THE OUTLANDISH COMPANION, VOLUME TWO (nonfiction)

THE EXILE (GRAPHIC NOVEL)

(in chronological order)

LORD JOHN AND THE HELLFIRE CLUB (novella)

LORD JOHN AND THE PRIVATE MATTER

LORD JOHN AND THE SUCCUBUS (novella)

LORD JOHN AND THE BROTHERHOOD OF THE BLADE

LORD JOHN AND THE HAUNTED SOLDIER (novella)

THE CUSTOM OF THE ARMY (novella)

LORD JOHN AND THE HAND OF DEVILS (collected novellas)

THE SCOTTISH PRISONER

A PLAGUE OF ZOMBIES (novella)

Other Outlander-related novellas

A LEAF ON THE WIND OF ALL HALLOWS

THE SPACE BETWEEN

✦ THE ✦
OUTLANDISH COMPANION
Volume Two

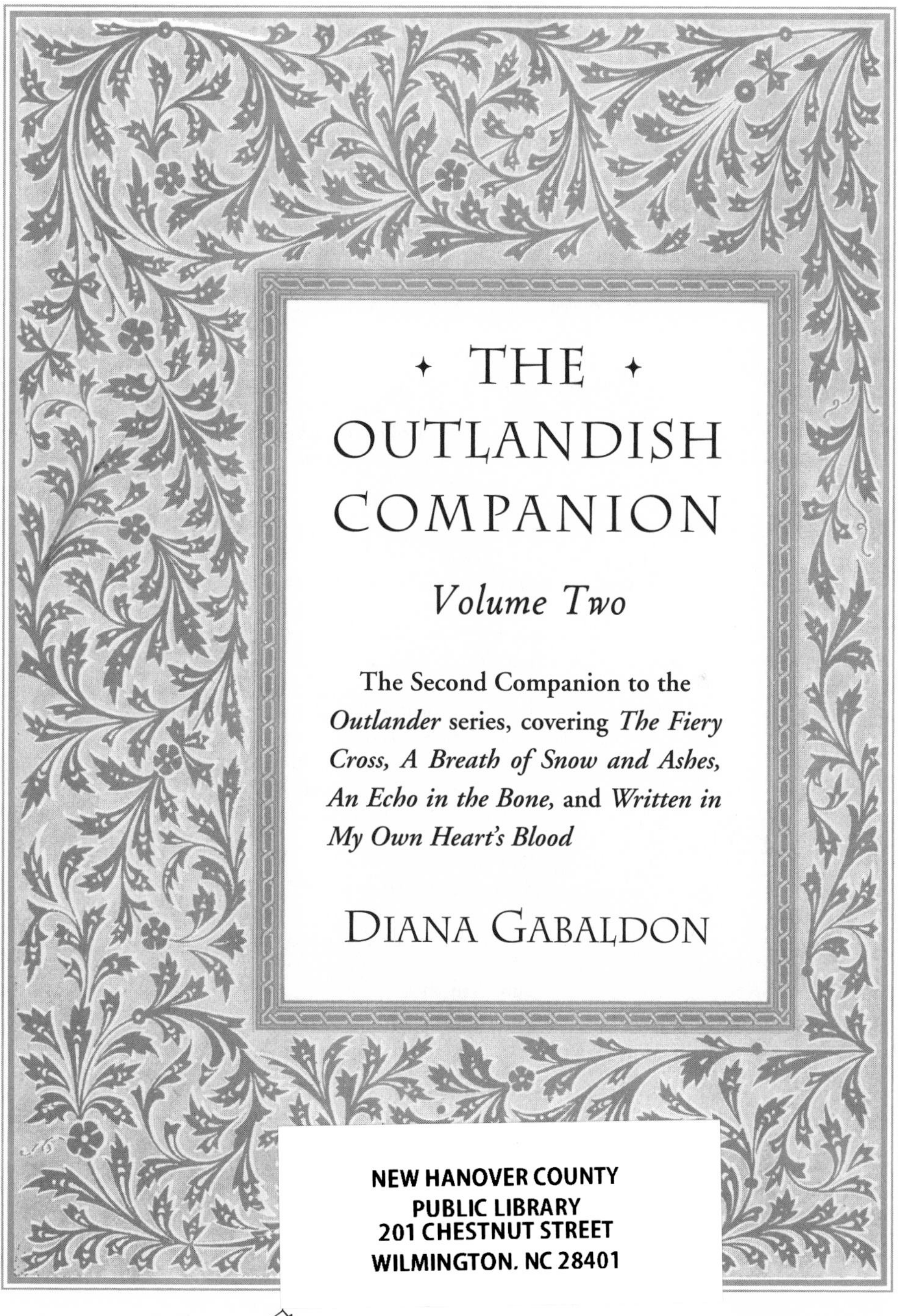

✦ THE ✦ OUTLANDISH COMPANION

Volume Two

The Second Companion to the *Outlander* series, covering *The Fiery Cross, A Breath of Snow and Ashes, An Echo in the Bone,* and *Written in My Own Heart's Blood*

DIANA GABALDON

DELACORTE PRESS / NEW YORK

The entries under the heading "An Outlandish Materia Medica" on pages 585–589 are offered to illustrate or provide background information relating to fictional references in the Outlander series to nine herbs. These entries are not offered to propose either a medical or nutritional regime or practice. Consult with a doctor before making any decisions that affect your health, particularly if you suffer from any medical condition or have any symptom that may require treatment.

Photographs by Barbara Schnell
Floor plans and diagrams by Virginia Norey
Maps on pages 606–607 by James Sinclair
Maps on pages 608–611 by Daniel R. Lynch
Endpaper design by Donna Sinisgalli

Published in the United States by Delacorte Press, an imprint of Random House, a division of Penguin Random House LLC, New York.

Delacorte Press and the House colophon are registered trademarks of Penguin Random House LLC.

Grateful acknowledgment is made to Orbit, an imprint of the Hachette Book Group USA Inc., for permission to reprint an excerpt from *The City Stained Red* by Sam Sykes, copyright © 2014 by Sam Sykes. All rights reserved. Reprinted by permission of Orbit, an imprint of the Hachette Book Group USA Inc.

ISBN 978-0-385-34444-9
eBook ISBN 978-0-440-24645-9

Printed in the United States of America on acid-free paper

randomhousebooks.com

2 4 6 8 9 7 5 3 1

First Edition

Book design by Virginia Norey

This book is dedicated to

Ronald D. Moore
Maril Davis
Terry Dresbach
Sam Heughan
Caitriona Balfe
Tobias Menzies
Ira Steven Behr
Anne Kenney
Matthew B. Roberts
Toni Graphia

And the rest of the cast and crew of the *Outlander*/Starz television production—my companions on the newest phase of this outlandish journey.

CONTENTS

✦ THE ✦
OUTLANDISH COMPANION

Volume Two

INTRODUCTION

. . . And what a long, strange trip it's been . . .

On March 6, 1988, I began writing what turned out to be *Outlander.* (I know this because my file names all include the date on which each was begun, and JAMIE.36 is the oldest file I have.)[1]

In the summer of 1998, *The Outlandish Companion* was published. The publisher was exceedingly dubious about there being any market—let alone a need—for such a book, despite my insistence that the readers really *did* care enough about the world of *Outlander* that they would enjoy reading information about its creation, trivia about its characters and settings, and miscellaneous related bits and pieces about history, Scotland, Celtic culture, and even the bibliographic references that had gone into the writing of the first four novels: *Outlander, Dragonfly in Amber, Voyager,* and *Drums of Autumn.*

In fact, I only succeeded in publishing that book because I refused to give them *The Fiery Cross* unless they let me have the *Companion,* too. But they did, tra-la, and all was sunshine and happiness—though I will say that if you think it's difficult to describe

---

[1] *No, that scene never ended up in the book. It wasn't even a complete scene (not surprising, as the only thing I knew about the book at that point was that it involved a Scotsman in a kilt), only a half page or so, in which Jamie (I did know his* first *name, at least) was having an argument with his sister (nameless at that point), who was chopping vegetables in a vehement manner. It was just my first experiment (bar Walt Disney comic books, which really don't work the same way) at putting fictional words on a page.*

It was nonetheless highly significant. At the conclusion of one paragraph, I'd just listed the ingredients of the dish Jamie's sister was making and—by academic reflex—began to put in the empty square brackets in which the bibliographic citation proving that those particular vegetables were indeed to be found in Scotland at that time in history and at that time of year would be placed. Then I stopped and, with a sense of joyous freedom, thought, I don't have to do that—it's FICTION!!! *Thus confirmed in my belief that I was indeed meant to be a novelist, I went happily on and never looked back.*

Outlander in twenty-five words or less,[2] just try explaining what a nonfiction book *about* a set of indescribable novels is.[3]

Still, people enjoyed it and that's all that really mattered. But . . . I kept on writing novels. And after *The Fiery Cross,* people began asking if I meant to provide them with an insert or something, giving them the same sort of background and information that was available on the first four novels. This kind of *ad hoc* demand increased with each new book, and several years ago I began thinking of writing *Volume Two* of this opus. I also realized that there were several bits of *Volume One* that could do with an update or revision—after all, the book has been out for seventeen years now, and Things (especially the Internet) have Changed.

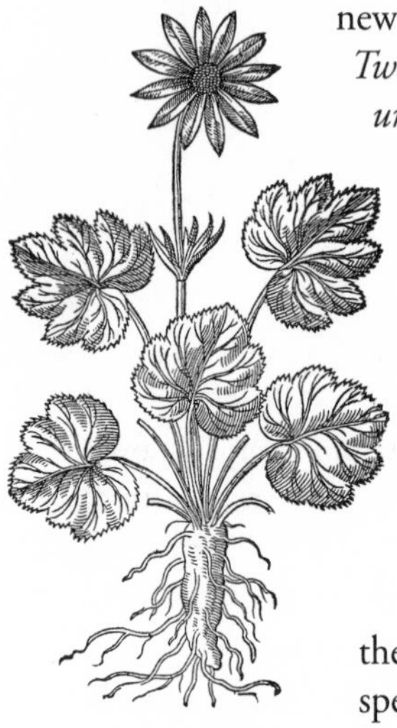

So I did both. I revised *The Outlandish Companion, Volume One,* removing obsolete sections, revising the FAQ, and adding in four new essays and a brand-new section about the Starz TV show (with photos kindly provided by Starz) and how *that* all came about.

And I put together *The Outlandish Companion, Volume Two,* which is the book you now hold in your hands.[4] I say "put together" because, while I did write most of it, I also had the kind assistance of several other talented people in supplying special articles (Terry Dresbach, costume designer for the TV show; Theresa Carle-Sanders, author of the *Outlander Kitchen,* website, and *The Outlander Kitchen Cookbook;* Bear McCreary, composer for the show; and Dr. Claire MacKay, who worked as a consulting herbalist for the show) and in doing the horrid drudgery involved in putting together lists (Susan Pittman-Butler, my

---

[2] *Frankly, it's flat-out impossible. I mean, try it. You can't exactly say it's historical fiction, because of the time travel (though the historical aspects are in fact as accurate as history itself—rather a large caveat, that . . .). You can't say it's fantasy, because people leap instantly to the conclusion that it has elves and dragons (the Loch Ness monster being rather a poor substitute, if you ask me). You can't say it's science fiction (even though it is, strictly speaking), because people start thinking of time machines and* War of the Worlds *and TARDIS, none of which are at all appropriate. And you really can't call it a romance, because a huge segment of the reading populace is disposed to think that most romance novels are illiterate bodice-rippers (they aren't, of course, but that's a common prejudice, ignorant as it is)—and, in fact, the book really isn't a romance, as it breaks just about every genre constraint there is.*

This is what happens when you write a book that you don't expect anyone ever to read, let alone publish. When I started writing, I just used any element or literary device that appealed to me—and I have very eclectic tastes.

[3] *The interviews resulting from the book tour for the* Companion *were especially bizarre.*

[4] *Now, I'm quite sure that you know that already—but the thing is, when* The OC, Volume One, *came out, there was quite a rash of indignant mail from readers who (in spite of my painstaking cover legend, which described exactly what the book was) had just grabbed it, ignoring cover, title, and flap copy, and then been incensed when it turned out not to be the next novel. I'm grateful for such enthusiasm, of course, but I do want to save people confusion and frustration, whenever possible.*

invaluable assistant, who compiled the enormous "Cast of Characters" and entered all the information for the monstrous bibliography on LibraryThing; and Àdhamh Ó Broin—Gaelic tutor and consultant for the TV show—who compiled the instructive and entertaining *Gàidhlig* glossary), to say nothing of the help of our wonderful book designer, Virginia Norey, who chose most of the illustrations (I put in a few . . .); Barbara Schnell, who gave me her amazing photographs of Scotland and Germany; and the mapmakers (James Sinclair and Daniel Lynch).

The general outline of this book is much like *The Outlandish Companion, Volume One,* with detailed synopses, a cast of characters, bibliography, and a lot of Highly

Opinionated Stuff by yours truly.[5] I didn't put in appendices, though, as no one seemed to take much notice of them in the earlier book, and I did (thanks to the marvels of social media) ask readers what sorts of things they'd especially like to see in this one. Hence the maps and floor plans and a few other interesting bits and pieces.

My husband remarked that the first *Companion* was "a great bathroom book—you can pick it up and open it anywhere," and I hope you'll find this second volume equally commodious.

Le meas agus,[6]

Diana Gabaldon

[5] *And footnotes, glorious footnotes . . . !*

[6] *That means "with deepest respect"—or "best wishes," as the case may be.*

Part One

Chronology

CHRONOLOGY OF THE *OUTLANDER* SERIES

The *Outlander* series includes three kinds of stories:

The Big, Enormous Books, which have no discernible genre (or all of them).

The Shorter, Less Indescribable Novels, which are more or less historical mysteries (though dealing also with battles, eels, and mildly deviant sexual practices).

And

The Bulges, these being short(er) pieces that fit somewhere inside the story lines of the novels, much in the nature of squirming prey swallowed by a large snake. These deal frequently—but not exclusively—with secondary characters, are prequels or sequels, and/or fill some lacuna left in the original story lines.

Now. Most of the shorter novels (so far) fit within a large lacuna left in the middle of *Voyager,* in the years between 1756 and 1761. Some of the Bulges also fall in this period; others don't.

So, for the reader's convenience, here is a detailed chronology, showing the sequence of the various elements in terms of the story line. *However, it should be noted that the shorter novels and novellas are all designed suchly that they may be read alone,* without reference either to one another or to the Big, Enormous Books—should you be in the mood for a light literary snack instead of the nine-course meal with wine pairings and dessert trolley.

Outlander (novel)—If you've never read any of the series, I'd suggest starting here. If you're unsure about it, open the book anywhere and read three pages; if you can put it down again, I'll give you a dollar. (1946/1743)

Dragonfly in Amber (novel)—It doesn't start where you think it's going to. And it doesn't end how you think it's going to, either. Just keep reading; it'll be fine. (1968/1744–46)

Voyager (novel)—This won an award from *EW* magazine for "Best Opening Line." (To save you having to find a copy just to read the opening, it was: *He was dead. However, his nose throbbed painfully, which he thought odd in the circumstances.*) If you're reading the series in order rather than piecemeal, you do want to read this book before tackling the novellas. (1968/1746–67)

Lord John and the Hand of Devils, "Lord John and the Hellfire Club" (novella)—Just to add an extra layer of confusion, *The Hand of Devils* is a collection that includes three novellas. The first one, "Lord John and the Hellfire Club," is set in London in 1756 and deals with a red-haired man who approaches Lord John Grey with an urgent plea for help, just before dying in front of him. [Originally published in the anthology *Past Poisons,* ed. Maxim Jakubowski, 1998.]

Lord John and the Private Matter (novel)—Set in London in 1757, this is a historical mystery steeped in blood and even less-savory substances, in which Lord John meets (in short order) a valet, a traitor, an apothecary with a sure cure for syphilis, a bumptious German, and an unscrupulous merchant prince.

Lord John and the Hand of Devils, "Lord John and the Succubus" (novella)—The second novella in the *Hand of Devils* collection finds Lord John in Germany in 1757, having unsettling dreams about Jamie Fraser, unsettling encounters with Saxon princesses, night hags, and a really disturbing encounter with a big blond Hanoverian graf. [Originally published in the anthology *Legends II,* ed. Robert Silverberg, 2003.]

Lord John and the Brotherhood of the Blade (novel)—The second full-length novel focused on Lord John (but it does include Jamie Fraser) is set in 1758, deals with a twenty-year-old family scandal, and sees Lord John engaged at close range with exploding cannon and even more dangerously explosive emotions.

Lord John and the Hand of Devils, "Lord John and the Haunted Soldier" (novella)—The third novella in this collection is set in 1758, in London and the Woolwich Arsenal. In which Lord John faces a court of inquiry into the explosion of a cannon and learns that there are more dangerous things in the world than gunpowder.

"The Custom of the Army" (novella)—Set in 1759. In which his lordship attends an electric-eel party in London and ends up at the Battle of Quebec. He's just the sort of person things like that happen to. [Originally published in *Warriors,* eds. George R. R. Martin and Gardner Dozois, 2010.]

The Scottish Prisoner (novel)—This one's set in 1760, in the Lake District, London, and Ireland. A sort of hybrid novel, it's divided evenly between Jamie Fraser and Lord John Grey, who are recounting their different perspectives in a tale of politics, corruption, murder, opium dreams, horses, and illegitimate sons.

"A Plague of Zombies" (novella)—Set in 1761 in Jamaica, when Lord John is sent in command of a battalion to put down a slave rebellion and discovers a hitherto unsuspected affinity for snakes, cockroaches, and zombies. [Originally published in *Down These Strange Streets,* eds. George R. R. Martin and Gardner Dozois, 2011.]

Drums of Autumn (novel)—This one begins in 1767, in the New World, where Jamie and Claire find a foothold in the mountains of North Carolina, and their daughter, Brianna, finds a whole lot of things she didn't expect, when a sinister newspaper clipping sends her in search of her parents. (1969–1970/1767–1770)

The Fiery Cross (novel)—The historical background to this one is the War of the Regulation in North Carolina (1767–1771), which was more or less a dress rehearsal for the oncoming Revolution. In which Jamie Fraser becomes a reluctant Rebel, his wife, Claire, becomes a conjure-woman, and their grandson, Jeremiah, gets drunk on cherry bounce. Something Much Worse happens to Brianna's husband, Roger, but I'm not telling you what. This won several awards for "Best Last Line," but I'm not telling you that, either. (1770–1772)

A Breath of Snow and Ashes (novel)—Winner of the 2006 Corine International Prize for Fiction and of a Quill Award (this book beat novels by both George R. R. Martin *and* Stephen King, which I thought Very Entertaining Indeed). All the books have an internal "shape" that I see while I'm writing them. This one looks like the Hokusai print titled "The Great Wave off Kanagawa." Think *tsunami*—two of them. (1773–1776/1980)

An Echo in the Bone (novel)—Set in America, London, Canada, and Scotland. The book's cover image reflects the internal shape of the novel: a caltrop. That's an ancient military weapon that looks like a child's jack with sharp points; the Romans used them to deter elephants, and the highway patrol still uses them to stop fleeing perps in cars. This book has four major story lines: Jamie and Claire; Roger and Brianna (and family); Lord John and William; and Young Ian, all intersecting in the nexus of the American Revolution—and all of them with sharp points. (1776–1778/1980)

Written in My Own Heart's Blood (novel)—The eighth of the Big, Enormous Books, it begins where *An Echo in the Bone* leaves off, in the summer of 1778 (and the autumn of 1980).

"A Leaf on the Wind of All Hallows" (novella)—Set (mostly) in 1941–43, this is the story of What Really Happened to Roger MacKenzie's parents. [Originally published in the anthology *Songs of Love and Death*, eds. George R. R. Martin and Gardner Dozois, 2010.]

"The Space Between" (novella)—Set in 1778, mostly in Paris, this novella deals with Michael Murray (Young Ian's elder brother), Joan MacKimmie (Marsali's younger sister), the Comte St. Germain (who is Not Dead After All), Mother Hildegarde, and a few other persons of interest. The space between *what*? It depends who you're talking to. [Originally published in 2013 in the anthology *The Mad Scientist's Guide to World Domination,* ed. John Joseph Adams.]

"Virgins" (novella)—Set in 1740 in France. In which Jamie Fraser (aged nineteen) and his friend Ian Murray (aged twenty) become young mercenaries. [Originally published in 2013 in the anthology *Dangerous Women,* eds. George R. R. Martin and Gardner Dozois.]

NOW, REMEMBER . . .

You can read the short novels and novellas by themselves, or in any order you like. I would recommend reading the Big, Enormous Books in order, though.

PART TWO

SYNOPSES

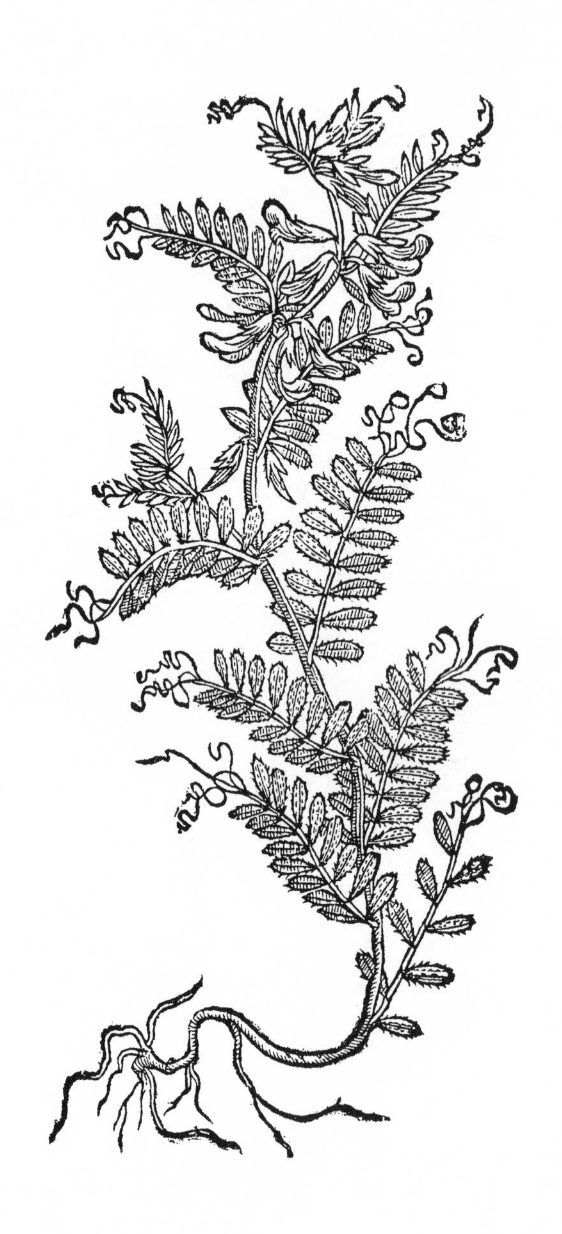

THE FIERY CROSS

I woke to the patter of rain on canvas,
with the feel of my first husband's kiss on my lips.

PART 1: *IN MEDIAS RES*

It's October of 1770, and the Frasers of Fraser's Ridge have come to a great Gathering on Mount Helicon (now known as Grandfather Mountain). In the morning, Claire wakes in a tent beside her husband, Jamie, from a dream of her first husband, Frank. It's her daughter Brianna's wedding day, and as Claire admits to herself, what could be more natural than that *both* her daughter's fathers should be there?

Brianna's wedding to Roger MacKenzie is not the only notable occurrence of the day. Claire has barely got her stockings on before a company of Highland soldiers, sent by the governor of the colony, William Tryon, is drawn up by the creek to issue a proclamation from the governor, demanding the surrender of persons known to have taken part in the Hillsborough riots—some of whom are in fact at the Gathering.

Thus begins a Very Long Day, during which all of the events and story lines that will be carried on through the book begin:

1. Brianna and Roger's relationship. They love each other madly and want nothing more than to be married and together forever. *But.* Brianna is hesitant about having more children; she doesn't know for sure who her son Jemmy's father is—it could be Roger, but she's terribly afraid that it might be Stephen Bonnet, the pirate who raped her. Roger has claimed Jemmy as his own—but he desperately wants another child, one he *knows* is his. Orphaned in infancy, he's been alone in the world for a long time.

Brianna's hesitation is twofold: She's a young woman; Jemmy would be self-sufficient in fifteen years; she *could* at that point try to return to the future, to the twentieth-century world that is hers by right. But not if she has more children, who would anchor her to the past. Also, childbirth is dangerous; one of the women at the Gathering has kindly given her some embroidery silk—with which to adorn her shroud, which by tradition she should begin making the day after the wedding. *"That way, I'll have it woven and embroidered by the time I die in childbirth. And if I'm a fast worker, I'll have time to make one for you, too—otherwise, your* next *wife will have to finish it!"*

But how can she deny Roger what she knows he wants so badly?

2. Jamie's relationship with Governor Tryon, which is delicate to begin with. The governor has given Jamie a large grant of land, on condition that he people it with settlers. One of Jamie's reasons for attending the Gathering is to recruit suitable immigrants from Scotland to come and homestead on his land—he's looking particularly for ex-Jacobite prisoners, especially men who were imprisoned with him at Ardsmuir after Culloden and who may have survived transportation.

The delicate bit is that Jamie is a Catholic and thus not allowed to own land grants under English law. Governor Tryon knows this but has chosen to look the other way, for the sake of getting the backcountry—always a volatile trouble spot, full of discontented hunters, trappers, and small farmers, all pushing against the Indian Treaty Line and none of them paying taxes regularly—settled and stabilized.

However, the unspoken fact of Jamie's Catholicism hangs over their dealings, and when Archie Hayes, commander of the company of Highland soldiers, presents Jamie with a letter from Tryon, appointing him colonel of militia and ordering him to collect *"so many Men as you Judge suitable to serve in a Regiment of Militia, and make Report to me as soon as possible of the Number of Volunteers that are willing to turn out in the Service of their King and Country, when called upon, and also what Number of effective Men belong to your Regiment who can be ordered out in case of an Emergency, and in case any further Violence should be attempted to be committed by the Insurgents,"* Jamie has no good way to refuse. As he tells Claire, *"I must. Tryon's got my ballocks in his hand, and I'm no inclined to see whether he'll squeeze."*

Tryon's concern with assembling a militia is the "Insurgents"—the Regulation, a growing movement of disaffected men in the mountainous western part of the state. What the Regulators want to regulate is government, which they see as abusive, non-representative, and generally a big nuisance. The governor, rather naturally, feels otherwise about the matter, but has no regular troops with which to impose his will.

3. Claire's expanding medical practice and the conflicts engendered thereby. After a successful morning removing nasal polyps, stitching up a mauled dog, and butting heads with one Murray MacLeod, a rival practitioner, Claire is somewhat taken aback when Jamie tells her that he's promised that she will remove Josiah Beardsley's tonsils.

Josiah is very young but a capable hunter. Jamie wants to recruit him to the new settlement at Fraser's Ridge, *because* of his youth. Men between sixteen and sixty are obliged to serve in the militia when summoned; Josiah is only fourteen and thus could remain behind to help provide the women and children of the Ridge with food and a stock of hides for later trading. Claire is a little dubious about performing a tonsillectomy *sans* anesthesia or operating facilities but agrees to try, once they're back home.

Her medical practice has other side benefits. She mends the arm and draws the tooth of a Mr. Goodwin, a solid citizen hurt in the Hillsborough riot, who later is of use to her in obtaining access to the priest, Father Kenneth. For Claire, her relationship with Jamie is drawing her further and further from her life in the modern world and her sense of identity; her ties to medicine and her destiny as a healer are what enable her to make that transition.

4. The brewing unrest in the backcountry. Several of the men who rioted in Hillsborough—tearing down houses, beating men who held public office, and driving the chief justice out of his courthouse and into hiding—are at the Gathering, and we hear their stories of dispossession for unpaid taxes (taxes must be paid in coin—despite the fact that there is virtually no cash money in the colony and most business is done by barter), oppression by the Crown (in the person of Governor Tryon), and death. This ferment will eventually erupt into what's known as the War of the Regulation, where "Regulators" from the mountain backcountry (taxes and representation being what they want to regulate) clash with the governor and the prosperous merchants and plantation owners of the coast.

The War of the Regulation is the beginning of the breakdown of law in the colony of North Carolina—and will provide fertile soil for the later Revolution.

5. Lizzie Wemyss and her father. Lizzie is the very young bond servant that Brianna brought from Scotland; Jamie has found her father—sold as an indentured servant—and purchased his indenture. He releases Joseph Wemyss from his bond but chooses not to make that fact publicly known, so that Mr. Wemyss will be not required to serve in the militia and can stay at home to help mind the property and people of the Ridge.

Lizzie has become a woman—i.e., had her menarche—at the Gathering and is thus now a prospect for love and marriage, as witnessed by her shy flirtation with one of the young soldiers.

6. Rosamund Lindsay and Ronnie Sinclair. Ronnie Sinclair is a cooper and one of the ex-Ardsmuir men whom Jamie invites to settle on the Ridge. Fiercely loyal to Jamie, he is constantly on the lookout for a wife and constantly at odds with Rosamund, a Bostonian lady of some two hundred pounds and decided opinions on most things, especially the proper way to cook barbecue.

7. Roger's relationship with Jamie. This has been strained, ever since Jamie and his nephew Young Ian gave Roger to the Mohawk as a slave (in *Drums of Autumn*), under the mistaken impression that *he* had raped Brianna. Roger was rescued and apologies given and accepted—but as a result of the unfortunate affair, Young Ian remained with the Mohawk, to be adopted by the Indians in replacement of a man Roger had killed. Jamie bitterly regrets the loss of his beloved nephew, and while he struggles to accept that it was not Roger's fault, the awareness lingers.

Beyond that—and the undeniable fact that Roger *did* take Brianna's virginity, albeit with her full consent (Jamie being somewhat more protective than the average eighteenth-century father, which is saying something)—Roger is keenly aware that he is a poor substitute for Young Ian, lacking most of the skills that are useful or valued in the eighteenth century. This is brought home to him forcefully when he learns that Jamie has engaged a man to be factor for the Ridge—the man who will take care of affairs there in Jamie's absence—and it isn't Roger. Normally, the "son of the house," whether true son, foster son, or son-in-law, would perform this office, and the fact that Roger has been passed over in this way seems a deliberate insult.

The only thing Roger has that seems useful in this present time is his ability to sing. A natural performer with a beautiful voice, he's called *A Smeòraich* ("Singing Thrush") by the Scots of the Ridge.

Jamie is not slow to exploit this ability of Roger's, but Roger can't help feeling that Jamie regards him as a hopeless numpty. Already sensitive about his lack of property and skill, Roger also finds himself in conflict with Jocasta Cameron, Jamie's aunt, who wants to make Brianna her heir. (Brianna's having none of it, as she refuses to own slaves—a good proportion of River Run plantation's wealth.)

8. Jocasta MacKenzie Cameron Cameron Cameron and Duncan Innes. Jamie's aunt Jocasta is the very rich, thrice-widowed owner of River Run Plantation. Blind and childless, she requires both a man to help with negotiations with the Royal Navy—who are the primary customers for River Run's valuable tar and timber—and an heir to whom the property can be bequeathed. A marriage has been arranged between Jocasta and Duncan Innes, a one-armed fisherman from Scotland, an ex-Jacobite comrade of Jamie's. It's principally a business arrangement, but there seems to be a true affection between Jocasta and Duncan, as well. This still leaves the question of inheritance, though.

Jocasta is the daughter and sister of MacKenzie chieftains and as proud—and as sly—as any of her clan. When Roger goes to call on her, to ask her help in providing for a family in dire poverty, she tells him she proposes to make Brianna's son, Jemmy, her heir, and then she goads Roger with remarks about fortune hunters, clearly implying that she thinks (or pretends to think) that Roger's chief motive in marrying Brianna is Jocasta's property and that Roger's only interest in Jem is the lad's prospects.

"Oh, I ken how it is," she assured him. "It's only to be understood that a man might not feel just so kindly toward a bairn his wife's borne to another. But if—"

He stepped forward then and gripped her hard by the shoulder, startling her. She jerked, blinking, and the candle flames flashed from the cairngorm brooch.

"Madam," he said, speaking very softly into her face. "I do not want your money. My wife does not want it. And my son *will not have it. Cram it up your hole, aye?"*

He let her go, turned, and strode out of the tent, brushing past Ulysses, who looked after him in puzzlement.

9. Ulysses. Jocasta's black butler, Ulysses is the true brains of River Run. Were he not black and a slave, he could manage everything—but since he is, Duncan Innes is needed to handle things like contracts with the Royal Navy and the external business of the plantation. Still, Ulysses is devoted to his mistress and has been her right hand for twenty years or more. He knows everything that happens at River Run—and controls almost everything.

10. Conflict between Claire and Jamie, Roger and Brianna, over Stephen Bonnet. Stephen Bonnet is the notorious pirate whose life Jamie saved (in *Drums of Autumn*) and who promptly repaid this debt by robbing the Frasers and later raping Brianna—thus causing doubt and friction between Bree and Roger, as they don't know for sure which man fathered little Jemmy.

Brianna reveals to Roger that she told Bonnet—facing imminent execution—that he was Jemmy's father, she thinking this likely at the time and wishing to give a doomed man some comfort in knowing that he left something of himself behind. Roger is angry—and alarmed—at the news. He feels that *he* is Jem's father and is disturbed to think that Bonnet, who escaped the noose, might at some point come to try to claim the child.

When Claire learns that Jamie is spreading the word through the Gathering that he wants to find Bonnet, she's both alarmed and annoyed, too. What is he doing, asking for the sort of trouble that's likely to result from finding Bonnet? He has more than enough trouble pending, what with the governor's appointment of him as a colonel of militia, the needs of the Ridge, and his quest for more settlers. And there's the question of Roger's feelings, too: it's one thing for Jamie to plan coldly to kill Bonnet; Roger is a man of peace, raised by a clergyman, and has never even thought of killing anyone. What will it do to *him* if Jamie either kills Bonnet himself (thus indicating that he doesn't think Roger can protect his family) or gets Roger killed in the process of hunting Bonnet?

Jamie is not swayed by Claire's arguments, stubbornly insisting that he needs to find and exterminate the man who not only raped his daughter and robbed the Frasers but who is also a continuing threat to the welfare of Brianna and little Jem—to say nothing of society as a whole.

Claire is not convinced, but neither can she sway Jamie from his path.

11. Religion. One of the further awkwardnesses between Jamie and Roger is the fact that Roger is a Presbyterian.

". . . well, you see, we're Catholics, and Catholics have priests, but Uncle Roger is a Presbyterian—"

"That's a heretic," Jamie put in helpfully.

"It is not *a heretic, darling, Grand-père is being funny—or thinks he is. Presbyterians are . . ."*

Regardless, Father Kenneth, a Catholic priest who has come to the Gathering to attend to the spiritual needs of the Catholic Highlanders there, has agreed to marry Roger and Brianna. The good father is not the only clergyman at the Gathering; there are preachers galore, of one persuasion or another, including the Rev. Mr. David Caldwell, a prominent (and real) Presbyterian.

In the midst of the Gathering, Jamie gets word that Father Kenneth has been arrested. Going to discover the difficulty, he finds that the priest has been arrested by David Anstruther, a county sheriff, and is being held in the tent of one Randall

Lillywhite, a magistrate from Hillsborough. This is baffling; while it's true that Catholics are officially discriminated against and that it is technically illegal for a Catholic priest to perform "ceremonials" in the colony, this isn't a legality that's often enforced—mostly because there are very few priests *in* the colony; in fact, Father Kenneth has been imported for the occasion, asked by Jocasta to come and perform both her marriage to Duncan and the marriage of Roger and Brianna.

The matter becomes still more baffling when Mr. Lillywhite refuses to release the priest into Jamie's custody—an apparently pointless insult to a prominent man. Jamie, however, has a greater concern than his daughter's or his aunt's marriage: he wants his grandchildren baptized. With considerable guile and Claire's help, he persuades the magistrate to allow him to speak privately with the priest, in order to have his confession heard, and then he smuggles in Jemmy, Germain, and Joan, whom the priest hastily baptizes in whisky, the "water of life" being all that's available.

Brianna and Roger, meanwhile, have spoken privately to the Rev. Mr. Caldwell and are married that evening after all—in a Presbyterian ceremony.

"You had your way over the baptism," I whispered. He lifted his chin slightly. Brianna glanced in our direction, looking slightly anxious.

"I havena said a word, have I?"

"It's a perfectly respectable Christian marriage."

"Did I say it was not?"

"Then look happy, *damn you!" I hissed. He exhaled once more, and assumed an expression of benevolence one degree short of outright imbecility.*

"Better?" he asked, teeth clenched in a genial smile.

* * *

Germain was paying no attention to my explanation, but instead had tilted his head back, viewing Jamie with fascination.

"Why Grand-père is making faces?"

"We're verra happy," Jamie explained, expression still fixed in a rictus of amiability.

"Oh." Germain at once stretched his own extraordinarily mobile face into a crude facsimile of the same expression—a jack-o'-lantern grin, teeth clenched and eyes popping. "Like this?"

"Yes, darling," I said, in a marked tone. "Just *like that."*

Marsali looked at us, blinked, and tugged at Fergus's sleeve. He turned, squinting at us.

"Look happy, Papa!" Germain pointed to his gigantic smile. "See?"

Fergus's mouth twitched, as he glanced from his offspring to Jamie. His face went blank for a moment, then adjusted itself into an enormous smile of white-toothed insincerity. Marsali kicked him in the ankle. He winced, but the smile didn't waver.

* * *

Reverend Caldwell stepped forward, a finger in his book at the proper place, put his spectacles on his nose, and smiled genially at the assemblage, blinking only slightly when he encountered the row of leering countenances.

12. Fergus, Jamie's adopted French son, his wife, Marsali (daughter of Jamie's ex-wife, Laoghaire), and their two children, Germain and Joan. Fergus, like Roger, has a few problems in finding status and self-worth in the environment where he finds himself. Intelligent, inventive, and artistic, but lacking one hand, he can't do many of the chores necessary on a frontier homestead, thus throwing a lot of the work onto his young wife. This causes him to feel guilty and creates friction between him and Marsali.

Still, in the present situation, Fergus's handicap is an advantage; lacking a hand, he is not obliged to serve with the militia, and while he will help in gathering the militia volunteers, if and when the militia is called to serve, he can remain on the Ridge to help defend and organize.

13. The Bugs. Jamie introduces Roger to an elderly but still strong and vigorous Highlander named Arch Bug, a recent immigrant to the colony with his wife, Murdina. Arch, Jamie informs Roger, will be the new factor for the Ridge, while Murdina will help with the cooking and household chores at the Big House.

Roger is outwardly cordial but inwardly fumes, This attitude undergoes an abrupt change when Jamie tells Roger *why* he's made Arch Bug factor:

"'Twas luck I should have come across auld Arch Bug and his wife today. If it comes to the fighting—and it will, I suppose, later, if not now—then Claire will ride with us. I shouldna like to leave Brianna to manage on her own, and it can be helped."

Roger felt the small nagging weight of doubt drop away, as all became suddenly clear.

"On her own. You mean—ye want me to come? To help raise men for the militia?"

Jamie gave him a puzzled look.

"Aye, who else?"

He pulled the edges of his plaid higher about his shoulders, hunched against the rising wind. "Come along, then, Captain MacKenzie," he said, a wry note in his voice. "We've work to do before you're wed."

14. The McGillivrays. Another of Jamie's Ardsmuir companions, Robin McGillivray is a talented gunsmith, married to an indomitable German lady named Ute, whose life is dedicated to making good matches for her children: her son, Manfred, but, more important, her three daughters, Hilda, Inga, and Senga. We meet the McGillivrays first at the Gathering, when John Quincy Myers, a trapping acquaintance, comes to tell Jamie that there is a certain amount of trouble with a thief-taker, who has just tried to arrest Manfred McGillivray for taking part in the Hillsborough riot. Manfred was *in* Hillsborough, his sisters admit, but they insist that he had nothing to do with the riots.

Going to investigate, Claire and Jamie find Manfred and a pair of manacles—but no thief-taker. Investigating more closely, they discover the thief-taker, one Harley Boble by name. He has been overpowered by the McGillivray women, who have him bound and gagged but are at something of a loss as to how to proceed.

Jamie deals with the immediate problem in his own inimitable fashion:

"Exactly what did Jamie tell him?" I asked Myers.

"Oh. Well." The mountain man gave me a broad, gap-toothed grin. "Jamie Roy told him serious-like that it was surely luck for the thief-taker—his name's Boble, by the way, Harley Boble—that we done come upon y'all when we did. He give him to understand that if we hadn't, then this lady here"—he bowed toward Ute—"would likely have taken him home in her wagon, and slaughtered him like a hog, safe out of sight."

Myers rubbed a knuckle under his red-veined nose and chortled softly in his beard.

"Boble said as how he didn't believe it, he thought she was only a-tryin' to scare him with that knife. But then Jamie Roy leaned down close, confidential-like, and said he mighta thought the same—only that he'd heard so much about Frau McGillivray's reputation as a famous sausage-maker, and had had the privilege of bein' served some of it to his breakfast this morning. Right about then, Boble started to lose the color in his face, and when Jamie Roy pulled out a bit of sausage to show him—"

The problem of the thief-taker thus disposed of, the McGillivrays accept Jamie's invitation to come and settle on the Ridge.

PART 2: *THE CHIEFTAIN'S CALL*

Once returned to the Ridge, Claire deals with a houseful of new immigrants—all staying with the Frasers while new cabins are hastily built—and pursues her most pressing order of business: the development of a usable form of penicillin. Jamie is busy settling his new tenants, drawing up property deeds, organizing labor, and—somehow—finding

the money to supply those tenants with the basic tools needed to carve homesteads out of the wilderness. As Claire pursues her chemical researches, so does Jamie: "somehow" is the clandestine making and selling of whisky.

Meanwhile, Roger and Brianna settle in the old cabin near the Big House, where Claire and Jamie live, and begin the adventurous if sometimes awkwardly bruising business of making a life together.

All this industry is abruptly interrupted by Governor Tryon's letter, sent to all the colonels of militia: There is a gathering of Regulators near Salisbury, and one General Waddell is heading there to disperse them. Jamie and the other militia commanders are to gather as many men as they can and join him.

Jamie begins the matter with a ceremonial supper, to which he summons all his tenants, inviting also the German settlers who live nearby. He erects a large wooden cross in the yard, causing Brianna to ask with nervous facetiousness whether he is starting his own religion. He explains the tradition of the "fiery cross"—a symbol used by the ancient clan chieftains to summon men to war—and gives Roger careful instruction as to which songs to sing and in what order. The event is carefully orchestrated, and when the cross blazes up, Jamie has the core of his militia, eager to follow him.

PART 3: *ALARMS AND EXCURSIONS*

More men are needed, though, and Jamie (with Claire, Roger, and Fergus) sets out with a party of forty men, intending to raise further recruits from the country through which they pass.

While Jamie and Roger are absent (with Claire as medico), Bree is left in charge of the teeming—and frequently riotous—household. Herself, if you would.

Herself flung open the study door and glowered at the mob. Mrs. Bug, red in the face—as usual—and brimming with accusation. Mrs. Chisholm, ditto, overflowing with maternal outrage. Little Mrs. Aberfeldy, the color of an eggplant, clutching her two-year-old daughter, Ruth, protectively to her bosom. Tony and Toby Chisholm, both in tears and covered with snot. Toby had a red handprint on the side of his face; little Ruthie's wispy hair appeared to be oddly shorter on one side than the other. They all began to talk at once.

". . . Red savages!"

". . . My baby's beautiful hair!"

"She started it!"

". . . dare to strike my son!"

"We was just playin' at scalpin', ma'am . . . "

". . . EEEEEEEEEEE!"

". . . and torn a great hole in my feather bed, the wee spawn!"

"Look *what she's done, the wicked auld besom!"*

"Look *what they've done!"*

"Look ye, ma'am, it's only . . . "

"AAAAAAAAAA!"

Escaping momentarily from the tumult, she shuts herself in her father's study and, while picking up a fallen ledger, discovers a letter from Lord John Grey, in which he tells Jamie of his inquiries regarding the whereabouts of Stephen Bonnet. He has news not only of Bonnet's continued presence in the Carolinas but also recounts a horrible incident in which Bonnet has maimed and blinded a man with whom he fought a duel. The news leaves Brianna chilled and shaking.

While camped one night, Jamie's militia are unexpectedly joined by Josiah Beardsley, the young hunter to whom Jamie had offered a place on the Ridge. Josiah is having an asthma attack, which Claire treats with hot coffee and breathing exercises. When recovered, Josiah says he will travel with the militia party for a bit, having "business" to conduct nearby.

The "business" turns out to be his twin brother, Keziah, whom Josiah has stolen from Aaron Beardsley's farm, where the two brothers were indentured servants—having been sold as such at the age of two, after their entire family died on the passage from England to the colonies.

Hearing this, Jamie is naturally reluctant to approach the Beardsley place but has to inquire whether Beardsley will join the militia. He and Claire decide to approach Mr. Beardsley on their own, in order to avoid Beardsley inadvertently learning of the boys having taken refuge with Jamie. They leave the rest of the party to continue to Brownsville, a nearby settlement, under Roger's command.

Roger is pleased—if a little nervous—at this sign of Jamie's confidence and rides into Brownsville at the head of his men, only to be confronted by the barrel of a gun sticking out the window of the house he's approached.

Isaiah Morton, one of the militiamen with Roger, has seduced Alicia, daughter of Lionel Brown, one of the two Brown brothers who founded the settlement. Hearing that Isaiah is unable to make an honest woman of Alicia, owing to his having a wife in Granite Falls, they're inclined to take Alicia's honor out of his hide—but Isaiah, with rare presence of mind, has vanished. Headed for the hills, Roger hopes—and, with the aid of Fergus and a barrel of whisky, pitches in to hold the Browns at bay, at least until Jamie can get there.

Meanwhile, Claire and Jamie discover an equally fraught situation at the Beardsley farm. They are greeted by Fanny Beardsley, who tells them that her husband is ill and tries to send them away. Claire's medical nose detects something rotten in the state of Denmark, though, and she insists on coming inside, where they discover Aaron Beardsley, helpless in the loft.

He has had a serious stroke and can neither move nor talk. His wife has made no effort to care for him—quite the opposite, as Claire can tell at once by the marks of torture on the man's wasted, filthy body. Fanny Beardsley claims that her husband has cruelly abused her—and she has clearly been getting a bit of her own back, wreaking vengeance on the helpless man, allowing him to die by inches.

Beardsley can't talk but indicates to Jamie that he wishes to die. Claire tells Jamie that he *will* certainly die; aside from the effects of the stroke that felled him, he has developed gangrene. Jamie reluctantly agrees and shoots Beardsley through the eye. He buries Beardsley, and Claire sees him first vomit and then weep silently, disturbed not only by the violence of what he's felt obliged to do but by thought of his own father, who died some days after a stroke many years before, with Jamie not present. Was his father in such dreadful case? he wonders. But he is estranged from his sister—the only one who could tell him—because of his having lost her youngest son to the Mohawk.

With Fanny Beardsley and the goats, the Frasers leave the ghastly farm, and on the way Fanny tells them about her dreadful marriage—revealing in the process that Aaron Beardsley had been married several times before and had (she says) killed his previous wives, whom he buried under a rowan tree in the yard. One of the dead wives appeared to her, she says casually, and urged her to flee. Disturbed by the woman's talk, the Frasers bed down some distance from her that night and discover in the morning that she *has* fled—but has left something behind: a small baby, newborn and bearing a Mongol spot—a pigmented mark at the base of the spine, common to children of African extraction. Whoever fathered Fanny's child, it wasn't her husband.

Back in Brownsville, Roger has succeeded in pacifying the Browns, at least to an extent, and is both proud and pleased when Jamie, arriving and assessing the situation, tells him he's done well. Jamie arranges for the Beardsley baby—now heir to Aaron Beardsley's farm and prosperous trading post—to be cared for by the Browns, and all looks good for an orderly recruitment and getaway, when Alicia Beardsley comes to talk with Claire privately. The girl is pregnant by the bigamous Isaiah and is on the verge of begging Claire to help her to terminate her pregnancy, when they are interrupted.

Later that night, Jamie and Claire are surprised in the makeshift stable by Isaiah himself; he's been lurking nearby, desperate to see Alicia. He attempts to hold Jamie at gunpoint, telling Claire to go get the girl, but Jamie is having no nonsense of that kind:

"Put it down, idiot," he said, almost kindly. "Ye ken fine ye willna shoot me, and so do I."

Claire sneaks into the house and up to Alicia's small room, where she finds the girl lying stark naked on the floor beneath an open window, letting snow drift in upon her.

"I've heard of a number of novel ways of inducing miscarriage," I told her, picking up a quilt from the cot and dropping it over her shoulders, "but freezing to death isn't one of them."

"If I'm d-dead, I won't need to m-m-miscarry," she said, with a certain amount of logic.

Jamie clutches his head over the situation but feels that the best he can do is to aid the absquatulation of Isaiah and Alicia, which he does, covering their escape by loosing the militia's horses in the midst of a snowstorm. In the aftermath of the confusion, as everyone is thawing out indoors, a messenger arrives with another letter from Governor Tryon. The Regulators have dispersed, and the militia is stood down.

PART 4: *I HEAR NO MUSIC BUT THE SOUND OF DRUMS*

Claire, Jamie, Roger, and Fergus return to the Ridge and the bosoms of their families. Brianna is delighted to have Roger safely home again—but rather miffed that he does not appreciate the work *she's* been doing in his absence. They make peace, though, and Christmas passes quietly, giving way to the more important—to Highlanders—occasion of Hogmanay (New Year's).

There is much festivity, dancing, fortune-telling, eating, and drinking. Jamie tells Claire that he used to be able to hear music, but since being struck in the head by an ax, he hears no music but the sound of drums. That sense of rhythm remains, though, and enables him to do the sword dance he once did as a young man, foretelling the fortunes of war on the eve of battle.

Another Highland Hogmanay custom is that of the "first-foot," wherein the first caller to cross a threshold after midnight on New Year's Eve brings gifts of salt, coal, and food—and brings luck to the household. A red-haired person as first-foot is ill luck, but a dark-haired man is a fortunate first-foot, and so Roger is pressed into service, first-footing the nearby houses. When a knock comes on the door of the Big House, therefore, Jamie and Claire open it expecting to see their son-in-law.

Instead of Roger and Brianna, two smaller figures stood on the porch. Skinny and bedraggled, but definitely dark-haired, the two Beardsley twins stepped shyly in together, at Jamie's gesture.

"A happy New Year to you, Mr. Fraser," said Josiah, in a bullfrog croak. He bowed politely to me, still holding his brother by the arm. "We've come."

With the twins both suffering terribly from chronic infections of tonsils and adenoids, Claire resumes her program of penicillin research. To find the right kind of bread mold, she uses the microscope from the medicine chest that Jamie gave her as an anniversary present, once the property of a Dr. Daniel Rawlings, whose casebook gives her the friendly feeling of companionship from a kindred practitioner. She makes good use of the microscope, trying it out on various things—including a sample of Jamie's semen, which horrifies but intrigues him.

"Oh, aye? And what then? What's the purpose of it, I mean?"

"Well, to help me diagnose things. If I can take a sample of a person's stool, for instance, and see that he has internal parasites, then I'd know better what medicine to give him."

Jamie looked as though he would have preferred not to hear about such things right after breakfast, but nodded. He drained his beaker and set it down on the counter.

"Aye, that's sensible. I'll leave ye to get on with it, then."

He bent and kissed me briefly, then headed for the door. Just short of it, though, he turned back.

"The, um, sperms . . ." he said, a little awkwardly.

"Yes?"

"Can ye not take them out and give them decent burial or something?"

I hid a smile in my teacup.

"I'll take good care of them," I promised. "I always do, don't I?"

Claire's penicillin experiments are successful, and she proceeds to remove the Beardsleys' tonsils, noting with interest how close the boys have grown to Lizzie in the short time they've been at the Ridge, following her like puppies.

A rare shipment of mail arrives at the Ridge, including ladies' magazines for Brianna, newspapers for Jamie—and a letter from Archie Hayes, intended for Jamie but opened by Brianna, in which the lieutenant tells Jamie the effect of *his* inquiries into the whereabouts and activities of one Stephen Bonnet. He has connections with a number of local merchants, particularly with a Mr. Butler, and warehouses in the Edenton area frequently have unusual goods, these goods coincidentally appearing at times when Bonnet has been in the vicinity. Hayes has made inquiries regarding one such warehouse and reports that it is jointly owned by "one Ronald Priestly and one Phillip Wylie."

Discovery of the letter leads to a discussion between Claire and Brianna, during which the former asks whether her daughter truly wants Stephen Bonnet dead.

"I can't," she said, low-voiced. "I'm afraid if I ever let that thought in my mind . . . I'd never be able to think about anything else, I'd want it so much. And I will be damned *if I'll let . . . him . . . ruin my life that way."*

Jemmy gave a resounding belch, and spit up a little milk. Bree had an old linen towel across her shoulder, and deftly wiped his chin with it. Calmer now, he had lost his look of vexed incomprehension, and was concentrating intently on something over his mother's shoulder. Following the direction of his clear blue gaze, I saw the shadow of a spiderweb, high up in the corner of the window. A gust of wind shook the window frame, and a tiny spot moved in the center of the web, very slightly.

"Yeah," Brianna said, very softly. "I do want him dead. But I want Da and Roger alive, more."

Roger, of course, knows none of this. But he returns late one night after singing for a wedding, and going to write down the lyrics of a new song he's heard, he comes across Brianna's dream-book—her description of various vivid dreams she's had. He is shaken by her description of one dream that makes it clear she has trouble reaching orgasm with him—and that her dreams are haunted by Stephen Bonnet.

PART 5: *'TIS BETTER TO MARRY THAN BURN*

Jocasta and Duncan's delayed wedding is finally to take place at River Run. A French priest from New Orleans has been imported to perform the ceremony, and the chief

question in everyone's mind is whether the bride (in her sixties) and groom (in his fifties) will share a bed, and much good-humored wagering is going on in consequence. Jamie backs Duncan at five to one—but Duncan is nowhere to be seen, and Jamie's money may be in danger, if the bridegroom can't be found.

The wedding is attended by everyone who is anyone, including Jocasta's old friend Farquard Campbell, a justice of the peace, and Lieutenant Wolff of the Royal Navy—the Navy's chief business contact with River Run and a rejected suitor of Jocasta's (his motive being, as she acerbically observes, desire of her property rather than her person). In addition, a military stranger appears—one Major Donald MacDonald, brought by Farquard Campbell.

"Everyone" includes both those in sympathy with the Regulation movement—and those emphatically opposed. A fight between two such men threatens to lead to a free-for-all but is stopped by Major MacDonald, at Claire's request. Hermon Husband, a prominent Quaker and leader of the Regulation, leaves the party, and James Hunter, another Regulator, tells Claire to tell Jamie that the Regulators are gathering at a big camp, up near Salisbury.

In conversation with MacDonald, Claire learns that he's a half-pay soldier, in search of professional engagement. With no war, pickings are slim—but perhaps Governor Tryon might see the virtue in engaging an officer of experience to help in the training and disposition of the militia? Claire, obliged to the major for his help in stopping the riot, assures him she will speak to Jamie about an introduction.

Their conversation is interrupted by Phillip Wylie, a rich young plantation owner from Edenton who attempts to flirt with Claire.

Phillip Wylie was a dandy. I had met him twice before, and on both occasions, he had been got up regardless: satin breeches, silk stockings, and all the trappings that went with them, including powdered wig, powdered face, and a small black crescent beauty mark, stuck dashingly beside one eye.

Now, however, the rot had spread. The powdered wig was mauve, the satin waistcoat was embroidered with—I blinked. Yes, with lions and unicorns, done in gold and silver thread. The satin breeches were fitted to him like a bifurcated glove, and the crescent had given way to a star at the corner of his mouth. Mr. Wylie had become a macaroni—with cheese.

She tries to shoo him off, but he insists upon showing her his Friesians, beautiful black horses with silky, floating hair, which are garnering much admiring attention from the wedding guests.

Jamie appears suddenly at Claire's side and detaches her from Wylie, then meets Major MacDonald, who begs a few moments' conversation. Once in private, he tells Jamie that he understands Jamie has been seeking news of Stephen Bonnet—and he has some. Bonnet, it appears, has close ties with a number of the coastal merchants, including a Mr. Butler. These men are likely protecting Bonnet's smuggling activities. This is interesting and perhaps ominous news to Jamie—for as MacDonald points out, while Jamie's inquiries have spread far enough to hear something of Bonnet, by the same token, this means Bonnet undoubtedly knows that Jamie is looking for him. In answer to MacDonald's matter-of-fact inquiry as to whether Jamie means to kill Bonnet, James tells MacDonald what Bonnet has done and agrees to give MacDonald a letter of introduction to the governor.

The news of Bonnet's influential connections gives Jamie pause for thought—but it's not a matter that can be dealt with at the moment, and the continued absence of Duncan is more pressing. So is Jamie's growing desire for his wife. What with travel and the press of wedding guests at River Run, he hasn't been able to bed her for a week.

Ever since she had shown him the sperms, he had been uncomfortably aware of the crowded conditions that must now and then obtain in his balls, an impression made forcibly stronger in situations such as this. He kent well enough that there was no danger of rupture or explosion—and yet he couldn't help but think of all the shoving going on.

Being trapped in a seething mass of others, with no hope of escape, was one of his own personal visions of Hell, and he paused for a moment outside the screen of willow trees, to administer a brief squeeze of reassurance, which he hoped might calm the riot for a bit.

He'd see Duncan safely married, he decided, and then the man must see to his own affairs. Come nightfall, and if he could do no better than a bush, then a bush it would have to be.

At last he discovers Duncan, pale and sweating, who tells him he must speak to him. Duncan is impotent, as the result of an accident suffered when a cart horse kicked him in the scrotum as a young man. He had been regarding the matter of his marriage as a matter of business and convenience; it hadn't dawned on him that Jocasta might expect . . . But having now heard the jests of the wedding guests, he's in a panic.

Jamie promises to attend to the matter—which he does by sexually blackmailing Claire into talking to his aunt about Duncan's problem.

He grinned down at me, stepping back and letting his kilt fall into place. His face was flushed a ruddy bronze with effort, and his chest heaved under his shirt ruffles. . . .

"I'll gie ye the rest when I'm ninety-six, aye?"

"You won't live that long! Come here!"

"Oh," he said. "So ye'll speak to my aunt."

"Effing blackmailer," I panted, fumbling at the folds of his kilt. "I'll get you for this, I swear I will."

"Oh, aye. You will."

Taking a break in the kitchen garden, Brianna is hailed by her father, lurking behind a bush. Jamie has found one of the servants, a black woman named Betty, out cold in the kitchen garden, reeking of drink, a fallen cup by her hand. The cup, however, contains not only the dregs of rum punch but also a strong whiff of laudanum. He fetches Brianna and, with her help, gets Betty up to the servants' attic, where they lay her on the bed, speculating about her situation. While any servant might take advantage of the party to sneak a drink, the laudanum casts another light on the matter. Did Betty take it herself? Or was it in the cup, intended for someone else, when she abstracted and drank it? If so—for whom was it meant, and why? The cup was special, one of a set made as a wedding present by Jocasta for Duncan.

While Jamie sends Roger and Brianna to check for bodies in the bushes, Phillip Wylie reappears, to invite Claire to see a surprise. She follows him into the stables, where he shows her a tiny Friesian colt, which he tells her he has named for her—then follows up promptly by making a pass at her, seizing and kissing her. She wrenches herself away and storms out, running into Jamie—who delicately removes Wylie's beauty mark from her face, demanding to know *what* she has been doing. Their incipient quarrel is aborted by spectators, and Jamie sends her off to speak to Jocasta.

I left Jamie in the parlor, and made my way up the stairs and along the hall toward Jocasta's room, nodding distractedly to friends and acquaintances encountered along the way. I was disconcerted, annoyed—and at the same time, reluctantly amused. I hadn't spent so much time in bemused contemplation of a penis since I was sixteen or so, and here I was, preoccupied with three of the things.

The objects in question belong to Jamie, Phillip Wylie, and Duncan Innes, of course, and Claire puts aside consideration of the first two in order to think about the third, wondering as to the physical basis of Duncan's incapacity and whether anything might be done about it. For the moment, though, such matters are hypothetical, and finding Jocasta alone with the French-speaking priest, she confides Duncan's problem, discovering both Jocasta and the priest sympathetic.

The priest inquires whether Jocasta still wishes to be married; impotence is a bar to marriage, since the sacrament can't be consummated—but in view of the parties' ages, clearly procreation is not God's will in this matter, so . . . ?

After only a moment, though, Jocasta stirred, letting out her breath in a deep sigh.

"Well, thank Christ I'd the luck to get a Jesuit," she said dryly. "One of them could argue the Pope out of his drawers, let alone deal wi' a small matter of reading the Lord's mind. Aye, tell him I do desire to be married, still."

This matter satisfactorily adjusted, Claire goes to attend the slave Betty, only to find her already attended, by Ulysses and one Dr. Fentiman, highlight of the medical profession of Fayetteville. The doctor is small, opinionated, and the worse for drink; he insults Claire and forces her to leave—but not before she's found out what she wanted to know: Betty *has* taken opium, whether deliberately or not.

The wedding hour is reached, and the wedding is quietly and movingly accomplished, with only Jocasta's immediate family as witnesses. The mostly Protestant friends and neighbors can join in the celebration of the marriage afterward, without the awkwardness of being compelled to witness a Popish ceremony.

Following the wedding, the festivities move into full swing. Jamie is thinking carnal thoughts of Claire—mingled with rage at Wylie—when he is approached by a man named Lyon, who, with singular ineptitude, tries to find out things about Jamie's militia unit and ends up baldly propositioning him regarding his whisky-making operations. Wondering who has set this incompetent intriguer on him, Jamie extricates himself and goes to find his wife.

Their tryst is interrupted, though, by the reappearance of a dangerously flushed Phillip Wylie, who invites—or challenges—Jamie to play whist with him. Jamie promptly accepts, despite Claire's certain knowledge that he hasn't any money with which to play high-stakes whist. He agrees with her and asks for her gold ring to use as a stake. Infuriated, she takes off *both* rings and drops them into his palm before stomping off.

Ignorant of all this tension, Roger and Brianna have been enjoying the party, Roger singing and accepting the applause of the multitudes, Brianna enjoying the momentary respite from motherhood, as Jocasta's body servant, Phaedre, is taking care of Jemmy. She and Roger meet outside the house and wander companionably toward the river.

"Did you find any of the guests passed out in the shrubbery?" she asked, her words muffled by a mouthful of mushroom pasty. She swallowed, and became more distinct. "When Da asked you to go and look this afternoon, I mean."

He snorted briefly, selecting a dumpling made of sausage and dried pumpkin.

"Ken the difference between a Scottish wedding and a Scottish funeral, do ye?"

"No, what?"

"The funeral has one less drunk."

While there may be a few feet sticking out of the shrubbery now, he says, none of the guests were missing or comatose during the afternoon. Their discussions, and their idyll, are rudely interrupted by a servant, rushing to find them; Jemmy has croup, and they hurry back to the house to take care of him.

Following all the alarms of the day, including Jemmy's attack of croup, Claire falls into bed and almost at once into sleep—from which she's roused by the feeling of someone playing "This Little Piggy" with her toes. The room is full of sleeping women, and the phantom foot-fondler disappears when some of them begin to stir. Claire rises and steals quietly out, to discover Jamie at the foot of the stair, in an advanced state of intoxication.

"What—" I began, whispering.

"Come here," he said. His voice was low, rough with sleeplessness and whisky.

I hadn't time either to reply or to acquiesce; he seized my arm and pulled me toward him, then swept me off the last step, crushed me to him, and kissed me. It was a most disconcerting kiss—as though his mouth knew mine all too well, and would compel my pleasure, regardless of my desires.

Jamie takes Claire to the barn, where, after a long-delayed and delightfully ferocious coupling, they fall asleep in the hay—though before doing so, Jamie returns both her rings, telling her that he's won Wylie's stallion, Lucas, at whist.

In the morning, he shows her the horse, telling her more about the evening's events. The conversation is interrupted, though, by a servant, summoning Claire—something's amiss with the slave Betty.

Something is more than amiss. The woman is hemorrhaging violently, in spite of the best efforts of Dr. Fentiman, and eventually dies messily. The two doctors stagger wearily downstairs, united in defeat, and have a moment of rapprochement despite their earlier mutual hostility. Phillip Wylie, red-eyed with sleeplessness and fury, pops up to denounce Claire for carrying on with Dr. Fentiman, who, outraged, dismisses Wylie as a puppy—thus enraging him more.

Claire has other things to think of than Wylie's offended pride, though. She's sure that Betty's death was not a natural one and persuades Jamie—much against his will and better judgment—to help her with a crude autopsy that night. She has almost finished her work by lantern light, when their grisly secrecy is interrupted by—who else—Phillip Wylie, who opens the shed door and is horribly shocked by what's going on inside.

He hasn't time for remonstrances, though, for another man looms out of the darkness just behind him: Stephen Bonnet.

"Jesus H. Roosevelt Christ," I said.

A number of things happened at that point: Jamie came out from under the table with a rush like a striking cobra, Phillip Wylie leaped back from the door with a startled cry, and the lantern crashed from its nail to the floor. There was a strong smell of splattered oil and brandy, a soft whoosh *like a furnace lighting, and the crumpled shroud was burning at my feet.*

The shed proceeds to catch fire and burn to the ground, incinerating Betty's body with it. Claire, hiding in the dark garden during the attendant confusion, succeeds in depositing in a jar what she has taken from the body—ground glass from Betty's stomach; the proof that the woman has been murdered. As the noise begins to die down, another sound is heard—Jocasta's voice from the house, screaming for help.

Jocasta is found in her bedroom, in her nightgown, bound hand and foot, with Duncan on the floor at her feet, out cold from a blow on the head with a candlestick. Freed, Jocasta explains that two or three men came into her room, knocked Duncan out, and then tied her up. The spokesman, "an Irishman," she says, demanded that she tell them the whereabouts of the gold.

What gold? The Frenchman's gold, replies Jocasta, and after checking to be sure that only her kin are present, she reluctantly tells them the story of the Jacobite gold: thirty thousand pounds in gold ingots, sent by the king of France to aid Charles Stuart's bid for the thrones of Scotland and England. The gold arrived too late to be of help to Charles but was divided in three parts for safekeeping by the three men who brought it ashore: Jocasta's brother Dougal MacKenzie, her husband, Hector Cameron—and a third man, who wore a mask and whose name she didn't know.

Following the disastrous battle at Culloden and the death of the Stuart cause, Hector Cameron had loaded his share of the gold into a coach, along with his wife, and fled the country, using part of the gold to finance his acquisition of River Run. For twenty-five years, that gold has been a secret—but, somehow, Stephen Bonnet has discovered the secret and come for the gold.

Jocasta tells her fascinated family that she told Bonnet the gold was buried under the floor of the shed—hoping that he and his mates would be shocked by finding a dead body inside the shed and sufficiently taken aback as to give her time to struggle free of her gag and shout for help. As it was . . .

There seemed no more to say or to do. Ulysses came back, sliding discreetly into the room with a fresh candlestick and a tray holding a bottle of brandy and several glasses. Major MacDonald reappeared briefly to report that indeed, they had found no sign of the miscreants. I checked both Duncan and Jocasta briefly, then left Bree and Ulysses to put them to bed.

Jamie and I made our way downstairs in silence. At the bottom of the staircase, I turned to him. He was white with fatigue, his features drawn and set as though he had been carved of marble, his hair and beard stubble dark in the shadowed light.

"They'll come back, won't they?" I said quietly.

He nodded, and taking my elbow, led me toward the kitchen stair.

After a brief stop by the kitchen for a jug of coffee and a crumb cake, Jamie leads Claire back to the stables, where they find Phillip Wylie locked in a loose-box, under Roger's guard. Roger and Jamie interrogate Wylie, who claims to have had nothing to do with Bonnet's sudden appearance and no knowledge whatever of the attack on Jocasta and Duncan. Naturally enough, Wylie resents the implications of this inquiry.

"You blackguard!" He rounded on Jamie, fists clenched. "You dare to imply that I am a thief?"

Jamie rocked back a little on his stool, chin lifted.

"Aye, I do," he said coolly. "Ye tried to steal my wife from under my nose—why should ye scruple at my aunt's goods?"

Wylie's face flushed a deep and ugly crimson. Had it not been a wig, his hair would have stood on end.

"You . . . absolute . . . cunt!*" he breathed. Then he launched himself at Jamie. Both of them went over with a crash, in a flurry of arms and legs.*

Claire, enormously irritated with both of them, puts a stop to the fight by emptying the jug of hot coffee over them. In subsequent, calmer conversation, Wylie repeats firmly that he has no knowledge of Stephen Bonnet. He had come to the stables the night before intending to say a private goodbye to his horse, Lucas; seeing the lantern in the shed, he then went to investigate, only to be shocked by finding Claire in mid-autopsy. But, he adds with an odd defiance, while he knows nothing of Bonnet, he thinks Jamie won't easily find him—Bonnet has absconded with Lucas.

Returning—somewhat worse for wear—to the house, everyone forgathers in Jocasta's rooms to discuss recent events, compare information, and try to make sense of things.

It's Roger who suggests that the key to the whole affair may be the priest. It looks very much as though someone had tried to poison Duncan—or at least to render him unconscious. Duncan is himself innocuous—but if he were dead (perhaps knocked on the head, or perhaps pushed into the river, to give the appearance of an accidental drowning), someone else might seize Jocasta, force the priest to marry her to the plotter, and thus gain ownership of River Run. That supposition focuses attention on Lieutenant Wolff, who had been present at the party but was seen leaving in a boat.

What if, Claire suggests, the lieutenant went downriver to meet Stephen Bonnet, coming back secretly with him? After all, someone's discovering the existence of the gold is one thing—disposing of it clandestinely is another, and who better to do that than a pirate and smuggler? And of the two men who attacked Jocasta and Duncan, one never spoke—presumably because Jocasta would have recognized his voice.

And why was the slave Betty (Phaedre's mother) murdered? Because, Claire suggests, she could—and would—have told who it was that gave her the cup of punch to give to Duncan; a cup he rejected because his stomach was upset from nervousness, leaving Betty to drink it herself. Nothing simpler than for the plotter—or one of them—to steal up to the slaves' attic and slip Betty a syllabub full of ground glass, assuming that her subsequent death from gastric hemorrhage would be put down to disease—as indeed it would have been, without Claire's midnight autopsy.

This all hangs together as a plausible theory—but as Claire points out, there's no way of proving it. The one thing they *do* know is that Stephen Bonnet will be back—a thought that makes Brianna go pale with fear.

Leaving Jocasta and Duncan to fortify the house and post guards, the Frasers and MacKenzies depart next day for the mountains. They are no more than five miles down the road, however, when Major MacDonald catches them up, delightedly brandishing a letter from the governor:

To the Commanding Officers of the Militia:

Sirs:

I Yesterday determined by Consent of His Majesty's Council to march with a Body of Forces taken from several Militia Regiments, into the Settlements of the Insurgents to reduce them to Obedience . . .

"Bloody, bloody, fucking hell," I said softly, again, with emphasis. Major MacDonald blinked. Jamie glanced at me, and the corner of his mouth twitched up.

"Aye, well," he said. "Nearly a month. Just time to get the barley in."

PART 6: *THE WAR OF THE REGULATION*

Tryon's troops gather, and so do the Regulators, the two bodies coming together near Alamance Creek. There are a good three thousand Regulators, irregularly armed, but armed nonetheless. The governor's troops are fewer in number and no better armed, being militia—but they have one vital thing the Regulators lack: leadership.

Roger MacKenzie has three important encounters on this momentous day: first with Hermon Husband, and then with Morag Gunn MacKenzie.

Husband, who has done his best to inflame the Regulators with his pamphleteering and public rabble-rousing, is appalled at the fruits of his labors. He has strong opinions regarding the rights of the colonists and the injustices of the Crown, but he *is* a Quaker; his sentiments stop well short of inciting actual violence. At the same time, he is the only thing approaching a leader that the Regulators have. If he leaves them without strong leadership, they *may* disperse peaceably—but if they don't, they may well be slaughtered by Tryon's troops.

He shuts himself in an abandoned cabin, agonized by the situation. Roger, sent by Jamie to see if Hermon will order his men to disperse before blood is shed, goes in to speak to him, and Husband asks him to pray with him. They do pray together, in the silent Quaker manner, and during the prayer Roger experiences a remarkable clarity of vision that both enlightens and shakes him. The visitation, if that's what it is, has also clarified things for Husband; he cannot stay and engage in or encourage physical violence—he exhorts his followers from horseback to disperse, and then he leaves, hoping they will follow.

They don't.

Making his way down the riverbank, Roger meets unexpectedly with Morag Gunn MacKenzie, the woman—his four-times great-grandmother—whom he'd met once before, aboard the *Gloriana,* when he saved her infant son from being thrown overboard by Stephen Bonnet. He stops to ask after her welfare, and that of her child, and experiences a sense of great tenderness and connection toward her—one that seems to be shared, although she urges him to go. He does but, in parting, kisses her.

Raising his head from this tender but chaste gesture, he has the third significant encounter of the day—with William Buccleigh MacKenzie, Morag's husband (and Roger's four-times great-grandfather).

Roger resisted his original impulse, which had been to say, "It's not what you think." It wasn't, but there weren't any plausible alternatives to suggest.

William Buccleigh launches himself at Roger, chasing him into the water. As he readies himself to lunge, there is a deep boom of cannon—the battle has begun.

Jamie and his militia are compelled to fight—reluctant as many of them are to fire on friends or neighbors. Jamie himself fires deliberately to miss, though he does run down and capture a man. Joe Hobson, one of the original Hillsborough rioters, is killed, mostly by mistake, and Claire, helped by Brianna, is busy treating the wounded in the aftermath of the short, chaotic battle.

Meanwhile, Roger is overpowered by William Buccleigh MacKenzie and one of Buccleigh's friends, who tie and gag him. They give him up to the governor, claiming that he is one James MacQuiston, a known Regulator.

Tryon, intending to quash the Regulation once and for all, makes a stern example, pardoning some of the apparent leaders but hanging another dozen outright. Claire is working with the wounded when Morag Gunn arrives, missing one shoe and breathless, and blurts out Roger's name, followed by, *"Hang . . . they . . . they are . . . hanging him! Gov-ner!"*

They are.

He dangled, kicking, and heard a far-off rumble from the crowd. He kicked and bucked, feet pawing empty air, hands clawing at his throat. Chest strained, back arched, and his sight had gone black, small lightnings flickering in the corners of his eyes. He reached for God and heard no plea for mercy deep within himself but only the shriek of no! *that echoed in his bones.*

And then the stubborn impulse left him and he felt his body stretch and loosen, reaching, reaching for the earth. A cool wind embraced him and he felt the soothing warmth of his body's voidings. A brilliant light blazed up behind his eyes, and he heard nothing more but the bursting of his heart and the distant cries of an orphaned child.

Jamie and the others arrive at the site of the hanging—too late. Bodies hang from the tree, all apparently lifeless. Jamie goes at once to take Roger's body, uncaring what the governor may do about it, and, seizing Roger, orders Brianna to cut him down. As Bree does so, though, Jamie realizes with shock that Roger is still alive—though his throat is so mangled by the rope that he won't be for more than a few moments longer.

Claire leaps into action and, by performing an emergency cricothrotomy with her scalpel, succeeds in saving Roger's life.

I must not stab too deeply. I felt the fibrous parting of skin and fascia, resistance, then the soft pop as the blade went in. There was a sudden loud gurgle, and a wet kind of whistling noise; the sound of air being sucked through blood. Roger's chest moved. I felt it, and it was only then that I realized my eyes were still shut.

Roger has survived being hanged and, very slowly, begins to recover. His voice, however, has been destroyed, and for months he is unable to talk. Brianna and Roger are houseguests of a prominent couple called the Sherstons, who engage Brianna to do a painting for them and go out of their way to give aid to Roger, who is famous as a result of his survival. Looking after him with fierce protectiveness mingled with fear, Brianna can only hope that her love, and the presence of Jemmy, will be enough to pull him out of his silent depression.

PART 7: *ALARMS OF STRUGGLE AND FLIGHT*

It is in fact Jemmy who causes Roger to speak—to save the little boy from being burned by a hot coffeepot.

"STOKH!" he roared.

It was a terrible cry, loud and harsh, but with a ghastly strangled quality to it, like a shout forced out around a fist shoved down his throat. It froze everyone in earshot—including Jemmy, who had abandoned the fireflies and stealthily returned to an investigation of the coffeepot. He stared up at his father, his hand six inches from the hot metal. Then his face crumpled, and he began to wail in fright.

In the aftermath of Alamance, Jamie confronts Governor Tryon over Roger's hanging, and in what is not quite an apology, Tryon gives Roger a land grant of five thousand acres. In hopes of giving Roger a sense of purpose—and time alone to heal—Jamie sends him out to survey both his new land and Jamie's; a good description of the land and a legal deed will be important to retaining or recovering the land, in the wake of the Revolution that Claire and the MacKenzies know is coming.

Roger takes the astrolabe sent by Lord John and goes out into the wilderness to survey. In the process, he meets with a band of runaway slaves living deep in the wood, who attack and take him prisoner. His life is saved by Fanny Beardsley, who is living with them—her lover (and her baby's father) being one of them. Roger returns home, sounder in mind, and with renewed appreciation for his family.

"You can talk," she said, wiping hastily at her eyes with the back of a wrist. "I mean—better." Once, she would have hesitated to touch his throat, fearful of his feelings, but instinct knew better than to waste the sudden intimacy of shock. The strain might come again, and they be strangers, but for a moment, for this moment in the dark, she could say anything, do anything, and she put her fingers on the warm ragged scar, touched the incision that had saved his life, a clean white line through the whiskers.

"Does it still hurt to talk?"

"It hurts," he said, in the faint croaking rasp, and his eyes met hers, dark and soft in the moonlight. "But I can. I will—Brianna."

She stepped back, one hand on his arm, unwilling to let go.

"Come in," she said. "It's cold out here."

Brianna is happy to have Roger back—but the burden of her dreaming returns; Stephen Bonnet haunts her. Roger, taking hold of himself and his position as protector of his family, becomes sure that he has to help Jamie find Bonnet—and kill him.

"Preacher's lad." That's what the other lads at school had called him, and that's what he was, with all the ambiguity the term implied. The initial urge to prove himself manly by means of force, the later awareness of the ultimate moral weakness of violence. But that was in another country—

He choked off the rest of the quotation, grimly bending to lever a chunk of rock free of moss and dirt. Orphaned by war, raised by a man of peace—how was he to set his mind to murder? He trundled the stone down toward the field, rolling it slowly end over end.

"You've never killed anything but fish," he muttered to himself. "What makes you

think . . ." But he knew all too well what made him think.

And so, knowing that his eyesight makes him uncertain with a pistol, he asks Jamie Fraser to teach him to fight with a sword.

Jamie and Roger are agreed about the need to remove Bonnet and begin to make their preparations. Jamie teaches Roger the rudiments of sword-fighting and takes him to buy a decent weapon. Leaving the smith's shop with the new sword, Roger encounters Dr. Fentiman, very drunk, and the doctor genially challenges him to a fight. *"A test of skill, sir?" The doctor whipped his sword to and fro, so the narrow blade sang as it cut the air. "First to pink his man, first to draw blood is the victor, what say you?"*

Roger has no choice but to accept and acquits himself creditably, though the fight is ended not by his skill but by the doctor's eagerness: *The doctor, sensing weakness, leapt forward, bellowing, blade pointed. Roger took a half-step sideways, and the doctor shot past, grazing the hock of the draft horse in his path.*

The horse emitted an outraged scream, and promptly sent swordsman and sword flying through the air, to crash against the front of the cobbler's shop. The doctor fell to ground like a crushed fly, surrounded by lasts and scattered shoes. Still, the fight has shown Roger something about himself and his own capabilities—and has shown the same things to Jamie. When Jamie asks Roger about the balance of the new sword, Roger replies, *"It will do."*

"Good," said Jamie. "So will you," he added casually, turning away to pay the smith.

PART 8: *A-HUNTING WE WILL GO*

Life doesn't stop for the making of war, and food is a necessity. Luckily, a small herd of buffalo (wood bison) has been spotted in the nearby mountains, and Jamie, with Roger, Fergus, and a few other men, set out hunting one bright morning.

There *are* buffalo, but while chasing the herd downhill, Jamie gets off a shot, then has the misfortune to step on a snake. Roger is nearby and rushes up just as Jamie kills the snake with the butt of his rifle. The other men had gone off to try to circle round the herd; Jamie and Roger are alone on the mountain, with night coming on—and Jamie has been bitten, his leg already beginning to swell.

Roger renders what first aid is possible, then settles down to build a fire, cook the snake, and lend what comfort he can, hoping that help will come in the morning. It's a long night, during which both men are faced with the stark fact that Jamie is very likely to die as his symptoms worsen. Jamie points out that if he does die, that will prove that history can be changed—for Roger and Brianna had found a news clipping in the future, stating that Jamie, Claire, and their family were all killed in a house fire—a fire that may or may not take place in three years.

An acerbic discussion regarding the philosophy of time travel, predestination, and choice takes place, during which Roger grapples with his fear of losing Jamie, realizes the depth of his love and respect for the man—and faces the even greater fear of being left to lead the family, the militia, and the Ridge by himself if Jamie dies.

Well aware of the gap he will leave, Jamie

takes pains to tell Roger everything he knows of the men on the Ridge, among the Indian villages, and the influential people of the colony. What to do, when to do it, how to manage.

"Tell Brianna I'm glad of her," Fraser whispered. "Give my sword to the bairn. . . ."

[Roger] waited as long as he thought he dared, the cold night creeping past in lonely minutes. Then leaned close, so Fraser could hear him.

"Claire?" he asked quietly. "Is there anything ye'd have me tell her?"

He thought he'd waited too long; Fraser lay motionless for several minutes. Then the big hand stirred, half-closing swollen fingers; the ghost of a motion, grasping after time that slipped away.

"Tell her . . . I meant it."

Jamie and Roger are found early the next day, and Jamie is taken home to the Ridge, where Claire is faced with treating an advanced case of rattlesnake bite, with concomitant infection—either of which may easily kill Jamie but won't do it quickly. While she's hastily making what preparations she can for treating his wounds, she sends Brianna out to look for maggots—and then sits down to look over her instruments, her heart cold in the knowledge that she may have no option but to amputate Jamie's leg, in spite of his insistence that he'd rather die.

Brianna is searching for maggots, but what shows up is somewhat larger—one of the buffalo the men were chasing days before has now wandered down the mountain and is in the yard of the house, where it looms over small Jemmy.

Swinging into mother-bear mode, Brianna rushes toward the beast and stuns it with an ax blow to the neck. This doesn't kill it, but Marsali, right behind, seizes a dyed petticoat hung on a bush to dry and flings it over the beast's head, blinding it. Claire, hearing the hullaballoo, rushes out of the house, amputation saw in hand, and, throwing herself on the beast, cuts its throat.

Brianna, backed up by Roger and Fergus, asserts her right to the kill and very competently oversees the butchering and distribution of the meat, while Claire tends Jamie. He asks to be taken up to his bed and for the windows to be left open, so that he can hear the festivities taking place outside over the buffalo's carcass. Then, as the night draws in, he asks Claire to come to bed with him, which she gingerly does.

She wakes in the night, alarmed by her physician's sense, realizing that Jamie is sinking and about to die. He asks her to touch him—and she does, with every bit of her healer's skill, and succeeds in drawing him back from the edge of death.

*"*You *bastard," I said, so relieved to feel the rise of his chest as he drew breath that my voice trembled. "You tried to die on me, didn't you?"*

His chest rose and fell, rose and fell, under my hand, and my own heart jerked and shuddered, as though I had been pulled back at the last moment from an unexpected precipice.

He blinked at me. His eyes were heavy, still clouded with fever.

"It didna take much effort, Sassenach," he said, his voice soft and husky from sleep. "Not dying was harder."

Claire, assisted by the Bugs, who bring her moldy garbage to be distilled into penicillin, and by Brianna, who devises a hypodermic syringe from a rattlesnake's fang, injects Jamie's leg in multiple places and succeeds against all odds in saving both his life *and* his leg.

With Jamie too ill to act as laird of the manor, Roger is called to greet a newcomer to the Ridge: another ex-Ardsmuir prisoner,

Tom Christie, who has come with his son and daughter to settle on the Ridge. Roger welcomes them and assigns them land, offering assistance with tools and building, then congratulates himself on handling things in Jamie's stead. Jamie, informed of this, is a little less enthusiastic. Tom Christie, he tells Claire, is a worthy man, though a stubborn one, and a Protestant. Beyond that . . . Jamie was compelled to kill a sadistic guard at Ardsmuir, strangling the man and throwing his body into the quarry there. There were only two witnesses to this: Duncan Innes and Tom Christie.

PART 9: *A DANGEROUS BUSINESS*

Returning to her medical practice on the Ridge, Claire is recording case notes in the book left by Dr. Daniel Rawlings, the original owner of her medical box. While doing so, she discovers Dr. Rawlings's notes of a visit to River Run Plantation and, within these notes, a clue suggesting that the doctor had heard of or seen the famous Frenchman's gold.

Jamie has for months been writing regularly to his sister and brother-in-law at Lallybroch, in Scotland. Ian, his brother-in-law, writes back cordially, but his sister has been silent—furious with him for his part in the loss of her youngest son, Young Ian. He is therefore surprised, though pleased, to get a letter from her, officially forgiving him.

> *. . . I see that it is cowardice indeed that I should go on blaming you for Young Ian. I have always kent what it is to love a man—be he husband or lover, brother or son. A dangerous business; that's what it is.*
>
> *Men go where they will, they do as they must; it is not a woman's part to bid them stay, nor yet to reproach them for being what they are—or for not coming back.*
>
> *I knew it when I sent Ian to France with a cross of birchwood and a lock of my hair made into a love knot, praying that he might come home to me, body and soul. I knew it when I gave you a rosary and saw you off to Leoch, hoping you would not forget Lallybroch or me. I knew it when Young Jamie swam to the seal's island, when Michael took ship for Paris, and I should have known it, too, when wee Ian went with you.*
>
> *But I have been blessed in my life; my men have always come back to me. Maimed, perhaps; a bit singed round the edges now and then; crippled, crumpled, tattered, and torn—but I have always got them back. I grew to expect that as my right, and I was wrong to do so.*

> *I have seen so many widows since the Rising. I cannot say why I thought I should be exempt from their suffering, why I alone should lose none of my men, and only one of my babes, my wee girl-child. And since I had lost Caitlin, I treasured Ian, for I knew he was the last babe I should bear.*
>
> *I thought him my babe still; I should have kent him for the man he was. And*

that being so, I know well enough that whether you might have stopped him or no, you would not—for you are one of the damnable creatures, too.

Now I have nearly reached the end of this sheet, and I think it profligate to begin another.

Mother loved you always, Jamie, and when she kent she was dying, she called for me, and bade me care for you. As though I could ever stop.

Your most Affectionate
and Loving Sister,
Janet Flora Arabella Fraser Murray

Jamie held the paper for a moment, then set it down, very gently. He sat with his head bent, propped on his hand so that I couldn't see his face. His fingers were splayed through his hair, and kept moving, massaging his forehead as he slowly shook his head, back and forth. I could hear him breathing, with a slight catch in his breath now and then.

Finally he dropped his hand and looked up at me, blinking. His face was deeply flushed, there were tears in his eyes, and he wore the most remarkable expression, in which bewilderment, fury, and laughter were all mingled, laughter being only slightly uppermost.

"Oh, God," he said. He sniffed, and wiped his eyes on the back of his hand. "Oh, Christ. How in hell does she do that?"

"Do what?" I pulled a clean handkerchief from my bodice and handed it to him.

"Make me feel as though I am eight years old," he said ruefully. "And an idiot, to boot."

He wiped his nose, then reached out a hand to touch the flattened roses, gently.

THE WEATHER THAWS into spring, and the Frasers and MacKenzies come down from their mountain once more, to do business in Wilmington. Jamie has heard no more from Mr. Lyon, and no further intrusions have disturbed River Run, but he is in hopes of learning more regarding the present whereabouts of Stephen Bonnet.

An ex-shipmate of Roger's, a Scot named Duff, proves to have such intelligence; he tells Roger and Jamie that Bonnet has a regular smuggling run, bringing in large loads of contraband every two weeks, on the coast between Virginia and Charleston. This argues a covert connection between Bonnet and someone in the Navy, because it would be hard for such a large operation to escape notice altogether.

Jamie leaves Duff with instructions to bring him any information that comes to hand regarding Bonnet's movements—and within a few days, such information is in hand. Roger and Jamie go together to a secluded landing, owned by Phillip Wylie, where Bonnet is expected to arrive with a load of contraband, intending there to meet and kill the man.

Instead of Stephen Bonnet, though, they discover a family of Russian immigrants, hiding in the sheds, they having arrived on a boat bringing Russian wild boar to stock Wylie's land for hunting and decided to stay. While they are interrogating the Russians, two boats arrive, filled with men who overcome the Russians and take control of the landing. But Stephen Bonnet isn't present; the invasive force is commanded by Sheriff Anstruther and magistrate Lillywhite, who have a pressing interest in Bonnet's contraband. They take Roger hostage, but Jamie hides on the roof of one of the sheds.

Jamie and Roger escape and, in so doing, meet Phillip Wylie, out spear hunting with several of his slaves. Wylie is incensed upon learning that his landing is being used for illicit purposes, and despite Jamie not being one of his favorite people, he at once agrees to help.

When they return to the landing, though, Anstruther and Lillywhite have taken a boat and disappeared. Heading back toward Wylie's house, Roger and Jamie are ambushed by Lillywhite and Anstruther, and in the mêlée, Roger accidentally kills Lillywhite. Jamie, much less accidentally, has already killed Anstruther. After Jamie and Roger pull themselves back together, Jamie speculates that Lillywhite and company have been trying to kill them at the behest of Stephen Bonnet—who plainly knows by this time that Jamie is after him and unlikely to be dissuaded from pursuit by anything short of death. He wonders aloud where Bonnet is just now, only to find that Roger has the answer.

"Wilmington."

Jamie swung round, frowning at him.

"What?"

"Wilmington," Roger repeated. He cautiously opened the other eye, but it seemed all right. Only one Jamie. "That's what Lillywhite said—but I thought he was joking."

Jamie stared at him for a moment.

"I hope to Christ he was," he said.

Jamie hopes Lillywhite was joking, because Wilmington is where the women are: Claire, Brianna, and Marsali, together with the children. The whole party is in fact out on the coastal flats near Wilmington, gathering wax myrtle berries for candle-making. Unfortunately, Lillywhite was *not* joking; Stephen Bonnet is in Wilmington, has heard about the presence of the Frasers, and follows the women, surprising Claire among the myrtle bushes.

"A homestead," he repeated, a muscle twitching in his cheek. "What business brings ye so far from home, and I might ask?"

"You might not," I said. "Or rather—you might ask my husband. He'll be along shortly."

I took another step backward as I said this, and he took a step toward me at the same time. A flicker of panic must have crossed my face, for he looked amused, and took another step.

"Oh, I doubt that, Mrs. Fraser dear. For see, the man's dead by now."

I squeezed Jemmy so hard that he let out a strangled squawk.

"What do you mean?" I demanded hoarsely. The blood was draining from my head, coagulating in an icy ball round my heart.

"Well, d'ye see, it was a bargain," he said, the look of amusement growing. "A division of duties, ye might say. My friend Lillywhite and the good sheriff were to attend to Mr. Fraser and Mr. MacKenzie, and Lieutenant Wolff was to manage Mrs. Cameron's end of the business. That left me with the pleasant task of makin' myself reacquainted with my son and his mother." His eyes sharpened, focusing on Jemmy.

"I don't know what you are talking about," I said, through stiff lips, taking a better grip on Jemmy, who was watching Bonnet, owl-eyed.

He gave a short laugh at that.

"Sure, and ye're no hand at lyin', ma'am; you'll forgive the observation. Ye'd never make a card player. Ye know well enough what I mean—ye saw me there, at River Run. Though I confess as how I should be obliged to hear exactly what you and Mr. Fraser was engaged in, a-butchering that Negro woman that Wolff killed. I did hear as how the picture of a murderer shows in the victim's eyes—but ye didn't seem to be looking at her eyes, from what I could see. Was it magic of a sort ye were after doing?"

"Wolff—it was him, then?" Just at the moment, I didn't really care whether Lieutenant Wolff had murdered scores of women, but I

was willing to engage in any line of conversation that offered the possibility of distracting him.

Distraction can't keep children quiet, though, and Bonnet ends up face-to-face with Brianna and Jem.

"He's not your son," Brianna said, low-voiced and vicious. "He'll never be yours."

He grunted contemptuously.

"Oh, aye? That's not how I heard it, in that dungeon in Cross Creek, sweetheart. And now I see him . . ." He looked at Jemmy again, nodding slowly. "He's mine, darlin' girl. He's the look of me—haven't ye, boyo?"

Jemmy buried his face in Brianna's skirts, howling.

Bonnet sighed, shrugged, and gave up any pretense of cajolement.

"Come on, then," he said, and started forward, obviously intending to scoop Jemmy up.

Brianna's hand rose out of her skirts, and aimed the pistol I had yanked out of his belt back at the place it had come from. Bonnet stopped in mid-step, mouth open.

"What about it?" she whispered, and her eyes were fixed, unblinking. "Do you keep your powder dry, Stephen?"

She braced the pistol with both hands, drew aim at his crotch, and fired.

BADLY WOUNDED BUT not dead, Bonnet flees, leaving the women to flee in the other direction, back to Wilmington, where they meet Roger and Jamie two days later, coming back from their expedition.

The party heads back toward the Ridge but stops at River Run Plantation, where they find matters in some disarray, Duncan suffering from a freshly broken leg. This injury was sustained during a fight with Lieutenant Wolff, who had come back for a fresh try. The lieutenant, though, suffered a fall and smacked his head on the walk. Whereupon . . .

"Ulysses killed him," Duncan said baldly, then stopped, as though appalled afresh. He swallowed, looking deeply unhappy. "Jo says as how she ordered him to do it—and Christ knows, Mac Dubh, *she might have done so. She's no the woman to be trifled with, let alone to have her servants murdered, herself threatened, and her husband set upon."*

I gathered from his hesitance, though, that some small doubt about Jocasta's part in this still lingered in his mind.

Jamie had grasped the main point troubling him, though.

"Christ," he said. "The man Ulysses will be hangit on the spot, or worse, if anyone hears of it. Whether my aunt ordered it, or no."

Duncan looked a little calmer, now that the truth was out. He nodded.

"Aye, that's it," he agreed. "I canna let him go to the gallows—but what am I to do about the Lieutenant? There's the Navy to be considered, to say nothing of sheriffs and magistrates."

That was a definite point. A good deal of the prosperity of River Run depended upon its naval contracts for timber and tar; Lieutenant Wolff had in fact been the naval liaison responsible for such contracts. I could see that His

Majesty's Navy might just possibly be inclined to look squiggle-eyed at a proprietor who had killed his local naval representative, no matter what the excuse.

Ulysses has prudently disappeared, leaving the Frasers and Duncan to consider how best to handle the lieutenant's death. Dispose of the body quietly, is the consensus, and after some discussion they decide to inter the lieutenant, at least temporarily, in Hector Cameron's mausoleum. In so doing, though, they make two shocking discoveries: one is the body of the late Dr. Rawlings, who presumably ran afoul of Ulysses while snooping round River Run and was killed. The other is Jocasta's coffin. Twin to Hector's, it is presumably awaiting receipt of its mistress's body—but the coffin is already full. The hiding place of the Frenchman's gold is a secret no more.

With the threats against them apparently ended, the Frasers and MacKenzies return to their home on the Ridge, to the settling of the new community, to tragedy (the death of Rosamund Lindsay, ironically killed by anaphylactic shock brought on by penicillin allergy), and to a surprising reunion.

Roger takes little Jem with him and Jamie on a small expedition into the woods. Things take a dangerous turn, though, when they meet with a wild boar, a huge feral pig that sees Jemmy as a tasty snack. The men fight off the boar but then hear the snarl and growl of a wolf, drawn by the scent of the injured pig's blood.

"WOLVES!" HE SHOUTED *to Jamie, and with a feeling that wolves on top of pigs was patently unfair, reached Jemmy, grabbed the knife, and threw himself on top of the boy.*

He pressed himself to the ground, feeling Jemmy squirm frantically under him, and waited, feeling strangely calm. Would it be tusk or tooth? he wondered.

"It's all right, Jem. Be still. It's all right, Daddy's got you." His forehead was pressed against the earth, Jem's head tucked in the hollow of his shoulder. He had one arm sheltering the little boy, the knife gripped in his other hand. He hunched his shoulders, feeling the back of his neck bare and vulnerable, but couldn't move to protect it.

He could hear the wolf now, howling and yipping to its companions. The boar was making an ungodly noise, a sort of long, continuous scream, and Jamie, too short of breath to go on shouting, seemed to be calling it names in brief, incoherent bursts of Gaelic.

There was an odd whirr overhead and a peculiar, hollow-sounding thump!, *succeeded by sudden and utter silence.*

Startled, Roger raised his head a few inches, and saw the pig standing a few feet before him, its jaw hanging open in what looked like sheer astonishment. Jamie was standing behind it, smeared from forehead to knee with blood-streaked mud, and wearing an identical expression.

Then the boar's front legs gave way and it fell to its knees. It wobbled, eyes glazing, and collapsed onto its side, the shaft of an arrow poking up, looking frail and inconsequential by comparison to the animal's bulk.

Jemmy was squirming and crying underneath him. He sat up slowly, and gathered the little boy up into his arms. He noticed, remotely, that his hands were shaking, but he felt curiously blank. The torn skin on his palms stung, and his knee was throbbing. Patting Jemmy's back in automatic comfort, he turned his head toward the wood and saw the Indian standing at the edge of the trees, bow in hand.

It occurred to him, dimly, to look for the wolf. It was nosing at the pig's carcass, no more than a few feet from Jamie, but his father-in-law was paying it no mind at all. He too was staring at the Indian.

"Ian," he said softly, and a look of incredulous joy blossomed slowly through the smears of mud, grass, and blood. "Oh, Christ. It's Ian."

The joy of Young Ian's return is not unalloyed. Lizzie Wemyss, once in love with Ian, is now betrothed to Manfred McGillivray but shows signs of wavering in her affections. Beyond that, Young Ian has brought with him the diary of Otter-Tooth, a Mohawk cast out of the tribe and killed some years before. The diary is written in Latin and makes it quite clear that Otter-Tooth was a time traveler; the diary is an account of his arrival in the past and his attempts to change history, with a number of companions, none of whom apparently survived the attempt.

Claire has a huge raw opal that once belonged to Otter-Tooth, given to her by Tewaktenyonh, one of the matriarchs of the Mohawk tribe that adoped Ian. She takes this down during the discussion, and in the course of the conversation, Jemmy takes the stone to play with.

I was opening my mouth to ask Ian about his wife, when I heard Jemmy. He had retired back under the table with his prize, and had been talking to it in a genially conversational—if unintelligible—manner for several minutes. His voice had suddenly changed, though, to a tone of alarm.

"Hot," he said, "Mummy, HOT!"

Brianna was already rising from her stool, a look of concern on her face, when I heard the noise. It was a high-pitched ringing sound, like the weird singing of a crystal goblet when you run a wet finger round and round the rim. Roger sat up straight, looking startled.

Brianna bent and snatched Jemmy out from under the table, and as she straightened with him, there was a sudden pow! *like a gunshot, and the ringing noise abruptly stopped.*

"Holy God," said Jamie, rather mildly under the circumstances.

Splinters of glimmering fire protruded from the bookshelf, the books, the walls, and the thick folds of Brianna's skirts. One had whizzed past Roger's head, barely nicking his ear; a thin trickle of blood was running down his neck, though he didn't seem to have noticed yet.

A stipple of brilliant pinpoints glinted on the table—a shower of the sharp needles had been thrust upward through the inch-thick wood. I heard Ian exclaim sharply, and bend to pull a tiny shaft from the flesh of his calf. Jemmy began to cry. Outside, Rollo the dog was barking furiously.

The opal had exploded.

Further cautious investigation makes it evident that Jemmy can indeed "hear" gemstones—and is likely therefore capable of time-travel, or may be when he's older.

This leads to a discussion of the possible genetics of Jem's inheritance—and to the re-

newed question of his paternity. Claire explains the nature of dominant and recessive genes and notes that Roger, for example, cannot roll his tongue. Neither can Brianna. Therefore, if Jemmy *can* . . . he must be Stephen Bonnet's son. An awkward silence ensues, broken by Jamie, who casually rolls his own tongue and asks Jem whether he can do that.

Roger looked up at Bree, and something seemed to pass through the air between them. He reached down and took hold of Jem's other hand, momentarily interrupting his song.

"So, a bhalaich, *can ye do it, then?"*

*"*FRÈRE *. . . do whats?"*

"Look at Grand-da." Roger nodded at Jamie, who took a deep breath and quickly put out his tongue, rolled into a cylinder.

"Can ye do that?" Roger asked.

"Chure." Jemmy beamed and put out his tongue. Flat. "Bleah!"

A collective sigh gusted through the room. Jemmy, oblivious, swung his legs up, his weight suspended momentarily from Roger's and Jamie's hands, then stomped his feet down on the floor again, recalling his original question.

"Grand-da gots balls?" he asked, pulling on the men's hands and tilting his head far back to look up at Jamie.

"Aye, lad, I have," Jamie said dryly. "But your Da's are bigger. Come on, then."

And to the sound of Jemmy's tuneless chanting, the men trundled him outside, hanging like a gibbon between them, his knees drawn up to his chin.

The next day, a small funeral ceremony takes place—for Otter-Tooth and his companions and for Dr. Rawlings, whose remains are buried now beneath a rowan tree on the Ridge.

It was nearly dark as we came down the narrow trail back to the house. I could see Brianna in front of me, though, leading the way; the men were a little behind us. The fireflies were out in great profusion, drifting through the trees, and lighting the grass near my feet. One of the little bugs lighted briefly in Brianna's hair and clung there for a moment, blinking.

A wood at twilight holds a deep hush, that bids the heart be still, the foot step lightly on the earth.

"Have ye thought, then, a cliamhuinn*?" Jamie said, behind me. His voice was low, the tone of it friendly enough—but the formal address made it clear that the question was seriously meant.*

"Of what?" Roger's voice was calm, hushed from the service, the rasp of it barely audible.

"Of what ye shall do—you and your family. Now that ye ken both that the wee lad can travel—and what it might mean, if ye stay."

What it might mean to them all. I drew breath, uneasy. War. Battle. Uncertainty, save for the certainty of danger. The danger of illness or accident, for Brianna and Jem. The danger of death in the toils of childbirth, if she was again with child. And for Roger—danger both of body and soul. His head had healed, but I saw the stillness at the back of his eyes, when he thought of Randall Lillywhite.

* * *

"Who knows? I know what's going on in England now—they are not ready, they've no notion of what they're risking here. If war were to break out suddenly, with little warning—if it had broken out, at Alamance—it might spread quickly. It might be over before the English had a clue what was happening. It might have saved years of warfare, thousands of lives."

"Or not," Jamie said dryly, and Roger laughed.

"Or not," he agreed. "But the point there is this; I think there are times for men of peace—and a time for men of blood, as well."

"Men of blood," Jamie repeated. "And I am one of those, ye think." It wasn't a question.

Brianna had reached the house, but turned and waited for the rest of us. She had been listening to the conversation, too.

"You are," Roger said. He looked up. Bright sparks flew from the chimney in a firework shower, lighting his face by their glow.

"Ye called me," he said at last, still looking up into the blazing dark. "At the Gathering, at the fire."

"Thig a seo, mac mo chinnich," *Jamie said quietly. "Aye, I did." Stand by my side, Roger the singer, son of Jeremiah.*

"Thig a seo, mac mo chinnich," *Roger said. "Stand by my side—son of my house. Did ye mean that?"*

"Ye know that I did."

"Then I mean it, too." He reached out and rested his hand on Jamie's shoulder, and I saw the knuckles whiten as he squeezed.

"I will stand by you. We will stay."

Beside me, Brianna let out the breath she had been holding, in a sigh like the twilight wind.

And later still, Claire and Jamie sit on the porch of their house, amid their family, their community, a temporary peace in the whirlwind of the coming war.

Jamie's hand still lay on mine. It tightened a little, and I glanced at him, but his eyes were still fixed somewhere past the dooryard; past the mountains, and the distant clouds. His grip tightened further, and I felt the edges of my ring press into my flesh.

"When the day shall come, that we do part," he said softly, and turned to look at me, "if my last words are not 'I love you'—ye'll ken it was because I didna have time."

THE END

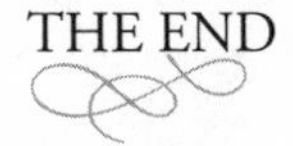

A Breath of Snow and Ashes

PART 1: *RUMORS OF WAR*

It is April of 1773, and Ian Murray is in the woods at night (accompanied by his dog, Rollo), engaged in an ongoing conversation with God, when he hears the sound of a number of men and horses, moving through the forest near him.

ELSEWHERE IN THE mountains, Jamie and Claire Fraser, their daughter, Brianna, and her husband, Roger, with other people from Fraser's Ridge, discover a remote cabin, apparently owned by Dutch settlers. The cabin has burned, but some of the inhabitants have not—they're dead of what appears to be poison. The Ridge people bury the dead, wondering what has happened.

RETURNING TO THE Ridge, the Frasers discover a visitor: one Major MacDonald, an involuntarily retired half-pay army officer, who comes bringing news of the colony's new governor, Josiah Martin, and his concerns about political unrest in the colony. Discussions of the recent news are interrupted by the sudden appearance of Rollo.

"Jesus H. Roosevelt Christ," I said. "Bloody Timmy's in the well!" I flew down the steps and ran for the path, barely registering the Major's startled oath behind me.

I found Ian a few hundred yards down the path, conscious, but groggy. He was sitting on the ground, eyes closed and both hands holding his head, as though to keep the bones of his skull from coming apart. He opened his eyes as I dropped to my knees beside him, and gave me an unfocused smile.

"Auntie," he said hoarsely. He seemed to want to say something else, but couldn't quite decide what; his mouth opened, but then simply hung that way, tongue moving thoughtfully to and fro.

"Look at me, Ian," I said, as calmly as possible. He did—that was good. It was too dark to see whether his pupils were unnaturally dilated, but even in the evening shadow of the pines that edged the trail, I could see the pallor of his face, and the dark trail of bloodstains down his shirt.

Ian thinks he's been shot by the men he heard in the wood, who fired at him—though upon close inspection, it appears that he's been struck in the head by a falling branch dislodged by a shot. Still, the fact that a band of violent men is abroad is a matter of concern.

ROGER AND BRIANNA return to their own cabin but feel uneasy. Their son, Jemmy, isn't there, having gone with Lizzie and her father, Mr. Wemyss, to an engagement party for Manfred's sister Senga. Impulsively, Roger and Brianna decide to walk the five miles to the McGillivrays', to get their son.

AT THE BIG House, Major MacDonald has stories that he's heard of young women and children kidnapped and sold to brothels, but he has a more pressing reason for his visit—he's brought Jamie news of a group of Scottish immigrants, fisher-folk from Thurso. Jamie needs tenants to settle his land, and the governor wants the backcountry settled; the immigrants have nowhere to go. So . . . ? Jamie is dubious, knowing the expense involved in settling new tenants and having no personal ties to the Thurso folk—but agrees. In further conversation, the major talks about the Committees of Safety that are springing up in the colony, impromptu assemblages of men who band together as substitute for the growing absence of law and law enforcement.

Inviting Jamie to set up a Committee of Safety meant that he would call upon those men who had served under him in the militia—but would commit the government to nothing, in terms of paying or equipping them—and the Governor would be clear of any responsibility for their actions, since a Committee of Safety was not an official body.

The danger to Jamie—and all of us—in accepting such a proposal, though . . . that was considerable.

Young Ian and Jamie converse about the coming war. Roger and Bree set out to retrieve Jemmy and are mistakenly attacked by the Beardsley twins, young men who are following Lizzie to protect her.

Roger tightened his grip on her arm in reflex.

"Whatever d'ye mean by that?"

"Just that if I were Manfred McGillivray, I'd take good care to be nice to Lizzie. Mama says the Beardsleys follow her around like dogs, but they don't. They follow her like tame wolves."

"I thought Ian said it wasn't possible to tame wolves."

"It isn't," she said tersely. "Come on, let's hurry, before they smoor the fire."

The engagement party is in full roar when the MacKenzies arrive, and they are made welcome. Ute McGillivray, Robin's German wife, is a warm and hospitable woman—but also one with a formidable personality and a determination to make good matches for her children. Her matchmaking extends also to Mr. Wemyss, whom she has introduced to the elderly Fraulein Berrisch, sister of a local pastor.

Jemmy, briefly reunited with his parents, goes off with his slightly older friend, Germain, son of Jamie's foster son and stepdaughter, Fergus and Marsali. Roger and Brianna relax in the hay with each other, only to be surprised by the eventual return of Jemmy, dead drunk on cherry bounce. The presence of a snoring three-year-old does not noticeably impair the sense of clandestine romance that permeates the party.

BACK AT THE Big House, Major MacDonald's real news is that Jamie is invited to become an Indian agent for the Southern Department. The job is to visit the nearby Indian villages and make sure they remain on good terms with—and amenable to advice from—the Indians' good friend King George. Claire and Jamie discuss this and segue from playful comment about Indian agents to seriousness and recollection of the Dutch settlers.

"The men came," he said softly, to the beams overhead. "He fought them, and they killed him there, on his own threshold. And when she saw her man was gone I think she told the men she must feed the weans first, before . . . and then she put toadstools into the stew, and fed it to the bairns and her mother. She took the two men with them, but I think it was that *that was the accident. She only meant to follow him. She wouldna leave him there, alone."*

I wanted to tell him that this was a rather dramatic interpretation of what we had seen. But I couldn't very well tell him he was wrong. Hearing him describe what he saw in thought, I saw it, too, all too clearly.

"You don't know," I said at last, softly. "You can't know." Unless you find the other men, *I thought suddenly,* and ask them. *I didn't say that, though.*

Neither of us spoke for a bit. I could tell that he was still thinking, but the quicksand of sleep was once more pulling me down, clinging and seductive.

"What if I canna keep ye safe?" he whispered at last. His head moved suddenly on the pillow, turning toward me. "You and the rest of them? I shall try wi' all my strength, Sassenach, and I dinna mind if I die doing it, but what if I should die too soon—and fail?"

And what answer was there to that?

"You won't," I whispered back. He sighed, and bent his head, so his forehead rested against mine. I could smell eggs and whisky, warm on his breath.

"I'll try not," he said, and I put my mouth on his, soft against mine, acknowledgment and comfort in the dark.

I laid my head against the curve of his shoulder, wrapped a hand round his arm, and breathed in the smell of his skin, smoke and salt, as though he had been cured in the fire.

"You smell like a smoked ham," I murmured, and he made a low sound of amusement and wedged his hand into its accustomed spot, clasped between my thighs.

I let go then, at last, and let the heavy sands of sleep engulf me. Perhaps he said it, as I fell into darkness, or perhaps I only dreamt it. "If I die," he whispered in the dark, "dinna follow me. The bairns will need ye. Stay for them. I can wait."

PART 2: *A GATHERING OF SHADOWS*

A letter comes from Lord John Grey, saying that his son, William, has returned to England to complete his education. He gives his (British) view of the recent Boston Massacre, mentioning that he has employed Bobby Higgins, the soldier who brought the letter. Bobby was convicted of manslaughter for his role in the massacre and branded on the cheek with an "M" for "murderer." Lord John thinks Higgins has been treated unjustly and mentions that he suffers from an indisposition, which he hopes Claire might be able to help.

EXAMINING BOBBY HIGGINS, Claire discovers that, among other things, he suffers severely from hemorrhoids, and she tells Jamie that she is doubtless unduly suspicious but wonders whether Lord John's motives in wanting Bobby to be treated are entirely altruistic. Jamie tells her that she *is* unduly suspicious and then tells her that when Lord John told him he would take William to raise, he—Jamie—had offered himself to Lord John, apparently in gratitude. But he tells her also why.

"Ye canna be so close to another," he said finally. "To be within each other, to smell their sweat, and rub the hairs of your body with theirs and see nothing of their soul. Or if ye can do that . . ." He hesitated, and I wondered whether he thought of Black Jack Randall, or of Laoghaire, the woman he had married, thinking me dead. "Well . . . that is a dreadful thing in itself," he finished softly, and his hand dropped away.

Claire repairs Bobby's hemorrhoids.

No man is really at his best with someone else's hand up his arse. I had noticed this before, and Robert Higgins was no exception to the general rule.

"Now, this won't hurt much at all," I said as soothingly as possible. "All you need to do is to keep quite still."

"Oh, I s'all do that, Mum, indeed I will," he assured me fervently.

But in the midst of the operation, Richard and Lionel Brown come to call and go to talk to Jamie. Bobby's run-in with the Browns' mule results in a nasty bite, which causes him to faint. Lizzie faints in turn from malaria, from which she suffers chronically, and Claire is out of Jesuit bark but makes gallberry syrup as a substitute.

The Browns have formed a Committee of Safety and want to arrest (and probably execute) Bobby Higgins as a murderer, to demonstrate their effectiveness. Jamie declines to allow them to take Bobby and decides to be an Indian agent, because if he doesn't, Richard Brown surely will.

JAMIE GOES TO ask Roger what he knows about the oncoming Revolution, in detail.

He'd rather bury the old privy pit or castrate pigs than go and ask Roger Mac what he kent about Indians and revolutions. He found it mildly gruesome to discuss the future with his son-in-law, and tried never to do it.

The things Claire told him of her own time seemed often fantastic, with the enjoyable half-real sense of faery tales, and sometimes macabre, but always interesting, for what he learned of his wife from the telling. Brianna tended to share with him small, homely details of machinery, which were interesting, or wild stories of men walking on the moon, which were immensely entertaining, but no threat to his peace of mind.

Roger Mac, though, had a cold-blooded way of talking that reminded him to an uncomfortable degree of the works of the historians he'd read, and had therefore a sense of concrete doom about it. Talking to Roger Mac made it seem all too likely that this, that, or the other frightful happenstance was not only indeed going *to happen—but would most likely have direct and personal consequences.*

It was like talking to a particularly evil-minded fortune-teller, he thought; one you hadn't paid enough to hear something pleasant. The thought made a sudden memory pop up on the surface of his mind, bobbing like a fishing cork.

The memory in question is of an old fortune-teller he'd met in Paris as a young student. The old woman told him, "You'll die nine times before you rest in your grave," and her words come back to him now, leaving him wondering, as he climbs toward Roger, just how many lives he has left.

CLAIRE SHOWS BOBBY the malaria parasites in Lizzie's blood and diagnoses Bobby with hookworms.

Bobby eyed me apprehensively.

"It's not exactly as I'm horrible shy, mum," he said, shifting gingerly. "You know that. But Dr. Potts did give me great huge clysters of mustard water. Surely that would ha' burnt they worms right out? If I was a worm, I s'ould let go and give up the ghost at once, did anyone souse me with mustard water."

"Well, you would think so, wouldn't you?" I said. "Unfortunately not. But I won't give you an enema," I assured him. "We need to see whether you truly do have the worms, to begin with, and if so, there's a medicine I can mix up for you that will poison them directly."

"Oh." He looked a little happier at that. "How d'ye mean to see, then, mum?" He glanced narrowly at the counter, where the assortment of clamps and suture jars were still laid out.

"Couldn't be simpler," I assured him. "I do a process called fecal sedimentation to concentrate the stool, then look for the eggs under the microscope."

He nodded, plainly not following. I smiled kindly at him.

"All you have to do, Bobby, is shit."

His face was a study in doubt and apprehension.

"If it's all the same to you, mum," he said, "I think I'll keep the worms."

LORD JOHN SENDS a present of white phosphorus to Brianna.

"And you intend to do . . . what *with it?" he asked, trying to keep any note of foreboding from his voice. He had the vaguest memories of hearing about the properties of phosphorus in his distant school days; he thought either it made you glow in the dark or it blew up. Neither prospect was reassuring.*

"Wellll . . . make matches. Maybe." Her upper teeth fastened momentarily in the flesh of her lower lip as she considered the jar. "I know how—in theory. But it might be a little tricky in practice."

"Why is that?" he asked warily.

"Well, it bursts into flame if you expose it to air," she explained. "That's why it's packed in water. Don't touch, Jem! It's poisonous." Grabbing Jemmy round the middle, she pulled him down from the table, where he had been eyeing the jar with greedy curiosity.

"Oh, well, why worry about that? It will explode in his face before he has a chance to get it in his mouth." Roger picked up the jar for safekeeping, holding it as though it might go off in his hands. He wanted to ask whether she were insane, but had been married long enough to know the price of injudicious rhetorical questions.

Jamie arrives to ask Roger to go to Cross Creek and collect the new tenants, with Arch Bug and Tom Christie—Tom Christie because Arch Bug is a Catholic, while the new tenants are all Protestants and fairly fierce about it.

Roger rubbed his chin, trying to think how to explain two centuries of Scottish religious intolerance in any way that would make sense to an American of the twentieth century. "Ahh . . . ye recall the civil-rights thing in the States, integration in the South, all that?"

"Of course I do." She narrowed her eyes at him. "Okay. So, which side are the Negroes?"

"The what?" Jamie looked entirely baffled. "Where do Negroes come into the matter?"

"Not quite that simple," Roger assured her. "Just an indication of the depth of feeling involved. Let us say that the notion of having a Catholic landlord is likely to cause our new tenants severe qualms—and vice versa?" he asked, glancing at Jamie.

CLAIRE IS EXHAUSTED from treating Bobby's hookworms and nursing Lizzie, who keeps throwing up the gallberry syrup. Claire finally tries rubbing the gallberry syrup mixed with goose grease into her skin. Jamie tells Claire about the "you'll die nine times" prophecy, and they disagree about how many lives he's got left.

"You're a very hard person to kill, I think," I said. "That's a great comfort to me."

He smiled, reluctant, but then reached out and lifted his glass in salute, touching it first to his own lips, then to mine.

"We'll drink to that, Sassenach, shall we?"

JAMIE, WITH IAN, visits a Cherokee village and talks to the leader of the band (which occupies several villages), Bird-who-sings-in-the-morning. Bird wants guns, as all the Indians do.

Jamie is somewhat uneasy about taking Ian, in spite of the lad's facility with various Indian languages.

The Cherokee welcomed them both with respect, but Jamie had noticed at once a particular edge in their response to Ian. They perceived Ian to be Mohawk—and he made them wary. In all honesty, he himself sometimes thought there was some part of Ian that had not come back from Snaketown, and perhaps never would.

What is somewhat more disturbing to Jamie, though, is Bird's idea of hospitality, which causes him to send two nubile maidens to warm Jamie's bed.

"Madam!" he said, disengaging his mouth with difficulty. He seized the lady by the shoulders and rolled her off his body with enough force that she whooped with surprise, bare legs flying—Jesus, was she naked?

She was. Both of them were; his eyes adapted to the faint glow of the embers, he caught the shimmer of light from shoulders, breasts, and rounded thighs.

He sat up, gathering furs and blankets round him in a sort of hasty redoubt.

"Cease, the two of you!" he said severely in Cherokee. "You are beautiful, but I cannot lie with you."

"No?" said one, sounding puzzled.

"Why not?" said the other.

"Ah . . . because there is an oath upon me," he said, necessity producing inspiration. "I have sworn . . . sworn . . ." He groped for the proper word, but didn't find it. Luckily, Ian leaped in at this point, with a stream of fluent Tsalagi, too fast to follow.

"Ooo," breathed one girl, impressed. Jamie felt a distinct qualm.

"What in God's name did ye tell them, Ian?"

"I told them the Great Spirit came to ye in a dream, Uncle, and told ye that ye mustn't go with a woman until ye'd brought guns to all the Tsalagi."

"Until I what?!"

"Well, it was the best I could think of in a hurry, Uncle," Ian said defensively.

AT JAMIE'S REQUEST, Roger has gone with Arch Bug and Tom Christie to collect the new tenants and has brought them as far as River Run, where he talks to Duncan about them.

"Ready to go, are they?" Duncan nodded toward the meadow, where the smoke of campfires hung in a low golden haze.

"Ready as they'll ever be. Poor things," Roger added, with some sympathy.

Duncan raised one shaggy brow.

"Fish out of water," Roger amplified, holding out his glass to accept the proffered refill. "The women are terrified, and so are the men, but they hide it better. Ye'd think I was taking them all to be slaves on a sugar plantation."

Duncan nodded.

"Or sell them to Rome to clean the Pope's shoon," he said wryly. "I misdoubt most of them had ever smelt a Catholic before embarking. And from the wrinkled noses, they dinna care so much for the scent now, I think. Do they so much as tak' a dram now and then, d'ye ken?"

"Only medicinally, and only if in actual danger of death, I think."

Jocasta arrives with her butler, Ulysses (whom she's got back after he fled the colony for killing Lieutenant Wolff). Ulysses has accompanied Jocasta shopping, along with Jocasta's body servant, Phaedre, and Jem. Phaedre takes Jem to bathe and put to bed but steps aside to speak privately with Roger—she tells him about the tall, light-haired man they met in Cross Creek, who showed an undue interest in little Jemmy.

Roger felt his bones strain in his flesh, urgent with desire to hunt and kill the man who had raped his wife, threatened his family. But there were seventy-six people depending on him—no, seventy-seven. Vengeance warred with responsibility—and most reluctantly, gave way.

He breathed slow and deep, feeling the knot of the rope scar tighten in his throat. No. He had to go, see the new tenants safe. The thought of sending them with Arch and Tom, while he remained behind to search for Bonnet, was tempting—but the job was his; he couldn't abandon it for the sake of a time-consuming—and likely futile—personal quest.

Nor could he leave Jem unprotected.

He must tell Duncan, though; Duncan could be trusted to take steps for the protection of River Run, to send word to the authorities in Cross Creek, to make inquiries.

And Roger would make sure that Jem was safe away, too, come morning, held before him on his saddle, kept in his sight every inch of the way to the sanctuary of the mountains.

"Who's your daddy?" he muttered, and a fresh surge of rage pulsed through his veins. "God damn it, I am, *you bastard!"*

PART 3: *TO EVERY THING THERE IS A SEASON*

Later in August, Claire tells Jamie about the state of the Ridge while he's been gone to the Cherokee villages. The new tenants arrived and were much taken aback by her, and vice versa. Grasshoppers got into the barley, causing Mrs. Bug and Claire to fire the field, which in turn caused the new tenants to regard their singed and reeking hostess with alarm.

JAMIE WRITES TO Lord John, telling him of his appointment as Indian agent, adding his contemplations of Committees of Safety and their possibilities for abuse of power and vigilantism, though the lack of law in the colony makes such committees seem attractive to the public. Jamie expresses wariness regarding the Browns of Brownsville and closes by mentioning that he's heard of an appearance by Stephen Bonnet, begging that Lord John advise him at once should he hear anything of the man.

"VROOM!"—

What I wonder is, these dreams I have about then—*they seem so vivid and detailed; more than the dreams I have about* now. *Why do I see things that don't exist anywhere except inside my brain?*

What I wonder about the dreams is—all the new inventions people think up—how many of those things are made by people like me—like us? How many "inventions" are really memories, of the things we once knew? And—how many of us are there?

So Brianna writes in the "dreambook" she keeps. Meanwhile, Roger is carving a toy for Jemmy, while listening to his wife contemplate aloud the project of getting hot running water to the house.

"Whatsit, Daddy, what's it?" Jemmy had recaptured the toy and ran up to him, clutching it to his chest.

"It's a . . . a . . ." he began, helpless. It was in fact a crude replica of a Morris Minor, but even the word "car," let alone "automobile," had no meaning here. And the internal combustion engine, with its pleasantly evocative noises, was at least a century away.

"I guess it's a vroom, honey," said Bree, a distinct tone of sympathy in her voice. He felt the gentle weight of her hand, resting on his head.

"Er . . . yeah, that's right," he said, and cleared a thickening in his throat. "It's a vroom."

"Broom," said Jemmy happily, and knelt to roll it down the hearth again. "Broom-broom!"

MAJOR MACDONALD RETURNS on the final day of haymaking and spots Bobby Higgins, with his "M" brand. He and Bobby warily observe and disapprove of each other. Bobby is exhibiting interest in Lizzie, and vice versa. Jamie blesses the gathering, and everyone gets more or less drunk.

Jamie sends Young Ian to distract Lizzie from Bobby. The men who have been haying—Jamie, Roger, most of the tenants—fall asleep with their beer in their hand, leaving Claire to talk to Major MacDonald, who tells her there have been other burnings of homesteads—he has a suspicion that some of the Cherokee might have been burning homesteads built over the Treaty Line.

The fireflies were coming out, drifting like cool green sparks in the shadows, and I looked upward involuntarily, to see a spray of red and yellow ones from the chimney. Whenever I thought of that gruesome clipping—and I tried not to, nor to count the days between now and January 21 of 1776—I had thought of the fire as occurring by accident. Such accidents were more than common, ranging from hearth fires run amok and candlesticks tipped over, to blazes caused by the summer lightning storms. It hadn't consciously occurred to me before that it might be a deliberate act—an act of murder.

I moved my foot enough to nudge Jamie. He stirred in his sleep, reached out one hand, and clasped it warmly round my ankle, then subsided with a contented groan.

"Stand between me and all things grisly," I said, half under my breath.

"Slàinte," said the Major, and drained his cup again.

PROPELLED BY MAJOR MacDonald's news, Jamie and Ian depart two days later for a visit to Bird-who-sings-in-the-morning, leaving Claire with Bobby Higgins for assistance. Bobby has brought several boxes from

Lord John, whose letter explains that he has sent not only the oil of vitriol that Claire asked for but also has managed the double-pelican retort.

Postscriptum: I have thus far restrained my sense of vulgar Curiosity, but I do venture to hope that on some future Occasion, you may possibly gratify me by explaining the Purpose to which you intend these Articles be put.

Claire unpacks with great excitement but is interrupted by Jamie and Ian's sudden return, with several Indians (some in need of medical treatment) following them.

"Duty calls," I said, a trifle breathless.

Jamie drew a deep breath of his own, squared his shoulders, and nodded.

"Well, I havena died of unrequited lust yet; I suppose I shallna do it now."

"Don't suppose you will," I said. "Besides, didn't you tell me once that abstinence makes . . . er . . . things . . . grow firmer?"

He gave me a bleak look.

"If it gets any firmer, I'll faint from a lack of blood to the heid. Dinna forget the eggs, Sassenach."

Claire deals with a broken tooth in an Indian woman, who says her family name is Wilson—much to the shocked displeasure of Hiram Crombie, leader of the Presbyterian fisher-folk, whose wife's family name is Wilson. Another Indian arrives sometime later, this one bearing a bundle on his shoulder—this containing a jumble of weathered bones, a hollow-eyed skull staring up from the midst of them.

These are the bones of the elderly man who owned the homestead that was burned inside the Treaty Line. The Indian says the man wasn't killed; he died of natural causes, and the Indian found his body. The Indian has brought it at Bird's request, in proof that the Indians didn't kill him (and, by extension, had nothing to do with the burning of the homestead). Bird also has a message for Jamie:

"Tsisqua says," he said, in the careful way of one who has memorized a speech in an unfamiliar tongue, "you re-mem-ber de guns." He nodded then decisively, and went.

Roger conducts a funeral for the owner of the bones. Afterward, Claire and Jamie find a little privacy, and he tells her the Scottish belief regarding the guardian of a graveyard:

"Did ye ken, Sassenach, that some folk believe the last person to lie in a graveyard becomes its guardian? He must stand on guard until the next person dies and comes to take his place—only then can he rest."

"I suppose our mysterious Ephraim might be rather surprised to find himself in such a position, when here he'd lain down under a tree all alone," I said, smiling a little. "But I do wonder: what is the guardian of a graveyard guarding—and from whom?"

He laughed at that.

"Oh . . . vandals, maybe; desecraters. Or charmers."

"Charmers?" I was surprised at that; I'd thought the word "charmer" synonymous with "healer."

"There are charms that call for bones, Sassenach," he said. "Or the ashes of a burnt body. Or soil from a grave." He spoke lightly enough, but with no sense of jesting. "Aye, even the dead may need defending."

"And who better to do it than a resident ghost?" I said. "Quite."

JAMIE LEADS HER to a secluded clearing where he has begun to fell logs—where the next house will stand, just in case there *is* anything to the newspaper clipping Brianna found in the future, stating that the Big House will burn, killing everyone in it.

They sit and talk about their family—

ought they insist that Roger and Bree and Jemmy all try to return through the stones, in order to escape the dangers of the coming war? This in turn leads to a discussion of their own relationship—for Claire will never think of leaving him.

"So what is *my most endearing trait?" I demanded.*

"Ye think I'm funny," he said, grinning.

"I . . . do . . . not . . ." I grunted, struggling madly. He merely lay on top of me, tranquilly oblivious to my pokings and thumpings, until I exhausted myself and lay gasping underneath him.

"And," he said thoughtfully, "ye like it verra much when I take ye to bed. No?"

"Er . . ." I wanted to contradict him, but honesty forbade. Besides, he bloody well knew I did.

"You are squashing me," I said with dignity. "Kindly get off."

"No?" he repeated, not moving.

"Yes! All right! Yes! Will you bloody get off*?!"*

He didn't get off, but bent his head and kissed me. I was close-lipped, determined not to give in, but he was determined, too, and if one came right down to it . . . the skin of his face was warm, the plush of his beard stubble softly scratchy, and his wide sweet mouth . . . My legs were open in abandon and he was solid between them, bare chest smelling of musk and sweat and sawdust caught in the wiry auburn hair. . . . I was still hot with struggling, but the grass was damp and cool around us. . . . Well, all right; another minute, and he could have me right there, if he cared to.

He felt me yield, and sighed, letting his own body slacken; he no longer held me prisoner, but simply held me. He lifted his head then, and cupped my face with one hand.

"D'ye want to know what it is, really?" he asked, and I could see from the dark blue of his eyes that he meant it. I nodded, mute.

"Above all creatures on this earth," he whispered, "you are faithful."

I thought of saying something about St. Bernard dogs, but there was such tenderness in his face that I said nothing, instead merely staring up at him, blinking against the green light that filtered through the needles overhead.

"Well," I said at last, with a deep sigh of my own, "so are you. Quite a good thing, really. Isn't it?"

Roger and Bree arrive for supper at the Big House, announcing that they have great news. By which they mean that Bree has succeeded in making workable Lucifer matches from Lord John's phosphorus, but before they can say that, Mrs. Bug leaps to the conclusion that Brianna is pregnant.

"You're wi' child again!" she cried, dropping a spoon in her excitement. She clapped her hands together, inflating like a birthday balloon. "Oh, the joy of it! And about time, too," she added, letting go her hands to wag a finger at Roger. "And here was me thinkin' as I should add a bit o' ginger and brimstone to your parritch, young man, so as to bring ye up to scratch! But ye kent your business weel enough in the end, I see. And you, a bhalaich, *what d'ye think? A bonny wee brother for ye!"*

Jemmy, thus addressed, stared up at her, mouth open.

"Er . . ." said Roger, flushing up.

"Or, of course, it might be a wee sister, I suppose," Mrs. Bug admitted. "But good news, good news, either way. Here, a luaidh, *have a sweetie on the strength of it, and the rest of us will drink to it!"*

Brianna is furious

"Sit down, darling," I said, in the tentative manner of one addressing a large explosive device. "You . . . um . . . had some news, you said?"

"Never mind!" She stood still, glaring. "Nobody cares, since I'm not pregnant. After all,

what else could I possibly do that anybody would think was worthwhile?" She shoved a violent hand through her hair, and encountering the ribbon tying it back, yanked this loose and flung it on the ground.

"Now, sweetheart . . ." Roger began. I could have told him this was a mistake; Frasers in a fury tended to pay no attention to honeyed words, being instead inclined to go for the throat of the nearest party unwary enough to speak to them.

"Don't you 'sweetheart' me!" she snapped, turning on him. "You think so, too! You think everything I do is a waste of time if it isn't washing clothes or cooking dinner or mending your effing socks! And you blame me for not getting pregnant, too; you think it's my fault! Well, it's NOT, and you know it!"

"No! I don't think that, I don't at all. Brianna, please . . ." He stretched out a hand to her, then thought better of the gesture and withdrew it, clearly feeling that she might take his hand off at the wrist.

Roger carries Bree out bodily, and the Frasers' subsequent discussion is interrupted by a knock on the door, which proves to be Thomas Christie, a bloodstained cloth wrapped round one hand.

Claire stitches up the gash, becoming aware as she does so of the oddly tense relations between Jamie and Tom, with small barbed comments from the latter. Claire notices that he has Dupuytren's contracture, a progressive clawing of the fingers on one hand, and urges him to let her operate on it. Jamie makes a number of small barbed comments in return, goading Christie with references to Jamie's own history of wounds, with the implication that it would be cowardly of Christie to avoid the surgery for fear of pain. This is too much for Christie, who agrees abruptly but gets in his own Parthian shot:

At the door, he paused, fumbling for the knob. Finding it, he drew himself up and turned back, looking for Jamie.

"At least," he said, breathing so hard that he stumbled over the words, "at least it will be an honorable scar. Won't it, Mac Dubh*?"*

Jamie straightened up abruptly, but Christie was already out, stamping down the corridor with a step heavy enough to rattle the pewter plates on the kitchen shelf.

"Why, ye wee pissant!" he said, in a tone somewhere between anger and astonishment. His left hand clenched involuntarily into a fist, and I thought it a good thing that Christie had made such a rapid exit.

This, Jamie explains, was a reference to the scars of flogging on his back; Christie had, of course, seen them at Ardsmuir. Claire inquires as to just why Jamie *wants* Tom Christie as a tenant, given their evident animosity.

"You aren't afraid of Tom Christie, are you?" I demanded.

He blinked, astonished, then laughed.

"Christ, no. What makes ye think that, Sassenach?"

"Well . . . the way the two of you act sometimes. It's like wild sheep, butting heads to see who's stronger."

"Oh, that." He waved a hand, dismissive. "I've a harder head by far than Tom, and he kens it well enough. But he's no going to give in and follow me round like a yearling lamb, either."

"Oh? But what do you think you're doing, then? You weren't just torturing him to prove you could, were you?"

"No," he said, and smiled faintly at me. "A man stubborn enough to speak English to Hieland men in prison for eight years is a man stubborn enough to fight beside me for the next eight years; that's what I think. It would be good if he were sure of it, himself, though."

I drew a deep breath and sighed, shaking my head.

"I do not *understand men."*

That made him chuckle, deep in his chest.

"Yes, ye do, Sassenach. Ye only wish ye didn't."

MEANWHILE, ROGER AND Bree have made up their differences.

Roger moved a little, and groaned.

"I think ye broke my leg."

"Did not," said his wife, calmer now, but still disposed to argument. "But I'll kiss it for you, if you want."

"That'd be nice."

Tremendous rustlings of the corn-shuck mattress ensued as she clambered into position to execute this treatment, ending with a naked Brianna straddling his chest, and leaving him with a view that caused him to wish they'd taken time to light the candle.

She was in fact kissing his shins, which tickled. Given the circumstances, though, he was inclined to put up with it. He reached up with both hands. Lacking light, Braille would do.

TOM CHRISTIE SENDS his daughter, Malva, for the ointment for his hand, and Malva shows great interest in Claire's surgery, her instruments and materials. She examines Dr. Rawlings's casebook with fascination.

She dimpled at me suddenly, gray eyes sparkling. "I'll tell him I've had a keek at your black book, and it's no by way of being spells in it, at all, but only receipts for teas and purges. I'll maybe not say about the drawings, though," she added.

"Spells?" I asked incredulously. "Is that what he thought?"

"Oh, aye," she assured me. "He warned me not to touch it, for fear of ensorcellment."

"Ensorcellment," I murmured, bemused. Well, Thomas Christie was a schoolmaster, after all. In fact, he might have been right, I thought; Malva glanced back at the book as I went with her to the door, obvious fascination on her face.

CLAIRE SUCCEEDS IN making ether. She wants to use it on Tom Christie but is cautious—both about the ether and about Tom. Visiting the Bugs' homestead, she overhears Jamie talking to Arch Bug about Christie—who had come to ask Arch whether it hurt a great deal when he lost the first two fingers of his right hand. She hears the story of just how he *did* lose his fingers—cut off by the Frasers of Glenhelm when they caught him, as a young man, trespassing on their lands.

When Claire goes to take the stitches out of Tom Christie's hand, he announces that he's changed his mind; he thinks the contracture of his right hand is God's will, and it would be wrong to seek to change it.

I suppressed the strong urge to say "Stuff and nonsense!" but with great difficulty.

"Sit down," I said, taking a deep breath. "And tell me, if you would, just why you think God wants you to go about with a twisted hand?"

He did glance at me then, surprised and flustered.

"Why . . . it is not my place to question the Lord's ways!"

"Oh, isn't it?" I said mildly. "I rather thought that's what you were doing last Sunday. Or wasn't it you I heard, inquiring as to what the Lord thought He was about, letting all these Catholics flourish like the green bay tree?"

The dull red color darkened substantially.

There is a rather spirited discussion of religion, God's will, and the nature of St. Paul's opinions on women, ending with Claire accusing Christie of cowardice.

"The truth of it is," I said severely, pointing a finger at him, "you're afraid."

"I am not!"

"Yes, you are." I got to my feet, replaced the workbasket on the table, and shoved the rag delicately over the puddle of milk with my foot. "You're afraid that I'll hurt you—but I won't," I assured him. "I have a medicine called ether; it will make you go to sleep, and you won't feel anything."

He blinked at that.

"And perhaps you're afraid that you'll lose a few fingers, or what use of your hand you have."

He was still kneeling on the hearth, staring up at me.

"I can't absolutely guarantee that you won't," I said. "I don't think *that will happen—but man proposes, and God disposes, doesn't He?"*

He reluctantly capitulates.

"All right," he said at last, hoarsely. He pulled his hand away from mine, not abruptly, but almost with reluctance, and stood cradling it in his sound one. "When?"

"Tomorrow," I said, "if the weather is good. I'll need good light," I explained, seeing the startled look in his eyes. "Come in the morning, but don't eat breakfast."

Claire wonders to Jamie the next day whether Tom will really come—but he does. Only to announce that he has changed his mind again, though—he will *not* allow her to use her foul potion (ether) on him. He will, however, let her mend his hand.

Jamie settles the impasse, lending Tom his support, his whisky, and his small Bible, holding his attention to various bits of Scripture while Claire works.

Jamie still held the bound arm tight, but had his other hand on Christie's shoulder, his own head bent near Christie's; his eyes, too, were closed, as he whispered the words.

"Yea, though I walk through the valley of the shadow of death, I will fear no evil . . ."

I knotted the last suture, clipped the thread, and in the same movement, cut through the linen bindings with my scissors, and let go the breath I'd been holding. The men's voices stopped abruptly.

I lifted the hand, wrapped a fresh dressing tightly around it, and pressed the clawed fingers gently back, straightening them.

Christie's eyes opened, slowly. His pupils were huge and dark behind his lenses, as he blinked at his hand. I smiled at him, and patted it.

"Surely goodness and mercy shall follow me all the days of my life," *I said softly.* "And I shall dwell in the house of the Lord forever."

Claire insists that Christie stay at the Big House overnight and goes up before bed to check the state of his wound; he criticizes her hair.

"Your hair." I looked up to see him staring at me, mouth curved downward in disapproval. "It's . . ." He made a vague movement round his own clipped poll. "It's . . ."

I raised my brows at him.

"There's a great deal of it," he ended, rather feebly.

She gives him wine, and a little the worse

for drink, he reveals his envy of Jamie's courage, even as he disparages him as a Catholic and a barbarian.

My personal barbarian was asleep, but woke, catlike, when I crawled into bed. He stretched out an arm and gathered me into himself with a sleepily interrogative "mmmm?"

I nestled against him, tight muscles beginning to relax automatically into his warmth.

"Mmmm."

"Ah. And how's our wee Tom, then?" He leaned back a little and his big hands came down on my trapezius, kneading the knots from my neck and shoulders.

"Oh. Oh. Obnoxious, prickly, censorious, and very drunk. Otherwise, fine."

They discuss Alex MacGregor's Bible—the small book belonging to a dead prisoner from Ardsmuir. Claire wakes from sleep a little later to find Jamie waking from a dream of Ardsmuir.

"In the dark . . ." he whispered at last, "there at Ardsmuir, we lay in the dark. Sometimes there was a moon, or starlight, but even then, ye couldna see anything on the floor where we lay. It was naught but black—but ye could hear."

Hear the breathing of the forty men in the cell, and the shuffles and shifts of their movement. Snores, coughing, the sounds of restless sleep—and the small furtive sounds from those who lay awake.

"It would be weeks, and we wouldna think of it." His voice was coming easier now. "We were always starved, cold. Worn to the bone. Ye dinna think much, then; only of how to put one foot in front of another, lift another stone . . . ye dinna really want *to think, ken? And it's easy enough not to. For a time."*

. . . "Did any of them ever . . . touch you?" I asked tentatively.

"No. None of them would ever think to touch me," he said very softly. "I was their chief. They loved me—but they wouldna think, ever, to touch me."

He took a deep, ragged breath.

"And did you want them to?" I whispered. I could feel my own pulse begin to throb in my fingertips, against his skin.

"I hungered for it," he said, so softly I could barely hear him, close as I was. "More than food. More than sleep—though I wished most desperately for sleep, and not only for the sake of tiredness. For when I slept, sometimes I saw ye.

"But it wasna the longing for a woman—though Christ knows, that was bad enough. It was only—I wanted the touch of a hand. Only that."

His skin had ached with need, 'til he felt it must grow transparent, and the raw soreness of his heart be seen in his chest.

He made a small rueful sound, not quite a laugh.

"Ye ken those pictures of the Sacred Heart—the same as we saw in Paris?"

I knew them—Renaissance paintings, the vividness of stained glass glowing in the aisles of Notre Dame. The Man of Sorrows, his heart exposed and pierced, radiant with love.

"I remembered that. And I thought to myself that whoever saw that vision of Our Lord was likely a verra lonely man himself, to have understood so well."

I lifted my hand and laid it on the small

hollow in the center of his chest, very lightly. The sheet was thrown back, and his skin was cool.

He closed his eyes, sighing, and clasped my hand, hard.

"The thought of that would come to me sometimes, and I would think I kent what Jesus must feel like there—so wanting, and no one to touch Him."

JAMIE AND ROGER head for the Cherokee villages, Jamie intending to introduce Roger, as he may need to know the Indians. Roger tells Jamie that Hiram Crombie has decided he must go and preach to the Cherokee, which Jamie considers funny, though seeing the potential for complications. The conversation is interrupted, though, by the smell of burning.

They find a homestead, freshly burned, two bodies hanging from a tree outside, with a notice accusing them of being Regulators. But Jamie is more concerned with what's *not* there—the children who belong to the homestead. They call through the woods, but the children are gone. Almost.

Roger thought it was a rock at first, half-hidden in the leaves that had drifted against the scorched cabin wall. He touched it, and it moved, bringing him to his feet with a cry that would have done credit to any of the corbies.

Jamie reached him in seconds, in time to help dig the little girl out of the leaves and cinders.

"Hush, a muirninn, *hush," Jamie said urgently, though in fact the child was not crying. She was maybe eight, her clothes and hair burned away and her skin so blackened and cracked that she might have been made of stone indeed, save for her eyes.*

"Oh, God, oh, God." Roger kept saying it, under his breath, long after it became clear that if it was a prayer, it was long past answering.

The child is burned beyond help; they cannot even take her to Claire.

Then they looked at each other, acknowledging necessity. Jamie was pale, sweat beading on his upper lip among the bristles of red beard. He took a deep breath, steeling himself, and lifted his hands, offering.

"No," Roger said softly. "I'll do it." She was his; he could no more surrender her to another than he could have torn off an arm. He reached for the handkerchief, and Jamie put it into his hand, soot-stained, still damp.

He'd never thought of such a thing, and couldn't think now. He didn't need to; without hesitation, he cradled her close and put the handkerchief over her nose and mouth, then clamped his hand tight over the cloth, feeling the small bump of her nose caught snug between his thumb and index finger.

Wind stirred in the leaves above, and a rain of gold fell on them, whispering on his skin, brushing cool past his face. She would be cold, he thought, and wished to cover her, but had no hand to spare.

His other arm was round her, hand resting on her chest; he could feel the tiny heart be-

neath his fingers. It jumped, beat rapidly, skipped, beat twice more . . . and stopped. It quivered for a moment; he could feel it trying to find enough strength to beat one last time, and suffered the momentary illusion that it would not only do so, but would force its way through the fragile wall of her chest and into his hand in its urge to live.

But the moment passed, as did the illusion, and a great stillness came. Near at hand, a raven called.

They bury the child but are interrupted by the arrival of Richard and Lionel Brown with some of their men. There is a not-quite confrontation between the Browns and Jamie, but the Browns back down and ride away.

PART 4: *ABDUCTION*

Roger returns, anxious about his family but glad to be home and have them safe. He relaxes, listening to Brianna's explanations of her plans: she's dug a kiln to fire pottery, with the intent of making clay pipe segments to carry warm air to make a hypocaust, and to carry water to the house.

DISTURBED BY HEARING that Marsali has bruises on her arm, Claire heads up the trail to the malting shed, where Marsali is working, intending to have a private conversation.

What ought I to say? I wondered. A straightforward "Is Fergus beating you?" *I couldn't quite believe that, despite—or perhaps because of—an intimate knowledge of emergency rooms filled with the debris of domestic disputes.*

It wasn't that I thought Fergus incapable of violence; he'd seen—and experienced—any amount of it from an early age, and growing up among Highlanders in the middle of the Rising and its aftermath probably did not inculcate a young man with any deep regard for the virtues of peace. On the other hand, Jenny Murray had had a hand in his upbringing.

I tried and failed to imagine any man who had lived with Jamie's sister for more than a week ever lifting his hand to a woman. Besides, I knew by my own observations that Fergus was a very gentle father, and there was usually an easiness between him and Marsali that seemed—

She is surprised by Germain, who drops out of a tree along her path and accompanies her to the malting floor, where Marsali sends him home. Claire interrogates her about Fergus; Marsali heatedly denies that he has been abusing her and tells Claire that it was a mistake, that Fergus grabbed her wrist when she tried to brain him with a stick of wood. She goes on to tell Claire about her mother, Laoghaire, and Laoghaire's husband, who was violent toward her. Claire offers to shovel the heavy grain, to let Marsali rest, as she's very pregnant.

I attacked them with a will, realizing as I did so that I was trying very hard not to think of the story Marsali had told me. I didn't want to like Laoghaire—and I didn't. But I didn't want to feel sympathy for her, either, and that was proving harder to avoid.

It hadn't been an easy life for her, apparently. Well, nor had it been for anyone else living in the Highlands then, I thought, grunting as I flung a shovelful of grain to the side. Being a mother was not that easy anywhere—but it seemed she had made a good job of it.

I sneezed from the grain dust, paused to wipe my nose on my sleeve, then went back to shoveling.

It wasn't as though she had tried to steal Jamie from me, after all, I told myself, striving for compassion and high-minded objectivity. Rather the reverse, in fact—or at least she might well see it that way.

The edge of the shovel gritted hard against the floor as I scraped up the last of the grain. I sent the grain flying to the side, then used the flat of the blade to shove some of the new-turned grain into the empty corner, and smooth down the highest hillocks.

I knew all the reasons why he said he'd married her—and I believed him. However, the fact remained that the mention of her name conjured up assorted visions—starting with Jamie kissing her ardently in an alcove at Castle Leoch, and ending with him fumbling up her nightgown in the darkness of their marriage bed, hands warm and eager on her thighs—that made me snort like a grampus and feel the blood throb hotly in my temples.

Perhaps, I reflected, I was not really a very high-minded sort of person. Occasionally quite low-minded and grudge-bearing, in fact.

Claire doesn't get the opportunity to consider her grudges at leisure, for the women are interrupted by the arrival of a gang of mounted men, who demand whisky. Told that there is only one small keg available, they threaten the women and end by shoving Marsali, knocking her out against the shed, and striking Claire, who falls stunned to the ground, the clay firepot she had thrown at the men starting a small grass fire. Marsali looks dead, but Claire has no chance to check, for the men seize her and bundle her onto a horse.

Frightened but able to think, Claire does her best to create a trail for Jamie, leaving hairs from her head tangled in bushes and ripping small branches as they pass.

The leader of the men is a British deserter named Hodgepile, who escaped from a warehouse fire at Cross Creek three years before, where he was presumed dead. He is now leading this band of brigands, occupied in plundering the countryside, burning houses, robbing and killing as they go.

I knew beyond the shadow of a doubt that Jamie would come. My job was to survive until he did.

Chances look worse when the band meets with more men—among them, Lionel Brown of Brownsville, who Claire fears will kill her to avoid her giving him away. She is saved by a mulatto man named Tebbe, who seems superstitious about her, but her life is hanging by a thread—a thread that grows thinner when night falls, finding her bound to a tree, gagged and helpless.

She is attacked by one of the young men in the party, though not injured. She barely has time to recover from this assault, though, when a new threat emerges from the darkness.

Here he came, a stealthy rustling in the bushes. I gritted my teeth on the gag and looked up, but the shadowy form in front of me wasn't one of the young boys.

The only thought that came to mind when I realized who the new visitor was was, Jamie Fraser, you bastard, where *are* you?

The newcomer is Harley Boble, a one-time thief-taker and a man with a severe grudge against both Jamie and Claire. He beats Claire viciously, kicking and hitting her, breaking her nose before committing a foul indecency.

I was frozen. Somewhere in the back of my mind, the detached observer wondered aloud whether this was in fact the single most disgusting thing I had ever encountered. Well, no, it wasn't. Some of the things I had seen at L'Hôpital des Anges, to say nothing of Father Alexandre's death, or the Beardsleys' attic . . . the field hospital at Amiens . . . heavens, no, this wasn't even close.

I lay rigid, eyes shut, recalling various nasty

experiences of my past and wishing I were in fact in attendance at one of those events, instead of here.

He leaned over, seized my hair, and banged my head several times against the tree, wheezing as he did so.

"Show you . . ." he muttered, then dropped his hand and I heard shuffling noises as he staggered away.

When I finally opened my eyes again, I was alone.

When another of the men approaches her, she is close to strangling on the gag and her own blood and is perfectly willing to accept rape in return for release. The man does remove her gag, but what's on his mind isn't sex.

He was saying something, whispering urgently. I didn't care, couldn't listen. All I heard was the grateful wheeze of my own breathing, and the thump of my heart. Finally slowing from its frantic race to keep oxygen moving round my starved tissues, it pounded hard enough to shake my body.

Then a word or two got through to me, and I lifted my head, staring at him.

"Whad?" I said thickly. I coughed, shaking my head to try to clear it. It hurt very much. "What did you say?"

He was visible only as a ragged, lion-haired silhouette, bony-shouldered in the faint glow from the fire.

"I said," he whispered, leaning close, "does the name 'Ringo Starr' mean anything to you?"

THE YOUNG MAN, Donner, is indeed a time traveler—one of the party of would-be time travelers who attempted to change the past of the Indian tribes in America, but their expedition went awry when some of the travelers were killed in the attempt and others went to different time periods.

Donner is afraid of his present companions and their violence and intends to get away. Claire insists he take her with him, and he reluctantly agrees but leaves her bound for the time being.

There comes a point when the body has simply had enough. It snatches at sleep, no matter what menace the future may hold. I'd seen that happen: the Jacobite soldiers who slept in the ditches where they fell, the British pilots who slept in their planes while mechanics fueled them, only to leap to full alert again in time to take off. For that matter, women in long labor routinely sleep between contractions.

In the same manner, I slept.

That kind of sleep is neither deep nor peaceful, though. I came out of it with a hand across my mouth.

The fourth man was neither incompetent nor brutal. He was large and soft-bodied, and he had loved his dead wife. I knew that, because he wept into my hair, and called me by her name at the end. It was Martha.

THE NEXT TIME Claire awakes, it is to hear the sound of a drum.

It wasn't an Indian drum. I sat up, listening hard. It was a drum with a sound like a beating heart, slow and rhythmic, then trip-hammer fast, like the frantic surge of a hunted beast.

I could have told them that Indians never used drums as weapons; Celts did. It was the sound of a bodhran.

What next? I thought, a trifle hysterically, bagpipes*?*

It was Roger, certainly; only he could make a drum talk like that. It was Roger, and Jamie was nearby.

Jamie is indeed nearby, with his men. The drums stampede the brigands, and Jamie's men attack the fleeing robbers. Hodgepile comes to get Claire, intending to use her as a hostage, but Jamie reaches her at the same time. He breaks Hodgepile's neck and seizes Claire in his arms.

He was saying something else, urgently, but I couldn't manage to translate it. Energy pulsed through him, hot and violent, like the current in a live wire, and I vaguely realized that he was still almost berserk; he had no English.

Ian, Fergus, and even old Arch Bug have come to rescue Claire. When Arch asks if she will take her vengeance on the men who abducted her, Jamie answers:

"There is an oath upon her," he said to Arch, and I realized dimly that he was still speaking in Gaelic, though I understood him clearly. "She may not kill, save it is for mercy or her life. It is myself who kills for her."

"And I," said a tall figure behind him, softly. Ian.

Arch nodded understanding, though his face was still in darkness. Someone else was there beside him—Fergus. I knew him at once, but it took a moment's struggle for me to put a name to the streaked pale face and wiry figure.

"Madame," he said, and his voice was thin with shock. "Milady."

Then Jamie looked at me, and his own face changed, awareness coming back into his eyes. I saw his nostrils flare, as he caught the scent of sweat and semen on my clothes.

"Which of them?" he said. "How many?" He spoke in English now, and his voice was remarkably matter-of-fact, as it might be if he were inquiring as to the number of guests expected for dinner, and I found the simple tone of it steadying.

"I don't know," I said. "They—it was dark."

He nodded, squeezed my arm hard, and turned.

"Kill them all," he said to Fergus, his voice still calm.

ROGER COMES BACK to Brianna, shocked by the night's work—and by the fact that he joined in the killing. He tells her what happened on the way home—Claire setting her broken nose, washing alone by the water; Jamie asking him—with apparent normality—whether he would feel differently about Jem if he knew that Jem was not his, explaining that he meant to take Claire to bed—if she would; in case she might be pregnant, there would be doubt as to the paternity of the child. Then Jamie wrapped Claire in his plaid and took her home.

The men did not kill Lionel Brown, only because he had been injured in a fall and was helpless when they attacked the camp. Instead, they have brought him back to the Ridge and confided him to Mrs. Bug's care, as Claire plainly can't take care of him.

Brianna goes to her mother, only to be assured that Claire is "perfectly fine."

Bree narrowed her eyes at me.

"Sure you are," she said. "You look like you've been run over by a locomotive. Two *locomotives."*

"Yes," I said, and touched my split lip gingerly. "Well. Yes. Other than that, though . . ."

Bree washes Claire's hair and cleans her up.

"Thank you, darling; that was wonderful," I said, with complete sincerity. "All I want just now is sleep," I added, with somewhat less.

I was still terribly tired, but now completely wakeful. What I did want was . . . well, I didn't know quite what I did *want, but a general absence of solicitous company was on the list. Besides, I'd caught a glimpse of Roger earlier, bloodstained, white, and swaying with weariness; I wasn't the only victim of the recent unpleasantness.*

"Go home, lass," Jamie said softly. He swung the cloak from its peg and over her shoulders, patting her gently. "Feed your man. Take him to bed, and say a prayer for him. I'll mind your mother, aye?"

Jamie explains his intent, to which Claire—rather dazed—assents.

"You—you're sure?" I asked, putting down the syringe.

"No," he said. "I'm not." He took a deep breath then, and looked at me, his face uncertain in the wavering candlelight. "But I mean to try. I must."

I smoothed the linen night rail down over my punctured thigh, looking at him as I did it. He'd dropped all his masks long since; the doubt, the anger, and the fear were all there, etched plain in the desperate lines of his face. For once, I thought, my own countenance was less easy to read, masked behind its bruises.

Something soft brushed past my leg with a small mirp! *and I looked down to see that Adso had brought me a dead vole, no doubt by way of sympathy. I started to smile, felt my lip tingle, and then looked up at Jamie and let it split as I did smile, the taste of blood warm silver on my tongue.*

"Well . . . you've come whenever I've needed you; I rather think you'll do it this time, too."

He looked completely blank for an instant, not grasping the feeble joke. Then it struck him, and blood rushed to his face. His lip twitched, and twitched again, unable to decide between shock and laughter.

I thought he turned his back then to hide his face, but in fact, he had only turned to search the cupboard. He found what he was looking for, and turned round again with a bottle of my best muscat wine in his hand, shining dark. He held it to his body with his elbow, and took down another.

"Aye, I will," he said, reaching out his free hand to me. "But if ye think either one of us is going to do this sober, Sassenach, ye're verra much mistaken."

MEANWHILE, ROGER MAKES his own confession and receives his own absolution from Brianna. Back in the Big House . . .

Not the kitchen, still strewn with emotional wreckage. Not the surgery, with all its sharp-edged memories. Jamie hesitated, but then nodded toward the stair, raising one eyebrow. I nodded, and followed him up to our bedroom.

They drink wine, groping emotionally for each other, forming tentative connections, until at last:

"The worst of it is," I said, into his shirt, "that I knew them. *Each one of them. And I'll remember them. And feel guilty that they're dead, because of me."*

"No," he said softly, but very firmly. "They are dead because of me, *Sassenach. And because of their own wickedness. If there is guilt, let it rest upon them. Or on me."*

"Not on you alone," I said, my eyes still closed. It was dark in there, and soothing. I could hear my voice, distant but clear, and wondered dimly where the words were coming from. "You're blood of my blood, bone of my bone. You said so. What you do rests on me, as well."

"Then may your vow redeem me," he whispered.

He lifted me to my feet and gathered me to him, like a tailor gathering up a length of fragile, heavy silk—slowly, long-fingered, fold upon fold. He carried me then across the room, and laid me gently on the bed, in the light from the flickering fire.

HE'D MEANT TO be gentle. Very gentle. Had planned it with care, worrying each step of the long way home. She was broken; he must go canny, take his time. Be careful in gluing back her shattered bits.

And then he came to her and discovered that she wished no part of gentleness, of courting. She wished directness. Brevity and violence. If she was broken, she would slash him with her jagged edges, reckless as a drunkard with a shattered bottle.

For a moment, two moments, he struggled, trying to hold her close and kiss her tenderly. She squirmed like an eel in his arms, then rolled over him, wriggling and biting.

He'd thought to ease her—both of them—with the wine. He'd known she lost all sense of restraint when in drink; he simply hadn't realized what she was restraining, he thought grimly, trying to seize her without hurting.

He, of all people, should have known. Not fear or grief or pain—but rage.

She raked his back; he felt the scrape of broken nails, and thought dimly that was good—she'd fought. That was the last of his thought; his own fury took him then, rage and a lust that came on him like black thunder on a mountain, a cloud that hid all from him and him from all, so that kind familiarity was lost and he was alone, strange in darkness.

It might be her neck he grasped, or anyone's. The feel of small bones came to him, knobbled in the dark, and the screams of rabbits, killed in his hand. He rose up in a whirlwind, choked with dirt and the scourings of blood.

Wrath boiled and curdled in his balls, and he rode to her spurs. Let his lightning blaze and sear all trace of the intruder from her womb, and if it burnt them both to bone and ash—then let it be.

* * *

Eyes puffed and bruised, clouded like wild honey, inches from his own.

"How do you feel?" she asked softly.

"Terrible," he replied with complete honesty. He was hoarse, as though he had been screaming—God, perhaps he had been. Her mouth had bled again; there was a red smear on her chin, and the taste of metal from it in his own mouth.

He cleared his throat, wanting to look away from her eyes, but unable to do it. He rubbed a thumb over the smear of blood, clumsily erasing it.

"You?" he asked, and the words were like a rasp in his throat. "How do ye feel?"

She had drawn back a little at his touch, but her eyes were still fixed on his. He had the feeling that she was looking far beyond him, through him—but then the focus of her gaze came back, and she looked directly at him, for the first time since he had brought her home.

"Safe," she whispered, and closed her eyes. She took one huge breath and her body relaxed all at once, going limp and heavy like a dying hare.

He held her, both arms wrapped around her as though to save her from drowning, but felt her sink away all the same. He wished to call out to her not to go, not to leave him alone. She vanished into the depths of sleep, and he yearned after her, wishing her healed, fearing her flight, and bent his head, burying his face in her hair and her scent.

The wind banged the open shutters as it passed, and in the dark outside, one owl hooted and another answered, hiding from the rain.

Then he cried, soundless, muscles strained to aching that he might not shake with it, that she might not wake to know it. He wept to emptiness and ragged breath, the pillow wet beneath his face. Then lay exhausted beyond the thought of tiredness, too far from sleep even to recall what it was like. His only comfort was the small, so fragile weight that lay warm upon his heart, breathing.

Then her hands rose and rested on him, the tears cool on his face, congealing, the white of her clean as the silent snow that covers char and blood and breathes peace upon the world.

THE FRAGILE IMITATION of normality next day is disturbed by a discussion as to what to do with Lionel Brown. Jamie has not decided whether to kill him or not, and if not, what else might be done with him, with no effective law, courts, or jails to which to commit him?

Claire is distressed at the thought of further violence—but on the other hand . . . They discuss the fate of the other men, and she tells Jamie about Donner; there's a possibility that he left the camp before Jamie's attack.

Troubled in mind but not allowed to visit Brown—in case Jamie decides to kill him—Claire sits down to read *Tom Jones.* Her reading is disturbed by the arrival of Tom Christie, who is much more disturbed by sight of her battered face. Seeking to distract him, she asks him if he's ever read *Tom Jones* and, in the subsequent conversation, learns that he burned his wife's books. She redresses his hand.

He nodded thanks to me, and donned his hat, turning to go. Upon a moment's impulse, I asked, "Did you ever have the chance to apologize to your wife?"

That was a mistake. His face tightened into coldness and his eyes went flat as a snake's.

"No," he said shortly. I thought for a moment that he would put the book down and refuse to take it. But instead, he tightened his lips, tucked the volume more securely under his arm, and left, without further farewell.

JAMIE AND IAN interrogate Lionel Brown, who tries to throw all blame on the dead Hodgepile, not only for abducting Claire and hurting Marsali (who is not dead, by the way) but for the string of house-burnings and other abductions.

"How long?" I said, appalled. "How many?" Children, young men, young women, wrenched from their homes and sold cold-bloodedly into slavery. No one to follow. Even if they were somehow to escape eventually, there would be no place—no one—to return to.

Jamie sighed. He looked unutterably tired.

"Brown doesna ken," Ian said quietly. "He says . . . He says he'd nothing to do with it."

"Like bloody hell he hadn't," I said, a flash of fury momentarily eclipsing horror. "He was with *Hodgepile when they came here. He knew they meant to take the whisky. And he must have been with them before, when they—did other things."*

Jamie nodded.

"He claims he tried to stop them from taking you."

"He did," I said shortly. "And then he tried to make them kill me, to stop me telling you he'd been there. And then he bloody meant to

drown me himself! I don't suppose he told you that."

"No, he didn't." Ian exchanged a brief look with Jamie, and I saw some unspoken agreement pass between them. It occurred to me that I might possibly just have sealed Lionel Brown's fate. If so, I was not sure I felt guilty about it.

Come nightfall, Jamie asks Claire if she wants him to come to her bed—to sleep. She does, and all is well—but Jamie dreams, of Culloden. And Black Jack Randall.

MALVA CHRISTIE COMES next day to help Claire in the surgery and to learn, but their conversation is interrupted by a thumping and dragging on the porch. This proves to be Lionel Brown, in a state of panic, who has dragged himself from the Bugs' cabin, to beg Claire not to let Jamie kill him. Claire isn't sure whether Jamie intends that or not—and is even less sure what her own feelings are in the matter. She can't let him lie wounded on the porch, though, and carries him inside, where she administers minimal first aid.

Claire goes out to the well to splash water on her face and returns to find Mrs. Bug in the act of smothering Lionel Brown with a pillow. Claire tries to stop her but fails. Mrs. Bug is distraught, as well she might be, once Jamie finds out about it.

"O, woman, how have you dared to lay hands upon a man who was mine?" he asked, very softly, in Gaelic.

"Oh, sir," she whispered. She was afraid to look up; she cowered under her cap, her face almost invisible. "I—I didna mean to. Truly, sir!"

Jamie glanced at me.

"She smothered him," I repeated. "With a pillow."

"I think ye do not do such a thing without meaning it," he said, with an edge in his voice that could have sharpened knives. "What were ye about, a boirean-nach, *to do it?"*

The round shoulders began to quiver with fright.

"Oh, sir, oh, sir! I ken 'twas wrong—only . . . only it was the wicked tongue of him. All the time I had care of him, he'd cower and tremble, aye, when you or the young one came to speak to him, even Arch—but me—" She swallowed, the flesh of her face seeming suddenly loose. "I'm no but a woman, he could speak his mind to me, and he did. Threatening, sir, and cursing most awfully. He said—he said as how his brother would come, him and his men, to free him, and would slaughter us all in our blood and burn the houses over our heids." Her jowls trembled as she spoke, but she found the courage to look up and meet Jamie's eyes.

"I kent ye'd never let that happen, sir, and did my best to pay him no mind. And when he did get under my skin enough, I told him he'd be deid long before his brother heard where he was. But then the wicked wee cur escaped—and I'm sure I've no idea how 'twas done, for I'd have sworn he was in no condition even to rise from the bed, let alone come so far—but he did, and threw himself upon your wife's mercy, and she took him up—I would have dragged his evil carcass away myself, but she wouldna have it—" Here she darted a briefly resentful glance at me, but returned an imploring gaze to Jamie almost at once.

"And she took him to mend, sweet gracious lady that she is, sir—and I could see it in her face, that having tended him so, it was coming to her that she couldna bear to see him killed. And he saw it, too, the gobshite, and when she went out, he jeered at me, saying now he was safe, he'd fooled her into tending him and she'd never let him be killed, and directly he was free of the place, he'd have a score of men down

upon us like vengeance itself, and then . . ." She closed her eyes, swaying briefly, and pressed a hand to her chest.

"I couldn't help it, sir," she said, very simply. "I really couldn't."

ASIDE FROM THE delicate questions of morality involved, Lionel Brown's death puts Jamie in an awkward position with regard to Richard Brown and the rest of Brownsville, since they will naturally want vengeance for Lionel's death.

With a little thought and the assistance of the Cherokee chief, Bird, though, Jamie and Roger succeed in returning Lionel's body to Brownsville in a ceremonial fashion, first telling Richard about Hodgepile's intrusion and abduction of Claire, noting that he, Jamie, found Lionel in Hodgepile's company and took him captive but did not slay him. Lionel suffered severe injuries in a fall before his capture, Jamie says—with complete truth—adding that they treated his injuries, but he died.

Jamie let a moment of stunned silence pass, before continuing.

"We have brought him to you, so that you may bury him." He made a small gesture, and Ian, who had dismounted, cut the ropes that held the travois. He and the two Cherokee pulled it to the porch and left it lying in the rutted road, returning silently to their horses.

Jamie inclined his head sharply, and swung Gideon's head around. Bird followed him, pleasantly impassive as the Buddha. I didn't know whether he understood enough English to have followed Jamie's speech, but it didn't matter. He understood his role, and had carried it out perfectly.

The Browns might have had a profitable sideline in murder, theft, and slavery, but their chief income lay in trade with the Indians. By his presence at Jamie's side, Bird gave clear warning that the Cherokee regarded their relationship with the King of England and his agent as more important than trade with the Browns. Harm Jamie or his property again, and that profitable connection would be broken.

* * *

"Will this be the end of it?" I asked. My voice felt thin in the cold air, and I wasn't sure he'd heard me. But he did. He shook his head slightly.

"There is never an end to such things," he said quietly. "But we are alive. And that is good."

PART 5: *GREAT UNEXPECTATIONS*

Claire returns with Jamie, determined to resume her life and her medical practice. The opportunity to do so arises at once, when she goes to check on the pregnant Marsali and detects something wrong with the baby's position. Not sure what the problem is, she doesn't know quite how to proceed: Induction of labor? Emergency cesarean? She brings Marsali to the Big House and summons Fergus.

LUCKILY, MARSALI'S CERVIX has begun to dilate, and the baby's heartbeat has settled down, so Claire opts for the least-risky procedure and—with some help from Fergus—induces labor. The child is safely born and healthy—but a dwarf. Little Henri-Christian is a healthy little boy, but his effect is out of all proportion to his size. His father is completely demoralized, and the superstitious fisher-folk think—and say—that he is demon spawn. Ian, though, comes to visit Marsali and give her comfort—and, holding Henri-Christian, tells Marsali that he had a child, among the Mohawk.

"Believe me, cousin," he said, very softly, "your husband grieves. But he will come back." Then he rose and left, silent as an Indian.

CLAIRE FINDS FERGUS skulking in the barn and reproaches him; he tells her about his experiences in the brothel where he was born and the experiences of dwarves in the milieus of Paris.

"They'll . . . get used to him," I said, as bravely as I could. "People will see that he isn't a monster. It may take some time, but I promise you, they'll see."

"Will it? And if they let him live, what then will he do?" He rose to his feet quite suddenly. He stretched out his left arm, and with a jerk, freed the leather strip that held his hook. It fell with a soft thump into the straw, and left the narrow stump of his wrist bare, the pale skin creased with red from the tightness of the wrappings.

"Me, I cannot hunt, cannot do a proper man's work. I am fit for nothing but to pull the plow, like a mule!" His voice shook with anger and self-loathing. "If I cannot work as a man does, how shall a dwarf?"

"Fergus, it isn't—"

"I cannot keep my family! My wife must labor day and night to feed the children, must put herself in the way of scum and filth who misuse her, who— Even if I was in Paris, I am too old and crippled to whore!" He shook the stump at me, face convulsed, then whirled and swung his maimed arm, smashing it against the wall, over and over.

"Fergus!" I seized his other arm, but he jerked away.

"What work will he do?" he cried, tears streaming down his face. "How shall he live? Mon Dieu! Il est aussi inutile que moi!*"*

He bent and seized the hook from the ground, and hurled it as hard as he could at the limestone wall. It made a small chiming sound as it struck, and fell into the straw, startling the nanny and her kids.

Fergus was gone, the Dutch door left swinging. The goat called after him, a long maaaah! *of disapproval.*

I held on to the railing of the pen, feeling as though it was the only solid thing in a slowly tilting world. When I could, I bent and felt carefully in the straw until I touched the metal of the hook, still warm from Fergus's body. I drew it out and wiped bits of straw and manure carefully off it with my apron, still hearing Fergus's last words.

"My God! He is as useless as I am!"

BRIANNA IS SPINNING with Marsali, trying not to discuss Fergus or Henri-Christian, while Roger is playing Vroom with Jem and Germain, when a young boy named Aidan McCallum comes to tell Roger that his mother wants him to come drive out "a de'il what's got intae the milk."

The Presbyterians on the Ridge are beginning to call upon Roger more and more often for the small ceremonies of life—buryings and blessings—but exorcism is a little out of his line. Still, he comes and does drive the "de'il"—a large frog—out of the milk. He stays to comfort the hysterical widow McCallum—thus putting himself in bad odor with Brianna, who is more than annoyed that he seems to spend more time with every other woman on the Ridge than he does with his own wife. He retorts that perhaps he'd spend more time with her if he had any notion that she needed him.

SOME WEEKS LATER, Hiram Crombie comes at dawn to inform Roger that his wife's old mother has "passed" in the night and to ask him to come and say a word at the grave. All the Frasers go to the wake, which is conducted with great propriety, including a hired wailer and a sin-eater—a strange, outcast man from somewhere in the wood, whose amber eye and mangled face disturb Claire. But they don't disturb her nearly as much as does the corpse—for when she rests a hand on old Mrs. Wilson's abdomen, she discovers that the woman is, in fact, not dead.

Mrs. Wilson recovers sufficiently to berate her son-in-law for providing a cheap funeral, but, as Claire is aware, it's a brief reprieve; the woman is suffering from an abdominal aneurysm, which has begun to separate, thus causing a loss of blood pressure and evident death. When it dissects and bursts, death will be more than evident.

She looked . . . peaceful, was the only word. It was no surprise whatever to feel the pulse beneath my hand simply stop. Somewhere deeper, in my own depths, I felt the dizzying rush of the hemorrhage begin, a flooding warmth that pulled me into it, made black spots whirl before my eyes, and caused a ringing in my ears. I knew to all intents and purposes she had now died for good. I felt her go. And yet I heard her voice above the racket, very small but calm and clear.

"I forgive ye, Hiram," she said. "Ye've been a good lad."

PART 6: *ON THE MOUNTAIN*

It's March of 1774, and with the melting of snow comes Major MacDonald, a red-coated bird of ill omen. He's brought newspapers, with the text of letters from Governor Martin to all sorts of people, from ex-Governor Tryon to General Gage, asking for help. Martin is losing his grip on the colony—what little he had—and is considering the desperate step of arming the Indians. As Indian agent, Jamie will have to go to the Cherokee villages to assess their readiness to undertake a fight on behalf of Governor Martin—if matters go so far.

"I'm guessing that he isn't actually going to do that," I said, finding the blue ribbon I was looking for, "because if he had—does, I mean—the Revolution would have got going in North Carolina right now, rather than in Massachusetts or Philadelphia two years from now. But why on earth is he publishing these letters in the newspaper?"

Jamie laughed. He shook his head, pushing back the disheveled hair from his face.

"He's not. Evidently, the Governor's mail is being intercepted. He's no verra pleased about it, MacDonald says."

MEANWHILE, FERGUS IS showing a little more animation and is earning a little money, teaching French to Hiram Crombie. Hiram has decided that he is called to go and preach Christianity to the Cherokee.

And Roger is helping Brianna to dig out her kiln, when Jamie comes to chat. He asks Roger again whether he is sure about staying in the past—war is getting closer and more distinct by the day, and Jamie is reaching the point where he must sell one or more of the gemstones he has.

"They're yours to sell," he replied, cautious. "Why now, though? Are things difficult?"

Jamie gave him an exceedingly wry look.

"Difficult," he repeated. "Aye, ye could say that." And proceeded to lay out the situation succinctly.

The marauders had destroyed not only a season's whisky in the making, but also the malting shed, only now rebuilding. That meant no surplus of the lovely drink this year to sell or trade for necessities. There were thirty more tenant families on the Ridge to be mindful of, most of them struggling with a place and a profession that they could never have imagined, trying merely to keep alive long enough to learn how to stay that way.

"And then," Jamie added grimly, "there's MacDonald—speak o' the devil."

The Major himself had come out onto the stoop, his red coat bright in the morning sun. He was dressed for travel, Roger saw, booted and spurred, and wearing his wig, laced hat in hand.

"A flying visit, I see."

Jamie made a small, uncouth noise.

"Long enough to tell me I must try to arrange the purchase of thirty muskets, with shot and powder—at my own expense, mind—to be repaid by the Crown, eventually," he added, in a cynic tone that made it obvious how remote he considered this eventuality to be.

"Thirty muskets." Roger contemplated that, pursing his own lips in a soundless whistle. Jamie had not been able even to afford to replace the rifle he had given Bird for his help in the matter of Brownsville.

Jamie shrugged.

"And then there are wee matters like the dowry I've promised Lizzie Wemyss—she'll be wed this summer. And Marsali's mother, Laoghaire—" He glanced warily at Roger, unsure how much he might know regarding Laoghaire. More than Jamie would be comfortable knowing, Roger thought, and tactfully kept his face blank.

"I owe a bit to her, for maintenance. We can live, aye, with what we've got—but for the rest . . . I must sell land, or the stones. And I willna give up the land." His fingers drummed restlessly against his thigh, then stopped, as he raised his hand to wave to the Major, who had just spotted them across the clearing.

"I see. Well, then . . ." Plainly, it had to be done; it was foolish to sit on a fortune in gems, merely because they might one day be needed for a far-fetched and risky purpose. Still, the notion made Roger feel slightly hollow, like rappelling down a cliff and having someone cut your safety line.

Roger agrees that Jamie should send a gem or two with Bobby Higgins to Lord John in Virginia, as Lord John will make sure to get a good price. Their discussion is cut short, though, by the approach of Major MacDonald, full of breakfast and bonhomie but oblivious to the presence of the white sow, who has emerged from her den beneath the foundation of the house and is about to spot the major. The white sow is not the only danger.

"Pit!" Roger shouted, only the word came out in a strangled croak. Nonetheless, MacDonald seemed to hear him, for a bright red face turned in his direction, eyes bulging. It must have sounded like "Pig!" for the Major glanced back over his shoulder then to see the

sow trot faster, small pink eyes fixed on him with murderous intent.

The distraction proved nearly fatal, for the Major's spurs caught and tangled, and he sprawled headlong in the grass, losing his grip on the laced hat—which he had held throughout the chase—and sending it pinwheeling through the air.

Roger hesitated for an instant, but then ran back to help, with a smothered oath. He saw Jamie running back, too, spade held at the ready—though even a metal shovel seemed pitifully inadequate to deal with a five-hundred-pound hog.

MacDonald was already scrambling to his feet, though; before either of them could reach him, he took off running as though the devil himself were breathing on his coattails. Arms pumping and face set in puce determination, he ran for his life, bounding like a jackrabbit through the grass—and disappeared. One instant he was there, and the next he had vanished, as though by magic.

Jamie looked wide-eyed at Roger, then at the pig, who had stopped short on the far side of the kiln pit. Then, moving gingerly, one eye always on the pig, he sidled toward the pit, glancing sideways, as though afraid to see what lay at the bottom.

Roger moved to stand at Jamie's shoulder, looking down. Major MacDonald had fallen into the deeper hole at the end, where he lay curled up like a hedgehog, arms clasped protectively over his wig—which had remained in place by some miracle, though now much bespattered with dirt and bits of grass.

"MacDonald?" Jamie called down. "Are ye damaged, man?"

"Is she there?" quavered the Major, not emerging from his ball.

Roger glanced across the pit at the pig, now some distance away, snout down in the long grass.

"Er . . . aye, she is." To his surprise, his voice came easy, if a little hoarse. He cleared his throat and spoke a little louder. "Ye needna worry, though. She's busy eating your hat."

JAMIE GOES TO see Robin McGillivray, the gunsmith, who has been talking with Brianna about her designs for a gun, then walks back, pondering the dilemma before him: knowing what he knows, he *must* declare himself a Rebel sooner or later—but when? And how? And what will the Scots who are his tenants, and the Indians who know him as the agent of the King, do when he does?

On the way, he meets Brianna, who gives him something else to worry about, by telling him about the Trail of Tears and what's going to happen to the Cherokee—not immediately, but eventually.

CLAIRE HAS SUCCEEDED in producing ether but requires a guinea pig, and she persuades first Lizzie and then Bobby Higgins to lend their services. Malva, who is present, is astonished.

———

JAMIE VISITS THE Cherokee again, to arrange a ransom for some Indian captives, and in so doing meets "Scotchee," Alexander Cameron, a Highlander who has married into the Cherokee and who seeks him out. From Cameron, he learns that Mr. Henderson, one of the justices who was chased out of Hillsborough during the riot a few years before, has retired into private life and is arranging the purchase of a large tract of land from the Cherokee, well inside the Treaty Line.

Jamie gave Cameron an eye, apprehending at once the complexity of the situation. For the one thing, the lands in question lay far, far inside the Treaty Line. For Henderson to instigate such dealings was an indication—had any been needed—of just how feeble the grasp of the Crown had grown of late. Plainly, Henderson thought nothing of flouting his Majesty's treaty, and expected no interference with his affairs as a result of doing so.

That was one thing. For another, though—the Cherokee held land in common, as all the Indians did. Leaders could and did sell land to whites, without such legal niceties as clear title, but were still subject to the ex post facto *approval or disapproval of their people. Such approval would not affect the sale, which would be already accomplished, but could result in the fall of a leader, and in a good deal of trouble for the man who tried to take possession of land paid for in good faith—or what passed for good faith, in such dealings.*

"John Stuart [the superintendent of the Southern Department] knows of this, of course," Jamie said, and Cameron nodded, with a small air of complacency.

"Not officially, mind," he said.

DURING THE SMOKING and drinking and feasting later, stories of battles are told, and Jamie—rather to his surprise—tells the assembly a story of Culloden, of the MacAllister who killed six enemies with the tongue of a wagon. One of the Indians asks how many men Jamie killed in this battle, and he finds himself suddenly on the field at Culloden.

The smoke burned in his chest, behind his eyes, and for an instant he tasted the bitter smoke of cannon fire, not sweet tobacco. He saw—he saw*—Alistair MacAllister, dead at his feet among the red-clothed bodies, the side of his head crushed in and the round curve of his shoulder shining solid through the cloth of the shirt, so wetly did it cling to him.*

He was there, on the moor, the wet and cold no more than a shimmer on his skin, rain slick on his face, his own shirt sopping and steaming on him with the heat of his rage.

And then he no longer stood on Drumossie, and became aware a second too late of the indrawn breaths around him. He saw Robert Talltree's face, the wrinkles all turned up in astonishment, and only then looked down, to see all ten of his fingers flex and fold, and the four fingers of the right extend again, quite without his meaning it. The thumb wavered, indecisive. He watched this with fascination, then, coming finally to his wits, balled his right hand as well as he could and wrapped the left around it, as though to throttle the memory that had been thrust with such unnerving suddenness into the palm of his hand.

Very late, he seeks out Bird and attempts to tell him what Brianna has revealed to him, regarding the Cherokees' fate:

"The women of my family are . . ." He groped, not knowing the Cherokee word. "Those who see in dreams what is to come." He darted a look at Cameron, who appeared to take this in his stride, for he nodded, and closed his eyes to draw smoke into his lungs.

"Have they the Sight, then?" he asked, mildly interested.

Jamie nodded; it was as good an explanation as any.

"They have seen a thing concerning the Tsalagi. Both my wife and my daughter have seen this thing."

Bird's attention sharpened, hearing this. Dreams were important; for more than one person to share a dream was extraordinary, and therefore most important.

"It grieves me to tell you," Jamie said, and meant it. "Sixty years from this time, the Tsalagi will be taken from their lands, removed to a new place. Many will die on this journey, so that the path they tread will be called . . ." He groped for the word for "tears," did not find it, and ended, "the trail where they wept."

* * *

"This wife you have," Bird said at last, deeply contemplative, "did you pay a great deal for her?"

"She cost me almost everything I had," he said, with a wry tone that made the others laugh. "But worth it."

Very late indeed, Jamie goes to his guesthouse, only to find a woman waiting for him, as per Bird's usual joke. But this one isn't a naked young nubile lass.

The firelight showed him an elderly woman, her hair in grizzled plaits, her dress of white buckskin decorated with paint and porcupine quills. He recognized Calls-in-the-Forest, dressed in her best. Bird's sense of humor had finally got completely out of hand; he had sent Jamie his mother.

All grasp of Tsalagi deserted him. He opened his mouth, but merely gaped at her. She smiled, very slightly, and held out her hand.

"Come and lie down, Bear-Killer," she said. Her voice was kind and gruff. "I've come to comb the snakes from your hair."

CLAIRE IS WORKING in her garden when she receives an unexpected visitor—Manfred McGillivray. He has come to say that he can't marry Lizzie and to confess the reason: he has contracted syphilis from a whore with whom he was carrying on an affair in Hillsborough.

Claire is about to inject him with penicillin when he takes alarm at someone coming, dives through the window, and runs. The someone coming is Young Ian, carrying Lizzie in his arms, she having collapsed with another malarial attack. Ian helps Claire to rub gallberry ointment into Lizzie's skin, while listening to Claire's tale of Manfred's trouble, then carries Lizzie up to bed.

"If you would, please, Ian." I hesitated, and his eyes met mine, deep brown and soft with worry and the shadow of remembered pain. "She'll be all right," I said, trying to infuse a sense of certainty into the words.

"Aye, she will," he said firmly, and stooped to gather her up, tucking the blanket under her. "If I've anything to say about it."

MANFRED DOESN'T COME back. Ian does, with a blackened eye, skinned knuckles, and the terse report that Manfred had declared a set intention of hanging himself, and good riddance to the fornicating son of a bitch, and might his rotten bowels gush forth like Judas Iscariot's, the stinking, traitorous wee turd. Ian then stamps upstairs to stand silently over Lizzie's bed.

The news of her son's trouble reaches Ute McGillivray, who responds with fury, accusing Claire of blackening Manfred's name, and storms off, declaring that she will stop anyone from trading with the Frasers.

Both Lizzie and her father miss the McGillivrays—for the severing of Lizzie's engagement has also severed the Wemysses from the large, warm family and ruined Joseph's budding romance with Monika Berrisch.

Malva Christie, however, is fascinated by the affair—and by Claire's explanation of "good bugs" and "bad bugs."

OUT GATHERING ON the hillside, Claire happens to oversee the Christies' yard and sees Tom Christie take a bundle of switches to his daughter. Rather shocked by this, she tells Jamie, but he declines to get involved, saying that it is, after all, Tom's business, so long as he isn't damaging his daughter.

"WOODEARS"—DESPITE HIS dismissal of the matter, though, Jamie promises Claire that he will look into it and finds an opportunity to speak with Malva by herself a few days later.

He learns a few more puzzling things about the family background from Malva, causing him to wonder about Tom's wife—or wives.

LATER, BRIANNA IS digging a channel from the nearest stream, and Jamie comes to help her. In the process, they find the remains of a sinister little fire on a stone on the bank—one including what looks like charred finger bones, as well as herbs. Jamie recognizes it as a Highland charm but doesn't know who left it or what its purpose is.

Brianna has her suspicions. Her father says to leave it alone, it's a private business—but Roger had come home well after dark the night before, whistling a song he said Amy McCallum had taught him, and the song was called "The Deasil Charm."

Brianna goes to consult Mrs. Bug, who listens to her description of the charm and tells her it's a love charm, one called "the Venom o' the North Wind."

"There are easier ways to make a lad fall in love wi' ye, lass," she added, pointing a stubby finger at Brianna in admonition. "Cook him up a nice plate o' neeps boiled in milk and served wi' butter, for one."

"I'll remember," Brianna promised, smiling, and excused herself.

She had meant to go home; there were dozens of things needing to be done, from spinning yarn and weaving cloth, to plucking and drawing the half dozen dead geese she had shot and hung in the lean-to. But instead she found her footsteps turning up the hill, along the overgrown trail that led to the graveyard.

Surely it wasn't Amy McCallum who'd made that charm, she thought. It would have taken her hours to walk down the mountain from her cabin, and her with a small baby to tend. But babies could be carried. And no one would know whether she had left her cabin, save perhaps Aidan—and Aidan didn't talk to anyone but Roger, whom he worshipped.

The sun was nearly down, and the tiny cemetery had a melancholy look to it, long shadows from its sheltering trees slanting cold and dark across the needle-strewn ground and the small collection of crude markers, cairns, and wooden crosses. The pines and hemlocks murmured uneasily overhead in the rising breeze of evening.

The sense of cold had spread from her backbone, making a wide patch between her shoulder blades. Seeing the earth grubbed up beneath the wooden marker with "Ephraim" on it didn't help.

ROGER HAS ENCOUNTERED an awkward situation. He came unexpectedly across Bobby Higgins, locked in embrace with Malva Christie, whose reponse was swift: *"Tell my father*, she'd said, *and I'll tell everyone I've seen you kiss Amy McCallum."* Too late, he becomes aware of what people in the mountains are saying: *"Everybody kens ye spend more time up at the notch wi' the widow McCallum than ye do with your own wife."*

Clearly, his visits to the McCallums must cease, for Amy's sake as much as his own. Going to explain matters to her, though, he finds a crisis in progress—Aidan has fallen seriously ill.

In fact, Aidan is suffering from appendicitis and becomes Claire's first real patient—and first success—for the use of ether. Roger forces Malva to come and help with the operation, which she reluctantly does—but her father notes her absence and appears during the operation, which shocks him.

"Did ye just raise that child from the dead?" he asked. His voice was almost conversational, though his feathery brows arched high.

I wiped a hand across my mouth, still tasting the sickly sweetness of the ether.

"I suppose so," I said.

"Oh."

He stared at me, blank-faced. The room reeked of alcohol, and it seemed to sear my nasal lining. My eyes were watering a little; I wiped them on my apron. Finally, he nodded, as though to himself, and turned to go.

I had to see to Aidan and his mother. But I couldn't let him go without trying to mend things for Malva, so far as I could.

"Tom—Mr. Christie." I hurried after him, and caught him by the sleeve. He turned, surprised and frowning.

"Malva. It's my fault; I sent Roger to bring her. You won't—" I hesitated, but couldn't think of any tactful way to put it. "You won't punish her, will you?"

The frown deepened momentarily, then lifted. He shook his head, very slightly, and with a small bow, detached his sleeve from my hand.

"Your servant, Mrs. Fraser," he said quietly, and with a last glance at Aidan—presently demanding food—he left.

MEANWHILE, A FIGHT breaks out between Roger and Brianna.

"You'll help any woman but me," she said, opening her eyes. "Why is that?"

He gave her a long, hard look, and she wondered for an instant whether there was such a thing as a black emerald.

"Maybe I didn't think ye needed me," he said. And turning on his heel, he left.

ROGER AND JAMIE go fishing, and alone together in the peace of the water, Roger tells Jamie that he feels he has a calling—that he is meant to be a minister. Rather to Roger's surprise, Jamie is less disconcerted by the admission than is Roger himself.

"Ye want to take care of them," Jamie said softly, and it wasn't a question, but rather an acceptance.

Roger laughed a little, unhappily, and closed his eyes against the sparkle of the sun off the water.

"I don't want to do it," he said. "It's the last

thing I thought of, and me growing up in a minister's house. I mean, I ken what it's like. But someone has *to do it, and I am thinking it's me."*

In fact, Jamie is very practical about the matter, asking whether Roger needs to be ordained and how this might be managed.

"Have ye spoken to your wife about it?"

"No," he said, staring across the pool.

"Why not?" There was no tone of accusation in the question; more curiosity. Why, after all, should he have chosen to talk to his father-in-law first, rather than his wife?

Because you know what it is to be a man, he thought, and she doesn't. What he said, though, was another version of the truth.

"I don't want her to think me a coward."

* * *

The mountains and the green wood rose up mysterious and wild around them, and the hazy sky unfurled itself over the hollow like angel's wings, silent and sunlit. But not peaceful; never peace, not here.

"Do you believe us—Claire and Brianna and me—about the war that's coming?"

Jamie laughed shortly, gaze fixed on the water.

"I've eyes, man. It doesna take either prophet or witch to see it standing on the road."

"That," said Roger, giving him a curious look, "is a very odd way of putting it."

"Is it, so? Is that no what the Bible says?

When ye shall see the abomination of desolation, standing where it ought not, then let them in Judaea flee to the mountains?"

Let him who readeth understand. *Memory supplied the missing part of the verse, and Roger became aware, with a small sense of cold in the bone, that Jamie did indeed see it standing on the road, and recognized it. Nor was he using figures of speech; he was describing, precisely, what he saw—because he had seen it before.*

* * *

"Your wife," he said thoughtfully, rising and hitching the strap of the creel onto his shoulder.

"Aye?" Roger picked up the battered hat, bestrewn with flies, and gave it to him. Jamie nodded thanks, and set it on his head.

"She has eyes, too."

"M-I-C"—TO ROGER'S further surprise, Brianna not only doesn't think him a coward but also seems very supportive of his desire to become a minister.

"I'll help," she said firmly. "You tell me how, and I'll help."

* * *

They sat silent for a little, the fireflies drifting down like slow green rain, their silent mating song lighting the darkening grass and trees. Roger's face was fading as the light failed, though she still saw the line of his jaw, set in determination.

"I swear to ye, Bree," he said. "Whatever I'm called to now—and God knows what that is—I was called to be your husband first. Your husband and the father of your bairns above all things—and that I always shall be. Whatever I may do, it will not ever be at the price of my family, I promise you."

Jamie, with Germain and Jemmy, joins them in the dark. Roger takes charge of the little boys, and Brianna tells Jamie about Disneyland and the magic of being there with her family, in a place outside time.

"A giant rat?" he said, sounding slightly stunned. "And they take the weans to play with it?"

"Not a rat, a mouse," she corrected him. "And it's really a person dressed up like a mouse."

"Oh, aye?" he said, not sounding terribly reassured. . . .

"You know what?" she said, and he made a small interrogatory noise in reply.

"It was nice—it was great—but what I really, really loved about it was that when we were there, it was just the three of us, and everything was perfect. Mama wasn't worrying about her patients, Daddy wasn't working on a paper—they weren't ever silent or angry with each other. Both of them laughed—we all laughed, all the time . . . while we were there."

He made no reply, but tilted his head so it rested against hers. She sighed again, deeply.

"Jemmy won't get to go to Disneyland—but he'll have that. A family that laughs—and millions of little lights in the trees."

PART 7: *ROLLING DOWNHILL*

Jamie writes a letter to Lord John, explaining his need for money from the gems he has confided to his friend. He has a matter of business in hand, he writes, concerning the acquisition of a number of guns. He had hoped to arrange the matter through a friend but must now explore other arrangements.

Since Manfred McGillivray's defection and the estrangement of the McGillivray family, Jamie can't get the muskets he needs for the Cherokee from Robin McGillivray, so he is hoping that Lord John knows a useful smuggler.

Meanwhile, the Frasers are coming down from the mountain to attend a barbecue at River Run, held in honor of Flora MacDonald, heroine of the Rising, who has recently moved to the colony with her husband and family.

Perhaps, though, the guns are not going to make it into the Indians' hands. Jamie shows Claire a letter from John Ashe, another militia colonel, regarding the North Carolina Committee of Correspondence and the formation of the new Continental Congress.

Everyone who is anyone in the colony attends the barbecue—including Neil Forbes, the local lawyer who once paid court to Brianna and who now approaches Claire privately.

"I hear that your husband is collecting guns, Mrs. Fraser," he said, his voice at a low and rather unfriendly pitch.

"Oh, really?" I was holding an open fan, as was every other woman there. I waved it languidly before my nose, hiding most of my expression. "Who told you such a thing?"

"One of the gentlemen whom he approached to that end," Forbes said. The lawyer was large and somewhat overweight; the unhealthy shade of red in his cheeks might be due to that, rather than to displeasure. Then again . . .

"If I might impose so far upon your good nature, ma'am, I would suggest that you exert your influence upon him, so as to suggest that such a course is not the wisest?"

"To begin with," I said, taking a deep breath of hot, damp air, "just what course do you think he's embarked upon?"

"An unfortunate one, ma'am," he said. "Putting the best complexion upon the matter, I assume that the guns he seeks are intended to arm his own company of militia, which is legitimate, though disturbing; the desirability of that course would rest upon his later actions.

But his relations with the Cherokee are well known, and there are rumors about that the weapons are destined to end in the hands of the savages, to the end that they may turn upon His Majesty's subjects who presume to offer objection to the tyranny, abuse, and corruption so rife among the officials who govern—if so loose a word may be employed to describe their actions—this colony."

I gave him a long look over the edge of my fan.

"If I hadn't already known you were a lawyer," I remarked, "that speech would have done it. I think that you just said that you suspect my husband of wanting to give guns to the Indians, and you don't like that. On the other hand, if he's wanting to arm his own militia, that might be all right—providing that said militia acts according to your desires. Am I right?"

A flicker of amusement showed in his deep-set eyes, and he inclined his head toward me in acknowledgment.

"Your perception astounds me, ma'am," he said.

Major MacDonald, needless to say, does not share Mr. Forbes's opinions. He is acting as impresario for Mrs. MacDonald, whom he's encouraging to make speeches supporting the Crown all through the colony. Jamie is outwardly composed, but Claire senses his inner disturbance and asks about it.

"I kent I should have to stand one day against a good many of them, aye? To fight friends and kin. But then I found myself standing there, wi' Fionnaghal's hand upon my head like a blessing, face to face wi' them all, and watching her words fall upon them, see the resolve growing in them . . . and all of a sudden, it was as though a great blade had come down from heaven between them and me, to cleave us forever apart. The day is coming—and I cannot stop it."

All political undercurrents come to an abrupt halt when Jocasta appears, in the grip of shattering pain from her eye. Claire, who has already privately diagnosed the probable cause of Jocasta's blindness as glaucoma, intercedes, puncturing Jocasta's eyeball with a sterile needle, thus draining away some of the fluid exerting pressure on the optic nerve.

When Jocasta has recovered enough to speak, she tells Jamie that the man has come back for the gold. He entered her sitting room and told her that he meant to take the gold back to its rightful owner. She recognized his voice, and when he seized her wrist and twisted it, trying to terrorize her, she reached into her workbag, pulled out her small, very sharp embroidery knife, and went for his balls. She succeeded in wounding him slightly, and he fled.

The man was not Stephen Bonnet, though; he was the third man who had brought the gold ashore from France, many years before.

At Jocasta's behest, Ulysses takes Jamie and Claire to show them the hiding place where half of a gold ingot had been kept—and is now gone.

Roger has gone to discover the requirements for ordination. Jamie and Claire send the Bugs back to the Ridge but remain at River Run for a while, in case either the mysterious man or Stephen Bonnet should return. Brianna also remains, and she undertakes a painting commission for one of Jocasta's friends. Chatting with her cousin Ian, though, she shows him two miniatures she's painted secretly—of her parents. She coaxes Ian to let her sketch him, and he reluctantly consents, but the sitting is interrupted when they hear someone on the terrace, whistling "Yellow Submarine."

It's Donner, the time traveler from

Hodgepile's band. He's come in search of Claire, wanting her to tell him how to get back to his own time—and is intrigued to meet Brianna, who he rightly surmises is also a traveler.

I was shocked, but less so than I might have been. I had felt that Donner was alive. Hoped he was, in spite of everything. Still, seeing him face to face, sitting in Jocasta's morning room, struck me dumb. He was talking when I came in, but stopped when he saw me. He didn't stand up, naturally, nor yet offer any observations on my survival; just nodded at me, and resumed what he'd been saying.

"To stop whitey. Save our lands, save our people."

"But you came to the wrong time," Brianna pointed out. "You were too late."

Donner gave her a blank look.

"No, I didn't—1766, that's when I was supposed to come, and that's when I came." He pounded the heel of his hand violently against the side of his head. "Crap! What was wrong with me?"

"Congenital stupidity?" I suggested politely, having regained my voice. "That, or hallucinogenic drugs."

The blank look flickered a little, and Donner's mouth twitched.

"Oh. Yeah, man. There was some of that."

Donner tells them more about the group of time travelers he belonged to, but the conversation is interrupted by Ulysses, accompanied by an incensed gentleman who claims that Donner stole his purse. He did and is summarily marched off to the jail in Cross Creek.

Ian's opinion is that the authorities will hang Donner, and Jamie, arriving belatedly, shares both this opinion and approval of the notion. He is reluctantly persuaded, though, that either Claire or Brianna needs to speak to the man at least once more and agrees to talk to the jailer. In the meantime, though, he has news: Manfred McGillivray has been spotted, in a brothel. No one knows quite where the brothel is but somewhere in the vicinity.

Claire is inclined to find this hopeful but is less sure about Jamie's other news. A local printer named Simms is having trouble because of his political sympathies and wishes to sell. Jamie has it in mind to buy the shop and set Fergus up in the printing business, that being a respectable trade that can be managed with one hand.

"That's a brilliant idea!" I said. "Only . . . what would Fergus use for money to buy it?"

Jamie coughed and looked evasive.

"Aye, well. I imagine some sort of bargain might be struck. Particularly if Simms is anxious to sell up."

"All right," I said, resigned. "I don't suppose I want to know the gory details. But, Ian—" I turned to him, fixing him with a beady eye. "Far be it from me to offer you moral advice. But you are not—repeat, not—to be questioning whores in any deeply personal manner. Do I make myself clear?"

"Auntie!" he said, pretending shock. "The idea!" But a broad grin spread across his tattooed face.

"TAR AND FEATHERS"—The acquisition of Fogarty Simms's printshop is a little more eventful than Jamie expects it to be—featuring an attempt to tar-and-feather the original proprietor, the appearance of Isaiah Morton—and Isaiah Morton's first wife, the musket-wielding Jezebel Hatfield—and Claire's acquisition of a penis syringe from Dr. Fentiman's maid.

The end of the riot is a blizzard of feathers over the downtown area and a call on the local brothel by Claire, who wishes to administer penicillin to the local whores, and Jamie—who does not want to accompany her but has been obliged to come against his will.

"Sassenach," he said, and I turned to find him regarding me with a bloodshot glint.

"Yes?"

"Ye'll pay for this."

Roger returns to the Ridge, to be greeted with delight by Brianna. He explains that while he's met most of the qualifications for ordination and is provisionally a minister of the Word, he does have to wait for a Presbytery Session before he can be ordained.

PART 8: *THE CALL*

Roger begins to work doggedly on improving his voice, knowing that he needs to preach. His first sermon is attended by everyone on the Ridge—including Claire and Jamie, who heroically snatches up a wandering snake (in spite of his rather natural horror of snakes), in order to keep it from ruining Roger's first appearance as a minister.

Roger and Brianna both savor his triumph—but Roger dreams that night of the *bodhrana* talking and of the man he clubbed to death during Claire's rescue.

LORD JOHN WRITES to Jamie, apologizing for having inadvertently given his name to one Josiah Quincy, who has sent out a list of the North Carolina Committee of Correspondence, showing Jamie's name as one of the members. Lord John warns Jamie of the dangers of this and urges him to make sure that there are no other seditious documents that could incriminate him as a Rebel.

In other news, he reports that his (and Jamie's) son, William, has purchased a lieutenant's commission and will take up service with his regiment more or less at once. Moving to more delicate matters, he notes that Bobby Higgins has apparently formed an attachment to *two* young ladies on Fraser's Ridge, and he, Lord John, wishes to engage in the preliminary negotiations necessary to secure marriage with either Lizzie Wemyss or Malva Christie—Lord John to provide various inducements to further Bobby's suit.

Claire is amused—and a little concerned—at Bobby's involvement with the two girls, and their discussion leads to a contemplation of Joseph Wemyss's situation; since the rupture of his daughter's betrothal and their relations with the McGillivrays (and the loss of Fraulein Berrisch, sent away to a distant relative), Joseph has taken to his bed in depression. Talk of marriage leads further, to Jamie's observation on Roger and the widow McCallum:

"Have ye not seen the way the widow McCallum looks at him?"

"No," I said, taken aback. "Have you?"

He nodded.

"I have, and so has Brianna. She bides her time for the moment—but mark my words, Sassenach: if wee Roger does not see the widow safely marrit soon, he'll find hell nay hotter than his own hearth."

"Oh, now. Roger isn't looking back *at Mrs. McCallum, is he?" I demanded.*

"No, he is not," Jamie said judiciously, "and that's why he's still in possession of his balls."

Malva, who has been helping Claire with herbal preparations, appears at this point, putting a stop to such discussions, and Claire goes to feed the pig—the notorious white sow, who has her den under the foundation of the house—wondering as she does so about the relations between Malva and

Young Ian, for he also seems smitten by the young woman.

Jamie undertakes to transmit Bobby's offer to Mr. Wemyss but meets with obdurate refusal. Joseph Wemyss admits that Bobby seems a good young man but is afraid of the effect of his murderer's brand; if Bobby should lose his lordship's patronage, the people of the community might easily turn on him—and on his wife and family.

Jamie is compelled to transmit this bad news to Bobby, who is downcast but in the course of the conversation mentions that he supposes Jamie will be going to the meeting.

What meeting? Jamie asks. A meeting of the Committee of Correspondence—one that Jamie has not been informed of, despite his writing several letters of inquiry to men he knows on the committee.

"When I heard nothing, I wrote myself, to the six men I know personally within the Committee of Correspondence. No answer from any of them." His stiff finger tapped once against his leg, but he noticed, and stilled it.

"They don't trust you," I said, after a moment's silence.

ON THE TWENTIETH *of September, Roger preached a sermon on the text,* God hath chosen the weak things of the world to confound the things which are mighty. *On the twenty-first of September, one of those weak things set out to prove the point.*

The weak thing in question is a microbe. An amoeba, to be exact, which lives in one of the springs on the Ridge and which afflicts a number of its inhabitants with a virulent flux.

"A NOISOME PESTILENCE"—The flux spreads through the community, exhausting Claire and those helping her. She tells Jamie, in the light of one surreal dawn, what she knows of this kind of warfare.

"The year after I was born," I said, "there was a great epidemic of influenza. All over the world. People died in hundreds and thousands; whole villages disappeared in the space of a week. And then came the other, my war."

The words were quite unconscious, but hearing them, I felt the corner of my mouth twitch with irony. Jamie saw it and a faint smile touched his own lips. He knew what I meant—that odd sense of pride that comes of living through a terrible conflict, leaving one with a peculiar feeling of possession. His wrist turned, his fingers wrapping tight around my own.

"And she has never seen plague or war," he said, beginning to understand. "Never?" His voice held something odd. Nearly incomprehensible, to a man born a warrior, brought up to fight as soon as he could lift a sword; born to the idea that he must—he would—defend himself and his family by violence. An incomprehensible notion—but a rather wonderful one.

"Only as pictures. Films, I mean. Television." That one he would never understand, and I could not explain. The way in which such pictures focused on war itself; bombs and planes and submarines, and the thrilling urgency of blood shed on purpose; a sense of nobility in deliberate death.

He knew what battlefields were really like—battlefields, and what came after them.

"The men who fought in those wars—and the women—they didn't die of the killing, most of them. They died like this—" A lift of my mug toward the open window, toward the peaceful mountains, the distant hollow where Padraic MacNeill's cabin lay hidden. "They died of illness and neglect, because there wasn't any way to stop it."

"I have seen that," he said softly, with a glance at the stoppered bottles. "Plague and ague run rampant in a city, half a regiment dead of flux."

"Of course you have."

Brianna is afraid—not for herself but for her children, trapped in a time when war and plague are both everyday disasters.

CLAIRE FINDS THE guilty amoeba, trapped in the objective of her microscope. With the help of Malva, among others, she is gradually winning the war against it; there are no new cases of dysentery on the Ridge, and the sick are beginning to recover. But not all recover, and at one funeral, Claire herself collapses.

Claire is deathly ill and, in the grip of fever and delirium, comes to the point where she sees death clearly—and can choose, as Jamie once chose. The thing that affects her decision is the sight of Jamie, standing by the window in the grip of sorrow and despair, Malva Christie standing near him, trying to comfort him.

Someone moved near him. A dark-haired woman, a girl. She came close, touched his back, murmuring something to him. I saw the way she looked at him, the tender inclination of her head, the intimacy of her body swaying toward him.

No, *I thought, with great calm.* That won't do.

I looked once more at myself lying on the bed, and with a feeling that was at once firm decision and incalculable regret, I took another breath.

CLAIRE SLOWLY RETURNS to consciousness, only to be horrified at the discovery that Mrs. Bug and Malva have cut off her hair, in the belief that it would lower her fever.

In point of fact, I looked like a skeleton with a particularly unflattering crew cut, as I learned when I finally gained sufficient strength as to force Jamie to bring me a looking glass.

"I dinna suppose ye'd think of wearing a cap?" he suggested, diffidently fingering a muslin specimen that Marsali had brought me. "Only until it grows out a bit?"

"I don't suppose I bloody would."

Shocked and self-conscious, she is supported by the realization that Jamie still loves her, and she gathers sufficient strength to ask him how the residents of the Ridge are faring. Mrs. Bug has her own idea of what constitutes proper care of an invalid and brings Claire food and gossip—telling her that the local boys tried to drown Henri-Christian, on the theory that he was the spawn of Satan, but that the baby was saved by Mr. Roger, who pulled him out of the water.

"I was just in time to see it," Jamie informed me, grinning at the memory. "And then to see Roger Mac rise out o' the water like a triton, wi' duckweed streaming from his hair, blood runnin' from his nose, and the wee lad clutched tight in his arms. A terrible sight, he was."

The miscreant boys had followed the basket's career, yelling along the banks, but were now struck dumb. One of them moved to flee, the others starting up like a flight of pigeons, but Roger had pointed an awful finger at them and bellowed, "Sheas!" *in a voice loud enough to be heard over the racket of the creek.*

Such was the force of his presence, they did *stay, frozen in terror.*

Holding them with his glare, Roger had waded almost to the shore. There, he squatted and cupped a handful of water, which he poured over the head of the shrieking baby—who promptly quit shrieking.

"I baptize thee, Henri-Christian," Roger had bellowed, in his hoarse, cracked voice. "In the name of the Father, and the Son, and the Holy Ghost! D'ye hear me, wee bastards? His name is Christian*! He belongs to the Lord! Trouble him again, ye lot of scabs, and Satan will pop up and drag ye straight down screaming—TO HELL!"*

* * *

"One of the lads asked me was it true, what Mr. Roger said, about the wean belonging to the Lord? I told him I certainly wouldna argue with Mr. Roger about that—but whoever else he belonged to, Henri-Christian belongs to me, as well, and best they should remember it."

The story has a more somber side, though—one Jamie tells her reluctantly. Fergus tried to kill himself, three days before, and was narrowly rescued by Jamie.

"But . . . how could *he?" I said, distressed. "To leave Marsali, and the children—how?"*

Jamie looked down, hands braced on his knees, and sighed. The window was open, and a soft breeze came in, lifting the hairs on the crown of his head like tiny flames.

"He thought they would do better without him," he said flatly. "If he was dead, Marsali could wed again—find a man who could care for her and the weans. Provide for them. Protect wee Henri."

"He thinks—thought—he couldn't?"

Jamie glanced sharply at me.

"Sassenach," he said, "he kens damn well he can't."

Jamie's answer to the difficulty is to send Fergus, Marsali, and the children away—to Cross Creek, Wilmington, or New Bern, where Fergus has a chance of finding self-respect and more security for his unusual son.

Jamie has accompanied Major MacDonald down from the Ridge and on the way meets five men on horseback—one of them Richard Brown. The men are members of the Committee of Correspondence, bound for a meeting in Halifax—and extremely suspicious of Jamie's political sympathies, owing to his having saved the life of Fogarty Simms, the printer from Cross Creek.

One of the strangers spat in the road.

"Not so innocent, if that's Fogarty Simms you're speakin' of. Little Tory pissant," he added as an afterthought.

"That's the fellow," Green said, and spat in agreement. "The committee in Cross Creek set out to teach him a lesson; seems Mr. Fraser here was in disagreement. Quite a scene it was, from what I hear," he drawled, leaning back a little in his saddle to survey Jamie from his superior height. "Like I said, Mr. Fraser—you ain't all that popular, right this minute."

* * *

Well, he'd known it was coming. Had now and then tried to imagine the circumstances of his declaration, in situations ranging from the vaingloriously heroic to the openly dangerous, but as usual in such matters, God's sense of humor trumped all imagination. And so he found himself taking that final step into irrevocable and public commitment to the Rebel cause—just incidentally being required to ally himself with a deadly enemy in the process—standing alone in a dusty road, with a uniformed officer of the Crown squatting in the bushes directly behind him, breeches round his ankles.

"I am for liberty," he said, in a tone indicat-

ing mild astonishment that there could be any question regarding his position.

The men don't believe him, and the discussion goes downhill rapidly, with accusations of Jamie's being a Loyalist owing to his connections with River Run, and reaches the point of threatened violence.

"Wait!" Wherry drew himself up, trying to quell them with a hand, though Jamie could have told him he was several minutes past the point where such an attempt might have had any effect. "You cannot lay violent hands upon—"

"Can't we, though?" Brown grinned like a death's head, eyes fixed on Jamie, and began to undo the leather quirt coiled and fastened to his saddle. "No tar to hand, alas. But a good beating, say, and send 'em both squealing home to the Governor stark naked—that'd answer."

The second stranger laughed, and spat again, so the gob landed juicily at Jamie's feet.

"Aye, that'll do. Hear you held off a mob by yourself in Cross Creek, Fraser—only five to two now, how you like them odds?"

Jamie liked them fine. Dropping the reins he held, he turned and flung himself between the two horses, screeching and slapping hard at their flanks, then dived headlong into the brush at the roadside, scrabbling through roots and stones on hands and knees as fast as he could.

In the confusion, Jamie escapes, collecting Major MacDonald as he passes through the wood.

"Verra unfortunate," MacDonald observed thoughtfully at one point. "That they should have met us together. D'ye think it's dished your chances of worming your way into their councils? I should give my left ball to have an eye and an ear in that meeting they spoke of, I'll tell ye that for nothing!"

With a dim sense of wonder, Jamie realized that having made his momentous declaration, overheard by the man whose cause he sought to betray, and then nearly killed by the new allies whose side he sought to uphold—neither side had believed him.

"D'ye ever wonder what it sounds like when God laughs, Donald?" he asked thoughtfully.

MacDonald pursed his lips and glanced at the horizon, where dark clouds swelled just beyond the shoulder of the mountain.

"Like thunder, I imagine," he said. "D'ye not think so?"

Jamie shook his head.

"No. I think it's a verra small, wee sound indeed."

HAVING HEARD THAT Tom Christie has also been ill, Claire goes to see him as soon as she's up and about. He is shocked at her appearance and at seeing her in a cap—he being an outspoken critic of her "wanton" hair.

MEANWHILE, JAMIE HAS brought thirty muskets to Bird-who-sings-in-the-morning—along with Hiram Crombie, who is almost as bemused by the Indians as they are by him.

Penstemon's nostrils flared delicately; Crombie was sweating with nervousness, and smelled like a goat. He bowed earnestly, and presented Bird with the good knife he had brought as a present, slowly reciting the complimentary speech he had committed to memory. Reasonably well, too, Jamie thought; he'd mispronounced only a couple of words.

"I come to b-bring you great joy," he finished, stammering and sweating.

Bird looked at Crombie—small, stringy, and dripping wet—for a long, inscrutable moment, then back at Jamie.

"You're a funny man, Bear-Killer," he said with resignation. "Let us eat!"

"It is good for men to eat as brothers," Hiram observed to Standing Bear, in his halting Tsalagi. Or rather, tried to. And after all, Jamie reflected, feeling his ribs creak under the strain, it was really a very minor difference between "as brothers" and "their brothers."

Standing Bear gave Hiram a thoughtful look, and edged slightly farther away from him.

Bird observed this, and after a moment's silence, turned to Jamie.

"You're a very funny man, Bear-Killer," he repeated, shaking his head. "You win."

Upon his return to the Ridge, Jamie sends a letter to the superintendent of the Southern Department, resigning his commission as Indian agent.

PART 9: *THE BONES OF TIME*

Jamie takes one of the remaining gems and gives it to Major MacDonald, to use in negotiating for the purchase of a printing shop in New Bern. MacDonald observes that he'd heard that Jamie had a cache of gems—a disquieting bit of gossip to have loose.

The deal is made, though, and Fergus and his family depart—to the great distress of Jem and Germain, who are fast friends.

Ian invites Brianna to go hunting with him, but it becomes apparent fairly quickly that he has something else in mind. It is a journey of several days before they reach what he means to show her—the bones of a huge animal, half buried in a cliff, exposed by a fall of rock.

"A mammoth," she said, and found that she was whispering, too. The sun had passed its zenith; already the bottom of the creekbed lay in shadow. Light struck the stained curve of ancient ivory, and threw the vault of the high-crowned skull that held it into sharp relief. The skull was fixed in the soil at a slight angle, the single visible tusk rising high, the eye socket black as mystery.

The shiver came again, and she hunched her shoulders. Easy to feel that it might at any moment wrench itself free of the clay and turn that massive head toward them, empty-eyed, clods of dirt raining from tusks and bony shoulders as it shook itself and began to walk, the ground vibrating as long toes struck and sank in the muddy soil.

"That's what it's called—mammoth? Aye, well . . . it is *verra big." Ian's voice dispelled the illusion of incipient movement, and she was able finally to take her eyes off it—though she felt she must glance back, every second or so, to be sure it was still there.*

ON THE WAY, camping at night, Ian has told Brianna a great deal about his time with the Mohawk and about his lost wife, Emily—about the loss of the children he gave her and her eventual turning away from him out of sorrow, to marry another man, Sun Elk. And now he's brought Brianna to see the mammoth.

"I needed ye to tell me, aye? Whether that's what it is, or no. Because if it was, then perhaps what I've been thinking is wrong."

"It's not," she assured him. "But what on earth have you been thinking?"

"About God," he said, surprising her again. He licked his lips, unsure how to go on.

"Yeksa'a—the child. I didna have her christened," he said. "I couldna. Or perhaps I could—ye can do it yourself, ken, if there's no priest. But I hadna the courage to try. I—never saw her. They'd wrapped her already. . . . They wouldna have liked it, if I'd tried to . . ." His voice died away.

"Yeksa'a," she said softly. "Was that your—your daughter's name?"

He shook his head, his mouth twisting wryly.

"It only means 'wee girl.' The Kahnyen'kehaka dinna give a name to a child when it's born. Not until later. If . . ." His voice trailed off, and he cleared his throat. "If it lives. They wouldna think of naming a child unborn."

"But you did?" she asked gently.

He raised his head and took a breath that had a damp sound to it, like wet bandages pulled from a fresh wound.

"Iseabàil," he said, and she knew it was the first—perhaps would be the only—time he'd spoken it aloud. "Had it been a son, I would ha' called him Jamie." He glanced at her, with the shadow of a smile. "Only in my head, ken."

He let out all his breath then with a sigh and put his face down upon his knees, back hunched.

"What I am thinking," he said after a moment, his voice much too controlled, "is this. Was it me?"

"Ian! You mean your fault that the baby died? How could it be?"

"I left," he said simply, straightening up. "Turned away. Stopped being a Christian, being Scots. They took me to the stream, scrubbed me wi' sand to take away the white blood. They gave me my name—Okwaho'kenha—and said I was Mohawk. But I wasna, not really."

He sighed deeply again, and she put a hand on his back, feeling the bumps of his backbone press through the leather of his shirt. He didn't eat nearly enough, she thought.

"But I wasna what I had been, either," he went on, sounding almost matter-of-fact. "I tried to be what they wanted, ken? So I left off praying to God or the Virgin Mother, or Saint Bride. I listened to what Emily said, when she'd tell me about her *gods, the spirits that dwell in the trees and all. And when I went to the sweat lodge wi' the men, or sat by the hearth and heard the stories . . . they seemed as real to me as Christ and His saints ever had."*

He turned his head and looked up at her suddenly, half-bewildered, half-defiant.

"I am the Lord thy God," *he said.* "Thou shalt have no other gods before me. *But I did, no? That's mortal sin, is it not?"*

IAN IS DESPERATE at thought of his dead daughter, adrift in limbo, unfound. Brianna holds him tightly against her and prays, calling on her father Frank.

"Daddy," she said, and her voice broke on the word, but she held her cousin hard. "Daddy, I need you." Her voice sounded small, and pathetically unsure. But there was no other help to be had.

"I need you to find Ian's little girl," she said, as firmly as she could, trying to summon her father's face, to see him there among the shifting leaves at the clifftop. "Find her, please. Hold her in your arms, and make sure that she's safe. Take—please take care of her."

She stopped, feeling obscurely that she should say something else, something more ceremonious. Make the sign of the cross? Say "amen"?

"Thank you, Daddy," she said softly, and cried as though her father were newly dead, and she bereft, orphaned, lost, and crying in the night. Ian's arms were wrapped around her, and they clung tight together, squeezing hard, the warmth of the late sun heavy on their heads.

WHILE CLAIRE IS making a black pudding, Ronnie Sinclair arrives, bearing a load of barrels for the whisky-making and a letter, meant for "the healer," bearing a cryptic message: *YU CUM.*

The note is from Phaedre, Jocasta's body servant, and in response to the mysterious plea, Jamie and Claire ride down from the Ridge to find out what is happening at River Run.

"Betrayals"—They arrive to discover that Phaedre has run away, and they learn from Jocasta that Phaedre is in fact the daughter of Hector Cameron and the slave Betty. Jocasta professes complete bafflement as to what might have made Phaedre leave—particularly after sending that cryptic message to Claire.

Jamie has no idea, either—but he and Claire go to talk to Duncan. Duncan confesses that, quite by accident, he discovered that his impotence was *not* purely physical.

"But I thought you couldn't—" I began.

"Oh, I couldna," he assured me hastily. "Only at night, like, dreaming. But not waking, not since I had the accident. Perhaps it was being so early i' the morning; my cock thought I was still asleep."

Jamie made a low Scottish noise expressing considerable doubt as to this supposition, but urged Duncan to continue, with a certain amount of impatience.

Phaedre had taken notice in her turn, it transpired.

"She was only sorry for me," Duncan said frankly. "I could tell as much. But she put her hand on me, soft. So soft," he repeated, almost inaudibly.

He had been sitting on his bed—and had gone on sitting there in dumb amazement, as she took away the breakfast tray, lifted his nightshirt, climbed on the bed with her skirts neatly tucked above her round brown thighs, and with great tenderness and gentleness, had welcomed back his manhood.

Knowing Jocasta as they do, this casts a different light on the matter for Jamie and Claire. She could not have sold the girl, as legally Phaedre is Duncan's property. But Jocasta *is* a MacKenzie of Leoch, and . . .

"Ulysses," I said, with certainty, and he nodded reluctantly. Ulysses was not only Jocasta's eyes, but her hands, as well. I didn't think he would have killed Phaedre at his mistress's command—but if Jocasta had poisoned the girl, for instance, Ulysses might certainly have helped to dispose of the body.

I felt an odd air of unreality—even with what I knew of the MacKenzie family, calmly discussing the possibility of Jamie's aged aunt having murdered someone . . . and yet . . . I did know the MacKenzies.

There is nothing they can do for Phaedre, save pray for her. Snow will fly soon in the mountains; they have to return to the Ridge. But just in case, Jamie goes first to speak to his aunt.

"Aunt," he said to Jocasta matter-of-factly, "I should take it verra much amiss were any harm to come to Duncan."

She stiffened, fingers halting in their work.

"Why should any harm come to him?" she asked, lifting her chin.

Jamie didn't reply at once, but stood regarding her, not without sympathy. Then he leaned down, so that she could feel his presence close, his mouth near her ear.

"I know, Aunt," he said, softly. "And if ye dinna wish anyone else to share that knowledge . . . then I think I shall find Duncan in good health when I return."

She sat as though turned to salt. Jamie stood up, nodding toward the door, and we took our leave. I glanced back from the hallway, and saw her still sitting like a statue, face as white as the linen in her hands and the little balls of colored thread all fallen from her lap, unraveling across the polished floor.

CLAIRE, WITH MRS. Bug's help, gets off the last malting of the season and then goes to help Jamie take some of his whisky casks to a secret cache. On the way there, though, they encounter Mr. Wemyss, in obvious distress.

"Are ye . . . quite well, Joseph?" Jamie came closer, extending a hand gingerly, as though afraid that Mr. Wemyss might crack into pieces if touched.

This instinct was sound; when he touched the little man, Mr. Wemyss's face crumpled like paper, and his thin shoulders began to shake uncontrollably.

"I am so sorry, sir," he kept saying, quite dissolved in tears. "I'm so sorry!"

Jamie gave me a "do something, Sassenach" look of appeal, and I knelt swiftly, putting my arms round Mr. Wemyss's shoulders, patting his slender back.

"Now, now," I said, giving Jamie a "now what?*" sort of look over Mr. Wemyss's matchstick shoulder in return. "I'm sure it will be all right."*

"Oh, no," he said, hiccuping. "Oh, no, it can't." He turned a face streaming with woe toward Jamie. "I can't bear it, sir, truly I can't."

Mr. Wemyss's bones felt thin and brittle, and he was shivering. He was wearing only a thin shirt and breeches, and the wind was beginning to whine through the rocks. Clouds thickened overhead, and the light went from the little hollow, suddenly, as though a blackout curtain had been dropped.

Jamie unfastened his own cloak and wrapped it rather awkwardly round Mr. Wemyss, then lowered himself carefully onto another boulder.

"Tell me the trouble, Joseph," he said quite gently. "Is someone dead, then?"

Mr. Wemyss sank his face into his hands, head shaking to and fro like a metronome. He muttered something, which I understood to be "Better if she were."

Mr. Wemyss has grounds for distress; he's just learned that Lizzie is pregnant. Worse, she's pregnant by one of the Beardsleys, those half-wild hunters. And worse still . . .

"Which Beardsley was it?" he asked, with relative patience. "Jo? Or Kezzie?"

Mr. Wemyss heaved a sigh that came from the bottoms of his feet.

"She doesn't know," he said flatly.

"Christ," said Jamie involuntarily. He reached for the whisky again, and drank heavily.

"Ahem," I said, giving him a meaningful look as he lowered the jug. He surrendered it to me without comment, and straightened himself on his boulder, shirt plastered against his

chest by the wind, his hair whipped loose behind him.

"Well, then," he said firmly. "We'll have the two of them in, and find out the truth of it."

"No," said Mr. Wemyss, "we won't. They don't know, either."

I had just taken a mouthful of raw spirit. At this, I choked, spluttering whisky down my chin.

"They what?*" I croaked, wiping my face with a corner of my cloak. "You mean . . . both of them?"*

Mr. Wemyss looked at me. Instead of replying, though, he blinked once. Then his eyes rolled up into his head and he fell headlong off the boulder, poleaxed.

Jamie meets one of the Beardsleys near the Big House and, after punching him in the stomach, orders him to find his twin and come back. Meanwhile, Claire speaks to Lizzie, who confides how it all came about—but defiantly refuses to see anything wrong with her three-cornered love knot.

The twins were still alive, but didn't look as though they were particularly glad of the fact. They sat shoulder to shoulder in the center of Jamie's study, pressed together as though trying to reunite into a single being.

Their heads jerked toward the door in unison, looks of alarm and concern mingling with joy at seeing Lizzie. I had her by the arm, but when she saw the twins, she pulled loose and hurried to them with a small exclamation, putting an arm about each boy's neck to draw him to her bosom.

I saw that one of the boys had a fresh black eye, just beginning to puff and swell; I supposed it must be Kezzie, though I didn't know whether this was Jamie's notion of fairness, or merely a convenient means of ensuring that he could tell which twin was which while talking to them.

Jamie, with all three miscreants—and Mr. Wemyss—before him, forces Lizzie to draw straws in order to choose one of the twins, declares her handfast with Keziah, and orders Jo to leave the Ridge until after the child is born.

Jamie and Claire usher out Mr. Wemyss, who is overcome, leaving the twins and Lizzie to their farewells. When they reenter the study, though, it's to find Keziah with a bloody handkerchief wrapped round his hand. The only way most people can tell the twins apart is by means of a round scar on Jo's thumb, where he cut away a branding that showed him a thief. Now Jo has pressed the hot knife blade to his brother's thumb; as soon as the wound heals, no one will be able to tell them apart—except Lizzie.

Roger and Brianna lie comfortably in bed, discussing whether—or, rather, when—to tell Jemmy about time travel and where they really come from. Their philosophical conversation is interrupted by a knock at the door, though, and Roger answers it to find Lizzie with the twins. They ask "Mr. Roger" if he would please marry Lizzie and Jo, because Lizzie is pregnant and they want to fix matters before anyone finds out. Roger, ignorant of what's been going on up at the Big House, and touched by their youth, agrees and does so, with Keziah and Bree as witnesses.

When Roger and Bree learn next day that there are *two* marriages, both apparently valid, there seems no way to deal with the situation save to keep quiet.

"Well, I don't suppose there's actually much anybody can do about it," Bree said practically. "If we say anything in public, the Presbyterians will probably stone Lizzie as a Papist whore, and—"

Mr. Wemyss made a sound like a stepped-on pig's bladder.

"Certainly no one will say anything." Roger fixed Mrs. Bug with a hard look. "Will they?"

"Well, I'll have to tell Arch, mind, or I'll burst," she said frankly. "But no one else. Silent as the grave, I swear it, de'il take me if I lie." She put both hands over her mouth in illustration, and Roger nodded.

"I suppose," he said dubiously, "that the marriage I performed isna actually valid as such. But then—"

"It's certainly as valid as the handfasting Jamie did," I said. "And besides, I think it's too late to force her to choose. Once Kezzie's thumb heals, no one will be able to tell . . ."

"Except Lizzie, probably," Bree said. She licked a smear of honey from the corner of her mouth, regarding Roger thoughtfully. "I wonder what it would be like if there were two of you?"

"We'd both of us be thoroughly bamboozled," he assured her. "Mrs. Bug—is there any more coffee?"

"Who's bamboozled?" The kitchen door opened in a swirl of snow and frigid air, and Jamie came in with Jem, both fresh from a visit to the privy, ruddy-faced, their hair and lashes thick with melting snowflakes.

"You, for one. You've just been done in the eye by a nineteen-year-old bigamist," I informed him.

CLAIRE IS BAKING cookies with Jem, when she discovers nits crawling in his hair. This is not a surprise—lice are endemic on the Ridge at the moment—but it is a cause for instant action. While Jem is having his head shaved, the cookies burn, a small fire is started—and extinguished—and Roger, who has returned in the midst of the chaos, notices that Jem has a small, perfectly round brown mark, called a nevus, behind one ear.

He assures Brianna that this is nothing to worry about; he has one himself, in . . . just . . . the . . . same . . . spot.

Jemmy was on his hands and knees now, trying to coax Adso out from under the settle. His neck was small and fragile, and his shaven head looked unearthly white and rather shockingly naked, like a mushroom poking out of the earth. Roger's eyes rested on it for a moment; then he turned to Bree.

"I do believe perhaps I've picked up a few lice myself," he said, his voice just a tiny bit too loud. He reached up, pulled off the thong that bound his thick black hair, and scratched his head vigorously with both hands. Then he picked up the scissors, smiling, and held them out to her. "Like father, like son, I suppose. Give us a hand here, aye?"

PART 10: *WHERE'S PERRY MASON WHEN YOU NEED HIM?*

From a letter from Lord John to Jamie:

Dear Mr. Fraser—

What in the Name of God are you about? I have known you in the course of our long Acquaintance to be many Things—Intemperate and Stubborn being two of them—but have always known you for a Man of Intelligence and Honor.

Yet despite explicit Warnings, I find your Name upon more than one List of suspected Traitors and Seditionists, associated with illegal Assemblies, and thus subject to Arrest. The Fact that you are still at Liberty, my Friend, reflects nothing more than the Lack of Troops at present available in North Carolina. . . .

Whatever else you may be, you are no Fool, and so I must assume you realize the Consequences of your Actions. But I would be less than a Friend did I not put the Case to you bluntly: you expose your Family to the utmost Danger by your Actions, and you put your own Head in a Noose.

For the Sake of whatever Affection you may yet bear me, and for the Sake of those dear Connexions between your Family and myself—I beg you to renounce these most dangerous Associations while there is still Time.

Jamie shows the letter to Claire, who is somewhat bemused by it.

"These lists he mentions—do you know anything about that?"

He shrugged at that, and poked through one of the untidy piles with a forefinger, pulling out a smeared sheet that had obviously been dropped in a puddle at some point.

"Like that, I suppose," he said, handing it over. It was unsigned, and nearly illegible, a misspelt and vicious denunciation of various Outrages and Debached Persons—*here listed—whose speech, action, and appearance was a threat to all who valued peace and prosperity. These, the writer felt, should be shown whats what, presumably by being beaten, skinned alive,* rold in bolling Tar and plac'd on a Rail, *or in particularly pernicious cases,* Hanged outright from there own Rooftrees.

"Where did you pick that *up?" I dropped it on the desk, using two fingers.*

"In Campbelton. Someone sent it to Farquard, as Justice of the Peace. He gave it to me, because my name is on it."

"It is?" I squinted at the straggling letters. "Oh, so it is. J. Frayzer. *You're sure it's you? There are quite a few Frasers, after all, and not a few named John, James, Jacob, or Joseph."*

"Relatively few who could be described as a Red-haired dejenerate Pox-ridden Usuring Son of a Bitch who skulks in Brothels when not drunk and comitting Riot in the Street, *I imagine."*

"Oh, I missed that part."

"It's in the exposition at the bottom."

Moving into seriousness, Jamie and Claire discuss the issue: plainly, the die is cast, and Jamie is a rebel, for good or ill.

He writes back to his good friend:

My dear John—

It is too late.

Our continued Correspondence cannot but prove a Danger to you, but it is with the greatest Regret that I sever this Link between us.

Believe me ever

Your most humble
and affectionate Friend,
Jamie

ON THE NIGHT before the eighteenth of April, Roger and Brianna lie in bed, talking about the Revolution. A child of Boston, Brianna knows only too well what is happening—or about to happen—as dawn breaks over Lexington and Concord on this day. She recites Longfellow's poem to Roger (*"Listen, my children, and you shall hear / Of the midnight ride of Paul Revere . . ."*), as he visualizes just what *is* happening, now, only a few hundred miles to the north.

"It was two by the village clock," *she repeated,*

"When he came to the bridge in Concord town.

He heard the bleating of the flock,
And the twitter of birds among the trees,
And felt the breath of the morning breeze
Blowing over the meadows brown.
And one was safe and asleep in his bed
Who at the bridge would be first to fall,
Who that day would be lying dead,
Pierced by a British musketball.

"You know the rest." *She stopped abruptly, her hand tight on his.*

From one moment to the next, the character of the night had changed. The stillness of the small hours had ceased, and a breath of wind moved through the trees outside. All of a sudden, the night was alive again, but dying now, rushing toward dawn.

If not actively twittering, the birds were wakeful; something called, over and over, in the nearby wood, high and sweet. And above the stale, heavy scent of the fire, he breathed the wild clean air of morning, and felt his heart beat with sudden urgency.

"Tell me the rest," he whispered.

He saw the shadows of men in the trees, the stealthy knocking on doors, the low-voiced, excited conferences—and all the while, the light growing in the east. The lap of water and creak of oars, the sound of restless kine lowing to be milked, and on the rising breeze the smell of men, stale with sleep and empty of food, harsh with black powder and the scent of steel.

And without thinking, pulled his hand from his wife's grasp, rolled over her, and pulling up the shift from her thighs, took her hard and fast, in vicarious sharing of that mindless urge to spawn that attended the imminent presence of death.

Lay on her trembling, the sweat drying on his back in the breeze from the window, heart thumping in his ears. For the one, he thought. The one who would be the first to fall. The poor sod who maybe hadn't swived his wife in the dark and taken the chance to leave her with child, because he had no notion what was coming with the dawn. This dawn.

Brianna lay still under him; he could feel the rise and fall of her breath, powerful ribs that lifted even under his weight.

"You know the rest," she whispered.

"Bree," he said very softly. "I would sell my soul to be there now."

The peace of dawn is shattered, a quarter of an hour later, by the arrival of one of the Beardsleys, shouting that "Lizzie's having the baby, come quick!" Brianna and Claire rush to the Beardsleys' cabin, only to find Lizzie and a small, round, blood-smeared baby, regarding each other with identical looks of astonished surprise.

Once things are cleaned up and settled, the male members of the Ridge come to pay their respects to the new mother and child.

"May the Blessing of Bride and of Columba be on you, young woman," Jamie said formally in Gaelic, bowing to her, "and may the love of Christ sustain you always in your motherhood. May milk spring from your breasts like water from the rock and may you rest secure in the arms of your"—he coughed briefly, glancing at the Beardsleys—"husband."

"If you can't say 'prick,' why can you say 'breasts'?" Jemmy inquired, interested.

"Ye can't, unless it's a prayer," his father informed him. "Grandda was giving Lizzie a blessing."

"Oh. Are there any prayers with pricks in them?"

"I'm sure there are," Roger replied, carefully avoiding Brianna's eye, "but ye don't say them out loud. Why don't ye go and help Grannie with the breakfast?"

BRIANNA IS MAKING paper, when Roger comes out to talk to her and mentions that he is founding a lodge of Freemasons on the Ridge, taking a page from Jamie's book when he started a lodge among the prisoners at Ardsmuir—to give men lacking the same religious background some common ground of idealism and camaraderie.

FERGUS AND MARSALI have begun a new life as printers; their maiden effort is a newspaper known as *L'Oignon-Intelligencer*: *distributed upon a Weekly Basis, with Extra Editions as events demand, these provided at a modest cost of One Penny. . . .*

Along with the initial edition of the new paper, Colonel John Ashe has sent a sheaf of other documents, including the Lexington Alarm—a note of the events surrounding the attack on Lexington.

COLONEL ASHE'S MESSENGER has also brought word of a Congress to be held in Mecklenburg County in mid-May, for the purpose of declaring the county's independence from King George. Aware that he is still regarded with skepticism by many in the rebellion, Jamie makes up his mind to attend this and takes Roger with him, to witness history in the making.

Before they can depart, a little local history is made: Tom Christie shows up at the Big House, dragging his daughter, Malva, who is pregnant, and insists that Jamie must help him force her to name the father. She does.

She took a huge gulp of air at that, and raised her head. Her eyes were reddened, but still very beautiful, and wide with apprehension.

"Oh, sir," she said, but then stopped dead.

Jamie was by now looking nearly as uncomfortable as the Christies, but did his best to keep his air of kindness.

"Will ye not tell me, then, lass?" he said, as gently as possible. "I promise ye'll not suffer for it."

Tom Christie made an irritable noise, like some beast of prey disturbed at its meal, and Malva went very pale indeed, but her eyes stayed fixed on Jamie.

"Oh, sir," she said, and her voice was small but clear as a bell, ringing with reproach. "Oh, sir, how can ye say that to me, when ye ken the truth as well as I do?" Before anyone could react to that, she turned to her father, and lifting a hand, pointed directly at Jamie.

"It was him," she said.

There is an understandable amount of confusion following Malva's statement. While Jamie follows Claire (who has fled, her usual behavior in times of emotional stress) and convinces her that Malva's statement is a lie, he also grimly notes that there are many, on the Ridge and elsewhere, who will believe it.

"They'll all believe it, Claire," he said softly. "I'm sorry."

JAMIE IS RIGHT. The devil of doubt has been set free in the world, and tongues wag merrily all over the Ridge. Even his own daughter is not immune to the poison.

"Bree," [Roger] said gently. "Jamie's an honorable man, and he loves your mother deeply."

"Well, see, that's the thing," she said softly. "I would have sworn Daddy was, too. And did."

Roger's own faith in Jamie is unshakable, but as a good minister, he must have care for his flock and, with that in mind, goes to talk to Malva Christie. He shows her sympathy and a willing ear, and she *may* just be about to confide in him when their conversation is interrupted by her brother, Allan, who drives Roger away with abuse, leaving him wondering whether he's made matters even worse.

Even the infant lodge is affected, so, far from bringing the men of the community together, it's now a ground for fights between Jamie's supporters and those eager to believe the worst.

CLAIRE IS WEEDING in her garden, trying to forget about the storm of troubles presently grumbling overhead, when Ian comes to talk to her. He's upset about Malva's accusation of Jamie.

His long, homely face was twisted with unhappiness, and it suddenly occurred to me that he might be having his own doubts about the matter.

"Ian," I said, with as much firmness as I could muster, "Malva's child could not possibly be Jamie's. You do believe that, don't you?"

He nodded, very slowly, but wouldn't meet my eyes.

"I do," he said softly, and then swallowed hard. "But, Auntie . . . it could be mine."

In the course of the subsequent discussion, Ian reveals that the baby might well be Bobby Higgins's, too—evidently, Malva has not been niggardly with her favors. Ian is willing to marry Malva if there's a good chance the child is his—for the child's sake, not his own. Claire tells him not to do anything hasty; there's still time.

Jamie and Roger ride to Mecklenburg, as much to escape the atmosphere on the Ridge as for political purposes. Politics there are, though, in abundance.

The one thing Roger had not envisioned about the making of history was the sheer amount of alcohol involved. He should have, he thought; if there was anything a career in academia had taught him, it was that almost all worthwhile business was conducted in the pub.

The public houses, taverns, ordinaries, and pothouses in Charlotte were doing a roaring business, as delegates, spectators, and hangers-on seethed through them, men of Loyalist sentiments collecting in the King's Arms, those of rabidly opposing views in the Blue Boar, with shifting currents of the unallied and undecided eddying to and fro, purling through the Goose and Oyster, Thomas's ordinary, the Groats, Simon's, Buchanan's, Mueller's, and two or three nameless places that barely qualified as shebeens.

Jamie visited all of them. And drank in all of them, sharing beer, ale, rum punch, shandy, cordial, porter, stout, cider, brandywine, persimmon beer, rhubarb wine, blackberry wine, cherry bounce, perry, merry brew, and scrumpy. Not all of them were alcoholic, but the great majority were.

In the course of the day, Roger also meets Davy Caldwell, the Presbyterian minister who married Roger and Bree. Caldwell tells him that there is to be a Presbytery Session soon—at which Roger may be ordained.

BACK ON THE Ridge, Claire discovers that someone has left the gate of her garden ajar, and a bear has evidently gotten in to raid her beehives—several are tipped over, and the air is full of angry bees. Whoever the intruder was, though, it wasn't a bear. Venturing into the garden, she discovers Malva Christie lying in a pool of blood, with her throat cut. Panicked but still possessed of her medical instincts, Claire hastily performs an emergency C-section with her garden knife and succeeds in delivering the child—a boy—alive, but it's too soon, and the premature infant dies in her hands.

"Don't go," I said, "don't go, don't go, please don't go." But the vibrancy faded, a small blue glow that seemed to light the palms of my hands for an instant, then dwindle like a candle flame, to the coal of a smoldering wick, to the faintest trace of brightness—then everything was dark.

I was still sitting in the brilliant sun, crying and blood-soaked, the body of the little boy in my lap, the butchered corpse of my Malva beside me, when they found me.

MALVA'S DEATH NATURALLY makes matters on the Ridge even worse. Suspicion shifts back and forth between Claire and Jamie, with occasional excursions in the direction of Ian or Bobby Higgins. After a week of shock, rumor, suspicion, speculation, and more rumor, Jamie has had enough.

"I have reached the mortal limit of endurance," he informed me. "One moment more of this, and I shall run mad. I must do something, and I will." Without waiting for any response to this statement, he strode to the office door, flung it open, and bellowed, "Joseph!" into the hall.

Mr. Wemyss appeared out of the kitchen, where he had been sweeping the chimney at Mrs. Bug's direction, looking startled, pale, soot-smudged, and generally unkempt.

Jamie ignored the black footprints on the study floor—he had burned the rug—and fixed Mr. Wemyss with a commanding gaze.

"D'ye want that woman?" he demanded.

"Woman?" Mr. Wemyss was understandably bewildered. "What—oh. Are you—might you be referring to Fraulein Berrisch?"

"Who else? D'ye want her?" Jamie repeated.

It had plainly been a long time since anyone had asked Mr. Wemyss what he wanted, and it took him some time to gather his wits from the shock of it.

Brutal prodding by Jamie forced him past deprecating murmurs about the Fraulein's friends no doubt being the best judge of her happiness, his own unsuitability, poverty, and general unworthiness as a husband, and into—at long last—a reckless admission that, well, if the Fraulein should not be terribly averse to the prospect, perhaps . . . well . . . in a word . . .

"Aye, sir," he said, looking terrified at his own boldness. "I do. Very much!" he blurted.

"Good." Jamie nodded, pleased. "We'll go and get her, then."

His notion of blowing off steam is to take Roger, Ian, and Mr. Wemyss and ride to find Fraulein Berrisch.

The departure of the men eases tension on the Ridge but does nothing to lessen the speculation. Claire, Brianna, Mrs. Bug, Lizzie, and Mrs. McCallum are engaged in just that when who should arrive, out of the blue, but Fraulein Berrisch, who has also reached the limit of endurance and left her sister-in-law's house in Halifax, walking to Fraser's Ridge to find Joseph. Her eye lights on little Rodney, Lizzie's baby, and Claire sees that there might just be a way in which Mr. Wemyss can be reconciled with his wayward daughter.

Roger and Bree pack to go to the Presbytery Session. She feels that she should stay to defend her parents from public opinion, but Roger is firm about her accompanying him; he wants her and little Jem safely away from the Ridge.

Roger has sound instincts; the Big House is in a state of moral siege. Jamie has sent Ian to the Cherokee villages, to keep him out of fights, and he and Claire are restless, helpless to resolve the external situation.

The situation becomes more exigent with the arrival of (who else?) Richard Brown, at the head of a party of men. Brown announces gloatingly that they've come to arrest Claire for Malva's murder. Armed confrontation ends with Claire shooting one of the men—not fatally—and Jamie barricading himself and Claire in the house. The men threaten to burn down the house, and there's some speculation as to whether this might be It, the ultimate cause of that sinister newspaper clipping. But the date is wrong . . . and perhaps Mrs. Bug, who Jamie sent off at the men's appearance, has succeeded in procuring help. . . .

Mrs. Bug has found help, but it's Hiram Crombie and some of the other fisher-folk; all of them are disposed to believe The Worst about Claire, Jamie, or both. Still, Hiram's unbending conscience won't stand for anything like a lynching. He *will* agree that Mrs. Fraser ought to be taken to Hillsborough and there committed to the proper authorities, but only with a guarantee of safety.

Richard Brown's idea of such a guarantee is enough to make Jamie start measuring the distance between him and Brown's throat, but Tom Christie steps out of the crowd and announces that he will accompany Mrs. Fraser to Hillsborough, to assure her safety (and, by implication, to assure that she doesn't try to escape). The other Protestants respect Christie and grudgingly agree that this can be done. Jamie, naturally, is not letting Claire go anywhere without him—and so Jamie, Claire, and Tom Christie set off willy-nilly with Brown and the Committee of Safety, bound for Hillsborough.

The journey is not without incident; Claire is now the main focus of suspicion, it being widely assumed that she killed her husband's pregnant mistress and cut the child from her womb. She is stoned, jeered at, and generally harassed along the way, though Jamie protects her from the worst of it.

Neither is she the only one having a difficult time. Watching Tom Christie at the campfire one night, Jamie sees him watching Claire and realizes that Christie is in love with her.

Poor bugger, he thought.

RICHARD BROWN, AFTER a murmured conversation with one of his lieutenants, decamps on some business of his own. The rest of the party pushes on to Brunswick, where they abruptly set upon Jamie, restraining him while they drag Claire away, riding hell-for-leather.

My throat was raw from screaming, and my stomach hurt, bruised and clenched in a knot of fear. Our speed had slowed, now that we had left Brunswick behind, and I concentrated on breathing; I wouldn't speak until I was sure I could do so without my voice trembling.

"Where are you taking me?" I asked finally. I sat stiff in the saddle, enduring an unwanted intimacy with the man behind me.

"New Bern," he said, with a note of grim satisfaction. "And then, thank God, we'll be shut of you at last."

CLAIRE IS DELIVERED to the sheriff in New Bern and locked up in a cell with a woman named Sadie Ferguson, a forger.

During the night, the women hear screaming from the kitchen on the other side of the wall, and they are released from their cell to help with the difficult birth of a slave woman—the sheriff's wife being incapable with drink and no hand at midwifery.

Meanwhile, Jamie has been bound and dumped in a boat shed near the shore. His nephew Ian had been traveling close behind Brown's party, keeping an eye on them, and Jamie hopes Ian was near enough to see what happened when he was separated from Claire. His only comfort at the moment is that Tom Christie was with the party that took Claire; he's sure that Christie would protect her, if he could.

Ian does show up to release his uncle—and brings news. He succeeded in following Richard Brown about his private business and managed to overhear a conversation between Brown and the lawyer Forbes.

Brown's aim was simple at this point—to rid himself of the encumbrance the Frasers had become. He knew of Forbes and his relations with Jamie, owing to all the gossip after the tar incident in the summer of last year, and the confrontation at Mecklenburg in May. And so he offered to hand the two of them over to Forbes, for what use the lawyer might make of the situation.

"So he strode to and fro a bit, thinking—Forbes, I mean—they were in his warehouse, ken, by the river, and me hiding behind the barrels o' tar. And then he laughs, as though he's just thought of something clever."

Forbes's suggestion was that Brown's men should take Jamie, suitably bound, to a small landing that he owned, near Brunswick. From there, he would be taken onto a ship headed for England, and thus safely removed from interference in the affairs of either Forbes or Brown—and, incidentally, rendered unable to defend his wife.

Claire, meanwhile, should be committed to the mercies of the law. If she were to be found guilty, well, that would be the end of her. If not, the scandal attendant upon a trial would both occupy the attention of anyone connected to her and destroy any influence they might have—thus leaving Fraser's Ridge ripe for the pickings, and Neil Forbes a clear field toward claiming leadership of the Scottish Whigs in the piedmont.

Jamie listened to this in silence, torn between anger and a reluctant admiration.

"A reasonably neat scheme," he said. He was feeling steadier now, the queasiness disappearing with the cleansing flow of anger through his blood.

"Oh, it gets better, Uncle," Ian assured him. "Ye recall a gentleman named Stephen Bonnet?"

"I do. What about him?"

He tries to think what he might have told Ian about Bonnet, but the pirate has vanished from their ken before Ian's return from the Mohawk—so far as he knows, Ian might have heard the name, but little else.

"Cousin Brianna told me about him," Ian says, his voice careful. Christ, has she told him Bonnet had raped her? Likely, given the way Ian is acting now.

"It's Mr. Bonnet's ship, Uncle, that's to take

ye to England." Amusement was beginning to show in his nephew's voice again. "It seems Lawyer Forbes has had a verra profitable partnership with Bonnet for some time—him and some merchant friends in Wilmington. They've shares in both the ship and its cargoes. And since the English blockade, the profits have been greater still; I take it that our Mr. Bonnet is a most experienced smuggler."

Jamie said something extremely foul in French. . . .

BACK AT THE jail, Claire and Sadie Ferguson have been released by Mrs. Tolliver, the sheriff's wife, to help with the laundry. Meanwhile, Mrs. Tolliver passes out in the shade of the house and is thus not available to deal with a gentleman who arrives, asking who is the midwife?

Claire admits that she is, whereupon the man asks what crime she's charged with.

The constable, a rather dim young man, pursed his lips at this, looking dubiously back and forth between us.

"Ahh . . . well, one of 'em's a forger," he said, "and t'other's a murderess. But as to which bein' which . . ."

"I'm the murderess," Sadie said bravely, adding loyally, "She's a very fine midwife!" I looked at her in surprise, but she shook her head slightly and compressed her lips, adjuring me to keep quiet.

Not until she is well away with the gentleman—who proves to be an aide to Governor Josiah Martin—does Claire learn that forgery is a capital offense; a murderess might well get off with whipping and being branded in the face. Still, she isn't being taken away for execution.

She's taken to Tryon's Palace, the governor's residence, where she is introduced to Mrs. Martin, the governor's wife, who is heavily pregnant—and most interested at meeting a murderess.

"Is it true?" Mrs. Martin asked suddenly, startling me.

"Is what true?"

"They say you murdered your husband's pregnant young mistress, and cut the baby from her womb. Did you?"

I put the heel of my hand against my brow and pressed, closing my eyes. How on earth had she heard that? When I thought I could speak, I lowered my hands and opened my eyes.

"She wasn't his mistress, and I didn't kill her. As for the rest—yes, I did," I said, as calmly as I could.

She stared at me for a moment, her mouth hanging open. Then she shut it with a snap and crossed her forearms over her belly.

"Trust George Webb to choose me a proper midwife!" she said—and much to my surprise, began to laugh. "He doesn't know, does he?"

"I would assume not," I said, with extreme dryness. "I didn't tell him. Who told you?"

"Oh, you are quite notorious, Mrs. Fraser," she assured me. "Everyone has been talking of it. George has no time for gossip, but even he must have heard of it. He has no memory for names, though. I do."

Claire looks for a means of escape but fails to find one. She tends Mrs. Martin, who has digestive difficulties, and bides her time.

An opportunity seems to present itself when the governor's aide, George Webb, comes to fetch her to the governor's office; the governor has lost his clerk.

"What, Webb?" he demanded, scowling at me. "I need a secretary, and you bring me a midwife?"

"She's a forger," Webb said baldly. That stopped whatever complaint the Governor had been going to bring forth. He paused, mouth slightly open, still frowning at me.

"Oh," he said, in an altered tone. "Indeed."

"Accused of forgery," I said politely. "I haven't been tried, let alone convicted, you know."

Martin is dubious but desperate, and discovering that Claire can in fact write a fair hand, he puts her to work copying official documents. She divides her time between copying documents and checking on Mrs. Martin, noticing as she passes the windows that the cannon that guard the palace are being dismounted. The governor says casually that they are being taken to be repaired in anticipation of the Queen's birthday salute, but Claire is bright enough to realize that he's afraid of the cannon being seized by the Rebels and turned on the palace.

The governor is *very* afraid. He has Claire dressed in one of his wife's outfits and takes her out in his carriage, as though he and his wife were merely going for a drive. Meanwhile, the faithful George Webb escapes from the palace with Mrs. Martin, taking her to a place of safety—and the governor's carriage suddenly speeds up, tearing out of the town of New Bern . . . and pursued by Jamie, who has sneaked into New Bern, having found out where Claire is and intending to rescue her.

He had never seen Josiah Martin, but thought the plump, self-important-looking gentleman must surely be the— His eye caught the merest glimpse of the woman, and his heart clenched like a fist. Without an instant's thought, he was pelting after the carriage, as hard as he could run.

In his prime, he could not have outrun a team of horses. Even so, he came within a few feet of the carriage, would have called, but had no breath, no sight, and then his foot struck a misplaced cobble and he fell headlong.

He lay stunned and breathless, vision dark and his lungs afire, hearing only the receding clatter of hooves and carriage wheels, until a strong hand seized his arm and jerked.

"We'll avoid notice, he says," Ian muttered, bending to get his shoulder under Jamie's arm. "Your hat's flown off, did ye notice that? *Nay, of course not, nor the whole street staring, ye crack-brained gomerel. God, ye weigh as much as a three-year bullock!"*

"Ian," he said, and paused to gulp for breath.

"Aye?"

"Ye sound like your mother. Stop." Another gulp of air. "And let go my arm; I can walk."

Ian gave a snort that sounded even more like Jenny, but did stop, and did let go. Jamie picked up his fallen hat and limped toward the printshop, Ian following in urgent silence through the staring streets.

Claire ends up on the *Cruizer,* a small ship on which the governor has taken refuge. He writes madly, begging England for help, trying vainly to manage a colony on which he dare not set foot—and Claire copies all his letters, wondering how on earth she is to escape now, but hoping that Jamie will find her.

He does and comes aboard, demanding an interview with the governor. He offers to ransom Claire with his remaining gems, and the governor is tempted but refuses. Jamie is forced to leave, though assuring Claire he *will* get her out, one way or another.

Escape comes, though, in the person of

Thomas Christie, who rows out to the *Cruizer* in order to present the governor with a signed confession, stating that he, Tom Christie, murdered his daughter, Malva, thus exonerating Claire. In the course of the conversation, he tells Claire that in fact Malva was not his daughter but was the daughter of his wife and his brother and that he was convinced Malva was a witch like her mother.

"I have written down my confession." He let go, and poked a hand into his pocket, fumbling a little, and pulled out a folded paper, which he clutched in his short, solid fingers.

"I have sworn here that it was I who killed my daughter, for the shame she had brought upon me by her wantonness." He spoke firmly enough, but I could see the working of his throat above the wilted stock.

"You didn't," I said positively. "I know you didn't."

He blinked, gazing at me.

"No," he said, quite matter-of-fact. "But perhaps I should have.

"I have written a copy of this confession," he said, tucking the document back into his coat, "and have left it with the newspaper in New Bern. They will publish it. The Governor will accept it—how can he not?—and you will go free."

Those last four words struck me dumb. He was still gripping my right hand; his thumb stroked gently over my knuckles. I wanted to pull away, but forced myself to keep still, compelled by the look in his eyes, clear gray and naked now, without disguise.

"I have yearned always," he said softly, "for love given and returned; have spent my life in the attempt to give my love to those who were not worthy of it. Allow me this: to give my life for the sake of one who is."

PART 11: *IN THE DAY OF VENGEANCE*

Jamie is waiting on the shore for Claire and takes her quickly away to an inn, where she can recover in privacy—and grieve for Tom Christie.

Meanwhile, Brianna is at River Run with Jem, preparing for a new painting commission, while Roger is in Edenton with the Presbytery Session. She becomes suddenly ill at the smell of the pigments she's grinding and faces the obvious conclusion:

"Congratulations, Roger," she said out loud, her voice sounding faint and uncertain in the close, damp air. "I think *you're going to be a daddy. Again."*

While Brianna is still coming to grips with her new discovery, Duncan comes to tell her that the gold is gone. All of it.

And in Edenton, Roger has been having a wonderful time in the company of his fellow Presbyterians. On the eve of his ordination, though, Jamie appears abruptly, to tell him that Brianna has been taken—Neil Forbes has arranged to have her kidnapped by Stephen Bonnet.

On board Bonnet's boat, Brianna decides that she won't be raped again, no matter what, and prepares to defend herself with a marlinespike. Upon discovering that she's pregnant, though, Bonnet abruptly withdraws—he has a horror of pregnant women, owing to an unfortunate occurrence some years earlier—and sends a sailor onshore to summon a whore, whom he promptly uses in Brianna's presence and then goes out, leaving the women together.

Brianna manages to give the whore, Hepzibah, a message for Jamie, giving her Jamie's ring as persuasion. From things Bonnet has said, Brianna knows he is heading for Ocracoke Island, for a rendezvous of some kind, at the dark of the moon. Hepzibah is uneasy at the thought of crossing Bonnet but says she will try.

The ship sails with the tide.

On shore, Neil Forbes sits in the parlor of the King's Inn, enjoying a glass of hard cider and the feeling that all's right with the world. This feeling proves to be temporary, when he lowers his glass to find himself facing Brianna's cousin—and her husband.

Roger and Ian demand to know where Stephen Bonnet is, but Forbes refuses to answer. He goes on refusing, though growing uneasy at the threatening manner of the two men facing him. His uneasiness increases substantially when a messenger appears with a small package containing his mother's favorite brooch—Jamie Fraser has waylaid the old lady and has her hostage.

"He would not harm an old woman," he said, with as much bravado as he could summon.

"Would he not?" Ian's sketchy brows lifted. "Aye, perhaps not. He might just send her awa', though—to Canada, maybe? Ye seem to ken him fair weel, Mr. Forbes. What d'ye think?"

The lawyer drummed his fingers on the arm of the chair, breathing through his teeth, evidently reviewing what he knew of Jamie Fraser's character and reputation.

"All right," he said suddenly. "All right!"

Forbes tells them the name of Bonnet's ship and when it sailed—two days before, from Edenton.

Roger nodded abruptly. Safe, he said. In Bonnet's hands. Two days, in Bonnet's hands. But he had sailed with Bonnet, he thought, trying to steady himself, keep a grip on his rationality. He knew how the man worked. Bonnet was a smuggler; he would not sail for England without a full cargo. He might— might*—be going down the coast, picking up small shipments before turning to the open sea and the long voyage for England.*

And if not—he might still be caught, with a fast ship.

No time to be lost; people on the docks might know where the Anemone *was headed next. He turned and took a step toward the door. Then a red wave washed through him and he whirled back, smashing his fist into Forbes's face with the full weight of his body behind it.*

The lawyer gave a high-pitched scream, and clutched both hands to his nose. All noises in the inn and in the street seemed to stop; the world hung suspended. Roger took a short, deep breath, rubbing his knuckles, and nodded once more.

"Come on," he said to Ian.

"Oh, aye."

Roger was halfway to the door when he realized that Ian was not with him. He looked back, and was just in time to see his cousin-by-marriage take Forbes gently by one ear and cut it off.

Jamie, Roger, and Ian have no trouble finding people familiar with Stephen Bonnet and his ship, the *Anemone.* Finding where it may be is another question, but Claire has encountered an unexpected visitor at the inn where they are staying—the long-lost Manfred McGillivray.

Manfred, it seems, is the lover of a whore named Hepzibah, and having heard her story and recognized Jamie Fraser's ring . . . he is able to tell them that Bonnet is heading for a rendezvous on Ocracoke. Jamie promptly hires a fishing boat to take them to their own rendezvous with the pirate.

The *Anemone* has not yet reached Ocracoke, though, and while Bonnet makes no sexual advances toward Brianna, he insists that she share his bed, as he suffers from nightmares of drowning. Moved by instinct, she comforts him following one of these dreams, assuring him that she will not let him drown.

The rescuers reach Ocracoke and proceed to search the island—Roger and Ian on shore, Jamie and Claire sailing round the island. Fighting his way through mangrove swamps, Roger discovers a primitive site—four stone pillars standing near a small creek—and recognizes the site as the one the Indian Donner had described to Brianna: the time portal he had come through. Roger backs carefully away.

Meanwhile, the fishing captain suggests that instead of trying to find the *Anemone* in one of the many creeks and inlets where it may be hidden, they keep an eye out for whatever ship Bonnet planned to rendezvous with. This strategy works—at the dark of the moon, a slave ship arrives, anchoring silently offshore.

At Stephen Bonnet's secret lair, Brianna discovers that while Neil Forbes may have meant her simply to be deported to London, Bonnet sees no reason to pass up profit and proposes to sell her to one of his private clients. She has a number of objections to this proposal but is physically overpowered by Bonnet's servant, a huge black man named Emmanuel, who locks her in an upper room to await the arrival of potential purchasers.

To Brianna's surprise, the slave who brings her food is Phaedre, Jocasta MacKenzie's missing body servant, abducted by Ulysses and sold to Bonnet.

A purchaser arrives, and Brianna undergoes a humiliating examination—but one that involves being dressed in fine clothes. When she is returned to her locked room, she has in her possession the pointed ivory busk from her stays.

Could she stab someone with it? Oh, yes, *she thought fiercely.* And please let it be Emmanuel.

It *is* Emmanuel. Escaping through the thatch of the roof, Brianna is pursued by Emmanuel but succeeds in stabbing him in the armpit with the busk, piercing a large artery and killing him. Meanwhile, Jamie, Roger, and Ian attack the house and succeed in overpowering and capturing Stephen Bonnet. However, the slave-ship captain escapes with a number of slaves, including Josh, one of the grooms from River Run.

It is unthinkable to return Phaedre to River Run, so the Frasers find her a place to live and work. Going to tell Duncan, Jamie hears that Duncan and Jocasta have decided to remove to Canada. With the bulk of the gold gone, they have just enough to live in modest comfort and feel that Canada will be a good deal safer for Loyalists.

And what of Jocasta's butler, Ulysses? Gone, apparently—but Jamie goes to wait in the stable and meets Ulysses, stealing in to abstract a horse. Ulysses has been Jocasta's lover for some twenty years, the man admits, and has done many things on her behalf—but has not stolen the gold.

"Will ye swear on my aunt's head?" he asked abruptly. Ulysses's eyes were sharp, shining in the lantern light, but steady.

"Yes," he said at last, quietly. "I do so swear."

Jamie was about to dismiss him, when one last thought occurred to him.

"Do you have children?" he asked.

Indecision crossed the chiseled face; surprise and wariness, mingled with something else.

"None I would claim," he said at last, and Jamie saw what it was—scorn, mixed with shame. His jaw tensed, and his chin rose slightly. "Why do you ask me that?"

Jamie met his gaze for a moment, thinking of Brianna growing heavy with child.

"Because," he said at last, "it is only the hope of betterment for my children, and theirs, that gives me the courage to do what must be

done here." Ulysses's face had gone blank; it gleamed black and impassive in the light.

"If you have no stake in the future, you have no reason to suffer for it. Such children as you may have—"

"They are slaves, born of slave women. What can they be, to me?" Ulysses's hands were clenched, pressed against his thighs.

"Then go," he said softly, and stood aside, gesturing toward the door with the barrel of his pistol. "Die free, at least."

THE FRASERS AND MacKenzies return to Fraser's Ridge, where they wait for the night of January 21, 1776, to see whether the newspaper clipping's prophecy will be fulfilled. To keep it from being fulfilled, they carefully extinguish all fires and then decamp to Roger and Brianna's cabin—where Adso the cat, stealing Major MacDonald's wig, upsets Brianna's white phosphorus and comes within inches of incinerating the cabin.

IN FEBRUARY, JAMIE receives word from Colonel Ashe that the militias are summoned to Wilmington—and goes, with those men who will follow him, and with Roger, with Ian, and with Claire, as always. They are headed for a place called Moore's Creek Bridge, where the Rebel militia will meet the Loyalists raised by the Crown—most of them Highlanders, including Flora MacDonald's husband and Major MacDonald. It will be the last Highland charge ever to take place in the world. But the Rebels have cannon.

Jamie, Caswell, and several of the other commanders were walking up and down the bank, pointing at the bridge and up and down the shore. The creek ran through a stretch of treacherous, swampy ground, with cypress trees stretching up from water and mud. The creek itself deepened as it narrowed, though—a plumb line that some curious soul dropped into the water off the bridge said it was fifteen feet deep at that point—and the bridge was the only feasible place for an army of any size to cross.

Which did a great deal to explain Jamie's silence over supper. He had helped to throw up a small earthwork on the far side of the creek, and his hands were smeared with dirt—and grease.

"They've cannon," he said quietly, seeing me eye the smudges on his hands. He wiped them absently on his breeks, much the worse for wear. "Two small guns from the town—but cannon, nonetheless." He looked toward the bridge, and grimaced slightly.

I knew what he was thinking—and why.

Ye were behind the cannon at Culloden, Donald, *he had said to the Major.* I was in front of them. With a sword in my hand. *Swords were the Highlanders' natural weapons—and for most, likely their only weapons. From all we had heard, General MacDonald had managed to assemble only a small quantity of muskets and powder; most of his troops were armed with broadswords and targes. And they were marching straight into ambush.*

"Oh, Christ," Jamie said, so softly I could barely hear him. "The poor wee fools. The poor gallant wee fools."

As the shadow of war comes ever closer, Jamie dreams more and more often of Culloden—and wakes with the feeling that his godfather, Murtagh, is near him—though Murtagh died at Culloden. And then the foggy dawn of battle comes.

They burst out of the mist a hundred feet from the bridge, howling, and his heart jumped in his chest. For an instant—an instant only—he felt he ran with them, and the wind of it snapped in his shirt, cold on his body.

But he stood stock-still, Murtagh beside him, looking cynically on. Roger Mac coughed, and Jamie raised the rifle to his shoulder, waiting.

"Fire!" *The volley struck them just before they reached the gutted bridge; half a dozen fell in the road, but the others came on. Then the cannon fired from the hill above, one and then the other, and the concussion of their discharge was like a shove against his back.*

He had fired with the volley, aiming above their heads. Now swung the rifle down and pulled the ramrod. There was screaming on both sides, the shriek of wounded and the stronger bellowing of battle.

"A righ! A righ!" *The King! The King!*

McLeod was at the bridge; he'd been hit, there was blood on his coat, but he brandished sword and targe, and ran onto the bridge, stabbing his sword into the wood to anchor himself.

The cannon spoke again, but were aimed too high; most of the Highlanders had crowded down to the banks of the creek—some were in the water, clinging to the bridge supports, inching across. More were on the timbers, slipping, using their swords like McLeod to keep their balance.

"Fire!" *and he fired, powder smoke blending with the fog. The cannon had the range, they spoke one-two, and he felt the blast push against him, felt as though the shot had torn through him. Most of those on the bridge were in the water now, more threw themselves flat upon the timbers, trying to wriggle their way across, only to be picked off by the muskets, every man firing at will from the redoubt.*

He loaded, and fired.

There he is, *said a voice, dispassionate; he had no notion was it his, or Murtagh's.*

McLeod was dead, his body floating in the creek for an instant before the weight of the black water pulled him down. Many men were struggling in that water—the creek was deep here, and mortal cold. Few Highlanders could swim.

He glimpsed Allan MacDonald, Flora's husband, pale and staring in the crowd on the shore.

Major Donald MacDonald floundered, rising halfway in the water. His wig was gone and his head showed bare and wounded, blood running from his scalp down over his face. His teeth were bared, clenched in agony or ferocity, there was no telling which. Another shot struck him and he fell with a splash—but rose again, slow, slow, and then pitched forward into water too deep to stand, but rose yet again, splashing frantically, spraying blood from his shattered mouth in the effort to breathe.

Let it be you, then, lad, *said the dispassionate voice. He raised his rifle and shot MacDonald cleanly through the throat. He fell backward and sank at once.*

JAMIE AND ROGER arrive in time to capture the fleeing Bonnet and offer Brianna the opportunity either to kill Bonnet herself or allow them to do it. She demurs, preferring to hand him over to an impersonal justice.

PART 12: *TIME WILL NOT BE OURS FOREVER*

Brianna and Roger's baby is born—a daughter that her father calls Amanda, "she who must be loved." She is loved—but there is something wrong, something that her grandmother Claire reluctantly diagnoses as a birth defect called patent ductus arteriosus: a hole in the heart. A simple matter to correct surgically—in the twentieth century, with anesthesia and modern instruments; impossible in the eighteenth.

And so the decision is made. The MacKenzies must go back. Perhaps not Jem—but certainly Brianna and Amanda. And Roger cannot let them go alone.

More gemstones must be found, for what safety they may offer the travelers. And there are a few last obligations to be met.

ON A CLEAR morning, the pirate Stephen Bonnet is taken out onto the mudflats near Wilmington and tied to a stake, to await the incoming tide. Brianna is ready. She has made her arrangements—but seeing Lord John Grey on the dock, she thinks to ask for his help, in case it's needed. Going to talk to him, though, she sees the young man he's conversing with and realizes with a sense of shock that she's looking at her brother.

She has no time to ask questions, though; she has a job to do.

At two o'clock in the afternoon, Roger helped his wife into a small rowboat, tied to the quay near the row of warehouses. The tide had been coming in all day; the water was more than five feet deep. Out in the midst of the shining gray stood the cluster of mooring posts—and the small dark head of the pirate.

Brianna was remote as a pagan statue, her face expressionless. She lifted her skirts to step into the boat, and sat down, the weight in her pocket clunking against the wooden slat as she did so.

Roger took up the oars and rowed, heading toward the posts. They would arouse no particular interest; boats had been going out ever since noon, carrying sightseers who wished to look upon the condemned man's face, shout taunts, or clip a strand of his hair for a souvenir.

He couldn't see where he was going; Brianna directed him left or right with a silent tilt of her head. She could see; she sat straight and tall, her right hand hidden in her skirt.

Then she lifted her left hand suddenly, and Roger lay on the oars, digging with one to slew the tiny craft around.

Bonnet's lips were cracked, his face chapped and crusted with salt, his lids so reddened that he could barely open his eyes. But his head lifted as they drew near, and Roger saw a man ravished, helpless and dreading a coming embrace—so much that he half welcomes its seductive touch, yielding his flesh to cold fingers and the overwhelming kiss that steals his breath.

"Ye've left it late enough, darlin'," he said to Brianna, and the cracked lips parted in a grin that split them and left blood on his teeth. "I knew ye'd come, though."

Roger paddled with one oar, working the boat close, then closer. He was looking over his shoulder when Brianna drew the gilt-handled pistol from her pocket, and put the barrel to Stephen Bonnet's ear.

"Go with God, Stephen," she said clearly, in Gaelic, and pulled the trigger. Then she dropped the gun into the water and turned round to face her husband.

"Take us home," she said.

Later, Brianna confronts Lord John and insists on knowing all about the young man; Lord John tells her the truth—or as much of it as he can. At the same time, he is horrified by her desire to tell her brother, William, the truth; a good many people have gone to a great deal of trouble over the last eighteen years to ensure that no one learns that the Ninth Earl of Ellesmere is actually the bastard of a Scottish Jacobite traitor, and Lord John is not disposed to let a young woman's whim destroy his son's life.

Jamie weighs in solidly on Lord John's side of the disagreement, and Brianna reluctantly agrees—but has a price. And so one afternoon the two estranged friends find themselves side by side in an upstairs room, watching the quay outside as brother and sister meet, for the first and last time.

And at last the fateful day comes, and the family makes its way to the stone circle on Ocracoke. Jamie holds his grandson's hand tightly, as his parents make their preparations.

Roger reached out a hand and rested it gently on Jemmy's head. "Know this, mo mac*—I shall love ye all my life, and never forget ye. But this is a terrible thing we're doing, and ye need not come with me. Ye can stay with your grandda and grannie Claire; it will be all right."*

"Won't I—won't I see Mama again?" Jemmy's eyes were huge, and he couldn't keep from looking at the stone.

"I don't know," Roger said, and I could see the tears he was fighting himself, and hear them in his thickened voice. He didn't know whether he would ever see Brianna again himself, or baby Mandy. "Probably . . . probably not."

Jamie looked down at Jem, who was clinging to his hand, looking back and forth between father and grandfather, confusion, fright, and longing in his face.

"If one day, a bhalaich,*" Jamie said conversationally, "ye should meet a verra large mouse named Michael—ye'll tell him your grandsire sends his regards." He opened his hand, then, letting go, and nodded toward Roger.*

Jem stood staring for a moment, then dug in his feet and sprinted toward Roger, sand spurting from under his shoes. He leaped into his father's arms, clutching him around the neck, and with a final glance backward, Roger turned and stepped behind the stone, and the inside of my head exploded in fire.

Mourning, the Frasers return to the Ridge once more. Claire goes one day to lay flowers on Malva's grave and finds Malva's brother, Allan, there, bent in sorrow. He tells Claire that he and his half sister had been lovers ever since she was a very young girl—and that the child she was carrying was his. He had told her to accuse Jamie of fathering the child, in hopes that Jamie would settle a large amount of money on her to keep quiet—then he and Malva could have gone away somewhere to live as man and wife. But Malva is gone, and he wishes to die, as well; he can't live. Malva had qualms, though, and had decided to tell the truth; Allan had no choice but to kill her.

Claire tries to dissuade him, but Ian, overhearing this confession from the wood, shoots Allan through the heart with an arrow.

"He's right, Auntie," Ian said quietly. "He can't."

Life is slowly returning to an approximation of normal when the Big House is invaded by a gang of men, led by Donner. They demand the gemstones that they are convinced Jamie has cached and ransack the house in search of wealth, breaking things with vicious abandon—including the carboy of ether in Claire's surgery; she can smell the fumes from the kitchen, where she and Jamie are being held hostage with Ian and Mrs. Bug.

The arrival of Scotchee Cameron with several Cherokee provides a distraction, and Jamie stabs Donner. A fight with the thugs ensues, but the bandits are quickly overpowered.

The kitchen was nearly dark now, the figures swaying like fronds of kelp in some underwater forest.

I closed my eyes for a second. When I opened them again, Ian was saying, "Wait, I'll light a candle." He had one of Brianna's matches in his hand, the tin in the other.

"IAN!" I shrieked, and then he struck the match.

There was a soft whoof! *noise, then a louder* whoomp! *as the ether in the surgery ignited, and suddenly we were standing in a pool of fire. For a fraction of a second, I felt nothing, and then a burst of searing heat. Jamie seized my arm and hurled me toward the door; I staggered out, fell into the blackberry bushes, and rolled through them, thrashing and flailing at my smoking skirts.*

Panicked and still uncoordinated from the ether, I struggled with the strings of my apron, finally managing to rip loose the strings and wriggle out of my skirt. My linen petticoats were singed, but not charred. I crouched panting in the dead weeds of the dooryard, unable to do anything for the moment but breathe. The smell of smoke was strong and pungent.

Mrs. Bug was on the back porch on her knees, jerking off her cap, which was on fire.

Men erupted through the back door, beating at their clothes and hair. Rollo was in the yard, barking hysterically, and on the other side of the house, I could hear the screams of frightened horses. Someone had got Arch Bug out—he was stretched at full length in the dead grass, most of his hair and eyebrows gone, but evidently still alive.

My legs were red and blistered, but I wasn't badly burned—thank God for layers of linen and cotton, which burn slowly, I thought groggily. Had I been wearing something modern like rayon, I should have gone up like a torch.

The thought made me look back toward the house. It was full dark by now, and all the windows on the lower floor were alight. Flame danced in the open door. The place looked like an immense jack-o'-lantern.

So the house *does* burn—but the resident Frasers are not dead. And in the aftermath of the disaster, Jamie discovers one of the missing ingots from the King of France's gold—in the possession of Arch Bug.

"I give ye the chance of explanation, man, not the choice." He'd dropped the pleasant tone. Jamie was smudged with soot, and scorched round the edges, but his eyebrows were intact and being put to good use. He turned to me, gesturing to the gold.

"Ye've seen it before, aye?"

"Of course." The last time I'd seen it, it had been gleaming in the lantern light, packed solid with its fellows in the bottom of a coffin in Hector Cameron's mausoleum, but the shape of the ingots and the fleur-de-lis stamp were unmistakable. "Unless Louis of France has been sending someone else vast quantities of gold, it's part of Jocasta's hoard."

"That it is not, and never was," Arch corrected me firmly.

"Aye?" Jamie cocked a thick brow at him. "To whom does it belong, then, if not to Jocasta Cameron? D'ye claim it as your own?"

"I do not." He hesitated, but the urge to speak was powerful. "It is the property of the

King," he said, and his old mouth closed tight on the last word.

"What, the King of—oh," I said, realizing at long last. "That *king."*

"Le roi, c'est mort," *Jamie said softly, as though to himself, but Arch turned fiercely to him.*

"Is Scotland dead?"

Jamie drew breath, but didn't speak at once. Instead, he gestured me to a seat on the stack of chopped cordwood, and nodded at Arch to take another, before sitting down beside me.

"Scotland will die when her last son does, a charaid,*" he said, and waved a hand toward the door, taking in the mountains and hollows around us—and all the people therein. "How many are here? How many will be? Scotland lives—but not in Italy." In Rome, he meant, where Charles Stuart eked out what remained to him of a life, drowning his disappointed dreams of a crown in drink.*

Arch narrowed his eyes at this, but kept a stubborn silence.

"Ye were the third man, were ye not?" Jamie asked, disregarding this. "When the gold was brought ashore from France. Dougal MacKenzie took one-third, and Hector Cameron another. I couldna say what Dougal did with his—gave it to Charles Stuart, most likely, and may God have mercy on his soul for that. You were tacksman to Malcolm Grant; he sent ye, did he not? You took one-third of the gold on his behalf. Did ye give it to him?"

Arch nodded, slowly.

"It was given in trust," he said, and his voice cracked. He cleared his throat and spat, the mucus tinged with black. "To me, and then to the Grant—who should have given it in turn to the King's son."

* * *

"You are free of your oath to me," Jamie said formally in Gaelic. "Take your life from my hand." And inclining his head toward the ingot, said, "Take that—and go."

Arch regarded him for a moment, unblinking. Then stooped, picked up the ingot, and went.

Jamie and Claire stand in the falling snow, looking at the burnt embers of their house.

"Ye can at least promise me the victory," he said, but his voice held the whisper of a question.

"Yes," I said, and touched his face. I sounded choked, and my vision blurred. "Yes, I can promise that. This time." No mention made of what that promise spared, of the things I could not guarantee. Not life, not safety. Not home, nor family; not law nor legacy. Just the one thing—or maybe two.

"The victory," I said. "And that I will be with you 'til the end."

He closed his eyes for a moment. Snowflakes pelted down, melting as they struck his face, sticking for an instant, white on his lashes. Then he opened his eyes and looked at me.

"That is enough," he said softly. "I ask no more."

He reached forward then and took me in his arms, held me close for a moment, the breath of snow and ashes cold around us. Then he kissed me, released me, and I took a deep breath of cold air, harsh with the scent of burning. I brushed a floating smut off my arm.

"Well . . . good. Bloody *good. Er . . ." I hesitated. "What do you suggest we do next?"*

He stood looking at the charred ruin, eyes narrowed, then lifted his shoulders and let them fall.

"I think," he said slowly, "we shall go—" He stopped suddenly, frowning. "What in God's name . . . ?"

Something was moving at the side of the house. I blinked away the snowflakes, standing on tiptoe to see better.

"Oh, it can't *be!" I said—but it was. With a tremendous upheaval of snow, dirt, and charred wood, the white sow thrust her way into daylight. Fully emerged, she shook her massive shoulders, then, pink snout twitching irritably, moved purposefully off toward the wood. A moment later, a smaller version likewise emerged—and another, and another . . . and eight half-grown piglets, some white, some spotted, and one as black as the timbers of the house, trotted off in a line, following their mother.*

"Scotland lives," I said again, giggling uncontrollably. "Er—where did you say we were going?"

"To Scotland," he said, as though this were obvious. "To fetch my printing press."

He was still looking at the house, but his eyes were fixed somewhere beyond the ashes, far beyond the present moment. An owl hooted deep in the distant wood, startled from its sleep. He stood silent for a bit, then shook off his reverie, and smiled at me, snow melting in his hair.

"And then," he said simply, "we shall come back to fight."

He took my hand and turned away from the house, toward the barn where the horses stood waiting, patient in the cold.

EPILOGUE: *THE DEVIL IS IN THE DETAILS*

"What's this, then?" Amos Crupp squinted at the page laid out in the bed of the press, reading it backward with the ease of long experience.

"It is with grief that the news is received of the deaths by fire . . . *Where'd that come from?"*

"Note from a subscriber," said Sampson, his new printer's devil, shrugging as he inked the plate. "Good for a bit of filler, there, I thought; General Washington's address to the troops run short of the page."

"Hmph. I s'pose. Very old news, though," Crupp said, glancing at the date. "January?"

"Well, no," the devil admitted, heaving down on the lever that lowered the page onto the plate of inked type. The press sprang up again, the letters wet and black on the paper, and he picked the sheet off with nimble fingertips, hanging it up to dry. "'Twas December, by the notice. But I'd set the page in Baskerville twelve-point, and the slugs for November and December are missing in that font. Not room to do it in separate letters, and not worth the labor to reset the whole page."

"To be sure," said Amos, losing interest in the matter, as he perused the last paragraphs of Washington's speech. "Scarcely signifies, anyway. After all, they're all dead, aren't they?"

THE END

An Echo in the Bone

Breath of Snow and Ashes ends (more or less) in 1777. *An Echo in the Bone* begins in 1776. (Well, we *are* playing fast and loose with time, pretty much all the time. Surely you've noticed that.)

We're seeing a scene that we've seen before—but this time it's from the point of view of Lieutenant William Ransom, Ninth Earl of Ellesmere. William is just eighteen, pleased to be back in the South, where he spent part of his youth, and excited at the prospect of his first military campaign. Still, he's not too distracted to notice the charms of the tall, red-haired young matron whom he meets on the quay in Wilmington—despite the presence of her husband and two children. The memory of the woman's dark-blue eyes, intent and slightly slanted, lingers pleasantly. It's been a long time since William's seen himself in a proper mirror, or he might think twice about those eyes.

As it is, the eyes and their owner depart, never to be seen again, and the memory vanishes, too, when William goes to take supper with his father, Lord John Grey, at a friend's house. The friend, Richard Bell, has two lovely—and single—daughters (William *is* only eighteen, after all). Bell also has an interesting guest: one Captain Ezekiel Richardson, who manages to get William's attention long enough to make him an interesting proposal: to wit, that William might undertake a small "intelligencing" job, carrying secret messages for Richardson and noticing anything helpful that might turn up along the way. (Intelligencing was what gentlemen did. Spying was vulgar—not something a gentleman would touch with his bare hands.) As reward, William would be attached to General Howe's staff up north—a much better prospect for military advancement.

William, always up for adventure and advantage, agrees, with his father's blessing. Lord John has private opinions (not all favorable) regarding the world of espionage, and a lot of experience to back them up. On the other hand, he has one urgent reason for wanting Willie out of town: the nearby presence of Jamie Fraser, William's *real* father. William may not have noticed the family resemblance when he met his half sister on the quay, but he can't miss it—and neither will anyone else—if he and Jamie ever come face-to-face. And a number of people have gone to a lot of trouble for some years now to conceal the fact that the Ninth Earl of Ellesmere is the bastard of a Scottish criminal.

Returning alone to his lodging, Lord John is distracted from his family complications when he's informed that "a Frenchman" is waiting in his room. He opens the door and comes face-to-face with an unexpected bit of his own past. The "Monsieur Beauchamp" who greets him is Perseverance Wainwright, his stepbrother and erstwhile (a long while erst) lover.

Lord John barely has time to absorb the shock of Percy's reappearance after nearly twenty years, or the knowledge that Percy has been working for the French government as an intelligence operative during those years, before Percy lays something even more disturbing at his feet: a suggestion that the French (or at least someone connected with the French military or government) would like to do a deal with the English. To wit, the French would like to get back the Northwest Territory, which they had ceded to Great Britain after the French and Indian War a decade earlier. In exchange for making this possible, Percy's masters—whomever they may be—will undertake to subvert one of Washington's highest officers and do anything else they can to cripple the infant rebellion and enable Britain to quash it before it grows into something large and expensive.

This suggestion is enough to make Lord John squint-eyed with suspicion, but when Percy casually mentions that he is looking for one James Fraser, and in the next breath mentions William, Lord John has had more than enough. He warns Percy roughly to keep his distance from William, then turns on his heel and leaves, hoping that Jamie Fraser *and* his daughter are both well on their way out of town.

Lest we forget the red-haired young woman with William's eyes . . .

This is, of course, Brianna Randall Fraser MacKenzie, daughter of Jamie Fraser and Claire Beauchamp Randall Fraser. She and her husband, Roger MacKenzie, together with their two children, Jem (for Jeremiah) and Mandy (Amanda), have returned through the stones to their proper future. We meet them in 1980 in the Scottish Highlands, where they have settled at Jamie's ancestral home, Lallybroch. Superficially, things seem to be going well: Jem is enrolled at the village school, where his exercise of some eighteenth-century skills—e.g., prowess at snaring and skinning rats—has gained him a certain amount of notoriety, and Mandy has recovered very well from the surgery needed to repair her heart and has developed a disturbing ability to take things apart. Brianna is contemplating a return to her engineering profession, and Roger . . . is not quite sure.

In the past, he was certain of his vocation as a minister but was never ordained. Now he *could* be—but is it still what he wants, what he feels is right? Things that he's seen and learned and thought, regarding his travels through time, have given him Doubts, and thinking how best to protect his children from the dangers of time travel has magnified them.

Still, for the moment, life is good for the MacKenzies at Lallybroch, and their focus of attention is on the box of letters left for them, in which Claire and Jamie recount their adventures after the MacKenzies' departure through the stones.

These adventures begin in late December of 1776, where we find Claire writing to her daughter late at night, with her husband sleeping curled against her knee, Jamie's nephew Ian out patrolling the frozen woods, and a dying stranger on the floor at her feet.

The stranger is an elderly woman, sick unto death, left with Claire by her grandsons, on their way to enlist in the militia. Ian and Jamie are taking turns in the woods at night, keeping watch over the ruins of the Big House, recently destroyed by fire. Someone has been creeping around at night, and that same someone has been trying to kill the White Sow, of whom Claire thinks: *The local Presbyterians would not have seen eye-to-eye with the Cherokee on any other spiritual matter you might name, but they were in decided agreement on the sow's demonic character.* Jamie and Ian suspect that the intruder is Arch Bug, who, while working as Jamie's factor, stole ten thousand pounds of Jacobite gold from Jamie's aunt Jocasta and spirited it away from her home at River Run. Jamie dismissed Arch and his wife, Murdina, but suspects that the gold is still somewhere on Fraser's Ridge.

The door opens and Ian and his dog, Rollo, appear, bidding Jamie come with them—something is up.

Something is: a black figure with a sack is prowling through the blackened timbers of the burnt Big House, and Jamie realizes that the gold was hidden under the foundations of the house, left under the guard of the White Sow, who makes her den there. Jamie hails the black figure, meaning to apprehend Arch Bug, but the figure turns and fires at him, wounding him slightly. Ian, defending his uncle, shoots the figure with his bow and arrow—realizing too late that the figure has fired the pistol with its right hand; Arch Bug can't hold a pistol in his right hand, having lost the first two fingers years before in Scotland.

Sure enough, the black figure proves to be not Arch but Murdina Bug, pierced through the throat with Ian's arrow. Claire ends the night holding a wake with Jamie over *two* bodies laid out on her porch (the stranger having died unnoticed in the midst of the excitement) and wondering what the morning will bring.

The morning brings two funerals—and further drama, as Arch Bug appears to attend his wife's burial and confront her killer. Ian, racked with guilt, offers his own life as payment for the killing of Mrs. Bug, but old Arch refuses.

"When you've something worth taking, boy—you'll see me again," he said quietly, then turned upon his heel and walked into the trees.

Jamie had already intended to leave the mountains as soon as spring and snowmelt made it possible, to find a ship that would carry the Frasers to Scotland, where he plans to reclaim the printing press he left there years before and bring it back to help wage war with words, rather than with sword and gun. He has two additional reasons for departure: years before, he had promised his sister that he would bring back her youngest son, Ian. Now looks like a really good time to keep that promise and get Young Ian out of Arch Bug's range. But beyond patriotic determination and family obligation, Jamie has a second reason—one that he doesn't discuss even with Claire. He's seen William and knows the boy is a lieutenant in the British army. Jamie suffers from recurrent nightmares, and the worst of these is the vision of himself facing his unacknowledged son across the barrel of a gun.

Leaving Fraser's Ridge—perhaps forever—

involves some preparation, and one of these preparations involves the Spaniard's Cave. This is a secret cave, deep in the woods, where Jamie and Young Ian have stashed the Jacobite gold for safekeeping. Jamie takes Claire to the cave so that she will know its location, should she ever come back without him, and there extracts a small amount of the gold to finance their expedition to Scotland.

Much needs to be done to ready the people of the Ridge, too. Claire delivers Lizzie's new baby—a dangerous transverse lie—and Jamie hands over responsibility for the tenants' physical welfare to Bobby Higgins and Hiram Crombie. But the most important part of leaving is, as always, finding a way to say goodbye.

I followed the calling of the jays uphill, away from the clearing. There was a pair nesting near the White Spring; I'd seen them building the nest only two days before. It wasn't far from the house site at all, though that particular spring always had the air of being remote from everything. It lay in the center of a small grove of white ash and hemlock, and was shielded on the east by a jagged outcropping of lichen-covered rock. All water has a sense of life about it, and a mountain spring carries a particular sense of quiet joy, rising pure from the heart of the earth. The White Spring, so called for the big pale boulder that stood guardian over its pool, had something more—a sense of inviolate peace.

The closer I came to it, the surer I was that that was where I'd find Jamie.

"There's something there that listens," he'd told Brianna once, quite casually. "Ye see such pools in the Highlands; they're called saints' pools—folk say the saint lives by the pool and listens to their prayers."

"And what saint lives by the White Spring?" she'd asked, cynical. "Saint Killian?"

"Why him?"

"Patron saint of gout, rheumatism, and whitewashers."

He'd laughed at that, shaking his head. "Whatever it is that lives in such water is older than the notion of saints," he assured her. "But it listens."

I walked softly, approaching the spring. The jays had fallen silent now. He was there, sitting on a rock by the water, wearing only his shirt. I saw why the jays had gone about their business—he was still as the white boulder itself, his eyes closed, hands turned upward on his knees, loosely cupped, inviting grace.

I stopped at once when I saw him. I had seen him pray here once before—when he'd asked Dougal MacKenzie for help in battle. I didn't know who he was talking to just now, but it wasn't a conversation I wished to intrude upon. I ought to leave, I supposed—but aside from the fear that I might disturb him by an inadvertent noise, I didn't want to go. Most of the spring lay in shadow, but fingers of light came down through the trees, stroking him. The air was thick with pollen, and the light was filled with motes of gold. It struck answering glints from the crown of his head, the smooth high arch of his foot, the blade of his nose, the bones of his face. He might have grown there, part of earth and stone and water, might have been himself the spirit of the spring.

I didn't feel unwelcome. The peace of the place reached out to touch me gently, slow my heart. Was that what he sought here, I wondered? Was he drawing the peace of the mountain into himself, to remember, to sustain him during the months—the years, perhaps—of coming exile?

I would remember.

The light began to go, brightness falling from the air. He stirred, finally, lifting his head a little.

"Let me be enough," he said quietly. I started at the sound of his voice, but he hadn't been speaking to me.

He opened his eyes and rose then, quiet as he'd sat, and came past the stream, long feet bare and silent on the layers of damp leaves. As he came past the outcropping of rock, he saw me and smiled, reaching out to take the plaid I held out to him, wordless. He said nothing, but took my cold hand in his large warm one and we turned toward home, walking together in the mountain's peace.

Claire too takes her own leave of the place she's lived in and loved for so long:

I looked last at the spot where I had planted salad greens; that's where she had died. In memory, I'd always seen the spreading blood, imagined it still there, a permanent stain soaked dark into the earth among the churned wreckage of uprooted lettuces and wilting leaves. But it was gone; nothing marked the spot save a fairy ring of mushrooms, tiny white heads poking out of the wild grass.

"I will arise and go now," *I said softly,* "and go to Innisfree, and a small cabin build there, of clay and wattles made; nine bean rows will I have there, a hive for the honey-bee, and live alone in the bee-loud glade." *I paused for a moment, and as I turned away, added in a whisper,* "And I shall have some peace there, for peace comes dropping slow."

I made my way briskly down the path then; no need to apostrophize the ruins of the house, nor yet the white sow. I'd remember them *without effort. As for the corncrib and hen coop—if you've seen one, you've seen them all.*

I could see the little gathering of horses, mules, and people moving in the slow chaos of imminent departure in front of the cabin. I wasn't quite ready yet for goodbyes, though, and stepped into the wood to pull myself together.

The grass was long beside the trail, soft and feathery against the hem of my weighted skirts. Something heavier than grass brushed them, and I looked down to see Adso. I'd been looking for him most of yesterday; typical of him to show up at the last minute.

"So there you are," I said, accusing. He looked at me with his huge calm eyes of celadon green, and licked a paw. On impulse, I scooped him up and held him against me, feeling the rumble of his purr and the soft, thick fur of his silvery belly.

He'd be all right; I knew that. The woods were his private game preserve, and Amy Higgins liked him and had promised me to see him right for milk and a warm spot by the fire in bad weather. I knew that.

"Go on, then," I said, and set him on the ground. He stood for a moment, tail waving slowly, head raised in search of food or interesting smells, then stepped into the grass and vanished.

I bent, very slowly, arms crossed, and shook, weeping silently, violently.

I cried until my throat hurt and I couldn't breathe, then sat in the grass, curled into myself like a dried leaf, tears that I couldn't stop dropping on my knees like the first fat drops of a coming storm. Oh, God. It was only the beginning.

I rubbed my hands hard over my eyes, smearing the wetness, trying to scrub away grief. A soft cloth touched my face, and I looked up, sniffing, to find Jamie kneeling in front of me, handkerchief in hand. "I'm sorry," he said, very softly.

"It's not—don't worry, I'm . . . He's only a cat," I said, and a small fresh grief tightened like a band round my chest.

"Aye, I know." He moved beside me and put an arm round my shoulders, pulling my head to his chest, while he gently wiped my face. "But ye couldna weep for the bairns. Or the house. Or your wee garden. Or the poor dead lass and her bairn. But if ye weep for your cheetie, ye know ye can stop."

"How do you know that?" My voice was thick, but the band round my chest was not quite so tight.

He made a small, rueful sound. "Because I canna weep for those things, either, Sassenach. And I havena got a cat."

BACK AT LALLYBROCH of the twentieth century, Roger rejoices with his wife at the message of survival in Claire's letter. But he can't help noticing the postscript to that letter, written in Jamie's hand:

> *I see I am to have the last Word—a rare Treat to a Man living in a House that contains (at last count) eight Women. . . .*
>
> *I wished to tell you of the Disposition of the Property which was once held in trust by the Camerons for an Italian Gentleman. I think it unwise to carry this with us, and have therefore removed it to a Place of Safety. Jem knows the Place. If you should at some Time have need of this Property, tell him the Spaniard guards it. If so, be sure to have it blessed by a Priest; there is Blood upon it.*

The past, though, is not the only element of disquiet at Lallybroch. Brianna is growing impatient—chafing at domesticity and troubled over Roger's indecision regarding his own career. Something else is going on, as well: Jem says he has met a Nuckelavee, out near the ancient broch behind the house. A Nuckelavee is one of the nastier forms of Scottish supernatural phenomena and nothing you'd want to meet, even in daylight. Roger doesn't *think* Jem's met one, but he goes to look and discovers that someone has certainly been living in the broch; there are small signs of occupancy. He buys a padlock and keeps a close eye on the broch, but there is no further sign of an intruder.

For her part, Brianna gets a job, as a safety inspector for the Highlands and Islands Development Board.

IN AUGUST OF 1776, Lieutenant William Ransom has successfully completed his first intelligencing assignment and made it to Staten Island, where he joins General Howe's staff—just in time to take ship next morning for the invasion of Long Island. William thirsts for battle and distinction but, like many another young soldier before him, finds the business not quite as he imagined it.

Pursuing the fleeing Americans through Jamaica Pass, the British are temporarily halted by heavy fog. William is summoned to headquarters but becomes lost in the fog and is captured by a pair of elderly, guntoting ladies, who more or less politely detain him, obliging him to sit on a rock, ignominiously witnessing the evacuation of the entire American army, who are headed for New York.

Released from captivity, he is forced to return to General Howe's headquarters, bearing the news that Washington's army has escaped.

"Heard of a lady called Cassandra?" one of

the older officers asks him. *"Some sort of Greek, I think. Not very popular."*

IN NEW BERN, Claire puts out her shingle at the printshop owned by Jamie's foster son and step-daughter, Fergus and Marsali. Jamie sets about the not-inconsequential problem of finding a ship. There's a British blockade of the southern colonies, and what few private ships are licensed by the Crown are not often willing to carry passengers. On the other hand, gold is a great persuader.

Jamie finds a man who knows a man who will take them—for a price—aboard his fishing ketch and thus outside the harbor, there to rendezvous with a privateer who will take them to Europe. Reluctant to entrust their welfare to a total stranger, Jamie insists upon meeting at least the first man in this chain—and in the process encounters a mention of the mysterious Mr. Beauchamp (aka Percy Wainwright).

From what Jamie can deduce, Percy is in search of one Fergus Fraser—who may be the missing heir to a great French family. Jamie scarcely knows what to do with this information, but asks Fergus if he wishes to meet with Monsieur Beauchamp.

"For a long time," he said at last, "when I was small, I pretended to myself that I was the bastard of some great man. All orphans do this, I think," he added dispassionately. "It makes life easier to bear, to pretend that it will not always be as it is, that someone will come and restore you to your rightful place in the world."

He shrugged.

"Then I grew older, and knew this was not true. No one would come to rescue me. But then—" He turned his head and gave Jamie a smile of surpassing sweetness.

"Then I grew older still, and discovered that, after all, it was true. I am the son of a great man."

The hook touched Jamie's hand, hard and capable.

"I wish for nothing more."

Underemployed following the battle of New York, and exiled to a customs checkpoint on remote Long Island as the result of a run-in with a fellow officer, William is chafing—and thus receptive to the advances of Captain Richardson, who reappears with an inviting prospect: a journey to Canada, acting as interpreter and aide to one Captain Denys Randall-Isaacs. William is cautious but lured by the thought of escape and adventure. Before he can depart for Canada, though, he accidentally makes the acquaintance of Captain Robert Rogers—leader of an elite if eccentric militia group. Rogers is on the track of an American spy reported to be on Long Island, and hearing that William has actually seen Captain Nathan Hale, who came through his checkpoint, he invites William to accompany his men to apprehend the spy.

Hale is captured without incident that night and promptly taken to General Howe in New York, who condemns him out of hand. Hale is hanged the next day, and as William watches the execution, he begins to take the risks of intelligence work a little more seriously.

Even so, he decides to accept Richardson's proposal.

Monsieur Beauchamp goes away, unsatisfied. Jamie is—reluctantly—satisfied as to the *bona fides* of the privateer, and so the Frasers, Young Ian, and the dog Rollo eventually find themselves aboard the *Tranquil Teal,* captained by a morose specimen named Captain Roberts and carrying cargo for delivery to the northern colonies before the ship turns toward Europe. Claire is intrigued to find that several of the boxes are addressed to Benedict Arnold, in care of his sister.

Jamie is deeply averse to boats at the best of times, though he's steeled himself for the rigors of an Atlantic voyage, with the help of Claire's acupuncture needles. Acupuncture, though, is no help against the Royal Navy, which shows up in the person of one Captain Stebbings, commander of the naval cutter *Pitt,* a bumptious officer with a ruthless streak, who tries to press hands from the *Teal*—including Jamie and Young Ian. This is a mistake, as the captain discovers more or less immediately.

Jamie and Ian (and Claire, who has followed them over the rail, desperate not to be abandoned on the high seas) take over the *Pitt,* and Jamie finds himself in the uncomfortable position of being an inadvertent pirate—and the still more uncomfortable position of being captain of a ship. Matters get worse when the *Teal,* now commanded by the enraged Captain Stebbings, pursues them, only to be intercepted by a third ship, the *Asp,* this captained by one (one of him was plenty, Claire reflects) Asa Hickman—a patriot, a smuggler, and a sworn enemy of Captain Stebbings, who was responsible for the death of Hickman's brother.

A three-sided sea battle ensues, though Claire sees little of it, locked in the hold with a cabin boy. Jamie and Captain Stebbings nearly succeed in killing each other, and Claire—to her intense annoyance—is obliged to stitch them both up. Captain Hickman is in command, though, and declares that they are now all going to keep *his* rendezvous—with the Continental army at Fort Ticonderoga, where he has a shipment of guns, ammunition—and now captives—to deliver.

———

LORD JOHN, HAVING seen William, Jamie and Claire, and Brianna's family all more or less safely disposed of for the moment, returns to London, where he visits an old connection from his days in the Black Chamber—the official center of diplomatic espionage. All major European capitals have their own Black Chambers, the inhabitants of which keep tabs on one another, and Lord John wants to know whether anything is known about Percy Wainwright (in his persona as Percival Beauchamp) or the Baron Amandine, whose sister Percy has married.

Lord John's connection has never heard of Amandine and has only a few obscure letters filed under *Beauchamp.* This intrigues and alarms Grey further, as he knows for a fact that there are—or *were*—extensive files of material on Beauchamp; Beauchamp was more or less his own opposite number when he himself was a member of the Black Chamber, and he knows Beauchamp's style well—though he had no idea at the time that Beauchamp was Percy Wainwright. Now that material has evidently disappeared.

His sense of disturbance is exacerbated by receipt of a letter from William, confessing that he, William, has fallen in love with Lady Dorothea Grey—Lord John's niece and William's cousin—and strongly implying that things between them had Gone Too

Far one romantic evening in a garden. Clearly they must be married. Will Lord John speak to Dottie's father? William asks.

Knowing William—and Dottie—as well as he does, Lord John finds this deeply suspicious. Whatever William may be up to, though, the next step is obvious: Lord John goes to Argus House to talk to his brother, Hal, Duke of Pardloe.

Hal is in poor health but brought to instant alertness by Lord John's news regarding Percy Wainwright. John decides not to speak to Hal regarding William's letter, though—not until he's had a chance to speak to Dottie. This he does, and she assures him that she and William are indeed in love, begging him to use his influence with her father to allow her to travel to America so they can be married, in case William is killed in the conflict.

Dottie is very convincing—but her uncle has been a soldier, a spy, and a parent for a long time and knows much too much about human nature—and Dottie—to believe her.

"Dorothea," he said firmly. "I will *discover what you're up to."*

She looked at him for a long, thoughtful moment, as though estimating the chances. The corner of her mouth rose insensibly as her eyes narrowed, and he saw the response on her face, as clearly as if she'd said it aloud.

No. I don't think so.

BACK IN SCOTLAND of 1980 . . . Prodded into fury by Brianna—but admitting to himself that she's *right,* which is even more galling—Roger goes to speak to the rector of St. Stephen's, in search of spiritual guidance regarding his vocation. He finds the rector's advice comforting—and the offer of employment as assistant choirmaster a welcome, if challenging, chance to do something useful while he looks for clarity in other matters. Having decided that confession is good for the soul, he makes up his mind to tell Brianna the source of his doubts.

Brianna returns from a successful job interview, hoping to celebrate with Roger, and is disturbed to find him not at home. He's gone to *England,* the housekeeper tells her, scandalized. A foreign country!

Bree can't imagine what he's doing in Oxford and is annoyed at his abrupt departure on the night of her triumph. Her annoyance fades at once, though, when he returns with a photocopied page—a reproduction of a news clipping from the *Wilmington Gazette,* telling of the death by fire of the Frasers of Fraser's Ridge. This was the clipping that sent Brianna—and then Roger—into the past, to find her family and, if possible, prevent the disaster. The disaster wasn't precisely prevented—the house did burn down, as they learned from Claire's letter—but Jamie and Claire escaped alive, and . . . the date on which the house burned was not the one given in the clipping.

But the date in the clipping has changed.

Roger is a Presbyterian, and one of the central tenets of his faith is a belief in predestination. The mere fact of time travel's existence is enough to shake that belief; the knowledge that history can apparently be altered knocks one or two important stones out of the foundation.

WILLIAM, MEANWHILE, WRITES to tell his father that he has enjoyed his intelligencing expedition into Canada but has now been abruptly and puzzlingly abandoned by his companion, Denys Randall-Isaacs. He spends a boring winter in Quebec, hunting and trapping ermine with an Indian scout and dining with the governor, and Lord

John is left to make inquiries regarding Randall-Isaacs—an evidently reputable soldier, but one about whom almost nothing is known. What is Randall-Isaacs's connection with Richardson?

ROGER IS IN better case than William; his job as assistant choirmaster is going well, and he has—to Brianna's joy—begun to sing again himself, though only with painful difficulty and only in private.

Brianna's job has also been going well—bar a certain amount of hazing from some of her male co-workers, who lock her into a maintenance tunnel for a joke. Fuming but level-headed, she boards the tiny electric train used to service the tunnel and drives toward the far end, where she knows there is a door into the service chamber of the dam. Somewhere in the darkness, though, something strikes her with the force of a garrote. Knocked half over and gasping, she realizes that whatever it was that nearly sliced through her, it had the same feel about it as the time passages she's encountered among the standing stones.

She tells Roger about it later, and they hypothesize that it may have been a ley line—a line of electromagnetic force in the earth's field. Roger is compiling something he ironically calls "The Hitchhiker's Guide"—this being a compendium of knowledge, guesses, and warnings about time travel, for the eventual use of his children.

LORD JOHN, SEEKING to establish the veracity—or otherwise—of Percy Wainwright's offer, goes to France to make inquiries. His lack of reception by officials who would normally see him causes him to think that there may just be something going on. Further investigations lead him to mention of the mysterious *Rodrigue Hortalez et Cie,* a Portuguese company whose directors and functions seem deliberately obscure. Finally, he goes to *Trois Flèches,* the estate of the Baron Amandine. He learns little from the baron, but there he meets another visitor—Dr. Benjamin Franklin. The doctor is pleasant company—but the presence of a prominent American at *Trois Flèches* convinces Lord John that there is indeed something going on, that the "something" concerns the American rebellion—and that Percy is in it up to his neck.

Lord John's brother, Hal, has been making his own inquiries in London and is able to assure John that Denys Randall-Isaacs is a "political," with ties to Lord Germain, the secretary of state—but knows very little of Captain Richardson, who seems to be lying low, somewhere in the colonies.

There is no time for further inquiries: news has come that Hal's youngest son, Henry, has been wounded and captured. Lord John and Dottie take ship at once, to find and rescue him.

BOUND FOR THE northern army under General Burgoyne, Willie detours—at Captain Richardson's request—into the Great Dismal Swamp, charged with the delivery of secret messages to several men in Dismal Town, a settlement in the center of the swamp. William is familiar with the Great Dismal, having hunted there frequently in his younger years. It is, however, a very large swamp. He loses his way, and then his horse, and is forced to spend the night in the swamp during a lightning storm, during which a large cypress tree is struck by lightning and explodes, a large splinter skewering William's arm. Alone, without food, and suffering from fever, William presses on toward the center of the swamp, where he knows Dismal Town is to be found along the shore of the lake there.

He runs into a poisonous snake and then into two Indians, who try to capture him to sell as a slave. Fleeing from these Indians, William runs head-on into another—a Mohawk who at once sends the first Indians on their way. But this man isn't exactly a Mohawk; he's Ian Murray (who has left Jamie and Claire at Ticonderoga and is traveling to rendezvous in the Great Dismal with some Mohawk hunters he knows, in hopes of learning the whereabouts and welfare of his Mohawk ex-wife). Ian has of course met William, seven years earlier at Fraser's Ridge. Any suspicions he entertained at that point regarding William's identity are settled permanently once he gets a good look at William's face—and his sprouting red beard.

Ian does his best to doctor Willie's arm, now badly infected, but when the other Mohawk hunters show up the next dawn, they agree that William needs more help than they can offer and suggest taking him to a small Quaker settlement not far away, where there is a doctor.

William awakes, after a period of delirium, in the house of Denzell Hunter, a young physician, and his younger sister, Rachel. William is weak and shaky but not too weak to appreciate Rachel, who is not only pretty but a girl of strong mind and undiluted opinions.

Neither is she shy. Having extracted enough information from William to suppose that he is a British deserter—but at least a capable man—she invites him to travel with her and her brother, to provide mutual protection on the road. They are going to join the Continental army, Denzell's convictions having led him to the firm conclusion that he must help the cause of liberty. Not by fighting—he *is* a Quaker—but by offering his medical services as an army surgeon.

William does not plan to get very close to the Continental army, but his way does lie north—and he may be able to pick up bits of intelligence along the way, in compensation for his failure to deliver messages to Dismal Town. He is somewhat uneasy about that mission, in fact; he's learned from Ian that all the men in Dismal Town are fervent Rebels, not the Loyalists he'd been led to expect. Can Captain Richardson have been so badly mistaken? Or . . . had he sent William deliberately into an ambush?

Meanwhile, Ian has learned from the other Mohawk that his wife is well and the mother of at least two children. She and her second husband, Sun Elk, have joined a group of Mohawk living in Unadilla, with the famous chief Thayendanegea, known to the English as Captain Joseph Brant.

Ian has unfinished business. He has some hope of perhaps finding a wife in Scotland—if they ever get there—but, as he tells Claire, he can't in good conscience wed a young woman if he knows he can never give her children. Claire questions him about the stillbirth and miscarriages suffered by his Mohawk wife and reassures him that it's probably not his fault and likely would not be a problem if he marries again. Still, he feels that he must see Works With Her Hands once more—if only to apologize.

He finds her—and her husband—in Unadilla. After a fight with Sun Elk, Ian succeeds in talking with Emily alone, and they make their peace with each other. She has in fact given birth a third time and offers Ian the naming of the new child—a great honor. Ian is deeply moved, but he has been talking with Emily's oldest son, a five-year-old who has told Ian that his great-grandmother says he is the child of Ian's spirit—but that it's probably best not to tell Sun Elk that. Ian gravely agrees—but when offered the chance to name the younger child, he tells Emily that the oldest son is his to name and gives him the name Swiftest of Lizards. Then, with a lighter heart, he returns to Ticonderoga.

On the road, William and the Hunters meet a man with a fractious cow, who offers them shelter from the driving rain—and a hot supper—if Denny and William will help him catch the cow. This they do, and after a terrible supper, they settle down to sleep by the farmer's hearth.

William suffers bad dreams and dreadful indigestion as a result of the foul stew served at supper, but this proves to be a blessing, as he wakes with griping in his guts just in time to avoid being brained by the ax-wielding farmer, bent on murder and robbery. Letting out a tremendous fart, William attacks the farmer and, after a bloody fight, succeeds in killing the man with his own ax, while the Hunters subdue his equally vicious wife.

Afterward, Willie rushes into the outdoor privy, from which he emerges some time later, pale of face and very shaken. He finds Rachel waiting for him and takes comfort in her presence, confessing to her that this was the first time he had ever killed a man. He'd thought about it, of course, but had expected such an event to occur in battle.

"Rachel." His own voice sounded odd to him, remote, as though someone else was speaking. "I've never killed anyone before. I don't—I don't quite know what to do about it." He looked up at her, searching her face for understanding. "If it had been—I expected it to be in battle. That—I think I'd know how. How to feel, I mean. If it had been like that."

She met his eyes, her face drawn in troubled thought. The light touched her, a pink softer than the sheen of pearls, and after a long time she touched his face, very gently.

"No," she said. "Thee wouldn't."

Sometime later, William parts from the Hunters to seek his own way, leaving them to head for Fort Ticonderoga. Along his road, he meets an old man, who holds his staff with a maimed hand, and who tells him he is in search of a man named Ian Murray—might William know him? Made uneasy by something in the old man's manner, William replies curtly that he does not and rides on toward his own rendezvous with General Burgoyne.

AT TICONDEROGA, CLAIRE has set up a medical practice—mostly among the women, as the army surgeons are extremely prejudiced against the intrusion of a woman onto their turf. An exception, though, is Captain Stebbings, now held as a prisoner. Stebbings refuses to be treated by anyone save Claire, nor will he allow his men to be treated by the other doctors. Claire meets Denzell Hunter over the amputation of a sailor's leg, and the two become friends at once, each recognizing the other as a real physician.

Jamie has taken responsibility for the volunteers from the *Asp* and formed them into a militia unit. The militia at the fort are all working under short-term contracts (most of which will not be paid), and Claire is keeping a line of notches on the doorpost of their room, counting the days until Jamie's enlistment will be up and they can leave. She only hopes that Young Ian will return from his errand before that day comes.

The matter is of some importance, because General Burgoyne's army is coming, and while the fort is well stocked and decently armed, its position is such that it can't be held for long against a besieging force. Everyone in the fort knows this—but the commander, Arthur St. Clair, is more than reluctant to evacuate the fort and thus fail in his duty and blemish his record—though, as Jamie points out rather acerbically, getting everyone in the fort killed or captured isn't going to do his record any good, either.

Still, St. Clair hesitates, and as news of Burgoyne's approach gets more and more exigent, and the protests of Jamie and other militia captains more urgent, the uneasiness of the fort's inhabitants explodes into panic. The British climb the small mountain opposite the fort and build an artillery emplacement, from which the whole fort can be enfiladed. Plainly, the time has come to evacuate. Luckily, Young Ian has returned and is able to help with the removal of the invalids and wounded.

The Battle of Ticonderoga is short and decisive—what battle there is, for most of the fort's inhabitants are already fleeing, by land or by boat. The refugees are closely pursued by the British army—and the army's Indian allies, who terrorize the fleeing Americans, killing and scalping in the dark.

Moving slowly, with a convoy of invalids, Claire is captured. Herded into a field with her patients, she meets a young British lieutenant with a familiar face—William. He doesn't at once recognize her, but when she explains that she'd met him several years before when he came with his father to Fraser's Ridge, he at once recalls the occasion and does his best to offer what help there is—precious little, as the British army has outstripped its baggage train and is seriously short of supplies.

Claire's concerns for her patients and worry over Jamie are cut short by the sudden appearance in the trees of Young Ian, come to rescue her. He's detected by William, who tries to stop him, but upon recognizing the man who saved his life in the swamp, William reluctantly lets Claire go.

She and Young Ian rejoin Jamie and continue the retreat south, drawing farther ahead of the British—who are still coming. As the refugees begin to coalesce into a unified body, some of the men begin to play the deserter game. This is a subterfuge in which an American pretends to desert to the British and, after being fed and having a good look around the camp, re-deserts back to his comrades.

One night, Claire discovers that Jamie has sent Denny out to play this game and is outraged, saying that Denny is not just a friend but also a trained physician—much too valuable to be risked in this way. Jamie tells her that he indeed tried to stop Denzell going, on just those grounds—but Denny is a Quaker, unable to fight, and therefore felt the need of contributing to the cause of liberty in whatever other way he could.

Some days later, Rachel comes in panic to find Jamie—her brother has played the deserter game again and had the misfortune to meet the same British officer to whom he had defected before; he's been captured and will surely hang if not rescued. Jamie and Ian go together to rescue Denny, but Ian is spotted in the process by William—who lets him go, this time out of obligation to Denzell, who saved William from dying of infection.

BACK AT THE ranch in the twentieth century, Jem is in hot water at school—for the mysterious crime of speaking Gaelic. Roger prevents Brianna from taking on the school's headmaster, fearing bloodshed, and goes himself to make inquiries. Lionel Menzies, the headmaster, tells Roger that Gaelic is a dying language because so many parents in the forties and fifties refused to teach it to their children, feeling that it was "backward" and would hinder the children in finding their place in the world.

Menzies and Roger have met before in the Inverness Masonic Lodge, but now take to each other, and Roger ends up with an invitation to come and teach a class in Gaelic at the school. A number of parents and grandparents attend and the class is a roaring success. Afterward, though, as he's leaving, he's stopped by Rob Cameron, the uncle of one of Jem's school-friends, and one of Brianna's co-workers, whom Roger knows slightly. Cameron, tells him that among the materials he'd handed out for the class to look at was this: *this* being "The Hitchhiker's Guide." Cameron thinks it's the draft of a science-fiction novel and assures Roger he'd love to read it when it's finished.

Building on their acquaintance, Rob mentions to Roger that he has an archaeologist friend who would be happy to come and look at the ruins of what might be an old Bronze Age fort on a hill near Lallybroch; Bree's told him about it. Roger accepts and, trembling inwardly at the near miss, takes his manuscript back home.

The archaeologist comes and pronounces the ruins to be an old—but not ancient—chapel, possibly built on the site of an older place of worship but probably not worth excavating.

Instead of excavating, Roger makes up his mind to rebuild the chapel, finding the slow, patient manual labor calming to his mind.

THE REFUGEES FROM Ticonderoga have reached the main body of the American army, under General Horatio Gates. There are a number of lesser generals present, too—including Major General Benedict Arnold, a courageous patriot and a gallant man. Claire makes his acquaintance one afternoon, not knowing whom he is, and is very much shaken on learning his identity. Once again, history is handing her a conundrum: Can the past be changed? If so, can *she* change it? And if so again—what might be the price of interference?

As usual, though, there are no answers—and the thing about history, as Claire's noted before, is that things just keep on happening. In the present instance, it's General John Burgoyne's attempt to cut the Colonies in two, severing the north from the south and thus starving the north of supplies.

The Battle(s) of Saratoga were the first major turning point of the American Revolution. These battles are also where the story lines of most of our characters collide: Jamie joins Daniel Morgan's elite corps of riflemen, while Claire sets up her triage tent; Denzell Hunter works as a surgeon, assisted by his sister, Rachel; and Young Ian (and Rollo) are foragers and scouts. On the British side, William takes command of a company under Brigadier Simon Fraser, with whom he has a close relationship.

Young Ian begins to notice Rachel Hunter as something more than a skilled nurse. When a minor accident befalls him, he heads for the tent where she is working, and there meets a Scotsman in a kilt, bringing in an injured friend. The man has red hair, and there is something vaguely familiar about him.

There should be. This is Hamish MacKenzie, son (so far as anyone other than Jamie and Claire knows) of the late Colum MacKenzie of Castle Leoch, and Jamie's cousin. He has come down from Canada with a company of MacKenzie volunteers to fight with the Continental army.

There is an emotional reunion between Jamie and Hamish, and we learn the fate of the exiled MacKenzies, who traveled to Prince Edward Island. Meanwhile, Ian finds himself drawn ineluctably back to Rachel Hunter, where he experiences a *coup de foudre.*

She reached to take the tin from him, and her fingers brushed his. The tin box was smeared with grease and slippery; it fell and both of them bent to retrieve it. She straightened first; her hair brushed his cheek, warm and smelling of her.

Without even thinking, he put both hands on her face and bent to her. Saw the flash and darkening of her eyes, and had one heartbeat, two, of perfect warm happiness, as his lips rested on hers, as his heart rested in her hands.

Then one of those hands cracked against his cheek, and he staggered back like a drunkard startled out of sleep.

Rachel is more than taken by surprise. She's a Quaker; how can she get involved in any way with a man of such violence? Still . . .

She ought to be putting coffee on to boil and getting up some supper; Denny would be back soon from the hospital tent, hungry and cold. She continued to sit, though, staring at the candle flame, wondering whether she would feel it were she to pass her hand through it.

She doubted it. Her whole body had ignited when he'd touched her, sudden as a torch soaked in turpentine, and she was still afire. A wonder her shift did not burst into flames.

Disturbed in mind, she tells her brother about the encounter. He sees clearly what she feels and sympathizes with her, though telling her plainly that it will not work for a Quaker to wed someone not a Friend. Rachel presses him, and he admits that he was in love with someone in London—but she was not a Friend, and he came away, back to America.

Jamie is wounded during the first battle of Saratoga, the Battle of Bemis Heights. Claire finds him unconscious on the field after the battle, on the verge of having his throat cut by a scavenging woman and child who are looting the dead—and the not-so-dead.

"He's mine," she said, thrusting her chin pugnaciously at me. "Go find yourself another." Another form slipped out of the mist and ma-

terialized by her side. It was the boy I had seen earlier, filthy and scruffy as the woman herself. He had no knife but clutched a crude metal strip, cut from a canteen. The edge of it was dark, with rust or blood.

He glared at me. "He's ours, Mum said! Get on wi' yer! Scat!" Not waiting to see whether I would or not, he flung a leg over Jamie's back, sat on him, and began to grope in the side pockets of his coat. "'E's still alive, Mum," he advised. "I can feel 'is 'eart beatin'. Best slit his throat quick; I don't think 'e's bad hurt."

I grabbed the boy by the collar and jerked him off Jamie's body, making him drop his weapon. He squealed and flailed at me with arms and elbows, but I kneed him in the rump, hard enough to jar his backbone, then got my elbow locked about his neck in a stranglehold, his skinny wrist vised in my other hand.

"Leave him go!" The woman's eyes narrowed like a weasel's, and her eyeteeth shone in a snarl. I didn't dare take my eyes away from the woman's long enough to look at Jamie. I could see him, though, at the edge of my vision, head turned to the side, his neck gleaming white, exposed and vulnerable.

"Stand up and step back," I said, "or I'll choke him to death, I swear I will!" She crouched over Jamie's body, knife in hand, as she measured me, trying to make up her mind whether I meant it. I did. The boy struggled and twisted in my grasp, his feet hammering against my shins. He was small for his age, and thin as a stick, but strong nonetheless; it was like wrestling an eel. I tightened my hold on his neck; he gurgled and quit struggling. His hair was thick with rancid grease and dirt, the smell of it rank in my nostrils. Slowly, the woman stood up. She was much smaller than I, and scrawny with it—bony wrists stuck out of the ragged sleeves. I couldn't guess her age—under the filth and the puffiness of malnutrition, she might have been anything from twenty to fifty.

"My man lies yonder, dead on the ground," she said, jerking her head at the fog behind her. "'E hadn't nothing but his musket, and the sergeant'll take that back." Her eyes slid toward the distant wood, where the British troops had retreated. "I'll find a man soon, but I've children to feed in the meantime—two besides the boy." She licked her lips, and a coaxing note entered her voice. "You're alone; you can manage better than we can. Let me have this one—there's more over there." She pointed with her chin toward the slope behind me, where the rebel dead and wounded lay.

My grasp must have loosened slightly as I listened, for the boy, who had hung quiescent in my grasp, made a sudden lunge and burst free, diving over Jamie's body to roll at his mother's feet. He got up beside her, watching me with rat's eyes, beady-bright and watchful. He bent and groped about in the grass, coming up with the makeshift dagger.

"Hold 'er off, Mum," he said, his voice raspy from the choking. "I'll take 'im."

From the corner of my eye, I had caught the gleam of metal, half buried in the grass. "Wait!" I said, and took a step back. "Don't kill him. Don't." A step to the side, another back. "I'll go, I'll let you have him, but . . ." I lunged to the side and got my hand on the cold metal hilt.

I had picked up Jamie's sword before. It was a cavalry sword, larger and heavier than the usual, but I didn't notice now. I snatched it up and swung it in a two-handed arc that ripped the air and left the metal ringing in my hands. Mother and son jumped back, identical looks of ludicrous surprise on their round, grimy faces. "Get away!" I said. Her mouth opened, but she didn't say anything. "I'm sorry for your man," I said. "But my man lies here. Get away, I said!" I raised the sword, and the woman stepped back hastily, dragging the boy by the arm. She turned and went, muttering curses at me over her shoulder, but I paid no attention to what she said.

The boy's eyes stayed fixed on me as he went, dark coals in the dim light. He would know me again—and I him.

They vanished in the mist, and I lowered the sword, which suddenly weighed too much to hold. I dropped it on the grass and fell to my knees beside Jamie. My own heart was pounding in my ears and my hands were shaking with reaction, as I groped for the pulse in his neck. I turned his head and could see it, throbbing steadily just below his jaw. "Thank God!" I whispered to myself. "Oh, thank God!"

Jamie's wound is not serious but is maiming: half his fourth finger is gone, and the sword cut has gone down into the palm of his hand, nearly bifurcating it. While Claire worries over the mending of the wound, Jamie suddenly asks her to amputate the mangled finger—it's been little use to him for the last twenty years and a constant source of pain and irritation.

When the other wounded have been cared for, and she has time to concentrate properly, she does as he asks.

A small scalpel, freshly sharpened. The jar of alcohol, with the wet ligatures coiled inside like a nest of tiny vipers, each toothed with a small, curved needle. Another with the waxed dry ligatures for arterial compression. A bouquet of probes, their ends soaking in alcohol. Forceps. Long-handled retractors. The hooked tenaculum, for catching the ends of severed arteries.

The surgical scissors with their short, curved blades and the handles shaped to fit my grasp, made to my order by the silversmith Stephen Moray. Or almost to my order. I had insisted that the scissors be as plain as possible, to make them easy to clean and disinfect. Stephen had obliged with a chaste and elegant design, but had not been able to resist one small flourish—one handle boasted a hooklike extension against which I could brace my little finger in order to exert more force, and this extrusion formed a smooth, lithe curve, flowering at the tip into a slender rosebud against a spray of leaves. The contrast between the heavy, vicious blades at one end and this delicate conceit at the other always made me smile when I lifted the scissors from their case.

Strips of cotton gauze and heavy linen, pads of lint, adhesive plasters stained red with the dragon's-blood juice that made them sticky. An open bowl of alcohol for disinfection as I worked, and the jars of cinchona bark, mashed garlic paste, and yarrow for dressing.

"There we are," I said with satisfaction, checking the array one last time. Everything must be ready, since I was working by myself; if I forgot something, no one would be at hand to fetch it for me.

"It seems a great deal o' preparation, for one measly finger," Jamie observed behind me. I swung around to find him leaning on one elbow, watching, the cup of laudanum undrunk in his hand.

"Could ye not just whack it off wi' a wee knife and seal the wound with hot iron, like the regimental surgeons do?"

"I could, yes," I said dryly. "But fortunately I don't have to; we have enough time to do the job properly. That's why I made you wait."

"Mmphm." He surveyed the row of gleaming instruments without enthusiasm, and it

was clear that he would much rather have had the business over and done with as quickly as possible. I realized that to him this looked like slow and ritualized torture, rather than sophisticated surgery.

"I mean to leave you with a working hand," I told him firmly. "No infection, no suppurating stump, no clumsy mutilation, and—God willing—no pain, once it heals."

His eyebrows went up at that. He had never mentioned it, but I was well aware that his right hand and its troublesome fourth finger had caused him intermittent pain for years, ever since it had been crushed at Wentworth Prison, when he was held prisoner there in the days before the Stuart Rising.

"A bargain's a bargain," I said, with a nod at the cup in his hand. "Drink it." He lifted the cup and poked a long nose reluctantly over the rim, nostrils twitching at the sickly-sweet scent. He let the dark liquid touch the end of his tongue and made a face.

"It will make me sick."

"It will make you sleep."

"It gives me terrible dreams."

"As long as you don't chase rabbits in your sleep, it won't matter," I assured him. He laughed despite himself, but had one final try.

"It tastes like the stuff ye scrape out of horses' hooves."

"And when was the last time you licked a horse's hoof?" I demanded, hands on my hips. I gave him a medium-intensity glare, suitable for the intimidation of petty bureaucrats and low-level army officials.

He sighed.

"Ye mean it, aye?"

"I do."

"All right, then." With a reproachful look of long-suffering resignation, he threw back his head and tossed the contents of the cup down in one gulp. A convulsive shudder racked him, and he made small choking noises.

"I did say to sip it," I observed mildly. "Vomit, and I'll make you lick it up off the floor." Given the scuffled dirt and trampled grass underfoot, this was plainly an idle threat, but he pressed his lips and eyes tight shut and lay back on the pillow, breathing heavily and swallowing convulsively every few seconds. I brought up a low stool and sat down by the camp bed to wait.

"How do you feel?" I asked, a few minutes later.

"Dizzy," he replied. He cracked one eye open and viewed me through the narrow blue slit, then groaned and closed it. "As if I'm falling off a cliff. It's a verra unpleasant sensation, Sassenach."

"Try to think of something else for a minute," I suggested. "Something pleasant, to take your mind off it." His brow furrowed for a moment, then relaxed.

"Stand up a moment, will ye?" he said. I obligingly stood, wondering what he wanted. He opened his eyes, reached out with his good hand, and took a firm grip of my buttock.

"There," he said. "That's the best thing I can think of. Having a good hold on your arse always makes me feel steady."

DURING THE SECOND battle, Morgan's Rifles are lurking in a wood at the foot of the battlefield, sniping at British officers, when Major General Benedict Arnold (still a patriot at that point) rides up and demands that someone shoot the British brigadier within range. This is General Simon Fraser, a distant cousin of Jamie's, and as Jamie thinks to himself, he'd *kill any other man on the field, but not that one*. He shoots deliberately high and wild, missing the general but knocking the hat off a young British officer, who shakes his fist and shouts, "You owe me a hat, sir!"

Other riflemen lack Jamie's inhibitions, though, and one of them shoots General Fraser, who is led off the field, seriously wounded. During the night following the battle, an emissary comes across the lines under a flag of truce, seeking Jamie. The general is dying, has heard of his kinsman in the American lines, and wishes to speak to him. Claire accompanies Jamie to the cabin of Baroness von Riedesel, where the general is indeed dying, laid out on the dining table. More alarming to Claire than the sight of the dying general, though, is the young officer crouching by his side—William, Lord Ellesmere.

In the flicker of firelight and the distraction of grief, neither Jamie nor William notices the other, though Claire is on tenterhooks lest anyone else notice the resemblance. No one does, though, and she is counting the moments until escape, as the officers stand outside the cabin in the dim, wet dawn, soberly discussing what to do with the general's body. Suddenly a voice from behind her inquires of Lieutenant Ransom as to what has become of his hat?

". . . rebel whoreson shot it off my head," mutters Lieutenant Ransom, in a deep, English-accented approximation of his father's voice. Distraction intervenes, though, and Claire is left palpitating, counting the seconds until they can make their escape. Jamie does take his leave of the British officers but is no more than few steps into the safety of the wood when he whirls suddenly on his heel, walks back, and, taking off his hat, thrusts it into William's hands, saying, *"I believe I owe ye a hat, sir."*

He then seizes Claire by the elbow and hastens her into the wood, where, once out of sight, he collapses onto a log, caught between laughter and tears. When Claire demands to know *what* he can have been thinking, he replies, *"I've lost a kinsman and found one, all in the same moment—and a moment later realize that for the second time in my life, I've come within an inch of shooting my son. . . . I shouldna have done it, I ken that. It's only—I thought all at once, What if I dinna miss, a third time? And—and I thought I must just . . . speak to him. As a man. In case it should be the only time, aye?"*

The death of General Fraser, significant as it is to the general, his men, and his kin, is minor by comparison with the other effects of the battles. The largest British army ever to be assembled in North America has been defeated—by a ragtag rebellion whose leaders have been nothing but gallows bait for the last year. No decent bookmaker would have given them odds of a hundred to one—and yet . . . they've won.

General Burgoyne has no option but to surrender and does so, reluctantly. The process is complex, though, and takes days, during which the Continental army relaxes in camp.

Claire's relaxation is disturbed by the sudden appearance of a strange Scotsman—a Lowlander in the uniform of a Continental officer, who inquires for Jamie and makes obnoxious innuendos. Claire walks away from him, which insult he repays by spitting in the soup she's making.

She's therefore less than pleased to see him return to her fireside that evening but is reassured by the presence of both Jamie and Ian. The stranger has more than innuendo on his mind this time; he means blackmail.

As an overseer on a West Indies plantation years before, he had taken delivery of a consignment of transported Jacobite prisoners. All the men were in poor condition and had died soon after arrival—but one man, Willie Coulter by name, had had a strange story to tell, regarding the death of his chieftain, Dougal MacKenzie. The overseer has noted the presence of Hamish MacKenzie and knows who he is. What if, he inquires pleasantly, Hamish were to learn what Willie Coulter had to say—i.e., that Dougal (Hamish's putative uncle; in fact, his father) didn't die on the field at Culloden but rather the night before, in the attics of Culloden House, killed by his other nephew, Jamie?

Ian, who had quietly excused himself a moment before, comes back at this delicate point in the conversation with his own point—which he drives between the stranger's ribs. Satisfying as this intervention is, it's unfortunately timed; someone sees and raises the cry of *"Murder!"*

Ian and Rollo are pursued through the camp, and Rollo is shot by one of the pursuers. Unwilling to leave his wounded dog, Ian hovers over him, torn between the desperate need to fly and the conviction that Rollo will be mistreated and killed if Ian leaves him. On the point of slitting the dog's throat himself, he's stopped by the breathless arrival of Rachel, who throws herself on Rollo, begs Ian to flee, and tells him she will mind his dog until he comes back. With little choice at this point, Ian vanishes into the dark.

Next day, Jamie is summoned once again by a British army emissary and taken to see General Burgoyne himself. Braced to hear that the army has captured or killed Ian, he's relieved—though taken aback—to have Burgoyne ask him, as General Fraser's nearest kinsman, to accompany the brigadier's body back to Scotland. Jamie swallows hard and says yes.

A few days later, the surrender is concluded. The British troops pile their weapons by the river and march off to captivity, parole, or eventual transport back to England; none will fight again in this war. The American victors line the road in salute, each man with his gun, silently watching the companies go past. From her vantage point behind Jamie, Claire sees William's company go past—and Jamie's head shift just slightly, watching his son out of sight. Then his shoulders slump a little, in relief.

William is safe. And the Frasers are bound—at last—for Scotland, including Ian, smuggled aboard the ship, disguised as an Indian scout accompanying the brigadier's body.

ROGER IS ALONE in the ruined chapel on the hill, putting stones in place and thinking:

Was God opening a door, showing him that he should be a teacher now? Was this, the Gaelic thing, what he was meant to do? He had plenty of room to ask questions, room and time and silence. Answers were scarce. He'd been at it most of the afternoon; he was hot, exhausted, and ready for a beer.

Now his eye caught the edge of a shadow in the doorway, and he turned—Jem or maybe Brianna, come to fetch him home to tea. It was neither of them.

For a moment, he stared at the newcomer, searching his memory. Ragged jeans and sweatshirt, dirty-blond hair hacked off and tousled. Surely he knew the man; the broad-boned, handsome face was familiar, even under a thick layer of light-brown stubble.

"Can I help you?" Roger asked, taking a grip on the shovel he'd been using. The man wasn't threatening but was roughly dressed and dirty—a tramp, perhaps—and there was something indefinable about him that made Roger uneasy.

"It's a church, aye?" the man said, and grinned, though no hint of warmth touched his eyes. "Suppose I've come to claim sanctuary, then." He moved suddenly into the light, and

Roger saw his eyes more clearly. Cold, and a deep, striking green.

"Sanctuary," William Buccleigh MacKenzie repeated. "And then, Minister dear, I want ye to tell me who ye are, who I am—and what in the name of God almighty are we?"

This is the Nuckelavee: the visitor who has been living in the broch, keeping an eye on Lallybroch, is none other than William Buccleigh MacKenzie, the son of Dougal MacKenzie and the witch Geillis Duncan, last seen at the battlefield of Alamance—in 1771.

SCOTLAND. AFTER A brief interlude in Edinburgh, during which Jamie is reunited with his beloved printing press (named, as he self-consciously admits to Claire, "Bonnie") and both Frasers buy spectacles, they journey at last into the barren Highlands, where they bury Simon Fraser in the presence of his family at the cairn of Corrimony. And then . . . it's time to go home. To Lallybroch.

Young Ian, unsure of his reception after his precipitous departure and long absence, has chosen to brazen it out and appears in full Mohawk dress, scalp lock and all. His mother, Jenny, takes one look at him, steps back, staggers—and bursts into laughter born of joy, relief, and astute recognition of her son's hesitance. This welcome disconcerts Ian but not nearly as much as her words of greeting as she embraces him: *"Oh, God, Ian. My wee lad. . . . Thank God ye've come in time."* Ian the elder is dying.

Phthisis, they called it now. Or doctors did. It meant "wasting," in the Greek. Laymen called it by the blunter name "consumption," and the reason why was all too apparent. It consumed its victims, ate them alive. A wasting disease, and waste it did. Ate flesh and squandered life, profligate and cannibal.

I'd seen it many times in England of the thirties and forties, much more here in the past. But I'd never seen it carve the living flesh from the bones of someone I loved, and my heart went to water and drained from my chest.

Winter lies cold on the Highlands and on the hearts of those at Lallybroch. Still, they *have* come in time. Time for Jamie to walk the hills—slowly—with the man who has always been closer than a brother, to share with him the burdens and secrets of his life. Time for Young Ian and his father to become close, in the way they never had—close enough to say the things that must be said.

In these close conversations, Young Ian tells his father everything—his short-lived marriage to a Mohawk woman, and the child she bore who is the child of his spirit, if not his body. His love for Rachel Hunter, and his fears that he may not prove worthy of her, either in soul or body.

The elder Ian listens, in sorrow and joy, and urges Young Ian not to hang about waiting for his own death but to return to America as soon as possible, find Rachel, and marry her.

The chance to return comes sooner than anyone expects. Since Jamie is making peace with his past, he determines to take care of one lingering loose end and goes one day to Balriggan, where Laoghaire lives. He means to make peace with her and to apologize for his part in their disastrous and ill-omened brief marriage. Things don't go quite as planned, but he does achieve the peace he sought—discovering in the process that Laoghaire has formed an attachment to her hired man.

While telling Claire about this interesting encounter, Jamie takes her up into the hills behind Lallybroch, to show her the cave where he hid for years after Culloden. Coming down from the cave, they meet Joan, Marsali's younger sister, Laoghaire's other daughter. Joan greets Jamie affectionately as a father—and tells him bluntly that he must do something about Laoghaire and Joey, the hired man.

Her mother feels she can't marry Joey, as remarriage would put an end to the money Jamie pays for her maintenance, and Joey, who is disabled, can't keep them. However, being unable to marry does not stop their feelings for each other, which manifest themselves in embarrassing physicality—embarrassing to Joan, whose strong desire is to become a nun but who feels that she can't leave home with her mother in such an immoral position. Rather bemused, Jamie promises to see what he can do about this.

Claire is inclined to find the whole situation more than funny, but her humor is quenched a few days later when her writing is interrupted by the abrupt appearance of Laoghaire herself.

"I've come to ask ye a favor," she said, and for the first time I heard the tremor in her voice. "Read that. If ye will," she added, and pressed her lips tight together.

Laoghaire has brought with her a letter from Marsali, who writes from the family's new home in Philadelphia, begging her mother to go to Claire, if Claire has in fact arrived at Lallybroch, and tell her of Henri-Christian's dire straits. Born a dwarf, the little boy suffers frequent respiratory problems; these have been increasingly aggravated by inflamed and overgrown tonsils and adenoids, which are blocking his throat to such a degree that he can only breathe when his head is upright—which means that he *stops* breathing several times each night and is only kept alive by one or the other of his family staying up with him, to wake him and readjust his position before he suffocates. Claire had told Marsali that the adenoids and tonsils could be removed surgically, but plainly there is no one in Philadelphia equipped to do this. Will Claire come back, as quickly as may be?

There is no ground on which Claire and Laoghaire are ever likely to see eye-to-eye—save the welfare of the grandchildren they share. Heart-struck at leaving Ian, in the certain knowledge that she'll never see him again, and agonized by parting from Jamie—who feels that he must stay and see his sister through Ian's passing—Claire packs her medical kit and returns to America with Young Ian, hoping she will be in time.

AT THE LALLYBROCH of 1980, the strange visitor is making himself at home. William Buccleigh MacKenzie tells Roger how he came to pass accidentally through the stones and, unable to get back, made his way to Inverness, where he sought help from the rector of the church he knew. Later, sitting dazed on the street as cars rushed past, he was shocked to recognize Roger, whom he followed to Lallybroch, where he took up residence in the broch, warily observing the family (and scaring the pants off Jem by claiming to be a Nuckelavee when the boy discovered him), until he could be sure that Roger was not in fact a supernatural being but a person like himself.

Brianna is more than suspicious of William B., who has quickly become "Uncle Buck" to the children—but even she is moved by his account of his difficulties and disasters in the past and his strong desire to return to his wife. She's a little less sympathetic when it comes to his interfering in *her* life, recalling the day he went with her to her work at Loch Errochty, where he met Rob Cameron and warned her against him.

"Yon man's got a hot eye for you. Does your husband know?"

Roger does not know, and Brianna has no intention of telling him Buck's opinion at the moment. Rob has become friendly with Roger, through the local Masonic lodge and through the children's choir, where Rob's fatherless nephew, Bobby, is a member. Jem and Bobby are friends, too, and Jem occasionally goes to the pictures with Bobby or to Bobby's house for supper. In fact, Jem is spending the night with Bobby.

At home that evening, the MacKenzies discuss William Buccleigh but put that subject aside until the morning, more interested in each other. Long before morning, though, Amanda wakes, screaming.

"Jemmy, Jemmy!" she sobbed. "He's gone, he's gone. He's GONE!"

No matter how her parents try to console her, she won't be comforted but keeps insisting that Jem is gone, thumping her head with her hand and insisting that he's *"Not* here . . . *Not here wif me!"*

Disquieted, Brianna goes to phone Bobby's mother—only to hear that Jemmy was not expected for the night; he isn't there. Really alarmed now, Bree asks Bobby's mother to go to her brother's house down the street and fetch Rob. Bobby's mother hurries back to report that Rob is not home—the old blue truck he drives is gone.

Amanda has suddenly stopped screaming and fallen asleep, but her parents—and William Buccleigh—are wide awake. Roger and William B. drive to the stone circle, where they find Cameron's blue truck, evidently abandoned on the road below. Panicked, Roger climbs frantically to the summit of the hill. The circle of stones is empty, but the stones themselves are live and screaming. He collapses in the circle, losing consciousness as the emptiness of time surrounds him.

He comes to himself some time later, outside the circle, having been pulled out by William Buccleigh, and they go home to tell Brianna—and to plan what to do next.

LORD JOHN HAS arrived in Philadelphia with his niece, Dottie, discovered the whereabouts of his wounded nephew Henry, and taken what steps are possible for Henry's treatment. The young man has been gutshot and retains two bullets deep in his abdomen. In his search for a doctor, Lord John sends William to the American camp at Valley Forge, twenty miles outside Philadelphia, to find Dr. Hunter and ask him whether he will come.

William is charmed afresh by Rachel Hunter, whom he insists upon bringing back into the city with her brother, not wanting her to suffer the privations of the derelict army. Denny Hunter succeeds in removing one bullet, thus saving Henry's life at least momentarily, but is unable to deal with the other.

One snowy night, while the Hunters are alone in the inn William has found for them, a visitor arrives. A woman, clad in ermine, and dazzlingly glamorous. She enters their room, drops her ermine cloak to disclose a shapeless gray dress, and announces that she has become a Quaker. Dottie has arrived.

Dazed by the appearance of his long-lost love, Denny Hunter tries to persuade Dorothea to leave, to go back to her uncle's house, but he's up against what may possibly be the most stubborn member of a famously strong-willed family. The Greys are also logical: Dorothea suggests that the three of them hold a Quaker meeting and allow God to speak to them on the matter. Denny is even more taken aback by this suggestion, but Rachel finds it sensible, and they sit in silence by the fire, waiting for discernment and wisdom to be found.

Rachel finds herself thinking not of her brother's situation but her own. Where is Ian? Will he ever come back—and if he does, what then? How can she think of marrying a man of blood and violence? For maybe Lady Dorothea Grey will make a Quaker, but Ian Murray never will.

She's pulled from these contemplations when her brother straightens a little on his stool.

"I love thee, Dorothea," he said. He spoke very quietly, but his soft eyes burned behind his spectacles, and Rachel felt her chest ache. "Will thee marry me?"

CLAIRE ARRIVES IN Philadelphia with Ian. Hurrying to the printshop where Fergus and Marsali live, Claire finds that she is, thank God, in time; Henri-Christian is alive and in sufficient health to survive the operation on his throat. However, Fergus has left home—not willingly but a half step ahead of arrest for sedition—and is living secretly, moving from one location to another in Philadelphia, passing information in and out of the British-occupied city.

Preparing for Henri-Christian's surgery, Claire goes in search of vitriol—the sulfuric acid she requires for the making of ether. Informed that there is none to be had in the city, she's told by one apothecary that the last of his own stock was sold to a British officer—Lord John Grey. Lord John is overjoyed to see Claire and instantly makes a bargain—she can have his vitriol and anything else she requires, if she will undertake to operate on Henry.

Henri-Christian's surgery goes successfully; then it's Henry's turn. Lord John insists on attending the operation—performed by Claire with Denzell Hunter assisting—and is struck both by the miraculous effects of ether and by the surgeon herself.

The air filled at once with a pungent, sweet aroma that clung to the back of Grey's throat and made his head swim slightly. He blinked, shaking his head to dispel the giddiness, and realized that Mrs. Fraser had said something to him.

"I beg your pardon?" He looked up at her, a great white bird with yellow eyes—and a gleaming talon that sprouted suddenly from her hand.

"I said," she repeated calmly through her mask, "you might want to sit back a little farther. It's going to be rather messy."

While the surgery is in progress, William sits on the stoop outside, with Rachel Hunter and his cousin Dorothea. He thinks to himself how strange this is: the three of them both friends and relatives, united in concern for Henry, and yet Rachel and Denny—and even Dorothea—are officially his enemies. These musings are interrupted, though, by Rollo, who stiffens, seeing a man down the street. The man—Arch Bug—vanishes, though, and the friends think no more of him, caught up in relief that the operation is over and Henry is alive.

Relaxing from the strain of surgery, Claire is further heartened by receipt of two letters from Jamie, one written from Lallybroch, with news of Ian's death, and another from Paris, telling her that he and Jenny will shortly be embarking aboard a ship called *Euterpe,* bound for America.

THINGS BEGIN TO move quickly.

Roger and William Buccleigh, after hasty preparations, go together to the stone circle near Inverness to rescue Jem, who has evidently been taken through the stones by Rob Cameron.

Shaken and grieving, Brianna sits alone in Roger's study, steeling herself for the unknown terrors of the future. Her meditations are interrupted, though, by footsteps in the hall and the unexpected advent of Rob Cameron—who is plainly *not* in the past, and for good reason: he couldn't pass through the stones. He tells Brianna that she must force Jem to reveal the location of the Jacobite gold (the secret of which he obtained from reading Claire and Jamie's letters).

JAMIE AND JENNY do indeed sail from Brest—but not aboard the *Euterpe,* which sailed abruptly, leaving them behind. Fuming, Jamie finds another ship that will take them to America. It will leave them at Charleston, and they'll have to make their way laboriously overland to Philadelphia, but he *will* get back to Claire, come hell, high water, or seasickness.

LORD JOHN ARRIVES suddenly at the printshop, startling Claire both by his presence and his appearance: he's red-eyed, disheveled, and plainly terribly upset. As well he might be; he's just heard from a friend that the *Euterpe* (which he knew to be carrying Jamie home) was sunk in a storm, with loss of all hands.

Claire is shattered by the news and barely pays attention when Lord John returns the next day to inform her that she is about to be arrested by Captain Richardson (the shady intelligence agent), who has been watching the printshop since Fergus's disappearance and has observed Claire passing packets of information and seditious documents in the streets of Philadelphia. She pays somewhat more attention when Lord John informs her further that she must marry him; he can protect her—and also Marsali and her family—if she is his wife.

Claire is barely conscious through the marriage ceremony; what does anything matter? Her state does not improve through the following days. She thinks of Jamie constantly, wracked not only by her own tearing grief but also by horrible thoughts of him drowning, pulled down by a vast, indifferent sea. She even thinks of suicide—she knows how.

I let my hand fall back, exposing my wrist, and placed the tip of the knife midway up my forearm. I'd seen many unsuccessful suicides, those who slashed their wrists from side to side, the wounds small mouths that cried for help. I'd seen those who meant it. The proper way was to slit the veins lengthwise, deep, sure cuts that would drain me of blood in minutes, assure unconsciousness in seconds.

The mark was still visible on the mound at the base of my thumb. A faint white "J," the mark he'd left on me on the eve of Culloden, when we first faced the stark knowledge of death and separation.

I traced the thin white line with the tip of the knife and felt the seductive whisper of metal on my skin. I'd wanted to die with him then, and he had sent me on with a firm hand. I carried his child; I could not die.

I carried her no longer—but she was still there. Perhaps reachable. I sat motionless for what seemed a long time, then sighed and put the knife back on the table carefully.

Perhaps it was the habit of years; a bent of mind that held life sacred for its own sake, or a superstitious awe of extinguishing a spark kindled by a hand not my own. Perhaps it was obligation. There were those who needed me—or at least to whom I could be useful. Perhaps it was the stubbornness of the body, with its inexorable insistence on never-ending process.

I could slow my heart, slow enough to count the beats . . . slow the flowing of my blood 'til my heart echoed in my ears with the doom of distant drums.

There were pathways in the dark. I knew; I had seen people die. Despite physical decay, there was no dying until the pathway was found. I couldn't—yet—find mine.

Unable to kill herself, she takes to drink as anodyne. She is not the only one left bereft and desperate by Jamie's death, though—nor the only one to seek surcease in brandy.

My glass was empty, the decanter halfway full. I poured another and took hold of the glass carefully, not wanting to spill it, determined to find oblivion, no matter how temporary.

Could I separate entirely? I wondered. Could my soul actually leave my body without my dying first? Or had it done so already?

I drank the glass slowly, one sip at a time. Another. One sip at a time.

There must have been some sound that made me look up, but I wasn't aware of having raised my head. John Grey was standing in the doorway of my room. His neckcloth was missing and his shirt hung limp on his shoulders, wine spilled down the front of it. His hair was loose and tangled, and his eyes as red as mine.

I stood up, slow, as though I were underwater.

"I will not mourn him alone tonight," he said roughly, and closed the door.

* * *

I was surprised to wake up. I hadn't really expected to and lay for a bit trying to fit reality back into place around me. I had only a slight headache, which was almost more surprising than the fact that I was still alive. Both those things paled in significance beside the fact of the man in bed beside me. "How long has it been since you last slept with a woman, if you don't mind my asking?"

He didn't appear to mind. He frowned a little and scratched his chest thoughtfully. "Oh . . . fifteen years? At least that." He glanced at me, his expression altering to one of concern. "Oh. I do apologize."

"You do? For what?" I arched one brow. I could think of a number of things he might apologize for, but probably none of those was what he had in mind. "I am afraid I was perhaps not . . ." he hesitated. "Very gentlemanly."

"Oh, you weren't," I said, rather tartly. "But I assure you that I wasn't being at all ladylike myself." He looked at me, and his mouth worked a bit, as though trying to frame some response to that, but after a moment or two he shook his head and gave it up.

"Besides, it wasn't me you were making love to," I said, "and both of us know it."

He looked up, startled, his eyes very blue. Then the shadow of a smile crossed his face, and he looked down at the quilted coverlet. "No," he said softly. "Nor were you, I think, making love to me. Were you?"

"No," I said. The grief of the night before had softened, but the weight of it was still there. My voice was low and husky, because my throat was halfway closed, where the hand of sorrow clutched me unawares.

Their brief encounter does little to cure grief for either Claire or Lord John, but the sense of a deeply shared grief does something to steady her, and make it possible for her at least to function.

MEANWHILE, JEM IS not in the past, but neither is he where Cameron left him. Locked into the maintenance tunnel under Loch Errochty while Cameron goes to speak to Brianna, he remembers his mother telling about the little train, and, discovering it in the dark, he starts it and trundles slowly into the blackness.

He's comforted by his sense of Mandy, who glows in his head like the small red light on the train's console. And pushing the power lever forward, he trundles a little faster, farther into the unknown.

IN PHILADELPHIA, RACHEL is buying bread when Rollo begins to act strangely. He's caught a scent, something that excites him, and he tears off in pursuit of it. Rachel runs after him but is unable to catch him. Instead, she runs smack into Arch Bug. Old Arch has evidently seen her with Rollo and demands to know what her relationship with Ian is. Does she love him?

Some distance away, Rollo finds Ian, whose scent he has been tracking, and there is a joyful reunion. Ian tries to persuade Rollo to backtrack, to find Rachel, but the dog is too delighted at being reunited with his master to think of anything else.

FERGUS IS IN hiding, moving from one location to another each night, but rousing one morning he hears that a tall, red-haired man with the bearing of a soldier has been asking for him in the outskirts of Philadelphia. Hardly daring to believe that it can be Jamie, he sets off to find the man.

WILLIAM COMES UPON Rachel, who is being threatened by Arch Bug, and pulls the old man away. A fight ensues, in which Arch strikes William in the head with his ax and leaves him bleeding on the ground as the old man flees.

Fortunately, William isn't dead, and Claire is able to stitch up his head. She then tells Rachel about Ian and Arch Bug.

"Then that is why—" she said, but stopped.

"Why what?"

She grimaced a little, but glanced at me and gave a small shrug.

"Why he said to me that he was afraid I might die because I loved him."

Worried about Rachel, Ian, and Arch Bug, Claire can do nothing about any of them. She accompanies Lord John to a "mischianza"—a gala ball put on by the British military and the local Loyalists in honor of General Howe, who has resigned as commander in chief of the army in America, to be replaced by General Clinton. At the ball, Claire meets a number of interesting people, but none more interesting than John André, the British officer who will conspire with Benedict Arnold—and hang for it.

IAN DECIDES THAT the logical place to begin his search for Rachel is probably Fergus's printshop, and he goes there. This is a good guess: she *is* there, minding the shop in Marsali's absence. Arch Bug is also there, ax in hand, and Rachel is struggling to get away from him. Ian—and Rollo—attack Arch, and there is a terrible fight. Arch is old but still strong, and quite mad. He succeeds in wounding Ian, and Rachel is sure he will kill him. But Arch was seen in the street going into the printshop, and William, who has been looking for him, was informed.

There seemed to be blood everywhere. Spattered against the counter and the wall, smeared on the floor, and the back of Ian's shirt was soaked with red and clinging so she saw the muscles of his back straining beneath it. He was kneeling half atop a struggling Arch Bug, grappling one-handed for the ax, his left arm hanging limp, and Arch was stabbing at his face with stiffened fingers, trying to blind him, while Rollo darted eel-like and bristling into the mass of straining limbs, growling and snapping. Fixed on this spectacle, she was only dimly aware of someone standing behind her, but looked up, uncomprehending, when his foot touched her bum.

"Is there something about you that attracts men with axes?" William asked crossly. He sighted carefully along his pistol's barrel, and fired.

CLAIRE AND LORD John are talking casually in his bedroom when a knock sounds on the door. Lord John calls to the knocker to come back later, only to be informed in a Scottish burr that he would, save that there's some urgency to the matter. Whereupon the door opens to reveal Jamie Fraser—who has, of course, found Fergus and inquired what the status of things in Philadelphia might be, before showing himself abroad. Fergus has told him how matters stand, including the news that he has been assumed to be dead and that Lord John has married Claire to protect her and the rest of the Fraser family. Jamie naturally then hastened to Lord John's house, to see Claire, but along the way has picked up unwelcome attention in the shape of a small patrol of English soldiers, who are on his heels.

Claire swoons into his arms, so shattered by his return that she can think of nothing but the fact that he's there. Lord John is nearly as happy, but the rejoicing is short-lived. Claire rushes out, intending to delay the soldiers while Jamie escapes, only to run smack into Willie on the stairs. And father and son find themselves suddenly face-to-face, no more than ten feet apart, staring into each other's eyes.

Jamie stood at the end of the hall, some ten feet away; John stood beside him, white as a sheet, and his eyes bulging as much as Willie's were. This resemblance to Willie, striking as it was, was completely overwhelmed by Jamie's own resemblance to the Ninth Earl of Ellesmere. William's face had hardened and matured, losing all trace of childish softness, and from both ends of the short hall, deep blue Fraser cat-eyes stared out of the bold, solid bones of the MacKenzies. And Willie was old enough to shave on a daily basis; he knew what he looked like.

William doesn't take the revelation of his true parentage well.

Willie's left hand slapped at his hip, reflex-

ively looking for a sword. Finding nothing, he slapped at his chest. His hands were shaking so badly that he couldn't manage buttons; he simply seized the fabric and ripped open his shirt, reached in and fumbled for something. He pulled it over his head and, in the same motion, hurled the object at Jamie.

Jamie's reflexes brought his hand up automatically, and the wooden rosary smacked into it, the beads swinging, tangled in his fingers.

"God damn you, sir," Willie said, voice trembling. "God damn you to hell!" He half-turned blindly, then spun on his heel to face John. "And you! You knew, *didn't you? God damn you, too!"*

There is no time for explanation or recrimination, though; the soldiers are in the house and storming the stair. Trapped, Jamie seizes Lord John and claps a pistol to his head, threatening to blow his brains out if the soldiers don't back off. William struggles with his emotions but tells them to hold—and Jamie retreats to the back stair with Lord John, escaping from the house with his hostage.

The two make their way out of Philadelphia, finally reaching refuge in the woods outside the city, where they stop for water. Lord John has been contemplating the state of things while they ride, and realizes a) that he will have to mention to Jamie, pretty much immediately, that he's slept with Claire—because Claire will certainly mention it at the first opportunity, and b) Jamie will undoubtedly kill him upon receipt of this news. Lord John is more or less resigned to this, merely wondering whether Jamie will shoot him or break his neck.

Likely bare hands, he thought. It was a visceral sort of thing, sex.

He therefore musters his courage and, at the first opportunity, blurts out, *"I have had carnal knowledge of your wife."* What he's not expecting is Jamie's reaction.

"Oh?" said Jamie curiously. "Why?"

MEANWHILE, BACK AT Lord John's house, William demands the truth from Claire—and gets it. He isn't pleased, and his shock rapidly turns to anger—both at the truth of his parentage and at the duplicity practiced upon him.

"Best for me," he repeated bleakly. "Right." His knuckles had gone white again, and he gave me a look through narrowed eyes that I recognized all too well: a Fraser about to go off with a bang. I also knew perfectly well that there was no way of stopping one from detonating but had a try anyway, putting out a hand to him.

"William," I began. "Believe me—"

"I do," he said. "Don't bloody tell me any more. God damn *it!" And, whirling on his heel, he drove his fist through the paneling with a thud that shook the room, wrenched his hand out of the hole he'd made, and stormed out. I heard crunching and rending as he paused to kick out several of the balusters on the landing and rip a length of the stair railing off, and I made it to the door in time to see him draw back a four-foot chunk of wood over his shoulder, swing, and strike the crystal chandelier that hung over the stairwell in an explosion of shattering glass. For a moment, he teetered on the open edge of the landing and I thought he would fall, or hurl himself off, but he staggered back from the edge and threw the chunk of wood like a javelin at the remnant of the chandelier with a burst of breath that might have been a grunt or a sob.*

Then he rushed headlong down the stairs, thumping his wounded fist at intervals against the wall, where it left bloody smudges. He hit the front door with his shoulder, rebounded, jerked it open, and went out like a locomotive.

I stood frozen on the landing in the midst of chaos and destruction, gripping the edge of the broken balustrade. Tiny rainbows danced on walls and ceiling like multicolored dragonflies sprung out of the shattered crystal that littered the floor.

Something moved; a shadow fell across the floor of the hall below. A small, dark figure walked slowly in through the open doorway. Putting back the hood of her cloak, Jenny Fraser Murray looked round at the devastation, then up at me, her face a pale oval glimmering with humor.

"Like father, like son, I see," she remarked. "God help us all."

SOMETIME LATER, WE join Ian and Rachel, on the banks of the Delaware River. The British are withdrawing from Philadelphia, and they are watching an artillery team removing the cannon that have guarded the city. The war and its outcome are not what concerns them just now, though. They are intensely conscious of each other, unsure how to say what they have to say. At last Ian takes the bit between his teeth, though, and, telling her that he thinks he cannot be a Quaker, asks whether she might ever be at peace with the idea of loving him.

She pointed at Rollo, who was lying couchant now, motionless but alert, yellow eyes following every movement of a fat robin foraging in the grass.

"That dog is a wolf, is he not?"

"Aye, well, mostly."

A small flash of hazel told him not to quibble.

"And yet he is thy boon companion, a creature of rare courage and affection, and altogether a worthy being?"

"Oh, aye," he said with more confidence. "He is."

She gave him an even look.

"Thee is a wolf, too, and I know it. But thee is my wolf, and best thee know that."

He'd started to burn when she spoke, an ignition swift and fierce as the lighting of one of his cousin's matches. He put out his hand, palm forward, to her, still cautious lest she, too, burst into flame.

"What I said to ye, before . . . that I kent ye loved me—"

She stepped forward and pressed her palm to his, her small, cool fingers linking tight.

"What I say to thee now is that I do love thee. And if thee hunts at night, thee will come home."

Under the sycamore, the dog yawned and laid his muzzle on his paws.

"And sleep at thy feet," Ian whispered, and gathered her in with his one good arm, blazing bright as day.

THE END

Written in My Own Heart's Blood

Each book in the series has a unique structure, tone, and voice (you may possibly have noticed this). This one consists of nine sections, seven of which are set in the American colonies in the eighteenth century and concern the adventures of Claire and Jamie Fraser, their friends and family.

These include Dr. Denzell Hunter and his sister, Rachel; Lord John Grey, his brother, Harold (Hal), who is the Duke of Pardloe, Dorothea (Dottie), Hal's daughter, and William, Lord John's stepson (and Jamie Fraser's natural son); also Fergus Fraser (Jamie's adopted son), his wife, Marsali (Jamie's foster daughter), and their four children: Germain, Joan, Félicité, and Henri-Christian; and also Jenny Murray, Jamie's sister, and her son, Young Ian Murray.

The other two sections (Parts Two and Six) are set in Scotland in the 1980s and concern the activities of Brianna and Roger MacKenzie and their two children, Jeremiah (Jemmy) and Amanda (Mandy). Also featuring William Buccleigh MacKenzie, Roger's great-great-great-great-grandfather.

(I tell you this for the sake of those readers who write to tell me that they "only want to read about Jamie and Claire!" and who may thus omit Parts Two and Six if they like. They'll regret it, but it's their choice.)

Now, as you may recall, *An Echo in the Bone* (Book 7) ended with a triple cliffhanger:

1. Jamie Fraser, who was thought to have perished at sea with his sister, Jenny, returns unexpectedly to find that his wife, Claire, has married his best friend, Lord John Grey. Jamie is grateful to Lord John for protecting Claire from arrest and prosecution as a Rebel spy. However, when he is obliged to abduct Lord John as a means of getting out of the city, he is somewhat taken aback to have his captive inform him, *"I have had carnal knowledge of your wife."* Knowing that John Grey is a) homosexual and b) in love with Jamie himself, all the bemused Mr. Fraser finds to say is, *"Oh? Why?"*

Naturally, we would like to hear the reply to this. . . .

2. William Ransom, Lord John's stepson, who to this point has believed himself to be the Ninth Earl of Ellesmere, leads a patrol of British soldiers in pursuit of a man suspected of passing seditious materials to a known Rebel printer. They follow the man (Jamie, but they don't know that yet) to Lord John's house, where they are delayed at the door but

finally force their way in. William rushes upstairs, knowing that his stepfather, Lord John, and stepmother, Claire, are up there—and comes face-to-face with Jamie Fraser.

The physical resemblance is sufficiently striking that William is brought to a screeching halt. The brief ensuing conversation makes it crystal clear that he is indeed the illegitimate son of this Scottish criminal traitor. Jamie takes Lord John hostage and decamps, whereupon William makes a dramatic—and destructive—exit himself.

Do we wonder where he's going and what he's going to do (to whom) when he gets there? Well, yes . . .

3. Meanwhile, back in Scotland in the twentieth century, young Jeremiah (Jemmy) MacKenzie has been abducted by one Rob Cameron, a co-worker of Jem's mother, Brianna. Cameron has accidentally stumbled on the MacKenzies' time-traveling secret and, in the course of further nosing around, has also discovered that Jemmy is the only person in the twentieth century to know the whereabouts of a large amount of gold, cached by Jem's grandfather in the eighteenth century. Rob stashes Jemmy in a tunnel under a hydroelectric dam and successfully decoys Jem's father, Roger, and Roger's ancestor, William Buccleigh, into thinking that he's taken Jem through the stones into the past. Cameron then heads back to Lallybroch, expecting to find Brianna MacKenzie alone with her small daughter and presumably at his mercy.

Mr. Cameron is sadly deluded—or at least we hope so.

So . . . what will William do with the blistering knowledge of his true paternity? What will Jamie do to Lord John—or to Claire? And what will become of little Jemmy, trapped in a long, dark tunnel and headed straight for a temporal vortex that might suck him away, either to times unknown or to a grisly end embedded in solid rock?

Naturally, *Written in My Own Heart's Blood* doesn't begin with the answers to any of these questions. (What fun would *that* be?) But we will get there in the end. So follow me like a leopard, if you will, and we will venture into the jungle of the Unknown.

PART ONE: *NEXUS*

Our story begins (or continues, depending how you want to look at it) with Young Ian Murray, alone in the forest outside Philadelphia, occupied in the heartbreaking work of building two cairns—a cairn being a pile of stones erected in memory of the dead—one for his mother, and one for his beloved uncle Jamie, both of whom have (so far as Ian knows) perished when their ship sank on the voyage to America.

He's thinking not only of his own loss and grief but of those others left behind. Because, with Jamie dead, who is there to be responsible for the family except Ian himself?

He crossed himself and bent to dig about in

the soft leaf mold. A few more rocks, he thought. In case they might be scattered by some passing animal. Scattered like his thoughts, which roamed restless to and fro among the faces of his family, the folk of the Ridge—God, might he ever go back there? Brianna. Oh, Jesus, Brianna . . .

He bit his lip and tasted salt, licked it away and moved on, foraging. She was safe with Roger Mac and the weans. But, Jesus, he could have used her advice—even more, Roger Mac's.

Who was left for him to ask, if he needed help in taking care of them all? . . .

Ian worked awhile longer and let the thoughts drain away with his sweat and his tears. He finally stopped when the sinking sun touched the tops of his cairns, feeling tired but more at peace. The cairns rose knee-high, side by side, small but solid.

He stood still for a bit, not thinking anymore, just listening to the fussing of wee birds in the grass and the breathing of the wind among the trees. Then he sighed deeply, squatted, and touched one of the cairns.

"Tha gaol agam oirbh, a Mhàthair," *he said softly. My love is upon you, Mother. Closed his eyes and laid a scuffed hand on the other heap of stones. The dirt ground into his skin made his fingers feel strange, as though he could maybe reach straight through the earth and touch what he needed.*

He stayed still, breathing, then opened his eyes.

"Help me wi' this, Uncle Jamie," he said. "I dinna think I can manage, alone."

Clearly Ian is the son of Jamie's heart and soul, his natural successor as head of the family. But what of William, Jamie's son by flesh and blood? He isn't having an easy time of it, either—though his problems are caused not by Jamie's death but by the big Scot being inconveniently alive:

William Ransom, Ninth Earl of Ellesmere, Viscount Ashness, Baron Derwent, shoved his way through the crowds on Market Street, oblivious to the complaints of those rebounding from his impact.

He didn't know where he was going, or what he might do when he got there. All he knew was that he'd burst if he stood still.

His head throbbed like an inflamed boil. Everything throbbed. His hand—he'd probably broken something, but he didn't care. His heart, pounding and sore inside his chest. His foot, for God's sake—what, had he kicked something? He lashed out viciously at a loose cobblestone and sent it rocketing through a crowd of geese, who set up a huge cackle and lunged at him, hissing and beating at his shins with their wings.

Feathers and goose shit flew wide, and the crowd scattered in all directions.

"Bastard!" shrieked the goose-girl, and struck at him with her crook, catching him a shrewd thump on the ear. "Devil take you, dreckiger Bastard!"

This sentiment was echoed by a number of other angry voices, and he veered into an alley, pursued by shouts and honks of agitation.

In the alley, William meets a young woman, a teenaged whore in a silk petticoat and no stays. Whether intrigued by his display of fury, attracted by his personal presence—which is considerable, even when boiling over—or merely in need of custom, Arabella (a *nom de guerre,* as she later informs William) invites the distraught young man inside her place of employment for a drink.

One thing leads to another, but not in a good way, and William ends up rushing out of the house minus his uniform coat, spattered with soap, pursued by the house's bouncer, and with the shrieks of Arabella ringing in his ears.

Leaving William to his own devices for

the nonce, we now enter Chapter 3, aptly entitled "In Which the Women, as Usual, Pick up the Pieces," and join Claire Randall Fraser, in *medias res.*

WILLIAM HAD LEFT *the house like a thunderclap, and the place looked as though it had been struck by lightning. I certainly felt like the survivor of a massive electrical storm, hairs and nerve endings all standing up straight on end, waving in agitation.*

Jenny Murray had entered the house on the heels of William's departure, and while the sight of her was a lesser shock than any of the others so far, it still left me speechless. I goggled at my erstwhile sister-in-law—though, come to think, she still was *my sister-in-law . . . because Jamie was alive.* Alive.

He'd been in my arms not ten minutes before, and the memory of his touch flickered through me like lightning in a bottle. I was dimly aware that I was smiling like a loon, despite massive destruction, horrific scenes, William's distress—if you could call an explosion like that "distress"—Jamie's danger, and a faint wonder as to what either Jenny or Mrs. Figg, Lord John's cook and housekeeper, might be about to say.

Mrs. Figg was smoothly spherical, gleamingly black, and inclined to glide silently up behind one like a menacing ball bearing.

"What's this?*" she barked, manifesting herself suddenly behind Jenny.*

"Holy Mother of God!" Jenny whirled, eyes round and hand pressed to her chest. "Who in God's name are you?"

"This is Mrs. Figg," I said, feeling a surreal urge to laugh, despite—or maybe because of—recent events. "Lord John Grey's cook. And, Mrs. Figg, this is Mrs. Murray. My, um . . . my . . ."

"Your good-sister," Jenny said firmly. She raised one black eyebrow. "If ye'll have me still?" Her look was straight and open, and the urge to laugh changed abruptly into an equally strong urge to burst into tears. Of all the unlikely sources of succor I could have imagined . . . I took a deep breath and put out my hand.

"I'll have you." We hadn't parted on good terms in Scotland, but I had loved her very much, once, and wasn't about to pass up any opportunity to mend things.

Her small firm fingers wove through mine, squeezed hard, and, as simply as that, it was done. No need for apologies or spoken forgiveness. She'd never had to wear the mask that Jamie did. What she thought and felt was there in her eyes, those slanted blue cat eyes she shared with her brother. She knew the truth now of what I was, and she knew I loved—and always had loved—her brother with all my heart and soul—despite the minor complications of my being presently married to someone else.

The men being conveniently absent for the moment, the women sit down with a cup of tea laced with brandy *(I thought it might take something stronger than brandy-laced tea to deal with the effect of recent events on my nerves—laudanum, say, or a large slug of straight Scotch whisky—but the tea undeniably helped, hot and aromatic, settling in a soft trickling warmth amidships),* and Claire brings Jenny and Mrs. Figg up to date on recent developments:

Jenny's eyes were disturbingly like Jamie's. She blinked at me once, then twice, and shook her head as though to clear it, accepting what I'd just told her.

"So Jamie's gone off wi' your Lord John, the British army is after them, the tall lad I met on the stoop wi' steam comin' out of his ears is Jamie's son—well, of course he is; a blind man could see that—and the town's aboil wi' British soldiers. Is that it, then?"

This isn't quite the half of it but will do to be going on with, and Claire does—go on, to the disquiet of Mrs. Figg, Lord John's devoted housekeeper.

Mrs. Figg made a deep humming noise of disapproval.

"And maybe [Mr. Fraser will] make for Valley Forge and turn [Lord John] over to the Rebels instead."

"Oh, I shouldna think so," Jenny said soothingly. "What would they want with him, after all?"

Mrs. Figg blinked again, taken aback at the notion that anyone might not value his lordship to the same degree that she did, but after a moment's lip-pursing allowed as this might be so.

"He wasn't in his uniform, was he, ma'am?" she asked me, brow furrowed. I shook my head. John didn't hold an active commission. He was a diplomat, though technically still lieutenant colonel of his brother's regiment, and therefore wore his uniform for purposes of ceremony or intimidation, but he was officially retired from the army, not a combatant, and in plain clothes he would be taken as citizen rather than soldier—thus of no particular interest to General Washington's troops at Valley Forge.

I didn't think Jamie was headed for Valley Forge in any case. I knew, with absolute certainty, that he would come back. Here. For me.

The thought bloomed low in my belly and spread upward in a wave of warmth that made me bury my nose in my teacup to hide the resulting flush.

Alive. *I caressed the word, cradling it in the center of my heart. Jamie was alive. Glad as I was to see Jenny—and gladder still to see her extend an olive branch in my direction—I really wanted to go up to my room, close the door, and lean against the wall with my eyes shut tight, reliving the seconds after he'd entered the room, when he'd taken me in his*

arms and pressed me to the wall, kissing me, the simple, solid, warm fact of his presence so overwhelming that I might have collapsed onto the floor without that wall's support.

Alive, *I repeated silently to myself.* He's alive.

Nothing else mattered. Though I did wonder briefly what he'd done with John.

We would all like to know that—and to find out the reply to Jamie's cliff-hanging question regarding John's bedding of his wife: *"Oh? Why?"* Fortunately, Lord John is still sufficiently healthy as to make that reply, which he does in Chapter Four, entitled "Don't Ask Questions You Don't Want to Hear the Answers To":

John Grey had been quite resigned to dying. Had expected it from the moment that he'd blurted out, "I have had carnal knowledge of your wife." *The only question in his mind had been whether Fraser would shoot him, stab him, or eviscerate him with his bare hands.*

To have the injured husband regard him calmly and say merely, "Oh? Why?" *was not merely unexpected but . . . infamous. Absolutely infamous.*

"Why?" John Grey repeated, incredulous. "Did you say 'Why?'"

"I did. And I should appreciate an answer."

Now that Grey had both eyes open, he could see that Fraser's outward calm was not quite so impervious as he'd first supposed. There was a pulse beating in Fraser's temple, and he'd shifted his weight a little, like a man might do in the vicinity of a tavern brawl: not quite ready to commit violence but readying himself to meet it. Perversely, Grey found this sight steadying.

"What do you bloody mean, *'Why?'" he said, suddenly irritated. "And why aren't you fucking dead?"*

"I often wonder that myself," Fraser replied politely. "I take it ye thought I was?"

"Yes, and so did your wife! Do you have the faintest idea what the knowledge of your death did *to her?"*

The dark-blue eyes narrowed just a trifle.

"Are ye implying that the news of my death deranged her to such an extent that she lost her reason and took ye to her bed by force? Because," he went on, neatly cutting off Grey's heated reply, "unless I've been seriously misled regarding your own nature, it would take substantial force to compel ye to any such action. Or am I wrong?"

Mr. Fraser has not been misled, but he *is* wrong, as Lord John wastes no time in pointing out. His subsequent explanations of the situation cause Mr. Fraser to slug him in the midriff, paste him in the eye, and abandon him to the mercies of a party of American militiamen who have interrupted this interesting *tête-à-tête.*

At this crux of his affairs, Lord John makes the inconvenient discovery that the letter he had so carelessly shoved into his pocket just before Jamie's abrupt arrival that morning is a warrant of commission with his name (and the royal seal) on it, with a note informing him that he has been recalled to service by the Duke of Pardloe, colonel and commander of his regiment—and, incidentally, John's elder brother.

Lord John's possession of these documents, while he's dressed in civilian clothes, gives the militiamen the reasonably founded notion that they have caught themselves a British spy, and they are prevented from hanging him on the spot only by their captain's desire to show off his catch to *his* commanding officer.

BACK AT CHESTNUT Street, the women's *tête-à-tête* is interrupted by a soldier come in search of Lord John, who is urgently wanted by Sir Henry Clinton, commander of His Majesty's troops in North America, and not a man to take "no" for an answer. Claire therefore dresses and accompanies the soldier to General Clinton's office, where she meets a stranger who seems oddly familiar:

"You're a relative of Lord John Grey's," I blurted, staring at him. He had to be. The man wore his own hair, as John did, though his was dark beneath its powder. The shape of his head—fine-boned and long-skulled—was John's, and so was the set of his shoulders. His features were much like John's, too, but his face was deeply weathered and gaunt, marked with harsh lines carved by long duty and the stress of command. I didn't need the uniform to tell me that he was a lifelong soldier.

He smiled, and his face was suddenly transformed. Apparently he had John's charm, too.

"You're most perceptive, madam," he said, and, stepping forward, smoothly took my limp hand away from the general and kissed it briefly in the continental manner before straightening and eyeing me with interest.

"General Clinton informs me that you are my brother's wife."

"Oh," I said, scrambling to recover my mental bearings. "Then you must be Hal! Er . . . I beg your pardon. I mean, you're the . . . I'm sorry, I know you're a duke, but I'm afraid I don't recall your title, Your Grace."

"Pardloe," he said, still holding my hand and smiling at me. "But my Christian name is Harold; do please use it if you like. Welcome to the family, my dear. I had no idea John had married. I understand the event was quite recent?" He spoke with great cordiality, but I was aware of the intense curiosity behind his good manners.

"Ah," I said noncommittally. "Yes, quite recent."

Hal is fascinated by his brother's new wife—and realizes instantly that there's something fishy going on:

"You're a very bad liar," he remarked with interest. "What are you lying about, though, I wonder?"

"I do it better with a little warning," I snapped. "Though, as it happens, I'm not *lying at the moment."*

Hal attempts to take Claire back to his inn in order to question her. This attempt is thwarted by an inopportune attack of asthma, which turns the tables on the duke and results in his being unwittingly kidnapped by Claire, who saves his life, puts him to bed, and, in the course of treating his breathing problems, ends up having a surprisingly intimate late-night conversation with him in a haze of ganja smoke.

MEANWHILE, A THOROUGHLY inflamed Jamie Fraser has turned his horse's head for Philadelphia, with no clear idea what he might say or do to his wife when he finds her but needing her like a castaway needs fresh water. He doesn't reach her, though, being intercepted by an old friend, Daniel Morgan, who persuades him (much against his will) to come for a moment to meet someone important.

"Someone important" proves to be General George Washington, who impresses Jamie by his personality and presence—and impresses Jamie bodily into the Continental army, appointing him a field general in command of militia, to replace a man who has just died. This is the last thing Jamie expected or wants, but he has no choice and can only hope that he'll have time to deal with Claire before reporting for duty—because if not, he'll be shot for desertion: nothing will keep him from her.

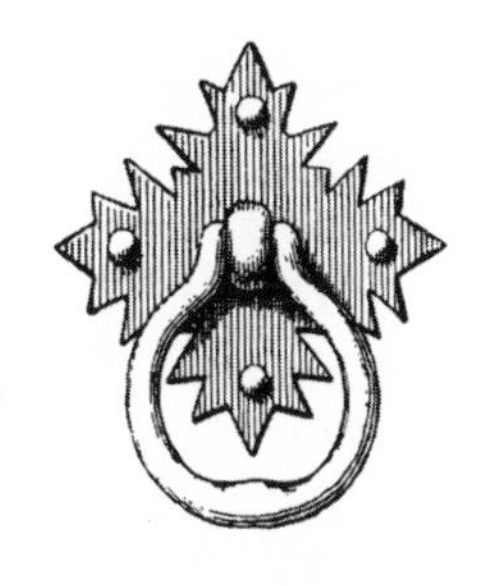

This hope, however, is stymied by a back spasm that temporarily immobilizes him, keeping him fuming and writhing in both physical and mental agony for two days at the home of Mrs. Hardman, the Quaker widow in whose cabin Washington was meeting with his generals.

JAMIE IS STUCK. Claire is stranded in Philadelphia with the British army leaving, the Americans about to invade the city, and a captive duke hidden in her house. Lord John, though, is having rather more-active adventures.

Despite John's assorted bruises and a badly injured eye, his militia captors take him to one Colonel Watson Smith—an erstwhile acquaintance of Grey's, now a turncoat in the service of the Continental army. This circumstance naturally causes a certain constraint between the men, which is deepened by Captain's Smith's observation that Grey is very likely to be hanged as a spy.

Though John is put in irons to prevent escape, his mood is lifted somewhat by hearing a voice in camp that he's sure belongs to his niece, Dorothea. Dottie is betrothed to Denzell Hunter, a Quaker physician in service with the Americans. Denzell and Dottie help Lord John escape during the night watches, and life, while still precarious, seems to be looking up.

But as Hal observe to John, "You have the greatest talent for awkward situations," and John, having gone to sleep in the hollow of a tree's roots, is rudely awakened by a party of American militia.

BY BREAKFAST ON *Thursday, I'd come to the firm conclusion that it was the Duke of Pardloe or me. If I stayed in the house, only one of us would remain alive by sundown. Denzell Hunter must have come into the city by now, I reasoned; he'd call in daily at Mrs. Woodcock's house, where Henry Grey was convalescing. A very kind and capable doctor, he could easily manage Hal's recovery—and perhaps his future father-in-law would be grateful for his professional attention.*

The thought made me laugh out loud, despite my increasing anxiety.

To Dr. Denzell Hunter
From Dr. C. B. R. Fraser

I am called away to Kingsessing for the day. I surrender His Grace the Duke of Pardloe to your most competent care, in the happy confidence that your religious scruples will prevent your striking him in the head with an ax.

Yours most sincerely,
C.

Postscriptum: I'll bring you back some asafoetida and ginseng root as recompense.

Post-postscriptum: Strongly suggest you don't bring Dottie, unless you possess a pair of manacles. Preferably two.

As Claire makes her way toward Kingsessing, she meets a carriage bearing General Benedict Arnold into Philadelphia as the new military governor of the city. The general offers her a lift to Bartram's Garden, and she accepts, though disquieted by her knowledge of what she believes will happen to Arnold at some not-very-distant date.

When? *I wondered uneasily. When would it begin to happen? Not yet; I was almost sure of that. What was it, what would it be, that turned this gallant, honorable man from patriot to traitor? Who would he talk to, what would plant the deadly seed?*

Lord, *I thought in a moment of sudden, horrified prayer,* please! Don't let it be something I said to him!

As she'd observed to herself earlier: *The hell of it was that I* liked *the man.*

But the man for whom she harbors a much deeper affection has recovered enough to make his way toward Philadelphia, desperate to reach her.

IN BETWEEN JAMIE and Claire, though, are Young Ian and his affianced, Rachel Hunter, who are walking through the woods toward the city, deep in conversation. Beyond the natural talk of an engaged pair who are much in love but facing complicated logistics concerning their marriage, Young Ian has a deeper motive for this conversation: he needs to confess a few things to Rachel.

"Did ye ken . . . I've been marrit before?"

Her face flickered, surprise overcome by determination so fast that he'd have missed it if he hadn't been watching so close.

"I did not," she said, and began to pleat the folds of her skirt, one-handed, clear hazel eyes fixed intently on his face. "Thee did say been married. Thee isn't now, I suppose?"

Rachel handles the news of Ian's earlier marriage to a Mohawk woman—and the news that Ian's ex-wife is still alive—with a reasonable amount of equanimity, but it isn't the marriage that's causing Ian's concern: it's the reason for the marriage ending.

"I couldna give her children," he blurted. "The first—we had a wee daughter, born too early, who died. I called her Iseabàil." He wiped the back of his hand viciously under his nose, swallowing his pain. "After that, she—Emily—she got wi' child again. And again. And when she lost the third . . . her heart toward me died with it."

Rachel made a small sound, but he didn't look at her. Couldn't. Just sat hunched on the log like a toadstool, shoulders drawn up around his ears, and eyes blurred with the tears he couldn't shed.

A small warm hand settled on his.

"And thy heart?" she asked. "Thine died, too?"

Ian tells Rachel that Claire thinks he *might* be able to have children with another woman—but he can't guarantee that.

He turned a little on the log, to look at her directly. "And I canna say that it would be different—with us. But I did ask Auntie Claire, and she told me about things in the blood . . . well, perhaps ye should ask her to explain it; I wouldna make a decent job of it. But the end of it was that she thought it might *be different wi' another woman. That I maybe could. Give ye bairns, I mean."*

He only realized that Rachel had been holding her breath when she let it out, a sigh that brushed his cheek.

"Do ye—" he began, but she had risen a little, into him, and she kissed him gently on the mouth, then held his head against her breast and took the end of her kerchief and wiped his eyes and then her own.

"Oh, Ian," she whispered. "I do love thee."

Back in Philadelphia, the British army is on the verge of departure, and William is having a very bad day. After overseeing the exodus of panicked Loyalists and repelling the overtures of Captain Richardson, the spy whose previous ventures came close to getting William captured or killed, William returns to his billet to find that his orderly has decamped, taking with him all of William's valuables, including a pearl-encrusted miniature of his two mothers.

This was so far over the bloody limit of what could be borne that he didn't even swear, merely sank down on the edge of the bed, closed his eyes, and breathed through clenched teeth until the pain in his stomach subsided. It left a raw-edged hollow.

William being a young male, the only thing that occurs to him to do is to fill the hollow with alcohol, and the end of the evening finds him accompanying his friends to a brothel, where he collapses into a chair and a near-stupor, in both of which he remains until he becomes slowly aware that a dragoon captain nearby—a Captain Harkness—is enjoying himself by describing various degrading things that he proposes to do to a young woman who works in the establishment.

William is roused from his stupor and revolted by this—and still more roused in the next instant, when he realizes that the young woman being threatened is the girl with whom he had the embarrassing and discreditable encounter the day before. With vague notions of gallantry and redeeming himself, he makes it to his feet and claims the girl for the night—hastily yanking off his silver gorget and handing it to the madam in payment, having belatedly remembered that he has no money.

Arabella (aka Jane; as she tells William, the "fancy pieces" are given ladies' names for marketing purposes) is more than wary of William—but he's definitely the lesser of two evils, and she takes him to her room, where he astonishes her by telling her that his intent is not what she supposes:

"My . . . um . . . my stepfather . . . told me once that a madam of his acquaintance said to him that a night's sleep was the best gift you could give a whore."

"It runs in the family, does it? Frequenting brothels?" She didn't pause for a response to that. "He's right, though. Do you really mean that you intend for me to . . . sleep?" From her tone of incredulity, he might have asked her to engage in some perversion well past buggery.

Arabella–Jane has a sense of honor, too, though, and succeeds in proving it.

"Unhand my . . ." Damn, what is the bloody word? *"Unhand my testicles if you please, madam."*

"Just as you like," she replied crisply, and, doing so, put her head back inside his damp, smelly shirt, seized one nipple between her teeth, and sucked so hard that it pulled every last word out of his head.

Matters thereafter were unsettled but largely pleasant, though at one point he found himself rearing above her, sweat dripping from his face onto her breasts, muttering, "I'm a bastard, I'm a bastard, *don't you understand?"*

She didn't reply to this but stretched up a long white arm, cupped her hand round the back of his head, and pulled him down again.

THE BRITISH EXODUS from Philadelphia begins the next day, with General Clinton's army proceeding in three separate bodies, shepherding a large number of Loyalists who feel unsafe remaining in the city and who evacuate on foot, carrying what they can of their possessions.

Ian and Rachel come upon the moving column of troops and camp followers as they reach the Philadelphia road. They also come upon William, hot, dusty, and clearly sharing the prevalent mood of disgruntlement.

While William's mood is momentarily lifted by sight of Rachel, things rapidly go downhill when she tells him that she and Ian are engaged—and things go from bad to worse when the name of Jamie Fraser enters the conversation:

Despite his resolve to be patient, Ian felt his own dander start to rise.

"Criminal, forbye!" he snapped. "Any man might be proud to be the son of Jamie Fraser!"

"Oh," said Rachel, forestalling William's next heated remark. "That."

"What?" He glared down at her. "What the devil do you mean, 'that'*?"*

"We thought it must be the case, Denny and I." She lifted one shoulder, though keeping a close watch on William, who looked as if he were about to go off like a twelve-pound mortar. "But we supposed that thee didn't wish the matter talked about. I didn't know that thee—how could thee not have known?" she asked curiously. "The resemblance—"

"Fuck the resemblance!"

Ian forgot Rachel and hit William on the head with a double-fisted thump that knocked him to his knees, then kicked him in the stomach. Had the kick landed where he'd meant it to, it would have finished the matter right there, but William was a good deal faster than Ian expected him to be. He twisted sideways, caught Ian's foot, and yanked. Ian hit the ground on one elbow, rolled up, and got hold of William's ear. He was dimly aware of Rachel screaming and was momentarily sorry for it, but the relief of fighting was too great to think of anything else, and she disappeared as his fury surged.

The fight ends with the advent of several of William's soldiers, who haul Ian off toward the column, presumably to be taken along to the evening camp, where punishment is routinely dealt out to those convicted of crimes such as assaulting an officer.

Rachel is horrified, outraged, and not inclined to take the situation lying down.

"If thee allow this to be done, William Ransom, I will—I will—"

William could feel the blood pool in his belly and thought he might faint, but not because of her threats.

"You'll what?" he asked, half breathless. "You're a Quaker. You don't believe in violence. Ergo, you can't—or at least won't"—he corrected himself, seeing the dangerous look in her eye—"stab me. You probably won't even strike me. So what did you have in mind?"

She did strike him. Her hand whipped out like a snake and slapped him across the face hard enough to make him stagger.

"So now thee has doomed thy kinsman, repudiated thy father, and caused me to betray my principles. What next?!"

"Oh, bloody hell," he said, and grabbed her arms, pulled her roughly to him, and kissed her. He let go and stepped back quickly, leaving her bug-eyed and gasping.

The dog growled at him. She glared at him, spat on the ground at his feet, then wiped her lips on her sleeve and, turning away, marched off, the dog at her heels casting a red-eyed look at William.

"Is spitting on people a part of your bloody principles?" he shouted after her.

She swung round, fists clenched at her sides.

"Is assaulting women part of thine?" she bellowed back, to the amusement of the infantrymen who had been standing still by the road, leaning on their weapons and gaping at the show provided.

Flinging her cap on the ground at his feet, she whirled on her heel and stamped away, before he could say more.

JAMIE, HAVING HITCHED a ride into Philadelphia on a wagon filled with cabbages, is startled to see his nephew Ian being dragged off by redcoats. Ian is more than startled to see his uncle apparently risen from a watery grave, but there is no opportunity for conversation. Jamie spots Rachel and Rollo, haring toward the city, and swings down to investigate.

Having ascertained the facts of the matter from Rachel, Jamie then goes to have a word with William:

He was reasonably sure Rachel hadn't told him everything about the recent stramash and wondered whether she herself had been partly the cause of it. She had *said the trouble began just after she'd told William about her betrothal to Ian. Her account had been slightly confused overall, but he'd got the gist of it well enough, and his jaw tightened as he came up to William and saw the look on his face.*

Christ, do I look like that in a temper? *he wondered briefly. It was off-putting to speak to a man who looked as though he asked nothing more of the world than the chance to rend someone limb from limb and dance on the pieces.*

"Well, rend away, lad," he said under his breath. "And we'll see who dances." He stepped up beside William and took off his hat.

"You," he said baldly, not wishing to call the lad by either title or name, "come aside wi' me. Now."

The look on William's face changed from incipient murder to the same look of startled horror Jamie had just surprised on Ian's. Had matters been otherwise, he'd have laughed. As it was, he gripped William hard by the upper arm, pushed him off-balance, and had him into the shelter of a scrim of saplings before he could set his feet hard.

WILLIAM IS, NOT surprisingly, in No Mood to have a conversation with his very unwelcome progenitor, let alone to do what he says—but Jamie has a fairly convincing argument:

"You're going to catch up the men ye sent Ian with and tell them to set him free," Jamie said evenly. "If ye don't, I go down under a flag of truce to the camp where they're taking him, introduce myself, tell the commander who you *are, and explain the reason for the fight. Ye'll be right there beside me. Do I make myself clear?" he asked, increasing the pressure of his fingers.*

"Yes!" The word came out in a hiss, and Jamie let go suddenly, folding his fingers into a fist to hide the fact that they were trembling and twitching from the effort.

"God damn you, sir," William whispered, and his eyes were black with violence. "God damn you to hell." His arm hung limp and must have hurt, but he wouldn't rub it, not with Jamie watching.

Jamie nodded. "Nay doubt," he said quietly, and went into the forest.

THE ATMOSPHERE OF Bartram's Garden is soothing to Claire's soul, and after restocking her supplies of herbs, seeds, and roots, she accepts Miss Bartram's invitation to dig her own arrowroot by the river.

I dug slowly and peaceably, lifting the dripping roots into my basket and packing each layer between mats of watercress. Sweat was running down my face and between my breasts, but I didn't notice it; I was melting quietly into the landscape, breath and muscle turning to wind and earth and water.

Cicadas buzzed heavily in the trees nearby, and gnats and mosquitoes were beginning to collect in uneasy clouds overhead. These were luckily only a nuisance when they flew up my nose or hovered too close to my face; apparently my twentieth-century blood wasn't attractive to eighteenth-century insects, and I was almost never bitten—a great blessing to a gardener. Lulled into mindlessness, I had quite lost track of time and place, and when a pair of large, battered shoes appeared in my field of view, I merely blinked at them for a moment, as I might at the sudden appearance of a frog.

Then I looked up.

What she sees, of course, is Jamie. And what ensues, of course, is a rather fraught conversation:

"Ye went to bed with John Grey, aye?"

I blinked, startled, then frowned at him. "Well, no, I wouldn't say that."

His eyebrows rose.

"He told me ye did."

"Is that what he said?" I asked, surprised.

"Mmphm." Now it was his turn to frown. "He told me he'd had carnal knowledge of ye. Why would he lie about such a thing as that?"

"Oh," I said. "No, that's right. Carnal knowledge is a very reasonable description of what happened."

"But—"

" 'Going to bed,' though . . . For one thing, we didn't. It started on a dressing table and ended—so far as I recall—on the floor." Jamie's eyes widened noticeably, and I hastened to correct the impression he was obviously forming. "For another, that phraseology implies that we decided to make love to each other and toddled off hand in hand to do so, and that wasn't what happened at all. Umm . . . perhaps we should sit down?" I gestured toward a rustic bench, standing knee-deep in creamy drifts of ranunculus.

I hadn't had a single thought of that night since learning Jamie was alive, but it was beginning to dawn on me that it might quite possibly seem important to Jamie—and that explaining what had happened might be somewhat tricky.

The succeeding conversation is indeed tricky, with a fair amount of justified high feeling on both sides.

"He did say there was drink taken," Jamie observed.

"Lots. He seemed nearly as drunk as I was, save that he was still on his feet." I could see John's face in memory, white as bone save for his eyes, which were so red and swollen that they might have been sandpapered. And the expression in those eyes. "He looked the way a man looks just before he throws himself off a cliff," I said quietly, eyes on my folded hands. I took another breath.

"He had a fresh decanter in his hand. He put it down on the dressing table beside me, glared at me, and said, 'I will not mourn him alone tonight.' *" A deep quiver ran through me at the memory of those words.*

"And . . . ?"

"And he didn't," I said, a little sharply. "I told him to sit down and he did, and he poured out more brandy and we drank it, and I have not one single notion what we said, but we were talking about you. And then he stood up, and I stood up. And . . . I couldn't bear to be alone and I couldn't bear for him *to be alone and I more or less flung myself at him because I very much needed someone to touch me just then."*

"And he obliged ye, I take it."

The tone of this was distinctly cynical, and I felt a flush rise in my cheeks, not of embarrassment but of anger.

"Did he bugger you?"

I looked at him for a good long minute. He meant it.

"You absolute bastard," I said, as much in astonishment as anger. Then a thought occurred to me. "You said he desired you to kill him," I said slowly. "You . . . didn't, did you?"

He held my eyes, his own steady as a rifle barrel.

"Would ye mind if I did?" he asked softly.

But Claire does at last find words to describe what it was that happened between her and Lord John:

"Triage," I said abruptly. "Under the numbness, I was . . . raw. Bloody. Skinned. *You do triage, you . . . stop the bleeding first. You stop it. You stop it, or the patient dies. He stopped it."*

He'd stopped it by slapping his own grief, his own fury, over the welling blood of mine. Two wounds, pressed together, blood still flowing freely—but no longer lost and draining, flowing instead into another body, and the other's blood into mine, hot, searing, not welcome—but life.

Jamie said something under his breath in Gaelic. I didn't catch most of the words. He sat with his head bent, elbows on his knees and head in his hands, and breathed audibly.

After a moment, I sat back down beside him and breathed, too. The cicadas grew louder, an urgent buzz that drowned out the rush of water and the rustling of leaves, humming in my bones.

"Damn him," Jamie muttered at last, and sat up. He looked disturbed, angry—but not angry at me.

"John, um, *is* all right, isn't he?" I asked hesitantly. To my surprise—and my slight unease—Jamie's lips twisted a little.

"Aye. Well. I'm sure he is," he said, in a tone admitting of a certain doubt, which I found alarming.

"What the bloody hell did you do to him?" I said, sitting up straight.

His lips compressed for an instant.

"I hit him," he said. "Twice," he added, glancing away.

"Twice?" I echoed, in some shock. "Did he fight you?"

"No," he said shortly.

"Really." I rocked back a bit, looking him over. Now that I had calmed down enough to take notice, I thought he was displaying . . . what? Concern? Guilt?

"Why did you hit him?" I asked, striving for a tone of mild curiosity, rather than one of accusation. Evidently I was less than successful with this, as he turned on me like a bear stung in the rump by a bee.

"*Why*? Ye dare to ask me *why*?"

"Certainly I do," I said, discarding the mild tone. "What did he do to make you hit him? And *twice*?" Jamie had no problem

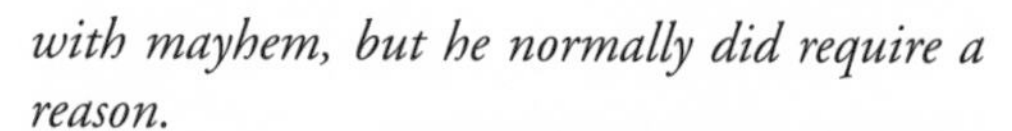

with mayhem, but he normally did require a reason.

He made a deeply disgruntled Scottish noise, but he'd promised me honesty a long time ago and hadn't seen fit to break that promise yet. He squared his shoulders and looked at me straight.

"The first was between him and me; it was a blow I've owed him for a good while."

"And you just seized the opportunity to punch him, because it was convenient?" I asked, a bit wary of asking directly what the devil he meant by "between him and me."

"I couldna help it," he said testily. "He said something and I hit him."

I didn't say anything but inhaled through my nose, meaning him to hear it. There was a long moment of silence, weighted with expectation and broken only by the shush of the river.

"He said the two of ye hadna been making love to each other," he finally muttered, looking down.

"No, we weren't," I said, somewhat surprised. "I told you. We were both—oh!"

He did look up at me then, glaring.

"Oh," he said, the word dripping with sarcasm. "Ye were both fucking me, he said."

"Oh, I see," I murmured. "Well. Um. Yes, that's quite true." I rubbed the bridge of my nose. "I see," I said again, and thought I probably did. There was a deep friendship of long standing between Jamie and John, but I was aware that one of the pillars it rested on was a strict avoidance of any reference to John's sexual attraction toward Jamie. If John had lost his composure sufficiently as to kick that pillar out from under the two of them . . .

"And the second time?" I asked, choosing not to ask him to elaborate any further on the first.

"Aye, well, that one was on your account," he said, both voice and face relaxing a little.

"I'm flattered," I said, as dryly as possible. "But you really shouldn't have."

"Well, I ken that now," he admitted, flushing. "But I'd lost my temper already and hadna got it back again. Ifrinn,*" he muttered, and, stooping, picked up the discarded digging knife and jammed it hard into the bench beside him.*

Despite the difficulties of the conversation, though, the basic fact is established beyond doubt:

"I wish to say something," he said, in the tone of one making a formal statement before a court. My heart had quieted while he held me; now it fluttered in renewed agitation.

"What?" I sounded so apprehensive that he laughed. Only a breath, but he did laugh, and I was able to breathe again. He took my hand firmly and held it, looking into my eyes.

"I don't say that I dinna mind this, because I do. And I don't say that I'll no make a fuss about it later, because I likely will. But what I do say is that there is nothing in this world or the next that can take ye from me—or me from you." He raised one brow. "D'ye disagree?"

"Oh, no," I said fervently.

He breathed again, and his shoulders came down a fraction of an inch.

"Well, that's good, because it wouldna do ye any good if ye did. Just the one question," he said. "Are ye my wife?"

"Of course I am," I said, in utter astonishment. "How could I not be?"

His face changed then; he drew a huge breath and took me into his arms. I embraced him, hard, and together we let out a great sigh, settling with it, his head bending over mine, kissing my hair, my face turned into his shoulder, openmouthed at the neck of his open shirt, our knees slowly giving way in mutual relief, so that we knelt in the fresh-turned earth, clinging together, rooted like a tree, leaf-tossed and multi-limbed but sharing one single solid trunk.

The first drops of rain began to fall.

Whereupon:

His face was open now and his eyes clear blue and free of trouble—for the moment, at least. "Where is there a bed? I need to be naked with ye."

BACK IN THE woods outside Philadelphia, Lord John's escape has been interrupted by another encounter with militiamen—but now attired in civilian clothes and fetters, he manages to convince them that he's an American who has escaped from British captors.

Well enough for the moment; his new acquaintances take him back to camp, get his fetters off, and feed him. But—

AND AS THE *sun set on the third day since he had left his home, Lord John William Bertram Amstrong Grey found himself once more a free man, with a full belly, a swimming head, a badly mended musket, and severely chafed wrists, standing before the Reverend Peleg Woodsworth, right hand uplifted, reciting as prompted:*

"I, Bertram Armstrong, swear to be true to the United States of America, and to serve them honestly and faithfully against all their enemies and opposers whatsoever, and to observe and obey the orders of the Continental Congress and the orders of the generals and officers set over me by them."

Bloody hell, *he thought.* What next?

What next, indeed? Part Two, that's what. Artfully titled . . .

PART 2: *MEANWHILE, BACK AT THE RANCH . . .*

Part Two takes up where we left Roger, Brianna, Jemmy, Mandy, and Roger's ancestor, William Buccleigh MacKenzie (aka "Buck").

Roger and Buck have gone through the stone circle at Craigh na Dun, in pursuit—they think—of Rob Cameron, one of Brianna's co-workers at the Highlands and Islands Development Board, who has kidnapped Jemmy and taken him into the past—they think—in an attempt not only to learn the secrets of time travel but also to find the gold that Jamie Fraser cached on Fraser's Ridge, the location known only to himself and to his grandson, Jemmy.

The passage through the stones is physically and emotionally shattering, and while Roger recovers fairly quickly, his four-times great-grandfather is not so fortunate. He's alarmingly debilitated by the crossing, having chest pains and symptoms of heart trouble. He does manage to get up, though, and the two men agree to separate and search in different directions for any sign of Rob Cameron and Jem, then meet again near Craigh na Dun in six days' time.

UNBEKNOWNST TO THE rescuers, though, neither Rob Cameron nor Jemmy is in the past. Cameron has decoyed them, in hopes of getting Brianna alone, and has stashed Jem for safekeeping in a hydroelectric service tunnel under the Loch Errochty dam.

Jem, who has visited the dam with his mother, is a little unnerved by the dark—and by thought of Mr. Cameron coming back—but he finds the small electric train that carries workers up and down the length of the tunnel and runs it slowly toward the farther end, hoping to find the service door there unlocked. As he passes through the dark, though, he's struck suddenly by *something* that knocks him flat, causing him to fall out of the train and lie stunned for a few moments.

Realizing that he isn't dead, as he'd first assumed, and is capable of movement, he gets up and looks at what hit him—or, rather, at the thing *he'd* hit.

He couldn't see it, *not with his eyes, not exactly. He squinted, trying to think how he* was *seeing it, but there wasn't a word for what he was doing. Kind of like hearing or smelling or touching, but not really any of those.*

But he knew where it was. It was right there, *a kind of . . . shiver . . . in the air, and when he stared at it, he had a feeling in the back of his mind like pretty sparkly things, like sun on the sea and the way a candle flame looked when it shone through a ruby, but he knew he wasn't really* seeing *anything like that.*

It went all the way across the tunnel, and up to the high roof, too, he could tell. But it wasn't thick at all; it was thin as air.

He guessed that was why it hadn't swallowed him like the thing in the rocks on Ocracoke had. At least . . . he thought it hadn't and, for an instant, worried that maybe he'd gone sometime else. But he didn't think so. The tunnel felt just the same, and so did he, now that his skin had stopped jumping. When they'd done it, on Ocracoke, he'd known right away it was different.

He stood there for a minute, just looking and think-

ing, and then shook his head and turned around, feeling with his foot for the track. He wasn't going back through that, no matter what. He'd just have to hope the door wasn't locked.

MEANWHILE, ROB CAMERON has gone to Lallybroch to confront Brianna, toward whom he's held a grudge—and considerable lust—since she was appointed supervisor over him. He wants information, about the stones, about time travel, and about the gold—but he also wants Brianna.

Brianna's hand closed on the letter opener, but even as she calculated the distance involved, the obstacle of the desk between Rob Cameron and herself, and the flimsiness of the wooden blade, she was reluctantly concluding that she couldn't kill the bastard. Not yet.

"Where's my son?"

"He's okay."

She stood up suddenly, and he jerked a little in reflex. His face flushed and he hardened his expression.

"He'd bloody well better *be okay," she snapped. "I said, where is he?"*

"Oh, no, hen," he said, rocking back on his heels, affecting nonchalance. "That's no how we're playing it. Not tonight."

God, why didn't Roger keep a hammer or a chisel or something useful *in his desk drawer? Did he expect her to* staple *this jerk? She braced herself, both hands flat on the desk, to keep from leaping over it and going for his throat.*

"I'm not playing," she said through her teeth. "And neither are you. Where's Jemmy?"

It won't be the first time Rob Cameron has underestimated a Fraser, but it might be the last. He tells Brianna to undress, intending to rape her. Knowing she can't possibly overpower him in a fight, Bree takes him by surprise, lashing her jeans across his face and then smashing the wooden box in which her parents' letters are kept over his head. He recovers and chases her down the hall, but she's in time to reach the hall tree, where the family sports equipment is kept.

There were weapons on the walls of the foyer, a few targes and broadswords kept for ornament, but all hung high, to be out of the children's reach. There was a better one easily to hand, though. She reached behind the coat rack and grabbed Jem's cricket bat.

You can't kill him, *she kept thinking, dimly surprised at the fact that her mind was still working.* Don't kill him. Not yet. Not 'til he says where Jemmy is.

"Fucking . . . bitch!*" He was nearly on her, panting, half blinded by blood running down his forehead, half sobbing through the blood pouring from his nose. "Fuck you, split you open, fuck you up the—"*

"Caisteal DOOON!*" she bellowed, and, stepping out from behind the coat rack, swung the bat in a scything arc that caught him in the ribs. He made a gurgling noise and folded, arms across his middle. She took a deep breath, swung the bat as high as she could, and brought it down with all her strength on the crown of his head.*

The shock of it vibrated up her arms to her shoulders and she dropped the bat with a clunk and stood there gasping, trembling and drenched with sweat.

"Mummy?" said a tiny, quavering voice from the foot of the stair. "Why is you not got pants on, Mummy?"

Needing to keep calm for three-year-old Mandy, Bree soothes the little girl, binds Cameron with duct tape, and dumps him into the priest's hole behind the kitchen. He refuses to tell her where Jemmy is, but she has a last resort: Mandy. When Jem was presumably spending the night with Cameron's nephew, Bobby—but in reality being forced to touch the rocks at Craigh na Dun—Mandy woke in hysterics, insisting that Jem was gone and that *"the wocks* ate *him!"* Her parents, knowing the threat of those rocks all too well, were frightened—and still more so upon learning of Jem's disappearance. In the chaos and hurry of trying to find him, and then of preparing for Roger and Buck to travel through the stones in search of him, no one had time to think about Mandy and what she'd said. But now she may be the only one who can find Jem.

"CAN YOU TELL *when Jem's at school?"*

"Yes. He goes on da bus." Mandy bounced a little on her booster seat, leaning to peer out the window. She was wearing the Halloween mask Bree had helped her make, this being a mouse princess: a mouse face drawn with crayons on a paper plate, with holes pierced for eyes and at either side for pink yarn ties, pink pipe cleaners glued on for whiskers, and a precarious small crown made with cardboard, more glue, and most of a bottle of gold glitter.

Scots celebrated Samhain with hollowed-out turnips with candles in them, but Brianna had wanted a slightly more festive tradition for her half-American children. The whole seat sparkled as though the car had been sprinkled with pixie dust.

She smiled, despite her worry.

"I meant, if you played warmer, colder with Jem, could you do it if he wasn't answering you out loud? Would you know if he was closer or farther away?"

Mandy kicked the back of the seat in meditative fashion.

"Maybe."

BACK IN THE past, Roger and Buck have split up, Buck going to Inverness, and Roger to Lallybroch, reasoning that Jem knows the way from Craigh na Dun to Lallybroch, and even though it's a long way, if he had escaped from Rob Cameron, he'd head for home.

"Jem!" He shouted now and then as he went, though the moors and mountains were empty save for the rustling of rabbits and stoats and silent but for the calling of ravens and the occasional shriek of a seagull winging high overhead, evidence of the distant sea.

"Jem!" *he called, as though he could compel an answer by sheer need, and in that need imagined sometimes that he heard a faint cry in response. But when he stopped to listen, it was the wind. Only the wind, whining in his ears, numbing him. He could walk within ten feet of Jem and never see him, and he knew that.*

His heart rose, in spite of his anxiety, when he came to the top of the pass and saw Lallybroch below him, its white-harled buildings glowing in the fading light. Everything lay peaceful before him: late cabbages and turnips in orderly rows within the kailyard walls, safe from grazing sheep—there was a small flock in the far meadow, already bedding for the night, like so many woolly eggs in a nest of green grass, like a kid's Easter basket. . . .

He hammered at the door, and a huge dog came galloping round the corner of the house, baying like the bloody hound of the Baskervilles. It slid to a stop in front of him but went on barking, weaving its huge head to and fro like a snake, ears cocked in case he might make a false move that would let it devour him with a clear conscience.

He wasn't risking any moves; he'd plastered himself against the door when the dog appeared and now shouted, "Help! Come call your beast!"

He heard footsteps within, and an instant later the door opened, nearly decanting him into the hall.

"Hauld your wheesht, dog," a tall, dark man said in a tolerant tone. "Come ben, sir, and dinna be minding him. He wouldna eat you; he's had his dinner."

"I'm pleased to hear it, sir, and thank ye kindly." Roger pulled off his hat and followed the man into the shadows of the hall. It was his own familiar hall, the slates of the floor just the same, though not nearly as worn, the darkwood paneling shining with beeswax and polishing. There was *a hall tree in the corner, though of course different to his; this one was a sturdy affair of wrought iron, and a good thing, too, as it was supporting a massive burden of jackets, shawls, cloaks, and hats, which would have crumpled a flimsier piece of furniture.*

He smiled at it, nonetheless, and then stopped dead, feeling as though he'd been punched in the chest.

The wood paneling behind the hall tree shone serene, unblemished. No sign of the saber slashes left by frustrated redcoat soldiers searching for the outlawed laird of Lallybroch after Culloden. Those slashes had been carefully preserved for centuries, were still there, darkened by age but still distinct, when he had owned—would own, he corrected mechanically—this place.

"We keep it so for the children," *Bree had quoted her uncle Ian as saying.* "We tell them, 'This is what the English are.'"

He had no time to deal with the shock; the dark man had shut the door with a firm Gaelic adjuration to the dog and now turned to him, smiling.

"Welcome, sir. Ye'll sup wi' us? The lass has it nearly ready."

"Aye, I will, and thanks to ye," Roger bowed slightly, groping for his eighteenth-century manners. "I—my name is Roger MacKenzie. Of Kyle of Lochalsh," he added, for no respectable man would omit to note his origins, and Lochalsh was far enough away that the chances of this man—who was he? He hadn't the bearing of a servant—knowing its inhabitants in any detail was remote.

He'd hoped that the immediate response would be, "MacKenzie? Why, you must be the father of wee Jem!" It wasn't, though; the man returned his bow and offered his hand.

"Brian Fraser of Lallybroch, your servant, sir."

Roger is—naturally—struck dumb upon realizing that he's just met Jamie Fraser's father. It's not merely the unexpected appearance of the man, let alone realization of who he is, that's disturbing Roger, though; it's the dawning horror that he's come to the wrong time. Or has he?

He's in 1739—nearly forty years earlier than he'd expected. He was concentrating, with Buck, on the name "Jeremiah" when they stepped through the stones. So have they come to this time because Jem is here—or has something gone terribly wrong?

SOMETHING *HAS* OBVIOUSLY gone wrong, but Jem is safe—for the moment. He reaches the end of the hydroelectric tunnel and—eureka!—the service door that leads up into the turbine chamber is unlocked. He makes his way through the sinister rumble of the darkened chamber, with its immense vibrating engines, and at last reaches the sanctum of the offices on the other side of the dam. A security guard named Jock MacLeod finds him, sits him down to recover with a can of warm Coke, and proceeds to phone his parents. Or tries to.

It was warm in the office, but he was starting to feel cold around his face and hands. Nobody was answering the phone.

"Maybe they're asleep," he said, stifling a Coke burp. Mr. MacLeod gave him a sideways look and shook his head, pushed down the receiver, and dialed the number again, making Jem say the numbers one at a time.

Breep-breep . . . breep-breep . . .

He was concentrating so hard on willing somebody to pick up the phone that he didn't notice anything until Mr. MacLeod suddenly turned his head toward the door, looking surprised.

"What—" the guard said, and then there was a blur and a thunking noise like when cousin Ian shot a deer with an arrow, and Mr. MacLeod made an awful noise and fell right out of his chair onto the floor, and the chair shot away and fell over with a crash.

Jem didn't remember standing up, but he was pressed against the filing cabinet, squeezing the can so hard that the bubbly Coke blurped out and foamed over his fingers.

"You come with me, boy," said the man who'd hit Mr. MacLeod. He was holding what Jem thought must be a cosh, though he'd never seen one. He couldn't move, even if he'd wanted to.

The man made an impatient noise, stepped over Mr. MacLeod like he was a bag of rubbish, and grabbed Jem by the hand. Out of sheer terror, Jem bit him, hard. The man yelped and let go, and Jem threw the can of Coke right at his face, and when the man ducked, he tore past him and out of the office and down the long hallway, running for his life.

JEM COULD USE some help, and, luckily, it's on the way. Mandy begins to sense Jem's presence, and the rescue party arrives at the road to the Loch Errochty dam. Heart in her mouth, Bree pulls up to the dam office just as all hell breaks loose—with motion-detector lights and sirens (these caused by Jem's having eluded his pursuer long enough to hit the emergency exit and escape the building). Seeing a big man thrashing his way through the bushes near the spillway with a stick, she leaps out, carrying Mandy, and bellows at the man, who whirls to confront her.

Bree had peeled Mandy off. Setting her daughter down behind her, she prepared to take the man apart with her bare hands, if necessary. Evidently this intent showed, because the man dropped the stick and abruptly vanished into the darkness.

Then flashing lights washed over the drive and she realized that it wasn't her own aspect that had frightened him. Mandy was clinging to her leg, too frightened even to wail anymore. Bree picked her up, patting her gently, and turned to face the two police officers who were advancing cautiously toward her, hands on their batons. She felt wobbly-legged and dreamlike, things fading in and out of focus with the strobing lights. The rush of tons of falling water filled her ears.

"Mandy," she said into her daughter's warm curly hair, her own voice almost drowned out by the sirens. "Can you feel Jem? Please tell me you can feel him."

"Here I am, Mummy," said a small voice behind her. Convinced she was hallucinating, she lifted a restraining hand toward the police officers and pivoted slowly round. Jem was standing on the drive six feet away, dripping wet, plastered with dead leaves, and swaying like a drunk.

Then she was sitting splay-legged on the

gravel, a child clutched in each arm, trying hard not to shake, so they wouldn't notice. She didn't start to sob, though, until Jemmy lifted a tearstained face from her shoulder and said, "Where's Daddy?"

DADDY IS STILL looking for Jem in the wrong place. In spite of his fear for Jem and his imminent worry, though, Roger finds support and friendship in Brian Fraser, who sends out word to his tenants, takes Roger round his lands to search—and finally suggests that they visit the garrison at Fort William, as the British soldiers may have picked up some useful news.

The commander, a Captain Buncombe, has no news of Jem but promises to put out word to his troops. As they leave Fort William, Roger and Brian are astonished to find Jenny, mounted and repelling the advances of soldiers at the fort's entrance. She's followed them, bringing urgent news: Buck has been found unconscious in the heather but came round sufficiently as to ask his rescuers to send to Lallybroch for Roger. Buck is presently abiding with a family of crofters named MacLaren but seems dangerously ill and may not live.

BACK AT LALLYBROCH, in the aftermath of Jem's rescue from the dam tunnel, Brianna finds Rob Cameron gone from the priest's hole, all the doors locked, and her .22 rifle gone as well. The conclusion is obvious: Cameron has associates—the man at the dam, and whoever let Cameron out of the priest's hole. And whoever these people are, they now have a key to Lallybroch.

Brianna takes what precautions she can, bringing the kids to Inverness to stay with her friend Fiona, who now runs a bed-and-breakfast establishment. Brianna then returns to her own house, shotgun in hand, and takes up station in the old broch tower, to see who might turn up.

As darkness begins to fall, she hears the phone ring inside the house—and hears the ringing stop as the phone is picked up.

Her immediate impulse was to go and flush out whoever was in her house and demand to know the meaning of this. Her money was on Rob Cameron, and the thought of flushing him like a grouse and marching him out at the point of a gun made her hand tighten on said gun with anticipation. She had Jem back; Cameron would know she didn't need to keep him alive.

But. She hesitated in the door of the broch, looking down.

But whoever was in the house had answered the phone. If I was a burglar, I wouldn't be answering the phone in the house I was burgling. Not unless I thought it would wake up the people inside.

Whoever was in her house already knew no one was home.

"Quod erat demonstrandum," *her father's voice said in her mind, with a grim satisfaction. Someone in the house was expecting a call.*

BACK IN INVERNESS, Jem and Mandy are passing the time pleasantly enough, playing with Fiona's three daughters. Finding the girliness a little overwhelming, Jem goes to bounce a ball on the landing. From there he has a good view of the front door, and when the bell rings, he looks up to discover Rob Cameron coming in.

Cameron has come, he tells Fiona, in the name of research, wanting information about the local group of dancers who call down the sun on Beltane at the nearby stone circle at Craigh na Dun. Fiona, knowing only too well who Rob is, distracts him briefly and runs to find Jem, whom she sends quickly out of the house, with instructions to run to a neighbor's house and call the police.

Jem does, but while waiting for the police to arrive, he sees Rob Cameron come hurriedly out of Fiona's place and drive off. A radio bulletin about Cameron (chief suspect in Jemmy's kidnapping) had come through while Cameron was talking to Fiona. Taking alarm, he'd hit Fiona and rushed out of the house.

Fiona's husband, Ernie Buchan, is also alarmed and decides to take Jem and Mandy back to their mother at Lallybroch, he fearing that their presence in his house will endanger his own family. He arrives with the children to find Brianna engaged in a standoff with unknown miscreants inside the house; reinforcements arrive shortly afterward, in a butcher's van. What ensues is a one-sided shoot-out at the O.K. Corral, with Brianna's shotgun shattering windows, shredding tires, and holding off the intruders long enough for her to reach Ernie's electrician's van.

The van's engine is flooded, though, and the bad guys, hooded with balaclava helmets, try to rush Ernie's stalled van. At this precarious point, the cavalry shows up, in the person of a dark-blue Fiat, which fiercely charges the bad guys and drives them back long enough for Ernie to get his engine going.

Ernie's van is badly damaged but limps down the highway toward the nearest truck stop, the blue Fiat following sedately behind. Taking temporary refuge in a Little Chef Café, Brianna discovers that her savior is Lionel Menzies—the principal of Jem's school (who has some reason to think there's something odd about the MacKenzie family, but who is also a friend of Roger's, by way of being a fellow Freemason of the same lodge).

Clearly there's more at work here than Rob Cameron and his personal malice. At her wits' end and badly needing an ally, Brianna confides as much of the truth as she can to Menzies—including Rob's possible motives but leaving out the mention of time travel, Spanish gold, or where Roger and Buck *really* are—and takes some comfort in his belief and support. He takes the MacKenzies home and leaves with the suggestion that Brianna might think of taking the children right away to America.

This is not something Bree hasn't thought of—but in light of recent events, it begins to look like more than a good idea. But what about Roger? She knows that he'll never give up looking for Jemmy, but she writes a letter for him, just in case, and conceals it in the ancient desk in the laird's study, knowing that Roger will look there sooner or later if he does return.

As she gropes for the secret recess, though, she dislodges another letter, shoved down in the innermost crevices of the desk. It's a letter from her father, Frank Randall, addressed to her and enclosing a brief family tree, along with Frank's speculations regarding his suspicions about undue interest in his family—Brianna, specifically.

Dearest Deadeye,

You've just left me, after our wonderful afternoon among the clay pigeons. My ears are still ringing. Whenever we shoot, I'm torn between immense pride in your ability, envy of it—and fear that you may someday need it.

What a queer feeling it is, writing this. I know that you'll eventually learn who—and perhaps, what—you are. But I have no idea how you'll come to that knowledge. Am I about to reveal you to yourself, or will this be old news when you find it? If we're both lucky, I may be able to tell you in person, when you're a little older. And if we're very lucky, it will come to nothing. But I daren't risk your life in that hope, and you're not yet old enough that I could tell you.

I'm sorry, sweetheart, that's terribly melodramatic. And the last thing I want to do is alarm you. I have all the confidence in the world in you. But I am your father and thus prey to the fears that afflict all parents—that something dreadful and unpreventable will happen to one's child, and you powerless to protect her.

The letter reinforces Brianna's feeling that there is in fact a conspiracy aimed at her and her children and that she must get the children away. *Right* away.

Shortly after the war ended, your mother and I came to Scotland. Something of a second honeymoon. She went out one afternoon to pick flowers—and never came back. I searched—everyone searched—for months, but there was no sign, and eventually the police stopped—well, in fact they didn't stop suspecting me of murdering her, damn them, but they grew tired of harassing me. I had begun to put my life back together, made up my mind to move on, perhaps leave Britain—and then Claire came back. Three years after her disappearance, she showed up in the Highlands, filthy, starved, battered—and pregnant.

Pregnant, she said, by a Jacobite Highlander from 1743 named James Fraser. I won't go into all that was said between us; it was a long time ago and it doesn't matter—save for the fact that IF your mother was telling the truth, and did indeed travel back in time, then you may have the ability to do it, too. I hope you don't. But if you should—Lord, I can't believe I'm writing this in all seriousness. But I look at you, darling, with the sun on your ruddy hair, and I see him. *I can't deny that.*

Well. It took a long time. A very long time. But your mother never changed her story, and though we didn't speak about it after a while, it became obvious that she wasn't mentally deranged (which I had rather naturally assumed to be the case, initially). And I began . . . to look for him.

Now I must digress for a moment; forgive me. I think you won't have heard of the Brahan Seer. Colorful as he was—if, in fact, he existed—he's not really known much beyond those circles with a taste for the more outlandish aspects of Scottish history. Reggie, though, is a man of immense curiosity, as well as immense learning, and was fascinated by the Seer—one Kenneth MacKenzie, who lived in the seventeenth century (maybe), and who made a great number of prophecies about this and that, sometimes at the behest of the Earl of Seaforth.

Naturally, the only prophecies mentioned in connection with this man are the ones that appeared to come true: he predicted, for instance, that when there were five bridges over the River Ness, the world would fall into chaos. In August 1939 the fifth bridge over the Ness was opened, and in September, Hitler invaded Poland. Quite enough chaos for anyone.

The Seer came to a sticky end, as prophets often do (do please remember that, darling, will you?), burnt to death in a spiked barrel of tar at the instigation of Lady Seaforth—to whom he had unwisely prophesied that her husband was having affairs with various ladies while away in Paris. (That one was likely true, in my opinion.)

Amongst his lesser-known prophecies, though, was one called the Fraser Prophecy. There isn't a great deal known about this, and what there is is rambling and vague, as prophecies usually are, the Old Testament notwithstanding. The only relevant bit, I think, is this: "The last of Lovat's line will rule Scotland."

Frank's explanation of the enclosed family tree makes it apparent that the conspirators—whoever they may be—do know about the possibility of time travel and do know that Brianna is the great-granddaughter of Lord Lovat, the Old Fox, whose legitimate line died out in the late eighteenth century. But do *prophecies* care about such issues as legitimacy?

If I find whoever drew this chart, I will question them and do my best to neutralize any possible threat to you. But as I say—I know the look of a conspiracy. Nutters of this sort thrive in company. I might miss one.

"Neutralize them," she murmured, the chill in her hands spreading through her arms and chest, crystallizing around her heart. She had no doubt at all what he'd meant by that, the bland matter-of-factness of the term notwithstanding. And had he found him—them?

Don't—I repeat, don't*—go anywhere near the Service or anyone connected with it. At best, they'd think you insane. But if you are indeed what you may be, the last people who should ever know it are the funny buggers, as we used to be known during the war.*

And if worse should come to worst—and you can do it—then the past may be your best avenue of escape. I have no idea how it works; neither does your mother, or at least she says so. I hope I may have given you a few tools to help, if that should be necessary.

And . . . there's him. Your mother said that Fraser sent her back to me, knowing that I would protect her—and you. She thought that he died immediately afterward. He did not. I looked for him, and I found him. And, like him, perhaps I send you back, knowing—as he knew of me—that he will protect you with his life.

I will love you forever, Brianna. And I know whose child you truly are.

With all my love,
Dad

BACK IN 1739, Brian takes Roger to the MacLaren croft, where he finds Buck plainly very ill with some sort of heart ailment. The MacLarens give Roger grudging accommodation for the night, remarking that they'll send for the healer in the morning—should Buck survive the night.

He does. And the healer, Dr. Hector

McEwan, is something of a revelation to Roger, from the moment he places his hands on Buck's chest and exclaims under his breath, *"Cognosco te!" I know you!*

The MacLarens all watched the healer work, with great respect and not a little awe. Roger, who had learned a good bit about the psychology of healing from Claire, was just as impressed. And, to be frank, scared shitless. . . .

All of them were breathing, hearts beating as one—and somehow they were supporting the stricken man, holding him as part of a larger entity, embracing him, bracing him. Buck's injured heart lay in the palm of Roger's hand: he realized it quite suddenly and, just as suddenly, realized that it had been there for some time, resting as naturally in the curve of his palm as rounded river rock, smooth and heavy. And . . . beating, in time with the heart in Roger's chest. What was much stranger was that none of this felt in any way out of the ordinary.

Odd—and impressive—as it was, Roger could have explained this. Mass suggestion, hypnosis, will and willingness. He'd done much the same thing himself any number of times, singing—when the music caught the audience up with him, when he knew they were with him, would follow him anywhere. He'd done it once or twice, preaching; felt the people warm to him and lift him up as he lifted them. It was impressive to see it done so quickly and thoroughly without any sort of warm-up, though—and much more disquieting to feel the effects in his own flesh. What was scaring him, though, was that the healer's hands were blue.

No one seems to see the faint blue glow but Roger. Unnerved by the sight but driven by the healer's words, Roger follows Dr. McEwan when he leaves the croft, stops him, and boldly says, *"Cognosco te."*

Hector McEwan is nearly as excited as Roger. Taking him off the road to a sheltered spot, he tells Roger his story—he traveled accidentally through the stones from 1841, where he was an Edinburgh physician—and asks eagerly after Roger's story. He also tells Roger the story of the half-burnt croft in which they've taken shelter, involving a mysterious death by hanging and an even more mysterious woman.

Roger is less interested in the man's stories than in his actions. McEwan puts his hand around Roger's damaged throat. *"Maybe, just maybe,"* he murmurs. Roger feels no more than a slight warmth—but over the subsequent days realizes gradually that his throat is better; it no longer hurts to swallow.

The MacLarens, who had been rattled by the arrival of the two strangers—and still more by the sight of the rope scar on Roger's throat, which makes them think that he may be the ghost of the hanged man—send for the authorities: Dougal MacKenzie, war chief of clan MacKenzie, who stops by with several of his henchmen.

"Good morn to ye, sir," the dark man said, with a courteous inclination of the head. "My name is Dougal MacKenzie, of Castle Leoch. And . . . who might you be?"

Dear Jesus bloody hell, *he thought. The shock rippled through him, and he hoped it didn't show on his face. He shook hands firmly.*

"I am Roger Jeremiah MacKenzie, of Kyle of Lochalsh," he said, keeping his voice mild and—he hoped—assured, as some compensation for his shabby appearance. His voice sounded nearly normal this morning; if he didn't force it, with luck it wouldn't crack or gurgle.

"Your servant, sir," MacKenzie said with a slight bow, surprising Roger with his elegant manners. He had deep-set hazel eyes, which looked Roger over with frank interest—and a faint touch of what appeared to be amusement—before shifting to Buck.

"My kinsman," Roger said hastily. "William Bu—William MacKenzie." When? *he thought in agitation.* Was Buck born yet? Would Dougal recognize the name William Buccleigh MacKenzie? But, no, he can't be born yet; you can't exist twice in the same time—can you?!?

Dougal finds the strangers interesting but no threat—either physically or supernaturally—and goes so far as to lend them horses to aid in their search. Roger wonders uneasily whether he should tell Buck the truth about his parentage, but this seems neither the time nor yet the place for it.

A toilsome search leads them eventually back to Lallybroch, where Brian Fraser greets them with the news that the garrison commander has sent an object found by one of his men, which may possibly have something to do with their search.

It does—but not in the way they expect.

"Captain Randall said that Captain Buncombe sent word out wi' all the patrols, and one of them came across this wee bawbee and sent it back to Fort William. None of them ever saw such a thing before, but because of the name, they were thinking it might have to do wi' your lad."

"The name?" Roger untied the cord and the cloth fell open. For an instant, he didn't know what the hell he was seeing. He picked it up; it was light as a feather, dangling from his fingers.

Two disks, made of something like pressed cardboard, threaded onto a bit of light woven cord. One round, colored red—the other was green and octagonal.

"Oh, Jesus," he said. "Oh, Christ Jesus."

J. W. MacKenzie *was printed on both disks, along with a number and two letters. He turned the red disk gently over with a shaking fingertip and read what he already knew was stamped there.*

RAF

He was holding the dog tags of a Royal Air Force flier. Circa World War II.

Have they been searching all along for the wrong Jeremiah? Is Roger's father, who disappeared during WWII, actually here, in 1739? It's a staggering and far-fetched possibility—but it's the only clue they have, and Roger insists on returning to the garrison in Fort William, to ask where the dog tags came from, in hopes of tracing their origin.

When they arrive at Fort William, though, they find that a new commander has succeeded the ailing Captain Buncombe: Captain Jonathan Randall. Shocked by meeting the man whose future actions he knows all too well, Roger expects a monster and is further shocked to find Randall curious, friendly, and helpful. The captain summons one of his soldiers, who can tell Roger where the dog tags came from.

During the conversation, Roger has been praying desperately, for help in their search and for a way—perhaps—to deal with what he knows Randall will do here in a few years' time. But talking to God is seldom a one-sided conversation, and he becomes aware—with considerable dismay—that there is more than one soul in danger here.

PRIVATE MACDONALD, ABASHED, *saluted and left. There was a moment's silence, during which Roger became aware of the rain, grown harder now, clattering like gravel on the large casement window. A chilly draft leaked around its frame and touched his face. Glancing at the window, he saw the drill yard below, and the whipping post, a grim crucifix stark and solitary, black in the rain.*

Oh, God.

Carefully, he folded up the dog tags again

and put them away in his pocket. Then met Captain Randall's dark eyes directly.

"Did Captain Buncombe tell you, sir, that I am a minister?"

Randall's brows rose in brief surprise.

"No, he didn't." Randall was plainly wondering why Roger should mention this, but he was courteous. "My younger brother is a clergyman. Ah . . . Church of England, of course." There was the faintest implied question there, and Roger answered it with a smile.

"I am a minister of the Church of Scotland myself, sir. But if I might . . . will ye allow me to offer a blessing? For the success of my kinsman and myself—and in thanks for your kind help to us."

"I—" Randall blinked, clearly discomfited. "I—suppose so. Er . . . all right." He leaned back a little, looking wary, hands on his blotter. He was completely taken aback when Roger leaned forward and grasped both his hands firmly. Randall gave a start, but Roger held tight, eyes on the captain's.

"Oh, Lord," he said, "we ask thy blessing on our works. Guide me and my kinsman in our quest, and guide this man in his new office. May your light and presence be with us and with him, and your judgment and compassion ever on us. I commend him to your care. Amen."

His voice cracked on the last word, and he let go Randall's hands and coughed, looking away as he cleared his throat.

Randall cleared his throat, too, in embarrassment, but kept his poise.

"I thank you for your . . . er . . . good wishes, Mr. MacKenzie. And I wish you good luck. And good day."

"The same to you, Captain," Roger said, rising. "God be with you."

PART 3: *A BLADE NEW-MADE FROM THE ASHES OF THE FORGE*

Valley Forge, that is. Washington's army is indeed coming out, headed toward Philadelphia with the intent of intercepting the retreating British army and engaging them in battle. This is the first—and maybe final—test of the newly trained American troops, and the battle—if it happens—may put paid once and for all to the rebellion, or may show the mettle of Washington's men and thus perhaps encourage vital support from France.

With the Continental regulars will be a good many companies of militia, drawn from Pennsylvania, New Jersey, and New York. And in command of ten of these companies will be the newly minted field general James Fraser. Much to the horror of his wife.

HE'D COME UP *to the loft and pulled the ladder up behind him, to prevent the children coming up. I was dressing quickly—or trying to—as he told me about Dan Morgan, about Washington and the other Continental generals. About the coming battle.*

"Sassenach, I had to," he said again, softly. "I'm that sorry."

"I know," I said. "I know you did." My lips were stiff. "I—you—I'm sorry, too."

I was trying to fasten the dozen tiny buttons that closed the bodice of my gown, but my hands shook so badly that I couldn't even grasp them. I stopped trying and dug my hairbrush out of the bag he'd brought me from the Chestnut Street house.

He made a small sound in his throat and took it out of my hand. He threw it onto our makeshift couch and put his arms around me, holding me tight with my face buried in his chest. The cloth of his new uniform smelled of fresh indigo, walnut hulls, and fuller's earth; it felt strange and stiff against my face. I couldn't stop shaking.

"Talk to me, a nighean,*" he whispered into my tangled hair. "I'm afraid, and I dinna want to feel so verra much alone just now. Speak to me."*

"Why has it always got to be you*?" I blurted into his chest.*

That made him laugh, a little shakily, and I realized that all the trembling wasn't coming from me.

"It's no just me," he said, and stroked my hair. "There are a thousand other men readying themselves today—more—who dinna want to do it, either."

"I know," I said again. My breathing was a little steadier. "I know." I turned my face to the side in order to breathe, and all of a sudden began to cry, quite without warning.

"I'm sorry," I gasped. "I don't mean—I don't want t-to make it h-harder for you. I—I—oh, Jamie, when I knew you were alive—I wanted so much to go home. To go home with you."

His arms tightened hard round me. He didn't speak, and I knew it was because he couldn't.

"So did I," he whispered at last. "And we will, a nighean. *I promise ye."*

It may be some time, though, before Jamie is able to keep that promise, and a long road lies ahead.

As they make their hurried preparations to leave Fergus and Marsali's printshop, Germain appears and makes an impassioned plea to accompany his grandfather to war.

"Bonjour, Grand-père," *he said, wiping a cobweb off his face as he landed and bowing to Jamie with great formality. He turned and bowed to me, as well.* "Comment ça va, Grand-mère?"

"Fi—" I began automatically, but was interrupted by Jamie.

"No," he said definitely. "Ye're not coming."

"Please, Grandda!" Germain's formality disappeared in an instant, replaced by pleading. "I could be a help to ye!"

"I know," Jamie said dryly. "And your parents would never forgive me if ye were. I dinna even want to know what your notion of help involves, but—"

"I could carry messages! I can ride, ye ken that, ye taught me yourself! And I'm nearly twelve!"

"Ye ken how dangerous that is? If a British sharpshooter didna take ye out of the saddle, someone from the militia would club ye over the head to steal the horse. And I can count, ken? Ye're no even eleven yet, so dinna be tryin' it on with me."

Germain is no match for his grandfather when it comes to stubbornness, and he retires, disgruntled.

JENNY HAD SENT *my medicine chest from Chestnut Street and with it the large parcel of herbs from Kingsessing, which had been delivered there the night before. With the forethought of a Scottish housewife, she'd also included a pound of oatmeal, a twist of salt, a package of bacon, four apples, and six clean handkerchiefs. Also a neat roll of fabric with a brief note, which read:*

Dear Sister Claire,

You appear to own nothing suitable in which to go to war. I suggest you borrow Marsali's printing apron for the time being, and here are two of my flannel petticoats and the simplest things Mrs. Figg could find amongst your wardrobe.

Take care of my brother, and tell him his stockings need darning, because he won't notice until he's worn holes in the heel and given himself blisters.

Your Good-sister,
Janet Murray

While their mood is anxious and somber, Claire is able to relieve at least one of Jamie's fears—that of meeting his son, William, on the field of battle.

"He can't fight," I said, letting out a half-held breath. "It doesn't matter what the British army is about to do. William was paroled after Saratoga—he's a conventioner. You know about the Convention army?"

"I do." He took my hand and squeezed it. "Ye mean he's not allowed to take up arms unless he's been exchanged—and he hasn't been, is that it?"

"That's it. Nobody can be exchanged, until the King and the Congress come to some agreement about it."

His face was suddenly vivid with relief, and I was relieved to see it.

"John's been trying to have him exchanged for months, but there isn't any way of doing it." I dismissed Congress and the King with a wave of my free hand and smiled up at him. "You won't have to face him on a battlefield."

"Taing do Dhia," *he said, closing his eyes for an instant. "I've been thinking for days—when I wasna fretting about* you, *Sassenach"—he added, opening his eyes and looking down his nose at me—"the third time's the charm. And that would be an evil charm indeed."*

"Third time?" I said. "What do you—would you let go my fingers? They've gone numb."

"Oh," he said. He kissed them gently and let go. "Aye, sorry, Sassenach. I meant—I've shot at the lad twice in his life so far and missed him by no more than an inch each time. If it should happen again—ye canna always tell, in battle, and accidents do happen. I was dreaming, during the night, and . . . och, nay matter." He waved off the dreams and turned away, but I put a hand on his arm to stop him. I knew his dreams—and I'd heard him moan the night before, fighting them.

"Culloden?" I said softly. "Has it come back again?" I actually hoped it was Culloden—and not Wentworth. He woke from the Wentworth dreams sweating and rigid and couldn't bear to be touched. Last night, he hadn't waked, but had jerked and moaned until I'd got my arms around him and he quieted, trembling in his sleep, head butted hard into my chest.

He shrugged a little and touched my face.

"It's never left, Sassenach," he said, just as softly. "It never will. But I sleep easier by your side."

IN ANOTHER PART of Philadelphia, Ian, Rachel, Denzell, and Dottie have things on their minds besides military affairs. They're collectively struggling with the logistics of Quaker marriage: Friends marry each other, without the need of ritual or clergy—but a marriage must take place before the Friends' meeting, approved, witnessed, and supported by said meeting. While it's known for a Friend to marry a non-Quaker, it's not common and usually results in the Friend being put out of his or her meeting.

The situation is made more complex by the fact that Rachel and Denny have already been put out of their home meeting in Virginia, in consequence of Denny deciding to join the Continental army. Dottie has become a Friend but has no home meeting, either. And Philadelphia Yearly Meeting, the "weightiest" meeting in the colonies, takes a dim view of the Revolution and has advised Friends to cleave to the Loyalist view, as being the most conducive to the preservation of peace.

All of which makes the question of marriage with a Mohawk scout and a Rebel physician highly questionable.

The future is murky and full of risk, but: *[Ian] had concerns himself, certainly, annoyances and worries. At the bottom of his soul, though, was the solid weight of Rachel's love and what she had said, the words gleaming like a gold coin at the bottom of a murky well.* "We will marry each other."

ON THE ROAD out of Philadelphia, William is riding the columns, carrying dispatches, taking note of incidents and emergencies, and handling as many of these as can be handled by one unarmed aide-de-camp.

The benefit of this occupation is that he's too busy to brood for very long over his anomalous situation. And thoughts of his paternity, his name, his title, and such future prospects as he has are all driven from his mind by the sudden appearance of one Denys Randall-Isaacs—or simply Denys Randall, as he's taken to calling himself, his Jewish stepfather being now dead.

Denys was last seen in Quebec, two years before, when he suddenly disappeared, abandoning William to a winter snowbound with nuns and voyageurs. This experience improved William's hunting and his French but not his temper. Still, he holds on to this, out of curiosity as to what Denys wants.

Denys gives away nothing regarding his own situation or immediate plans but inquires as to whether William has spoken recently with Captain Richardson; upon hearing the answer, he strongly advises William to have nothing whatever to do with Richardson—and if possible to avoid even speaking with the man. Whereupon Denys spurs up and rides off, leaving William still more baffled.

THE CONTINENTALS ARE massing, militia troops arriving from Pennsylvania, New Jersey, and New York to join Washington's army. Among these is the 16th Pennsylvania, and, with them, Bert Armstrong, aka Lord John Grey.

His lordship's ribs are not troubling him much, but his injured eye is; seemingly frozen in its socket, its attempts to focus with its fellow are giving him double vision and chronic, crippling headaches that make him grateful to stop for the night, able at last to lie down and rest his throbbing cranium.

Feeling too ill to eat, he puts his journeycake aside, only to hear a small, hungry voice inquire as to whether he means to eat that. He turns to discover a young boy, disheveled and tearstained—and as his wavering vision focuses on the boy's face, he recognizes Germain Fraser. Who had—of course—defied parents and grandparents and come to join Jamie and the army, riding Clarence, the family mule.

A pair of no-goods came upon him in the wood, though, pulled him off and stole

Clarence, leaving Germain to wander alone, until he saw the militia's fire and—to his amazement—recognized Lord John, his erstwhile stepgrandfather. Despite shock, distress, and hunger, Germain is canny enough to say nothing, until he and Lord John are able to step away from camp together.

Still in the shelter of the woods, Grey put his hand on Germain's shoulder and squeezed. The boy stopped dead.

"Attendez, monsieur," *Grey said, low-voiced. "If the militia learn who I am, they'll hang me. Instantly. My life is in your hands from this moment.* Comprenez-vous?*"*

There was silence for an unnerving moment.

"Are you a spy, my lord?" Germain asked softly, not turning round.

Grey paused before answering, wavering between expediency and honesty. He could hardly forget what he'd seen and heard, and when he made it back to his own lines, duty would compel him to pass on such information as he had.

"Not by choice," he said at last, just as softly.

A cool breeze had risen with the setting of the sun, and the forest murmured all around them.

"Bien," *Germain said at last. "And thank ye for the food." He turned then, and Grey could see the glint of firelight on one fair brow, arched in inquisitiveness.*

"So I am Bobby Higgins. Who are you, then?"

"Bert Armstrong," Grey replied shortly. "Call me Bert."

He led the way then toward the fire and the blanket-humped rolls of sleeping men. He couldn't quite tell, above the rustling of the trees and the snoring of his fellows, but he thought the little bugger was laughing.

AS THE COLONIALS begin to converge on the rendezvous point at Coryell's Ferry, Clinton's troops and the Loyalist refugees hurry onward, hoping to outrun danger. William, pausing to refresh himself in a creek, is taken unawares by a familiar voice: Jane, the young whore from Philadelphia, and her younger sister, Frances, known as Fanny. Jane tells him that the nasty Captain Harkness, who had threatened her, came back, and that the girls had therefore decided to flee with the army.

Jane returns William's gorget—given by him to hire her for the night and save her from Harkness—and then suggests that he might show his gratitude by offering her and Fanny his protection and helping them to find a secure place once the army reaches New York.

"Don't want much, do you?" he said. On the one hand, if he didn't give her some assurance of help, he wouldn't put it past her to fling his gorget into the water in a fit of pique. And on the other . . . Frances was a lovely child, delicate and pale as a morning-glory blossom. And on the third hand, he hadn't any more time to spare in argument.

"Get on the horse and come across," he said abruptly. "I'll find you a new place with the baggage train. I have to ride a dispatch to von Knyphausen just now, but I'll meet you in General Clinton's camp this evening—no, not this evening, I won't be back until tomorrow. . . ." He fumbled for a moment, wonder-

ing where to tell her to find him; he could not have two young whores asking for him at General Clinton's headquarters. "Go to the surgeons' tent at sundown tomorrow. I'll—think of something."

REACHING CORYELL'S FERRY at last, Jamie prepare to confer with Washington, his second-in-command, General Charles Lee, and the other generals. Claire has other immediate concerns:

My chief concern was to get some food into Jamie before he met with General Lee, if the aforementioned indeed had a reputation for arrogance and short temper. I didn't know what it was about red hair, but many years' experience with Jamie, Brianna, and Jemmy had taught me that while most people became irritable when hungry, a redheaded person with an empty stomach was a walking time bomb.

While strolling the camp in search of food, she encounters an unexpected young Frenchman.

"Nonsense," I said in French, laughing. "You aren't a turnip at all."

"Oh, yes," he said, switching to English. He smiled charmingly at me. "I once stepped on the foot of the Queen of France. She was much less gracious, sa Majesté,*" he added ruefully. "She called me a turnip. Still, if it hadn't happened—I was obliged to leave the court, you know—perhaps I would never have come to America, so we cannot bemoan my clumsiness altogether,* n'est-ce pa*?"*

He was exceedingly cheerful and smelled of wine—not that that was in any way unusual. But given his exceeding Frenchness, his evident wealth, and his tender age, I was beginning to think—

"Have I the, um, honor of addressing—" Bloody hell, what was his actual title? Assuming that he really was—

"Pardon, madame!" *he exclaimed, and, seizing my hand, bowed low over it and kissed it.* "Marie Joseph Paul Yves Roch Gilbert du Motier, Marquis de La Fayette, à votre service!"

I managed to pick "La Fayette" out of this torrent of Gallic syllables and felt the odd little thump of excitement that happened whenever I met someone I knew of from historical accounts—though cold sober realism told me that these people were usually no more remarkable than the people who were cautious or lucky enough not *to end up decorating historical accounts with their blood and entrails.*

This encounter ends with the Marquis inviting Claire to join him at dinner—this proving to be a dinner for Washington, his second-in-command, Charles Lee, and the other generals, including Jamie, who is attended by Young Ian and Rollo. Claire's opinion of the generals in general is favorable, though she is somewhat bemused by General Lee:

"Good Christ!" Lee apparently hadn't noticed the dog before this and flung himself to one side, nearly ending in Jamie's lap. This action distracted Rollo, who turned to Lee, sniffing him with close attention.

I didn't blame the dog. Charles Lee was a tall, thin man with a long, thin nose and the most revolting eating habits I'd seen since Jemmy had learned to feed himself with a spoon. He not only talked while he ate and chewed with his mouth open, but was given to wild gestures while holding things in his hand, with the result that the front of his uniform was streaked with egg, soup, jelly, and a number of less identifiable substances.

Despite this, he was an amusing, witty man—and the others seemed to give him a certain deference. I wondered why; unlike some of the gentlemen at the table, Charles Lee never attained renown as a Revolutionary figure. He treated them *with a certain . . . well, it wasn't scorn, certainly—condescension, perhaps?*

The dinner party concludes and Claire is sent off to sleep at a nearby house, while the officers make plans for what will likely be battle on the morrow. Unsettled by the tension running like a bowstring through the camp, Claire is unable to sleep and ventures out into the dark, where she runs into Denzell Hunter, out fetching a pitcher of beer for Dottie, who is attending a patient. Claire accompanies him back to the tent, and a period of medical adventure ensues, when the extremely intoxicated patient turns out to be pregnant. When things settle again, Denzell goes in search of the patient's husband, leaving Claire, Dottie, and Rachel watching over the comatose woman.

At Dottie's request, Claire gives the young women the benefit of a little premarital counseling.

". . . and if he says, 'Oh, God, oh, God,' at some point," I advised, "take note of what you were just doing, so you can do it again next time."

Rachel laughed, but Dottie frowned a little, looking slightly cross-eyed.

"Do you—does thee—think Denny would take the Lord's name in vain, even under those circumstances?"

"I've heard him do it on much less provocation than that," Rachel assured her, stifling a burp with the back of her hand. "He tries to be perfect in thy company, thee knows, for fear thee will change thy mind."

"He does?" Dottie looked surprised but rather pleased. "Oh. I wouldn't, thee knows. Ought I to tell him?"

"Not until he says, 'Oh, God, oh, God,' for thee," Rachel said, succumbing to a giggle.

"I wouldn't worry," I said. "If a man says, 'Oh, God,' in that situation, he nearly always means it as a prayer."

Dottie's fair brows drew together in concentration.

"A prayer of desperation? Or gratitude?"

"Well . . . that's up to you," I said, and stifled a small belch of my own.

The return of the men—with Jamie and with Mr. Peabody, the patient's husband—breaks up the hen party, and the four young people carry Mrs. Peabody home, accompanied by her husband, leaving Jamie and Claire to share a precious half hour of solitude in the darkness of the medical tent.

"How long do you think we have?" I asked, undoing his flies. His flesh was warm and hard under my hand, and his skin there soft as polished silk.

"Long enough," he said, and brushed my nipple with his thumb, slowly, in spite of his own apparent urgency. "Dinna hurry yourself, Sassenach. There's no telling when we'll have the chance again."

He kissed me lingeringly, his mouth tasting of Roquefort and port. I could feel the vibration of the camp here, too—it ran through both of us like a fiddle string pegged tight.

"I dinna think I've got time to make ye scream, Sassenach," he whispered in my ear. "But I've maybe time to make ye moan?"

"Well, possibly. It's some time 'til dawn, isn't it?"

Whether it was the beer and premarital explanations, the late hour and lure of secrecy—or only Jamie himself and our increasing need to shut out the world and know only each other—he had time, and to spare.

"Oh, God," he said at last, and came down slowly on me, his heart beating heavy against my ribs. "Oh . . . God."

I felt my own pulse throb in hands and bones and center, but couldn't manage any response more eloquent than a faint "Ooh." After a bit, though, I recovered enough to stroke his hair.

"We'll go home again soon," I whispered to him. "And have all the time in the world."

That got me a softly affirmative Scottish noise, and we lay there for a bit longer, not wanting to come apart and get dressed, though the packing cases were hard and the possibility of discovery increasing with each passing minute.

At last he stirred, but not to rise.

"Oh, God," he said softly, in another tone altogether. "Three hundred men." And held me tighter.

NEXT MORNING, WE find William in conversation with his groom, Zebedee, who has a festering wound in his arm from a horse bite. No sooner does William instruct Zeb to go straight to the surgeons' tent and have it seen to than the groom's place is taken by the ubiquitous Captain Richardson. William neatly evades the captain's *pourparlers,* but the captain has mentioned Lady John—and the mention of his erstwhile (and present, as he realizes with a sense of shock) stepmother brings fresh awareness of his impossible situation—and sudden strong memories of Mac, the groom whom he had loved at Helwater and who had given William a wooden rosary, and his own name:

He took a long, slow breath and pressed his lips together. Mac. The word didn't bring back a face; he couldn't remember what Mac had looked like. He'd been big, that was all. Bigger than Grandfather or any of the footmen or the other grooms. Safety. A sense of constant happiness like a soft, worn blanket.

"Shit," he whispered, closing his eyes. And had that happiness been a lie, too? He'd been too little to know the difference between a groom's deference to the young master and real kindness. But . . .

"You are a stinking Papist," he whispered, and caught his breath on something that might have been a sob. "And your baptismal name is James."

"It was the only name I had a right to give ye."

He realized that his knuckles were pressed against his chest, against his gorget—but it wasn't the gorget's reassurance that he sought. It was that of the little bumps of the plain wooden rosary that he'd worn around his neck for years, hidden under his shirt where no one would see it. The rosary Mac had given him . . . along with his name.

With a suddenness that shocked him, he felt his eyes swim. You went away. You left me!

"Shit!" he said, and punched his fist so hard into the saddlebag that the horse snorted and shied, and a bolt of white-hot pain shot up his arm, obliterating everything.

PREPARATIONS CONTINUE ON both sides of the coming conflict. Jamie gives Ian his own pre-wedding advice, and William meets Jane and Fanny in camp and agrees to give them his protection, in return for their care of his young groom and orderly.

Lord John and Germain, entering the American camp with their militia company, are both surprised to see a familiar figure: Percival Beauchamp, aka Perseverance Wainwright.

He hadn't seen Percy—ex-lover, ex-brother, French spy, and all-around shit—since their last conversation in Philadelphia, some months before. When Percy had first reappeared in Grey's life, it had been with a last attempt at seduction—political rather than physical, though Grey had an idea that he wouldn't have balked at the physical, either. . . . It was an offer for the British government: the return to France of the valuable Northwest Territory, in return for the promise of Percy's "interests" to keep the French government from making an alliance with the American colonies.

He had—as a matter of duty—conveyed the offer discreetly to Lord North and then expunged it—and Percy—from his mind.

CLAIRE, IN HER position as surgeon to Jamie's troops, prepares to inspect the new arrivals for suitability but also offers medical advice and minor treatment to the camp followers, the women and children accompanying the Continental army and militia. Going to her tent to fetch medicine, she discovers a young Continental surgeon named Captain Leckie rifling her medicine chest.

The ensuing conversation begins with Leckie's conviction that Claire is a laundress and goes downhill from there:

"He is teething," I agreed, shaking out a quantity of crumbled willow bark into my mortar. "But he also has an ear infection, and the tooth will come through of its own accord within the next twenty-four hours."

He rounded on me, indignant and astonished.

"Are you contradicting me?"

"Well, yes," I said, rather mildly. "You're wrong. You want to have a good look in his left ear. It's—"

"I, madam, am a diplomate of the Medical College of Philadelphia!"

"I congratulate you," I said, beginning to be provoked. "You're still wrong."

This conversation is still fresh in Claire's mind when she joins Jamie to conduct the inspection of his troops.

There were three hundred men, he'd told me, and most of them were quite all right. I kept walking and nodding, but wasn't above beginning to fantasize some dangerous circumstance in which I found Captain Leckie writhing in pain, which I would graciously allay, causing him to grovel and apologize for his objectionable attitude. I was trying to choose between the prospect of a musket ball embedded in his buttock, testicular torsion, and something temporarily but mortifyingly disfiguring, like Bell's palsy, when my eye caught a glimpse of something odd in the lineup.

The man in front of me was standing bolt upright, musket at port arms, eyes fixed straight ahead. This was perfectly correct—but no other man in the line was doing it. Militiamen were more than capable, but they generally saw no point in military punctilio. I glanced at the rigid soldier, passed by—then glanced back.

"Jesus H. Roosevelt Christ!" I exclaimed, and only sheer chance kept Jamie from hearing me, he being distracted by the sudden arrival of a messenger.

I took two hasty steps back, bent, and peered under the brim of the dusty slouch hat. The face beneath was set in fierce lines, with a darkly ominous glower—and was completely familiar to me.

"Bloody effing hell," I whispered, seizing him by the sleeve. "What are you doing *here?"*

"You wouldn't believe me if I told you," he whispered back, not moving a muscle of face or body. "Do walk on, my dear."

Such was my astonishment, I might actually have done it, had my attention not been drawn by a small figure skulking about behind the line, trying to avoid notice by crouching behind a wagon wheel.

"Germain!" I said, and Jamie whirled about, eyes wide.

Lord John, with some presence of mind, surrenders to Jamie—as does Germain. Jamie is about to dispatch the prisoners to custody, but Claire objects, on grounds that Lord John's eye is clearly in need of attention.

As Claire is contemplating ways and means, though, she is interrupted by the appearance of Percy Wainwright Beauchamp, who wants to talk to Lord John. Lord John doesn't wish to talk to Percy, though, and when Jamie enters and orders Percy to sit down, the quasi-Frenchman rises smoothly and exits, saying he is required to attend upon the Marquis de La Fayette, with whose entourage he is associated.

With help from a slightly squeamish Jamie, Claire manages to free Lord John's frozen eyeball and anoints it with honey, that substance being both antibacterial and slippery. John refuses to answer any questions, and Jamie leaves him, having other urgent things to do.

Claire return to her other patients but finds them hovering anxiously, making way for a dangerous-looking mule skinner, who is nursing a nasty bite and threatening to beat to death the mule responsible. Germain recognizes the man as the thief who stole Clarence—obviously the mule in question.

As Claire is wondering exactly what to do with her patient, Germain steals away—with the obvious intent of reclaiming Clarence. Terrified that Germain will be noticed and harmed by the other mule skinners, Claire takes advantage of the appearance of Percy Beauchamp, asking him in French to go and see if he can retrieve the boy safely—which Percy gallantly does.

The reappearance of Percy with Germain *and* Clarence leads to a major scene with the irate mule skinner, this broken up by the appearance of Fergus, who stops the fight by firing his pistol into the air.

Everything stopped, for a split second, and then the shouting and screaming started again, everyone surging toward Clarence and his companions to see what had *happened. For a long moment, it wasn't apparent what had happened. The teamster had let go his grip in astonishment and turned toward Fergus, eyes bulging and blood-tinged saliva running down his chin. Germain, with more presence of mind than I would have had in such a situation, got hold of the reins and was hauling on them with all his strength, trying to turn Clarence's head. Clarence, whose blood was plainly up, was having none of it.*

Fergus calmly put the fired pistol back into his belt—I realized at this point that he must have fired into the dirt near the teamster's feet—and spoke to the man.

"If I were you, sir, I would remove myself promptly from this animal's presence. It is apparent that he dislikes you."

The shouting and screaming had stopped, and this made several people laugh.

"Got you there, Belden!" a man near me called. "The mule dislikes you. What you think of that?"

Not much, is the answer, but Percy has a better one.

But Percy had managed to get to his feet and, while still somewhat hunched, was mobile. Without hesitation, he walked up and kicked the teamster smartly in the balls.

This went over well. Even the man who appeared to be a friend of Belden's whooped with laughter. The teamster didn't go down but curled up like a dried leaf, clutching himself. Percy wisely didn't wait for him to recover, but turned and bowed to Fergus.

"À votre service, monsieur. *I suggest that you and your son—and the mule, of course—might withdraw?"*

"Merci beaucoup, *and I suggest you do the same,* tout de suite," *Fergus replied.*

Percy is in agreement but lingers long enough to ask to speak with Fergus—who grimaces but agrees to do so later.

PREPARATIONS FOR THE coming battle go on:

Three hundred men. Jamie stepped into the darkness beyond the 16th New Jersey's campfire and paused for a moment to let his eyes adjust. Three hundred bloody men. He'd never led a band of more than fifty. And never had much in the way of subalterns, no more than one or two men under him.

Now he had ten militia companies, each with its own captain and a few informally appointed lieutenants, and Lee had given him a staff of his own: two aides-de-camp, a secretary—now, that *he could get used to, he thought, flexing the fingers of his maimed right hand—three captains, one of whom was striding along at his shoulder, trying not to look worrit, ten of his own lieutenants, who would serve as liaison between him and the companies under his command, a cook, an assistant cook—and, of course, he had a surgeon already.*

His own men are Jamie's major concern but scarcely the only one. Washington's plan calls for a foray by a thousand men, to come round Clinton's flank and attack from the far side. Charles Lee is to lead this but declines—on the grounds that a thousand men is not a large enough number to be a suitable command to an officer of his reputation. La Fayette is put in command instead. But discussions go on all night, and in the end, Lee takes command of five thousand men—a sufficient number to satisfy the general's ego—while La Fayette will still keep his lesser command but under Lee, as are General Fraser and his militia companies.

Jamie is less than impressed with Charles Lee as a man but hopes that his European reputation as a good soldier and officer is true.

His thoughts are interrupted by the appearance of the Reverend Woodsworth, captain of the 16th Pennsylvania, the militia company that brought John Grey into camp. The reverend is concerned:

"They are saying—the men from Dunning's company—that Armstrong is a government spy, that he is a British officer who concealed himself among us. That they found a commission upon him, and correspondence. I—" He paused and gulped breath, the next words coming out in a rush. "I cannot believe it of him, sir, nor can any of us. We feel that some mistake must have been made, and we—we wish to say that we hope nothing . . . hasty will be done."

"No one has suggested anything of the sort, Captain," Jamie assured him, alarm running down his spine like quicksilver. Only because they haven't had time. *He'd been able to ignore the thorny problem Grey presented as a prisoner, in the fierce rush of preparation and the fiercer rush of his own feelings, but he couldn't ignore it much longer. He should have notified La Fayette, Lee, and Washington of Grey's presence immediately, but had gambled on the confusion of imminent battle to disguise his delay.*

There's nothing to be done about Grey

now, though Jamie regrets having asked Lord John to give his parole; if he hadn't, Grey might easily—and honorably—escape in the bustle of the army's departure. Right now, all Jamie can do is reassure Wordsworth that Lord John is being cared for and that nothing hasty will be done.

With preparations as much in hand as is possible, Jamie seeks out Claire. Despite the lateness of the hour and her own long and arduous day, she's relieved and happy to see Jamie, and they steal a brief hour's respite alone together by the water.

"You . . . all right?" I murmured, thick-tongued with drowsiness.

"Aye, fine," he whispered, and his hand smoothed the hair from my cheek. "Go back to sleep, Sassenach. I'll wake ye when it's time."

My mouth was sticky, and it took a moment to locate any words.

"You need to sleep, too."

"No," he said, soft but definite. "No, I dinna mean to sleep. So close to the battle . . . I have dreams. I've had them the last three nights, and they get worse."

My own arm was lying across his midsection; at this, I reached up involuntarily, putting my hand over his heart. I knew he'd dreamed—and I had a very good idea what he'd dreamed about, from the things he'd said in his sleep. And the way he'd wakened, trembling. "They get worse."

"Shh," he said, and bent his head to kiss my hair. "Dinna fash, a nighean. *I want only to lie here wi' you in my arms, to keep ye safe and watch ye sleep. I can rise then with a clear mind . . . and go to do what must be done."*

What must be done involves his own spiritual preparations, washing and speaking to his own dead—the men who have stood with him in battle—or the ones he trusts to be with him in this one.

Jamie is not the only one making ceremonial preparations. Young Ian is preparing for battle in the Mohawk way, putting on his war paint. When his uncle emerges from the trees near the river, Ian invites him to do the same; Jamie declines but helps Ian to put on his own.

"I can, aye." Jamie's head was bent over the paint dishes, hand hovering. "Did ye not tell me once the white is for peace, though?"

"Aye, should ye be going to parley or trade, ye use a good deal of white. But it's for the mourning, too—so if ye go to avenge someone, ye'd maybe wear white."

Jamie's head came up at that, staring at him.

"This one's no for vengeance," Ian said. "It's for Flying Arrow. The dead man whose place I took, when I was adopted." He spoke as casually as he could, but he felt his uncle tighten and look down. Neither one of them was ever going to forget that day of parting, when he'd gone to the Kahnyen'kehaka, and both of them had thought it was forever. He leaned over and put a hand on Jamie's arm.

"That day, ye said to me, 'Cuimhnich,' *Uncle Jamie. And I did."* Remember.

"So did I, Ian," Jamie said softly, and drew the arrow on his forehead, his touch like a priest's on Ash Wednesday, marking Ian with the sign of the cross. "So did we all. Is that it?"

Ian touched the green stripe gingerly, to be sure it was dry enough.

"Aye, I think so. Ken Brianna made me the paints? I was thinking of her, but then I thought I maybe shouldna take her with me that way."

He felt Jamie's breath on his skin as his uncle gave a small snort and then sat back.

"Ye always carry your women wi' ye into battle, Ian Òg. They're the root of your strength, man."

"Oh, aye?" That made sense—and was a relief to him. Still . . . "I was thinkin' it maybe

wasna right to think of Rachel in such a place, though. Her being Quaker and all."

Jamie dipped his middle finger into the deer fat, then delicately into the white clay powder, and drew a wide, swooping "V" near the crest of Ian's right shoulder. Even in the dark, it showed vividly.

"White dove," he said with a nod. He sounded pleased. "There's Rachel for ye."

He wiped his fingers on the rock, then rose and stretched. Ian saw him turn to look toward the east. It was still night, but the air had changed, just in the few minutes they'd sat. His uncle's tall figure was distinct against the sky, where a little before he'd seemed part of the night.

"An hour, nay more," Jamie said. "Eat first, aye?" And, with that, turned and walked away to the stream and his own interrupted prayers.

ON THE OTHER side of the night, William is also wakeful, if a good deal less spiritual. He's lying on his cot, sweating and irritable, not looking forward to the coming battle, as he isn't going to fight in it. His grim ruminations are interrupted by the sudden appearance of Jane, who indicates her intent of offering aid and comfort in a physical way. He goes outside with her, to prevent his tentmates from hearing, but declines her offer, with some difficulty, leaving Jane as annoyed as he is.

"You're going to fight tomorrow, aren't you?" There was enough light to see the shine of her eyes as she glared at him. "Soldiers always want to fuck before a fight! They need it."

He rubbed a hand hard over his face, palm rasping on his sprouting whiskers, then took a deep breath.

"I see. Yes. Very kind of you." He suddenly wanted to laugh. He also—very suddenly—wanted to take advantage of her offer. But not enough to do it with Merbling on one side and Evans on the other, ears flapping.

"I'm not going to fight tomorrow," he said, and the pang it caused him to say that out loud startled him.

"You're not? Why not?" She sounded startled, too, and more than a little disapproving.

"It's a long story," he said, struggling *for patience. "And it's not your business. Now, look. I appreciate the thought, but I told you: you're not a whore, at least not for the time being. And you're not* my *whore." Though his imagination was busy with images of what might have happened had she stolen into his cot and taken hold of him before he was fully awake . . . He put the thought firmly aside and, taking her by the shoulders, turned her round. . . .*

"When we get to New York," he whispered, bending to speak in her ear, "I'll think again."

She stiffened, her buttock rounding hard in his hand, but didn't pull away or try to bite him, which he'd half-expected.

"Why?" she said, in a calm voice.

"That's a long story, too," he said. "Good night, Jane." And, releasing her, stalked away into the dark. Nearby, the drums of reveille began.

PART 4: *DAY OF BATTLE*

And at last, the day of battle dawns. Jamie gathers his men to ride out, and Claire joins Denny, with Rachel and Dottie, taking Denzell's wagon full of medical supplies. Lord John, left behind, receives an unwelcome visitor—Percy Beauchamp, who gives Lord John even more unwelcome news: that the suspicious Captain Richardson intends to abduct William, with the notion of using him as a hostage to influence the Greys' political actions regarding the war.

Ian is out before first light, scouting the

land, and William is dressing, still sore in spirit—a state not relieved by a note from Sir Henry Clinton, ordering him to remain in camp with the clerks. Before he can obey this order, though, Captain John André appears with a dispatch to be delivered to Colonel Banastre Tarleton, commander of the new British Legion.

Scouting in advance of the Continental army, Ian attracts the notice of two Abenaki scouts in the employ of the British army. They taunt him with cries of "Mohawk" and shoot arrows at him, but he escapes, returning to his scouting with one eye over his shoulder.

William yields to temptation and rides out in search of Tarleton, who receives the

dispatch but then mentions Jane to William, expressing admiration of her person and essentially asking William if the girl is his. William replies that Jane and her sister are under his protection—rashly telling Tarleton to keep away from her.

Tarleton isn't the sort to be told things. He offers to fight William for Jane's favors, and a fight ensues, but it's interrupted by the sudden appearance of a company of American militia. Dragged off Tarleton, William manages to mount his horse and escape.

Jamie's militia companies come under fire, and things become serious in short order. Meanwhile, Claire and her companions have reached Tennent Church, which the Continental army has commandeered as a hospital. Unfortunately, the uncivil Captain Leckie is in charge and refuses to have some ignorant "cunning-woman" taking up valuable space. Claire doesn't waste time arguing but tells Denzell to work inside; she'll set up her tent outside and do triage for incoming patients.

I DON'T KNOW *when physicians began calling it "the Golden Hour," but surely every battlefield medic from the time of the* Iliad *onward knows about it. From the time of an accident or injury that isn't immediately fatal, the victim's chances of living are best if he receives treatment within an hour of sustaining the injury. After that, shock, continued loss of blood, debility due to pain . . . the chance of saving a patient goes sharply downhill.*

Add in blazing temperatures, lack of water, and the stress of running full out through fields and woods, wearing wool homespun and carrying heavy weapons, inhaling powder smoke, and trying either to kill someone or avoid being killed, just prior to being injured, and I rather thought we were looking at a Golden fifteen minutes or so.

Jamie receives an order from La Fayette to take some of his men and try to dispose of a British artillery company that has taken over a strategically placed cider orchard. And Lord John escapes from the American camp, in search of William.

FOUR BLOODY HOURS. *Hours spent slogging through an undulant countryside filled with mobs of Continental soldiers, clots of militia, and more bloody rocks than anyplace required for proper functioning, if you asked Grey. Unable to stand the blisters and shreds of raw skin any longer, he'd taken off his shoes and stockings and thrust them into the pockets of his disreputable coat, choosing to hobble barefoot for as long as he could bear it.*

Should he meet anyone whose feet looked his size, he thought grimly, he'd pick up one of the omnipresent rocks and avail himself.

After a considerable amount of travail, Lord John finds himself in earshot of British artillery, recognizable from the frequency and routine of their firing. This is, of course, the artillery company that Jamie's men are trying to extirpate, and Lord John runs afoul of a couple of American teenagers whose father has just been killed by a cannonball and who are thus not inclined to handle an Englishman gently.

Jamie arrives in time to prevent the boys from killing Grey—or, more likely, Grey killing them. He revokes Lord John's parole, thus gracefully saving him from the dishonor of breaking it, and sends him off under the nominal guard of the two boys—in the full expectation that he'll promptly escape. His mind thus relieved of responsibility for *one* man, Jamie returns to increasingly heated battle.

The day of the battle is the hottest day of the year, and soldiers are dropping from heatstroke faster than from wounds. Claire treats everything from minor gashes to blown-off hands, dripping with sweat and keeping up her own level of hydration with water laced with brandy.

Meanwhile, in the larger scheme of things, General Lee has been screwing things up. Having haughtily neglected to send out scouts, he's running into trouble.

So is William. His horse having thrown a shoe, he approaches a company of German grenadiers, asking them where the nearest farrier might be. One soldier courteously replies that there are hussars two companies behind and they will likely be accompanied by a farrier. But William overhears a whispered fragment of panicked conversation behind him: "He speaks German! He knows, he heard!" Before he can make sense of this, one of the grenadiers picks up a rock and brains him with it.

Ian is also having trouble. He's been harassed all day by the two Abenakis, who finally manage to trap him in the bottom of a watercourse, after he's rushed down to see if the long-legged, red-coated soldier lying in the bottom might be his cousin William. It is, but before he can determine more than the basic fact that William is still alive, Ian finds himself fighting for his own life.

Ian breaks away from his assailants and gains temporary refuge in the branches of a tree. Before the Abenaki can figure out how to get at him, they're interrupted by the sounds of a large body of men approaching and decide that discretion is the better part of valor, decamping with Ian's mare.

Ian manages to crawl up the bank and into hiding, and after resting for a bit, he goes to find Jamie, in order to get another mount and to procure help for William. On his way, he runs into General Lee's main body, swirling in disorder, but can't take time to worry about it. He manages to tell Jamie about William—but an arrow coming out of nowhere strikes him in the upper arm, and he keels over.

He struggles up again, though, insisting that he must take men to rescue William, and Jamie reluctantly agrees, breaking off the arrow so that Ian can move with less difficulty. Meanwhile some of Jamie's men have caught up with the Abenakis and bring back one of the Indians, dead.

Jamie takes what hasty measures he can, but he can't take long about it; Lee's disorganization is fast turning into a panicked rout.

Everything teeters on a razor's edge—and then George Washington comes galloping up on his white horse to demand to know the meaning of this. Failing to get a satisfactory answer from Lee, he relieves the general of command and rallies the troops single-handedly, riding through the companies, waving his hat and shouting for men to follow him.

There was barely time to summon Corporal Greenhow and detail him to take five men and accompany Ian, before Washington came close enough to spot Jamie and his companies. The general's hat was in his hand and his face was afire, anger and desperation subsumed in eagerness, and the whole of his being radiating something Jamie had seldom seen, but recognized. Had felt himself, once. It was the look of a man risking everything, because there was no choice.

"Mr. Fraser!" Washington shouted to him, and his wide mouth stretched wider in a blazing grin. "Follow me!"

Ian and his men find William and load him onto a horse, meaning to carry him back to the American camp, but are interrupted by a party of British soldiers, who retrieve William but capture Ian in the process.

Lord John has succeeded in escaping from his own captors and has finally located a British company, to whom he promptly surrenders. They give him badly needed water and make him sit down with some other prisoners, until someone has time to decide what to do with him; his attempts to explain himself to the very young lieutenant in charge of prisoners earn him nothing but a probably broken arm. Among the other prisoners, though, is a wounded Mohawk scout, whom Lord John recognizes as Ian Murray, Jamie's nephew.

Ian and Lord John exchange coded remarks in Latin, and Ian stands up and informs the young lieutenant of Grey's identity.

Back at the British camp, whence William has been removed, he wakes to find his uncle Hal beside his cot.

"Papa . . ." he whispered.

"No, but the next best thing," said his uncle Hal, taking a firm hold on the groping hand and sitting down beside him. "How's the head?"

William closed his eyes and tried to focus on something other than the pain.

"Not . . . that bad."

"Pull the other one, it's got bells on," his uncle murmured, cupping William's cheek and turning his head to the side. "Let's have a look."

* * *

"It will likely come back to you." His uncle paused. "Do you happen to remember where you last saw your father?"

His defenses down, William reveals the Awful Truth:

William felt an unnatural calm come over him. He just bloody didn't care anymore, he told himself. The whole world was going to know, one way or another.

"Which one?" he said flatly, and opened his eyes. His uncle was regarding him with interest, but no particular surprise.

"You've met Colonel Fraser, then?" Hal asked.

"I have," William said shortly. "How long have you *known about it?"*

"Roughly three seconds, in the sense of certainty," his uncle replied. He reached up and unfastened the leather stock around his neck, sighing with relief as it came off. "Good Lord, it's hot." The stock had left a broad red mark; he massaged this gently, half-closing his eyes. "In the sense of thinking there was something rather remarkable in your resemblance to the aforesaid Colonel Fraser . . . since I met him

again in Philadelphia recently. Prior to that, I hadn't seen him for a long time—not since you were very small, and I never saw him in close conjunction with you then, in any case."

While William gathers the scattered pieces of his wits and his life, the battle rages on. Unlike most eighteenth-century battles, this one is not a matter of massed armies meeting each other. Sir Henry Clinton's army is moving in three separate bodies, each under a different commander; Washington's troops are likewise divided; and, most important, the ground is chopped and riven by several creeks and their ravines. The day is a series of vicious pitched battles, fought wherever enemies catch sight of each other.

Swaying with weariness and heat, Claire notices the fighting only by its results: a constant flood of wounded and men suffering—and dying—from heatstroke. Alarm breaks through her exhaustion, though, when a young man she recognizes from one of Jamie's companies appears. His wound is minor, but his presence means that the fighting she hears nearby involves Jamie.

Corporal Greenhow assures her that General Fraser was neither dead nor wounded when last seen, which is comforting so far as it goes. But the fighting is not only nearby—soldiers are running through the tombstones of the extensive churchyard, and Claire sees a British officer fall, wounded, and be killed. A peculiar fight ensues over the body, with Americans and British troops, apparently crazed by heat and battle, each trying to seize the fallen officer.

Jamie is in the fighting nearby and sees the unseemly struggle over the fallen officer's body. He sees something more alarming, too: Claire's white canvas tent, and Claire herself outside it, a basin of bloodstained bandages at her feet. Random shots are being fired all round.

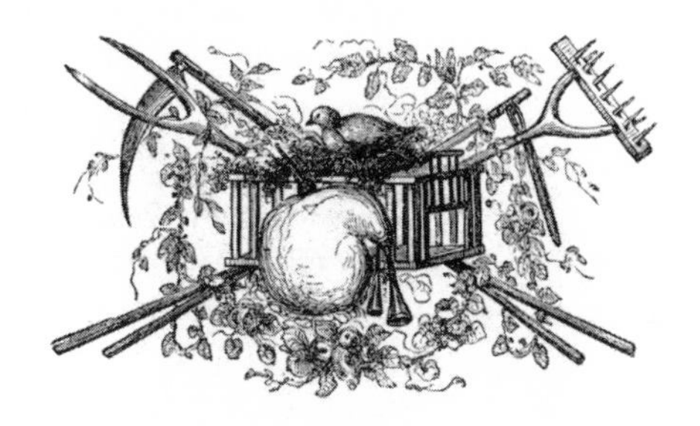

He was already following Bixby toward the road but glanced back. Yes, the men who had the dead British officer were taking him into the church, and there were wounded men sitting near the door, more of them near a small white—God, that was Claire's tent, was she—

He saw her at once, as though his thought had conjured her, right there in the open. She was standing up, staring openmouthed, and no wonder—there was a Continental regular on a stool beside her, holding a bloodstained cloth, and more such cloths in a basin at her feet. But why was she out here? She—

And then he saw her jerk upright, clap a hand to her side, and fall.

A SLEDGEHAMMER HIT *me in the side, making me jerk, the needle dropping from my hands. I didn't feel myself fall but was lying on the ground, black and white spots flashing round me, a sense of intense numbness radiating from my right side. I smelled damp earth and warm grass and sycamore leaves, pungent and comforting.*

Shock, *I thought dimly, and opened my mouth, but nothing but a dry click came out of my throat. What . . . The numbness of the impact began to lessen, and I realized that I had curled into a ball, my forearm pressed by reflex over my abdomen. I smelled burning, and fresh blood, very fresh. I've been shot, then.*

"Sassenach!" I heard Jamie's bellow over the roaring in my ears. He sounded far off, but I heard the terror in his voice clearly. I wasn't disturbed by it. I felt very calm.

"Sassenach!" The spots had coalesced. I was looking down a narrow tunnel of light and spinning shadow. At the end of it was the shocked face of Corporal Greenhow, the needle dangling by its thread from the half-sewn gash in his forehead.

PART 5: *COUNTING NOSES*

Jamie falls to his knees beside Claire, terrified that she's dying. He's interrupted by a messenger with an urgent summons from General Lee. Jamie's response to this is to make the messenger remove his coat and waistcoat, whereupon:

Stooping swiftly, he scooped a handful from the horrifying puddle of bloody mud and, standing, wrote carefully on the messenger's white back with a finger:

I resign my commission. J. Fraser.

He made to fling the remnants of mud away but, after a moment's hesitation, added a smeared and reluctant "Sir" at the top of the message, then clapped the boy on the shoulder.

"Go and show that to General Lee," he said. The lieutenant went pale.

"The general's in a horrid passion, sir," he said. "I dassen't!"

Jamie looked at him. The boy swallowed, said, "Yes, sir," shrugged on his garments, and went at a run, unbuttoned and flapping.

Unexpected succor comes from the church: Captain Leckie approaches at a run, hurdling tombstones, and with Jamie's help succeeds in stanching the bleeding, at least temporarily.

As evening falls, Claire is lying on a kitchen table in the township of Freehold, and Denzell Hunter is laying out his knives, preparing to remove the musket ball from her side. Jamie is present, silent and anguished as he watches, praying that she won't die and wishing with all his heart that he could somehow spare her the agonies of the next half hour.

His prayers are answered by the appearance of Dorothea Grey, in company with some American soldiers. She's carrying a basket, sent by the Marquis de La Fayette, containing all manner of French goodies for the nourishment of Mrs. Fraser: jellies, fruits, cheeses . . . and . . .

"And he sent this," she said, a rather smug look on her face as she held up a squat green-glass bottle. "Thee will want this first, I think, Denny."

"What—" Denny began, reaching for the bottle, but Dorothea had pulled the cork, and the sweet cough-syrup smell of sherry rolled out—with the ghost of a very distinctive herbal scent beneath it, something between camphor and sage.

"Laudanum," said Jamie, and his face took on such a startling look of relief that only then did I realize how frightened he had been for me. "God bless ye, Dottie!"

"It occurred to me that Friend Gilbert might just possibly have a few things that might be useful," she said modestly. "All the Frenchmen I know are dreadful cranks about their health and have enormous collections of tonics and pastilles and clysters. So I went and asked."

But La Fayette's basket contains something else helpful, as Claire realizes when she smells Roquefort cheese. The mold that makes that sort of cheese is *Penicillium,* and before she falls into a laudanum swoon, she instructs Denny to pack the wound with cheese, once the ball is removed.

"Again, Sassenach," Jamie whispered, lifting my head and putting the spoon to my lips, sticky with sherry and the bitter taste of opium. "One more." I swallowed and lay back. If I died, would I see my mother again? I wondered, and experienced an urgent longing for her, shocking in its intensity.

I was trying to summon her face before me, bring her out of the floating horde of strangers, when I suddenly lost my grip on my own thoughts and began to float off into a sphere of dark, dark blue.

"Don't leave me, Claire," Jamie whispered, very close to my ear. "This time, I'll beg. Dinna go from me. Please." I could feel the warmth of his face, see the glow of his breath on my cheek, though my eyes were closed.

"I won't," I said—or thought I said—and went. My last clear thought was that I'd forgotten to tell him not to marry a fool.

Denzell's surgery is successful, but Claire has lost a lot of blood; Jamie sits up with her through the night and the next day and night, sponging her and giving her water and praying. The fate of the Continental army and the outcome of the battle mean nothing to him—though he does spare a thought now and then for Ian . . . and William.

At nightfall on the day of battle, Lord John Grey walks into the British camp, accompanied by a wounded Mohawk. As they pass one of the campfires, his companion spots an Abenaki scout and, to Grey's astonishment, attacks him. The fight is brutal and brief; Ian overpowers his enemy and holds a knife to his throat, but then—with regard for Rachel and her principles—with an effort, lets the man go, telling him that he gives him back his life.

In the excitement, most of the crowd likely didn't hear the Indian's reply, but Grey and André did. He sat up, very slowly, hands shaking as they pressed a fold of his shirt to the shallow cut across his throat, and said, in an almost conversational tone, "You will regret that, Mohawk."

Murray was breathing like a winded horse, his ribs visible with each gasp. Most of the paint had gone from his face; there were long smears of red and black down his glistening chest, and only a horizontal streak of some dark color remained across his cheekbones—that and a smudge of white on the point of his shoulder, above the arrow wound. He nodded to himself, once, then twice. And, without haste, stepped back into the circle of firelight, picked up a tomahawk that was lying on the ground, and, swinging it high with both hands, brought it down on the Indian's skull.

The sound froze Grey to the marrow and silenced every man present. Murray stood still for a moment, breathing heavily, then walked away. As he passed Grey, he turned his head and said, in a perfectly conversational tone of voice, "He's right. I would have," before disappearing into the night.

William's fretting is relieved by the appearance of his father—battered and bruised, but alive and plainly glad to see William in a similar condition:

"If you and I have things to say to each other, Willie—and of course we do—let it wait until tomorrow. Please. I'm not . . ." He made a vague, wavering gesture that ended nowhere.

The lump in William's throat was sudden and painful. He nodded, hands clenched tight on the bedding. His father nodded, too, drew a deep breath, and turned toward the tent flap—where, William saw, Uncle Hal was hovering, eyes fixed on his brother and brows drawn with worry.

William's heart seized, in a lump more painful than the one in his throat.

"Papa!" His father stopped abruptly, turning to look over his shoulder.

"I'm glad you're not dead," William blurted.

A smile blossomed slowly on his father's battered face.

"Me, too," he said.

MEANWHILE, IAN MAKES his way alone out of the British camp and heads in the general direction of the American lines. Wounded and with a nascent fever, he walks through the night in conversation with his dead father, finally stumbling off the trail with the knowledge that he can go no farther. He manages to pull a layer of pine needles over himself and surrenders to the night.

Hal tends to John's cut and battered feet, gets him food, and fills him in on recent events: notably the revelation regarding William's paternity and the outcome of the battle.

"How long have you known?" Hal asked curiously.

"For certain? Since Willie was two or three." He suddenly gave an enormous yawn, then sat blinking stupidly. "Oh—meant to ask. How did the battle go?"

Hal looked at him with something between affront and amusement. "You were bloody in it, weren't you?"

"My part of it didn't go that well. But my perspective was somewhat limited by circumstance. That, and having only one working eye," he added, gently prodding the bad one. A good night's sleep . . . Longing for bed made him sway, narrowly catching himself before simply falling into Hal's cot.

"Hard to tell." Hal fished a crumpled towel out of a basket of laundry lurking disreputably in a corner and, kneeling down, lifted Grey's feet out of the oil and blotted them gently. "Hell of a mess. Terrible ground, chopped up by creeks, either farmland or half covered in trees . . . Sir Henry got away with the baggage train and refugees all safe. But as for Washington . . ." He shrugged. "So far as I can tell from what I saw and heard, his troops acquitted themselves well. Remarkably well," he added thoughtfully. He rose to his feet. "Lie down, John. I'll find a bed somewhere else."

As Hal is leaving his brother, though, he quietly remarks that he's had news himself—his eldest son, Benjamin, is dead.

Lord John awakes next morning, wondering whether he dreamed that last bit—but he didn't. Hal explains that his eldest son had been captured at the battle at Brandywine Creek and was held in a prisoner-of-war camp in the Watchung Mountains of New Jersey. Hal has now received a letter telling him that Benjamin died in the camp. He firmly tells John that he doesn't believe it and proposes to find out the truth.

This belief is enhanced by what John tells him about the reappearance of Captain Richardson and his interest in William—it's Richardson who brought Hal the news about Benjamin. The Grey brothers speculate that Richardson's news may well be a trap, designed to get Hal away from the safety of the army, either to abduct or threaten him. Beyond these considerations, though, John is worried about William; Percy Beauchamp told him that Richardson had designs on the Grey family in general, and while he wouldn't touch Percy with a ten-foot pole (*Something shorter, though . . .* he thinks), in this instance he's inclined to give Percy, rather than Richardson, the benefit of the doubt.

The Grey brothers separate, to look for Richardson and William, respectively. They reconvene several hours later with no results; both William and Richardson are gone, and it seems more than likely that William has gone with the duplicitous captain, whether willingly or not.

In fact, William has had a visit from Banastre Tarleton, who fills him in on the German deserters who bashed him on the head, informs him that he (Tarleton) has William's missing horse, and also mentions that the Captain Harkness for whom William was looking has turned up AWOL. As he was talking of going back to the brothel to *"give some whore a proper seeing-to,"* the assumption is that he's done just that and is in Philadelphia.

Jane and her sister, Fanny, had been knocked out of William's head, but this story brings them back with a jolt.

He had an immediate impulse to get up and go find her, make sure they were all right. The fugitive Loyalists and camp followers would have been well clear of the actual battle, of course—but the violence and agitation that attended fighting didn't simply stop when the fighting did. And it wasn't only deserters and scavengers who looted, raped, and hunted among the hapless sheep.

William does go in search of Jane and Fanny, but they have left the camp, according to his groom. William has been relieved of duty and has no role to play in the army's movements; he manages to borrow a mule and cart from the teamsters and goes in search of the girls; how far could they get?

Farther than he bargains for, and it's not until the next day that he finds them—and rescues them from a small party of German deserters, with the timely assistance of Rachel Hunter, out on a mule looking for Ian.

Jane attempts to flee. Chasing after her into the brush, Fanny reappears to tell William that she has found an Indian lying in the wood.

This is, of course, Ian, in a state of high fever and dehydration, with his arrow wound beginning to go bad. Plainly, he has to be taken to a doctor—preferably Claire. William is disturbed at hearing that Claire has been shot, but there's nothing he can do about that, and he has a young murderess and her even younger sister on his hands.

Rather to his indignant surprise, Jane refuses to come back with him, telling him that Banastre Tarleton had approached her in the bread line. He had visited the brothel in Philadelphia where she worked and was bound to recall where he had seen her before. She can't risk being suspected of Captain Harkness's murder—the more so because, in fact, she *has* killed him.

Ultimately, Rachel takes the girls in the cart, headed for a small Quaker settlement that will give them shelter until William is able to make provisions for them to go to New York. Leaving Ian in his state nearly kills her, but she entrusts his life and safety to William.

"This man is my heart and my soul," she said simply, looking up into his face. "And he is thy own blood, whatever thee may presently feel about the fact. I trust thee to see him safe, for all our sakes."

William gave her a long look, thought of several possible replies, and made none of them, but gave a curt nod.

Ian is in bad shape but not quite unconscious, and he and William have a barbed but civil conversation as they head toward Freehold, where—with luck—Denny Hunter is still working on the wounded from the battle.

"D'ye want me to tell ye, or no?" Murray said suddenly.

"Tell me what?"

There was a brief sound that might have been either amusement or pain.

"Whether ye're much like him."

Possible responses to this came so fast that they collapsed upon themselves like a house of cards. He took the one on top.

"Why do you suppose I should wonder?" William managed, with a coldness that would have frozen most men. Of course, Murray was blazing with such a fever, it would take a Quebec blizzard to freeze him.

"I would, if it was me," Murray said mildly.

That defused William's incipient explosion momentarily.

"Perhaps you think so," he said, not trying to hide his annoyance. "You may know him, but you know nothing whatever about me."

This time, the sound was undeniably amusement: laughter, of a hoarse, creaking sort.

"I helped fish ye out of a privy ten years ago," Murray said. "That was when I first kent it, aye?"

BACK IN FREEHOLD, Claire has survived her wound, the subsequent operation, and a rising fever; though still very weak, she is able to receive a pair of unlikely callers: Lord John Grey and his brother, the Duke of Pardloe. They've come, out of uniform and unarmed save for a flag of truce, to ask a favor of Jamie: will he write a note to Benedict Arnold, his friend and now military governor of Philadelphia, asking him to allow the Greys to remain in the city for a time in order to search for William (not mentioning the elusive Captain Richardson, though they definitely want to catch up to that gentleman).

Jamie is both suspicious and aloof with the man who's had sexual relations with his wife, but William *is* his son, and he writes the requested letter.

Worn out by long vigil, Jamie sleeps, and so does Claire—but she awakens at the sound of a knock below and staggers to the window.

There was a handsome bay mule in the dooryard, with a half-naked body laid over the saddle. I gasped—and immediately doubled in pain, but didn't let go the sill. I bit my lip hard, not to call out. The body was wearing buckskins, and his long brown hair sported a couple of bedraggled turkey feathers.

"Jesus H. Roosevelt Christ," I breathed, through gritted teeth. "Please, God, don't let him be—" But the prayer was answered before I'd finished speaking it; the door below opened, and in the next moment William and Lieutenant Macken walked out and lifted Ian off the mule, put his arms about their shoulders, and carried him into the house.

I turned, instinctively reaching for my medical bag—and nearly fell. I saved myself by a grab at the bed frame but let out an involuntary groan that brought Jamie up into a crouch, staring wildly about.

"It's . . . all right," I said, willing my belly muscles into immobility. "I'm fine. It's—Ian. He's come back."

Jamie sprang to his feet, shook his head to clear it, and at once went to the window. I saw him stiffen and, clutching my side, followed him. William had come out of the house and was preparing to mount the mule. He was dressed in shirt and breeches, very grubby, and the sun licked his dark chestnut hair with streaks of red. Mrs. Macken said something from the door, and he turned to answer her. I don't think I made a noise, but something made him look up suddenly and he froze. I felt Jamie freeze, too, as their eyes met.

William's face didn't change, and after a long moment he turned to the mule again, mounted, and rode away. After another long moment, Jamie let out his breath.

"Let me put ye back to bed, Sassenach," he said calmly. "I'll have to go and find Denny to put Ian right."

Denny does put Ian right, removing the arrow and treating the wound, and Ian comes round in a cow byre, with Rachel tending him. She asks him about the horrible nightmares he was evidently having while under the influence of laudanum—about a green-eyed woman named Geillis, among other things. With some reluctance, Ian tells her about his abduction and captivity on Jamaica and the deaths of the other boys held captive with him, whom he still sees sometimes in his dreams.

Finally a shiver went over Rachel, as though she shook herself awake, and she put a hand on his forehead, smoothing back his hair as she looked into his eyes, her own now soft and fathomless. Her thumb came down and traced the tattooed line across his cheekbones, very slowly.

"I think we can't wait any longer to be married, Ian," she said softly. "I will not have thee face such things alone. These are bad times, and we must be together."

He closed his eyes and all the air went out of him. When he drew breath again, it tasted of peace.

"When?" he whispered.

"As soon as thee can walk without help," she said, and kissed him, lightly as a falling leaf.

WHILE THE AMERICANS slowly gather up the pieces, the brothers Grey reach Philadelphia, and after a chilly but civil reception by Benedict Arnold, are given leave to search for William. They begin at Lord John's house on Chestnut Street.

The housekeeper, Mrs. Figg, has not seen William and is disturbed at the news that he's missing. However, she informs Hal that his daughter, Dottie, is at the house, and there is a tender meeting between them—tender in spite of Dottie's bringing up the matter of her marriage to Denzell Hunter. She asks Lord John if they might use his house for the wedding, whereupon Mrs. Figg offers the use of her husband's church—in view of the fact that Lord John provided part of the money to build it, she thinks this only right, and surely they will need more room than the house on Chestnut Street can provide.

Discussion of the wedding is abruptly interrupted, though, by a visitor:

Not bothering to complete her thought, she flew to the unbolted door and yanked it open, revealing a startled William on the stoop.

"Dottie!" he said. "What—" And then caught sight of John and Hal. William's face underwent a lightning shift that made a frisson *run straight down John's back to his tailbone. He'd seen that exact expression on Jamie Fraser's face a hundred times, at least—but had never before seen it on William's.*

It was the look of a man who doesn't like his immediate prospects one bit—but who feels himself entirely capable of dealing with them. William stepped inside, repelling by force of will Dottie's abortive attempt to embrace him. He removed his hat and bowed to Dottie, then, punctiliously, to John and Hal.

"Your servant, ma'am. Sirs."

William and his stepfather and uncle exchange what knowledge they have of Captain Richardson—unfortunately very little—and William learns about Ben. At the conclusion of his visit, he offers to go and make inquiries regarding Ben in New Jersey; he is, after all, at loose ends, having now resigned his commission.

Lord John is somewhat rocked by this and asks why William has come to Philadelphia.

"I came on a personal matter," William said, in a tone suggesting that the matter was still personal and was going to remain that way. "But also . . ." He pressed his lips together for a moment, and again John had that odd sense of dislocation, seeing Jamie Fraser. "I was going to leave this here for you, in case you came back to the city. Or ask Mrs. Figg to send it to New York, if . . ." His voice trailed away, as he pulled a letter from the breast of his dark-blue coat.

"But I needn't now," he concluded firmly, and put it away again. "It's only saying what I've already told you." A slight flush touched his cheekbones, though, and he avoided John's eye, turning instead to Hal.

"I'll go and find out about Ben," he said simply. "I'm not a soldier any longer; there's no danger of my being taken up as a spy. And I can travel much more easily than you can."

"Oh, William!" Dottie took the handkerchief from her father and blew her nose with a small, ladylike honk. She looked at him with brimming eyes. "Will you, really? Oh, thank *you!"*

That was not, of course, the end of it. But it was no revelation to Grey that William possessed a stubbornness so obviously derived from his natural father that no one but Hal would even have thought of arguing with him. And even Hal didn't argue long.

In due course, William rose to go.

"Give Mrs. Figg my love, please," he said to John, and, with a small bow to Dottie, "Goodbye, cousin."

John followed him to the door to let him out, but at the threshold put a hand on his sleeve.

"Willie," he said softly. "Give me the letter."

For the first time, William looked a little less than certain. He put his hand to his breast, but left it there, hesitant.

"I won't read it—unless you don't come back. But if you don't . . . I want it. To keep."

William drew breath, nodded, and, reaching into his coat, removed a sealed cover and handed it over. Grey saw that it had been sealed with a thick daub of candle wax and that William hadn't used his signet, preferring instead to stamp it with his thumbprint, firm in the hot wax.

"Thank you," he said through the lump in his throat. "Godspeed. Son."

CHAPTER 94, "THE Sense of the Meeting," concludes Part Five, describing the double wedding between Rachel and Ian and Dottie and Denzell before a motley congregation consisting of Quaker witnesses and family of all sorts:

Hal, who had flushed at Dottie's remarks, went somewhat redder at Denny's and breathed in a menacing rasp, but didn't say anything further. Hal and John were both wearing full dress uniform and far outshone the two brides in splendor. I thought it rather a pity that Hal wouldn't get to walk Dottie down the aisle, but he had merely inhaled deeply when the form of the marriage was outlined to him and said—after being elbowed sharply in the ribs by his brother—that he was honored to witness the event.

Jamie, by contrast, did not wear uniform,

but his appearance in full Highland dress made Mrs. Figg's eyes bulge—and not only hers.

"Sweet Shepherd of Judea," she muttered to me. "Is that man wearing a woolen petticoat? And what sort of pattern is that cloth? Enough to burn the eyes out your head."

"They call it a Fèileadh beag*," I told her. "In the native language. In English, it's usually called a kilt. And the pattern is his family tartan."*

She eyed him for a long moment, the color rising slowly in her cheeks. She turned to me with her mouth open to ask a question, then thought better and shut it firmly.

"No," I said, laughing. "He isn't."

She snorted. "Either way, he's like to die of the heat," she predicted, "and so are those two gamecocks." She nodded at John and Hal, glorious and sweating in crimson and gold lace. Henry had also come in uniform, wearing his more modest lieutenant's apparel. He squired Mercy Woodcock on his arm and gave his father a stare daring him to say anything.

"Poor Hal," I murmured to Jamie. "His children are rather a trial to him."

"Aye, whose aren't?" he replied. "All right, Sassenach? Ye look pale. Had ye not best go in and sit down?"

* * *

Both curiosity and conversation rose to a much higher pitch when Ian walked in. He wore a new shirt, white calico printed with blue and purple tulips, his buckskins and breechclout, moccasins—and an armlet made of blue and white wampum shells, which I was reasonably sure that his Mohawk wife, Works With Her Hands, had made for him.

"And here, of course, is the best man," I heard John whisper to Hal. Rollo stalked in at Ian's heel, disregarding the further stir he *caused. Ian sat down quietly on one of the two benches that had been set at the front of the church, facing the congregation, and Rollo sat at his feet, scratched himself idly, then collapsed and lay panting gently, surveying the crowd with a yellow stare of lazy estimation, as though judging them for eventual edibility.*

Quaker weddings are a matter of witness and discussion, just like any other meeting of Friends, and there's a good bit of both in the preliminaries:

"Now, pardon me for interrupting, but from what I understand, you Friends think a woman's equal to a man, is that right?"

"It is," Rachel and Dottie said firmly together, and everyone laughed.

Mrs. Figg flushed like a ripe black plum, but kept her composure. "Well, then," she said. "If these ladies want to marry with you gentlemen, why do you think you got any business trying to talk them out of it? Have you maybe got your own reservations about the matter?"

A distinctly feminine murmur of approval came from the congregation, and Denny, who was still standing, seemed to be struggling for his own composure.

"Does he have a cock?" came a French-accented whisper from behind me and an unhinged giggle from Marsali in response. "You can't get married without a cock."

This reminiscence of Fergus and Marsali's unorthodox wedding on a Caribbean beach made me stuff my lace handkerchief into my mouth. Jamie shook with suppressed laughter.

"I do have reservations," Denzell said, taking a deep breath. "Though not," he added

hastily, with a glance at Dottie, "regarding my desire to wed Dorothea or the honor of my intentions toward her. My reservations—and perhaps Friend Ian's, though I must not speak for him—lie entirely the other way. That is, I—we, perhaps—feel that we must lay bare our failings and limitations as . . . as husbands—" And for the first time, he, too, blushed. "That Dorothea and Rachel may . . . may come to a proper—er . . ."

"That they know what they may be getting into?" Mrs. Figg finished for him. "Well, that's a fine sentiment, Dr. Hunter—"

"Friend," he murmured.

"Friend *Hunter," she said, with a minimal roll of the eyes. "But I tell you two things. One, your young lady probably knows more about you than you do." More laughter. "And two—speaking as a woman with some experience—I can tell you that nobody knows what being married's going to be like until you find yourself in the midst of it." She sat down with an air of finality, to a hum of approbation.*

A good many things are said, and much thought given, and finally a silence falls. Claire, like many others, is thinking of her own marriages.

Frank. John. Jamie. Sincerity of intention wasn't always enough, I thought, looking at the young people on the benches at the front of the church, none of them now looking at one another but staring at their folded hands, the floor, or sitting with closed eyes. Perhaps realizing that, as Mrs. Figg had said, a marriage is made not in ritual or in words but in the living of it.

A movement pulled me out of my thoughts; Denny had risen to his feet and held out a hand to Dottie, who rose as though mesmerized and, reaching out, clasped both his hands in hers, hanging on for dear life.

"Does thee feel the sense of the meeting clear, Dorothea?" he asked softly, and at her nod, spoke:

"In the presence of the Lord, and before these our Friends, I take thee, Dorothea, to be my wife, promising, with divine assistance, to be unto thee a loving and faithful husband so long as we both shall live."

Her voice was low but clearly audible as, face shining, she replied:

"In the presence of the Lord, and before these our Friends, I take thee, Denzell, to be my husband, promising, with divine assistance, to be unto thee a loving and faithful wife so long as we both shall live."

I heard Hal catch his breath, in what sounded like a sob, and then the church burst into applause. Denny looked startled at this but then broke into a brilliant smile and led Dottie, beaming on his arm, out through the congregation to the back of the church, where they sat close together on the last bench.

People murmured and sighed, smiling, and the church gradually quieted—but not to its former sense of contemplation. There was now a vibrant sense of expectation, tinged perhaps with a little anxiety, as attention focused on Ian and Rachel—no longer looking at each other but down at the floor.

Ian took a breath audible to the back benches, raised his head, and, taking the knife from his belt, laid it on the bench beside him.

"Aye, well . . . Rachel kens I was once married, to a woman of the Wolf clan of the Kahnyen'kehaka. And the Mohawk way of marriage is maybe none so different from the way Friends do it. We sat beside each other before the people, and our parents—they'd adopted me, ken—spoke for us, sayin' what they kent of us and that we were of good character. So far as they *knew," he added apologetically, and there was a breath of laughter.*

"The lass I was to wed had a basket on her lap, filled wi' fruit and vegetables and other bits o' food, and she said to me that she promised to feed me from her fields and care for me.

And I—" He swallowed and, reaching out, laid a hand on his knife. "I had a knife, and a bow, and the skins of some otters I'd taken. And I promised to hunt for her and keep her warm wi' my furs. And the people all agreed that we should be married, and so . . . we were."

He stopped, biting his lip, then cleared his throat and went on.

"But the Mohawk dinna take each other for as long as they live—but only for as long as the woman wishes. My wife chose to part wi' me—not because I hurt or mistreated her, but for . . . for other reasons." He cleared his throat again, and his hand went to the wampum armlet round his biceps.

"My wife was called Wakyo' teyehsnonhsa, which means 'Works With Her Hands,' and she made this for me, as a love token." Long brown fingers fumbled with the strings, and the strip of woven shells came loose, slithering into his hand. "Now I lay it down, as witness that I come here a free man, that my life and my heart are once more mine to give. And I hope I may be allowed now to give them forever."

The blue and white shells made a soft clicking noise as he laid them on the bench. He let his fingers rest on them for a moment, then took his hand away.

I could hear Hal's breathing, steady now but with a faint rasp. And Jamie's, thick in his throat.

I could feel all sorts of things moving like wraiths in the thick, still air of the church. Sentiment, sympathy, doubt, apprehension . . . Rollo growled very softly in his throat and fell silent, yellow-eyed and watchful at his master's feet.

We waited. Jamie's hand twitched in mine, and I looked up at him. He was looking at Ian, intent, his lips pressed tight, and I knew he was wondering whether to stand up and speak on Ian's behalf, to assure the congregation—and Rachel—of Ian's character and virtue. He caught my glance, though, shook his head very slightly, and nodded toward the front. It was Rachel's part to speak, if she would.

Rachel sat still as stone, face bleached as bone and her eyes on Ian, burning. But she said nothing.

Neither did she move, but something moved in her; I could see the knowledge of it cross her face, and somehow her body changed, straightening and settling. She was listening.

We all listened with her. And the silence kindled slowly into light.

There was a faint throb in the air then, not quite a sound, and people began to look up, called from the silence. A blur appeared between the benches at the front, and a hummingbird materialized, drawn through the open window, a tiny blur of green and scarlet hovering beside the coral trumpets of the native honeysuckle.

A sigh came from the heart of the church, and the sense of the meeting was made clear.

Ian rose, and Rachel came to meet him.

"THE SENSE OF the Meeting" is followed by "A Coda in Three-Two Time." This is an account of three wedding nights: Dottie and Denzel, Ian and Rachel—and Jamie and Claire. You'll find an annotated version of this coda elsewhere in this book.

PART 6: *THE TIES THAT BIND*

Back in America, Brianna has fled with her children to California, there to reckon the odds and make a fateful decision: whether to take Jem and Mandy through the stones in hopes of finding Roger or remain in hiding and try to discover the true nature of the threat to her family.

While thinking, she adds some notes to the time-traveler's guide that Roger had begun compiling: a collection of all the information and speculations available regarding the nature of travel and what it might do to those reckless enough to undertake it. Going through the stones is plainly an enormous danger—how can she be thinking of doing such a thing, particularly with her children? And yet . . .

And yet . . . in the end, her decision doesn't rest on any reckoning of relative dangers but on her clear perception that the family must be together, and as Roger can't come to them . . .

IN SCOTLAND, ROGER is also searching for family—at present, for the owner of the RAF identity disks. Following the information given to them by Captain Randall, Roger and Buck head south, finding the dealer of odd bits and pieces from whom the soldier got the disks. Mr. Cumberpatch, the dealer, tells them he got the disks in trade from someone living near the wall—Hadrian's Wall, that is.

As they take their leave, Roger sees a cracked and tarnished pendant with an undamaged garnet, and he buys it—just in case.

Camping in the rain, Buck and Roger talk about the possibility of finding Jerry MacKenzie, and on impulse Roger tells Buck the truth about his own parentage:

"Your father was Dougal MacKenzie of Castle Leoch—war chieftain of the clan MacKenzie. And your mother was a witch named Geillis."

Buck's face was absolutely blank, the faint firelight shimmering on the broad cheekbones that were his father's legacy. Roger wanted suddenly to go and take the man in his arms,

smooth the hair back from his face, comfort him like a child—like the child he could so plainly see in those wide, stunned green eyes. Instead, he got up and went off into the night, giving his four-times great-grandfather what privacy he could in which to deal with the news.

Roger wakes, coughing, and is surprised to realize that his throat doesn't hurt. Neither does clearing his throat hurt. Perhaps—just perhaps—Dr. McEwan's laying-on of hands has helped.

FROM CALIFORNIA, BRIANNA takes the children to Boston, seeking help from her mother's oldest friend, Joe Abernathy. The Abernathys welcome the little family warmly, and over two bottles of wine, with Jem a sober spectator, Bree tells Joe the truth.

"Leave them, darlin'. Come talk to me in the den. Bring the rest of the wine," he added, then smiled at Jem. "Jem, whyn't you go up and ask Gail can you watch TV in the bedroom?"

Jem had a smudge of spaghetti sauce at the corner of his mouth, and his hair was sticking up on one side in porcupine spikes. He was a little pale from the journey, but the food had restored him and his eyes were bright, alert.

"No, sir," he said respectfully, and pushed back his own chair. "I'll stay with my mam."

"You don't need to do that, honey," she said. "Uncle Joe and I have grown-up things we need to talk about. You—"

"I'm staying."

She gave him a hard look, but recognized instantly, with a combination of horror and fascination, a Fraser male with his mind made up.

His lower lip was trembling, just a little. He shut his mouth hard to stop it and looked soberly from her to Joe, then back.

"Dad's not here," he said, and swallowed. "And neither is Grandda. I'm . . . I'm staying."

Joe is interested in the fact that Jem and Mandy are aware of each other, even at a distance, and wonders how far that phenomenon can work—and whether it might be of use in the family's journey.

"I don't think I can feel her when I'm at school," Jem said, anxious to be helpful. "But I'm not sure, 'cause I don't think about her at school."

"How far's the school from your place?" Uncle Joe asked. "You want a Pop-Tart, princess?"

"Yes!" Mandy's buttery round face lighted up, but Jem glanced at Mam. Mam looked as if she wanted to kick Uncle Joe under the counter for a second, but then she glanced down at Mandy and her face went all soft.

"All right," she said, and Jem felt a fluttery, excited sort of feeling in his middle. Mam was telling Uncle Joe how far the school was, but Jem wasn't paying attention. They were going to do it. They were really going to do it!

Because the only reason Mam would let Mandy eat Pop-Tarts without a fuss was because she figured she'd never get to eat another one.

"Can I have one, too, Uncle Joe?" he asked. "I like the blueberry ones."

REACHING HADRIAN'S WALL is only the first hurdle for Roger and Buck. The inhabitants speak an impenetrable Northumbrian dialect, more like Middle English than anything else, and are more than suspicious of outsiders. They persevere, though, and eventually find the small stone circle where they think Jerry must have passed through. Inquiring locally, they find proof that he did.

"Be those thy be-asts?" the boy asked, grinning at Roger. He pointed at the stones, explaining—Roger thought—the local legend that the stones were in fact faery cattle, frozen in place when their drover had too much drink betaken and fell into the lake.

"Sooth," the boy assured them solemnly, making a cross over his heart. "Mester Hacffurthe found es whip!"

"When?" Buck asked sharply. "And where liveth Mester Hacffurthe?"

A week ago, maybe twa, said the boy, waving a hand to indicate that the date was not important. And he would take them to Mester Hacffurthe, if they liked to see the thing.

Despite his name, Mester Hacffurthe proved to be a slight, light-haired young man, the village cobbler. He spoke the same impenetrable Northumbrian dialect, but with some effort and the helpful intervention of the boy—whose name, he said, was Ridley—their desire was made clear, and Hacffurthe obligingly fetched the faery whip out from under his counter, laying it gingerly before them.

"Oh, Lord," Roger said at sight of it—and, with a raised brow at Hacffurthe to ask permission, touched the strip carefully. A machine-woven, tight-warped strip some three inches wide and two feet long, its taut surface gleaming even in the dim light of the cobbler's shop. Part of the harness of an RAF flier. They had the right stones, then.

Further inquiry leads them to a remote farm, where they believe Jerry may be being held prisoner. Despite vicious dogs and similarly antisocial farmers, they persist, stealing onto the premises on a moonless night.

"He'll get out of it soon enough," Roger whispered back. "He's no need of it. Meanwhile, where the devil d'ye think they've got him?"

"Someplace that's got a door ye can bolt." Buck rubbed his palms together, brushing off the dirt. "They'd no keep him in the house, though, would they? It's no that big."

It wasn't. You could have fitted about sixteen farmhouses that size into Lallybroch, Roger thought, and felt a sudden sharp pang, thinking of Lallybroch as it was when he had—he would—own it.

Buck was right, though: there couldn't be more than two rooms and a loft, maybe, for the kids. And given that the neighbors thought Jerry—if it was Jerry—was a foreigner at best, a thief and/or supernatural being at worst, it wasn't likely that the Quartons would be keeping him in the house.

"Did ye see a barn, before the light went?" Buck whispered, changing to Gaelic. He had risen onto his toes, as though that might help him see above the tide of darkness, and was peering into the murk. Dark-adapted as Roger's eyes now were, he could at least make out the squat shapes of the small farm buildings. Corncrib, goat shed, chicken coop, the tousled shape of a hayrick . . .

"No," Roger replied in the same tongue. The goose had extricated itself and gone off making disgruntled small honks; Roger bent and retrieved his cloak. "Small place; they likely haven't more than an ox or a mule for the plowing, if that. I smell stock, though . . . manure, ken?"

"Kine," Buck said, heading abruptly off toward a square-built stone structure. "The cow byre. That'll have a bar to the door."

It did. And the bar was in its brackets.

* * *

*The door swung open as Buck set down the bar, and light shot out of the lantern's open slide. A slightly built young man with flyaway fair hair—*the same color as Buck's, *Roger thought—blinked at them, dazzled by the light, then closed his eyes against it.*

Roger and Buck glanced at each other for an instant, then, with one accord, stepped into the byre.

He is, *Roger thought.* It's him. I know it's him. God, he's so young! Barely more than a boy. *Oddly, he felt no burst of dizzying excitement. It was a feeling of calm certainty, as though the world had suddenly righted itself and everything had fallen into place. He reached out and touched the man gently on the shoulder.*

"What's your name, mate?" he said softly, in English.

"MacKenzie, J. W.," the young man said, shoulders straightening as he drew himself up, sharp chin jutting. "Lieutenant, Royal Air Force. Service Number—" He broke off, staring at Roger, who belatedly realized that, calmness or no, he was grinning from ear to ear. "What's funny?" Jerry MacKenzie demanded, belligerent.

"Nothing," Roger assured him. "Er . . . glad—glad to see you, that's all."

Time is short, and the farmer and his family may wake at any moment. They leave, heading as fast as possible for the stone circle by the lake—Jerry's only means of escape.

"Take this; it's a good one. When ye go through," Roger said, and leaned toward him,

trying to impress him with the importance of his instructions, "think about your wife, about Marjorie. Think hard; see her in your mind's eye, and walk straight through. Whatever the hell ye do, though, don't think about your son. Just your wife."

"What?" Jerry was gobsmacked. "How the bloody hell do you know my wife's name? And where've ye heard about my son?"

"It doesn't matter," Roger said, and turned his head to look back over his shoulder.

"Damn," said Buck softly. "They're still coming. There's a light."

There was: a single light, bobbing evenly over the ground, as it would if someone carried it. But look as he might, Roger could see no one behind it, and a violent shiver ran over him.

"Thaibhse," *said Buck, under his breath. Roger knew that word well enough—spirit, it meant. And usually an ill-disposed one. A haunt.*

"Aye, maybe." He was beginning to catch his breath. "And maybe not." He turned again to Jerry. "Either way, ye need to go, man, and now. Remember, think of your wife."

Jerry swallowed, his hand closing tight around the stone.

"Aye. Aye . . . right. Thanks, then," he added awkwardly.

Roger couldn't speak, could give him nothing more than the breath of a smile. Then Buck was beside him, plucking urgently at his sleeve and gesturing at the bobbing light, and they set off, awkward and lumbering after the brief cooldown.

Bree . . . *He swallowed, fists clenched. He'd got a stone once, he could do it again. . . . But the greater part of his mind was still with the man they had just left by the lake. He looked over his shoulder and saw Jerry beginning to walk, limping badly but resolute, thin shoulders squared under his pale khaki shirt and the end of his scarf fluttering in the rising wind.*

Then it all rose up in him. Seized by an urgency greater than any he'd ever known, he turned and ran. Ran heedless of footing, of dark, of Buck's startled cry behind him.

Jerry heard his footsteps on the grass and whirled round, startled himself. Roger grabbed him by both hands, squeezed them hard enough to make Jerry gasp, and said fiercely, "I love you!"

That was all there was time for—and all he could possibly say.

* * *

The night shivered. The whole *night. The ground and the lake, the sky, the dark, the stars, and every particle of his own body. He was scattered, instantly everywhere and part of everything. And part of* them. *There was one moment of an exaltation too great for fear and then he vanished, his last thought no more than a faint,* I am . . . *voiced more in hope than declaration.*

Roger came back to a blurred knowledge of himself, flat on his back under a clear black sky whose brilliant stars seemed pinpoints now, desperately far away. He missed them, missed being part of the night. Missed, with a brief rending sense of desolation, the two men who'd shared his soul for that blazing moment.

They've found Jerry—but not Jem. And so they turn northward once more, to search for both Jem . . . and Buck's mother, Geillis Duncan.

BACK IN SCOTLAND now, Brianna makes her final preparations, writing in her "Practical Guide for Time Travelers":

It's almost time. The winter solstice is day after tomorrow. I keep imagining that I can feel the earth shifting slowly in the dark, tectonic plates moving under my feet and . . . things . . . invisibly lining up. The moon is waxing, nearly a quarter full. Have no idea whether that might be important.

In the morning, we'll take the train to Inverness. I've called Fiona; she'll meet us at the station, and we'll eat and change at her house—then she'll drive us to Craigh na Dun . . . and leave us there. Keep wondering if I should ask her to stay—or at least to come back in an hour, in case one or more of us should still be there, on fire or unconscious. Or dead.

IN CRANESMUIR, ROGER and Buck reach the fiscal's house and ask for Mrs. Duncan. The mistress, it seems, is at home but has a visitor: Dr. McEwan. She'll see the new visitors, though, and the men go up, each wondering what they may find.

Roger felt Buck stiffen slightly, and no wonder. He hoped he wasn't staring himself.

Geillis Duncan was maybe not a classic beauty, but that didn't matter. She was certainly good-looking, with creamy-blond hair put up under a lace cap, and—of course—the eyes. Eyes that made him want to close his own and poke Buck in the back to make him do the same, because surely she or McEwan would notice. . . .

McEwan had noticed something, all right, but it wasn't the eyes. He was eyeing Buck with a small frown of displeasure, as Buck took a long stride forward, seized the woman's hand, and boldly kissed it.

"Mrs. Duncan," he said, straightening up and smiling right into those clear green eyes. "Your most humble and obedient servant, ma'am."

She smiled back, one blond brow raised, with an amused look that met Buck's implied challenge—and raised it. Even from where he was standing, Roger felt the snap of attraction between them, sharp as a spark of static electricity. So had McEwan.

"How is your health, Mr. MacKenzie?" McEwan said pointedly to Buck. He pulled a chair into place. "Do sit down and let me examine you."

Buck either didn't hear or pretended not to. He was still holding Geillis Duncan's hand, and she wasn't pulling it away.

The obvious sense of electric attraction between Buck and Geillis horrifies both Roger and Dr. McEwan—albeit for different reasons. Geillis takes Buck up to her herb attic, leaving the other two aghast.

"Stop, man," he said, keeping his voice pitched as low and evenly as he could, in hopes of soothing McEwan. "Ye'll do yourself no good. Sit down, now. I'll tell ye why it—why he—why the man's interested in her."

"For the same reason every dog in the village is interested *in a bitch in heat," McEwan said venomously. But he let Roger take the poker from his hand, and while he wouldn't sit down, he did at least take several deep breaths that restored a semblance of calm.*

"Aye, tell me, then—for all the good it will do," he said.

It wasn't a situation that allowed for diplomacy or euphemism.

"She's his mother, and he knows it," Roger said bluntly.

Whatever McEwan had been expecting, that wasn't it, and for an instant, Roger was gratified to see the man's face go absolutely blank with shock. Only for an instant, though.

It was likely going to be a tricky bit of pastoral counseling, at best.

Roger does his best, listening to McEwan's miserable confessions regarding his relationship with Geillis—and tries to distract him from what he hopes *isn't* happening upstairs, by asking the doctor to look at his throat again. This McEwan does, explaining as much as he knows about the blue light and what he thinks might happen with regard to healing. But distraction is not enough; plainly the man is fatally engaged.

At last Buck returns, and Roger gets him away. Buck is quiet, though admitting—to Roger's relief—that while Geillis made advances to him, they . . . didn't. Later, over a campfire outside Cranesmuir, Buck tells Roger the story of his own wife and why he felt he oughtn't try to return to her—instead, he offers to go back to Brianna, to tell her what's happened and where Roger is.

"So ye see," he said. "If I go back and tell your wife what's to do—and, with luck, come back to tell you—it's maybe the one good thing I could do. For my family—for yours."

It took some time for Roger to get his voice sufficiently under control as to speak.

"Aye," he said. "Well. Sleep on it. I mean to go up to Lallybroch. Ye'll maybe go and see Dougal MacKenzie at Leoch. If ye think ye still . . . mean it, after . . . there's time enough to decide then."

BRIANNA AND THE kids have reached Inverness and completed their preparations. She fears that they may have been seen, though, in spite of her precautions, and as they climb Craigh na Dun, she hears footsteps behind her and is sure that Rob Cameron and his companions are in pursuit.

Turning on the pursuer, though, she finds Lionel Menzies, distraught and urgent. Needing help, she'd told him about the venture, and he's been watching out. They *have* been spotted, he says; Rob and others are on their way—they must go at once.

But while they've been conversing, Mandy has been climbing, up into the stone circle.

But Mandy, little fist clutching her emerald, had turned toward the biggest of the standing stones. Her mouth drooped open for a moment, and then suddenly her face brightened as though someone had lit a candle inside her.

"Daddy!" *she shrieked, and, yanking her hand out of Brianna's, raced directly toward the cleft stone—and into it.*

"Jesus!" Brianna barely heard Menzies's shocked exclamation. She ran toward the stone, tripped over Esmeralda, and fell full length in the grass, knocking out her wind.

"Mama!" Jem paused for a moment beside her, glancing wildly back and forth between her and the stone where his little sister had just vanished.

"I'm . . . okay," she managed, and with that assurance, Jem charged across the clearing, calling back, "I'll get her, Mam!"

Jem does get Mandy back, both children popping out of the stone whole and unhurt, though shocked and nauseated by the passage. One problem: the emeralds they were carrying for passage have burned up. Lionel Menzies saves the day, knocking a small diamond out of his Masonic ring for Jem and giving the ring (with its other diamond) to Mandy.

"Lionel," she said, and he reached out and touched her cheek.

"Go now," he said. "I can't leave until ye go. Once you're gone, though, I'll run for it."

She nodded jerkily, once, then stooped and took the children's hands. "Jem—put that in your other pocket, okay?" She gulped air and turned toward the big cleft stone. The racket of it hammered at her blood and she could feel it pulling, trying to take her apart.

"Mandy," she said, and could barely hear her own voice. "Let's find Daddy. Don't let go."

It was only as the screaming began that she realized she'd not said "Thank you," and then she thought no more.

Brianna, Jem, and Mandy reach what they hope is the right time—they know they're in the right place. Brianna heads for Lallybroch; that's the only place she knows for sure that Roger has been, and is the logical place to ask after him. She approaches cautiously from the back of the house, though, still worried about the possibility of changing the future by meeting people she knows from a different time. What if her father, aged eighteen, is here? If so, will meeting him now mean she *won't* meet him at forty-six in North Carolina?

But her need to find Roger impels her, and she comes slowly down the hill toward the house, through the small family burying ground, leaving the kids at the broch above. Jem rushes down after her, though, saying he sees a man coming up—a black-haired man. Bree's heart leaps, but, no, it can't be Roger; Jem would know his father. . . .

She ducks back out of sight and sees the man come up among the graves, with a bit of greenery in his hand. He kneels beside one grave—one she knows is that of Ellen MacKenzie Fraser, and she realizes with a shock that the man is Brian Fraser, Jamie's father.

She shifted her weight, uncertain whether to call out or wait 'til he'd finished his business with the dead. But the small stones under her feet shifted, too, rolling down with a click-clack-click that made him look up and, seeing her, rise abruptly to his feet, black brows raised.

Black hair, black brows. Brian Dubh. *Black Brian.*

I met Brian Fraser (you would like him, and he, you) . . .

Wide, startled hazel eyes met hers, and for a second that was all she saw. His beautiful deep-set eyes, and the expression of stunned horror in them.

"Brian," she said. "I—"

"A Dhia!" *He went whiter than the harled plaster of the house below. "Ellen!"*

Astonishment deprived her of speech for an instant—long enough to hear light footsteps scrambling down the hill behind her.

"Mam!" Jem called, breathless.

Brian's glance turned up, behind her, and his mouth fell open at sight of Jem. Then a look of radiant joy suffused his face.

"Willie!" he said. "A bhalaich! Mo bhalaich!" *He looked back at Brianna and stretched out a trembling hand to her.* "Mo ghràidh . . . mo chridhe . . ."

"Brian," she said softly, her heart in her voice, filled with pity and love, unable to do anything but respond to the need of the soul that showed so clearly in his lovely eyes. And with her speaking of his name for the second time, he stopped dead, swaying for a moment, and then the eyes rolled up in his head and he fell.

Brianna fears for a moment that they've killed him, but it's all right; he's only fainted from the shock. She hesitates but can't bring herself to rouse him and introduce herself; having seen the joy on his face at sight of what he thought were his wife and son, she can't deprive him of the knowledge that Ellen and Willie are waiting for him.

As she begins to steal away, though, Jem rushes up to tell her that Mandy has run off, saying she hears her daddy.

Daddy is indeed close by, also headed for Lallybroch, to rendezvous with Buck. He's disturbed in mind, worried about Buck—and what he might or might not do with regard to his very unorthodox mother.

The presence of the gull broke his sense of isolation, at least. He rode on in a calmer frame of mind, resolved only not to think about things until he had to.

He thought he was close to Lallybroch; with luck, would reach it well before dark. His belly rumbled at the prospect of tea, and he felt happier. Whatever he could and couldn't tell Brian Fraser, just seeing Brian and his daughter, Jenny, again would be a comfort.

*The gulls cried high overhead, still wheeling, and he looked up. Sure enough: he could just make out the low ruins of the Iron Age hill fort up there, the ruins he'd rebuilt—would rebuild? What if he never got back to—*Jesus, don't even think about it, man, it'll drive you crazier than you are already.

He nudged the horse and it reluctantly accelerated a bit. It accelerated a lot faster in the next moment, when a crashing noise came from the hillside just above.

"Whoa! Whoa, you eedjit! Whoa, I said!" These adjurations, along with a heave of the reins to bring the horse's head around, had an effect, and they ended facing back the way they'd come, to see a young boy standing, panting, in the middle of the road, his red hair all on end, nearly brown in the muted light.

"Daddy," he said, and his face lit as though touched by a sudden sun. "Daddy!"

Roger hadn't any memory of leaving his horse or running down the road. Or of anything else. He was sitting in the mud and the mist in a patch of wet bracken with his son hugged tight to his chest, and nothing else mattered in the world.

With the family reunited, the MacKenzies find temporary refuge with Dr. McEwan in Cranesmuir. The doctor leaves the four of them to share his bed, while he says he will find a bed "with a friend." With the children safely asleep, Roger and Bree go into the doctor's surgery to make love . . . and talk, after so long apart.

"I thought I might never see you again," she whispered.

"Aye," he said softly, and his hand stroked her long hair and her back. "Me, too." They were silent for a long moment, each listening to the other's breath—his came easier than it had, she thought, without the small catches—and then he finally said, "Tell me."

She did, baldly and with as little emotion as she could manage. She thought he might be emotional enough for both of them.

He couldn't shout or curse, because of the sleeping children. She could feel the rage in him; he was shaking with it, his fists clenched like solid knobs of bone.

"I'll kill him," he said, in a voice barely pitched above silence, and his eyes met hers, savage and so dark that they seemed black in the dim light.

"It's okay," she said softly, and, sitting up, took both his hands in hers, lifting one and then the other to her lips. "It's okay. We're all right, all of us. And we're here."

He looked away and took a deep breath, then looked back, his hands tightening on hers.

"Here," he repeated, his voice bleak, still hoarse with fury. "In 1739. If I'd—"

"You had to," she said firmly, squeezing back hard. "Besides," she added, a little diffidently, "I sort of thought we wouldn't stay. Unless you've taken a great liking to some of the denizens?"

ROGER FELT HER *begin to relax, and quite suddenly she let go her stubborn hold on consciousness and fell asleep like someone breathing ether. He held her and listened to the tiny sounds that made up silence: the distant hiss of the peat fire in the bedroom, a cold wind rattling at the window, the rustling and breathing of the sleeping kids, the slow beating of Brianna's valiant heart.*

Thank you, *he said silently to God.*

He had expected to fall asleep himself at once; tiredness covered him like a lead blanket. But the day was still with him, and he lay for some time looking up into the dark.

He was at peace, too tired to think coherently of anything. All the possibilities drifted round him in a slow, distant swirl, too far away to be troublesome. Where they might go . . . and how. What Buck might have said to Dougal MacKenzie. What Bree had brought in her bag, heavy as lead. Whether there would be porridge for breakfast—Mandy liked porridge.

The thought of Mandy made him ease out of the quilts to check on the children. To reassure himself that they were really there.

They were, and he stood by the bed for a long time, watching their faces in wordless gratitude, breathing the warm childish smell of them—still tinged with a slight tang of goat.

At last he turned, shivering, to make his way back to his warm wife and the beckoning bliss of sleep. But as he reentered the surgery, he glanced through the window into the night outside.

Cranesmuir slept, and mist lay in her streets, the cobbles beneath gleaming with wet in the half-light of a drowning moon. On the far side of the square, though, a light showed in the attic window of Arthur Duncan's house.

And in the shadow of the square below, a small movement betrayed the presence of a man. Waiting.

Roger closed his eyes, cold rising from his bare feet up his body, seeing in his mind the sudden vision of a green-eyed woman, lazy in the arms of a fair-haired lover . . . and a look of surprise and then of horror on her face as the man vanished from her side. And an invisible blue glow rose in her womb.

With his eyes tight shut, he put a hand on the icy windowpane, and said a prayer to be going on with.

PART 7: *BEFORE I GO HENCE*

And now we rejoin Claire and Jamie in Philadelphia, with Fergus, Marsali, and their children. Things have quieted, with the exodus of the British army, but there is still substantial unrest; the Loyalists who have *not* left the city haven't surrendered their opinions, either, and a small stream of threats flows under the door of the Rebel printshop.

Lord John has offered the use of his house on Chestnut Street to Claire, but Jamie declines, saying he will take care of his own family, thank you. So the printshop is crowded but happy, despite the sort of disturbing news that occurs during a war. In this instance, it's an account of a massacre at a place in New York called Andrustown. Joseph Brant, a Mohawk (known as Thayendanegea) is fighting with and for the British, and his warriors have attacked a settlement called Andrustown, massacring the inhabitants.

She stood watching until Joanie had gone out through the back door, then turned to me and handed me the letter.

It was from a Mr. Johansen, apparently one of Fergus's regular correspondents, and the contents were as Marsali had said, though adding a few gruesome details that she hadn't men-

tioned in Joanie's hearing. It was fairly factual, with only the barest of eighteenth-century ornaments, and the more hair-raising—literally, I thought; some of the Andrustown residents had been scalped, by report—for that.

Marsali nodded as I looked up from the letter.

"Aye," she said. "Fergus wants to publish the account, but I'm nay so sure he ought to. Because of Young Ian, ken?"

"What's because of Young Ian?" said a Scottish voice from the printshop doorway, and Jenny came through, a marketing basket over one arm. Her eyes went to the letter in my hand, and her sharp dark brows rose.

"Has he told ye much about her?" Marsali asked, having explained the letter. "The Indian lass he wed?"

Jenny shook her head and began taking things out of her basket.

"Nay a word, save for his telling Jamie to say he wouldna forget us." A shadow crossed her face at the memory, and I wondered for a moment how it must have been for her and Ian, receiving Jamie's account of the circumstances in which Ian had become a Mohawk. I knew the agony with which he'd written that letter, and doubted that the reading of it had been done with less.

She laid down an apple and beckoned to me for the letter. Having read it through in silence, she looked at me. "D'ye think he's got feelings for her still?"

"I think he does," I answered reluctantly. "But nothing like his feelings for Rachel, surely." I did recall him, though, standing with me in the twilight on the demilune battery at Fort Ticonderoga, when he'd told me about his children—and Emily, his wife.

"He feels guilty about her, does he?" Jenny asked, shrewdly watching my face. I gave her a look, but nodded. She compressed her lips, but then handed the letter back to Marsali.

"Well, we dinna ken whether his wife has anything to do wi' this Brant or his doings, and it's no her that's been massacred. I'd say let Fergus print it, but"—and she glanced at me—"show the letter to Jamie and have him talk to wee Ian about it. He'll listen." Her expression lightened a little then, and a slight smile emerged. "He's got a good wife now, and I think Rachel will keep him to home."

IAN AND RACHEL are indeed happy in their marriage. Though saddened by the death of Ian's dog, Rollo, the news that Rachel is pregnant fills Ian with both joy and terror; his children with his first wife were stillborn or miscarried—will it be the same this time?

LORD JOHN WRITES to Claire, offering his house again—but this time for use as a surgery, he knowing full well that she'll be attending the sick and injured, no matter where she is, and wanting the house to be occupied and used. Given the state of crowding in the printshop, Jamie reluctantly agrees to this use—feeling that in any case, the situation will be temporary. For now that Jamie is out of the army—for good—he and Claire are free to do what they've longed to do since being reunited: go home to Fraser's Ridge.

Given the unsettled state of things in the north, Jamie urges Fergus and Marsali to come with them, moving the press south, perhaps to Wilmington or Savannah. Marsali and Fergus are still considering the idea when tragedy makes their minds up for them.

Fire breaks out in the printshop one night. Perhaps an accident; perhaps not. All is chaos, and as the adults hastily count noses, they discover that the boys are missing. Germain and Henri-Christian had gone out through a loft door to sleep on the roof, because of the heat. Roused belatedly by the shouts and noise, they've made their way back through the lofts, to the loading door used to raise bales of paper and barrels of ink. A rope hangs down to the alley, where the family and all the neighbors have gathered.

Henri-Christian, dizzy from the smoke, had fallen against the doorframe and was clinging to it. He was too frightened to move; I could see him shaking his head as Germain pulled at him.

"Throw him, Germain! Throw your brother!" Fergus was shouting as loudly as he could, his voice cracking with the strain, and several other voices joined in. "Throw him!"

I saw Germain's jaw set hard, and he yanked Henri-Christian loose, picked him up, and clutched him with one arm, wrapping the rope around the other.

"No!" Jamie bellowed, seeing it. "Germain, don't*!" But Germain bent his head over his brother's, and I thought I saw his lips move, saying,* "Hold on tight!" *And then he stepped out into the air, both hands clinging to the rope, Henri-Christian's stocky legs wrapped round his ribs.*

It happened instantly and yet so slowly. Henri-Christian's short legs lost their grip. Germain's grab failed, for the little boy was already falling, arms outstretched, in a half somersault through the smoky air.

He fell straight through the sea of upraised hands, and the sound as his head struck the cobbles was the sound of the end of the world.

Shocked and gutted by Henri-Christian's death, the small family makes ready to depart.

There were two large cairns there, knee-high. And a smaller one, at the edge of the clearing, under the branches of a red cedar. A flat stone lay against it, the word ROLLO scratched into it.

Fergus and Jamie set down the little coffin, gently. Joanie and Félicité had stopped crying during the long walk, but seeing it there, so small and forlorn, facing the thought of walking away . . . they began to weep silently, clinging hard to each other, and at the sight of them, grief rose in me like a fountain.

Germain was holding hard to his mother's hand, mute and jaw-set, tearless. Not seeking support, giving it, though the agony showed clear in his eyes as they rested on his brother's coffin.

Ian touched Marsali's arm gently.

"This place is hallowed by my sweat and my tears, cousin," he said softly. "Let us hallow it also by our blood and let our wee lad rest here safe in his family. If he canna go with us, we will abide with him."

He took the sgian dubh *from his stocking and drew it across his wrist, lightly, then held his arm above Henri-Christian's coffin, letting a few drops fall on the wood. I could hear the sound of it, like the beginning of rain.*

Marsali drew a shattered breath, stood straight, and took the knife from his hand.

PART 8: *SEARCH AND RESCUE*

The story reopens with the move of the family—Jamie and Claire, Marsali, Fergus, and their children, Jenny, and Ian and Rachel—to Savannah, in search of Jamie's printing press. This was saved from a fire in Edinburgh and dispatched to America in the care of one Richard Bell, a Loyalist merchant from Wilmington who had been forcibly deported by the local Sons of Liberty.

Jamie pays the cost of his passage back to his family, in return for Bell's seeing to the safe transport and keeping of his press.

Richard Bell is reunited with his family, but as the political climate in Wilmington is unfriendly to Loyalists, the Bells have removed south to Savannah, and Jamie and Fergus decide to see whether the city is a decent place to resume the printing business.

MEANWHILE, HAL RECEIVES a letter from his nephew, William:

Dear Uncle Hal,

You will be gratified to know that your paternal Instinct was correct. I am very pleased to tell you that Ben probably isn't dead.

On the other hand, I haven't the slightest Idea where the devil he is or why he's there.

I was shown a Grave at Middlebrook Encampment in New Jersey, purported to be Ben's, but the Body therein is not Ben. (It's probably better if you don't know how that bit of information was ascertained.)

Clearly someone in the Continental army must know something of his whereabouts, but most of Washington's troops who were at the Encampment when he was captured have gone. There is one Man who might possibly yield some Information, but beyond that, the only possible Connection would seem to be the Captain with whom we are acquainted.

I propose therefore to hunt the Gentleman in question and extract what Information he may possess when I find him.

Your most obedient nephew,
William

William has, in fact, visited the prisoner-of-war camp—now occupied only by the residents of Middlebrook and a few token soldiers—found the grave of Benjamin Grey, and, upon a midnight investigation of same, discovered that the body buried there is missing both ears—a thief, and by no means his cousin.

Another letter apprises Hal that John and Dottie have reached Charleston—the last known residence of Amaranthus Grey née Cowden, Benjamin's presumed wife and mother of his presumed child.

Some progress is made with their inquiries, but Dottie proves to be pregnant, and Lord John, totally unwilling to be midwife at an unexpected birth, insists on taking her back to New York, where Denzell is working as a surgeon with the Continental army, and where Hal can see that she's taken care of.

THE FRASERS BEGIN to settle in Savannah, the men working at whatever occupation they find, while finding quarters to re-establish the printing business, and Claire running a small surgery in one of the city's famous squares.

She encounters a wide variety of patients, from the city's prostitutes to a young girl suffering from a ghastly condition.

"You are a female physician?" she asked, in a tone just short of accusation.

"I am Dr. Fraser, yes," I replied equably. "And you are . . . ?"

She flushed at that and looked disconcerted.

Also very dubious. But after an awkward pause, she made up her mind and gave a sharp nod. "I am Sarah Bradshaw. Mrs. Phillip Bradshaw."

"I'm pleased to meet you. And your . . . companion?" I nodded at the young woman, who stood with her shoulders hunched and her head bent, staring at the ground. I could hear a soft dripping noise, and she shifted as though trying to press her legs together, wincing as she did so.

"This is Sophronia. One of my husband's slaves." Mrs. Bradshaw's lips compressed and drew in tight; from the lines surrounding her mouth, she did it routinely. "She—that is—I thought perhaps—" Her rather plain face flamed crimson; she couldn't bring herself to describe the trouble.

"I know what it is," I said, saving her the difficulty. I came round the table and took Sophronia by the hand; hers was small and very callused, but her fingernails were clean. A house slave, then. "What happened to the baby?" I asked her gently.

A small, frightened intake of breath, and she glanced sideways at Mrs. Bradshaw, who gave her another sharp nod, lips still pursed.

"It died in me," the girl said, so softly I could scarcely hear her, even though she was no more than an arm's length from me. "Dey cut it out in pieces." That had likely saved the girl's life, but it surely hadn't helped her condition.

Despite the smell, I took a deep breath, trying to keep my emotions under control.

"I'll need to examine Sophronia, Mrs. Bradshaw. If you have any errands, perhaps you'd like to go and take care of them . . . ?"

She unzipped her lips sufficiently as to make a small, frustrated noise. Quite obviously, she would like nothing better than to leave the girl and never come back. But just as obviously, she was afraid of what the slave might tell me if left alone with me.

"Was the child your husband's?" I asked baldly. I didn't have time to beat around the bush; the poor girl was dripping urine and fecal matter on the floor and appeared ready to die of shame.

I doubted that Mrs. Bradshaw meant to die of that condition, but she plainly felt it almost as acutely as did Sophronia. She went white with shock, then her face flamed anew. She turned on her heel and stamped out, slamming the door behind her.

"I'll take that as a 'yes,' then," I said to the door, and turned to the girl, smiling in reassurance. "Here, sweetheart. Let's have a look at the trouble, shall we?"

Vesicovaginal fistula and *rectovaginal fistula. I'd known that from the first moment; I just didn't know how bad they might be or how far up the vaginal canal they'd occurred. A fistula is a passage between two things that ought never to be joined and is, generally speaking, a bad thing.*

Claire can repair the damage, but lacking twentieth-century instruments and given the girl's age, she needs to perform the surgery abdominally—which means making ether again. This is terribly dangerous—but necessary.

As she walks the streets of Savannah, considering the prospect, she runs into William Ransom, who is surprised but grudgingly glad to see her, nonetheless. He explains his business—and that he is tracking Captain Ezekiel Richardson, whom he strongly suspects of having something to do with his cousin's disappearance.

"I've been searching for him for the last three months," he said, putting down his cup and wiping his mouth with the back of his hand. "He's an elusive scoundrel. And I don't know that he's in Savannah at all, for that matter. But the last hint I had of him was in Charleston, and he left there three weeks ago, heading south.

"Now, for all I know, the fellow's bound for Florida or has already taken ship for England. On the other hand . . . Amaranthus is here, or at least I believe so. Richardson seems to take an inordinate interest in the Grey family and its connections, so perhaps . . . Do you know Denys Randall yourself, by the way?"

He was looking at me intently over his cup, and I realized, with a faint sense of amusement mingled with outrage, that he had thrown the name at me suddenly in hopes of surprising any guilty knowledge I might have.

Why, you little scallywag, *I thought, amusement getting the upper hand.* You need a bit more practice before you can pull off that sort of thing, my lad.

Claire knows a few things about Denys Randall—including a few things that Denys himself doesn't know—but none of these is likely to be helpful to William's inquiries, and they part with an exchange of addresses, just in case.

The males of the family supplement their meager income by fishing and hunting in the nearby swamps—where one night they witness a sinister arrival:

"I got it, I got it!" [Germain] shouted, and splashed into the water, heedless of the alligator. He bent to see that his prey was firmly transfixed, let out another small whoop, and pulled up his spear, displaying a catfish of no mean size, belly showing white in its frantic flapping, blood running in trickles from the holes made by the tines.

"More meat on that than on yon wee lizard there, aye?" Ian took the spear, pulled the fish off, and bashed its head with the hilt of his knife to kill it.

Everyone looked, but the alligator had departed, alarmed by the kerfuffle.

"Aye, that's us fettled, I think." Jamie picked up both bags—one half full of bullfrogs, and the other still squirming slightly from the inclusion of a number of shrimp and crayfish netted from the shallows. He held open the one with the frogs for Ian to toss the fish inside, saying a verse from the Hunting Blessing, for Germain: "Thou shalt not eat fallen fish nor fallen flesh / Nor one bird that thy hand shall not bring down / Be thou thankful for the one / Though nine should be swimming."

Germain was not paying attention, though; he was standing quite still, fair hair lifting in the breeze, his head turned.

"Look, Grand-père,*" he said, voice urgent. "Look!"*

They all looked and saw the ships, far out beyond the marsh but coming in, heading for the small headland to the south. Seven, eight, nine . . . a dozen at least, with red lanterns at their masts, blue ones at the stern. Jamie felt the hair rise on his body and his blood go cold.

"British men-of-war," Fergus said, his voice empty with shock.

"They are," Jamie said. "We'd best get home."

With battle impending and a British occupation of the city imminent, Fergus and Jamie hide the printing press at a distant farm. Military matters make little difference to medical urgencies, though, and Claire has fortunately discovered a source of ether. She is preparing for the operation on Sophronia when she receives an unexpected visitor—Captain, now Colonel, Richardson, late of the British army and now in the employ of the Americans.

"Your most humble servant, ma'am. Have no alarm; I merely wished to make sure we weren't interrupted."

"Yes, that's what I'm alarmed about,*" I said, taking a firm grip on the saw. "Unbolt that bloody door this minute."*

He looked at me for a moment, one eye narrowed in calculation, but then uttered a short laugh and, turning, pulled the bolt. Folding his arms, he leaned against the door.

"Better?"

"Much." I let go the saw but didn't move my hand far from it. "I repeat—what do you want?"

"Well, I thought perhaps the time had come to lay my cards upon your table, Mrs. Fraser—and see whether you might want to play a hand or two."

"The only thing I might be inclined to play with you, Colonel, is mumblety-peg," I said, tapping my fingers on the handle of the saw. "But if you want to show me your cards, go right ahead. You want to be quick about it, though—I have an operation to conduct in less than an hour."

* * *

"For the third—and last—time," I said. "What do you bloody want?"

"Your help," he said promptly. "I'd originally had it in mind to use you as an agent in place. You could have been very valuable to me, moving in the same social circles as the British high command. But you seemed too unstable—forgive me, ma'am—to approach immediately. I hoped that as your grief over your first husband faded, you would come to a state of resignation in which I might seek your acquaintance and by degrees achieve a state of intimacy in which you could be persuaded to discover small—and, at first, seemingly innocent—bits of information, which you would pass on to me."

"Just what do you mean by 'intimacy'?" I said, folding my arms. Because while the word in current parlance often meant merely friendship, he hadn't used it with that intonation at all.

"You're a very desirable woman, Mrs. Fraser," he said, looking me over in an objectionably appraising way. "And one who knows her desirability. His lordship obviously wasn't obliging you in that regard, so . . ." He lifted a shoulder, smiling in a deprecating fashion. "But as General Fraser has returned from the dead, I imagine you're no longer susceptible to lures of that kind."

I laughed and dropped my arms.

"You flatter yourself, Colonel," I said dryly. "If not me. Look: why not stop trying to fluster me and tell me what you want me to do and why on earth you think I'd do it."

Richardson reveals that he is well aware of Lord John's homosexuality and that he is seeking to control Hal's influence in the House of Lords by controlling as many members of Hal's family as possible—either by blackmail or more directly.

"Were he fiercely committed to one extreme or the other, he would be difficult to . . . influence. While I don't know His Grace well, everything I know of him indicates that he values his sense of honor—"

"He does."

"—almost as much as he values his family," Richardson finished. He looked directly at me, and for the first time I felt a flicker of real fear.

"I have for some time been working to acquire influence—whether direct or otherwise—over such members of the duke's family as are within my reach. With, say, a son—a nephew?—perhaps even his brother in my control, it would then be possible to affect His Grace's public position, in whatever way seemed most advantageous to us."

"If you're suggesting what I think you're suggesting, then I suggest you leave my sight this instant," I said, in what I hoped was a

tone of calm menace. Though I spoiled whatever effect there might have been by adding, "Besides, I have absolutely no connection with any of Pardloe's family now."

He smiled faintly, with no sense of pleasantry at all.

"His nephew, William, is in the city, ma'am, and you were seen speaking with him nine days ago. Perhaps you are unaware, though, that both Pardloe and his brother are here, as well?"

"Here?" My mouth hung open for an instant and I closed it sharply. "With the army?"

He nodded.

"I gather that in spite of your recent . . . marital rearrangement? . . . you remain on good terms with Lord John Grey."

"Sufficiently good that I would do nothing whatever to deliver him into your bloody hands, if that's what you had in mind."

"Nothing so crude, ma'am," he assured me, with a brief flash of teeth. "I had in mind only the transmission of information—in both directions. I intend no damage at all to the duke or his family; I only wish to—"

Whatever his intentions, they were interrupted by a tentative knock on the door, which then opened to admit Mrs. Bradshaw's head. She looked apprehensively at me and suspiciously at Richardson, who cleared his throat, stood up, and bowed to her.

"Your servant, ma'am," he said. "I was just taking my leave of Mrs. Fraser. Good day to you." He turned and bowed to me, more elaborately. "Your most humble servant, Mrs. Fraser. I look forward to seeing you again. Soon."

"I'll just bet you do," I said, but far enough under my breath that I doubted he heard me.

A BRIEF, DECISIVE battle has ended with the British—as expected—in control of the city. While billeting arrangements are made, though, the army, under Lieutenant Colonel Archibald Campbell, is camped over several acres outside the city. William, headed for Saperville, where the elusive Amaranthus Cowden is said to be living, debates the wisdom of walking through the camp but, with a mental shrug, decides that the risk of being recognized is low—and even if someone he knows should pop up, what of it? He's no longer a soldier.

He would have passed right by her, thinking she was a part of the bog, for she was curled over in a tight ball and the hood of her sad-colored cloak covered her head. But she made a tiny sound, a heartbroken whimper that stopped him in his tracks, and he saw her then, crouched in the mud at the foot of a sweet gum.

"Ma'am?" he said tentatively. She hadn't been aware of him; she uncurled suddenly, her white face staring up at him, shocked and tear-streaked. Then she gulped air and leapt to her feet, throwing herself at him.

"Wiyum! Wiyum!" It was Fanny, Jane's sister, alone, daubed with mud, and in a state of complete hysteria. She'd catapulted into his arms; he gripped her firmly, holding her lest she fly to pieces, which she looked very like doing.

"Frances. Frances! It's all right; I'm here. What's happened? Where's Jane?"

At her sister's name, she gave a wail that made his blood go cold and buried her face in his chest. He patted her back and, this failing to help, then shook her a little.

"Frances! Pull yourself together. Sweetheart," he added more gently, seeing her swimming, red-rimmed eyes and swollen face. She'd been weeping for a long time. "Tell me what's happened, so I can help you."

"You can't," she blubbered, and thumped her forehead hard against his chest, several times. "You can't, you can't, nobody can, you can't*!"*

In fact, Fanny is very likely right. The girls, growing restive at the Quaker settlement and feeling that Harkness's death is safely distant, have taken up with the army again—after all, the only profitable occupation Jane has is as a whore. But she has been recognized and arrested, and Fanny fears that Jane is about to be hanged.

William tells Fanny to take refuge with her friends, while he goes to find his stepfather and uncle. This he does, but Hal is on bad terms with Colonel Campbell, and Jane has already confessed to Harkness's murder; even Lord John's famous diplomatic skills are futile.

William, having no idea where else to go for help, goes to Jamie. Leaving Fanny in Claire's care, the two men set out to rescue Jane from the house where she's being held.

"Is the young woman's life worth yours?" Fraser asked. "Because I think that consideration is likely what lies behind your—your other kinsmen's"—the corner of his mouth twitched, though William couldn't tell whether with humor or distaste—"failure to help ye."

William felt hot blood rise in his face, anger supplanting desperation.

"They didn't fail *me. They couldn't help. Are you saying that you will not help me, either, sir? Or can't? Are you afraid of the venture?"*

Fraser gave him a quelling look; William registered this but didn't care. He was on his feet, fists clenched.

"Don't bother, then. I'll do it myself."

"If ye thought ye could, ye'd never have come to me, lad," Fraser said evenly.

They succeed in disabling the sentry, breaking into the house and into the room where Jane is being held—but too late.

The candle was standing on a small bureau, its flame flickering wildly in the draft from the open door. There was a strong smell of beer; a broken bottle lay on the floor, brown glass a-glitter in the wavering light. The bed was rumpled, bedclothes hanging half off the mattress . . . Where was Jane? He whirled, expecting to see her cowering in the corner, frightened by his entrance.

He saw her hand first. She was lying on the floor by the bed, beside the broken bottle, her hand flung out, white and half open as though in supplication.

"A Dhia," *Fraser whispered behind him, and now he could smell the cut-steel reek of blood, mingled with beer.*

He didn't remember falling on his knees or lifting her up in his arms. She was heavy, limp and awkward, all the grace and heat of her gone and her cheek cold to his hand. Only her hair was still Jane, shining in the candlelight, soft against his mouth.

"Here, a bhalaich.*" A hand touched his shoulder, and he turned without thought.*

Fraser had pulled the mask down around his neck, and his face was serious, intent. "We havena much time," he said softly.

Lord John manages the claiming of Jane's body on behalf of her sister and arranges a private funeral.

We buried Jane on the morning of a dull, cold day. The sky was sodden with low gray clouds, and a raw wind blew in from the sea.

It was a small private burying ground, belonging to a large house that stood outside the city.

All of us came with Fanny: Rachel and Ian, Jenny, Fergus and Marsali—even the girls and Germain. I worried a bit; they couldn't help but feel the echoes of Henri-Christian's death. But death was a fact of life and a common one, and while they stood solemn and pale amongst the adults, they were composed. Fanny was not so much composed as completely numb, I thought; she'd wept all the tears her small body could hold and was white and stiff as a bleached stick.

John came, dressed in his uniform (in case anyone became inquisitive and tried to disturb us, he explained to me in an undertone). The coffin-maker had had only adult coffins to hand; Jane's shrouded body looked so like a chrysalis, I half-expected to hear a dry rattling sound when the men picked it up. Fanny had declined to look upon her sister's face one last time, and I thought that was as well.

There was no priest or minister; she was a suicide, and this was ground hallowed only by respect. When the last of the dirt had been shoveled in, we stood quiet, waiting, the harsh wind flurrying hair and our garments.

Jamie took a deep breath and a step to the head of the grave. He spoke the Gaelic prayer called the Death Dirge, but in English, for the sake of Fanny and Lord John.

Thou goest home this night to thy home of winter,
To thy home of autumn, of spring, and of summer;
Thou goest home this night to thy perpetual home,
To thine eternal bed, to thine eternal slumber.

Sleep thou, sleep, and away with thy sorrow,
Sleep thou, sleep, and away with thy sorrow,
Sleep thou, sleep, and away with thy sorrow,
Sleep, thou beloved, in the Rock of the fold.

The shade of death lies upon thy face, beloved,
But the Jesus of grace has His hand round about thee;
In nearness to the Trinity farewell to thy pains,
Christ stands before thee and peace is in His mind.

Jenny, Ian, Fergus, and Marsali joined in, murmuring the final verse with him.

Sleep, O sleep in the calm of all calm,
Sleep, O sleep in the guidance of guidance,
Sleep, O sleep in the love of all loves,
Sleep, O beloved, in the Lord of life,
Sleep, O beloved, in the God of life!

It wasn't until we turned to go that I saw William. He was standing just outside the wrought-iron fence that enclosed the burying ground, tall and somber in a dark cloak, the wind stirring the dark tail of his hair. He was holding the reins of a very large mare with a back as broad as a barn door. As I came out of the burying ground, holding Fanny's hand, he came toward us, the horse obligingly following him.

"This is Miranda," he said to Fanny. His face was white and carved with grief, but his

voice was steady. "She's yours now. You'll need her." He took Fanny's limp hand, put the reins into it, and closed her fingers over them. Then he looked at me, wisps of hair blowing across his face. "Will you look after her, Mother Claire?"

"Of course we will," I said, my throat tight. "Where are you going, William?"

He smiled then, very faintly.

"It doesn't matter," he said, and walked away.

In the aftermath of Jane's death, some things are decided. Claire has told Lord John about Richardson the turncoat and the threat he poses to the Grey family—and to Lord John himself. With the city occupied for the foreseeable future, there's no chance of re-establishing the printing business; the family will go north, with Fergus and Marsali taking up residence in Charleston, and Jamie and Claire, with Ian, Rachel, Jenny, Fanny, and Germain (at Marsali's request, she fearing lest he be caught up in war) proceeding on to Wilmington, where they can equip themselves for the final journey up into the mountains—home.

With the city safely occupied, Lord John and Hal can turn their attention once more to personal matters, and they pay a call on the house in Saperville where William has told them the mysterious Amaranthus lives.

It was a good, solid door; Hal flung himself at it shoulder-first and rebounded as though made of India rubber. Barely pausing, he raised his foot and slammed the flat of his boot sole against the panel, which obligingly splintered but didn't break inward.

Wiping his face on his sleeve, he eyed the door and, catching the flicker of movement through the splintered paneling, called out, "Young woman! We have come to rescue you! Stand well away from the door!

"Pistol, please," he said, turning to John with his hand out.

"I'll do it," John said, resigned. "You haven't any practice with doorknobs."

Whereupon, with an air of assumed casualness, he drew the pistol from his belt, aimed carefully, and shot the doorknob to pieces. The boom of the gun evidently startled the room's inhabitants, for a dead silence fell. He gently pushed the stem of the shattered knob through the door; the remnants of the knob thunked to the floor on the other side, and he pushed the door cautiously open.

Hal, nodding his thanks, stepped forward through the wisps of smoke.

It was a small room, rather grimy, and furnished with no more than a bedstead, stool, and washstand. The stool was particularly noticeable, as it was being brandished by a wild-eyed young woman, clutching a baby to her breast with her other hand.

An ammoniac reek came from a basket in the corner, piled with dirty clouts; a folded quilt in a pulled-out drawer showed where the baby had been sleeping, and the young woman was less kempt than her mother would have liked to see, her cap askew and her pinny stained. Hal disregarded all matters of circumstance and bowed to her.

"Do I address Miss Amaranthus Cowden?" he said politely. "Or is it Mrs. Grey?"

John gave his brother a disparaging look and turned a cordial smile on the young woman.

*"*Viscountess *Grey," he said, and made a leg in courtly style. "Your most humble servant, Lady Grey."*

The young woman looked wildly from one man to the other, stool still raised, clearly unable to make head or tail of this invasion, and finally settled on John as the best—if still dubious—source of information.

"Who are *you?" she asked, pressing her back against the wall. "Hush, darling." For the baby, recovered from shock, had decided to grizzle.*

John cleared his throat.

"Well . . . this is Harold, Duke of Pardloe, and I am his brother, Lord John Grey. If our information is correct, I believe we are, respectively, your father-in-law and your uncle by marriage. And, after all," he remarked, turning to Hal, "how many people in the colonies do you think there could possibly be named Amaranthus Cowden?"

"She hasn't yet said she is *Amaranthus Cowden," Hal pointed out. He did, however, smile at the young woman, who reacted as most women did, staring at him with her mouth slightly open.*

"May I?" John reached forward and took the stool gently from her unresisting hand, setting it on the floor and gesturing her to take a seat. "What sort of name is Amaranthus, may I ask?"

She swallowed, blinked, and sat down, clutching the baby.

"It's a flower," she said, sounding rather dazed. "My grandfather's a botanist. It could have been worse," she added more sharply, seeing John smile. "It might have been Ampelopsis or Petunia."

"Amaranthus is a very beautiful name, my dear—if I may call you so?" Hal said, with grave courtesy. He wiggled a forefinger at the baby, who had stopped grizzling and was staring at him warily. Hal pulled his officer's gorget off over his head and dangled the shiny object, close enough for the child to grab—which he did.

"It's too large to choke him," Hal assured Amaranthus. "His father—and his father's brothers—all teethed on it. So did I, come to that." He smiled at her again. She was still white-faced but gave him a wary nod in response.

"What is the little fellow's name, my dear?" John asked.

"Trevor," she said, taking a firmer hold on the child, now completely engrossed in trying to get the demilune gorget—half the size of his head—into his mouth. "Trevor Grey." She looked back and forth between the Grey brothers, a frown puckering her brows. Then she lifted her chin and said, enunciating clearly, "Trevor . . . Wattiswade *. . . Grey. Your Grace."*

"So you are Ben's wife." A little of the tension left Hal's shoulders. "Do you know where Ben is, my dear?"

Her face went stiff, and she clutched the baby tighter.

"Benjamin is dead, Your Grace," she said. "But this is his son, and if you don't mind . . . we should quite like to come with you."

WILLIAM IS FINISHED. With the army, with women, with his family—with one exception. There is one small item of business to be accomplished before he leaves Savannah. He comes to the warehouse where James Fraser is at work, to take his leave—and ask one question.

"I want to know what happened," William said. "When you lay with my mother. What happened that night? If it was *night," he added, and then felt foolish for doing so.*

Fraser eyed him for a moment.

"Ye want to tell me *what it was like, the first time ye lay with a woman?"*

Jamie declines entirely to tell William the details of his conception but does tell him what he really wants to know.

". . . But that's not what ye want *to know, in any case," he said. "Ye want to know, did I force your mother. I did not. Ye want to know, did I love your mother. I did not."*

William let that lie there for a moment, controlling his breathing 'til he was sure his voice would be steady.

"Did she love you?" It would have been easy to love him. *The thought came to him unbidden—and unwelcome—but with it, his own memories of Mac the groom. Something he shared with his mother.*

Fraser's eyes were cast down, watching a trail of tiny ants running along the scuffed floorboards.

"She was verra young," he said softly. "I was twice her age. It was my fault."

And in the course of the conversation, they reach the bottom line:

"Are you sorry?" he said, and made no effort to keep his voice from shaking. "Are you sorry for it, damn you?"

Fraser had turned away; now he turned sharply to face William but didn't speak at once. When he did, his voice was low and firm.

"She died because of it, and I shall sorrow for her death and do penance for my part in it until my own dying day. But—" He compressed his lips for an instant, and then, too fast for William to back away, came round the table and, raising his hand, cupped William's cheek, the touch light and fierce.

"No," he whispered. "No! I am not sorry." Then he whirled on his heel, threw open the door, and was gone, kilt flying.

PART 9: "*THIG CRIOCH AIR AN T-SAOGHAL ACH MAIRIDH CEOL AGUS GAOL.*" ("THE WORLD MAY COME TO AN END, BUT LOVE AND MUSIC WILL ENDURE.")

The Frasers, at last, are coming home. As they climb higher and higher into the mountains, Claire feels herself surrounded by the scents and sights of the wilderness, and the feel of home rises in her blood. As they come to the head of the pass into Fraser's Ridge, they find Joseph Wemyss, an old friend and tenant, waiting for them, with his eldest grandson, Rodney; Joseph and Rodney welcome the Frasers and share the news of the Ridge and its people as they walk on, past the places they have known, past the place where the Big House once stood, before it burned.

Just before we came to the spot where the trail ended above the clearing, Jamie and Mr. Wemyss stopped, waiting for Rodney and me to catch up. With a shy smile, Mr. Wemyss kissed my hand and then took Rodney's, saying, "Come along, Roddy, you can be first to tell your mam that Himself and his lady have come back!"

Jamie took my hand and squeezed it hard. He was flushed from the walk, and even more from excitement; the color ran right down into the open neck of his shirt, turning his skin a beautiful rosy bronze.

"I've brought ye home, Sassenach," he said, his voice a little husky. "It willna be the same—and I canna say how things will be now—but I've kept my word."

He has, and nothing else seems needed. But something else is given, nonetheless:

My throat was so choked that I could barely whisper "Thank you." We stood for a long moment, clasped tight together, summoning up the strength to go around that last corner and look at what had been, and what might be.

Something brushed the hem of my skirt, and I looked down, expecting that a late cone from the big spruce we were standing by had fallen.

A large gray cat looked up at me with big, calm eyes of celadon green and dropped a fat, hairy, very dead wood rat at my feet.

"Oh, God*!" I said, and burst into tears.*

The Frasers and their entourage settle quickly into the life of the North Carolina mountains: there's much to be done before summer fades and the autumn comes. A new Big House to raise, food to gather, hunt, and preserve—and a few small, necessary things.

Fanny's frenulum, for one. The frenulum, a small band of elastic tissue that fastens the tongue to the floor of the mouth, is what's causing Fanny to be tongue-tied. Claire luckily can put this right with a tiny snip of scissors—and does, freeing Fanny and welcoming her to her new home and family.

But not everything can be gathered or made. Claire and Jenny, with Ian, Rachel (very pregnant), and Germain, make the four-day trip to Beardsley's trading post, to buy necessities like salt and needles and luxuries like barley sugar and pickles.

But a trading post provides more than goods for sale or barter; it's a gathering place, where one might meet friends—or some long-lost echo of the past. Ian meets Mrs. Sylvie, a prostitute of his acquaintance, along with her two young bodyguards.

He'd thought they were boys when he'd met them: a pair of feral Dutch orphans named—they said—Herman and Vermin, and they thought *their last name was Kuykendall. In the event, they'd turned out to be in actuality Hermione and Ermintrude. He'd found them a temporary refuge with . . . oh, Christ.*

"God, please, no!" he said in Gaelic, causing Rachel to look at him in alarm.

Surely they weren't still with . . . but they were. He saw the back of a very familiar head—and a still more familiar arse—over by the pickle barrel.

He glanced round quickly, but there was no way out. The Kuykendalls were approaching fast. He took a deep breath, commended his soul to God, and turned to his wife.

"Do ye by chance recall once tellin' me that ye didna want to hear about every woman I'd bedded?"

"I do," she said, giving him a deeply quizzical look. "Why?"

"Ah. Well . . ." He breathed deep and got it out just in time. "Ye said ye did *want me to tell ye if we should ever meet anyone that I . . . er—"*

"Ian Murray?" said Mrs. Sylvie, turning round. She came toward him, a look of pleasure on her rather plain, bespectacled face.

"Her," Ian said hastily to Rachel, jerking his thumb in Mrs. Sylvie's direction before turning to the lady.

"Mrs. Sylvie!" he said heartily, seizing her by both hands in case she might try to kiss him, as she had occasionally been wont to do upon their meeting. "I'm that pleased to see ye! And

even more pleased to present ye to my . . . er . . . wife."

Ian is not the only one surprised by an old acquaintance, though. As Claire and Jenny stroll the grounds, considering the purchase of chickens or a couple of young goats, Claire sees a man.

At first, I had no idea who he was. None. But the sight of the big, slow-moving man froze me in my tracks and my stomach curled up in instant panic.

No, *I thought.* No. He's dead; they're all dead.

He was a sloppily built man, with sloping shoulders and a protruding stomach that strained his threadbare waistcoat, but big. Big. I felt again the sense of sudden dread, of a big shadow coming out of the night beside me, nudging me, then rolling over me like a thundercloud, crushing me into the dirt and pine needles.

Martha.

A cold wind swept over me, in spite of the warm sunshine I stood in.

"Martha," *he'd said. He'd called me by his dead wife's name and wept into my hair when he'd finished.*

This is the man who raped her during her abduction nearly six years before—a man she thought had been killed, along with the other kidnappers. Finding him alive, well—and right in front of her—is more than she can deal with. But deal with it she does.

I was not going to be bloody sick. I wasn't. With that decision made, I calmed a little. I hadn't let him or his companions kill my spirit at the time; whyever would I let him harm me now?

He moved away from the pigs, and I followed him. I wasn't sure why *I was following him but felt a strong compulsion to do so. I wasn't afraid of him; logically, there was no reason to be. At the same time, my unreasoning body still felt the echoes of that night, of his flesh and fingers, and would have liked to run away. I wasn't having that.*

She follows the man, steeling herself, becoming accustomed to the sight of him—thinking, all the time, what will happen if she tells Jamie that one man escaped. She concludes that she can live with the knowledge of this man; he's no threat to her now, and she doesn't want to be responsible for Jamie having to kill the man—she knows he won't consider any other form of action—and risk possible repercussions, or spiritual damage, for that matter.

But Claire has a glass face, and a sharp-eyed sister-in-law. On the way back, Jenny and Claire are separated for a while from Ian and Rachel, and Jenny worms the truth out of Claire.

She sipped and nodded approvingly. "Who was the dirty fat lumpkin that scairt ye at Beardsley's?"

I choked on the whisky, swallowed it the wrong way, and nearly coughed my lungs out in consequence. Jenny put down the flask, kirtled up her skirts, and waded into the creek, sousing her hankie in the cold water; she handed it to me, then cupped water in her hand and poured a little into my mouth.

"Lucky there's plenty of water, as ye said," she remarked. "Here, have a bit more." I nodded, eyes streaming, but pulled up my skirts, got down on my knees, and drank for myself, pausing to breathe between mouthfuls, until I stopped wheezing.

"I wasna in any doubt, mind," Jenny said, watching this performance. "But if I had been, I wouldn't be now. Who is he?"

"I don't bloody know," I said crossly, climbing back on my rock. Jenny wasn't one to be daunted by tones of voice, though, and merely raised one gull-wing-shaped brow.

CLAIRE IS OBLIGED to explain the circumstances, and Jenny understands. She tells Claire about one of her daughters and how they dealt with an instance of rape—in that case, her daughter chose to keep the secret and bear the resulting child as her husband's, because the rapist was her husband's brother, and to do otherwise would tear the entire family apart, as well as risk her husband's life. This, she observes, is rather different.

I thought about it, after everyone had rolled up in their blankets and begun snoring that night. Well . . . I hadn't stopped *thinking about it since I'd seen the man. But in light of the story that Jenny had told me, my thoughts began to clarify, much as throwing an egg into a pot of coffee will settle the grounds.*

The notion of saying nothing was of course the first one to come to my mind and was still my intent. The only difficulty—well, there were two, to be honest. But the first one was that, irritating as it was to be told so repeatedly, I couldn't deny the fact that I had a glass face. If anything was seriously troubling me, the people I lived with immediately began glancing at me sideways, tiptoeing exaggeratedly around me—or, in Jamie's case, demanding bluntly to know what the matter was.

Jenny had done much the same thing, though she hadn't pressed me for details of my experience. Quite plainly, she'd guessed the outlines of it, though, or she wouldn't have chosen to tell me Maggie's story. It occurred to me belatedly to wonder whether Jamie had *told her anything about Hodgepile's attack and its aftermath.*

The underlying difficulty, though, was my own response to meeting the dirty fat lumpkin. I snorted every time I repeated the description to myself, but it actually helped. He was a man, and not a very prepossessing one. Not a monster. Not . . . not bloody worth *making a fuss about. God knew how he'd come to join Hodgepile's band—I supposed that most criminal gangs were largely composed of feckless idiots, come to that.*

And . . . little as I wanted to relive that experience . . . I did. He hadn't come to me with any intent of hurting me, in fact hadn't hurt me (which was not to say that he hadn't *crushed me with his weight, forced my thighs apart, and stuck his cock into me . . .).*

I unclenched my teeth, drew a deep breath, and started over.

He'd come to me out of opportunity—and need.

"Martha," *he'd said, sobbing, his tears and snot warm on my neck.* "Martha, I loved you so."

Could I forgive him on those grounds? Put aside the unpleasantness of what he'd done to me and see him only as the pathetic creature that he was?

If I could—would that stop him living in my mind, a constant burr under the blanket of my thoughts?

I put back my head, looking up at the deep black sky swimming with hot stars. If you knew they were really balls of flaming gas, you could imagine them as van Gogh saw them, without difficulty . . . and looking into that illuminated void, you understood why people have always looked up into the sky when talking to God. You need to feel the immensity of something very much bigger than yourself, and there it is—immeasurably vast, and always near at hand. Covering you.

Help me, *I said silently.*

I never talked to Jamie about Jack Randall. But I knew from the few things he told me—and the disjointed things he said in the worst of his dreams—that this was how he had chosen to survive. He'd forgiven Jack Randall. Over and over. But he was a stubborn man; he could do it. A thousand times, and still one more.

Help me, *I said, and felt tears trickle down my temples, into my hair.* Please. Help me.

For a time, Claire's resolve works. Aided by the distractions of life—such as pinworm infestations and the work of building the new house—she's able to forgive, and forgive, and sometimes to forget. But Jamie knows her far too well.

"THERE'S NOTHING WRONG," *I said, for probably the tenth time. I picked at a scab of bark still clinging to the timber I sat on. "It's perfectly all right. Really."*

Jamie was standing in front of me, the cove and the clouded sky bright behind him, his face shadowed.

"Sassenach," he said mildly. "I'm a great deal more stubborn than you are, and ye ken that fine. Now, I know something upset ye when ye went to Beardsley's place, and I know ye dinna want to tell me about it. Sometimes I ken ye need to fettle your mind about a matter before ye speak, but you've had time and more to do that—and I see that whatever it is is worse than I thought, or ye'd have said by now."

Well aware that Jamie can't let such a matter lie, Claire asks him instead not to force her to tell him, to accept that it's her responsibility to forgive injustice—she thinks she can—and leave things there.

He unwillingly agrees—for the moment—and things seem to be at rest. But as Jenny warned Claire during their conversation, *"Ye canna have been marrit to a Hieland man all these years and not ken how deep they can hate."*

THE NEXT EVENING, Jamie and Claire come up to their building site, for a bit of privacy. They make tender love to each other and fall asleep enmeshed—but when Claire wakes in the morning—

I BLOODY KNEW. *From the moment I woke to birdsong and a cold quilt beside me, I knew. Jamie often rose before dawn, for hunting, fishing, or travel—but he invariably touched me before he left, leaving me with a word or a kiss. We'd lived long enough to know how chancy life could be and how swiftly people could be parted forever. We'd never spoken of it or made a formal custom of it, but we almost never parted without some brief token of affection.*

And now he'd gone off in the dark, without a word.

"You bloody, bloody man!*" I said, and thumped the ground with my fist in frustration.*

The birth of Rachel's baby—a boy—is a considerable distraction, and when Jamie returns three days later with a large buck behind his saddle, Claire is able to greet him with a fair show of equanimity. But neither has ever been able to lie to the other, even by omission, and an honest conversation ensues:

"And if ye could forgive him, he needn't die,

ye're saying? That's like a judge lettin' a murderer go free, because his victim's family forgave him. Or an enemy soldier sent off wi' all his weapons."

"I am not a state at war, and you are not my army!"

He began to speak, then stopped short, searching my face, his eyes intent.

"Am I not?" he said quietly.

I opened my mouth to reply but found I couldn't. The birds had come back, and a gang of house finches chittered at the foot of a big fir that grew at the side of the clearing.

"You are," I said reluctantly, and, standing up, wrapped my arms around him. He was warm from his work, and the scars on his back were fine as threads under my fingers. "I wish you didn't have to be."

"Aye, well," he said, and held me close. After a bit, we walked hand in hand to the biggest pile of barked timber and sat down. I could feel him thinking but was content to wait until he had formed what he wanted to say. It didn't take him long. He turned to me and took my hands, formal as a man about to say his wedding vows.

"Ye lost your parents young, mo nighean donn, *and wandered about the world, rootless. Ye loved Frank"—his mouth compressed for an instant, but I thought he was unconscious of it—"and of course ye love Brianna and Roger Mac and the weans . . . but, Sassenach—I am the true home of your heart, and I know that."*

He lifted my hands to his mouth and kissed my upturned palms, one and then the other, his breath warm and his beard stubble soft on my fingers.

"I have loved others, and I do love many, Sassenach—but you alone hold all my heart, whole in your hands," he said softly. "And you know that."

They work in close amity through the day, building, and sit down in the afternoon, surveying the Ridge below them and resting in the sense of being home at last. On the far side of the clearing below, four people emerge from the head of the wagon road, on foot. A tall man, a tall woman, and two children, one a boy with bright-red hair.

"Look, the lad's got red hair," Jamie said, smiling and raising his chin to point. "He minds me of Jem."

"So he does." Curious now, I got up and rummaged in my basket, finding the bit of silk in which I kept my spectacles when not wearing them. I put them on and turned, pleased as I always was to see fine details spring suddenly into being. Slightly less pleased to see that what I had thought was a scale of bark on the timber near where I'd been sitting was in fact an enormous centipede, enjoying the shade.

I turned my attention back to the newcomers, though; they'd stopped—the little girl had dropped something. Her dolly—I could see the doll's hair, a splotch of color on the ground, even redder than the little boy's. The man was wearing a pack, and the woman had a large bag over one shoulder. She set it down and bent to pick up the doll, brushing it off and handing it back to her daughter.

The woman turned then to say something to her husband, throwing out an arm to point to something—the Higginses' cabin, I thought. The man put both hands to his mouth and shouted, and the wind carried his words to us, faint but clearly audible, called out in a strong, cracked voice.

"Hello, the house!"

I was on my feet, and Jamie stood and grabbed my hand, hard enough to bruise my fingers.

Movement at the door of the cabin, and a small figure that I recognized as Amy Higgins appeared. The tall woman pulled off her hat and waved it, her long red hair streaming out like a banner in the wind.

"Hello, the house!" she called, laughing.

Then I was flying down the hill, with Jamie just before me, arms flung wide, the two of us flying together on that same wind.

THE END

Grey Family Tree

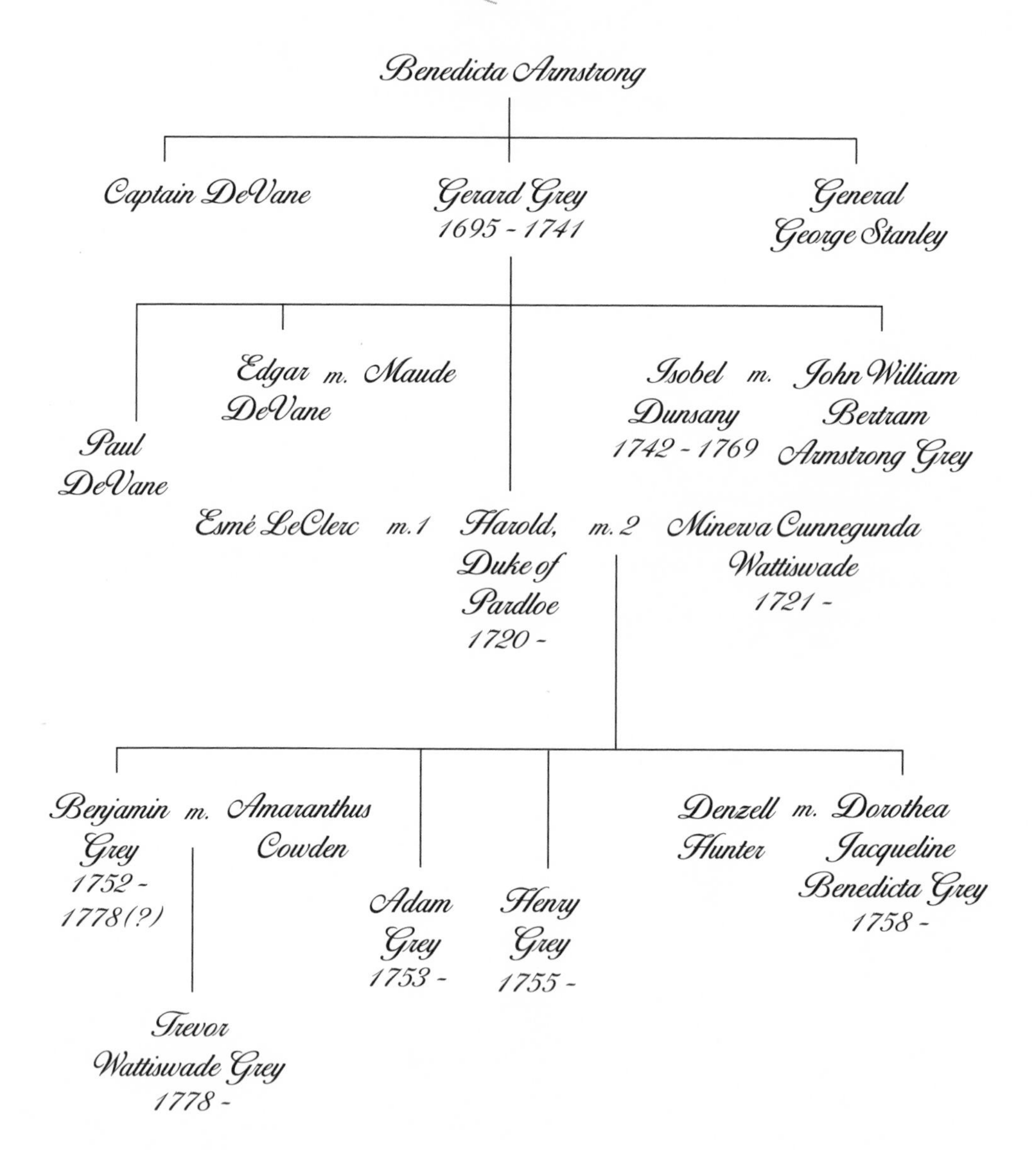

The Lord John Series

I always have mixed feelings about referring to these books as a separate "series." The Lord John novels and novellas are very much an integral part of the bigger, overall *Outlander* story. At the same time, these books are undeniably shaped and focused differently than are the "Jamie and Claire" (to simplify the references) Big Books.

As the name suggests, Lord John Grey is the central figure (though not always the only one) in these stories, and for various reasons his novels are structured roughly as historical mysteries. He isn't himself a time traveler, nor does he—at this point in his career, at least—believe in any such far-fetched notions, so his books don't have the science-fiction component[1] that the Big Books do. They do, however, tend to have disconcerting whiffs of the supernatural; Lord John is one of those very rational men whose sense of logic and order attracts things likely to disturb rationality, logic, and order.

Still, he's a man of his time, that time being the second half of the eighteenth century. A time of intellectual ferment, geographic exploration, and wild social upheavals. Who better to deal with such things than the educated younger son of a noble house, who's taken up the traditional second son's profession of soldiering?

Lord John appeared for the first time—briefly, but memorably—in *Dragonfly in Amber,* the second of the main *Outlander* novels. He was sixteen at the time, a very young soldier on his first campaign with his elder brother's regiment, in search of Highland rebels.

He finds one, in the person of the notorious "Red Jamie" Fraser. This Highland brigand is engaged in conversation with an obviously well-born Englishwoman, whom the Highlander has presumably kidnapped, either for ransom or immoral purposes—possibly both, the reputation of Hielandmen being what it is.

With no help to hand, the young man determines to kill or disable Fraser and rescue this woman, as is his honorable duty. He hasn't actually tried to kill anyone before, though, and his first effort is less successful than he anticipates. He ends up with a broken arm, the captive of a disheveled and rather irritated Highlander, who wants answers and wants them now. As a British soldier, Lord John naturally refuses to tell this Jacobite scoundrel anything, though the

[1] *And I do indeed mean science fiction, not fantasy. The time travel in the* Outlander *series has a (theoretical) scientific basis and works on standard principles of energy and space; it's not "magic," as various ill-informed reviewers and copywriters are prone to put it.*

man threatens him and goes so far as to burn him with the hot blade of a dirk. These are the risks of war, after all.

The man has even less conscience than Grey assumed, though, and declares that he will ravish the Englishwoman right before John's eyes if John doesn't start talking. He then ties up the woman and rips the bodice off her shoulders, exposing her breasts.

Dreadfully shocked by this behavior, as well as physically shocked and in pain, John gives the necessary information: who he is (though some instinct of concealment makes him use his first middle name of William, just in case this poltroon has heard of Lord John Grey . . .), where his brother's troops are, and what they're doing—i.e., bringing cannon to the aid of General Cope, who proposes to engage the Highland army in battle.

It then turns out that the Englishwoman is actually Fraser's *wife,* and while she does talk Fraser out of killing John, the humiliation of having been hoodwinked into betraying his brother, his regiment, and his king is enough that John would much prefer to have been shot. Fraser, though, directs his men to tie John to a tree along the direction of march of his brother's regiment, ensuring that he'll be found in the morning. And while John is thus unavoidably detained and unable to warn anyone, Fraser and his men raid the camp, steal the wheels of the caissons required to transport the cannon, and burn them.

Understandable, then, that the next time we meet John Grey in the context of the main novels (early in *Voyager*), some ten years later, his feelings toward Jamie Fraser are exigent and hostile. The situation is complicated by the fact that John is now the governor of Ardsmuir Prison, a remote and desolate pile of rock used for the incarceration of Jacobite prisoners—and Jamie Fraser is one of those prisoners.

This is a cleft stick for a man of honor: to have a man for whom he feels the deepest hatred completely at his mercy—but to be prevented by his office and sense of duty from taking revenge on a helpless prisoner, whose care is his responsibility. At first, the situation is eased a bit by Fraser's apparent lack of recognition of Grey—he is, after all, ten years older, no longer a callow boy—and Grey manages to treat the man with a decent respect as the *de facto* leader of the Jacobite prisoners. And while Grey keeps Fraser in irons, they develop a wary cooperation, meeting weekly over dinner in Lord John's quarters to discuss problems and needs of the prisoners.

As his knowledge of and respect for Fraser deepen, though, John is disquietingly aware that something else is deepening, as well. John is homosexual, a condition punishable by death in England at the time, and has in fact been exiled to Ardsmuir as a means of getting him out of London in the wake of a near scandal. He's almost forgotten George Everett, the man with whom he was involved in London—but his physical attraction to Jamie Fraser is becoming alarmingly intense. The emotional tenor of their relationship has also changed, with Fraser's revelation that he did indeed recognize John—and that he had honored his bravery and sense of duty when they met those years before, in the darkness of the Carryarrick Pass.

Things come to a head one evening when the atmosphere of congeniality over their usual game of chess leads John to take a major risk:

The bishop made a soft thump as he set the felted base down with precision. Without stopping, his hand rose, as though it moved without his volition. The hand traveled the short distance through the air, looking as though it knew precisely what it wanted, and set itself on Fraser's, palm tingling, curved fingers gently imploring.

The hand under his was warm—so warm—but hard, and motionless as marble. Nothing moved on the table but the shimmer of the flame in the heart of the sherry. He lifted his eyes then, to meet Fraser's.

"Take your hand off me," Fraser said, very, very softly. "Or I will kill you."

This encounter irrevocably—or so it seems—changes the relationship between the two men. Still, when the prison is closed and the prisoners transported to the sugar plantations of the West Indies, Jamie Fraser is not among them. John Grey arranges a situation for him as groom at a large estate in the Lake District. He will still be a prisoner, kept captive by his word rather than by walls, but at least he will have space, air, decent food, and horses. Jamie fails to appreciate the magnanimity of John's gesture; he's deeply depressed by the loss of the men whose care has kept him alive during the last few years. Now they've all been sent off to the equivalent of a slow—or not so slow—death sentence, leaving him racked with both survivor's guilt and loneliness. And an abiding resentment of Lord John Grey.

John, released from his own sentence as governor of Ardsmuir, returns to London—and that is where his own separate story begins:

LORD JOHN AND THE HELLFIRE CLUB

[Author's Note: Like most of the critical events of my literary life, the Lord John stories began by accident. In this instance, the accidental agency was a British editor named Maxim Jakubowski, who invited me to write a short story for his upcoming anthology of historical crime, this to feature such stars of the genre as Anne Perry, Steven Saylor, and Ellis Peters.

Well, I thought, the company is flattering, and it would be an interesting technical challenge to see if I can write something shorter than 300,000 words. Sure—why not?[2] *And so I wrote "Hellfire" for the anthology* Past Poisons, *published in 2001.]*

"Hellfire" (later retitled as *"Lord John and the Hellfire Club"*) begins in 1756, shortly after Lord John's return to London in the wake of the closing of Ardsmuir Prison. Not surprisingly, Jamie Fraser is still somewhat on his mind, and thus he's taken by surprise (and an instant sense of attraction) when he glimpses a red-haired man in the hallway of his club, the Society for Appreciation of the

[2] *I was born with a couple of risky genes: one of them causes a reflexive "Says who?" in response to any statement of a personally questionable nature, and the other causes an equally reflexive "Why not?" in response to any invitation that seems certain to offer challenge and/or bizarre complexity.*

English Beefsteak. The man is having a disagreement with an older man, which ends in the red-haired young man turning his back and stamping into the club's drawing room, where he encounters Lord John and his good friend Harry Quarry, a colonel of his regiment.

The red-haired man is Robert Gerald, Harry's cousin, and a junior secretary to the prime minister. He pushes aside Harry's questions regarding his conversation with Bubb-Dodington, the man he was arguing with in the corridor.

"Bubb-Dodington, surely? The man's a voice like a costermonger."

"I—he—yes, it was." Mr. Gerald's pale skin, not quite recovered from its earlier excitement, bloomed afresh, to Quarry's evident amusement.

"Oho! And what perfidious proposal has he made you, young Bob?"

"Nothing. He—an invitation I did not wish to accept, that is all. Must you shout so loudly, Harry?" It was chilly at this end of the room, but Grey thought he could warm his hands at the fire of Gerald's smooth cheeks.

Quarry snorted with amusement, looking around at the nearby chairs.

"Who's to hear? Old Cotterill's deaf as a post, and the General's half dead. And why do you case in any case, if the matter's so innocent as you suggest?" Quarry's eyes swiveled to bear on his cousin by marriage, suddenly intelligent and penetrating.

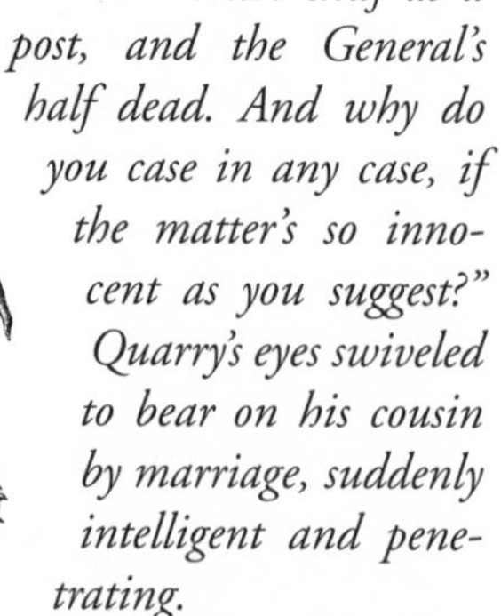

"I did not say it was innocent," Gerald replied dryly, regaining his composure. "I said I declined to accept it. And that, Harry, is all you will hear of it, so desist this piercing glare you turn upon me. It may work on your subalterns, but not on me."

The conversation turns to other matters, but Lord John is aware that Mr. Gerald's attention is drawn to him—and that the junior secretary is debating some course of action. As the men take leave of each other later, Gerald draws Lord John aside.

"I impose intolerably, sir," Gerald said, moving close enough to keep his low-voiced words from the ears of the servant who kept the door. "I would ask your favor, though, if it be not entirely unwelcome?"

"I am completely at your command, I do assure you," Grey said, feeling the warmth of claret in his blood succeeded by a rush of deeper heat.

"I wish—that is, I am in some doubt regarding a circumstance of which I have become aware. Since you are so recently come to London—that is, you have the advantage of perspective, which I must necessarily lack by reason of familiarity. There is no one . . ." He fumbled for words, then turned eyes grown suddenly and deeply unhappy on Lord John. "I can confide in no one!" he said in a sudden, passionate whisper. He gripped Lord John's arm, with surprising strength. "It may be nothing, nothing at all. But I must have help."

"You shall have it, if it be in my power to give." Grey's fingers touched the hand that grasped his arm; Gerald's fingers were cold. Quarry's voice echoed down the corridor behind them, loud with joviality.

"The 'Change, near the Arcade," Gerald said rapidly. "Tonight, just after full dark." The grip on Grey's arm was gone, and Gerald vanished, the soft fall of his hair vivid against his blue cloak.

Lord John sets about doing necessary errands, awaiting darkness with keen anticipation. However, his anticipation is forestalled; while he and Harry Quarry are having a drink at the Beefsteak, their attention is drawn suddenly to an altercation in the street outside. A snarl of traffic has stranded several sedan chairs, and a man emerging from one of these is attacked, stabbed by someone in the crowd. The victim is Robert Gerald, and while Harry and Lord John rush out to render assistance, their help comes too late. John is only in time to hold the dying man in his arms.

Brown eyes fixed wide on his, a spark of recognition deep behind the shock and pain. He seized the dying man's hand in his, and chafed it, knowing the futility of the gesture. Gerald's mouth worked, soundless. A bubble of red spittle swelled at the corner of his lips.

"Tell me." Grey bent urgently to the man's ear, and felt the soft brush of hair against his mouth. "Tell me who has done it—I will avenge you. I swear it."

He felt a slight spasm of the fingers in his, and squeezed back, hard, as though he might force some of his own strength into Gerald; enough for a word, a name.

The soft lips were blanched, the blood bubble growing. Gerald drew back the corners of his mouth, a fierce, tooth-baring rictus that burst the bubble and sent a spray of blood across Grey's cheek. Then the lips drew in, pursing in what might have been the invitation to a kiss. Then he died, and the wide brown eyes went blank.

John's quest to discover the truth of Gerald's death leads him through the tangles of London politics and then into the catacombs of Medmenham Abbey, where the notorious Sir Francis Dashwood's Hellfire Club holds court—and where the secrets of his own life prove as dangerous as those of the mad monks of Medmenham.

LORD JOHN AND THE PRIVATE MATTER

London, June 1757

The Society for the Appreciation of the English Beefsteak, a Gentlemen's Club

It was the sort of thing one hopes momentarily that one has not really seen—because life would be so much more convenient if one hadn't.

What Lord John Grey has just seen (while engaged in a private moment behind the screen that hides the chamber pots) is incontrovertible evidence that the Honorable Joseph Trevelyan is suffering from the French pox—syphilis. While this would ordinarily be reason for mild shock and perhaps sympathy, in the present instance it's rather a problem for his lordship. Trevelyan is engaged to Grey's young cousin, Olivia.

While wondering what the devil to do about the situation, Grey runs into Malcolm Stubbs, a member of his regiment, who tells him that he, Stubbs, is on the way to visit the widow of one Sergeant Timothy O'Connell, recently killed in a street brawl. While mildly surprised—knowing O'Connell, Grey would have given long odds on him in a fight that was even halfway fair—his lordship has other things to think about.

He discusses the matter with his good friend Harry Quarry, who has a few suggestions, these of varying appeal:

Quarry raised both brows.

"The first thing is make certain of it, eh, before you stink up the whole of London with a public accusation. I take it you don't want to make overtures to the man yourself, in order to get a better look."

Quarry grinned widely, and Grey felt the blood rise in his chest, washing hot up his neck. "No," he said shortly. Then he collected himself and lounged back a little in his chair. "Not my sort," he drawled, flicking imaginary snuff from his ruffle.

Quarry guffawed, his own face flushed with a mixture of claret and amusement. He hiccuped, chortled again, and slapped both hands down on the table.

"Well, whores ain't so picky. And if a moggy will sell her body, she'll sell anything else she has—including information about her customers."

Grey stared blankly at the Colonel. Then the suggestion dropped into focus.

"You are suggesting that I employ a prostitute to verify my impressions?"

"You're quick, Grey, damn quick." Quarry nodded approval, snapping his fingers for more wine. "I was thinking more of finding a girl who'd seen his prick already, but your way's a long sight easier. All you've got to do is invite Trevelyan along to your favorite convent, slip the lady abbess a word—and a few quid—and there you are!"

What with one thing and another, Lord John is not much in the habit of visiting brothels—at least, not the sort in which female flesh is purveyed. Still, he's reluctant to cause a huge scandal without absolute certainty . . .

The discovery that Sergeant O'Connell was murdered comes as almost a relief—though the concomitant revelations of spying and the theft of secret military requisitions are worrying. They become much more so when Grey is charged with investigating both matters. Distracted by such urgencies, Grey is reluctantly reminded that he must do Something about Olivia's fiancé.

"Speakin' of Cornishmen, what have you done about your putative cousin-in-law? Arranged to take him to a brothel yet?"

"He says he doesn't go to brothels," Grey replied tersely, recalled unwillingly to the matter of his cousin's marriage. Christ, weren't spies and suspected murder enough?

"And you're letting him marry your cousin?" Quarry's thick brows drew down. "How d'ye know he's not impotent, or a sodomite, let alone diseased?"

"I am reasonably sure," Lord John said, repressing the sudden insane urge to remark that, after all, the Honorable Mr. Trevelyan had not been watching him *at the chamber pot.*

He had called on Trevelyan earlier in the day, with an invitation to supper and various libidinous "amusements" to bid a proper farewell to Trevelyan's bachelorhood. Trevelyan had agreed with thanks to a cordial supper, but claimed to have promised his mother upon her deathbed to have nothing to do with prostitutes.

Quarry's shaggy brows shot up.

"What sort of mother talks about whores on her deathbed? Your mother wouldn't do that, would she?"

"I have no idea," Grey said. "The situation has fortunately not arisen. But I suppose," he said, attempting to divert the conversation, "that surely there are *men who do not seek such recreation. . . ."*

Quarry gave him a look of jaundiced doubt. "Damn few," he said. "And Trevelyan ain't one of 'em."

"You seem sure of it," Grey said, slightly piqued.

"I am." Quarry settled back, looking pleased with himself. "Asked around a bit—no, no, I was quite discreet, no need to fret. Trevelyan goes to a house in Meacham Street. Good taste; been there meself."

Aided by his new valet, a resourceful young gent named Tom Byrd (who has his own reasons for wanting to find out more about the Honorable Mr. Trevelyan), a fourteen-year-old whore named Agnes (who appreciates a man who'd rather sleep with her than fornicate with her), Harry, and young Malcolm Stubbs, Lord John sets out boldly to learn the truth—and as so often happens in such cases, learns a great deal more than he's bargained for.

There's the heel print on Sergeant O'Connell's face, for starters—and the black eyes and split lip on Mrs. O'Connell's face. Then there's the dead woman in a green velvet dress, found in St. James's Park—and later found to be a man. In the end, money and love are at the root of things—but a very unexpected love indeed.

LORD JOHN AND THE SUCCUBUS

[Author's Note: In 2003, I was invited to write a novella for an anthology edited by Robert Silverberg, titled *Legends II: New Short Novels by the Masters of Modern Fantasy.* I had slight reservations—as my World of Warcraft–playing son asked, seeing the contract, "Since when are you a master of modern fantasy, Mom?"—but a) was very flattered to be asked to share a volume with George R. R. Martin, Terry Brooks, and Orson Scott Card, and b) I'm inclined to regard the notion of literary genres in the same light as a Chinese menu, and c) if I had a family motto, it would probably be "Why Not?" (The accompanying coat of arms being a stone circle quartered on a field of azure and crimson with rampant hippogriffs.) So I did.

However, I had the same concerns regarding the main characters of the *Outlander* books that obtained when I wrote "Hellfire." Reflecting that it had worked once, so why not?, I decided to call Lord John into active duty once more.

The difficulty being, of course, that Lord John is not a time traveler, a telepath, a shape-shifter, or even an inhabitant of an alternate universe loosely based on the history and culture of Scotland or Turkestan. But, on the other hand, there was no requirement that the main character of this putative novella be himself a creature of fantasy—and a story in which a perfectly normal (well, more or less) hero comes into conflict with supernatural creatures is a solid archetype. Hey, if it was good enough for Homer, it's good enough for me.

Set in Germany (which didn't exist in a political sense but was a recognizable geographical region) during the early phases of the Seven Years' War, "Succubus" is a supernatural murder mystery with military flourishes.]

GREY'S SPOKEN GERMAN *was improving by leaps and bounds, but found itself barely equal to the present task.*

After a long, boring day of rain and paperwork, there had come the sound of loud dispute in the corridor outside his office, and the head of Lance-Korporal Helwig appeared in his doorway, wearing an apologetic expression.

"Major Grey?" he said. "Ich habe ein kleines Englische problem."

A moment later, Lance-Korporal Helwig had disappeared down the corridor like an eel sliding into mud, and Major John Grey, English liaison to the Imperial Fifth Regiment of Hanoverian Foot, found himself adjudicating a three-way dispute among an English private, a gypsy prostitute, and a Prussian tavern owner.

Having resolved the situation, Major

Grey resumes a quick letter to his brother, outlining his present situation:

. . . I am quartered with several other English and German officers in the house of a Princess Louisa von Lowenstein . . .

We have two English regiments quartered here: Sir Peter Hicks's 35th, and half of the 52nd—I am told Colonel Ruysdale is in command, but have not yet met him . . .

French forces are reported to be within twenty miles, but we expect no immediate trouble. Still, so late in the year, the snow will come soon and put an end to the fighting; they may try for a final thrust before the winter sets in. Sir Peter begs me send his regards . . .

Lord John is up to his neck in requisitions when a welcome interruption occurs.

Captain Stephan von Namtzen, Landgrave von Erdberg, poked his handsome blond head through the doorway, ducking automatically to avoid braining himself on the lintel. The gentleman following him had no such difficulty, being a foot or so shorter.

"Captain von Namtzen," Grey said, standing politely. "May I be of assistance?"

"I have here Herr Blomberg," Stephan said in English, indicating the small, round, nervous-looking individual who accompanied him. "He wishes to borrow your horse."

Grey was sufficiently startled by this that he merely said, "Which one?" rather than "Who is Herr Blomberg?" or "What does he want with a horse?"

* * *

"Herr Blomberg is the bürgermeister of the town," Stephan explained, taking matters in a strictly logical order of importance, as was his habit. "He requires a white stallion, in order that he shall discover and destroy a succubus. Someone has told him that you possess such a horse," he concluded, frowning at the temerity of whoever had been bandying such information.

"A succubus?" Grey asked, automatically rearranging the logical order of this speech, as was his *habit.*

With Stephan's assistance, Lord John learns that the town of Gundwitz has been suffering mysterious and disturbing events: numbers of young men (many of them soldiers quartered in the town) have been claiming to have been victimized in their sleep by a young woman of demonic aspect. By the time these events made their way to the attention of Herr Blomberg, the situation was serious. A man had died.

Not only a man but a soldier, and not merely a soldier but one of the Prussian cavalrymen under Stephan's command. Obviously, something must be done.

The unraveling of the mystery of the night hag (as the Germans refer to the succubus) leads to murder, spying, military maneuvers (as the French troops nearby begin to move, threatening Schloss Lowenstein), ancient evil, and present treachery—to say nothing of Lord John's personal entanglements, between his growing (and possibly mutual) attraction to Stephan von Namtzen and the evident attraction of the Princess Louisa to *him.* Add in the penis of St. Orgevald, and you have more than enough to keep one British major busy.

LORD JOHN AND THE BROTHERHOOD OF THE BLADE

London, January 1758

The Society for Appreciation of the English Beefsteak, A Gentlemen's Club

To the best of Lord John Grey's knowledge, stepmothers as depicted in fiction tended to be venal, evil, cunning, homicidal, and occasion-

ally cannibalistic. Stepfathers, by contrast, seemed negligible, if not completely innocuous.

"Squire Allworthy, do you think?" he said to his brother. "Or Claudius?"

Hal stood restlessly twirling the club's terrestrial globe, looking elegant, urbane, and thoroughly indigestible. He left off performing this activity, and gave Grey a look of incomprehension.

"What?"

"Stepfathers," Grey explained. "There seem remarkably few of them among the pages of novels, by contrast to the maternal variety. I merely wondered where Mother's new acquisition might fall, along the spectrum of character."

Hal's nostrils flared. His own reading tended to be confined to Tacitus and the more detailed Greek and Roman histories of military endeavor. The practice of reading novels he regarded as a form of moral weakness; forgivable, and in fact, quite understandable in their mother, who was, after all, a woman. That his younger brother should share in this vice was somewhat less acceptable.

However, he merely said, "Claudius? From Hamlet*? Surely not, John, unless you happen to know something about Mother that I do not."*

Grey was reasonably sure that he knew a number of things about their mother that Hal did not, but this was neither the time nor place to mention them.

A "brother of the blade" was eighteenth-century slang for a soldier—and the Greys have been soldiers since Hal and John's father raised a regiment to defend his king against the Jacobites in 1715, receiving a dukedom in reward for his loyalty.

But it's been seventeen years since Lord John's late father, the Duke of Pardloe, was found dead, a pistol in his hand and accusations of his role as a Jacobite agent staining his family's honor. Hal refuses to use his father's tainted title, keeping instead the earlier family title, Earl of Melton. But now Hal has mysteriously received a page of their late father's missing diary—and John is convinced that someone is taunting the Grey family with secrets from the grave.

And there's also a new brother to consider: Percy Wainwright, who John had met briefly (in *Lord John and the Private Matter*) in circumstances making it clear that Percy shares John's own proclivities in the matter of sexual attraction. Percy's stepfather is now marrying Benedicta Grey, dowager Duchess of Pardloe, and Hal and John's mother.

By the time the pudding arrived, though, cordial relations appeared to have been established on all fronts. Sir George had replied satisfactorily to all Hal's questions, seeming quite untroubled by the intrusive nature of some of them. In fact, Grey had the feeling that Sir George was privately rather amused by his brother, though taking great care to ensure that Hal was not aware of it.

Meanwhile, he and Percy Wainwright had discovered a mutual enthusiasm for horse-racing, the theater, and French novelists—a discussion of this last subject causing his brother to mutter, "Oh, God!" beneath his breath and order a fresh round of brandy.

Snow had begun to fall outside; in a momentary lull in the conversation, Grey heard the whisper of it against the window, though the heavy drapes were closed against the winter's chill, and candles lit the room. A pleasant shiver ran down his back at the sound.

"Do you find the room cold, Lord John?" Wainwright asked, noticing.

He did not; there was an excellent fire, roaring away in the hearth and constantly kept up by the ministrations of the Beefsteak's servants. Beyond that, a plentitude of hot food, wine, and brandy ensured sufficient warmth. Even now, the steward was bringing in cups of mulled wine, and a Caribbean hint of cinnamon spiced the air.

"No," he replied, taking his cup from the proffered tray. "But there is nothing so pleasant as being inside, warm and well-fed, when the elements are hostile without. Do you not agree?"

"Oh, yes." Wainwright's eyelids had gone heavy, and he leaned back in his chair, his clear skin flushed in the candlelight. "Most . . . pleasant." Long fingers touched his neckcloth briefly, as though finding it a little tight.

Awareness floated warm in the air between them, heady as the scents of cinnamon and wine. Hal and Sir George were beginning to make noises indicative of leave-taking, with many expressions of mutual regard.

Percy's long dark lashes rested for a moment on his cheek, and then swept up, so that his eyes met Grey's.

"Perhaps you would be interested to come with me to Lady Jonas's salon—Diderot will be there. Saturday afternoon, if you are at liberty?"

So, shall we be lovers, then?

"Oh, yes," said Grey, and touched the linen napkin to his mouth. His pulse throbbed in his fingertips. "I think so."

Well, *he thought,* I don't suppose it's really incest, *and pushed his chair back to arise.*

Percy joins the family regiment, as well as the family, and John's relationship with him deepens—only to come apart disastrously in Germany, where the regiment has been sent to fight. Percy is arrested for the crime of sodomy, threatened with hanging if convicted.

John's anguish over the situation is superseded, though, by more-pressing matters: the Battle of Crefeld, in the course of which he's separated from his troops, nearly captured, and ends up taking command of a cannon crew whose captain has just been spectacularly decapitated by a bouncing enemy cannonball. Lord John and his crew fight their gun heroically, until said gun explodes, killing part of the crew and ending John's further involvement in the battle.

As he slowly recovers from his wounds, John returns to his interrupted investigations into his father's death and wrestles with the dilemma of what—if anything—to do about Percy. At last, he turns to the only man who—ironically—he can speak to frankly: his prisoner, Jamie Fraser.

He's well aware that Fraser hates him. At the same time, Fraser is the only man who knows the truth of John's sexuality—but cannot reveal it to anyone—and who John knows to be an honest man who will give him an honest answer. Jamie *does* give John the honesty he requires to make the necessary difficult decisions he's facing—but the subsequent exchange of frankness results in an explosion that apparently ruptures the fragile relations between the two men for good.

Still, John now sees the path before him and manages both to save Percy and to discover the ultimate truth behind his father's death.

Reginald Holmes, head steward of White's Chocolate House, was spending a peaceful late evening in going over the members' accounts in his office. He had just rung the bell for a waiter to bring him another whisky to facilitate this task when the sounds of an ungodly rumpus reached him from the public rooms below, shouts, cheers, and the noise of overturning furniture causing him to upset the ink.

"What's going on now, *for God's sake?" he asked crossly, mopping at the puddle with his handkerchief as one of the waiters appeared in his doorway. "Do these men never sleep? Bring me a cloth, Bob, will you?"*

"Yes, sir." The waiter bowed respectfully. "The Duke of Pardloe has arrived, sir, with his brother. The duke's respects, sir, and he would like you to come and witness the settling of a wager in the book."

"The Duke of—" Holmes stood up, forgetting the ink on his sleeve. "And he wants to settle a wager?"

"Yes, sir. His Grace is very *drunk, sir," the waiter added delicately. "And he's brought a number of friends in a similar condition."*

"Yes, I hear." Holmes stood for a moment, considering. Disjoint strains of "For He's a Jolly Good Fellow" reached him through the floor. He took up his accounts ledger and his quill, and turned to the page headed Earl of Melton. *Drawing a neat line through this, he amended the heading to* Duke of Pardloe, *and with a flourish, inserted beneath it a new item reading,* Breakages.

LORD JOHN AND THE HAUNTED SOLDIER

[Author's Note: I'm indebted to Outlander *Wiki for the first part of this excellently concise summary.]*

In November 1758, following the events of June in *Brotherhood of the Blade,* the surviving members of the gun crew manning the cannon "Tom Pilchard" at Crefeld are brought before a board of inquiry, including Lord John Grey.

Grey, who commanded the cannon crew upon the abrupt death of Lt. Philip Lister, is both troubled and insulted by the questioning, and stalks out of the inquiry. He does see the remains of the burst cannon, and briefly presents a missing piece; shrapnel from the gun that had been removed from his chest by surgeons, but Grey refuses to surrender it. Eventually, this piece will be the only remaining evidence that the cannons were poorly manufactured. At least one piece of metal remains in Grey's chest, and this along with residual damage leave Grey with severe chest pains and uncontrolled shaking.

Harry Quarry warns Grey about Col. Twelvetrees's willingness to use the cannon inquiry to goad John into action that will be used to discredit either him, his brother Hal, or both. He suggests Grey be seconded to the 65th or 78th regiments temporarily to stay out of Twelvetrees's way for a while, but Grey instead begins to investigate the cannon failures himself.

When Grey returns Lt. Lister's sword to the man's father, the elder Lister begs Grey's assistance in locating the missing fiancée and child of his late son. While on these tasks, he discovers political intrigue surrounding his half-brother's government contract for supplying black powder to the military, and meets Captain Fanshawe and the other members of Edgar's consortium.

GREY WRITES ON two occasions to his paroled charge, James Fraser; starkly honest confessions of his cares and worries that are never sent, but serve to help ground Grey's thoughts and emotions. Here is an excerpt from *Lord John and the Haunted Soldier*:

It was very late, but John Grey was not yet asleep. He sat by the fire in his quarters in the barracks, the distant sounds of the night watch outside his window, writing steadily.

. . . and so it is ended. You may imagine the difficulties of discovering a wet-nurse in an army barracks in the middle of the night, but Tom Byrd has arranged matters and the child is cared for. I will send to Simon Coles tomorrow, that he may undertake the business of bringing the boy to his family—perhaps such an ambassage will pave the way for him in his courtship of Miss Barbara. I hope so.

I cling to the thought of Simon Coles. His goodness, his idealism—foolish though it may be—is a single bright spot in the dark quagmire of this wretched business.

God knows I am neither ignorant nor innocent of the ways of the world. And yet I feel unclean, so much evil as I have met tonight. It weighs upon my spirit; thus I write to cleanse myself of it.

He paused, dipped the pen, and continued.

I do believe in God, though I am not a religious man such as yourself. Sometimes I wish I were, so as to have the relief of confession. But I am a rationalist, and thus left to flounder in disgust and disquiet, without your positive faith in ultimate justice.

Between the cold consciencelessness of the government and the maniac passion of Marcus Fanshawe, I am left almost to admire the common, ordinary, self-interested evil of Neil Stapleton; he is so nearly virtuous by contrast.

He paused again, hesitating, bit the end of the quill, but then dipped it and went on.

A strange thought occurs to me. There is of course no point of similarity between yourself and Stapleton in terms of circumstance or character. And yet there is one peculiar commonality. Both you and Stapleton know. And for your separate reasons, cannot or will not speak of it to anyone. The odd result of this is that I feel quite free in the company of either one of you, in a way that I cannot be free with any other man.

You despise me; Stapleton would use me. And yet, when I am with you or with him, I am myself, without pretense, without the masks that most men wear in commerce with their fellows. It is . . .

He broke off, thinking, but there really was no way to explain further what he meant.

. . . most peculiar, *he finished, smiling a little despite himself.*

As for the army and the practice of war, you will agree, I think, with Mr. Lister's assertion that it is a brutal occupation. Yet I will remain a soldier. There is hard virtue in it, and a sense of purpose that I know no other way of achieving.

He dipped the pen again, and saw the slender splinter of metal that lay on his desk, straight as a compass needle, dully a-gleam in the candlelight.

My regiment is due to be reposted in the spring; I shall join them, wherever duty takes me. I shall, however, come to Helwater again before I leave.

He stopped, and touched the metal splinter with his left hand. Then wrote,

You are true north.

Believe me ever your servant, sir,
John Grey

He sanded the letter and shook it gently dry, folded it, and taking the candlestick, dripped wax upon the edge and pressed his ring into the warm soft wax to seal it. The smiling crescent moon of his signet was sharp-cut, clear in the candlelight. He set down the candlestick, and after weighing the letter in his hand for a moment, reached out and touched the end of it to the flame.

It caught, flared up, and he dropped the flaming fragment into the hearth. Then, standing, shucked his banyan, blew out the candle, and lay down, naked in the dark.

THE SCOTTISH PRISONER

There are only two compensations to Jamie Fraser's life as a paroled Jacobite prisoner of war in the remote Lake District: he's not cutting sugar cane in the West Indies, and he has access to William, his illegitimate (and very secret) son, otherwise known as the Ninth Earl of Ellesmere. His quiet life comes suddenly apart with the appearance of Tobias Quinn, an Irishman and an erstwhile comrade from the Rising.

Some Jacobites were killed; others, like Jamie, imprisoned or transported. Others escaped. And many of them didn't give up. Quinn still burns with passion for the Stuart cause, and he has a Plan. A singularly dangerous plan, involving Jamie Fraser and an ancient relic of Irish kingship—the sacred cup of the Druid king.

Jamie has had enough of politics, enough of war—and more than enough of the Stuarts. He's having none of it.

IN LONDON, LORD John Grey has brought home from Quebec a packet of papers that might as well have come equipped with a fuse, so explosive are their contents. Material collected by a recently deceased friend, the papers document a damning case of corruption and murder against a British officer, Major Gerald Siverly. For the sake of his friend, and his own honor as a soldier, John is determined to bring Siverly to justice.

John's brother, Hal, the Duke of Pardloe, takes this cause as his own and enlists the help of his wife, Minnie, a retired spy in her own right. The Greys show Minnie a mysterious document from the dangerous docket—what appear to be verses, written in a language they don't recognize. Minnie does recognize the language. It's Erse, she tells the brothers. The language spoken by Irishmen and Scottish Highlanders.

Erse. The word gave Grey a very odd sensation. Erse was what folk spoke in the Scottish Highlands. It sounded like no other language he'd ever heard—and barbarous as it was, he was rather surprised to learn that it existed in a written form.

Hal was looking at him speculatively. "You must have heard it fairly often, at Ardsmuir?"

"Heard it, yes. Almost all the prisoners spoke it." Grey had been governor of Ardsmuir prison for a brief period; as much exile as appointment, in the wake of a near scandal. He disliked thinking about that period of his life, for assorted reasons.

"Did Fraser speak it?"

Oh, God, *Grey thought.* Not that. Anything but that.

"Yes," he said, though. He had often overheard James Fraser speaking in his native tongue to the other prisoners, the words mysterious and flowing.

"When did you see him last?"

"Not for some time." Grey spoke briefly, his voice careful. He hadn't spoken to the man in more than a year.

Not careful enough; Hal came round in front of him, examining him at close range, as though he might be an unusual sort of Chinese jug.

"He is still at Helwater, is he not? Will you go and ask him about Siverly?" Hal said mildly.

"No."

"No?"

"I would not piss on him was he burning in the flames of hell," Grey said politely.

One of Hal's brows flicked upward, but only momentarily.

"Just so," he said dryly. "The question, though, is whether Fraser might be inclined to perform a similar service for you."

Grey placed his cup carefully in the center of the desk.

"Only if he thought I might drown," he said, and went out.

But needs must when the devil drives—and Lord John and Jamie are shortly unwilling companions on the road to Ireland, a country whose dark castles hold dreadful secrets and whose bogs hide the bones of the dead.

THE CUSTOM OF THE ARMY

London, 1759

All things considered, it was probably the fault of the electric eel. John Grey could—and for a time, did—blame the Honorable Caroline Woodford, as well. And the surgeon. And certainly that blasted poet. Still . . . no, it was the eel's fault.

After a high society electric-eel party leads to a duel that ends badly, Lord John Grey feels the need to lie low for a while. Conveniently, before starting his new commission in His Majesty's army, Lord John receives an urgent summons. An old friend from the military, Charlie Carruthers, is facing court-martial in Canada and has called upon Lord John to serve as his character witness. Grey voyages to the New World—a land rife with savages (many of them on his own side) and cleft by war—where he soon finds that he must defend not only his friend's life but his own.

Not that the New World does not offer its own interesting opportunities.

He woke abruptly, face-to-face with an Indian. His reflexive flurry of movement was met with a low chuckle and a slight withdrawal, rather than a knife across the throat, though, and he broke through the fog of sleep in time to avoid doing serious damage to the scout Manoke.

"What?" he muttered, and rubbed the heel of his hand across his eyes. "What is it?" And why the devil are you lying on my bed?

In answer to this, the Indian put a hand behind his head, drew him close, and kissed him. The man's tongue ran lightly across his lower lip, darted like a lizard's into his mouth, and then was gone.

So was the Indian.

He rolled over onto his back, blinking. A dream. It was still raining, harder now. He breathed in deeply; he could smell bear grease, of course, on his own skin, and mint—was there any hint of metal? The light was stronger—it must be day; he heard the drummer passing through the aisles of tents to rouse the men, the rattle of his sticks blending with the rattle of the rain, the shouts of corporals and sergeants—but still faint and gray. He could not have been asleep for more than half an hour, he thought.

"Christ," he muttered, and, turning himself stiffly over, pulled his coat over his head and sought sleep once again.

AS USUAL IN the life of a soldier, though, war tends to intrude upon one's personal affairs, and Lord John finds himself in a barque upon the night-black waters of the mighty St. Lawrence, assisting General James Wolfe and an officer named Simon Fraser, in command of a party of Highlanders, who plan to make a daring assault on the Citadel of Quebec by climbing a sheer cliff—in the dark.

The scrabblings and gruntings grew fainter and abruptly ceased. Wolfe, who had been sitting on a boulder, stood up, straining his eyes upward.

"They've made it," he whispered, and his fists curled in an excitement that Grey shared. "God, they've made it!"

Well enough, and the men at the foot of the cliff held their breaths; there was a guard post at the top of the cliff. Silence, bar the everlasting noise of tree and river. And then a shot.

Just one. The men below shifted, touching their weapons, ready, not knowing for what.

Were there sounds above? Grey could not tell and, out of sheer nervousness, turned aside to urinate against the side of the cliff. He was fastening his flies when he heard Simon Fraser's voice above.

"Got 'em, by God!" he said. "Come on, lads—the night's not long enough!"

The next few hours passed in a blur of the most arduous endeavor Grey had seen since he'd crossed the Scottish Highlands with his brother's regiment, bringing cannon to General Cope. No, actually, he thought, as he stood in darkness, one leg wedged between a tree and the rock face, thirty feet of invisible space below him and rope burning through his palms with an unseen deadweight of two hundred pounds or so on the end, this was worse.

The Highlanders had surprised the guard, shot their fleeing captain in the heel, and made all of them prisoner. That was the easy part. The next thing was for the rest of the landing party to ascend to the cliff top, now that the trail—if there was such a thing—had been cleared. There they would make preparations to raise not only the rest of the troops now coming down the river aboard the transports but also seventeen battering cannon, twelve howitzers, three mortars, and all of the necessary encumbrances in terms of shell, powder, planks, and limbers necessary to make this artillery effective. At least, Grey reflected, by the time they were done, the vertical trail up the cliff side would likely have been trampled into a simple cow path.

As the sky lightened, Grey looked up for a moment from his spot at the top of the cliff, where he was now overseeing the last of the artillery as it was heaved over the edge, and saw the bateaux coming down again like a flock of swallows, they having crossed the river to collect an additional 1,200 troops that Wolfe had directed to march to Levi on the opposite shore, there to lie hidden in the woods until the Highlanders' expedient should have been proved.

A head, cursing freely, surged up over the edge of the cliff. Its attendant body lunged into view, tripped, and sprawled at Grey's feet.

"Sergeant Cutter!" Grey said, grinning as he bent to yank the little sergeant to his feet. "Come to join the party, have you?"

"Jesus fuck," replied the sergeant, belligerently brushing dirt from his coat. "We'd best win, that's all I can say." And, without waiting for reply, turned round to bellow down the cliff, "Come ON, you bloody rascals! 'Ave you all eaten lead for breakfast, then? Shit it out and step lively! CLIMB, God damn your eyes!"

The net result of this monstrous effort being that, as dawn spread its golden glow across the Plains of Abraham, the French sentries on the walls of the Citadel of Quebec gaped in disbelief at the sight of more than four thousand British troops drawn up in battle array before them.

A PLAGUE OF ZOMBIES

Lord John Grey, a lieutenant-colonel in His Majesty's army, arrives in Jamaica with orders to quash a slave rebellion brewing in the mountains. But a much deadlier threat lies close at hand. The governor of the island is being menaced by zombies, according to a servant. Lord John has no idea what a zombie is, but it doesn't sound good. It sounds even worse when hands smelling of grave dirt come out of the darkness to take him by the throat. Between murder in the governor's mansion and plantations burning in the mountains, Lord John will need the wisdom of serpents and the luck of the devil to keep the island from exploding.

A FOOTNOTE ON CHRONOLOGY AND OTHER NOVELLAS

The Lord John novellas and novels[3] are sequential but are built to stand alone; you don't need to read them in order.

In terms of their relationship to the larger *Outlander* novels: These books are part of the overall series but are focused for the most part on those times in Lord John's life when he's not "onstage" in the main novels. *The Scottish Prisoner,* in particular, focuses also on a part of Jamie Fraser's life not covered in the main novels.

All of the Lord John novels take place between 1756 and 1761 and in terms of the overall *Outlander* novels/timeline, they thus occur more or less in the middle of *Voyager.* So you can read any of them, in any order, once you've read *Voyager,* without getting lost.

---

[3] *There are also a couple of short stories—and will eventually be more—dealing with minor events, minor characters, and/or lacunae in the main books. These are presently published in various anthologies but will eventually be collected in book form.*

"A Leaf on the Wind of All Hallows" appears in the anthology Songs of Love and Death *(edited by George R. R. Martin and Gardner Dozois). This is a short story set in WWII that tells the story of what really happened to Roger MacKenzie's parents, Jerry and Dolly.*

"The Space Between" is a novella that appears in an anthology titled The Mad Scientist's Guide to World Domination *(edited by John Joseph Adams). This story is set mostly in Paris and involves Joan McKimmie (Marsali's younger sister), Michael Murray (Young Ian's older brother), the Comte St. Germain (no, of course he's not dead, don't be silly), and Mother Hildegarde.*

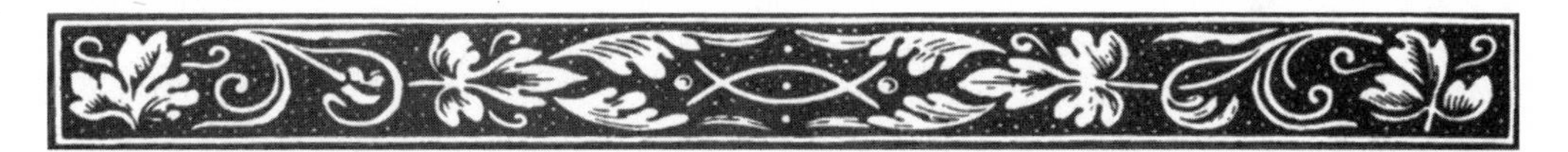

Lord John's Character

Well, the man's got a ruthless streak, though owing to being a younger brother, he observes this in full flower in his brother, Hal, and keeps his own in better check. He *doesn't* check his capacity for violence but has had either the good fortune or the good sense to let it loose (for the most part) in appropriate circumstances, such as on battlefields. He's very impulsive, but since he's usually acting from decent motives and is quick in his perceptions and actions, this usually doesn't lead him into serious trouble. ("Usually." *Vide* what he does when confronting a killer in *Brotherhood*.)

He's vulnerable to the sexual attraction of violence, too—see the chapter titled "Shame" in *Brotherhood*—but *is* ashamed when he gives way to it. I.e., he certainly has flaws but is also very self-aware (doubtless because of his double identity; *he* has to know who he really is, particularly since the world can't ever know), and that self-awareness usually preserves him from giving way to them. Not always, though. There are a couple of scenes in "The Custom of the Army" where he lets his impulses overpower his judgment—but, by and large, he knows what he's doing and takes the rap for it.

There are several threads that lead through John's life, regardless of where he is and what he's doing. Love of his family and fierce loyalty to them; a strong sense of duty, to his regiment, his country, and the king. And . . . Jamie Fraser. From the first moment these two men met, John remained intensely aware of Jamie, whether the awareness was hatred, sexual attraction, or (much later) the deepening of a solid friendship. But as he thinks to himself (in *A Plague of Zombies*):

> *He had lost one lover to death, another to betrayal. The third . . . His lips tightened. Could you call a man your lover, who would never touch you—would recoil from the very thought of touching you? No. But at the same time, what would you call a man whose mind touched yours, whose prickly friendship was a gift, whose character, whose very existence, helped to define your own?*

John isn't a victim, pining away from unrequited love. He finds love, as well as physical gratification, where he can. But he understands the need *to* love—to give of himself, rather than to demand the gift of another.

Like anyone, he has his flaws—but he has a good heart.[4]

[4] *(BTW, the fact that a particular person doesn't act in a given situation as* you *would doesn't necessarily mean they're wrong.)*

Part Three

Cast of Characters

This list includes all the characters from the second four novels and from the Lord John books, with brief notes as to which book each character is introduced in, who they are, their role in the story, and whether they're fictional or real historical persons (indicated by an "x").

All Big Books [All]

All Lord John [All LJ]

The Fiery Cross [*Fiery Cross*]

A Breath of Snow and Ashes [*Ashes*]

An Echo in the Bone [*Echo*]

Written in My Own Heart's Blood [*MOBY*]

Lord John and the Hellfire Club [*HF*]

Lord John and the Private Matter [*PM*]

Lord John and the Succubus [*SU*]

Lord John and the Brotherhood of the Blade [*BL*]

Lord John and the Haunted Soldier [*HS*]

The Custom of the Army [*CA*]

The Scottish Prisoner [*SP*]

A Plague of Zombies [*PZ*]

A Leaf on the Wind of All Hallows [*LW*]

The Space Between [*SB*]

A

Abbott, Mrs. Madge—Brothel owner in Philadelphia and Jane's former employer. [*MOBY*]

Abercrombie, Mrs.—A member of Reverend Wakefield's congregation, who runs to the Reverend (and Roger) for help when she thinks she's killed her husband with the steam iron he presented her with as an anniversary gift, causing Roger to think carefully about his wedding gift to Brianna. [*Fiery Cross*]

Aberfeldy, Billy—One of the tenants who accompanies the Frasers to the Ridge to homestead. [*Fiery Cross*]

Aberfeldy, Ruth, Mrs.—The wife of Billy Aberfeldy, newly arrived tenants who are living in cramped conditions with the Frasers and two other families, until a cabin can be built for the growing family. [*Fiery Cross*]

Abernathy, Arabella (aka Grannie Belly)—The granddaughter-in-law of Old Grannie Abernathy, family matriarch of the Abernathys on Fraser's Ridge. [*Ashes*]

Abernathy, Barnabas—Jamaican plantation owner of Rose Hall, supposedly killed by rioting slaves. [*PZ*]

Abernathy, Gail—Joe Abernathy's wife. [*MOBY*]

Abernathy, Geillis—See "Geillis Duncan."

Abernathy, Hugh—Member of the extensive Abernathy clan on Fraser's Ridge, he stands by Jamie's side during the heinous accusations voiced by Allan Christie regarding the murder of his sister, Malva. [*Ashes*]

Abernathy, Jocky—One of the extensive Abernathy clan on Fraser's Ridge and Roger's fishing companion. [*Ashes*]

Abernathy, Joseph, Dr. (aka Uncle Joe)—Claire's best friend in the twentieth century, whom she met in medical school, later left in charge of Brianna when Claire returned to Jamie, and who helped establish twentieth-century credentials for Brianna and Roger MacKenzie and the children when they returned from the past; he also helped Brianna through Mandy's medical issue. [*Fiery Cross, Echo, MOBY*]

Abernathy, Mrs.; Young Grannie—Daughter-in-law of long-lived Old Grannie, the Abernathy clan matriarch, and mother of Arabella. Young Grannie is in her seventies and lives with other members of the Abernathy clan. [*Ashes*]

Abernathy, Old Grannie—Family matriarch of the Abernathy clan on Fraser's Ridge; she confides to Claire that she was actually born a Fraser. Almost one hundred years old, her family's longevity lets her live with her daughter-in-law and granddaughter-in-law. [*Ashes*]

Abram—A member of Jamie's militia and part of a three-man hunting party searching for game before the Battle of Alamance. [*Fiery Cross*]

Absolute, Lieutenant—A literary reference and professional nod to author C. C. Humphreys and his own literary character "Jack Absolute" (himself a reference to a character of the same name in Sheridan's play *The Rivals*), an eighteenth-century British soldier; also in attendance at the Battle of Bemis Heights during the Saratoga Campaign. [*Echo*]

x **Accompong, Captain**—The head of the maroons on Jamaica, he helps keep the peace between settlers and the escaped/freed blacks. [*PZ*]

Adams, Bernard Donald—First Secretary of the Ministry of Ordnance and a secret Irish Jacobite and cousin to the Twelvetrees brothers; an investigation by Lord John proves him to be the Irish Jacobite who killed Gerard Grey, Lord John's father, when he discovered the identity of key Jacobite members in London society. He confesses to the murder of Gerard Grey (first Duke of Pardloe) and is hanged for the crime. [*BL, CA, SP*]

Adams, Billy, Private—Young soldier at Battle of Monmouth. Claire treats his wounded arm. [*MOBY*]

x **Adams, John**—(1735–1826) Patriot statesman, signer of the Declaration of Independence, and VP under the first U.S. president, George Washington; elected as the second U.S. president and noted for the abundance of letters and documents pertaining to the formation of the first American government. [*Fiery Cross, Ashes, Echo*]

Adams, Private—Lord John's military orderly, he assists Lord John with military business, as well as caring for his uniforms and personal needs—that is, until Tom Byrd appears. [*PM*]

x **Adams, Samuel**—(1722–1803) Radical patriot, political agitator, master propagandist, and signer of the Declaration of Independence; he was the founder of the Committee of Safety and reported to be in danger of arrest on the night of Paul Revere's famous ride. [*Ashes, Echo, MOBY*]

Adso—Claire's beloved gray cat, given to her by Jamie, who found the wild kitten ("cheetie") on their trek to Fraser's Ridge after the Gathering at Mount Helicon and the aborted double wedding. [*All*]

Agnes-Maria—A young Prussian schoolgirl who, at Tom Byrd's urging, enlists Lord John to help her with a school assignment by providing her with a narrative on his travels in Scotland, a place far from Prussia. [*BL*]

Agrippa—Roger's horse, named for the first-century Roman statesman and general Marcus Vipsanius Agrippa (63 B.C.–12 B.C.), who was a close confidant and military strategist for Roman emperor Octavian. [*Ashes*]

Ahkote'ohskennonton—See "Sun Elk."

Alderdyce, Mrs.—A friend of Jocasta Cameron's and the widowed mother of Judge Alderdyce, she's eager to see her son wed to Brianna, in hopes of obtaining a grandchild. [*Fiery Cross*]

Alexander—Stephan von Namtzen's young son. [*BB*]

Alfred—The pet bulldog belonging to Lord John's cousin Olivia; his undershot-jaw makes him resemble Captain Jones from the Royal Armory. [*HS*]

Alice—A young Cross Creek prostitute who is abused by her client and then offered to a pub's common room for sport; Jamie wins the girl in a game of cards and mercifully returns her to Cross Creek's most popular brothel, run by Mrs. Sylvie. [*Ashes*]

x **Allen, Ethan**—(1738–1789) Colonel for Continental forces, led Vermont's Green Mountain Boys to capture Fort Ticonderoga in 1775. Claire describes his exploits and consequent disgrace in a letter to Brianna. [*Echo*]

Almerding, Viscount—Owner of a game preserve near Earlingden and a friend of Benjamin Grey, who often hunted there with his cousin William Ransom. [*MOBY*]

Amandine, Baron—Percy Wainwright/Beauchamp's brother-in-law and one of *Trois Flèches*. [*Echo*]

Anderson, Corporal—Soldier who helps William on the quay during the evacuation of Philadelphia. [*MOBY*]

Anderson, Mr.—One of the *Teal*'s displaced crewmen, now with the Continental army and Jamie's unofficial corporal during the evacuation of Ticonderoga. [*Echo*]

x **André, John**—(1750–1780) British officer hanged by Continentals in collusion with American General Benedict Arnold, for espionage to surrender the American fortification known as West Point to the British army. Claire meets him at the Mischianza ball in Philadelphia in May of 1778, and he later brings William a note for Banastre Tarleton, just prior to the Battle of Monmouth in June. [*Echo, MOBY*]

Andrews—A footman at Argus House, the London residence of the Duke and Duchess of Pardloe. [*SP*]

Andrews, Private—An infantryman in one of Lord John's companies. He loses his hat marching to battle, but Lord John deftly spears it with his sword and drops the hat onto Andrews's head, to the cheers of his companions. [*BL*]

Angelica—Newborn baby of Jenny and Ian Murray's eldest daughter, Maggie. [*Fiery Cross*]

Angelina (slave)—One of Jocasta Cameron-Innes's slaves at River Run; Claire gives her orders for supplies when she is required to treat Jocasta's painful eye condition during the party held for Flora MacDonald. [*Ashes*]

Angie—Possibly a member of clan Campbell, she is the young apprentice (helot) to the builder hired by Brianna to renovate and make repairs to Lallybroch, the Fraser homestead purchased by Roger and Brianna upon their return to the twentieth century. [*Ashes*]

Angus Mhor—Colum MacKenzie's body servant, bodyguard, and general factotum of justice at Leoch, and the one Jamie took a beating from in front of the entire clan to save a very young Laoghaire MacKenzie from punishment for wantonness, thus impressing Claire with his bravery, as well. N.B.: "Mhor" is not a last name but rather a Gaelic adjective. [*Echo*]

Anna—The English name of one of the Cherokee women Claire and Jamie meet upon visiting the village of the nearest Cherokee leader, Tsatsa'wi, while hunting for the white bear. [*Fiery Cross*]

Annabelle—The Frasers' new jenny mule and companion to Clarence. [*MOBY*]

Annie and Senga—Housemaids in Brian Fraser's home, Lallybroch. [*MOBY*]

Annie and Tab—Two servants from Cheapside working in Mayrhofer's house; both are aware of their employer's fetish for being totally shaven. [*PM*]

Anstruther, David—The sheriff of Orange County (North Carolina) and one of the men detaining Father Donahue at the Gathering on Mount Helicon, effectively preventing the priest from performing the marriage ceremony of Jocasta Cameron and Duncan Innes. [*Fiery Cross*]

Anthony, Lady—One of Benedicta Grey's close friends in attendance at her wedding. Lord John discreetly attempts to get Lady Anthony's attention by throwing a small candy at her back, but it hits her husband instead. [*BL*]

Anthony, Paul, Sir—Husband to Lady Anthony, Benedicta's close friend, he becomes the unfortunate victim of Lord John's candy missiles, tossed from the church balcony to garner attention—and help—for Olivia's plight. [*BL*]

Appledore—A bosun's mate onboard the *Sunrise,* he was part of the secret theft of the stolen copper and kidnapped Gormley from the Royal Arsenal when he came too close to discovering the truth. [*HS*]

Arabella—See "Jane Pocock."

Arbuthnot, Victor—An astronomer friend of the Duke of Pardloe; the duke suspects him to be one of a group of secret London Jacobite sympathizers. [*BL, CA*]

x **Archie Bell and the Drells**—Twentieth-century R&B musical group (1960s) whose hit song "Tighten Up," which supplies the phrase describing the movement of the Bell women. [*Echo*]

Armstrong, Bertram—Lord John's alias when disguised in the militia. [*MOBY*]

Armstrong, Nicodemus Patricius Marcus; Uncle Nick—A great-uncle of Lord John's, one of his mother's relatives, and a Jacobite supporter, as well as a heavy investor in the South Sea Bubble prior to its collapse in 1719. [*BL*]

x **Arnold, Benedict, Colonel**—(1741–1801) Later promoted to major general and a victor at Ticonderoga; became disgruntled with the Continental army and, with Major André's help, attempted to surrender West Point, the fort under his command, to the British. Claire meets him at Saratoga and forms a friendship with him, despite her knowledge of his eventual treason. They meet again when Arnold becomes military governor of Philadelphia in June of 1778 and he offers Claire a ride to Bartram's Garden. [*Echo, MOBY*]

Arthur—The footman for Hal, the Duke of Pardloe. [*Echo*]

x **Ashe, John, Colonel**—(1720–1781) A member of both the Committee for Correspondence and Committee of Safety, as well as a leader of the Sons of Liberty, he instigated the burning of Fort Johnson after North Carolina governor Josiah Martin fled, forcing Martin to direct the Loyalists from aboard his ship, the *Cruizer.* [*Fiery Cross, Ashes, Echo*]

Asher, Viscount—See "Henry Grey."

x **Atterbury, Francis**—(1663–1732) The Bishop of Rochester, he was banished for attempting to exploit the already disgruntled public feelings regarding the South Sea collapse, by staging an invasion by James Stuart (the Old Pretender) and dethroning the king. Since he was a close friend of Gerard Grey (the first Duke of Pardloe), Pardloe was deemed guilty by association of also being a Jacobite. [*BL*]

Augustus—One of the horses in the stable of Lord Dunsany at Helwater. [*SP*]

Auld John—See "John Murray."

Aunt Burton—Relative with whom the Bell women live in New Bern. [*Echo*]

Auntie Darla—The abusive Scottish aunt of Malva and Allan Christie; after forcing them to watch their mother being hanged as a witch, she performed her Christian duty and kept the children while their father, Tom Christie, was imprisoned at Ardsmuir after Culloden. [*Ashes*]

Auntie Gertrud—One of the names mentioned by matchmaker Ute McGillivray and family as a possible wife for Joseph Wemyss. [*Ashes*]

x **Avery, Waightstill**—(1741–1821) Opposed to the Regulator movement because of what he perceived as a mob mentality, Avery was nonetheless a signer of the Mecklenburg Declaration of Independence for North Carolina in 1775. An extract from his deposition regarding the behavior of Regulators who arrested him is quoted. [*Fiery Cross*]

Azeel—A young slave girl employed in the Jamaican governor's house and in love with Rodrigo. She is abused by the governor and flees, paying a witch doctor to curse the governor for his crimes against her. [*PZ*]

B

Babette—A former mistress of Michael Murray's close friend Charles Pépin. [*SB*]

Bacon, Eglantine and Pansy—A pair of young girls at the Gathering on Mount Helicon who present Claire with an overly large and garishly embellished mobcap, made by their grandmother, Grannie Bacon, to cover Claire's hair. [*Fiery Cross*]

Bacon, Grannie—An elderly resident from Edenton who deems it unseemly and amoral for a woman of Claire's age to not only have her head uncovered but to wear her hair loose about her shoulders; to repay Claire for medical treatment, she sends Claire a cap that is obviously several sizes too large. [*Fiery Cross*]

Bacon, Polly—Grannie Bacon's daughter-in-law and mother to Eglantine and Pansy; she gives Claire the first supply of *dauco* seeds—an Indian remedy for preventing pregnancy—which Polly has possibly used with success. [*Fiery Cross*]

Bad Sweat—The name applied to an Indian agent who visited Ian's Mohawk village of Snaketown. He was a fearful man who reeked of body odor and fear and expected to be killed by the Mohawk at any moment; Ian was required to act as translator but preferred to think himself Mohawk rather than acknowledge any kinship with the white Indian agent. [*Ashes*]

Bailey, Emmanuel—A Jewish banker living in Philadelphia, also the owner of three ships, including the *Asp,* with regular runs to the West Indies; he obtained the letter of marque from Congress for Captain Hickman. [*Echo*]

x **Balcarres, Sixth Earl of**—See "Alexander Lindsey."

x **Baldwin, Jeduthan**—(1732–1788) Engineer who constructed fortifications for Boston Siege, New York City, and Ticonderoga. [*Echo*]

x **Baldwin, Nathan**—(unknown) Town clerk for the city of Worcester, he was one of many clerks who copied General J. Palmer's missive, later known as the "Lexington Alarm," for distribution to militia companies throughout the colonies by order of Colonel Ashe. [*Ashes*]

Bampton-Howard, Colonel—A British leader present near Crefeld; his men beat Ruysdale's men in a game of bowls, or skittles. [*SU*]

Banquo—One of the characters in Shakespeare's "Scottish play," *Macbeth,* and the secret name given to George Longstreet by other conspirators involved in the Jacobite plot to kill King George and set James Stuart in his place. [*BL*]

Baragwanath, Colenso—A Cornish stableboy employed in Lord John Grey's home in Philadelphia during the wake of the British defeat at Saratoga. He becomes William's groom and accompanies him to the Battle of Monmouth, where he forms a friendship with Jane and Fanny [*Echo, MOBY*]

Barlow, Robert—A heavyset merchant opposed to the Regulators. As a guest at Jocasta Cameron's wedding, he gets in a physical altercation with old Ninian Hamilton and several other guests, until Major MacDonald and Hermon Husband bring a peaceful end to the conflict. [*Fiery Cross*]

x **Baron de Tollendal**—See "Thomas Lally."

x **Bartram, John**—(1699–1777) Founder of Bartram's Garden, outside Philadelphia; known as the father of American botany. Bartram's Garden was the site of Jamie and Claire's reunion following his escape from Philadelphia with Lord John Grey. [*MOBY*]

Bartram, Sissy—Daughter of John Bartram. [*MOBY*]

Bartram, Young Mr.—Son of John Bartram. [*MOBY*]

Bates, Ezekial, General—Father of the traitorous Michael Bates, and close friend of General Stanley, who was stepfather to Hal and John Grey and Percy Wainwright. [*BL*]

Bates, Michael, Captain—Son of esteemed General Ezekial Bates; General Stanley's chief aide-de-camp for a time; was secretly obtaining military information and selling it to the French through his connections with Private Otway and Mr. Ffoulkes. Hanged on a false charge of sodomy. [*BL*]

Batty—A sneaky-tempered cat at Magda's brothel, Batty is very likely to bite in return for affection. [*PM*]

Baudry, the Widow—A woman from Brownsville with whom Wendigo Donner stays after arriving with Hodgepile and company. [*Ashes*]

x **Baum, Friedrich, Lieutenant Colonel**—(1727–1777) Commander of approximately six hundred "Hessian" dragoons serving under General Riedesel; was defeated at the Battle of Bennington by the larger and battle-proven forces of John Stark. Had Baum's request for enforcements been expedited by Colonel Breymann (who didn't like Baum, so marched slowly to assist him), the outcome might have been different. [*Echo*]

Bear Cub—Indian name Glutton gives to William after he is injured in the Great Dismal Swamp. A fitting name, since the Cherokee gave Jamie the Indian name "Bear Killer." [*Echo*]

Beardsley, Aaron—Owner of a trading post deep within the Treaty Line, he bought identical twin boys, Keziah and Josiah, as bond servants to cover the passage for the rest of their family, who died on the journey to America. Abusive to his servants, Beardsley was also possibly a murderer who killed several wives; he suffered a debilitating stroke before he could murder his fifth wife, Fanny, who left him to die a slow death while she tortured him. Jamie found him and helped give him a swift death instead of allowing him to linger painfully as his vengeful—and insane—wife had intended. [*Fiery Cross, Ashes*]

Beardsley, Alicia—See "Alicia Beardsley Brown."

Beardsley, Frances; Fanny—The widow and fifth wife of Mr. Beardsley, she has apparently lived a life of isolation and abuse and is mentally unstable, her only friends being the goats in her care. After being discovered in horrible conditions by Jamie and Claire, she travels with the Frasers toward Brownsville, to live where there are other people; during the night, she quietly delivers a mixed-blood child, then disappears, abandoning the child to Jamie and Claire. [*Fiery Cross*]

Beardsley, Josiah; Jo—Though Jo is a wayward youth, Jamie picks him as a tenant for Fraser's Ridge. Because he is under sixteen, he can't be conscripted into the militia, which leaves one more male figure on the Ridge to help the women who are staying behind, and he is a capable hunter. In exchange for Jo joining Fraser's Ridge, Jamie offers to have Claire remove the youth's badly infected tonsils and adenoids. He will be joined later by his identical-twin brother, Keziah, both of whom become Lizzie Wemyss's husbands. [*All*]

Beardsley, Keziah; Kezzie—One of a pair of identical twins whom Jamie takes in as a resident for the Ridge, Keziah is exempt from the militia call-up, leaving another able-bodied male on the Ridge to hunt and provide food and protection for the women and to help with chores in the men's absence. Later, Keziah and his brother, Josiah, become partners in a bigamous marriage with Lizzie Wemyss. [*All*]

Beardsley, Lizzie Wemyss—See "Lizzie Wemyss."

Beardsley, Mary Ann—The fourth dead wife of Mr. Beardsley. Her ghostly apparition appears periodically to Fanny Beardsley, warning the lonely, abused woman that she'll be the fifth wife buried in the woods if she doesn't get away. [*Fiery Cross*]

Beardsley, Rodney—The first child of Lizzie Wemyss Beardsley and one of the

Beardsley-twin husbands. [*Ashes, Echo, MOBY*]

Beardsley Brown, Alicia (aka Alicia Beardsley)—The nameless child Fanny Beardsley delivers on the journey to Brownsville, then abandons to the Frasers' care. Jamie notices a small bluish discoloration above the newborn's buttocks, which Claire calls a "Mongol spot," indicating that the child is of mixed blood—part African, or "mulatto"—and therefore cannot be the child of Fanny Beardsley's recently deceased husband. Richard Brown and his family agree to adopt the infant and name her Alicia; the girl is the sole heir to not only her dead (legal) father's farm but also to the considerable trade goods stored there. [*Fiery Cross, Ashes, MOBY*]

Bear-Killer—The name given to Jamie Fraser by the Tuscarora in consequence of his having killed a black bear single-handedly, with only a knife. [*Fiery Cross, Ashes, Echo*]

Beasley, Mr.—Hal's elderly clerk and the only one able to understand the orderly chaos on Hal's desk at the regimental offices. [*BL, SP*]

Beathag—One of three small sisters who were the children of tenants of Lallybroch. The croft in which she lived was burned after Culloden. [*SP*]

Beauchamp, Amelie Élise LeVigne—The missing younger sister of Baron Amandine, last heard to have been living in a Paris brothel and quite possibly the mother of Fergus "Claudel" Fraser. Along with her brother and her sister, she is one of the *Trois Flèches* Lord John is investigating. [*Echo*]

Beauchamp, Cecile—Percival Beauchamp's wife, sister of Baron Amandine, and one of the *Trois Flèches.* [*Echo*]

Beauchamp, Percival—see "Percy Wainwright."

Beauchamp, Quentin Lambert (aka Uncle Lamb)—Claire's paternal uncle, who raised her from childhood following the death of her parents in a car accident. [*Fiery Cross, Echo, MOBY*]

x **Beaumarchais, Pierre**—(1732–1799) French playwright (*The Barber of Seville, The Marriage of Figaro*), U.S. sympathizer, and founder of Hortalez et Cie exports—a front for a joint French–Spanish arms/ammunitions supplier to the Continental army. [*Echo*]

Beckett, Moira—Daughter of the landlord at the public house in the village near Siverly's Irish estate; she catches the eye of Tom Byrd, Lord John's valet. [*SP*]

Beckett, Mr.—Landlord of the public house in the village near Siverly's Irish estate. [*SP*]

Bedelia—A horse at the inn near Siverly's estate. [*SP*]

Behan, Rose—The downstairs neighbor of Kitty O'Donnell; she requests that the O'Higgins brothers put an end to the wake. [*BL*]

Belcher, Tod—The incorrect name of the cannon "Tom Pilchard," listed in a Sussex newspaper article that was rife with exaggerations and inaccuracies, except for the name of the commander, called the Hero of Crefeld—Lord John Grey. [*HS*]

Belden, Mr.—Mule skinner who stole Clarence from Germain and who suffers a nasty bite from the mule. [*MOBY*]

Bell, Abigail—Wife of Richard Bell, the man in charge of keeping Jamie's printing press safe; she appeals to Jamie to find her husband in Scotland. [*Echo*]

x **Bell, Andrew; Andy**—(1726–1809) Scottish engraver and co-founder of the Encyclopedia Britannica. He has been storing

Jamie's printing press in Edinburgh since Jamie left there so many years ago. Richard Bell of Wilmington is his fictitious kinsman. [*Echo*]

Bell, Lillian—Richard Bell's daughter, who shares a kiss with William after a dinner meeting between William and Captain Richardson. [*Echo*]

Bell, Miriam—Richard Bell's other daughter, also enamored of William. [*Echo*]

Bell, Richard—Wilmington merchant and father of two attractive daughters, both admired by William Ransom. He is abducted by the Sons of Liberty and forcibly deported to London; Jamie hires him to look after his printing press, Bonnie. [*Echo, MOBY*]

Bella—One of Lord Dunsany's older, sedate, and sensible horses, who is chosen for two-year-old William's first horseback ride. [*SP*]

Bellman, Edwin, Sir—A suspected Jacobite and one of the men who thought to protect his own secret by supporting the false accusations of treason and Jacobitism directed at Lord John's father. [*CA*]

Benedicta, Lady Stanley—See "Benedicta Grey."

Benjamin, Mr.—Owner of a Cross Creek warehouse; while he's conducting business with Jocasta Cameron, Stephen Bonnet appears briefly and frightens Phaedre and wee Jem. [*Ashes*]

Berculi, Signor—A small Sicilian gentleman who is the senior swordsman and fencing instructor to the Duke of Pardloe and Lord John; he includes Percy as a new student since he will become one of the family. [*BL*]

Berrisch, Monika, Fraulein (aka Monika Wemyss)—German Pastor Berrisch's spinster sister; while attending the engagement party between Lizzie Wemyss and Manfred McGillivray, she catches the eye of Lizzie's father, Joseph, eventually becoming his wife and grandmother to Lizzie's future children. (Monika is one of the Real People—friends or acquaintances of mine gracious enough to allow me to make free with their names and/or personae.) [*Ashes, Echo, MOBY*]

Berrisch, Pastor—Protestant pastor for the German population near Salem and brother to Monika, Joseph Weymss's future wife. [*Ashes*]

Betty—A River Run slave found drunk and unconscious during Jocasta's wedding reception. She dies after being fed ground glass, which Claire discovers when she performs a nocturnal autopsy; the Frasers and Jocasta wonder why someone would go to great lengths to kill the woman, who happened to be Phaedre's mother. [*Fiery Cross*]

Beverley, Lady—A woman attending Lady Joffrey's salon, who Lord John knows is a flirt and woman of easy virtue, even though she is respectably married. [*BL*]

Bewlie, Peter—Resident of Fraser's Ridge, married to a Cherokee woman. He brings news of a ghostly white bear that's been terrorizing Indian villages and enlists the aid of Jamie and Claire to hunt the bear. [*Fiery Cross*]

Billings—An under-footman at Helwater. [*SP*]

Billman, Captain—The captain of the English horse soldiers present at dinner at Schloss Lowenstein, where the succubus is discussed. [*SU*]

Bingham—A member of Hal's regiment and one of the piquet players meeting at Almack's gentlemen's club. [*SP*]

Bird-who-sings-in-the-morning; Bird (aka Tsisqua)—The Cherokee war chief's English name. He asks Jamie to provide his tribe with guns so they might be able to defend their homes and fight opposing tribes; in turn, Jamie warns Bird about a "dream" his daughter, Brianna, has had regarding the future fate of the Cherokee people and gives him instructions to avoid what will become known as the Trail of Tears. [*Ashes*]

x **Bissell, Israel**—(1752–1823) Bissell was a post rider who rode 345 miles from Boston to Philadelphia, alerting the American colonists of the British attack on April 19, 1775. [*Ashes*]

x **Bishop of Ely**—(1683–1770) Matthias Mawson, an academic and churchman, he was also a friend of Lord John's mother, Benedicta Grey. [*HF*]

Bishop of York—Second-highest-ranking cleric in the Church of England; a highly honored guest at Benedicta Grey's party celebrating Clive's victory over the Nawab of Bengal. [*PM*]

Bixby, Judah—One of the lieutenants under Jamie's command at Monmouth. [*MOBY*]

Black-beard—One of the scruffy Regulators from Hermon Husband's encampment. He blames Roger for Husband's departure from the camp, leaving the Regulators without leadership, and is instrumental in helping Buck MacKenzie turn Roger in as a traitor to Tryon's army at the Battle of Alamance. [*Fiery Cross*]

Black Hugh—Jocasta Cameron's second husband; he fathered her daughter Seonag. [*Fiery Cross*]

Black Jack—See "Jonathan Wolverton Randall."

Bledsoe, Miss—An elderly guest at Jocasta Cameron's wedding. [*Fiery Cross*]

Bledsoe, Tench—Edward Shippen's young cousin. Benedict Arnold, a friend of the Shippen family, comes on their behalf to ask Claire to tend Mr. Bledsoe, who has been attacked by the Sons of Liberty. She saves his life, though she is forced to amputate his shattered leg. [*MOBY*]

Blogweather, Mr.—Glassmaker from Williamsburg, Virginia; contracted by Lord John Grey to manufacture the delicate equipment for Claire's distillation of ether from the dangerous oil of vitriol, also known as sulfuric acid. [*Ashes*]

Blomberg, Agathe; Old Agathe—Deceased mother of Herr Blomberg, the mayor of Gundwitz; her body is suspected to house a demon spirit, since the white horse stopped at her grave during the nocturnal search through the graveyard. [*SU*]

Blomberg, Herr—The bürgermeister, or mayor, of the Prussian village of Gundwitz, who seeks to borrow Lord John's white stallion to locate a succubus. [*SU*]

Bob—A waiter employed at White's Chocolate House in London. [*BL*]

Boble, Harley—Thief-taker and member of a group of bandits who abduct and abuse Claire and the one who savagely beats Claire in retaliation for a personal humiliation at the Mount Helicon Gathering; Roger kills Boble after he and the tenants of Fraser's Ridge track the bandits down and rescue Claire. [*Fiery Cross, Ashes, Echo*]

Bodger, Private—An English private who has an altercation with a gypsy whore and is later found dead—allegedly killed by a marauding female demon intent on seducing men. [*SU*]

Bodley, Mr.—The chief steward at the Society for Appreciation of the English Beefsteak, the gentlemen's club where Lord John is a longtime member. [*HS, Echo*]

Boggs—The young clerk employed by Sussex lawyer Simon Coles. [*HS*]

Bogle—Harry Quarry's predecessor as governor of Ardsmuir Prison; put Jamie Fraser in irons. [*Fiery Cross*]

Bogues, Miranda; Randy—Ten-year-old daughter of the Cross Creek apothecary Ralston Bogues; Claire finds her upset about moving to England and having to sell the family's wagon horse, Jack, who is her particular pet. [*Ashes*]

Bogues, Melanie—Wife of the Cross Creek apothecary, she is terrified that her husband will be caught up in the mob that Jamie is holding off. [*Ashes*]

Bogues, Ralston—The Cross Creek apothecary who is closing shop and returning with his family to England, as the population is becoming more patriotic and hostile to anyone harboring Tory sensibilities; he helps Jamie fight off a mob intent on tarring-and-feathering local printer Fogarty Simms. [*Ashes*]

Bonham, Colonel—A military officer in charge of the Fifty-first Regiment stationed in London during 1758. [*BL*]

Bonham, Viscount—Fictitious nobleman and one of the guests at Benedicta Grey's party celebrating Clive's victory over the Nawab of Bengal. [*PM*]

Bonnet, Stephen—An Irishman orphaned young, he is a sociopath and notorious pirate, who escaped hanging once and played upon the Frasers' sympathies to aid his escape from the British; he promptly returned their generosity by ambushing and robbing their party, taking Claire's gold wedding ring. Brianna later recognizes the ring and meets with Bonnet in an attempt to buy it back, but his price is rape. Brianna finds out she's pregnant with a child that could belong to either the rapist Bonnet or Roger MacKenzie, with whom she is handfasted. Bonnet finally meets his fate after raising the ire of the entire Fraser clan by kidnapping and attempting to sell Brianna as a sex slave. He's sentenced to drown for piracy, but Brianna shoots him out of mercy. [*All*]

Bonnie—The name Jamie sheepishly admits to Claire that he has given his beloved printing press, left behind in Edinburgh in the care of his printing associate, Andrew Bell. [*Echo, MOBY*]

Bork, Lieutenant—The commanding officer in Scotland who inadvertently directs Hector and Meadows into an enemy's path; his direction forces Hector to kill his first man by running a bayonet through the Scot who had just felled Meadows with a rock. [*PM*]

Borthy, Robert—One of the commanders of militia present at the Battle of Moore's Creek Bridge, who briefs Jamie on the status of the opposing Emigrant Highland Regiment led by Fraser's old acquaintance and friend Donald MacDonald and Alexander McLean. [*Ashes*]

Bouton—While we see the original Bouton only in *Dragonfly in Amber*, Mother Hildegarde's later canine companions share the same name. Claire meets one of these incumbents when she visits L'Hôpital many years later. [*SB*]

Bowen, Zeke—A householder outside Philadelphia, to whose house Natty Bumppo takes Corporal Woodbine's militia company while Woodbine himself escorts his prisoner, Lord John Grey, to Colonel Smith. [*MOBY*]

Bowles, Hubert—The head of a classified British government organization that engages in intercepting and decrypting diplomatic dispatches; the organization is only known as the Black Chamber. He is an unnerving character since he has informants in many areas of the government and among London society and is willing to use anyone in the protection of England from its enemies, domestic or abroad. [*PM, BL, HS, SP, Echo*]

Brabham-Griggs—One of the junior officers in the Duke of Pardloe's Forty-sixth Regiment of soldiers. [*BL*]

Bracknell, Lady—A London socialite and the hostess of the salon where Joseph Trevelyan meets Maria Mayrhofer. [*PM*]

Bradbury, Captain—An English officer who interrogates Denzell Hunter for information after he pretends to desert the Continental army. The "deserter game" was practiced on both sides during the war, with soldiers pretending to desert and giving false information but getting a look at the other side's encampment, before "re-deserting" to report back to their own commanding officers. Anyone caught was executed as a spy. [*Echo*]

Bradshaw, Mrs. Phillip; Sarah—Wife of a slave owner, she brings her very young house slave, Sophronia, to Claire for treatment after a childbirth injury. [*MOBY*]

x **Brant, Joseph** (aka Thayendanegea, "Two Wagers")—(1742–1807) Mohawk chief educated by whites, staunch Loyalist sympathizer, fought with British against Patriots so well that he received the commission of Colonel of Indians from King George I. [*Echo, MOBY*]

Brennan, Mr.—A resident of Cross Creek, whose wife has requested Dr. Fentiman's aid in delivering her child. [*Ashes*]

Brett, Richard—The fifteen-year-old ensign assisting Lord John near the Drachenfels in the Rhine Valley during the Seven Years' War. [*BL*]

Brewer, Joseph—Dr. McEwan's friend and shooting companion. [*MOBY*]

Brewster, Neph—A Continental soldier recuperating after the Battle of Saratoga and suffering from a bad case of diarrhea, which leaves him raw and uncomfortable but still with a sense of humor and the ability to flirt with Claire. [*Echo*]

Broch Tuarach, Lord—see "Jamie Fraser."

Brother Bertram—One of the monks at the Irish monastery of Inchcleraun, in charge of cooking for the monks and guests. [*SP*]

Brother Daniel—One of the monks at the Irish monastery of Inchcleraun, also the clerk. [*SP*]

Brother Infirmarian—One of the monks trained in healing at the Irish monastery of Inchcleraun; he treats a wounded Tom Byrd after Lord John's rescue from Athlone Prison. [*SP*]

Brother Mordecai—One of the German residents of Salem, he is an accomplished potter and knowledgeable about the ceramic process; Brianna wishes to speak with him regarding kiln-building but is unable to because of the rift between the Frasers and most of the Salem community. [*Ashes*]

Brother Polycarp—One of the monks at the Abbey of St. Anne in France, he told a young Jamie Fraser stories of various saints while Jamie recuperated from injuries. [*Ashes*]

Brown, Aaron—One of Richard Brown's nephews and part of the kidnapping party that includes Lionel Brown and Harley Boble. [*Ashes*]

Brown, Alicia—Lionel Brown's daughter, and the second wife of bigamist Isaiah Morton. [*Fiery Cross*]

Brown, Christopher—Jemima Brown's three-month-old son, who shares his mother's milk with the orphaned Beardsley child. [*Fiery Cross*]

Brown, Lionel—The stupider and more impulsive pair of the Brown brothers;

after the Regulation is put down, the Browns form a Committee of Safety to help police the Ridge from bandits. However, suspicions arise in Jamie's mind that the Browns *are* the bandits. Lionel is injured during Claire's abduction and brought back to the Ridge, where Mrs. Bug kills him by suffocating him with a pillow. [*Fiery Cross, Ashes*]

Brown, Meg—Richard Brown's wife. [*Fiery Cross*]

Brown, Moses—One of Richard Brown's nephews and part of the kidnapping party that includes Lionel Brown and Harley Boble. [*Ashes*]

Brown, Mrs.—The high-strung pregnant wife of a colonel of militia at the Fort Ticonderoga encampment, noted as "an hysteric" by Denzell Hunter. [*Echo*]

Brown, Richard—Leader of a small, close-knit community called Brownsville. While hotheaded and vengeful, Richard is the more calculating of the two Brown brothers. After the War of Regulation is put down, he and his brother form a Committee of Safety to help police the Ridge from bandits. Following Malva Christie's accusation and subsequent murder, Richard Brown and his Committee arrest Claire by force and take her to stand trial for the murder. [*Fiery Cross, Ashes*]

Brown, Thomasina—Richard Brown's sister. [*Fiery Cross*]

x **Bruce, Nigel**—British source of information on Colonel Richardson, who died before importing it. The name is my nod to the British actor famous for his role as Doctor Watson in the series of Sherlock Holmes films of the 1930–'40s. [*Echo*]

Brugge—A Moravian gunsmith near Salem who Robin McGillivray thinks will be able to assemble a gun per Jamie's requirements. [*Ashes*]

Brunton—The butler employed in Benedicta Grey's Jermyn Street residence. [*BL*]

x **Bryan, Colonel**—(unknown) Militia leader of the Rowan County, N.C.; Governor Tryon's combined forces gathered at Bryan's plantation near New Bern before marching toward Alamance in May 1771. [*Fiery Cross*]

Bryan, Mrs.—Colonel Bryan's wife, who offers Claire a bed in her plantation house during the army and militia rendezvous before Alamance. [*Fiery Cross*]

x **Bubb-Dodington, George**—(1691–1762) An English politician and nobleman said to have been part of a spy ring collecting information regarding Jacobite activities in the years after Culloden. [*HF*]

Bubbles—See "Henri-Christian Fraser."

Buchan—A butcher in Campbelton who, because of the terrible writing and spelling, Jamie suspects is the author of a note sent to Farquard Campbell, denouncing Jamie as a seditionist and traitor who should be hanged or at the least tarred and sent out of town on a rail. [*Ashes*]

Buchan, Ernie—Fiona's husband. While a friend to Brianna and Roger, he grows alarmed at the threat to his own family when Rob Cameron comes to his house in search of Jem. Ernie returns Jem and Mandy to Lallybroch, only to run straight into an ambush. He inadvertently provides rescue for Brianna and gets her and the children away to a place of safety. [*MOBY*]

Buchan, Fiona Graham—Auntie Fiona to Jem and Mandy. Granddaughter of Mrs. Graham, the Reverend's housekeeper, who succeeds her grandmother as housekeeper and as the "caller"—the leader of the women who dance on Craigh na Dun, calling down the sun on the feast days. Fiona is a good friend to both

Roger and Brianna and gives Jem and Mandy a place to stay while Brianna is trying to track down the criminals who are threatening her family. While Fiona is harboring the children, Rob Cameron shows up and—spooked by a radio report giving his name—hits Fiona and rushes out. [*All*]

Buchan, Ginger, Tisha, and Sheena—Children of Fiona and Ernie. [*MOBY*]

Buchan, Seaumais—An elderly resident of the Ridge who has been in ill health, but his family chose not to seek out Claire to treat him; according to folklore, when he dies, he will guard the graveyard until the next burial. [*Ashes*]

Buchanan, Alexander; Sawny—A pipe-smoking acquaintance of Duncan Innes, staying at River Run and possibly mistaken for a ghost by wee Jem. [*Ashes*]

Buchanan, DeWayne—Ninian Hamilton's son-in-law, who attempts to help his father-in-law in a fight; his involvement is curtailed by Major MacDonald firing his gun into the air, which startles all the participants into a momentary lull. [*Fiery Cross*]

Buchanan, Dougie—A friend from Roger's youth and one of his gang of friends in Inverness. [*Ashes*]

Buchanan, Mrs.—One of the attendees at the Gathering, she presents Brianna with a wedding gift of embroidery thread, to decorate her funeral clothes in the event Brianna should die in childbirth. [*Fiery Cross*]

Buckman, Joe—A militiaman. [*MOBY*]

Bug, Arch—The factor hired to oversee the smooth running of the farm on Fraser's Ridge, former tacksman of Clan Grant but displaced after the Highland Clearances. He later proves to be a treacherous foe to the Frasers, especially Young Ian. Blaming Ian for his wife's death (with reason), he vows vengeance on the young man and tracks him ultimately to Philadelphia, where he nearly makes good on his threats. But he's prevented by Rollo from killing either Rachel or Ian and is then killed by William. [*All*]

Bug, Murdina—Arch Bug's beloved wife, housekeeper and cook for the Frasers, and general busybody of the Big House on Fraser's Ridge. While presumably fond of the Frasers, her only true devotion is to her husband—and thus to his desire to recover the Jacobite gold. While attempting to help him do this, she is discovered in the dark by Jamie and Ian and fires at them. Not knowing who their adversary is, Young Ian shoots an arrow at the shadowy figure—and is appalled to find that he has killed Mrs. Bug. [*Fiery Cross, Ashes, Echo*]

Bulstrode—Young butler at Gerald Siverly's estate in Ireland. [*SP*]

Bumppo, Natty; Hawkeye—A reference to James Fenimore Cooper's famous literary figure "Leatherstocking" (known also as "Hawkeye," as well as his given name of Nathaniel Bumppo). If one charts the travels and adventures of Mr. Bumppo through Cooper's novels, it's entirely possible (and even likely) that he might have been where fortune (and this author) placed him in the summer of 1778. [*MOBY*]

Buncombe, Captain—Jack Randall's predecessor as garrison commander at Fort William. [*MOBY*]

x **Burgoyne, General John** (aka Gentleman Johnny)—(1722–1792) One of the British generals under Lord Germain's command. He was victorious at Fort Ticonderoga but, due to miscommunication and overconfidence, was forced to surrender his entire army of 5,800 to the larger, better equipped Patriot army led by Horatio Gates. [*Echo, MOBY*]

Burkhardt, Herr—The butler at Mayrhofer's home, who notices the new English servant hired to apparently "guard" Frau Mayrhofer. [*PM*]

Burns, Annie—The daughter of a Wilmington landlady, her claim of seeing poisonous snakes while berry-picking causes her mother to offer the use of a flintlock to the Fraser/MacKenzie berry-picking party. [*Fiery Cross*]

Burns, Mrs.—The landlady in Wilmington with whom the Fraser women remain while the men are off hunting Stephen Bonnet. [*Fiery Cross*]

Butler, Gilbert—Local Edenton smuggler and an associate of Neil Forbes. He assists Forbes in abducting Brianna to give to Bonnet and sells Jocasta Cameron's slave Phaedre to Bonnet, as well. [*Ashes*]

Byrd, Jack—Older brother to Lord John's valet, Tom, and formerly a footman for Joseph Trevelyan. He has assisted Lord John in London detective work. [*PM, HS*]

Byrd, Tom—Lord John's valet, a young man previously unskilled as a personal servant; through his diligence and willingness to learn, he becomes a loyal friend and servant to Lord John, accompanying him on his frequent military postings. [*PM, SU, BL, HS, CA, PZ*]

Byrnes, Rob—A member of Jamie's militia at Alamance. (Also a crime novelist friend of the author.) [*Fiery Cross*]

C

Cairistiona—One of three sisters who were tenants of Lallybroch; the croft in which she lived was burned out after Culloden. [*SP*]

Calder, Henry, Sir—Commander of the Forty-ninth Regiment. [*MOBY*]

x **Caldwell, Reverend**—(1725–1824) David Caldwell, a moderate Presbyterian preacher from Greensboro, performs the marriage ceremony between Brianna and Roger at the Gathering, after Catholic priest Father Kenneth Donahue is arrested by powerful political factions. Later, Caldwell assists Roger in his own endeavors in becoming a Presbyterian minister. [*Fiery Cross, Ashes*]

Callahan, Michael—Rob Cameron's archaeologist friend from Orkney, who is interested in excavating the stone church at Lallybroch, deeming it an old site, possibly Pictish; also one of the gang who attempt to kidnap Brianna and the children. [*Echo, MOBY*]

Calls-in-the-Forest—The Cherokee mother of Bird, she is sent to help Jamie relax and be at peace; after instructing Jamie to talk to ease his mind, she combs his hair while burning sweet herbs. [*Ashes*]

Calvert—Soldier from Quarry's regiment whom Lord John wishes to accompany him while investigating Sergeant O'Connell's death. [*PM*]

x **Cameron, Alexander** (aka Scotchee)—(ca. 1730–1781) Loyalist and deputy to the Southern Superintendent of Indian Affairs, Cameron was an influential man among the Cherokee; under British authority, he influenced the Cherokee to side with the Loyalists but had to maintain a delicate balance between the Indians and settlers so as not to inflame Patriot sentiments through indiscriminate attacks from the Indians on whites, which could possibly push settlers toward the Rebel cause. [*Ashes*]

Cameron, Clementina—Jocasta's widowed eldest daughter by John Cameron. Jocasta never knew if Clementina and her family were burned out or starved out of the Scottish home she shared with her sister Seonag during the months following Culloden. [*Fiery Cross*]

Cameron, Hector—Jamie Fraser's uncle by marriage; husband to Jocasta MacKenzie Cameron, Jamie's aunt. He is one of three men who each receive ten thousand pounds of gold meant for Bonnie Prince Charlie's army; Hector secretly transports his from Scotland to the colonies after the fall of Culloden, using it frugally to set up his plantation, River Run, near Cross Creek. [*All*]

Cameron, Janie—One of the children attending Bree's school lessons at her cabin on the Ridge. [*Fiery Cross*]

Cameron, Jocasta Isobeail MacKenzie—see "Jocasta Innes."

Cameron, John—Jocasta Cameron's first husband. She was wed to him while no more than a child herself; he fathered her daughter Clementina. [*Fiery Cross*]

Cameron, Morna—Hector Cameron's only daughter and Jocasta's youngest daughter, who was accidentally shot in the head by Hector after their coach was accosted by a party of British soldiers. [*Fiery Cross*]

Cameron, Rob—Brianna's insubordinate co-worker at the hydroelectric dam, uncle of one of Jem's classmates, and the instigator of nasty tricks on Brianna and Jem; he's a dangerous (and possibly unhinged) man, who needs to be watched. This assumption is borne out when he kidnaps Jem, having learned that Jem is the only person (in 1980) who knows the location of the Spaniard's gold—and, even more intriguingly, may be able to time-travel. He successfully decoys Roger and his ancestor, Buck MacKenzie, into the stones by making them think he has taken Jem through into the past. Meanwhile, he stashes Jem under the Loch Errochty dam and goes to Lallybroch to settle a few personal scores with (who he assumes is) a helpless Brianna. He's wrong in this assumption but escapes from the priest's hole at Lallybroch (after Brianna has clubbed him with a cricket bat and put him there) and makes another try, with reinforcements. The danger he poses to her children causes Brianna to flee Scotland with them and finally to decide to leave the twentieth century in search of Roger. [*Echo,MOBY*]

Cameron, Seonag—Jocasta's daughter by her third husband, Black Hugh. Jocasta never knew if she and her family were burned out or starved out of their Scottish home during the months following Culloden. [*Fiery Cross*]

Campbell, Angus Og—One of the residents on Fraser's Ridge. While too old to join the militia Jamie is forced to gather, he has several nephews who will be mustered for the cause. [*Fiery Cross*]

x **Campbell, Archibald, Lt. Col.**—(unknown) Commander of the Seventy-first Foot, Fraser's Highlanders, during the brief Battle of Savannah. [*MOBY*]

x **Campbell, Farquard**—(unknown) A prominent member of Cape Fear's Scottish community and a close friend to Jocasta Cameron. A law-abiding man with a scrupulous conscience, he is a local magistrate, as well as a planter; at the Mount Helicon Gathering he is asked to meet with Lieutenant Hayes and other powerful leaders of the region. [*Fiery Cross, Ashes, Echo*]

Campbell, Jenny ban—A neighbor woman of the Frasers who has outlived two husbands and safely delivered eight children. [*Fiery Cross*]

Campbell, Mr.—The personnel manager at the hydroelectric authority office, who is shocked that Brianna—a woman—insists on applying for the position of plant inspector rather than secretary. [*Echo*]

x **Campbell, Mr.**—(1705–1780) Rev. James Campbell of the Barbecue Church in Sanford was the first official Presbyterian minister in North Carolina who accepted a call to minister from the parishioners and stayed. [*Fiery Cross*]

Campbell, Rabbie—Farquard Campbell's youngest son. At his father's request, he summons Jamie and Claire and shows them the location of the missing priest, Father Kenneth, at the Gathering. [*Fiery Cross*]

Campbell, Rachel—Farquard Campbell's young and rather muddleheaded wife and mistress of his Cross Creek plantation. Her husband dotes on her and teases her about her excitement in meeting Flora MacDonald at River Run plantation. [*Fiery Cross, Ashes*]

Campbell, Ronnie—One of Farquard Campbell's numerous offspring, and an exuberant guest at Jocasta and Duncan's wedding; after too many celebratory drinks, he accidentally shoots DeWayne Buchanan in the arm. After the victim is treated, a remorseful Ronnie proceeds to ply him with alcohol for an effective painkiller. [*Fiery Cross*]

x **Carleton, Guy, Sir**—(1724–1808) After Cornwallis's surrender at Yorktown, Carleton was appointed Britain's commander in chief for all North America forces during the Revolutionary War; he led the defense of Quebec in 1775, then later oversaw the evacuation of British citizens from New York in 1783. [*Echo*]

x **Carmichael, Alexander, Reverend**—(1832–1912) Scottish writer and folklorist who traveled around the country collecting traditional songs, prayers, and chants; he compiled them into a multivolume written work titled *Carmina Gadelica,* which helped preserve the ancient (often pre-Christian) Celtic culture from an oral history to a written one. [*Echo*]

Carmichael, Geordie—The man who raped Jenny's daughter, Maggie, and brother to Maggie's husband, Paul. [*MOBY*]

Carmichael, Paul—Maggie Murray's lawful husband. [*MOBY*]

Carmichael, Wally—The child conceived through rape but raised as Maggie and her husband Paul's true child. [*MOBY*]

Carruthers, Captain Charles; Charlie—A former sexual partner and military comrade of Lord John's during his wild period of grieving after Hector's death at Culloden; an honor-bound man much like Lord John and his brother, Charlie was notable for a rare deformity: he had a second small hand growing out of the palm of one hand—which was functional in movement, something Lord John remembers erotically. [*CA, SP*]

Castellotti, Duc di—A dissipated Italian nobleman, he accompanied Charles Stuart on his drunken ramblings through Paris in the months before the Rising. [*SP*]

x **Caswell, George**—A guest at Jocasta's wedding and the son of Richard Caswell. Both Caswells are drawn into a brawl between Ninian Hamilton and Robert Barlow. [*Fiery Cross*]

Caswell, Mrs.—The wife of wedding combatant George Caswell, she escorts him from the brawl while applying a cloth to his bleeding nose. [*Fiery Cross*]

Caswell, Richard—Father of George Caswell and also a guest at Jocasta's wedding.

He is drawn into the brawl between Ninian Hamilton and Robert Barlow. [*Fiery Cross*]

Caswell, Richard; Dickie; "Mother"—The proprietor of Lavender House, a meeting place for homosexual men; he can provide the information Lord John seeks—for a price. He is also a moneylender and associate of Captain Bates. [*PM, BL*]

Caulfield, Phineas Graham—A prominent Philadelphia Loyalist who tries to come to Hal's aid when the latter has an asthma attack in the street. Claire tries to dissuade him, but the ruckus attracts a hostile crowd, from which Claire and Hal barely escape. [*MOBY*]

Cawdor, Bobby—A friend from Roger's youth and one of his gang of friends in Inverness. [*Ashes*]

Chemodurow, Iva—Wife of swineherd Mikhail. (The Chemodurows are Real People: friends or acquaintances written in—with their permission—for fun.) [*Fiery Cross*]

Chemodurow, Karina—Daughter of Russian immigrants Iva and Mikhail. When Roger crashes into her in the darkness of Wylie's boathouse, she thinks he's assaulting her, then eagerly complies and is almost disappointed when Roger declines her charms. [*Fiery Cross*]

Chemodurow, Mikhail—Russian swineherd hired by Phillip Wylie to transport Russian boars to Wylie's plantation, where the boars would be released to reproduce for sport hunting. [*Fiery Cross*]

Chenowyth, Mr. and Mrs.—The Chenowyths are the family with whom Claire is temporarily billeted at Coryell's Ferry, when she and Jamie rendezvous there with Washington's troops. [*MOBY*]

Cherry, Captain Robert; Bob—Adjutant officer for Lord John's regiment in Jamaica. [*PZ*]

Chester, Mr.—The owner of a brig in Wilmington harbor that carried Lord John Grey and his stepson, William, from Virginia to North Carolina for William's first military posting. [*Ashes*]

x Chew, Miss—(unknown) One of the daughters of prominent Philadelphia lawyer and Loyalist Benjamin Chew. She flirts with William Ransom at the mischianza held at the Chews' large home in honor of General Howe, who was being replaced by Sir Henry Clinton. [*Echo*]

Chinless Ned, the Ponce—See "Edward Markham."

Chisholm, Charley—One of Geordie Chisholm's teenage sons. [*Fiery Cross*]

Chisholm, Geoff—One of the Chisholm children. [*Fiery Cross*]

Chisholm, Geordie—An ex-prisoner from Ardsmuir; at the end of the Gathering, he and his family travel back to the Ridge, where they take up residence with the Frasers and two other families until a cabin can be built for the growing family. [*Fiery Cross*]

Chisholm, Grannie—The elderly mother of Geordie Chisholm; while traveling with the Frasers from the Gathering to Fraser's Ridge, she narrowly escapes being trampled by Jamie's high-strung horse, Gideon. [*Fiery Cross*]

Chisholm, Mrs.—Geordie Chisholm's wife and the mother of five. [*Fiery Cross*]

Chisholm, Thomas, Anthony, and Toby—Geordie Chisholm's younger sons, ranging in age from five through eight and dubbed "the spawn of Satan" by Mrs. Bug. They ransack Claire's surgery and cause mayhem in the Big House while Geordie and his older sons are off with Jamie and the militia. [*Fiery Cross*]

Chrissy—A maidservant in the Shippen household. [*MOBY*]

Christie, Allan—An immigrant from Scotland with his father, Tom, and sister, Malva. He puts Malva up to accusing Jamie as the father of Malva's unborn child, hoping to gain some Fraser wealth to support himself and his sister away from Fraser's Ridge. After Malva is murdered, Claire finds a suicidal Allan by her graveside, and he confesses to having impregnated his sister and then killed her, Ian, hiding in the nearby woods, shoots and kills Allan with his bow and arrow. [*All*]

Christie, Edgar—Tom Christie's brother in Scotland and Malva's true father, he cared for Tom's wife, Mona, and his son, Allan, while Tom was imprisoned in Ardsmuir after the Rising; in return, Mona killed him. [*Ashes*]

Christie, Malva—Daughter of Tom Christie and sister of Allan. After showing great interest in medicine, she becomes Claire's apprentice—then uses her newfound knowledge to almost kill Claire and her own father, before destroying Claire's trust in her by exposing her secret pregnancy and naming Jamie as the father. Jamie and Claire both know Malva is lying but don't know why. Malva's loose ways eventually become known and she is mysteriously murdered in Claire's garden. Claire finds her moments after the crime is committed and performs a cesarean delivery, but the child also dies within moments. Claire is then accused of Malva's murder and mutilating the corpse for revenge. [*All*]

Christie, Mona—Tom Christie's wife and Malva's mother, suspected of being a witch. When Tom was sent to Ardsmuir, he entrusted his wife to his brother Edgar's care; Mona seduced Edgar, who impregnated her; she later killed him. She was found guilty of murder and sentenced to hang for her crimes while her children were forced to watch. [*Ashes*]

Christie, Thomas; Tom—One of the former Ardsmuir prisoners who locates Jamie on Fraser's Ridge after being transported; he volunteers his services as schoolmaster. There are two concerns with Christie's residence on the Ridge: he is an ardent Protestant, and he harbors a grudge against Jamie from their time in Ardsmuir. As time goes by, despite his gruff demeanor he develops feelings for Claire and acts bravely on her behalf. [*Fiery Cross, Ashes, Echo*]

Cinnamon, John—The child of Malcolm Stubbs (husband to Lord John's cousin Olivia) and an Indian mistress; Lord John gives the child to the Catholic mission near Quebec to raise, and he agrees to provide funds for the child's welfare as long as a lock of hair is sent annually. William encounters Cinnamon years later in Quebec, where the latter is working as a guide, and the two spend the winter together, snowbound. [*CA, Echo*]

Cirencester, Duke of; Jacob Cirencester—One of the guests at Benedicta Grey's party celebrating Clive's victory over the Nawab of Bengal. [*PM*]

Clarence—Jamie's mule; a sociable creature, given to loud greetings. [*All*]

Clellan, Kimmie—A roving singer of Scottish ballads and an acquaintance of Roger's. His song repertoire has given Roger the idea to write down the old ballads and tunes for future generations. [*Fiery Cross*]

x **Clerke, Francis, Captain, Sir**—(1748–1777) General Burgoyne's aide-de-camp at Ticonderoga and Saratoga; killed with

General Simon Fraser by Patriot sniper Tim Murphy. [*Echo*]

Clifford, Captain Leo—An officer from Hal's regiment and one of the piquet players meeting at Almack's gentlemen's club. [*SP*]

X Clinton, Henry, General, Sir—(1730–1795) A field strategist at the Battle of Bunker Hill and second in command to General Howe at Battle of New York; Clinton replaced General Howe as commander in chief upon Howe's resignation after the surrender of Saratoga to the Continental army. [*Echo, MOBY*]

x Clive, Robert—(1725–1774) Also known as "Clive of India," he was a British military officer who established the military and political supremacy of the East India Company in India and a key figure in establishing British India. [*PM*]

Cobb, Reverend Mr.—Curate of St. Giles and part of the Church of England; Miss Stokes brings the Protestant Reverend Cobb to collect the body of Tim O'Connell for burial at St. Giles. An argument ensues, which Lord John is forced to resolve. [*PM*]

Cochrane, Rabbie—One of the residents on Fraser's Ridge. While he's too old to join the militia Jamie is forced to gather, some of his eleven grown children scattered across the mountains will be mustered for Jamie's forces. [*Fiery Cross*]

Coinneach, Mrs.—One of the Protestant residents of Fraser's Ridge, she attends Roger's first sermon and notices that he seems nervous, as he's sweating quite a bit. [*Ashes*]

Coles, Simon—Lawyer to the Thackerays. He receives a message from Anne Thackeray for her sister, Barbara; the letter offers limited information regarding her situation and gives a location somewhere in Southwark. [*HS*]

x Collet, Captain—(unknown) John Collet was a Swiss mapmaker who joined the British army and eventually became the commanding officer at Fort Johnston. [*Ashes*]

Collet, Corporal—After working under Lord John's command for more than two years, he and his company function like a well-oiled machine. [*BL*]

Colson, Lieutenant—A junior officer in William's regiment, in charge of the men while William dines with Lord John and Captain Richardson. [*Echo*]

x Comte St. Germain—See "Robert François Quesnay de St. Germain."

Congreve, Mr.—One of the wine-sellers employed by Fraser et Cie, an importer known for selling a rare German red wine. [*PM*]

x Cope, General—(1690–1760) John Cope was commander-in-chief of Scotland during the Jacobite uprising of 1745; he was defeated by Bonnie Prince Charles's forces during an early-morning surprise attack at Prestonpans. He is forever remembered in a Scottish folk song depicting his defeat and the triumph of the Scots over the English forces. [*BL, HS, CA*]

Corey, Lieutenant—A Middlebrook Encampment officer who may have lied about Benjamin Grey's death while a prisoner at the encampment. [*MOBY*]

x Cornbury, Lord—(1710–1753) Heir to the Earl of Clarendon. He tried to persuade the French to support an invasion to install the Old Pretender and overthrow King George; the French withdrew support, but the Jacobite association followed Cornbury even as he became godfather to Lord John's eldest stepbrother, Paul DeVane. [*BL*]

x **Cornell, Samuel**—(1731–1781) Member of the Governor's Royal Council and wealthy merchant from Edenton. Cornell was included in a council of war held by Governor Tryon and other leaders prior to the Battle of Alamance; he passed information to Jamie about Stephen Bonnet's possible activities near the Outer Banks, most notably just where the contraband was supposedly unloaded. [*Fiery Cross*]

x **Cornwallis, Charles, General, Lord**—(1738–1805) Famous general under Howe, he saw several victories and defeats in the Americas but suffered his greatest humiliation during the Battle of Yorktown, when combined Patriot and French forces surrounded his army and forced him to surrender, thus ending a great deal of the fighting in the North American theater. [*Ashes, Echo, MOBY*]

Coulter, Willie—The only person other than Claire to witness Jamie killing Dougal MacKenzie on the evening before Culloden. [*Echo*]

Cowden, Amaranthus—Benjamin Grey's alleged wife, and mother to his supposed son, Trevor Wattiswade Grey. [*MOBY*]

x **Cowley, Hannah, Mrs.**—(1743–1809) London playwright William met prior to arriving in America and whose work largely revolved around marriage and women's social roles. [*Echo*]

Crabbot, Old—One of Lord John's senior contacts within the Black Chamber, possibly retired from active duty. [*Echo*]

Craddock, Captain—One of the captains under Jamie's command at Monmouth. [*MOBY*]

Crawford, Mrs.—One of Wilmington's prominent hostesses, her musical evenings are in direct competition with those of Mrs. Dunning, and while her assembly lacked a poet of comic verse, lovely-smelling wax-myrtle candles were burned, prompting Claire and company to go on an outing to locate wax-myrtle berries. [*Fiery Cross*]

Crenshaw—One of the junior officers in Lord John's regiment. [*PM*]

Cresswell, Captain—The white superintendent appointed by the Crown to oversee the maroons living on Jamaica; he disappeared prior to Lord John's arrival and his whereabouts are unknown. [*PZ*]

Crombie, Hiram—A dour Scots Protestant immigrant and leader of the Protestant fisher-folk who settled on Fraser's Ridge, he doesn't always see eye to eye with the Catholic Frasers. Hiram studies the Indian languages from Ian and Jamie so he may minister God's word to the tribes near the Ridge. [*All*]

Crombie, Mairi—Wife of Presbyterian settler Hiram Crombie and daughter of old Mrs. Wilson, who dies twice in one day. [*Ashes*]

Crosbie, Captain—One of General Clinton's aides. [*MOBY*]

Crossley, Mr.—A botanist friend of Mr. Stanhope, Crossley possesses an extensive ornamental garden in England. Stanhope wishes to exchange the roots and seeds of the North Carolina native flora for some of Crossley's herbal garden specimens and offers to share the forthcoming specimens with Claire for use in medicines and healing. [*Fiery Cross*]

Crupp, Amos—Proprietor of the Wilmington newspaper, the *Gazette,* and the printer who changed the date of the fire on Fraser's Ridge to save space, inevitably causing Brianna and Roger to travel to the eighteenth century. [*Ashes, Echo*]

Crusoe—A stable-hand at Lord Dunsany's estate, Helwater, located in the Lake District of England. [*SP*]

Culper, Abel—The citizen with whom William is billeted after being sent to Long Island for fighting with Lieutenant "Chinless Ned" Markham over a crude cartoon. [*Echo*]

Culper, Abigail—One of Abel Culper's elderly sisters, who dote on William; he returns the favor by bringing gifts of food or drink. [*Echo*]

Culper, Beulah—The second of Abel Culper's elderly sisters and the keeper of the noisy goats; she insists that their braying keeps thieves from the corncrib. [*Echo*]

x **Cumberland**—(1721–1765) Prince William Augustus, Duke of Cumberland, and younger son of King George II; leader of the King's forces during the Forty-five, bent on subduing the Jacobite Rising and stamping out its remains. He involves himself in a court-martial in which Lord John and his brother, Hal, have an interest. [*FC, SP*]

Cumberpatch, Anthony—The farmer who won J. W. MacKenzie's dog tags in a dice game. [*MOBY*]

Cumberpatch, Mrs.—The wife of Anthony Cumberpatch. [*MOBY*]

Custis, Captain—An officer from the Ninth Regiment, commanded by John's friend Colonel Jeffreys. He accompanies Lord John to his quarters to retrieve a book that Jeffreys wishes to borrow from Lord John and is one of the officers present to witness Percy's act of sodomy with a German soldier. [*BL*]

Cutter, Sergeant Aloysius—A military comrade of Lord John Grey during the Battle of Quebec, his commanding voice encourages the British troops in their victory over the French; Lord John's stepson, William, later encounters Sergeant Cutter when he reaches America. [*CA, Echo*]

D

x **Dacres, Lieutenant James**—(1749–1810) Captain of British schooner *Carleton* at the Battle of Lake Champlain; after the heavy battle, which he survived in real life, went on to lead a distinguished British naval career. [*Echo*]

Daisy—A camp prostitute at Saratoga, who brings Claire some meat pies in return for healing, the medical issue being something Claire deems unmentionable while Jamie is eating. [*Echo*]

Dalrymple, Hector—John Grey's first lover; killed at Culloden at age eighteen, only two years older than John. [*PM, BL, CA, SP*]

Danner—One of the regimental surgeons assigned to Hal's regiment in Prussia. [*BL*]

Darcy, Hugh—A stable owner in Dublin who outfits Jamie and Lord John with horses for their journey to Athlone. [*SP*]

x **Dartmouth, Lord; William Legge**—(1731–1801) Second Earl of Dartmouth, secretary of state for the colonies during the early part of the Revolution, and a proponent of educating and Christianizing the Indians. He helped finance a charitable Indian school in Connecticut but refused to be coerced into financially backing the New Hampshire college that its founder named in the earl's honor. [*Ashes*]

x **Dashwood, Francis, Sir**—(1708–1781) An English libertine with powerful political connections and the founder of the notorious Hellfire Club, located in underground caves in West Wycombe. [*HF, PM*]

Davies, Andy—One of Brianna's co-workers at the hydroelectric dam, and the thief who leaves her without a flashlight during the trick played on her first day on the job. [*Echo*]

Davison, Mr. and Mrs.—Loyalist stable owners in Philadelphia. [*MOBY*]

Dawes, Gideon—The secretary for Governor Warren, and Lord John's adviser regarding the events in the governor's household and on the island of Jamaica. [*PZ*]

Deacon/Deke—An elderly horse belonging to the Dunsany stables; William is introduced to him by Jamie. [*SP*]

x **Deane, Silas**—(1737–1789) American merchant and lawyer, agent sent to France to seek military assistance; conspired with Beaumarchais to use the fictitious Hortalez et Cie company to import weapons and ammunition into America for the Continental army. He was later accused of treason for unknowingly sharing information with British double agent Edward Bancroft but was not prosecuted, due to a lack of evidence at the time of the indiscretion. [*Echo*]

Deborah—Brianna's twentieth-century friend who performed tarot readings when Brianna was at college; though Brianna would never let Deb read her cards, she dreams of a reading where the Hanged Man card keeps appearing, making her reflect on Roger's dilemma. [*Fiery Cross*]

x **de Chaulnes, Duchess**—(unknown) The duke's considerably older wife, host of several notable literary salons in Paris; Jamie attends one of these and entertains the crowd with stories of the American colonies and how he lost his finger. [*Echo*]

x **de Chaulnes, Duke**—(1741–1792) A young French noble with a much older wife, interested in science and the Americas—especially the Indians; also a close friend of Beaumarchais, the founder of the French-based supply company Hortalez & Cie, a joint French–Spanish arms/ammunitions supplier to the Continental army. [*Echo*]

x **de Clermont, Comte**—(1709–1771) Louis de Bourbon, he took over command of the French forces during the Seven Years' War when the Duc de Richelieu abruptly resigned his commission and returned to France. [*BL*]

x **de Lamerie, Paul**—(1688–1751) A famous London-based silversmith, noted by some as the greatest silversmith of the eighteenth century. One of his pieces is stolen by the Comte St. Germain on one of his time-traveling forays. [*SB*]

de Marillac, Annalise—Woman Jamie dueled over in Paris. [*MOBY*]

Denys—One of Stephen Bonnet's seamen, he helps row the boat containing a kidnapped Brianna to Bonnet's hideout on Ocracoke Island. [*Ashes*]

x **DeRosset, Lewis**—(unknown) Adjutant general of Governor Tryon's army; DeRosset was included in a council of war held by Governor Tryon and other leaders prior to the Battle of Alamance. [*Fiery Cross*]

Desplains, Colonel—William's senior officer. [*MOBY*]

x **d'Estaing, Admiral**—(1729–1794) An admiral of the French navy sailing to aid the Continental forces. [*MOBY*]

DeVane, Captain—Benedicta Grey's first husband and father of her two elder sons, Edgar and Paul, half brothers to Lord John and Hal. [*PM, HS*]

DeVane, Edgar—One of Lord John's older half brothers from his mother's first marriage. Edgar resembles his handsome father; he is owner of a gunpowder mill and is the largest shareholder in a consortium with other Sussex gunpowder producers selling their products to the Royal Ordnance Office. [*PM, BL, HS*]

DeVane, Maude—Wife of Edgar Devane and sister-in-law to Lord John Grey. [*HS*]

DeVane, Paul—The elder of Lord John's two half brothers residing in Sussex; considered a strikingly handsome man who resembles his father but is not altogether very bright. [*PM, HS*]

DeVries—One of the junior officers in Lord John's regiment, who helps spread the rumor that the regiment was posting back to Calais in France. [*PM*]

Dewhurst, Lord—A nobleman Lord John and Harry Quarry observe returning after using the chamber pot at the Beefsteak. [*PM*]

x **Diderot, Denis**—(1713–1784) French philosopher, writer, frequent guest of intellectual salons in France during the Enlightenment period of the eighteenth century, and a member of the salon Jamie attends in Paris with Mr. Lyle. [*BL, SP, Echo*]

Dietrich, Lieutenant—The Hanovarian officer in charge of an artillery crew guarding the bridge. Grey gives him the dispatch from von Namtzen regarding the questionable movements of the French troops. [*SU*]

Digger—See "Swiftest of Lizards."

Dilman—A frightened young maidservant in Governor Josiah Martin's home; she escorts Claire—the midwife—to the side of the governor's very pregnant wife in New Bern. [*Ashes*]

Dobbs—Horace Suddfield's assistant at Lady Joffrey's electric-eel party, who announces there are forty-five people connected and awaiting the performance. [*CA*]

Dobbs, Mr.—The strong-arm employed by the Beefsteak to keep ruffians and miscreants from entering and disturbing the peace and harmony of the club's members, as well as to keep the peace between members themselves. He was not easily intimidated. [*HS*]

Dobson, Harry—Another junior officer in William's regiment in Wilmington, caught ogling Brianna. [*Echo*]

Dolly—See "Marjorie MacKenzie."

Donahue, Father Kenneth—The traveling Catholic priest at Mount Helicon, who is forbidden to perform the sacraments after his arrest by local officials, leaving Jocasta and Brianna unwed; the priest performs secretive christenings on Jamie's grandchildren after Jamie creates a diversion and the young mothers and Claire sneak the children into Father Donahue's tent. [*Fiery Cross*]

Donner, Wendigo—One of the Montauk Five, Donner is a time traveler from the 1960s, who was with the group that abducted Claire. [*Ashes, Echo*]

Donoghue, Mrs.—The housekeeper at Nessie's new house at the end of Brydges Street. [*SP*]

Doreen—A housemaid at Lord John's residence on Chestnut Street in Philadelphia. [*MOBY*]

x **d'Orléans, Louis, Duc**—(1703–1752) Cousin of Louis XV and the King of France's heir apparent (until the King's own son was born). [*SP, Echo*]

Dornan, Gully—A youth living on Fraser's Ridge and practical joker; his favorite joke was sneaking a snake into church services, he was apprehended by Hiram Crombie before his mischief could take place. [*Ashes*]

Dottie—see "Lady Dorothea Grey."

Dottie—One of the prostitutes at Mrs. Sylvie's establishment, Dottie is said to have a partiality for women in her bed. [*Ashes*]

Doyle, Father—The Catholic parish priest in London's Irish area near Clare Market. He weds Finbar Scanlon and the Widow O'Connell shortly after her husband is found murdered and attempts to gain possession of O'Connell's body for burial, although Widow O'Connell thinks her former husband is already in hell. [*PM*]

x **Drummond, Duncan, Captain**—One of Sir Henry Clinton's senior aides-de-camp, who berates William for the loss of William's gorget. [*MOBY*]

x **Drummond, William, Governor**—(1617–1677) First governor of North Carolina, who discovered a huge natural lake within the Great Dismal Swamp. Lake Drummond was named in his honor. [*Echo*]

Dubois—A comrade of Jamie's at the university in Paris, he urges Jamie to have his palm read by a gypsy woman, teasing Jamie with meowing and yowling when she calls him a "little red cat"—complete with nine lives. [*Ashes*]

x **Duchess of Kendal**—(unknown) A recently deceased society dowager, to whom Horace Walpole compares Lord John based on John's sickly complexion while recovering from wounds suffered at the Battle of Crefeld. [*BL*]

Duff—An acquaintance of Roger's and former deckhand on the *Gloriana*—Stephen Bonnet's ship. The grizzled old man is hired to row the Frasers and MacKenzies to view a dead whale grounded on an island near Wilmington Harbor, while giving Jamie and Roger valuable information on Bonnet's whereabouts. [*Fiery Cross*]

Dugan, Patrick, Reverend—One of the religious leaders present at Reverend McMillan's home in Edenton when Roger is studying for his ordination as a Presbyterian minister. [*Ashes*]

x **Duke of Gloucester**—(1743–1805) Prince William Henry of Hanover, the younger brother of King George III, third son of Frederick, Prince of Wales. [*PM*]

Duke of Pardloe—See "Harold Grey."

x **Dunbonnet**—Jamie's identity for the seven years after Culloden when he was hiding from the English; based on a real person named James Fraser of Foyers, who actually lived in a small cave for seven years post-Culloden. [*Echo*]

Duncan, Arthur—Procurator fiscal in Cranesmuir, and husband to Geillis. Roger and Buck see him briefly when they visit Cranesmuir in 1739. [*MOBY*]

Duncan, Geillis (aka Geilie, Geillis Abernathy, and Gillian Edgars)—A mysterious young woman and fellow time traveler from the twentieth century, whom Claire meets upon her arrival in the eighteenth century. Accused of being a witch and murderess in Scotland, Geillis is sentenced to be burned but is given a temporary reprieve by reason of pregnancy; she bears a child to Dougal MacKenzie. With his help, she escapes to Paris, then makes her way to the West Indies, soon becoming the rich widow of plantation owner Mr. Abernathy. She attempts to travel back to her own time, which leads her to a final confrontation with Claire in the cave of Abandawe. [*All, PZ*]

Dundas, Christopher, Lieutenant—A young Scottish officer in charge of a survey party assigned to spy on the French forces to ascertain the size and quantity of the enemy's artillery. [*SU*]

Dunkling, Lieutenant—One of Lord

Dunsmore's young officers in Virginia, who will sell Duncan Innes guns and powder to pass on to General Donald MacDonald for his Highland regiment, to help crush the militia. [*Ashes*]

x **Dunmore, Lord**—(1730–1809) John Murray, Fourth Earl of Dunmore and last royal governor of Virginia. In order to allay plantation owners' fears of slave uprisings within the colonies, he passed a freedom proclamation for all slaves and indentured men who agreed to join the royal militia and defend against the Patriot forces. [*Ashes*]

Dunning, Mrs.—Another of Wilmington's prominent hostesses, her musical evenings are in direct competition with those of Mrs. Crawford; Mrs. Dunning also utilizes a local poet to recite phrases both tragic and comedic. [*Fiery Cross*]

Dunphy, Mr.—Former Philadelphia resident and Loyalist printer, was Fergus's competition. [*MOBY*]

Dunsany, Geneva; Lady Geneva—Eldest daughter of the Dunsany family of Helwater, she takes a shine to Jamie Fraser while he's a paroled groom there and blackmails him into sharing her bed before her marriage to a nobleman twice her age; Geneva becomes pregnant after their one night together and dies soon after giving birth to Jamie's son, William Ransom. [*BL, SP, Ashes, Echo, MOBY*]

Dunsany, Gordon—The only son of Lord and Lady Dunsany and heir to Helwater; a close friend of Lord John, he was killed during the Rising. [*BL, SP*]

Dunsany, Isobel—Younger daughter of Lord and Lady Dunsany of Helwater, younger sister to Geneva. Following the death of her sister in childbed, Isobel becomes foster mother to Geneva's child, William, and later marries Lord John Grey, who thus becomes the boy's stepfather and guardian. [*BL, SP, Ashes, Echo, MOBY*]

Dunsany, Lady—Wife of Lord Dunsany, mother of Geneva and Isobel, and grandmother to William—the Ninth Earl of Ellesmere. Acute observation causes her to suspect the actual parentage of her grandchild; thus she offers to arrange Jamie's pardon so that he can leave Helwater. He declines her offer, wishing to stay near the infant William. [*BL, SP*]

Dunsany, Lord—A minor aristocrat and friend of Lord John Grey who accepts Jamie Fraser (under the alias Alexander MacKenzie) as a groom on his estate, Helwater, as a favor to Lord John. He arranges his daughter Geneva's marriage to the elderly Earl of Ellesmere, hoping this will ensure her shortly becoming a wealthy young widow and a countess. [*BL, SP, Ashes*]

E

x **Earl of Orford**—(1701–1751) Robert Walpole, eldest son of the first prime minister, who gave his word to recommend clemency should Percy Wainwright be condemned in his court-martial trial. [*BL*]

Eats Turtles—A Mohawk man Ian knows from his time in Snaketown; he finds Ian after the stillbirth of Ian's daughter. [*Ashes, Echo, MOBY*]

Edgars, Gillian—See "Geillis Duncan."

Eevis—Large, aggressive farm dog set on Roger and Buck by a farmer while they're hunting Roger's dad. [*MOBY*]

Elise—Stephan von Namtzen's young daughter, who, along with her brother, is forced to live with Stephan's mother while he is fulfilling his military duty. [*SU, SP*]

Ellesmere, Earl of (Old)—Ludovic, the Eighth Earl of Ellesmere; the elderly husband to Geneva Dunsany and putative father of William, Viscount Ashness. Killed by Jamie Fraser while threatening the life of the newborn infant whom he knows to be the result of cuckoldry. [*BL, SP*]

Ellesmere, Ninth Earl of—See "William Ransom."

Elliott, Miss—One of the impressionable ladies present at the Duke de Chaulnes's Paris salon, where Jamie recounts his story of the Iroquois amputating and eating his finger. [*Echo*]

Elspeth, Nanny—Geneva and Isobel Dunsany's elderly nurse, she accompanies Geneva to her new marriage home but returns to Helwater to help raise the child when Geneva and Lord Ellesmere both die on the same day. [*BL, SP*]

Emile—The sub-gardener and lover of Percival Beauchamp at Baron Amandine's estate, *Trois Flèches.* He apparently reminds Percy of a younger Lord John. [*Echo*]

Emily (aka Wakyo'teyeshsnonhsa, "Works With Her Hands")—Ian's Mohawk wife, unable to carry a pregnancy to term with Ian; devastated, Ian is forced to leave the Mohawk after the third miscarriage. Emily turns to Sun Elk, full-blood Mohawk brave, and is finally able to have children. [*Echo*]

Emmanuel—Stephen Bonnet's butler and bodyguard, one of the Ibo tribe of Africa; he believes in the superstitions of his homeland. A large man with a cruel streak, he keeps Brianna under guard and beats her. She later stabs him to death with an ivory corset busk. [*Ashes*]

Endicott, Anne—Elder daughter of the Endicotts. [*MOBY*]

Endicott, Margaret; Peggy—Age nine, the youngest of the Endicott children. [*MOBY*]

Endicott, Mr.—Loyalist traveling out of Philadelphia with the British army. [*MOBY*]

Endicott, Mrs.—Wife of Mr. Endicott. [*MOBY*]

Endicott, Sally—Middle daughter of the Endicotts. [*MOBY*]

Entwidge—One of the regimental surgeons assigned to Hal's regiment in Prussia. [*BL*]

Erlande, Mademoiselle—One of the ladies present at the Duke de Chaulnes's Paris salon where Jamie recounts his entertaining story of the Iroquois amputating and eating his finger; she is observed in some sort of wanton behavior with Mr. Lyle, the man Jamie accompanied to the salon. [*Echo*]

Esmé—Hal's first wife, a beautiful French woman who was seduced by Nathaniel Twelvetrees and died in childbirth along with her first child. [*BL, SP*]

Esmeralda—Mandy's red-haired rag doll. [*MOBY*]

Ethan and Johnny—Two children Lord John witnesses running loose on the Philadelphia docks when a small riot breaks out among British soldiers and local citizens waiting for the ferry. Lord John is despondent over recent bad news and, instead of taking charge of the situation, walks away. [*Echo*]

Eugenie—One of the grooms at Helwater. [*SP*]

Eulalie, Madame—An upper-scale seamstress in Charleston, South Carolina, hired to sew maternity clothes for Amaranthus Grey. [*MOBY*]

Eustace—Benedicta Grey's favorite dog, an elderly spaniel. [*PM*]

Evans, Corporal—An enlisted man in William's regiment on Long Island when William becomes lost in the fog. [*Echo*]

Evans, Mr.—Mrs. Raven's first husband, who had been a fisherman and violent drunkard; he would cut off the noses or ears of those who displeased him and nail them to the goat shed, which, according to Mrs. Raven, caused said parts to shrivel up like dried mushrooms. [*Echo*]

Evans, Thomas, Captain—One of William's fellow officers and tentmates on the road to Monmouth. [*MOBY*]

Everett, Colonel—An officer at Saratoga who promises Claire two assistants to help her with any battle injuries. [*Echo*]

Everett, George—A young dark-haired London contemporary of Lord John's; a brief affair with him caused the scandal that sent Lord John to Scotland as the governor of Ardsmuir Prison. He extends an invitation to Lord John to become a member of the Hellfire Club. [*HF, PM*]

Everett, Mr.—The South Carolina plantation owner to whom Tom Christie was indentured as a schoolteacher after being transported from Scotland when Ardsmuir was closed. After Everett's death from influenza, Christie was forced to look for employment elsewhere. [*Fiery Cross*]

Ezra—A member of Richard Brown's gang that arrests Claire for the alleged murder of Malva Christie, and Jamie as an accessory; Claire shoots Ezra during the arrest, and even though she offers to treat his wound, he refuses. During the trek toward Wilmington to find a justice to try Jamie and Claire, his wound festers and he falls from his horse, dead. [*Ashes*]

F

x **Fanning, Edmund**—(1739-1808) Crown attorney and clerk of the Superior Court of Orange County, N.C.; Fanning was a close friend of Governor Tryon's and received several select positions due to those allegiances. He was attacked by Regulators for his close association with the governor as well as the public's belief in his malfeasance. [*Fiery Cross*]

Fanny—A Belgian draft horse belonging to Lord Dunsany, she goes missing, only to be found with Isobel's maid Betty Mitchell upon her back. [*SP*]

Fanshawe, Douglas—Owner of Mudlington, his gunpowder mill comprises one-third of the Sussex consortium headed by Edgar DeVane; his only son is Marcus who was severely injured during an explosion at the gunpowder mill. [*HS*]

Fanshawe, Marcus, Captain—The only son of gunpowder-mill owner Douglas Fanshawe, he is critically injured during an explosion at one of the manufacturing sheds; the severe disfigurement of his head and face causes him to wear a black silk mask. [*HS*]

Father Alexandre—A Jesuit priest cruelly killed by the Iroquois after fathering a child with a maiden, then refusing to baptize the child. [*Echo*]

Father Anselm—A priest visiting Ste. Anne de Beaupré while Jamie is recovering from his treatment by Jack Randall. Father Anselm keeps Jamie company on nights when his ordeal prevents him from sleeping; he also counsels Claire on the morality of time travel. [*Ashes*]

Father Fenstermacher—A priest in Hanover who Stephan von Namzten indicates is strict when handing out penance for sinners. [*SP*]

Father Gehring—A priest near von Namtzen's home who is not as liable to hand down strict penance as is Father Fenstermacher. [*SP*]

Father Jim—An Irish priest in the London slum called the Rookery, he is to aid the O'Higgins brothers in procuring a body to substitute for Percy's, thereby completing Percy's escape from Newgate. [*BL*]

Father McCarthy—The elderly Catholic priest at Lallybroch who performed the wedding ceremony between Laoghaire and Jamie. [*Echo*]

Faydree—See "Phaedre."

Fentiman, Charles, Dr.—A surgeon from Cross Creek and Claire's medical rival. While not always medically adept—too ready to "bleed" his patients and not very sanitary—he is a sensitive man who genuinely cares for his patients; he is the first to treat the doomed glass-ingesting slave woman at River Run, then later treats Stephen Bonnet for a bullet hole through the testicle. [*All*]

x **Ferdinand, Duke**—(1735–1806) A Prussian field marshal with Frederick during the Seven Years' War. Hal's regiment is ordered to join him in Prussia. [*BL*]

Ferguson, Mr.—The solicitor who employs young Buck MacKenzie as his clerk. [*MOBY*]

Ferguson, Sadie, Mrs.—A woman with whom Claire shares a jail cell while in New Bern following Malva's death. A convicted forger who's addicted to gin and card-playing, Mrs. Ferguson falsely claims to be Malva's murderer, as the sentence for murder is less severe than that for forgery. [*Ashes*]

x **Fermoy, Matthias, General**—(ca. 1737–ca. 1780) French soldier of fortune at Fort Ticonderoga who claimed to be an engineer. Upon General Gates's decision to withdraw quietly and secretly from Burgoyne's advancing army, Fermoy failed to deliver the message to his entire regiment on Mount Independence and, against orders, set fire to his lodging upon leaving. The fire acted as a bright light to expose the secret withdrawal of the Continental forces. [*Echo*]

Fettes, Major—One of Lord John's officers while on Jamaica. [*PZ*]

Ffoulkes, Melchior—A solicitor in Lincoln's Inn, married to a French woman, and the recipient of military secrets forwarded by Captain Bates, who had been chief aide to General Stanley, Lord John's new stepfather, prior to a transfer. [*BL*]

x **Fielding, John, Sir**—(1721–1780) The social reformer some called "the Blind Beak," he was appointed as London chief magistrate and head of the Bow Street Runners when his older brother, Henry, founder of that first paid law-enforcement squad, died. Due to artistic license, a small detail regarding Fielding's title has changed because John Fielding was not knighted until 1761, four years after *Private Matter* takes place. [*PM*]

Figg, Jerusha, Mrs.—The large, round, free-black woman of uncertain temper and a gift for foul language was hired by Lord John to be his cook at his home in Philadelphia. [*Echo, MOBY*]

Figg, Reverend Mortimer—Husband of Mrs. Figg, Lord John's housekeeper in Philadelphia. [*MOBY*]

Filmer, Corporal—One of the militia company belonging to Captain Craddock (who is killed in the Battle of Monmouth).[*MOBY*]

Findlay, Annie—Joanie Findlay's elder daughter, summoned to fetch Joanie's brothers to speak to Roger regarding their joining the militia. [*Fiery Cross*]

Findlay, Hugh—One of Joan Findlay's teenage sons, prepared to join Fraser's militia. [*Fiery Cross*]

Findlay, Iain Óg—One of Joan Findlay's

teenage sons, prepared to join Fraser's militia. [*Fiery Cross*]

Findlay, Joan; Auld Joan—Sister to Iain Mhor; one of the residents on Fraser's Ridge with two capable brothers and two sons old enough to fight with Jamie's militia. [*Fiery Cross*]

Findlay, Joanie; Wee Joanie—Joan Findlay's younger daughter, who takes over the pot-stirring while her mother takes Roger to meet Iain Mhor regarding the Findlay sons joining the militia. [*Fiery Cross*]

Findlay, Major—A British army officer who sends William's groom, Colenso Baragwanath, in search of William. [*MOBY*]

Findlay, Tom—Another of Joanie Findley's male relatives who join the militia and is in camp after Alamance. [*Fiery Cross*]

Finlay, Mary—The young girl caught in a compromising position with Donald McAllister. [*MOBY*]

Firouz—The Persian manservant of field professor Quentin Lambert Beauchamp. Firouz helps with Claire's unconventional upbringing after she is adopted by "Uncle Lamb," her late father's only brother. [*Fiery Cross*]

FitzGibbons, Michael, Father—Cousin to Jamie Fraser's godfather, Murtagh, and abbot of Inchcleraun in Ireland. [*SP*]

Fitzwalter, Hugh, Sir—An elderly baronet with estates in Sussex, apparently oblivious to the publicly flirtatious actions of his wife. [*HF*]

Fitzwalter, Lady—The wife of an elderly baronet from Sussex, she flirts shamelessly with Harry Quarry, who has no qualms about her marital status. [*HF*]

Flying Arrow—Mohawk warrior killed during Roger's rescue from the Kahnyen'kehaka and whose place Ian takes. [*MOBY*]

Flynn, Jack—A notorious Irish highwayman scheduled to be hanged at Tyburn. The crush of a "leave-taking" party of well-wishers and friends flooding into Newgate prison prior to his hanging is sure to cause confusion and distraction while Percy Wainwright is spirited out of the prison. [*BL*]

Follard, Captain—Captain of the *Cruizer,* the British ship anchored at the mouth of the Cape Fear River. Governor Josiah Martin retreats to the ship, with Claire still in custody, when the Patriots overrun New Bern and set fire to Fort Johnston. [*Ashes*]

Forbes, Elspeth—Neil Forbes's elderly mother, whom he loves dearly; Jamie and Roger use Mrs. Forbes as leverage to discover Brianna's whereabouts after Neil has her kidnapped by Stephen Bonnet's men. [*Ashes*]

Forbes, Neil—A prominent resident and lawyer in Cross Creek; he brought four gemstones to assist his suit when paying court to Brianna but was rejected and lost the stones to Jamie in a high-stakes card game. Constantly seeking retribution for his imagined slights, he has Brianna kidnapped and given to the pirate Stephen Bonnet. As revenge, Ian cuts Forbes's ear off, then smokes the ear and carries it in his sporran. (Introduced as Gerald in *Drums of Autumn,* his name was changed in subsequent books to "Neil.") [*Fiery Cross, Ashes, Echo*]

Fortescue, Mamie, Mrs.—A striking blond woman whom Harry Quarry claims—along with a bottle of wine—at Benedicta Grey's party celebrating Clive's victory over the Nawab of Bengal. [*PM*]

Fortnum, Anthony, Lieutenant—One of William Ransom's roommates during the New York occupation with General Howe's army. [*Echo*]

Foster, Harry, Lieutenant—Foster delivers an order from Sir Henry Clinton to William, who decides to ignore said order. [*MOBY*]

x **Foster, Jedidiah, Colonel**—(1726–1779) Harvard-educated lawyer and militia leader from Brookfield, Massachusetts, his regiment was present at the Battle of Lexington on April 19, 1775, and he was an elected delegate for the First Provincial Congress. [*Ashes*]

Fowles, Hugh—Joe Hobson's young son-in-law, who participates in the Hillsborough riots after being put out of his house by the British sheriff for non-payment of taxes. [*Fiery Cross*]

x **Fox, George**—(1624–1691) Founder of the Quaker religion, or Religious Society of Friends, whose purpose was to live by following examples in the Bible, forsaking violence, and seeking a peaceful life; he believed that women had souls and that personal faith, not education, was all that was required to become a member of the clergy, even for women and children. [*Fiery Cross, MOBY*]

x **Franklin, Benjamin**—(1706–1790) Scientist, writer, printer, politician, and first postmaster general; one of the Founding Fathers of the United States, minister to France, also noted ladies' man who practiced nude sunbathing in the belief it was beneficial for various health reasons. Lord John observes him doing this during a visit to the *Trois Flèches* estate. [*Echo, MOBY*]

Franz—The young soldier who meets fellow soldier Samson under the bridge to become his lover; later, Lord John pulls him from a badger hole and learns from him of the Austrian forces gathering near. [*SU*]

Fraser, Alexander—Brother to Jamie's father, Brian; abbot of Ste. Anne de Beaupré priory in France. [*SP*]

x **Fraser, Archibald**—(unknown) Younger brother and Young Simon's heir, also died childless. [*MOBY*]

Fraser, Bobby—One of the Frasers of Glenhelm, not Lovat, a very distant clansman to Jamie; he was the man who caught young Arch Bug and cut off his bow fingers when the young man was on a raid against the Frasers at Glenshiels; later both Bobby of Glenhelm and his nephew Leslie were found dead in a ditch—their heads caved in by an ax. [*Ashes*]

Fraser, Brian; Black Brian; Brian Dubh—Husband to Ellen MacKenzie; father of Jamie Fraser and Jenny Fraser Murray; he was the illegitimate—but recognized—son of Lord Lovat, Simon Fraser. [*All*]

Fraser, Claire Elizabeth Beauchamp Randall—Born Oct. 20, 1918; World War II army nurse. On a second honeymoon in Scotland with her husband, historian and former MI6 agent Frank Randall, she walks through a circle of standing stones and straight into the eighteenth century—where she's obliged to rely on wit, courage, and her noticeable skill with healing in order to survive. In the course of events, she's forced to marry a young clansman named James Fraser in order to avoid falling into the hands of the dangerous Black Jack Randall, after which things become Much More Complicated. [Author's Note: it might be argued that if you've bought this particular book, you already know everything there is to know about Claire, but, what the heck, we aim for completeness. . . .] Joining Claire's story at the beginning of *The Fiery Cross* (her adventures through the earlier novels are synopsized in *The Outlandish Companion,*

Volume One), we find her at a Gathering on Mount Helicon in North Carolina, sleeping next to one husband and dreaming of another. It's her daughter Brianna's wedding day; no wonder that Claire should think of her first husband, Frank Randall, who was Brianna's father for all of her childhood and adolescence. But sentiment is fleeting when it's been raining for three days, the food is running short, eight—no, nine—people are coming for dinner, there are no clean diapers, and you've started your period. Whisky helps. So does a husband who knows to give you some if you threaten to bite him if he kisses you. Beyond the domestic issues, Claire is dealing with her usual round of medical cases; there's nothing like a large public gathering for injuries and contagious illnesses—and that's *before* a Highland regiment of the British army shows up. Another thing that happens at large gatherings with a lot of alcohol is politics, and the backcountry of North Carolina is simmering with resentment of taxes and social injustices perpetrated by British rule. Claire, who knows all too well where this sort of thing is leading, is scared stiff at the idea of Jamie (and Roger, and Young Ian, and the other men of the Ridge) being caught up in such things. She's right to be scared; in the fullness of time, as the Regulator movement grows, Jamie is obliged to bring men to back up the royal governor as he attacks the Regulators, and Claire finds herself, along with Brianna, in the vicinity of the Battle of Alamance. She's patching up the wounded when a woman rushes up, looking for Jamie, and gasps out that they (Tryon's troops) are hanging Roger MacKenzie! Through chance or the grace of God (not always separate things), Roger survives the hanging, and Claire narrowly manages to save his life with an emergency tracheotomy. But his voice is gone. The important thing, though, is that the family is preserved: the new young marriage of the MacKenzies, Jamie and Claire's larger inclusive family—and the community of Fraser's Ridge. But it's not a peaceful time, and threats are constant. Some threats are external, as the process that will lead to rebellion and independence gathers steam, and some are internal. One of the external threats is the existence of lawless bandit gangs that roam the mountains, burning and looting. One of these gangs comes upon Marsali and Claire at the malting shed, and leaving the pregnant Marsali knocked out, they take Claire with them, with some idea of ransoming her to Jamie, who is perceived to be wealthy. One of the bandits warns them that this is a Bad Idea, but being Bad People, they naturally don't listen. They should have. . . . They also shouldn't have beaten and raped Claire, but they did. Jamie, with Roger, Ian, and the other men of the Ridge, tracks and rescues her, and deals out justice ("Kill them all") to the perpetrators. Still, his only real focus is Claire. He knows too well what kind of lasting wounds such experiences leave and is racked with fear of losing her soul, even though he's recovered her body. But he's willing to relive his own hell to get her back, and she recognizes his courage and meets it with her own. *("I have lived through a fucking world war," I said, my voice low and venomous. "I have lost a child. I have lost two husbands. I have starved with an army, been beaten and wounded, been patronized, betrayed, imprisoned, and at-*

tacked. And I have fucking survived!" My voice was rising, but I was helpless to stop it. "And now should I be shattered because some wretched, pathetic excuses for men stuck their nasty little appendages between my legs and wiggled *them?!" I stood up, seized the edge of the washstand and heaved it over, sending everything flying with a crash—basin, ewer, and lighted candlestick, which promptly went out.*

"Well, I won't," I said quite calmly.

"Nasty little appendages?" he said, looking rather stunned.

"Not yours," I said. "I didn't mean yours. I'm rather fond of yours." Then I sat down and burst into tears.)

Part of her recovery is her determination to resume doing what she needs to do, being who she's always known she is: a healer. As to the internal threats to the peace of the Ridge: one of the new tenants, Thomas Christie, has a nubile young daughter named Malva, who seems to take to Claire and shows signs of becoming her much-longed-for apprentice. These hopes go up in flames when Malva turns up pregnant and—dragged in front of Jamie by her father—accuses Jamie of being the father. Talk and suspicion begin to split the community—which ruptures when Claire finds Malva in Claire's own garden, her throat freshly cut. Claire tries to save the unborn child with a cesarean performed with her gardening knife, but the child dies in her hands—just as she in turn is discovered. Talk grows worse, and the Browns—a belligerent family from a nearby settlement—press to have Claire tried for murder. They organize a posse and take her from the house, delivering her to a jail in New Bern to await trial. Mistaken as a forger, she becomes the governor's unwilling amanuensis and goes with him when he's obliged to flee the governor's palace and take refuge aboard a ship in the harbor. Here Jamie finds her but is unable to convince the governor to release her. He leaves and finds Thomas Christie. Christie comes aboard and confesses that he murdered his daughter out of shame and disgust at her scandalous behavior. He surrenders himself to the governor's justice—but alone with Claire, he confesses that he's in love with her and feels that saving her is one of the few truly good things he's done in his life; he's not afraid to die for her. Emotionally shattered by all of this, Claire goes home with Jamie to the Ridge, where she eventually learns the last part of Malva's story. The final trauma of the book, though, is Amanda's heart defect and Claire's anguish at being unable to heal her granddaughter. She is forced to tell Bree that while the child could easily be cured in the twentieth century, there is no hope for her in the eighteenth—and thus Claire's knowledge sends the young MacKenzie family back through the stones, in a dangerous bid to save their daughter, leaving Jamie and Claire thinking that they will never see their beloved family again. But there are more family members to be considered. The British army has landed in force, and the Revolution is fully under way. William Ransom has come, as a young lieutenant; his stepfather, Lord John Grey, is also in the colonies—though retired from the army, he still has one foot in the world of espionage. Claire has always been suspicious, if not outright hostile, to Lord John, knowing what his feelings are for Jamie. But as the two men's friendship continues, mostly through letters, she begins to see why they *are* friends and to value John for himself. Which is rather a Good Thing later on. In between though, quite a number of things happen, including the Battle of Saratoga, Claire's amputating Jamie's ruined ring finger, and Jamie being asked to escort the body of Brigadier General Simon Fraser (a distant kinsman) home to Scotland, as part of the complex arrangements for the British surrender. Claire is relieved at being back in Scotland, away from the war, but there are private wars to be fought, too. The elder Ian Murray, Jamie's best friend and brother-in-law, is dying of consumption—a fatal and nontreatable disease. Beyond Claire's distress at being unable to help Ian and her further distress at Jamie's sorrow is a rupture of relations with Jenny, Jamie's sister—and a good friend/sister to Claire during her first sojourn at Lallybroch. Jenny is more than suspicious of Claire's long absence and feels utterly betrayed by what she sees as Claire's refusal to help save Ian's life. When news comes from Marsali in Philadelphia, begging Claire to come home and save little Henri-Christian, Marsali and Fergus's youngest son, Claire's distress at leaving Jamie to face Ian's dying without her is at least slightly tempered by the relief of being away from Jenny. Back in Philadelphia, her operation on Henri-Christian's enlarged tonsils and adenoids is successful, and things seem to be at least superficially normal, despite the British occupation of Philadelphia, which causes Fergus to live in hiding. Claire undertakes to carry messages and writings to and from Fergus and the printshop, using her basket of medical supplies as cover. She doesn't realize that she's been rumbled in this activity until sudden devastating news arrives: the ship Jamie and Jenny were sailing on has sunk, with all souls lost. Crushed by this tragedy, Claire has no attention to pay to small matters like being suspected of spying or arrested for passing seditious materials—but Lord John, devastated himself, feels that the last thing he can do for Jamie is to safeguard Jamie's wife. Knowing that Claire is about to be arrested, he insists that she marry him, so he can protect not only her but Fergus and Marsali, as well. Distraught, she does. The marriage doesn't last long—Jamie reappears, alive and well, only a couple of months later. But in the interim, Claire and Lord John have shared a bed, briefly, offering each other comfort. Which Lord John mentions to Jamie, as soon as the two of them have left the city. *"I have had carnal knowledge of your wife,"* he says. To which Jamie replies (rather calmly under the circumstances), *"Oh? Why?"* The answer to that question takes a good bit of unraveling, which leads us into the heart of the rebellion and the Battle of Monmouth; this ends—for Claire—with her being shot while tending the wounded. She comes close to dying but is saved by Denzell Hunter's skill and recovers to see further adventures, including the double marriage of Young Ian and Rachel Hunter, and Dorothea Grey and Denzell Hunter. Happiness is succeeded by tragedy, though, when little Henri-Christian dies in a fire at the printshop. Gutted by this, the family leaves Philadelphia and goes to Savannah to retrieve Jamie's printing press—and, in the fullness of time, return at last to Fraser's Ridge. Here, the peace of the mountains enables Claire to ignore things like war for at least a little while—until she unexpectedly sees a man she recognizes at the local trading post: the man who raped her during her abduction by the bandit gang. She doesn't want to tell Jamie, knowing that he'll feel he has to do something about it—but he sees that something is amiss, winkles the truth out of Jenny . . . and goes to take care of the matter. Claire is torn between gratitude that the man is dead, distress that Jamie had to kill him, and a nagging burden of guilt at having been responsible—if indirectly—for the man's death. But marriage means bearing each other's burdens, and Claire and Jamie are rather good at that by now. They resume their building of the new Big House and are sharing a companionable moment at the site, when they see four strangers arrive in the clearing below: a tall, dark-haired man, a tall woman with long, flowing red hair, a redheaded boy, and a small girl with a redheaded doll. As anyone with an ounce more brain than a cuckoo clock would instantly realize, the MacKenzies have come home, and Claire follows Jamie at a run down the hill to meet them, flying on the wind of happiness. [*All, SU, SP*]

Fraser, Claudel—see "Fergus Fraser."

Fraser, Ellen Caitriona Sileas MacKenzie—Mother of Jamie Fraser and Jenny Fraser Murray, also William and Robert, both deceased; wife to Brian Fraser; elder sister to Colum, Dougal, and Jocasta MacKenzie. [*All*]

Fraser, Faith—Claire and Jamie's first child, stillborn at L'Hôpital des Anges following a miscarriage after Jamie's duel with Jack Randall. [*All*]

Fraser, Félicité—Second daughter of Marsali and Fergus Fraser; along with her elder sister, Joanie, they are known as "the hell-kittens." [*Ashes, Echo, MOBY*]

Fraser, Fergus (aka Claudel)—Jamie's foster son, rescued from a Paris bordello as a child. Possibly the missing heir to the fortune of the French aristocrat, the Comte St. Germain. Married to Jamie's stepdaughter Marsali and father to Germain, Joanie, Félicité, and Henri-Christian. [*All*]

Fraser, Germain Alexander Claudel MacKenzie—Marsali and Fergus's precocious eldest son. Born in America but decidedly a unique combination of Scots and French, he is fiercely protective of his family and very loyal to his grandfather, Jamie. He comes to live on Fraser's Ridge with his grandparents following the death of his younger brother, Henri-Christian. [*All*]

Fraser, Henri-Christian—Marsali and Fergus's younger son, a dwarf but much loved and protected by his siblings; his "stage name" is Bubbles when performing in front of Claire's Wilmington surgery or Fergus's printshop. His accidental death during a fire at the printshop devastates his family, particularly his elder brother, Germain. [*Ashes, Echo, MOBY*]

x **Fraser, Hugh**—(unknown) Older brother of Brigadier General Simon Fraser, named after their father, and still living at Balnain. He helps settle the general's body in its (fictitious?) final resting place at Corrimony, Scotland. [*Echo*]

Fraser, Jamie; James Alexander Malcolm MacKenzie (aka "Seaumais Ruaidh")—Born May 1, 1721; former Laird of Broch Tuarach in Scotland, son of Ellen MacKenzie and Brian Fraser, illegitimately descended (though legitimately born) grandson of Lord Lovat, Simon

Fraser (the Old Fox). He is the father (by Claire Beauchamp Randall Fraser) of Faith (stillborn in France) and Brianna Ellen Randall Fraser MacKenzie, and (by Geneva Dunsany) William Ransom. After leaving Scotland and finding a new life in the New World, Jamie establishes a small settlement called Fraser's Ridge, in the mountains of North Carolina. Though remote, the Ridge is not immune to the turmoil of the times, and Jamie's life is often a balance of joy in his wife and family and the constant strains of being leader and protector. While he's seen enough of war not to want to see more, he knows from the time travelers in his family that war can't be avoided—the only question is what path to take through the oncoming carnage. As the first rumbles of the Revolution begin to be felt in North Carolina, he's obliged to pick his way between the royal governor, who gave him his land grant and is tacitly blackmailing him by not revealing Jamie's illegal Catholicism, and the growing pressure of the Regulators—the men of the backcountry who oppose what they see as increasing tyranny and corruption. Obliged to form his own militia group, Jamie takes reluctant part in the Battle of Alamance, at which his son-in-law, Roger MacKenzie, is hanged and permanently damaged. Still, he manages despite everything to see that the important things are done: his daughter is married and his grandchildren are baptized. As Fraser's Ridge continues to grow, so does the danger from the incipient—though so far undeclared—rebellion. As the royal institutions crumble and governors flee, bandits and violent elements spring up in their wake. Jamie protects his own, whatever the price—and sometimes the price is high. His wife is abducted by a band of roving brigands who attack his homestead, and he musters his tenants to rescue her. He finds her and kills (he thinks) all of those involved in the crime, but Claire has been badly abused and raped—something he knows much too much about. But he's walked through hell for this woman before and has no hesitation in doing it again. *(He'd meant to be gentle. Very gentle. Had planned it with care, worrying each step of the long way home. She was broken; he must go canny, take his time. Be careful in gluing back her shattered bits.*

And then he came to her and discovered that she wished no part of gentleness, of courting. She wished directness. Brevity and violence. If she was broken, she would slash him with her jagged edges, reckless as a drunkard with a shattered bottle.

For a moment, two moments, he struggled, trying to hold her close and kiss her tenderly. She squirmed like an eel in his arms, then rolled over him, wriggling and biting.

He'd thought to ease her—both of them—with the wine. He'd known she lost all sense of restraint when in drink; he simply hadn't realized what she was restraining, he thought grimly, trying to seize her without hurting.

He, of all people, should have known. Not fear or grief or pain—but rage.

She raked his back; he felt the scrape of broken nails, and thought dimly that was good—she'd fought. That was the last of his thought; his own fury took him then, rage and a lust that came on him like black thunder on a mountain, a cloud that hid all from him and him from all, so that kind familiarity was lost and he was alone, strange in darkness.

It might be her neck he grasped, or anyone's. The feel of small bones came to him, knobbled in the dark, and the screams of rabbits, killed in his hand. He rose up in a whirlwind, choked with dirt and the scourings of blood.

Wrath boiled and curdled in his balls, and he rode to her spurs. Let his lightning blaze and sear all trace of the intruder from her womb, and if it burnt them both to bone and ash—then let it be.)

A reluctant Rebel, he nonetheless finds a sense of idealism that resonates with the principles of the new Revolution. But if war is not a respecter of private life, the opposite is true, as well, and everything he's built is threatened when Malva Christie turns up pregnant and identifies Jamie as the father. The ensuing brouhaha splits Fraser's Ridge, particularly when Claire finds the young woman freshly murdered and is suspected of having killed the girl and her child. Nearby troublemakers take advantage of the situation to have Claire arrested, which also removes Jamie from the Ridge, as he's obliged to find and rescue her from the ship to which the ex-royal governor has fled with her. Beyond politics and violence, though, there is a deeper threat to the family's happiness: Jamie and Claire's daughter, Brianna, gives birth to an enchanting baby girl named Amanda—but Mandy suffers from a birth defect of the heart. It's a defect easily cured by surgery—in the twentieth century. And with much anguish, the young MacKenzie family decides to risk the journey through the stones to save the child's life. They leave, taking half of Jamie's heart with them. But Brianna is not Jamie's only child, and with the onset of the war itself, Jamie finds himself in close proximity to William, his illegitimate son, who believes himself to be the Ninth Earl of Ellesmere and is now in the colonies as an officer in His Majesty's Army. Jamie has a terrible premonition that he will one day face his son across the barrel of a gun—and does, at the Battle of Saratoga, where he narrowly misses killing William by accident. At his side through the travails of battle and travel, though, are both his beloved wife and Young Ian, his nephew and the son of his heart. Ian's own life has been a troubled one, but his return from the Mohawk heartens Jamie and provides him with an invaluable ally on the road to war. Following Saratoga, Jamie is asked to go to Scotland, accompanying the body of a distant kinsman, Brigadier General Simon Fraser, who was killed in the battle. Ian accompanies Jamie and Claire and thus arrives with them at Lallybroch in time to bid his father farewell. The elder Ian is dying slowly of consumption, and the loss of the man who has been more than a brother to Jamie is almost more than he can bear. But he has a small space of precious time with Ian, and when Claire is obliged to return to North Carolina for a medical emergency, Jamie stays, to see his friend decently buried and take care of his sister Jenny, Ian's wife. Jenny declares her intent to travel to North Carolina with Jamie after the funeral, determined to look after Ian, her youngest child. By mischance and miscommunication, Claire and Lord John Grey are informed that the ship on which Jamie and Jenny sailed has sunk. Thus, when they arrive on a different ship, Jamie discovers that Claire has married Lord John Grey, which is something of a shock. So is his coming face-to-face unexpectedly with his son, William, who sees the marked resemblance and who immediately Draws Conclusions. The still-greater shock, though, is to have Lord John inform Jamie that *"I have had carnal knowledge of your wife."* To which Jamie can only manage to say, *"Oh? Why?"* The answer to that, plus the Battle of Monmouth, Claire's nearly fatal wound, and a few other things, keep him from thinking too much about William. But when William comes to him for help in rescuing a young woman under his protection, Jamie assures his son that he's entitled to Jamie's help for any worthy purpose he intends. Through deaths and weddings and war and births, the Frasers at last manage to return to the Ridge, where Jamie begins to rebuild their house and their lives. [*All, HF, PM, SU, BL, HS, SP, PZ*]

Fraser, Jared—Successful expatriate Scottish wine merchant, with ships and warehouses in Le Havre and a mansion in Paris. Jamie's cousin and a strong Jacobite supporter. Later, his cousin Michael Murray (Jenny and Ian's son) moves to Paris to learn the wine business from him. [*Fiery Cross, Ashes, Echo, SB*]

Fraser, Joan Laoghaire Claire; Joanie—Marsali and Fergus's oldest daughter; one of the "hell-kittens," along with her sister, Félicité. [*All*]

Fraser, Laoghaire MacKenzie (pronounced "Leery," "L'heer," or "L'heery," depending on regional usage)—First seen as a young girl at Castle Leoch with designs on Jamie Fraser. In later years, following Culloden and Claire's disappearance through the stones, she marries Jamie, at Jenny Fraser's instigation. The marriage is unsuccessful, though, and following Jamie's departure for Edinburgh, Laoghaire takes up with a crippled hired man named Joey—as Jamie discoveres, to his intense (and surprising) discomposure. But as Laoghaire tells Jamie, during their final conversation, when he demands to know why, "Because he needs me. And you, ye bastard, never did!" She is mother to Marsali and Joan. [*All*]

Fraser, Leslie—Nephew of Bobby Fraser of Glenhelm, who was with him when they caught young Arch Bug and cut off his bow fingers; later, both Frasers of Glenhelm were found dead in a ditch, their heads caved in by an ax. [*Ashes*]

Fraser, Marsali—Laoghaire's eldest daughter by Simon MacKimmie; Jamie's stepdaughter and Fergus's wife; mother of Germain, Joanie, Félicité, and Henri-Christian. [*All*]

Fraser, Murtagh FitzGibbons—Jamie Fraser's godfather, killed at Culloden while saving Jamie's life. [*SP*]

Fraser, Robert Brian Gordon MacKenzie—Jamie's infant brother who died with his mother, Ellen, in childbed. [*Fiery Cross, Echo, MOBY*]

Fraser, Ronnie—The young son of Vhairi Fraser, a tenant of Balriggan. He was crushed to death by an ox; his death was predicted in the second vision that appeared to Joan. [*SB*]

x **Fraser, Simon, Brigadier General**—(1729–1777) From Balnain, Scotland, and cousin to the Frasers of Lovat. In command of combined forces at Saratoga and as a prominent general leading his troops in the Battle of Bemis Heights, he was targeted by Morgan's sharpshooter Tim Murphy. General Fraser was nursed through the night but died at dawn. He requested that his body be buried in the Great Redoubt at Saratoga, but General

Burgoyne asked Jamie to take the brigadier's body back to Scotland, thus allowing Jamie, Claire, and Ian to leave the Continental army. [*CA, Echo, MOBY*]

x **Fraser, Simon; Lord Lovat; the Old Fox**—(1667–1747) Eleventh Lord Lovat and chief of clan Fraser, he was Jamie Fraser's paternal grandfather but was beheaded for his underhanded—and treasonous—actions during the '45. [*All*]

Fraser, Vhairi—A tenant near Balriggan, mother to a young child who met an early death; the child was the second person Joan MacKimmie's visions indicated would die. [*SB*]

Fraser, William Simon Murtagh MacKenzie; Willie—Jamie's older brother who died of smallpox when Jamie was six. He carved the cherrywood snake with "Sawny," his nickname for Jamie, on the backside of it. [*Echo, MOBY*]

x **Fraser, Young Simon; Lord Lovat; the Young Fox**—(1726–1782) Son of the executed Lord Lovat and younger half brother to Jamie Fraser's father, Brian. He led Fraser clansmen at Culloden but escaped execution, though suffering the loss of most of his family property. As the nineteenth chief of clan Fraser, he was known as the MacShimidh but was unable to reclaim the title of Lord Lovat. He later regained much of his property through both legal channels and as a reward for his own efforts in raising two Highland regiments to fight in the colonies during the French and Indian War, notably the 78th Fraser Highlanders. [*Fiery Cross, MOBY*]

x **Frederick, King of Prussia; Frederick the Great**—(1712–1786) A bold military tactician, he won military acclaim for himself and Prussia by his attack on Austria. He was also lauded for physically uniting his kingdom by conquering Polish territories after making a political and military alliance with Britain in 1756 during the Seven Years' War; his conquests turned Prussia into an economically strong and politically reformed country. [*HS, BL*]

Frobisher, Mr.—A London legal adviser for Stephan von Namtzen, involved with settling Stephan's motherless children to live with his sister in London. [*SP*]

Frye, Theo—One of the residents of Fraser's Ridge who help to build various businesses, including Ronnie Sinclair's cooperage, a smithy, and a general store. [*Fiery Cross*]

G

Gabriel—Young soldier in love with and accompanying Sally-Sarah and her brother, Phillip. [*MOBY*]

x **Gage, Thomas, General**—(ca. 1720–1787) Commander in chief of the British forces in North America from 1763–1775; after being appointed the military governor of Massachusetts Bay, he was instructed to implement several severe acts to punish Massachusetts for the Boston Tea Party and attempted to seize stores from the militia; his actions sparking several notable battles. He was replaced as the commander in chief by General Howe after the Battle of Bunker Hill in 1775. [*Ashes*]

Gainsborough, Mr.—(1727–1788) Thomas Gainsborough, the portrait artist commissioned to commemorate the christening of Lady Dorothea Grey, Lord John's niece. [*BL*]

Galantine, Madame Eugenie—Léonie's and Lillie's aunt—Lillie being the deceased young wife of Michael Murray. [*SB*]

Gallagher—A member of White's wagering that the person lying in the gutter outside the club is dead. [*BL*]

Gallegher, Henry (aka "The Glaswegian")—A recent immigrant to the Ridge and member of Jamie's militia unit. Not much is known about him except that his distinctive manner of speech marks him as being from or near Glasgow, with an accent so marked that others on the Ridge have a difficult time understanding him. [*Fiery Cross*]

Gardner, Mrs. and Miss Gardner—dependents of British military evacuating Philadelphia. [MOB*Y*]

Garlock, Eldon—An ensign and the youngest member of the court hearing the court-martial case against Gerald Siverly. (Eldon was a good friend of mine from the Compuserve Literary Forum, who passed away some years ago. RIP.) [*SP*]

x **Garrick, Mr.**—(1717–1779) Influential London playwright and actor David Garrick, who helped make acting "respectable" and whom William Ransom met briefly in London. [*BL, Echo*]

Gaskins, Lieutenant—One of the soldiers sent by the Duke of Pardloe to bring Jamie to London. [*SP*]

x **Gates, Horatio, General**—(ca. 1728–1806) Washington's adjutant general (chief of staff) after the fall of Fort Ticonderoga. He was promoted to commander of the Northern Department under General Burgoyne, and his army combined with those of General Benedict Arnold to force the surrender of Burgoyne's larger British army at Saratoga. Arnold disparagingly called him "Granny Gates," due to his indecisiveness and lack of swift action in most military matters. [*Echo*]

Gaugh, Barney—The train stationmaster in Inverness since Roger's arrival as a child, and a member of Roger's twentieth-century Masonic lodge. [*Echo*]

The General—An elderly unnamed military leader and patron of Lord John's favorite London club, the Beefsteak. [*HF*]

x **Gentleman Johnny**—See "General John Burgoyne."

Geordie—One of Dougal's men. [*MOBY*]

x **George III**—(1738–1820) King of England from 1760–1820. Thoughts during the funeral of the King's father, George II, cause Lord John to realize the truth about Jamie Fraser's paternity of William. While the king was on the throne throughout the American Revolution, he has relatively little to do with our story. [*BL, All*]

Gerald, Robert; Bob—Harry Quarry's cousin by marriage, who is killed outside the Beefsteak after declining an invitation to join the Hellfire Club. [*HF*]

x **Germain, George, Sir**—(1716–1785) British secretary of state for America in Lord North's cabinet, Germain failed to understand both the geography and the colonists' determination. He was Lord John's superior during his years of espionage. [*Echo*]

Gershon—One of the American militia under the command of Corporal Woodbine. [*MOBY*]

Gibbs—Whisky maker from Aberdeenshire in Scotland. (Named in compliment to Mike Gibb, creator and lyricist of *Outlander: The Musical* CD.) [*MOBY*]

Gideon—Jamie's foul-tempered horse, who dislikes being ridden and is prone to bite and kick. Temperament notwithstanding, he is highly desired by the North Carolina Indians as a sire for their own ponies. [*Fiery Cross, Ashes*]

Gill, Captain—A friend of Lord John Grey, and captain of the sloop where Bobby

Higgins attempts to work as a sailor. [*Ashes*]

x **Gillespie**—(unknown) One of the Regulators identified by Waightstill Avery in his deposition before Justice William Harris. [*Fiery Cross*]

Gillespie, Graham—A Scottish soldier who died at Culloden, shot through the head. Jamie tells Claire that he saw him sit up while on a burning funeral pyre; Claire explains to Jamie that there are medical reasons for reactions like this in a corpse, i.e., postmortem contracture. [*Fiery Cross*]

Gist, George—A member of the Cherokee hunting party that sets out to find the mysterious white "ghost" bear, which Jamie and Claire eventually locate after a violent mountaintop thunderstorm. [*Fiery Cross*]

Glasscock, Jimmy—Jem's classmate in twentieth-century Inverness who claims Jem, Mandy, and their mother will burn in hell for being Catholic. [*Echo*]

Glaswegian (the)—See "Henry Gallegher."

Glendenning, Miss—Jem's teacher in twentieth-century Inverness. A city woman from Aberdeen, she grabs Jem by the ear and scolds him for speaking Gaelic; he reacts by swearing at her in Gaelic—and is overheard by the headmaster, Mr. Menzies. [*Echo*]

Glory—Young patient with extremely bad dentition, whom Claire attempts to help through multiple extractions; the anesthetic of choice is whisky, which almost kills the young girl when her mother forces a bit too much down her throat. [*Echo*]

Glutton (aka Walking Elk)—Ian's Mohawk friend who helps take care of William in the Great Dismal; Glutton received the name for killing one with his bare hands and carries the scars as signs of his totem. [*Echo*]

Goldie-Locks—See "Neil Stapleton."

Goodwin, Mr.—A resident of Hillsborough who becomes embroiled in the local politics. While trying to protect his friend Edmund Fanning from the rioters, he is assaulted himself, forcing him to seek out medical treatment from Claire at the Gathering. [*Fiery Cross*]

x **Goodwin, Samuel**—(ca. 1775–unknown) Loyalist mapmaker in Maine who provided Benedict Arnold's Continental army with incorrect maps for the march to British-held Quebec City; the information delayed Arnold's troops so badly that, instead of marching 180 miles, they actually marched about 350, and winter found them well short of their goal. [*Echo*]

Goose—Tuscarora brave who escaped an attack by the Cherokee; more specifically, the Cherokee with whom Jamie has a friendship. [*Ashes*]

Gore, Joe—A farmhand at Helwater. He was charged with bringing in Fanny, one of the farm horses, left in the field when a wagon wheel was damaged. [*SP*]

Gormley, Herbert; Gormless—An employee of the royal laboratory at the Arsenal who is investigating the cause of the recent catastrophic cannon explosions among the royal artillery. [*HS*]

Gowan, Ned—A lawyer from Edinburgh; he handles the negotiations resulting from Jamie Fraser's invalid marriage to Laoghaire MacKenzie and the terms of cancellation of the agreement years later, as well as settling the dowries of both Marsali and Joan (Laoghaire's daughters). [*Fiery Cross, Echo*]

Graf von Erdberg—See Stephan von Namtzen.

Gräfin von Erdberg—See Princess Louisa von Lowenstein.

Graham, Fiona—See "Fiona Buchan."

Graham, Mrs.—Reverend Wakefield's housekeeper, Roger's foster mother, and grandmother to Fiona, she was the leader and "caller" of the secret Craigh na Dun dancers. [*All*]

Gran (née Wakefield)—Roger's grandmother, mother of Marjorie "Dolly" MacKenzie, and sister to Reverend Reginald Wakefield, who adopted Roger after his parents were killed. [*Fiery Cross, LW*]

Grannie Belly—See "Arabella Abernathy."

x **Grant, James, Colonel**—(1720–1806) One of General Howe's leaders during the Long Island invasion; also one of the officers present at General Simon Fraser's death, and the officer who tells William he has been promoted to the rank of captain at General Fraser's recommendation after William's actions at Ticonderoga. [*Echo*]

Grant, Malcolm—Chieftain of clan Grant; rejected suitor of Ellen MacKenzie; received one-third of the French gold for Bonnie Prince Charlie, which his tacksman, Arch Bug, picked up in his place. [*Fiery Cross, Ashes, Echo*]

Graves, Colonel—Author of a very interesting note that Lord John receives in Philadelphia, just moments before Jamie returns from the dead. [*Echo, MOBY*]

x **Gray, Thomas**—(1716–1771) English poet, classical scholar, and Cambridge professor and close friend to Horace Walpole; he was suspected by some to be Walpole's lover, but the unspoken allegations were never proven. [*BL*]

Green, Amos—An ex-Regulator from Salisbury in the company of Richard Brown and others, whom Jamie meets on the road to Halifax while on his way to attend the meeting for the Committee of Correspondence. [*Ashes*]

x **Greene, Gen. Nathanael**—Washington's quartermaster, an important Revolutionary general, and a friend of Jamie's. A lapsed Quaker, he advises Jamie on the form and customs of Quaker weddings. [*MOBY*]

Greenhow, Corporal Joshua—One of Jamie's militiamen who is injured. [*MOBY*]

Greenleaf, Lieutenant—A British engineer with General Simon Fraser's regiment who is surveying the American fortifications at Fort Ticonderoga shortly before the battle. [*Echo*]

Gregory—The mechanic at the airfield near Northumbria who assures Jerry that his beloved plane, Dolly, will be back in the air in no time. [*LW*]

Grendel—The calm-mannered but alert horse Lord John rides when out on patrol with Percy's company after they're posted to Prussia's Rhine Valley; the horse's keen senses prevent the patrol from blundering into a French foraging party. [*BL*]

x **Grenville, George**—(1712–1770) Treasurer of the British navy, he was in attendance at the funeral for King George III, under whom Grenville had succeded to the office of prime minister. [*SP*]

Gretchen—One of several German women in Frau Ute McGillivray's schemes for making a match with resident Ronnie Sinclair of Fraser's Ridge. [*Ashes*]

Grey, Adam—Hal's middle son (born 1754), Lord John's nephew, William's cousin, and Dottie's older brother, also with the British army in America; goes out on a night of drinking with William and friends, only to quickly sober at witnessing the beating and burning alive of a "fireship"—a whore infected with the pox (syphilis). Later, he sends a letter to his brother Henry, telling that their other brother, Benjamin, isn't dead. [*BL, SP, Echo, MOBY*]

Grey, Benedicta; Lady Stanley—Dowager Countess of Melton, formerly Dowager Duchess of Pardloe; widow of Gerard Grey; mother to John and Harold Grey, and Paul and Edgar DeVane; married to her third husband, General Sir George Stanley. [*PM, BL, SP, Echo*]

Grey, Benjamin—Lord John's nephew (born 1752) and eldest son and heir to Hal, the Duke of Pardloe. Presumably married to Amaranthus Cowden, and the father (alleged) of Trevor, he was taken prisoner at the Battle of the Brandywine and later reported to have died in captivity. However, his cousin William investigates and finds a stranger in his grave. [*BL, SP, MOBY*]

x Grey, Charles Major General—(1729–1807) British leader of a nocturnal attack at Paoli, where he ordered his men to fix bayonets and remove the flints from their muskets to avoid firing accidentally. Grey allegedly showed no quarter and many Americans were bayoneted in their beds. The Paoli Massacre, as the engagement became known, is still fresh in the minds of the Continental army and militia when Lord John is arrested; hence the militia's acute suspicion upon hearing his surname. [*Echo, MOBY*]

Grey, Dorothea Jacqueline Benedicta; Lady Dorothea; Dottie—Lord John's niece; William Ransom's cousin; youngest child (born 1758) and only daughter of Hal and Minnie. As a young woman she travels to America in search of her beloved, a young Quaker doctor serving with the Continental army. In the course of events, she serves with the army, helping both her fiancé, Denzell Hunter, and later Claire, at the Battle of Monmouth. Eventually, she marries Denzell. Hearing that her brother Benjamin is dead, though, she sets out with her uncle, Lord John, in search of Benjamin's theoretical wife, but is obliged to go back to Denzell when she realizes she is pregnant. [*HS, SP, Echo, MOBY*]

Grey, Gerard; Gerry—The Duke of Pardloe (deceased), Benedicta's second husband, father of Harold and John. He died under suspicious circumstances while accused of treason, so his sons embark on a mission to restore honor to their father's name. [*BL, CA*]

Grey, Harold; Hal (aka the Duke of Pardloe)—Formerly Lord Melton, upon his father's death Hal inherits the ducal title but refuses to use it, owing to the stain left on the family honor by the circumstances of his father's death. He is John Grey's older brother; a colonel and commander of his own infantry regiment, which takes part in the American Revolution. Hal leaves his regiment temporarily to visit his son and brother in Philadelphia, where he meets Claire, who saves his life during an asthma attack and then kidnaps him. [*PM, BL, HS, CA, SP, PZ, Echo, MOBY*]

Grey, Henry—Hal's youngest son (born 1755) and Lord John's nephew. Severely wounded during a battle in America, he's near death but is saved by Claire, who uses ether to perform a risky operation on him. As he recovers, he falls in love with the free black woman who has been caring for him, Mercy Woodcock. [*Echo, MOBY*]

Grey, Lord John—(aka "William Grey" in Dragonfly) Younger brother of Harold,

Duke of Pardloe, retired (theoretically) from his brother's regiment. In the wake of the discovery of Jamie Fraser's death at sea, he marries Claire in order to save her from being arrested as a spy. Both devastated and grieving Jamie, John and Claire share a very drunken evening—and a bed, despite John's being homosexual. This incident causes some friction when Jamie turns out not to be dead, after all. However, Claire is not the only bond between the two men; there's William, Jamie's illegitimate son (by Geneva Dunsany) and Lord John's stepson (by Isobel Dunsany). Whatever Jamie's feelings about Lord John, he's obliged to suppress them when William's welfare is at stake. [*Breath, Echo, MOBY*]

Grey, Minnie; Minerva Wattiswade—Hal's devoted wife, the Duchess of Pardloe (formerly Lady Melton), and the mother of Benjamin, Adam, Henry, and Dottie. Previously was a Jacobite spy, which is known only by her husband and a few others.[*PM, BL, CA, SP, Echo*]

Grey, Trevor Wattiswade—Benjamin Grey's alleged son by Amaranthus Cowden. [*MOBY*]

x Gridley, Captain Richard—(1710–1796) An engineer in the company of Colonel Prescott, charged with building a redoubt fortification at Breed's Hill shortly before the battles of Breed Hill and Bunker Hill. [*Ashes*]

Grieves, Mr.—The factor, or foreman, for the Dunsany's estate, Helwater. [*SP*]

x Grimes/Graham, James—(unknown) One of the Regulators identified by Waightstill Avery in his deposition before Justice William Harris. [*Fiery Cross*]

Griswold, Captain—One of General Howe's senior staff members on Long Island, and the one who lent William a mount to lead his four companies in the invasion. [*Echo*]

Gruenwald, Ober-Leftenant—German soldier contracted to the British army. William befriends him on a foraging mission near Bennington with Hessian Colonel Baum, when they are ambushed by the Americans in what is known as the Battle of Bennington. [*Echo*]

Grume, Joe—An acquaintance of Germain's, who (with his friend Shecky Loew) throws rocks and dirt clods at the Duke of Pardloe's sedan chair, until Germain threatens them. [*MOBY*]

Guinea Dick—Crewman of the *Pitt* who was "involuntarily drafted" from a Guinea pirate ship and becomes Captain Stebbings's fierce protector; his appearance is frightening, as his teeth are filed into points and he has elaborate facial tattoos on his black skin. Although he assures Ian and company he is not a cannibal, there's no guarantee he's harmless. [*Echo*]

Gunn, Ephraim—An Edinburgh lawyer; brother of William Buccleigh MacKenzie's wife, Morag Gunn. [*Echo*]

Gussie—One of Jocasta Cameron's house slaves, present at the death of Betty the slave. She asks permission from Claire to tell Phaedre of Betty's death, since Betty was Phaedre's mother. [*Fiery Cross*]

Gustav—The good-natured short-legged hound von Namtzen has bred. Gentle but fierce in battle, Gustav follows badgers into their burrows and eliminates the varmints (named in memory of my own late Gus). [*BL*]

Guthrie, Captain Bob—One of the captains under Jamie's command at Monmouth. [*MOBY*]

Guthrie, Mr.—Thurlo Guthrie's elderly father, who produces a set of small uilleann pipes for the Hogmanay celebration at the Big House. [*Fiery Cross*]

Guthrie, Thurlo—One of the residents of Fraser's Ridge, who helps celebrate Hogmanay at the Big House by having his elderly father play his small pipes. [*Fiery Cross*]

Gwilty, Mr.—A small, wizened man accompanying Mrs. Gwilty—who was either his wife or daughter-in-law—to Roger's first sermon on the Ridge. [*Ashes*]

Gwilty, Mrs.—The official "mourning woman" for Scottish funerals on Fraser's Ridge; her duty is to walk behind the coffin wailing (keening) her mourning song, which she does at the funeral for Hiram Crombie's mother-in-law. [*Ashes*]

Gwilty, Olanna—Mrs. Gwilty's niece, whom she is training to be the next generation's mourning or keening woman. Olanna is admonished for not wailing loud enough but keeps on trying. [*Ashes*]

Gwynne, Oliver—A London friend of Lord John's, he is a natural philosopher and very interested in snakes, owning several different varieties, both harmless and venomous. [*PZ*]

H

Hacffurthe, Mester—The Northumbrian man who found part of Jerry MacKenzie's flight harness. [*MOBY*]

x **Hale, Nathan, Captain**—(1755–1776) Member of Knowlton's Rangers who volunteered to gather British military intelligence for Washington; Hale was found with incriminating documents, out of uniform behind enemy lines, and arrested as a spy. Taken before General William Howe, he was sentenced to hanging; it is said he uttered the famous line, "I only regret that I have but one life to lose for my country." William witnesses the hanging. [*Echo*]

Hall, DeLancey—Owner of a fishing ketch and small-time smuggler in New Bern, who secures Jamie, Claire, and Ian passage to Scotland on the ship *Tranquil Teal.* [*Echo*]

Halloran, Bartholomew—The adjutant of Hal's regiment and a close informant of Gerald Siverly; he has a membership at Almack's, where Lord John and Hal meet him for an evening of cards and information. [*SP*]

x **Hamilton, Ninian Bell**—An elderly Scottish guest at River Run plantation, who jokes with Jamie over the possible causes for Duncan to be running frequently to the outhouse on the morning of his wedding to Jocasta Cameron; he gets into an altercation with James Hunter regarding the Regulators, but the fight is stopped by the Quaker Hermon Husband. [*Fiery Cross*]

x **Hamilton, Thomas**—(unknown) One of the Regulators identified by Waightstill Avery in his deposition before Justice William Harris. [*Fiery Cross*]

Hammond, Lieutenant—An officer who accompanied William through the open gates into the abandoned Fort Ticonderoga. He is amazed to find that the Continentals had not only not set fire to the fort but had left in such a hurry that much of their personal belongings remained behind, ready for the British army to utilize. [*Echo*]

x **Hancock, John**—(1737–1793) Merchant and millionaire, he gained prominence after his ship *Liberty* was seized and he was charged with smuggling by vengeful customs officials in Boston, who claimed that the duty on a cargo of wine was unpaid; the charges were dropped, but the incident set the stage for the Boston Massacre. One of the Founding Fathers and president of the Continental Congress in 1776, he was the first signer of the Declaration of Independence. [*Ashes*]

Hanks—A stable-hand at Helwater; possibly a poor relation of the Dunsanys' butler of the same name. [*SP*]

Hanks, Captain—An officer on Long Island who sends William's detail in search of a smuggler's cache of contraband. [*Echo*]

Hanley, Lord—One of the prominent members of the English Beefsteak gentlemen's club; an associate of William Pitt and Trevelyan. [*PM*]

Hanlon, Seamus—The Irish fiddler with the music ensemble hired to play at Jocasta and Duncan's wedding, he invites Roger to sing with them during the evening. [*Fiery Cross*]

Hanson, Captain—The unsuspecting captain of the naval ship *Sunrise,* he is unwittingly drawn into the scandal of the stolen copper when Stoughton takes refuge aboard his ship—with a letter of safe passage signed by a prominent admiral of the Royal Navy. [*HS*]

Hardman, Gabriel—Missing husband of Silvia Hardman. [*MOBY*]

Hardman, Prudence, Patience, and Chastity—Children of Silvia. [*MOBY*]

Hardman, Silvia—A Quaker widow who reluctantly hosts a meeting of George Washington's generals before the Monmouth campaign. Jamie, who has been reluctantly compelled to attend the meeting by Dan Morgan, and even more reluctantly compelled to accept appointment as a field general by Washington himself, rises to leave the meeting only to find himself immobilized by a back spasm. He remains with Friend Silvia and her three young daughters for two days before recovering enough to make his way to Philadelphia and Claire. [*MOBY*]

Hardy—A footman at the Jermyn Street home of Benedicta Grey, Lord John's mother. [*PM*]

Harkness, Captain—A captain of dragoons with depraved tastes. On a drunken evening before the British army leaves Philadelphia, William rouses from a stupor to hear Harkness regaling his companion with comments regarding what he intends to do to one of the young whores present. Revolted by the man's crudeness and open cruelty, William is further shocked to realize that the target of Harkness's desires is Arabella-Jane, the whore with whom William suffered an unfortunate encounter the day before. Moved by a mixture of chivalry and guilt, William takes Jane for the night in order to keep her out of Harkness's clutches. Much later in the story, William meets Jane and her younger sister, Frances (Fanny), and learns that Harkness had contracted with the madam of the brothel for Fanny's maidenhead. Unable to bear the thought of her sister being defiled by Harkness, Jane stabbed the brute and fled with her sister. [*MOBY*]

x **Harnett, Cornelius**—(1723–1781) A prominent Revolutionary from North Carolina, he was the head of the Sons of Liberty and an outspoken opponent and leader against the Stamp Act. A friend of Jocasta's, we meet him at a party at River Run. [*Ashes*]

x **Harris, William**—(unknown) Justice of the peace in Mecklenburg who witnessed Waightsill Avery's deposition regarding his arrest and detainment by a mob of Regulators. [*Fiery Cross*]

Harry and Allan—Two men, one with a Scottish voice, who assault William on Long Island when he becomes lost in the fog, taking not only his horse and weapons but further humiliating him by cutting off his pigtail as a sign of his helplessness. [*Echo*]

Harte, Bob—A former English soldier; according to Nessie (aka Agnes)—a prostitute of Lord John's acquaintance—he took advantage of her mother, whose husband and sons had been killed at Culloden, and set her up as a prostitute. He may have forced Nessie into the life of prostitution as well, when she reached adolescence. [*PM*]

Hartsell, Mr. and Mrs.—A couple present at an evening event hosted by Benedicta Grey at Jermyn House. [*PM*]

Haseltine, Mrs.—One of the ladies present at an evening event hosted by Benedicta Grey, and to whom von Namtzen replies in answer to what the French think of the English army. [*PM*]

Hatfield, Jemima—A guest at Jocasta Cameron's wedding, she is one of many women sharing sleeping space with Claire in the overcrowded house and nearly awakes during a provocative nighttime assault on Claire's bare feet. [*Fiery Cross*]

Hatfield, Jezebel; Jessie—Isaiah Morton's first lawful wife from Granite Falls. She is a rough woman—rugged, loyal, fiercely jealous—and unforgiving of her husband eloping with another woman. She is in attendance when Jamie attempts to save a Wilmington printer from tar-and-feathering. [*Fiery Cross, Ashes*]

Hauptmann, Herr—A Prussian infantry captain, he accompanies Captain Custis and Lord John to John's quarters, to retrieve a book Colonel Jeffreys wishes to borrow, and is the other officer present to witness Percy's act of sodomy with a German soldier. [*BL*]

Hawkins, Mary—Daughter of a minor English baronet, niece to Silas Hawkins. She becomes pregnant by her lover, Alex Randall (brother of Jonathan "Black Jack" Randall), but is obliged to marry Jonathan for protection, as Alex is dying of consumption. Years later, William Ransom finds himself bound for Canada on an intelligence-gathering mission with another young officer named Denys Randall-Isaacs. The two young men become friends, and Denys tells William that he was adopted by his mother's second husband, a Jewish merchant named Robert Isaacs—thus the hyphenated last name. This means nothing in particular to William, but it does to us. [*Echo*]

x **Hayes, Archibald, Lieutenant; Archie**—(unknown) Wounded and captured at Culloden—where his father, Gavin, was killed—Archie Hayes joined the English army as an alternative to transportation and achieved the rank of lieutenant. With his regiment of Scottish Highlanders, he takes part in the attempted "pacification" of the incipient rebellion in North Carolina. [Fiery Cross]

Hebden, Mr.—A volunteer under Jamie's command at Monmouth. [*MOBY*]

Hebdy, Dr.—A Philadelphia physician, summoned by a bystander when the Duke of Pardloe suffers an asthma attack in the street. Claire, who knows the man for a quack, shoves Hal into his sedan chair and makes off with him to Lord John's house. [*MOBY*]

Hector—See "Hector Dalrymple."

Helwig, Lance-Korporal—An officer in Stephan von Namtzen's Imperial Fifth

Regiment of Hanovarian Foot, assigned to protect the area of Gundwitz during the Seven Years' War. [*SU*]

Hempstead, Mary—Mrs. Hempstead's young daughter, she receives a message for Fergus from her playmate, Tommy Wilkins, who in turn received the message from Mr. Jessop, saying that a tall Scottish man was looking for Fergus. [*Echo*]

Hempstead, Mrs.—A widow and laundress whose husband was killed during the Battle of Paoli, she helps hide Fergus at a bolt-hole in Philadelphia when things get too heated at the printship due to his inflammatory writing. [*Echo*]

Henderson—The deckhand on Trevelyan's ship, the *Nampara,* on which Trevelyan and Maria are making their escape. [*PM*]

Henderson, Anne and Kate—Two children who attend Brianna's impromptu school in her cabin on the Ridge; living a bit farther away, they're escorted to the school by their older brother, Obadiah. [*Fiery Cross*]

x Henderson, Richard, Chief Justice—(1734–1785) Presiding judge in Hillsborough, N.C., who condemned captured tax resistors to death during the War of the Regulation. Viewed as a member of the gentry, he had been a target of Regulator violence and in 1770 was attacked and whipped at the courthouse. [*Fiery Cross*]

Henderson, Obadiah—A possible suitor for Malva Christie; older brother of Anne and Kate. He escorts his sisters to lessons at the cabin belonging to Brianna and Roger; after watching Brianna for months, he tries to accost her, but Jamie stops him and tells him to never come to the Big House again. [*Fiery Cross, Ashes*]

Hennings, Mr.—A Philadelphia Loyalist who tries to persuade William to allow his bond servants to be removed on the single, very crowded ship available during the evacuation of Philadelphia. [*MOBY*]

Henry—The first man Percy had sex with; he did it for the price of three shillings—a fortune to a starving fourteen-year-old and his mother. [*BL*]

x Henry, Patrick—(1736–1799) One of the best-known rabble-rousers of the Revolution, remembered particularly for his famous "Give me liberty or give me death" speech. Fergus comes to the attention of the authorities for printing one of Henry's seditious speeches. [*Echo*]

Hepzibah/Eppie—A dockside prostitute in Roanoke, who Brianna meets while on board Bonnet's ship, the *Anemone.* Bree pays Eppie with Jamie's cabochon ruby ring to get word to her family of the island location where Bonnet is taking her. Eppie is also the love of Manfred McGillivray; both are infected with syphilis, but Claire can treat it successfully with her penicillin. [*Ashes*]

Herbert, George—One of a delegation of New Bern residents who notice that the cannons at the Governor's Palace have been removed and wish to know why; Governor Martin gives them a false story about the wood caissons being rotted and needing to be replaced. In actuality, the cannons were unmounted to leave them inoperable in case the Patriots tried to seize the palace and the armory. [*Ashes*]

Herbert, Lieutenant—One of the officers under Jamie's command at Monmouth. [*MOBY*]

Hercules—The popular pug dog owned by Dr. Gilbert Rigby. Sporting a black velvet jacket and small hat, the little dog charms attendees at the artistic fundraiser Lord John and Percy attend together. [*BL*]

Herman; Hermione Kuykendall—One of two young ragamuffin boys who attempt to rob the Frasers on their way to New Bern; Ian is nominated to try to locate their relatives near Bailey Camp. During the journey, it's discovered that the boys are actually girls in disguise. When Ian can't find any relations of the children, he takes them to Mrs. Sylvie's brothel in Cross Creek and pays her to "tame" the girls and make them housemaids. Hermione swears revenge upon Ian if she or her sister end up being whores after all. In fact, the girls do *not* become whores, as Ian learns when he meets them a few years later; they have become small, wiry, ferocious teenaged enforcers for the brothel, adopting male dress and names ("Herman" and "Trask" Wurm). [*Echo, MOBY*]

Hetty—The personal maid to the Princess von Lowenstein. [*SU*]

Heughan—Blacksmith in Freehold; named in compliment to actor Sam Heughan after he was cast as Jamie Fraser in the Starz TV show. [*MOBY*]

Hickman, Asa, Captain—American ship captain of the *Asp.* On his first voyage with an American "letter of marque," he attacks the British cutter *Pitt.* After conquering the British ship in vengeance for the death of his brother, Theo, he sends the British crew ashore as prisoners of war, to be exchanged later. [*Echo*]

Hickman, Theo—Dead brother of Asa Hickman and captain of the *Annabelle.* He was killed when Captain Stebbings attempted to press crewmen from the *Annabelle* into the British navy and Hickman and his crew resisted. [*Echo*]

Hicks, Corporal—The horse-master for Lord John's regiment; he is horrified that his hay shed is temporarily being used to house a dead body. [*PM*]

Hicks, Sir Peter—Chief officer for the Thirty-fifth Regiment while Lord John is a liaison in Prussia. [*SU*]

Higgins, Aidan McCallum—Oldest son of Amy McCallum Higgins; Claire removes his appendix using her homemade ether. [*Ashes, Echo, MOBY*]

Higgins, Amy McCallum—Fraser's Ridge widow, single mother to Aidan and Orrie, and in desperate need of someone to help her. She marries Bobby Higgins, former British soldier and employee of Lord John Grey, and has a son named Rob by him [*Ashes, Echo, MOBY*]

Higgins, Corporal—Soldier who helps William on the quay during the evacuation of Philadelphia. [*MOBY*]

Higgins, Orrie McCallum—The younger of Amy McCallum Higgins's children fathered by Orem McCallum. [*Ashes, Echo, MOBY*]

Higgins, Robert; Bobby—Former British soldier, present and convicted during the Boston Massacre; he is branded with the letter "M" on his cheek. He finds employment with Lord John Grey as a courier to deliver goods and mail to Fraser's Ridge. During his visits, he becomes acquainted with Amy McCallum. When his employment with Lord John ends due to the political upheavals in Virginia, he moves to Fraser's Ridge and weds Amy, and Jamie appoints him as the new factor of the Ridge. He has a son with Amy, named Robert. [*Ashes, Echo, MOBY*]

Higgins, Wee Rob—The son born to Amy and Bobby Higgins. [*MOBY*]

Hilde—Mayrhofer's parlor maid, who receives the explanation of why Waldemar needs so much shaving soap and imparts the information to the other household staff. [*PM*]

Hiltern, Captain Benjamin—One of Ruysdale's officers, who shares a drink and information with Lord John, before directing John to the surgeon's assistant. [*SU*]

x **Hinton, John, Colonel**—(1715–1784) One of Wake County's leading citizens and largest landholders, Hinton led the county militia to the Battle of Alamance, but his unit arrived after the brief battle. When the Revolutionary War broke out, Hinton changed sides to support the Patriot cause; he fought at the Battle of Moore's Creek Bridge. [*Fiery Cross, Ashes*]

Hiram and Beckie—Two of the goats brought from the Beardsley farm with Fanny and the Frasers; Beckie is carried off in an attack by a panther, while Hiram charges the panther to protect the rest of his harem, receiving a broken leg and Jamie's admiration for his heroic efforts. [*Fiery Cross*]

Hobson, Janet—Resident of Drunkard's Creek and wife of Joe Hobson, possible member of the Regulation. [*Fiery Cross*]

Hobson, Joe—A resident of Drunkard's Creek, near Fraser's Ridge, who was in attendance at the Gathering on Mount Helicon; possibly a member of the Regulation, the North Carolina organization vehemently opposed to British taxation practices. Father-in-law of Hugh Fowles. Killed during the Battle of Alamance. [*Fiery Cross*]

Hodgepile, Arvin; Hodge—A former English soldier, he is presumed dead in a warehouse fire but has disappeared into the backcountry and a life of crime. He becomes the leader of a large gang of bandits who invade Fraser's Ridge, assault Marsali, steal the whisky from the malting shed, and abduct Claire. Later killed by Jamie, who breaks Hodgepile's neck and orders his men to kill all of the bandits. [*Ashes, MOBY*]

Hognose—One of Lord John's horses during his Prussian military campaign, a steady, sure-footed bay who carries John on a scouting expedition when he declines to risk Karolus's legs in the boggy terrain. [*SU*]

x **Holmes, Charles, Admiral**—(1711–1761) A career navy man. During the Seven Years' War, Holmes was part of Admiral Saunders's forces that sailed up the St. Lawrence River to get a squadron of ships past the guns at Quebec City. [*CA*]

Holmes, Reginald—The head steward at White's Chocolate House, a London gentlemen's club. [*BL*]

x **Holt, Michael, Captain**—(1723–1799) Captain of the Alamance County Militia, and owner of the plantation where the Battle of Alamance took place. [*Fiery Cross*]

Honey, Captain Joseph—An officer of the Lancers and Edward Twelvetrees's second at the duel between John Grey and Twelvetrees. [*SP*]

Hoskins, William; Bill—Overseer of Edgar DeVane's gunpowder mill in Sussex. [*HS*]

Houvener, Monsieur—One of several guests invited to attend Stephen Bonnet's special slave auction, which includes Brianna. [*Ashes*]

Howard, Mister—One of several guests invited to attend Stephen Bonnet's special slave auction, which includes Brianna; objecting to Howard's inspection of her, Bree assaults him but is punished by Bonnet's servant Emmanuel. [*Ashes*]

Howard, Willie—An older soldier in Lord John's regiment, who tells DeVries that the regiment will be posting back to Calais. [*PM*]

x **Howe, Richard, Admiral; Dick**—(1726–1799) British commander in chief on American seas; brother to army General William Howe. He provided naval support during the Battle of Long Island but resigned his command in support of his brother: both were upset with the way London had handled their requests for reinforcements and now blamed them for several defeats. [*Echo*]

x **Howe, Robert, Colonel**—(1732–1786) During the War of the Regulation, he served as Governor Tryon's colonel of artillery for the North Carolina militia's expeditions against the Regulators. As a Colonial supporter, he was elected to the provincial Congress and was appointed colonel of the Second North Carolina Regiment; he marched his troops into Virginia to occupy Norfolk, the last Loyalist stronghold. [*Ashes*]

x **Howe, William, Lieutenant General, Sir**—(1729–1814) Assisted General Wolfe's attack on Quebec in 1759; was appointed commander of the British army in North America after taking over forces from General Gage. After a successful victory at the Battle of Long Island, his refusal to attack Washington's smaller forces allowed the Americans a nighttime escape in the dense fog. This missed opportunity was considered to be the greatest of the war and would haunt Howe. After several other military mistakes, including the loss of Saratoga under General Burgoyne's command, Howe resigned and returned to England. [*Echo, MOBY*]

Howell, Davis—A wealthy ship owner and member of Governor Tryon's Royal Council. He hosts an evening of gaming in New Bern, where Major MacDonald learns a great deal about Stephen Bonnet—information MacDonald later shares with Jamie, in exchange for a small favor. [*Fiery Cross*]

Howlat, Johnnie—A reclusive old man who lived near a village in Scotland where the Bugs once resided; filthy and unkempt, he was known as a sort of charmer or witch who would sell herbs, charms, and spells as well as tell fortunes for those willing—or brave enough—to peer into their futures. Mrs. Bug once sought him out for a charm to aid her in carrying a child to term, but after scrying her future, he warned that a living child would be the death of her husband, Arch. [*Fiery Cross*]

Hubert—The butler at the home of Léonie and Lillie's aunt, Madame Eugenie. [*SB*]

Huckabee, Morris—A local resident near Lord Dunsany's estate who, unbeknownst to his neighbors, lives in a common-law incestuous relationship with his own daughter and has sired a child—his own grandchild; the convoluted relationship is the talk of the county near Helwater. [*SP*]

Hückel, Herr—The landlord—a dwarf—where Private Koenig last rented a room. [*SU*]

Hückel, Margarethe—The landlord Herr Hückel's normal-sized—and quite pretty—wife. [*SU*]

Hudson, Private—An illiterate British private in William's unit, questioned regarding Nathan Hale's passage through a checkpoint the previous day. [*Echo*]

Humber, Misses—A couple of unmarried young ladies present at an evening event hosted by Benedicta Grey at Jermyn House. [*PM*]

Humberto—The Italian shed-master for Jared Fraser's wine importing business, Fraser et Cie. [*SB*]

Humphries, George—Amos Crupp's business partner in Wilmington's defunct *Gazette*. [*Echo*]

Hunnicut, Joseph—Medical dowser called in by Mrs. Mercy Woodcock to locate the metal balls in Henry Grey's belly by divination of the metal's radiation or aura through the flesh; the practice was deemed a bit occult but sometimes proved successful—perhaps it was just coincidental. [*Echo*]

Hunter, Denzell, Dr.; Denny—A young Quaker doctor living near the Great Dismal Swamp with his sister, Rachel. He is against violence but his support of the Patriot cause is at odds with his religious beliefs. He joins the Continental army as a doctor, having trained in England with his relative, the great surgeon John Hunter. He loves Lady Dorothea Grey, Lord John's niece and William Ransom's cousin, but feels that being a Quaker makes him unacceptable to someone of Dottie's social standing. Circumstances—and Dottie—contrive to overcome his scruples, and they are married in Philadelphia, after the Battle of Monmouth. [*Echo, MOBY*]

x **Hunter, James**—(ca. 1740–1820) One of the leaders of the Regulation movement in North Carolina, commonly referred to as the General of the Regulators. [*Fiery Cross, Ashes*]

x **Hunter, John, Dr.**—(1728–1793) Prominent Scottish surgeon and anatomist, founder of experimental pathology in England; his study of dissection and anatomy put surgical practices on the scientific pathway, laying the groundwork for twentieth-century developments. It is rumored that he inoculated himself with both syphilis and gonorrhea to prove that two diseases cannot exist at the same time; unfortunately, his theory was disproven and it took three years for the "cure" to become effective. [*CA, SP, Echo, MOBY*]

Hunter, Mrs.—The wife of Dr. John Hunter and a supporter of the arts, her London salons were renowned for the celebrity poets often in attendance. [*CA*]

Hunter, Rachel—An opinionated young Quaker woman living near the Great Dismal Swamp with her brother, Denzell, a physician. After Ian Murray delivers an injured and delirious William Ransom to their door, Rachel and her brother assist in William's recovery. While she clearly likes William, it's Ian Murray to whom she's truly drawn, and after considerable difficulties caused by her being a Quaker and Ian a man of blood, they are married in Philadelphia, at the same ceremony that unites Denzell and Dorothea. Returning to a semblance of peaceful life, Rachel becomes pregnant and later gives birth to their son—so far unnamed but going by the nickname "Oggy" (for "Oglethorpe")—at Fraser's Ridge. [*Echo, MOBY*]

x **Hunter, Theophilus, Major**—(1735–1798) Pioneer settler of Wake County and early political leader in Raleigh, he was an officer of the Wake regiment of colonial militia during the War of the Regulation; he served the county as a land surveyor and its first tax assessor, as well as holding a seat in the House of Commons. [*Fiery Cross*]

Hunter, William, Dr.—Another distant relative to Denzell and Rachel. He is also midwife to Charlotte, the Queen of England. [*MOBY*]

Hurragh, Bobby—Rob Cameron's nephew, a member of the children's choir Roger MacKenzie is directing, and a friend of Jem MacKenzie. [*Echo, MOBY*]

Hurragh, Martina—Rob Cameron's sister and mother of Bobby Hurragh, Jem MacKenzie's twentieth-century best friend. [*Echo*]

x **Husband, Hermon**—(1724–1795) One of the leaders of the Regulator movement in North Carolina; a Quaker, and thus opposed to violence, but a man of principle who cannot abide the malfeasance of corrupt officialdom. [*Fiery Cross, Ashes*]

I

Iain Mhor—Brother of Auld Joan Findlay; Iain Mhor, who suffers from severe cerebral palsy, "has nay speech," but is still the head of the Findlay family. [*Fiery Cross*]

Ilse—One of the kitchen maids at Schloss Lowenstein, Princess Louisa's home, who takes a liking to young Tom Byrd, Lord John's valet. [*SU, PZ*]

Innes, Duncan—Onetime fisherman, part-time smuggler, ex-Ardsmuir prisoner, and Jamie's friend, he marries Jocasta Cameron, Jamie's aunt and owner of the North Carolina plantation River Run. [*Fiery Cross, Ashes, Echo*]

Innes, Jocasta (aka Jocasta Cameron, Jocasta Isobeail MacKenzie)—The late Hector Cameron's wife and Jamie Fraser's aunt, owner of a large plantation in Cross Creek, which she runs with the aid of her black butler, Ulysses. She is also keeper of the Frenchman's gold, a treasure transported to the colonies by Hector Cameron after the fall of Culloden; her fourth husband, Duncan Innes, is a former Ardsmuir inmate and friend of Jamie. She and Duncan emigrate to Canada when the gold is stolen and the Loyalists lose power in North Carolina. [*All*]

Innes, Margaret—The sister of Duncan Innes's grandfather, she was executed by drowning during the seventeenth century for being a Scottish Covenanter. The Covenanters were Scottish Episcopalians, but, far more extreme in their beliefs than their English counterparts, they rejected the Anglican Book of Common Prayer, claiming it was too similar to the Catholic liturgy. [*Ashes*]

Iredell, Samuel—A prominent rebel leader in Edenton and business associate of Neil Forbes. [*Ashes*]

Iris—A tall, thin black whore in Savannah, who accompanies her colleague Molly to Claire for pox cures. [*MOBY*]

Isaacs, Robert—Jewish merchant and part owner of a warehouse in the French coastal town of Brest. He marries Mary Hawkins Randall after Jonathan Randall is killed at Culloden and is the stepfather to her son, Denys Randall-Isaacs. Isaacs is dead when Denys meets William again during the British retreat from Philadelphia, and Denys tells William that he has dropped "Isaacs" from his own name, presumably to avoid any opprobrium due to the Jewish connection. [*Echo, MOBY*]

Isbister, Geillis—The name used by Geillis Duncan before marrying. [*MOBY*]

Iseabaìl—Ian and Emily's stillborn daughter. [*Ashes, Echo, MOBY*]

Ishmael—The *houngan* who worships snakes and creates "zombies," including Rodrigo. [*PZ*]

Isobeaìl, Alasdair, and Elspeth—The names given to the chickens by Mrs. Bug. [*Echo*]

J

Jackson, Captain—The captain of the slave ship sitting offshore from Stephen Bonnet's hideout on Ocracoke Island. [*Ashes*]

Jackson, Jolly—The Indian shaman at the Cherokee village known as Raventown; his invocations could be boring, even to the village inhabitants, but his spiritual guidance was required by the Cherokee in order that the hunt for the ghost bear be successful. [*Fiery Cross*]

Jacob Ruaidh—See "Jacob MacKenzie."

Jakob—One of Princess von Lowenstein's footmen. [*SU*]

Jameson, Mr.—Elderly apothecary in Savannah with a pleasant working relationship with Claire and a good memory of his customers. [*MOBY*]

Jameson, Nigel, Mr.—Grandson of the apothecary's founder, he lets Claire know that pre-made ether is available for her surgery and is a great cure for seasickness. [*MOBY*]

Jameson, Silas—Owner of an ordinary in Cross Creek, located in front of Mrs. Sylvie's brothel. [*Ashes*]

x **Jane (McCrea)**—(1752–1777) A Loyalist resident living in the woods near Ticonderoga, engaged to a British soldier. She was abducted, killed, and scalped; her long locks were recognized when Wyandot Indians, hired by General Burgoyne to terrorize the colonists, brought her scalp to camp for their bounty. [*Echo*]

Janie; "Oor Janie"—One of the prostitutes employed in the MacNabs' brothel, she is noted for her energetic romps and sometimes-vocal declarations of pleasure in her job. [*BL*]

Jean-Baptiste—Michael Murray's butler. [*SB*]

Jeffers, Zebedee—William's new groom. [*MOBY*]

x **Jefferson, Thomas**—(1743–1826) Founding Father, chief author of the Declaration of Independence, and third U.S. president, Jefferson promoted the idea of republicanism in opposition to the imperialistic ideas prominent in Europe. [*Ashes, Echo*]

Jeffords—A lawyer who was also part of the spy ring, along with Ffoulkes, Bates, and Otway, but was arrested on a variety of other charges, from lewd conduct to sodomy, conspiracy to commit unnatural acts, and possibly conspiracy to assassinate public officials. [*BL*]

Jeffries—The Dunsanys' elderly former coachman and witness to the death of old Ellesmere on the day William was born. He was pensioned off to Ireland to prevent his testimony from causing a scandal. [*SP*]

Jeffries, Corporal—A corporal leading one of the companies in William's regiment at the Battle of Long Island. [*Echo*]

Jemima—A cousin to Alicia Brown and Richard Brown, she is the woman who offers to nurse Baby Beardsley along with her own three-month-old son when Jamie and Claire bring the orphaned child to Brownsville. [*Fiery Cross*]

Jenkins, Major—A soldier who recognizes Arabella-Jane from the Philadelphia brothel where fellow soldier Harkness was killed; he has her arrested for murder. [*MOBY*]

Jenks—Lord John's young comrade at Prestonpans. They are patrolling together before the battle, and Jenks dismisses John's hints of enemies near Carryarick Pass. [*BL*]

Jeremy, Atta, and Jojo—Three members of the Montauk Five, a group of time travelers from the 1960s, who apparently failed to make the journey through the time passage safely, as they were never seen again. [*Ashes*]

Jernigan, Dr.—A Philadelphia Loyalist. [*MOBY*]

Jernigan, Mary—Daughter of Dr. Jernigan, she is also a friend of Anne Endicott and is described by William as "a flirtatious blond piece." [*MOBY*]

Jerusha—The quiet but plump mare (also known affectionately as Mistress Piggy, due to her appetite) that Hermon Husband leaves for Jamie and Claire when he is forced to flee in the face of the upcoming confrontation with the Regulators. [*Fiery Cross*]

Jess—A soldier wounded by a panther prior to the Battle of Saratoga; his cousin Lester—who is also Claire's triage aide—applied a tourniquet to his leg to stanch the blood flow. [*Echo*]

Jessop, Mr.—A neighbor of Mrs. Hempstead, he informs her—through the gamut of local child messengers—that a tall Scottish man is looking for Fergus. [*Echo*]

Jocelyn, Ralph—One of Lieutenant Ransom's roommates during the New York occupation with General Howe's army. [*Echo*]

Joe—A footman employed at Argus House, the home of Benedicta Grey. He brings the refreshments Lord John's cousin Olivia apparently insisted that he needs. [*BL*]

Joey—See "Joseph Boswell Murray."

Joffrey, Lucinda, Lady (introduced as "Amanda" in *PM;* renamed in subsequent books)—Wife of Sir Richard Joffrey and Harry Quarry's sister-in-law. She regards Lord John not only as a close friend but also as a possible marriage prospect to one of her many unmarried sisters and cousins. [*HF, PM, BL, HS, CA*]

Joffrey, Richard, Sir—Harry Quarry's half brother and husband to Lady Lucinda (Amanda) Joffrey. [*HF, PM, BL HS, CA*]

Johansen, Mr.—One of Fergus's correspondents, who regularly provides news for *L'Oignon.* [*MOBY*]

Johnny—William Buccleigh MacKenzie's other friend present when Roger is accosted by Buccleigh and Black-beard. He is instructed to escort Morag back to their camp while Buck deals with Roger MacKenzie. [*Fiery Cross*]

Johnson, Antioch—Sinister host and axwelding madman who invites Denzell, Rachel, and William to spend the night at his home after they take a wrong turn on the road to Albany; the wrong turn nearly costs the trio their lives. [*Echo*]

Johnson, Micah, Colonel—Commander of the company that was saved during the Battle of Saratoga, when Jamie broke the British charge and suffered a severe injury to his hand, forcing Claire to finally remove Jamie's broken finger. [*Echo*]

Johnson, Mrs.—The split-tongued wife of Antioch Johnson, who makes Rachel uneasy by staring at her shoes; she helps her husband try to murder the travelers, as they've apparently done to others in the past. [*Echo*]

x **Johnson, Samuel, Doctor**—(1709–1784) English author of several published essays and *A Dictionary of the English Language* (1755), also known as "Johnson's Dictionary," he was a popular guest at various literary salons and other social settings. [*PM*]

Johnston, Private—One of the soldiers in Percy's company, who was slightly injured during a brief skirmish with a French foraging party in the Rhine Valley near Crefeld. [*BL*]

Jonas, Lady—A popular London socialite

with whom Percy Wainwright and Lord John are acquainted. She is a hostess of literary salons, her interesting guests including poets, philosophers, and novelists of the time. [*BL, SP*]

Jones, Dai—The blacksmith in the small community where the McGillivrays live, about five miles from the Ridge. [*Ashes*]

x Jones, David, Lieutenant—(ca. 1752–after 1778) Loyalist soldier near Ticonderoga who discovers the long-haired scalp of his murdered Loyalist fiancée, Jane McCrea, being submitted as a "bounty" to General Burgoyne by the Wyandot Indians. [*Echo*]

Jones, Egbert—A homosexual man known among his comrades as "Miss Irons," but during the day he's a cheerful young Welsh blacksmith employed to work on the fence surrounding Benedicta's Jermyn Street house. [*PM*]

Jones, Reginald, Captain—An officer of the Royal Artillery, assigned by the Royal Ordnance Office to determine the cause of the explosions among the cannons; he tries to confiscate the bit of cannon shrapnel Lord John possesses—which was removed from his chest. [*HS*]

Jones, Wilbraham—A mild-mannered, effeminate smuggler of tea and other luxury items, who Brianna knows has been supplying Jocasta Cameron with many of her contraband luxuries. [*Ashes*]

Jones-Osborn, Colonel—An infantry colonel in attendance at the ordnance meeting, who misinterprets Lord John's nervous hand-clenching as impatience and agrees that the speaker has droned on long enough. [*BL*]

Joseph—See "Ulysses."

Josephine—A prostitute at Magda's, possibly experienced in erotic punishment as part of sex. [*PM*]

Josephine from Cornwall—The fictional name Lord John gives to the mollies at Lavender House when trying to track the "woman in green." [*PM*]

Joshua; Josh—One of Jocasta Cameron's grooms; a slave born in North Carolina, but he speaks both Gaelic and Scots-accented English, as a result of being born on a plantation owned by a man from Aberdeen. He is kidnapped by slave traders on the same night that Phaedre disappears from River Run. [*Fiery Cross, Ashes*]

Jowett, Corporal—Soldier from Quarry's regiment whom Lord John wishes to accompany him while investigating Sergeant O'Connell's death. [*PM*]

Jurgen—Soldier who suggests that the sound of the "crying child" is only wind moaning through a hole in the bridge. [*SU*]

K

Karolous—The large, attractive white stallion belonging to Lord John, given to him as a gift by Landgrave Stephan von Namtzen. [*SU, BL*]

Karònya (Mohawk for "Looking at the Sky")—Karònya was a young maiden from Ian's Mohawk village who was taken captive by the Abenaki, an enemy tribe to the Mohawk. [*Ashes*]

Kebbits, Mrs.—Wife of one of the New Hampshire militiamen, who feeds Ian and Claire after a sinister stranger, looking for Jamie, insults Claire and ruins her kettle of soup by spitting in it. [*Echo*]

Keeble, Sergeant—The soldier who was to have drilled Percy on use of a musket but has another commitment; instead, Lord John gives the instruction. [*BL*]

Keegan, Mr.—The surgeon's assistant assigned to Ruysdale's campaign; he's put in charge of the surgeon's tent after the surgeon dies of flux. He cleverly advances the idea that if the troops take matters "into their own hands" prior to sleeping, it will keep the succubus at bay. [*SU*]

Kelleher, Mrs.—Fiona and Ernie Buchan's elderly neighbor in Inverness. Fiona sends Jem running to Mrs. Kelleher's house to call the police when Rob Cameron shows up at the Buchans' house. [*MOBY*]

Keren-happuch—A Welsh kitchen maid employed at Helwater, who carries a message from Jamie to Betty. (A Real Person, named in compliment to my friend Karen Henry, Queen of the Nitpickers.) [*SP*]

Kerr, Duncan—A MacKenzie tacksman, he dies shortly after being found wandering near Ardsmuir, sea-soaked, demented, and babbling of white witches and hidden gold. Jocasta Cameron remembers him as a servant of the mysterious man who received one-third of the gold meant for Charles Stuart and his army during the '45. [*Fiery Cross*]

Keyes—A homosexual man and briefly the cellmate of Captain Bates, who has been accused of sodomy, during his confinement in Newgate Prison; he attempts to force his attentions on Bates but is rebuffed. [*BL*]

x **King James** (James Francis Edward Stuart of Scotland)—(1688–1766) Also called the "Old Pretender," the Prince of Wales, James VIII of Scotland, and James III of England, he was heir to the exiled Catholic royal dynasty. In 1708 and 1715, he attempted to invade and overthrow British rule in Scotland; he was forced to retreat and live in exile in Italy. [*Fiery Cross*]

x **King Louis XV**—(1710–1774) A Jacobite sympathizer before the '45 Rising, he had Jamie imprisoned for a duel but set him free after Claire went to the King and begged for Jamie's release, trading a brief sexual favor for Jamie's life. [*BL, Ashes, Echo*]

x **King, the** (King George VI of England; Bertie)—(1895–1952) In a discussion with Roger, Claire mentions that she briefly met King George VI during the war when she was a nurse, when he was visiting injured troops. [*Echo*]

x **Kingston, Robert, Major**—(unknown) General Burgoyne's aide-de-camp after the Battle of Bemis Heights, he relinquished proposals to General Gates and the American army for the British surrender at Saratoga. Jamie comments on Kingston's red-faced complexion, which was flushed due to the humiliation of being blindfolded and marched through the American camp while carrying the proposal for surrender. [*Echo*]

Kirby, Captain—One of the captains under Jamie's command at Monmouth. [*MOBY*]

x **Knox, Henry, General**—(1750–1806) Chief of artillery under General George Washington, Knox moved more than sixty tons of heavy artillery three hundred miles, from Ticonderoga to Boston, in midwinter, forcing the British army to evacuate Boston. [*Echo*]

Koenig, Hanna—Nursemaid to young Siegfried Lowenstein and wife to the dead soldier Private Koenig; she disappears the night the supposed witch visits young Siegfried's room. [*SU*]

Koenig, Private—A Prussian soldier found dead in the barracks, with suspicious marks on his body; his death is attributed to a nocturnal visit by a succubus, or female demon. [*SU*]

Kolodziewicz, Andrej—A former crew member and fellow pilot of Jerry's "Green

Flight," and his good friend who taught him a smattering of Polish during their off-duty time; he died when his plane was shot down in battle. [*LW*]

x **Kościuszko, Tadeusz, Colonel** (pronounced "kohs-CHOOSH-koh")—(1746–1817) "Kos" was a Polish émigré and volunteer in the Continental army before being noticed and commissioned as a colonel of engineers by the Continental Congress. Kos was instrumental in his strategic placement and defenses of several forts, bridges, and roadways, including the impregnable fortifications at Saratoga, which ultimately forced the British forces under General John Burgoyne to surrender. [*Echo*]

L

Lachlan, Isaiah—Jacky Lachlan's father and a member of Roger MacKenzie's new congregation on Fraser's Ridge. [*Ashes*]

Lachlan, Jacky—One of the young boys on Fraser's Ridge, who tries to disrupt Roger's first sermon by setting loose a snake among the parishioners. [*Ashes*]

Lachlan, Stuart—Fellow historian and friend of Reverend Wakefield, who shares an interest in the Lovat family. He somehow comes into a possession of a hand-drawn family tree, showing Jamie, Claire, and Brianna; this tree is discovered by Frank Randall, who encloses it with a note of warning to Brianna. [*MOBY*]

Lady Belvedere—The hostess of a ball where William claims to have "dishonored" his cousin Dottie, therefore imploring Lord John to convince Hal to allow Dottie and William to wed. Since Dottie and William's stories don't match, John knows they're both lying and means to find out why. [*Echo*]

Lady Jane—Dr. Joe Abernathy's affectionate name for Claire, due to her cultured British accent. [*Fiery Cross*]

x **Lady Seaforth**—(unknown) The earl's wife who had the Brahan Seer burned to death. [*MOBY*]

Lady Windermere—The hostess of a musicale where Dottie claims to have fallen in love with William, therefore imploring Lord John to convince Hal to allow Dottie and William to wed. Since Dottie and William's stories don't match, John knows they're both lying and means to find out why. [*Echo*]

x **La Fayette, Marquis de** (aka Wee Gilbert)—(1757–1834) Marie Joseph Paul Yves Roch Gilbert du Motier. The young marquis was a favorite of George Washington's and accompanied him on the Monmouth campaign, where he first meets and befriends Claire. He commands a body of troops during the battle, but his true importance is the friendship that causes him to send Claire a basket of French goodies when he hears that she's been wounded. Among the contents of the basket are a much-needed bottle of laudanum and a chunk of Roquefort cheese, which Claire instructs Denzell to pack into her wound (she realizing that the strain of mold that makes Roquefort cheese is a variety of *Penicillium*). [*MOBY*]

x **Lally, Thomas Arthur** (aka Baron de Tollendal)—(1702–1766) One of Charles Stuart's former aides-de-camp, captured after the Rising but paroled in London under the watchful eyes of the English. [*SP*]

Lambert, Widow—The young owner of a home near a mission church in Canada, she rents a room to Charlie Carruthers while he is awaiting trial in a court-martial. [*CA*]

Landringham, Miss—A reference to General James Wolfe's real-life fiancée, Katherine Lowther (1736–1809), who was depicted in a miniature he carried; upon his death at the Battle of Quebec, a request was made to return the small portrait to Katherine's parents. [*CA*]

Landrum, Mrs.—The Fraser family's landlady in Savannah. [*MOBY*]

Latham, Dr.—The official military surgeon for Hal and John's regiment, called in to stitch Lord John's wounds after a duel. [*SP*]

Laughlin, Constable—WPC Laughlin escorts Brianna and her children back to Lallybroch after the attack by Rob Cameron and his companions. [*MOBY*]

Launfal, Private—A private under William's command on Long Island, placed under arrest by William for attempting to bargain for contraband brandy at a checkpoint the men were supposed to be guarding. [*Echo*]

x **Learned, Ebenezer, General**—(1728–1801) Commander of the Third Continental Regiment. Acting as intermediary, Learned helped negotiate the British evacuation of Boston and took control of the city; he later combined forces with General Benedict Arnold at Bemis Heights, where they charged the Hessians and broke through the enemy lines. [*Echo*]

x **Leatherlips**—(1732–1810) A chief of the Wyandot Indians, one of the tribes employed by General Burgoyne to intimidate the colonists by raids on their homesteads, often killing livestock and setting fire to homes and outbuildings. [*Echo*]

LeCarré, Father—The Catholic priest who accepts the mixed-blood child of Malcolm Stubbs—husband to Lord John's cousin Olivia—and his Indian mistress. [*CA*]

Leckie, Jared, Captain—Surgeon with the Second New Jersey. Dr. Leckie gets off on the wrong foot with Claire when he high-handedly tries to appropriate her stock of medical supplies and later denies her entrance to the church where the surgeons are tending the wounded from the Battle of Monmouth. He redeems himself by racing to her rescue when she's shot outside the church and saves her life by preventing her bleeding to death on the spot. He then infuriates Jamie by abruptly abandoning Claire to go back to his work—but she *is* alive. [*MOBY*]

LeClerc, Father—A French-speaking Jesuit priest on his way from New Orleans to Quebec, with a tendency to shout the only English he knows: "Tally-ho!" He is waylaid to perform the sanctioned wedding ceremony for Jocasta Cameron and Duncan Innes—by a sizable donation from Jocasta to the Society of Jesus. [*Fiery Cross*]

x **Lee, Charles, Major General**—(1732–1782) Known as Ounewaterika, or "Boiling Water," by his wife's family, the Mohawk. A career soldier with a mixed reputation, he takes service with the Continental army and, on the strength of his experience and undoubted bravery, becomes Washington's second in command prior to the Battle of Monmouth. Owing to his part in the events of that battle, Lee is court-martialed for incompetence but is eventually acquitted. [*MOBY*]

Lee, Warren—Secretary to the Reverend Doctor McCorkle, he is present at the Reverend McMillan's home and relates a story of his time spent with the Massachusetts militia during the Battle of

Breed's Hill and how he shot a British officer during the battle. He confesses to Roger privately that, even though he didn't know if the soldier lived or died, he prayed for him every night anyway. [*Ashes*]

LeGrand, Jeanne (aka Madame Jeanne)—French madame of Edinburgh brothel, partner and customer of "Jamie Roy" during his time in the brandy-smuggling business. Through her many clients, the madame has a strong sense of just about any happenings in Edinburgh. [*Echo*]

Lenny, Jr.—Joe Abernathy's grandson. [*MOBY*]

Léonie—The late Lillie Murray's sister, she becomes pregnant by a married lover and attempts to seduce a drunken Michael Murray to save her honor and that of her child. When that fails, she purchases an abortifacient to rid herself of the child. [*SB*]

Leopold—A large albino python with a voracious appetite and nasty attitude, brought from the West Indies by Madame Fabienne many years ago; she claims that her pet is a spirit, or *Mystère,* a mediary between God and man. [*SB*]

LeRoi—Stephen Bonnet's closest companion, one with whom Brianna is acquainted and would like to forget. I.e., Bonnet's pet name for his penis. [*Ashes*]

Lester—Claire's cheerful triage aide at the Battle of Saratoga, familiar with tourniquets as well as the blood and filth of war. [*Echo*]

Lethbridge-Stewart, Brigadier—A British officer present at Wolfe's storming of the Citadel at Quebec. (Also the name of a fictional character more commonly known as "The Brigadier" from the modern science-fiction television show *Doctor Who*.) [*CA*]

Lewis, Mr.—The Edinburgh spectacle-maker whom Claire and Jamie visit upon their arrival in Scotland while transporting home the body of General Simon Fraser. Jamie and Claire both invest in eyeglasses—a serviceable pair for reading for Jamie; a slightly stronger and gold-rimmed pair for Claire. [*Echo*]

Light, Mrs.—The wife of the Tuscarora brave Light on Water, she is abducted by the Cherokee tribe governed by Bird/Tsisqua, with whom Jamie and Ian have a tenuous alliance; Jamie and Ian assist with the ransom to return her to her husband. [*Ashes*]

Light on Water—Tuscarora brave who escapes an attack by the Cherokee with whom Jamie has a friendship; his wife is taken captive, but Jamie and Ian, through their diplomacy, help Light to retrieve her, and the Tuscaroras are adopted into the Cherokee. [*Ashes*]

Lillington, Alexander—Cousin to Randall Lillington; leader of the Patriot forces at the Battle of Moore's Creek Bridge. As they face MacDonald and McLeod's combined Highland and British forces across the waterway, Lillington questions Jamie's loyalty to the cause since Jamie, too, is a Highlander. [*Ashes*]

Lillington, Randall (identified in early editions as "Lillywhite")—A magistrate of the circuit court and personal friend of Governor Tryon, he is asked to meet with Lieutenant Hayes and other powerful men of the region. Later, he enters into a smuggling contract with other local businessmen and the notorious pirate, Stephen Bonnet, and is killed by Roger during a scuffle. [*Fiery Cross, Ashes*]

Lind, Mrs.—An apparently well-endowed woman whom a very drunk William Ransom and Sandy Lindsay are discussing following a dinner party with fellow officers and several young ladies. [*Echo*]

x **Lindsay, Alexander, Major; Sandy**—(1752–1825) The Sixth Earl of Balcarres, Sandy is a fellow officer and friend of William's, who was also with Burgoyne during the surrender at Saratoga. At Ticonderoga, he and William have a philosophical discussion comparing the Indian savages to Scots and their trainability as soldiers. Later, just prior to the British withdrawal from Philadelphia in June of 1778, Sandy takes William out for an evening of drinking and women; William ends up at Madge's brothel, where he again meets Jane and has a confrontation with Captain Harkness. [*Echo, MOBY*]

Lindsay, Bobby, Grace, Hugh, Caitlin—Evan Lindsey's children, some of whom fell sick or died during the breakout of bloody flux on the Ridge. [*Ashes*]

Lindsay, Evan—One of Kenny Lindsay's brothers, who has decided to settle on Fraser's Ridge and whom Jamie calls to his side as one of his followers to provide mutual protection against whatever may come. [*Fiery Cross, Ashes*]

Lindsay, Gordon—A shy young man on the Ridge who is betrothed to a Quaker girl from Woolam's Mill; Brianna jokingly asks Roger if he's throwing a stag party for Gordon when Roger asks her to stay at the Big House for the night so he can have a male-only meeting in their cabin. [*Ashes*]

Lindsay, Kenny—One of Jamie's comrades from Ardsmuir Prison, who settles on Fraser's Ridge with his common-law wife, Rosamund. [*Fiery Cross, Ashes*]

Lindsay, Mrs.—Wife of Evan Lindsay, one of the settlers on Fraser's Ridge. [Fiery Cross]

Lindsay, Murdo—One of Kenny Lindsay's brothers, who has decided to settle on Fraser's Ridge. Claire sets fire to his barley field in order to extirpate a plague of locusts. [*Fiery Cross, Ashes*]

Lindsay, Rosamund—The common-law wife of Kenny Lindsay, who threatens to kill Ronnie Sinclair if he doesn't stop bedeviling her while at the Gathering; after waiting too long to seek treatment for an open cut on her hand—opting first to wrap a dead pigeon around the wound, which only causes the infection to get worse—she finally seeks treatment but dies suddenly of an unfortunate allergic reaction to Claire's penicillin. [*Fiery Cross*]

x **Linzee, Captain John**—(1743–1798) Captain of the British schooner HMS *Falcon;* while attempting to run down and capture two American ships on their way back from the Caribbean, his own ship runs aground and is instead captured by the local militia of Gloucester, Massachusetts, one of the inciting incidents of the early Revolution [*Ashes*]

Lister, Mr.—Grieving father of Lieutenant Philip Lister. Opposed to his son's chosen profession, he comes to Lord John to ask for assistance in locating the grandchild Philip fathered when he eloped with the local minister's daughter; their actions created such a scandal that the girl's family was dismissed from the congregation. [*HS*]

Lister, Philip, Lieutenant—The dead officer in charge of the cannon that exploded during the Battle of Crefeld; he is decapitated by a cannon shot shortly before Lord John takes over. Lister is survived by his pregnant wife in Sussex. [*HS*]

Liston, Captain—A military acquaintance of Lord John's who witnesses an incident concerning Stephen Bonnet; the incident is related to Jamie in a letter from Lord John. [*Fiery Cross*]

Little Otto—The private name Roger and Brianna give their unborn child. [*Ashes*]

Lloyd—One of the survey party assigned to spy on the French forces and killed during a skirmish with the Austrians, allies of the French forces. [*SU*]

Lockett, Friend—A Quaker farmer who gives Denzell, Rachel, and William vague directions north toward Albany, where the Continental army might be found, but instead the trio find themselves dinner guests of some strange hosts. [*Echo*]

Loew, Shecky—An acquaintance of Germain's, who joins his friend Joe Grume in throwing dirt clods and stones at the Duke of Pardloe's sedan chair (and, incidentally, at Claire), until Germain threatens them off. [*MOBY*]

Longfield, Herbert—The owner of the land and the shop that housed Wilmington's newspaper, the *Gazette,* before the shop was burned and the printer run out of town. [*Echo*]

Longstreet, Arthur, Dr.—The English surgeon who operates on Lord John after the Battle of Crefeld, removing the fragments of the demolished cannon from Grey's chest; also cousin to George Longstreet. [*BL, HS, CA*]

Longstreet, George; Lord Creemore—One of the men who support the accusations of treason and Jacobitism directed at Lord John's father, Gerard, the Duke of Pardloe; he also courts Benedicta after the death of her husband. Because he dies childless, the title passes to his dying cousin, Dr. Arthur Longstreet. [*BL, CA*]

Looking at the Sky—A Mohawk woman who was Sun Elk's wife and Emily's sister; when Looking at the Sky is kidnapped by an opposing tribe, Sun Elk begins his pursuit to win Emily from Ian. [*Ashes*]

Lossey, Captain—One of the officers in Lord John's regiment, he makes sure Lord John has enough supplies and horses for his trek into the Jamaican uplands to the plantation called Twelvetrees. [*PZ*]

x Louis of France—(1729–1765) The eldest son and heir apparent of King Louis XV, he was known as the Dauphin of France. He died before he could inherit the French throne from his father; his eldest son became Louis XVI upon the King's death in 1774. [*BL*]

x Lovat, Lord—See "Simon Fraser."

Lowens, Mr.—A neighboring farmer acquaintance of Lord Dunsany. [*SP*]

Lowry, John—A bewildered young farmer from Woolam's Mill who is the object of admiration by a group of young unmarried girls playing a marriage prediction game during Hogmanay at the Big House. [*Fiery Cross*]

Lucianne—Cecile Beauchamp's cousin, who—according to Cecile's husband, Percy—shares an intimate relationship with Cecile. [*Echo*]

Lucy—One of Hal's dogs, a spaniel with a new litter of pups. [*SP*]

Ludgate, Captain—One of two former superintendents appointed by the Crown to oversee the maroons and act as their emissary with the British settlers. [*PZ*]

Lyle, Mr.—Mysterious man Jamie meets while in Paris with Jenny, after Ian's death. He invites Jamie to attend a salon, where Jamie entertains the crowd with tales of the Americas, much to the amusement and horror of the salon attendees. [*Echo*]

Lyon, Milford (identified in early editions as George Lyon)—A neighbor of Phillip Wylie, he proposes a discreet business arrangement with Jamie for the secret sale and distribution of illegal whisky in the colonies. [*Fiery Cross*]

Lyons, William—Local Edenton smuggler and associate of Neil Forbes, he meets with Forbes shortly before Roger and Ian find Forbes demanding information on the abducted Brianna's whereabouts. [*Ashes*]

M

MacAllister, Alistair—One of Jamie's comrades who died on Culloden Moor; during a conversation with the Cherokee, Jamie recalls his name and the manner of his death, envisioning MacAllister's broken body lying in front of him. [*Ashes*]

MacAllister, Mr.—One of the Lallybroch tenants, living near Broch Mordha. [*Echo*]

MacArdle, Maisie—One of the fisher-folk and mother of six children, she is married to a former boat builder and is the great-niece of Seaumais Buchan. [*Ashes*]

MacBean—Scottish settlers who proclaim themselves in attendance at the bonfire on the final night of the Gathering. [*Fiery Cross*]

Macbeth and Fleance—Two characters in Shakespeare's "Scottish play," *Macbeth,* and the secret names given to conspirators involved in the Jacobite plot to kill King George and sit James Stuart in his place. [*BL*]

MacBeth, Grannie—One of Claire's patients on Fraser's Ridge, who has a long list of recorded medical complaints. [*Ashes*]

MacCammon, Robert, Major—One of the officers under Jamie's command at Monmouth. [*MOBY*]

x **MacDonald, Allan**—(ca. 1720–1792) Seventh of the Kingsburgh MacDonalds and husband of famous Scottishwoman Flora MacDonald, who helped Prince Charles escape after Culloden. In Scottish fashion. the owner of a plantation or estate was sometimes referred to by the estate name; hence Allan is sometimes referred to as "Kingsburgh." [*Ashes*]

x **MacDonald, Anne and Fanny**—(unknown) The adult daughters of Flora and Allan MacDonald, who attended Jocasta's barbecue with their famous mother. [*Ashes*]

MacDonald, Annie—The girl Roger and Brianna hire at Lallybroch in the twentieth century to help take care of the children and house; she is technically Fiona's replacement now that Fiona has a home and family of her own. [*Echo*]

MacDonald, Donald, Major—A semi-retired Scottish officer with the British army, the soon-to-be-unemployed major uses Jamie's influence to help him secure a position with Governor William Tryon as the commander of the North Carolina militia. To Jamie's regret, he and MacDonald meet as enemies at Moore's Creek Bridge, where he shoots the gravely wounded MacDonald to save him from drowning. [*Fiery Cross, Ashes*]

x **MacDonald, Flora**—(1722–1790) The famous Scotswoman who helped Prince Charles escape Scotland after the defeat at Culloden by disguising him as her maid Betty. Later she was a British Loyalist who moved to North Carolina; her husband fought for the Crown and was captured during the Battle of Moore's Creek Bridge. Claire meets her at River Run, where a barbecue is being held in Flora's honor. [*Ashes*]

x **MacDonald, Hugh**—(ca. 1700–1780) Flora MacDonald's stepfather, whom Jamie met once on Skye when he and his father, Brian, went there on a matter of sheep. [*Ashes*]

MacDonald, Matthew—The young man with whom Rachel and Ian are staying on the Ridge; he notifies Claire that Rachel's water has broken. [*MOBY*]

MacDonald, Private—One of the soldiers of the Fort William garrison, whom Roger and Brian meet on their visit to the fort. The private is suffering from a bad cold. [*MOBY*]

MacDonald, Robert—Major MacDonald's father from Stornoway on the Isle of Harris, he was a Scottish acquaintance of the late Hector Cameron. [*Fiery Cross*]

MacDowell, Widow—A resident of Fraser's Ridge with whom Jenny Murray, Germain, and Fanny will stay when the family returns to the Ridge. [*MOBY*]

MacDuff, Mr.—One of the residents of Fraser's Ridge, whose wife and sister were both stricken by the bloody-flux epidemic. [*Ashes*]

MacFreckles, Dr.—A young freckled Scottish surgeon with the British army, so called by William. [*MOBY*]

MacGregor, Alexander—A young Scottish man imprisoned at Fort William by Captain Jonathan Randall, he took his own life rather than suffer further abuse—both physical and emotional—as Randall's captive. Upon his death, his small Bible was given to Jamie by the prison surgeon. [*Ashes*]

MacGregor, Mairi—Young Alexander's long-lost sister, Jamie vowed after Culloden that he would find her and give her Alexander's Bible and tell her that Alexander had been avenged. [*Ashes*]

Macken, Mrs.—Wife of a Continental officer engaged in the Battle of Monmouth. Jamie carries a wounded Claire to Mrs. Macken's door, and that startled lady gives them shelter. Denzell Hunter uses her kitchen table for his surgery on Claire, and Jamie and Claire occupy a small attic room while Claire recovers. [MOBY]

MacKenzie, Alexander—Jamie Fraser's alias while employed at Helwater, although the family knows his true identity as a paroled Jacobite prisoner. Known to young William as "Mac," the kind Scottish groom. [*BL, SP, Echo*]

MacKenzie, Amanda Claire Hope; Mandy—Daughter of Brianna and Roger MacKenzie, sister to Jem, granddaughter to Jamie and Claire Fraser. Born in the eighteenth century with a serious heart defect, her survival through advanced medical intervention is the pivotal point in the family's decision to return to the twentieth century. [*Ashes, Echo, MOBY*]

MacKenzie, Brianna Ellen Randall Fraser MacKenzie; Bree—Daughter of Claire and Jamie Fraser; stepdaughter of Frank Randall. Married to Roger MacKenzie, mother of Jeremiah/Jem and Amanda/Mandy MacKenzie. Having followed her mother into the past in hopes of saving her parents from a reported house fire, Brianna runs headfirst into life in the eighteenth century. In short order, she acquires a maid, becomes handfast with Roger, who has followed her, runs afoul of the pirate Stephen Bonnet and is raped by him, and becomes pregnant with a child whose father is unknown—all before she actually finds either of her parents. But find them she does, and she reunites with Roger, who is rescued from the Indians Jamie and Ian gave him to under the mistaken impression that *he* was the rapist. Now she and Roger MacKenzie hope to be formally married at the Gathering at Mount Helicon (there being few Catholic priests in the colonies, and even fewer in the Carolina backcountry) and eventually are—but the rising tide of politics threatens their happiness, and when Roger is hanged at the Battle of Alamance, Brianna struggles to help him heal and overcome the depression of losing his voice. An ongoing conflict between them concerns children: Roger, an orphan, has always wanted children of his own, and Brianna knows he still does, in spite of having taken Jeremiah as his son. Brianna, though, knows that having more children is a) a dangerous proposition in this place and time, and b) would likely tie her permanently to the past. Their relationship also has problems owing to the fact that she's much better at eighteenth-century skills, like hunting, than Roger is—and he's struggling hard to find a place and a sense of purpose in the past. Eventually, they find their way together; Roger discovers his true vocation as a minister, and Brianna risks becoming pregnant again for his sake. At this point, she's kidnapped by Stephen Bonnet, who has a small but profitable sideline in slaves and has several potential buyers for a white woman of known breeding potential. She escapes Bonnet, and he's captured by Jamie and Roger, then sentenced to drown as a pirate. Knowing that Bonnet fears drowning more than anything, Brianna shoots him out of mercy. The child she's carrying is born—a lovely little girl named Amanda—but has a serious birth defect of the heart: something easily correctible in the twentieth century with a modern hospital's facilities but impossible in the eighteenth century. In anguish, Claire tells Brianna that she can't help, and Roger and Bree make the desperate decision to travel through the stones again, with their children. The journey is successful, and so is Amanda's surgery. The MacKenzies settle down at Lallybroch, and Brianna begins to forge a career as an engineer, while Roger, once more dislocated in time and place, begins to pick up the pieces of his life and vocation. One of the men at Brianna's work, though, Rob Cameron, accidentally discovers the family's secrets. He kidnaps Jem, and after verifying that the boy probably really can pass through the stones, secrets him in a maintenance tunnel under the Loch Errochty dam. Cameron then decoys Roger and his ancestor Buck into actually going through the stones to rescue Jem, while Cameron goes to Lallybroch to take care of what he sees as unfinished business with Brianna, against whom he has a grudge for her superseding him at work. Left alone to protect her children from what appears to be an increasing threat (Cameron has colleagues), and fearing that she'll never see Roger again, Bree flees Scotland for America, where she asks her mother's old friend Joe Abernathy for help. Finally, she makes the dangerous decision to return to Scotland and take Jem and Mandy through the stones to find Roger. Safely arrived in the past, they go to Lallybroch as a place to begin their search; Bree and Jem encounter Brian Fraser in the graveyard, and Brian is overcome with joy, thinking that he's seeing his wife, Ellen, and their eldest boy, Willie, again. He passes out from the shock, and Brianna leaves, feeling that she can't bear to destroy his happiness. Shortly thereafter, she finds Roger and the family is reunited—but then the question is: where shall they go, and how? Through space, from Scotland to the New World? Through time, either back to the 1980s, where Cameron is still a danger, or to 1779, where Jamie and Claire theoretically are? The decision is made, and at the end of *Written in My Own Heart's Blood,* we see them arrive on Fraser's Ridge, the family completely reunited. [*All*]

MacKenzie, Colum—Chief of the MacKenzies of Leoch, brother to Ellen, Dougal, Jocasta, Flora and Janet; uncle to Jamie Fraser. Father (presumably) to Hamish, heir to the leadership of the clan. Intelligent and cunning although crippled as a young man by disease, Colum leads the clan in everything except war—in those instances he leaves matters in the hands of his younger brother, Dougal. Suspicious of Claire and who she might or might not represent, Colum dies shortly before Culloden and before his suspicions are made known to anyone, even his own brother. [*All*]

MacKenzie, Dougal—War chieftain of Clan MacKenzie, brother to Colum, Ellen, Jocasta, Flora, and Janet; uncle to Jamie Fraser. Father to four daughters: Margaret, Eleanor, Molly, and Tabitha (Tibby), unacknowledged father of Hamish MacKenzie, and secret father of the bastard child (later known as William Buccleigh MacKenzie) born to Geillis Duncan. Jamie kills Dougal the night before Culloden, to prevent Dougal from killing Claire as a witch. [*All*]

MacKenzie, Hamish—Jamie's cousin, claimed to be the son of Colum but actually the unacknowledged son of Dougal. Post Culloden, he is forced from his home and country, conscripted into the British army at age twelve, and sent to Nova Scotia to fight for a king who killed his clan and kin. He later finds his way to the Patriot side to take up arms against the British. [*Echo*]

MacKenzie, Jacob (aka Jacob Ruaidh, or Red Jacob, and Seaumais Ruaidh)—Late chieftain of clan MacKenzie; father of Ellen, Colum, Dougal, Jocasta, Flora, and Janet; grandfather of Jamie Fraser and Jenny Murray. According to Young Ian, he was reputed to be a fierce warrior, able to put the Iroquois to shame for pure cruelty. [*Ashes, Echo*]

MacKenzie, Jeremiah Alexander Ian Fraser; Jem; Jemmy—The precocious oldest child of Brianna and Roger MacKenzie, grandson of Claire and Jamie Fraser, born in the eighteenth century to twentieth-century parents, he is fiercly protective of his family and is quite resilient on his own merits. [*All*]

MacKenzie, Jeremiah Buccleigh; Jemmy—Son of William Buccleigh MacKenzie and Morag Gunn, he is Roger MacKenzie's great-great-great-grandfather. As an infant, he narrowly escapes death from smallpox and drowning on the *Gloriana,* where Roger helps to hide him, thereby saving his life and future generations. [*Fiery Cross, Echo, MOBY*]

MacKenzie, Jeremiah Walter; Jerry—Roger MacKenzie's father, a WWII hero who was supposedly shot down in his RAF Spitfire over the English Channel in 1941. Married to Marjorie Wakefield MacKenzie. In fact, Jerry was being trained for a secret mission to Poland and, in the course of this, crashed near a stone circle in Northumbria. Staggering into the circle, he ends up in 1739 and in the hands of the hostile inhabitants—from whom he is eventually rescued by two mysterious strangers (Roger and Buck), who take him back to the stone circle and urge him to go through, clinging to the thought of his wife, Marjorie. He does and arrives safely in 1945, where he finds himself in the middle of an air raid. Rushing down into a subway-station shelter, he sees Marjorie coming down the stairs, little Roger in her arms. The roof begins to cave in, and Marjorie, catching sight of Jerry, heaves the child over the railing to safely. Jerry catches the boy, but his bad knee gives way and he falls onto the Tube tracks, fracturing his skull but preserving the boy in his arms. [*All, LW*]

x **MacKenzie, Kenneth**—(unknown) Known as the Brahan Seer. A famous Highland seer, born in the seventeenth century, he made numerous prophecies. He made one too many true ones, though, and was burned to death in a spiked barrel filled with tar by the wife of a Scottish nobleman who the Seer had prophesied was having affairs with other women. Among his lesser-known prophecies is a fragmentary reference to the Frasers of Lovat, with the cryptic statement that "the last of Lovat's line will rule Scotland." It's this statement that leads Geillis Duncan to decide to go after Brianna, once she's learned of Jamie's daughter's existence. [*MOBY*]

MacKenzie, Marjorie (aka "Dolly")—Jerry's wife and young Roger's mother, noted for her dark, curly locks; she and Jerry have a deep and abiding love for each other. Her nickname is reminiscent of the name written on his plane—*Rag Doll*—complete with an image of a doll with dark ringlets. She bids farewell to Jerry, a Spitfire pilot, and never sees him again—until they meet moments before the bombing collapse of the Bethnal Green Tube station, which kills them both. But by their joint actions, they save the life of their small son, Roger. [*Echo, LW*]

MacKenzie, Morag Gunn—Wife of William Buccleigh (Buck) MacKenzie, Roger MacKenzie's five-times grandmother, and mother of Jeremiah. Roger helps save young Jeremiah from drowning while on Bonnet's ship, but his kindness is seen as something else by Morag's jealous husband. Morag, however, sees Roger about to be hanged and runs to tell Jamie Fraser, who arrives too late to stop the hanging but in time to save Roger's life by cutting him down. [*All*]

MacKenzie, Roger—Great-nephew of the Reverend Wakefield, adopted as a child by the Reverend following the death of Roger's parents during World War II. A historian, talented musician, and charming Scottish folk singer. Father of Jemmy and Mandy MacKenzie; Jamie's nickname for him is Roger Mac. Having followed Brianna into the past, married her, and claimed her son, Jeremiah, as his own (which indeed he is), he becomes a "son of the house" to Jamie and the Fraser family, and a valuable help to Jamie in the work of raising a militia company, which Roger does by singing rousingly emotional songs as a prelude to Jamie's exhortations. He accompanies Jamie to Alamance, where, through a series of unfortunate misunderstandings, he is hanged as one of the ringleaders of the Regulation. Roger narrowly survives the hanging—Claire saves his life with an emergency tracheotomy—but has lost his beautiful singing voice. With the help of Brianna and the family, he also survives the depression caused by this loss and slowly realizes his vocation as a minister. On the verge of Roger's ordination, though, Brianna is kidnapped by Stephen Bonnet, and Roger and Jamie go to rescue her. A few months later, Brianna and Roger's daughter, Amanda, is born—with a serious heart defect. The MacKenzies make the agonizing choice to leave Fraser's Ridge and venture through the stones with their two children, in hopes of making it to the future, where the defect can be easily cured by surgery. They do make it, the surgery is successful, and they begin to build a new life for themselves at the Lallybroch of 1980. This life is interrupted when Rob Cameron kidnaps Jem and tricks Roger and William Buccleigh ("Buck") into thinking that he has taken Jem into the past. The two men resolve to go after Jem; however, upon arriving in the past, they discover that they've come to the wrong time—they're in 1739! In the course of the fruitless search for his son, Roger discovers evidence of his father, also named Jeremiah MacKenzie. Roger and Buck find Jerry, rescue him, and take him to the stone circle where his Spitfire crashed during WWII. They then resume their search for the other Jeremiah and are at last reunited with Brianna and the two children, who have come in search of Roger. The family then makes it from the Scotland of 1739 to Fraser's Ridge in 1779, where they finally rejoin Jamie and Claire. [*All*]

MacKenzie, Rupert—A tacksman of clan MacKenzie and distant cousin to Dougal and Colum MacKenzie. He helps Claire rescue Jamie from Wentworth Prison; later, in great pain from wounds suffered at the Battle of Falkirk, he makes a request to die quickly and mercifully by Dougal's hand instead of suffering a painful, lingering death. [*All*]

MacKenzie, William and Sarah—The adoptive parents of William Buccleigh MacKenzie. The child's real father, Dougal MacKenzie, gave him to them to raise after their own child died; the child's real mother, Geillis Duncan, escaped to France, with Dougal's help, after nearly being burned as a witch. [*Fiery Cross*]

MacKenzie, William Buccleigh; Buck; "the Changeling"—The five-times grandfather of Roger MacKenzie; illegitimate son of Geillis Duncan and Dougal MacKenzie; fostered to a family who had lost a child of the same age and given the same name as the dead child. He later emigrates to America with his wife, Morag, and infant son, Jeremiah. He's a jealous man and through a severe misunderstanding causes Roger to nearly be killed; years later, he discovers his own ability to time-travel and must ask Roger and Brianna for assistance when he finds himself accidentally in the twentieth century. (See further details in entry for "the Nuckelavee.") He repays the favor by joining Roger in the search for Jem, which takes them back through the stones, ending up in 1739. He is deeply intrigued by Roger's telling him who his real parents were—and are. He insists on meeting his real mother, Geillis Duncan—to whom he is strongly sexually attracted, much to Roger's horror. Later, when Roger is finally reunited with his family, Buck goes to Castle Leoch, meaning to learn more about his father, Dougal MacKenzie. [*All*]

MacKimmie, Joan (aka Sister Gregory)—Laoghaire's younger daughter by Simon MacKimmie, sister to Marsali, and stepdaughter to Jamie Fraser; she wishes to join a convent and enlists Jamie's aid in obtaining her goal. Traveling to France under the protection of Michael Murray, she finds herself attracted to him—but still desirous of joining the convent, in hopes that spiritual company and practice will help her to stop the voices in her head. [*Fiery Cross, Echo, SB*]

MacKimmie, Simon—Laoghaire's second husband; father of Marsali and Joan. Died in prison, following the Rising. [*Ashes, Echo*]

MacLachlan, Captain—An officer of the Scotch Greys, who rescues Lord John from the mobs present at Tyburn during the public hanging of Captain Bates. [*BL*]

MacLaren, Allie, Robby, Sandy, Stuart, and Josephine—Children of Angus and Maggie MacLaren. [*MOBY*]

MacLaren, Angus—The reluctant host of Roger and Buck when Buck suffers a heart-related collapse during the search for Jem. MacLaren summons the local healer, Dr. Hector McEwan—who proves to be something more than just a healer. [*MOBY*]

MacLaren, Annie—A Balriggan tenant, beside herself with fear for her overly large pregnant belly and terrified that she and her child will die in childbirth; one of Joan's inner "voices" tells her to assure young Annie that all will be well and that she will safely deliver a son—the voices don't tell Joan that Annie will also safely deliver a twin daughter. [*SB*]

MacLaren, Maggie—Wife of Angus. [*MOBY*]

MacLennan, Abel—An elderly resident of Drunkard's Creek, near Fraser's Ridge, who was in attendance at the Gathering on Mount Helicon. The British put the MacLennans out of their house for nonpayment of taxes, whereupon Abel's wife took ill and died, leaving him alone in the world. [*Fiery Cross*]

MacLennan, Abigail; Abby—The elderly wife of Abel MacLennan, she dies after suffering from hypothermia when she and her husband are put out of their home by the local sheriff. [*Fiery Cross*]

MacLeod, Angus—From Skeabost, Skye; a Scottish man at the Gathering who wishes to hire Roger to sing at his cousin's wedding in Spring Creek. [*Fiery Cross*]

MacLeod, Duncan—A homesteader near the Ridge and kin to Rabbie Cochrane; he and his brother are summoned by Roger to join Jamie's regiment of militia. [*Fiery Cross*]

MacLeod, Grannie—Elderly resident of Fraser's Ridge, brought to the Frasers in a comatose state; Claire is unable to do anything except sit with her until she dies, after which Claire prepares her body for burial in the deep of winter. [*Echo*]

MacLeod, Jock—The night watchman at the Loch Errochty Dam offices. Jem runs into him (literally) when he escapes from the tunnel. Mr. MacLeod is trying to phone Jem's parents when they are suddenly attacked by one of Rob Cameron's buddies. Jock is hit on the head but Jem escapes, running out of the building and hiding on the ladder in the dam's spillway, where Brianna finds him a short time later. [*MOBY*]

MacLeod, John Robert—The man from Killicrankie with whom sixteen-year-old Laoghaire played loose, thereby warranting a public punishment at Castle Leoch for her wanton behavior. After Jamie gallantly took the beating in her stead but married Claire anyway, a broken-hearted Laoghaire turned to McLeod for comfort—giving up her virginity—only to discover he was a married man with a family. [*Echo*]

MacLeod, Mrs.—The wife of one of the MacLeod brothers and a new tenant on the Ridge. [*Fiery Cross*]

MacLeod, Murray—A traveling apothecary in attendance at the Mount Helicon Gathering. He is not sanitary in his person or practice, is not educated in medicine, and is viewed by Claire as a charlatan and nuisance; as a member of the New Light Church, he's also considered a bit of a heretic by more-conservative Presbyterians. [*Fiery Cross*]

MacLeod, Robert; Bobby—One of Jamie's comrades from Ardsmuir and a resident of the Ridge. He spots a herd of forest bison and alerts Jamie and the other men of the Ridge so a hunting party can be organized. [*Fiery Cross*]

MacLeod, Siegfried—The twentieth-century choirmaster at the Old High Church of St. Stephen's in Inverness; Roger speaks to him about teaching the children's choir. [*Echo*]

MacMahon, Old Alec—Colum MacKenzie's master of horse (lead groom) at Castle Leoch, he was an admirer of Jamie's mother, Ellen, and took Jamie under his wing during his time at Castle Leoch; among other things, he tells Jamie the importance behind the old custom of "the fiery cross." [*Fiery Cross*]

MacMillan, Gerry—A friend from Roger's youth and one of his gang of friends in Inverness. [*Ashes*]

MacNab, Grannie—An elderly resident on Lallybroch estate; mother of Ronnie and grandmother of Rabbie. She asks Jamie to take Rabbie in as stable-lad, to remove him from his abusive father. [*Ashes*]

MacNab, Mary—The widow of Ronald MacNab of Lallybroch and mother to Rabbie, she is offered a position as a Lallybroch maid after her husband's death. She offered comfort (and sex) to Jamie when he was in hiding in the cave, the night before his surrender to the English; Jamie confesses this event to Claire after he's accused of seducing Malva Christie. [*Ashes*]

MacNab, Nessie; Mrs. MacNab; Agnes—A young Scottish prostitute-madame married to Rab MacNab, she is an acquaintance of Lord John Grey. They first meet when she's new at the profession and he's trying to hide his predilections from his companions, and they form a friendship of sorts. Although they do not share physical pleasures, Lord John enjoys her straightforwardness and her skill as an intelligence agent, and she enjoys the sweets and candies that he brings her. [*PM, BL, SP, Echo*]

MacNab, Rabbie—A former stable-boy at Lallybroch and young Fergus's best friend; after the fall of Culloden, he moves to London and finds employment carrying a hired sedan-chair (a sort of taxi). He eventually meets and marries Nessie, the young Scottish prostitute, and they end up running a brothel together. [*PM, SP, Echo*]

MacNab, Ronald—A tenant at Lallybroch, he's a drunken sot who abuses his son, Rab, who is rescued by Jamie. Ronald is later suspected of betraying Jamie to the Watch, and he dies when someone sets fire to his house, presumably in revenge for the betrayal. [*SP*]

MacNair, Corporal—One of the aids accompanying Lieutenant Hayes's military division to the Gathering. He requests that Jamie and other powerful men of the area meet with him to discuss the formation of a militia to protect the citizens against mob actions such as the Regulators. [*Fiery Cross*]

MacNeil, Misses—Two elderly women in attendance at the reception for Jocasta Cameron's wedding to Duncan Innes. [*Fiery Cross*]

MacNeil, Mr.—One of Brianna and Roger's neighbors at Lallybroch, possibly a farmer. [*Echo*]

MacNeil, Mrs.—Staunch member of the Ladies' Altar and Tea Society at the Free North Church in Inverness, concerned about Brianna's mortal soul since she is a Papist and doesn't attend services with Roger. [*Echo*]

MacNeill, Alex—One of Jamie's comrades from Ardsmuir and a resident of the Ridge. Tom Christie insists that Alex can vouch for his character if needed. [*Fiery Cross*]

MacNeill, Andrew—A plantation owner and local magistrate who lives near Cross Creek; a friend of Jocasta's. [*Fiery Cross*]

MacNeill, Angelica—Infant daughter of Hortense MacNeill, she and her mother were among the first vicitims of the fatal epidemic of bloody flux on Fraser's Ridge. [*Ashes*]

MacNeill, Captain—An officer of the Scotch Greys who rescues Lord John from the mobs present at Tyburn during the public hanging of Captain Bates. [*BL*]

MacNeill, Hortense—Resident of Fraser's Ridge and wife to Padraic, she and her family are the first victims of the bloody flux that sweeps the Ridge; she and her infant daughter are also the first fatalities of the epidemic. [*Ashes*]

MacNeill, John—A resident of the Ridge, he is in attendance the day Richard Brown and company attempt to arrest Claire for the murder of Malva Christie. [*Ashes*]

MacNeill, Padraic—Resident of Fraser's Ridge and husband to Hortense, he and his family are the first victims of the bloody flux that sweeps the Ridge; he survives, but his wife and youngest daughter do not. After Malva's accusations are made, Claire retreats to MacNeill's home to treat him for a bad lung infection. [*Ashes*]

x **MacQuiston, James**—(1736–1804) Native of Pennsylvania, MacQuiston was a spy on the western frontier of the colonies; he was affiliated with the Regulators, and his two brothers were present at the Battle of Alamance. This is also the name Buck MacKenzie gives to Governor Tryon after the Battle of Alamance when he turns over a bound and gagged Roger, falsely marking him as the notorious MacQuiston. [*Fiery Cross*]

MacWheen, Angus—An elderly tenant near Balriggan, known by many to be ill and often drunk, but he was the first person Joan's visions indicated would die shortly. [*SB*]

Madame Brechin—Wife of Monsieur Brechin, who thinks her husband's comment unseemly toward a nun but accepts his behavior nonetheless. [*SB*]

x **Madame de la Tourelle; Marie Anne de Mailly**—(1717–1744) A French courtier and the widow of the Marquis de la Tourelle. She became one of Louis XV's favorite mistresses before dying at the relatively young age of twenty-seven. [*Fiery Cross*]

Madame Fabienne—Owner of a Paris brothel located on the Rue Antoine, she has known the Comte for many years and knows of Master Raymond, as well. [*SB*]

Madame Hortense—Michael Murray's cook at his Paris house. [*SB*]

Madame Jeanne—See "Jeanne LeGrand."

Madame Mags; Magda—A German brothel owner and seller of information, also a good friend of Harry Quarry. [*PM, BL*]

Maddox, Mr.—A volunteer under Jamie's command at Monmouth. [*MOBY*]

Madeleine—A pretty blond prostitute with green eyes employed by Madame Fabienne, she fancies herself in love with the Comte, who can see the blue aura that surrounds her. He wishes to impregnate her and reserves her "favors" from Madame Fabienne for four months in order to do so. [SB]

Madge—Madame at the brothel where William meets Arabella-Jane. [*MOBY*]

Madras—One of William's horses. [*MOBY*]

Magruder, Constable—Constable of the day for the Bow Street Runners, the first formal organization of law-enforcement officers, paid through the local magistrate by funds allocated from the central government. [*PM*]

Maguire, Dr.—Duke of Pardloe's family doctor, called in to treat Lord John's wounds after his duel with Edward Twelvetrees. [*SP*]

Mairi—One of three sisters who were tenants of Lallybroch; the croft in which she lived burned out after Culloden. [*SP*]

Maisie—A co-worker of Marjorie MacKenzie. Due to the shortage of "luxury items" during the war, she innovatively uses an eyebrow pencil to draw a line up the back of her legs, giving the impression of wearing seamed stockings. [*LW*]

x **Malan, Sailor; Adolph Malan**—(1910–1963) The captain for Jerry's flight group, he recommends MacKenzie for the special work needed by Captain Randall. [*LW*]

Malcolm, Alexander—Jamie Fraser's alias when he was a printer in Edinburgh; he uses it again at a roadside inn after retrieving Claire from Governor Josiah Martin's care on the *Cruizer*. [*Ashes*]

Malcolm, Captain—One of Governor Tryon's aides-de-camp, who accompanies the Orange County sheriff to meet with the Regulators regarding a peaceful surrender. [*Fiery Cross*]

Manoke—An Indian guide whom Lord John meets and becomes sexually involved with during his time in Canada; Manoke later becomes Lord John's cook in Virginia, but their relationship remains one of sex and friendship, not of love. [*CA, PZ, Ashes, Echo*]

Mansel, Captain—A British officer used as a courier for messages between British General Burgoyne and American General Gates while the terms of surrender were being settled after Saratoga, as well as one of Jamie's poorly skilled card opponents. [*Echo*]

x **Mar, Earl of**—(1705–1766) Thomas Erskine, an intimate of Charles Stuart and the heir to the Scottish earldom of Mar; due to his father's participation in the Jacobite rebellion of 1715, the title and lands attached to the Earl of Mar had become forfeit, on charges of treason. [*SP*]

Marchmont, Lord—One of the three members of the military tribunal investigating Lord John's part in the explosion of a cannon during the Battle of Crefeld; he holds a personal grudge toward Lord John, whose previous investigation resulted in the arrest of Marchmont's cousin on the charge of treason. [*HS*]

Margery—A prostitute at Mrs. McNab's establishment on Brydges Street in London, where Lord John takes sixteen-year-old William after William and friends are caught looking at a scandalous book of London's women of pleasure. Margery gives William his first lesson in the art of love, and he promptly falls in love with her. [*Echo*]

Margrave, Mr. Justice—A magistrate and member of Lord John's favorite club, the Beefsteak, and a good friend of Lord John's family; he is highly opinionated on the subject of sodomy, declaring that castration should be practiced on those found to practice it. [*HF*]

Mariah—One of Jocasta Cameron's house slaves, she brings a drink to Betty, the slave who later dies of eating ground glass. [*Fiery Cross*]

Marilyn—A friend of Mrs. Abernathy, Uncle Joe's wife. [*MOBY*]

Markham, Edward, Lieutenant; Marquis of Clarewell—Known as Chinless Ned, or the Ponce, he offers William a suck of his sour pickle as a cure for seasickness upon the water landing on Long Island. [*Echo*]

Marks—Lord John's current valet, adequate but not the same high caliber as Tom Byrd. [*MOBY*]

Marquis of Banbury—An English nobleman, fierce Catholic, and Jacobite, known by Arthur and George Longstreet to belong to the plot to assassinate King George and install the Catholic James Stuart as King of England. [*BL*]

Marquise of Pelham—A noblewoman in London who is apparently involved with Thomas Lally—deeply enough to keep him from starving, anyway. [*SP*]

Marsden, Bill; Jonah (aka John Smith)—An earring-decorated deserter from the Royal Navy, he earns the name "Jonah" from crewmates on board the *Tranquil Teal* for his skills in surviving so many naval sinkings. [*Echo*]

Marsden, Captain—A half-pay army captain, known to be a good swordsman. After being disarmed in a duel and honorably yielding the victory, he is cruelly blinded and permanently disfigured by the dishonorable Stephen Bonnet. [*Fiery Cross*]

Martha—The dead wife of the only man to actually rape Claire during her abduction, she was loved by her husband, who weeps and calls her name when he is finished with Claire. [*Ashes, MOBY*]

x **Martin, Abraham**—(1589–1684) The fisherman and river pilot who owned a plot of grazing land atop the cliffs near the fortress of Quebec on the St. Lawrence River; these heights were later named for Abraham, because this is where the French forces holding Quebec City were defeated by the British army during the Seven Years' War. [*CA*]

Martin, Colonel—An officer with the Vermont militia who plays cards with Jamie after the battles of Saratoga. He later witnesses Ian murder the soup-spitter, Mr. X; after almost shooting Ian during the chase to capture him, Martin wounds Rollo instead but is prevented from finishing off the big dog when Rachel prostrates herself across Rollo's body. [*Echo*]

x **Martin, Elizabeth; Betsy**—(unknown) The governor's wife and cousin; Claire is released from the New Bern jail to care for the very pregnant woman, who has a history of childbearing problems. The governor later uses Claire as a decoy, in order to get his wife out of an increasingly dangerous New Bern and to her family in New York. [*Ashes*]

x **Martin, Josiah, Governor**—(1737–1786) The last colonial governor of North Carolina, who holds Claire prisoner on his ship, the *Cruizer,* after Claire's arrest for Malva Christie's murder. [*Fiery Cross, Ashes, Echo*]

Martin, Miss—The young and rather plain companion of elderly Miss Bledsoe at Jocasta Cameron's wedding. Miss Martin very much enjoys watching Roger sing with the Irish musicians at the reception. [*Fiery Cross*]

Martin, Mrs.—One of the attendees at the Gathering, who has apparently helped Claire with her clinic patients. [*Fiery Cross*]

Martin, Sam—One of Governor Martin's children, he died of a fever in the Governor's Palace at age eight. [*Ashes*]

Martine—A servant employed in the house of the widow Lambert, she is sent to bring more beer for Carruthers and Lord John. [*CA*]

Masonby, Doctor—A nerve doctor residing on Smedley Street, whom Trevelyan insultingly recommends to Lord John when John confronts Trevelyan about his syphilitic condition. [*PM*]

Master Raymond; Maître Raymond—Also called Maître Grenouille, or "the Frog." A small, mysterious apothecary whose facial features resemble those of a frog, he seems to know a great deal regarding secret matters, both political and occult. [*SB*]

Matilda—The laundress at River Run, Jocasta Cameron Innes's plantation, to whom Jem takes a paint-stained shirt. [*Ashes*]

Maxim Le Grand—Son of el Maximo, also a dwarf, he has taken over his late father's business; he is mistaken for his father by the Comte St. Germain, who has not been in Paris for many years. [*SB*]

Maximilian the Great; Maximiliano el Maximo—A deceased Spanish dwarf and bar owner in Paris, known to the Comte St. Germain during earlier times. [*SB*]

Maxwell, Viscount—A noble whom William mentions in a letter to Lord John, as he attempts to convince John to assist his own suit for Dottie's hand. [*Echo*]

Maybelle—One of the prostitutes in Nessie's London establishment. [*Echo*]

Mayrhofer, Maria—Reinhardt Mayrhofer's wife. After being infected with syphilis by her philandering husband, she bears a child deformed from the ravages of the disease; the baby is quickly smothered by her husband. She falls in love with Joseph Trevelyan, unwittingly infects him with the disease, and, at his urging, attempts a cure by deliberately infecting herself with malaria; the high fever of malaria was thought to "burn out" the syphilitic infection. (*Author's Note: There is some modern evidence that this actually works. We will hope that it did for Maria and Joseph.*) [*PM*]

Mayrhofer, Reinhardt—A cousin and heir to the wealthy Austrian Hungerbach family, progenitors of the lovely red wine known as Schilcher. Riddled with syphilis, he infects his pregnant wife, Maria, then murders their child when it is born deformed by the ravages of the disease. [*PM*]

McAfee, Rab—Father of one of the young boys on Fraser's Ridge who try to disrupt Roger's first sermon by setting loose a snake among the parishioners. [*Ashes*]

McAllister, Donald—The man Buck's wife, Morag, was really in love with and who loved her in return. [*MOBY*]

McAllister, Georgiana—Mother of twins delivered at the Gathering. After her older daughter finds a watch chain belonging to Presbyterian minister Reverend Caldwell in Jemmy's diaper, Georgiana and her husband relate to Claire their opinions and the merits of

several noted Presbyterian ministers present at the Gathering. [*Fiery Cross*]

McAllister, Mr.—Georgiana McAllister's husband, who, along with his wife and Claire, discuss the merits of several noted Presbyterian ministers who have spoken at the Gathering. [*Fiery Cross*]

McCallum, Orem—The late husband of Amy McCallum Higgins, father to Aidan and Orrie. After building the cabin on Fraser's Ridge for his family, he took a misstep and fell into the rock-filled ravine, breaking his neck and leaving his young family alone. [*Ashes*]

McCann, Geordie, Auld and Young—Auld Geordie is the twenty-five-year-old man that Laoghaire wishes her daughter Joan to marry; Young Geordie is the three-year-old nephew of Auld Geordie. Joan does not want to wed either of them. [*Echo*]

x McCartny, Rev. James—(unknown) Presbyterian minister hired as a chaplain to Governor Tryon's forces; he performs a sermon the evening before Alamance on the topic chosen to encourage Tryon's troops: "If you have no sword, sell your garment and buy one." [*Fiery Cross*]

McCarty, Craig—One of Brianna's co-workers at the hydroelectric dam, and the one who borrows her keys and removes the one to the electrical panel during a trick played on her first day on the job. [*Echo*]

McCaskill, Angus—The local proprietor of the largest ordinary in Wilmington and an expressive orator of poetry—both tragic and comic—at the social evenings held by Mrs. Dunning. [*Fiery Cross*]

McCorkle, Captain—One of the captains under Jamie's command at Monmouth. [*MOBY*]

x McCorkle, Reverend Doctor—(1746–1811) Presbyterian minister and educator, he was ordained as minister in Rowan County in 1777, at the same ordination that Roger attended prior to leaving to rescue Brianna. [*Ashes*]

McCrea, William—A Scotsman from Balgownie, who fought with Arch Bug at the bloody Battle of Sheriffmuir in November 1715; he lost part of his jaw and nose to an English pikesman, yet lived. [*Ashes*]

McCreary, Mr.—A man from the town of Brownsville who told Tom Christie of the fire on Fraser's Ridge, in which all of the Frasers perished. [*Echo*]

McEwan, Hector, Dr.—Time-traveling doctor from the year 1841. Roger and Buck encounter him when Buck collapses during the search for Jem and is taken in by the MacLaren family, who summon Dr. McEwan. Roger is startled to observe a faint blue light playing about McEwan's hands while he heals Buck, and he's even more shocked to hear the doctor say softly (and delightedly) to Buck, *"Cognosco te"—I know you.* Boldly approaching the doctor afterward, Roger says the same to him and hears McEwan's own tale. Later, when Roger and Buck visit Geillis Duncan—Buck's real mother—they meet the doctor again and discover that he is Geillis's lover. [*MOBY*]

McGillis, Dr.—A doctor with the Colonial army. [*MOBY*]

McGillivray, Hilda—A daughter of Ute and Robin McGillivray. She and her sisters are used as pawns in arranged marriages by their domineering mother, in an attempt to bring land and prosperity to the McGillivray family. [*Fiery Cross, Ashes*]

McGillivray, Inga—A daughter of Ute and Robin McGillivray. She and her sisters are used as pawns in arranged marriages by their domineering mother, in an attempt to bring land and prosperity to the McGillivray family. [*Fiery Cross, Ashes*]

McGillivray, Manfred—Ute and Robin McGillivray's son, who narrowly escapes arrest by the thief-taker Harley Boble. After a successful matchmaking by his mother, he becomes engaged to Lizzie Weymss, but then is infected with syphilis through an encounter with a Wilmington prostitute. In his shame, he breaks off the engagement to Lizzie; before Claire can explain to him that she can cure him with penicillin, he disappears. [*Fiery Cross, Ashes*]

McGillivray, Robin; Robbie—A talented gunsmith and ex-prisoner from Ardsmuir, he and his family move to Fraser's Ridge at the offer of a permanent home on Jamie's land. [*Fiery Cross, Ashes*]

McGillivray, Senga—Another daughter of Ute and Robin McGillivray. Her domineering mother attempts to contract a marriage for her that will bring land and prosperity to the McGillivray family, but Senga ("Agnes" spelled backward) is also possessed of strong opinions and a lack of inhibition in expressing them, traits she inherited from her mother. [*Fiery Cross, Ashes*]

McGillivray, Ute—Robin McGillivray's German wife; a domineering known matchmaker who is fiercely protective of her family. [*Fiery Cross, Ashes*]

McIver, Nelson—A settler on Fraser's Ridge involved in a conflict with another settler, Alex MacNeill. [*Fiery Cross*]

McLanahan, Mrs.—Proprietor of the King's Inn in Cross Creek. [*Ashes*]

McLaughlin, Joey—A resident of Fraser's Ridge who, young Aidan claims, has seen the ghost of Malva Christie. Roger states that McLaughlin was most likely drunk and probably saw Ian's dog, Rollo, instead. [*Ashes*]

x McLean, Alexander—(ca. 1735–1785) Captain in the British army and aide to General Donald MacDonald, assigned to recruit Loyalists prior to the Battle of Moore's Creek Bridge. Although he submitted a long list of names to his commanders, many of the Highlanders and Scots-Irish failed to join him, preferring instead to side with the Patriots. [*Ashes*]

McLehose, Sergeant—A British army soldier at the garrison commanded by Jack Randall. At dice, he wins a strange ornament bearing the name *J. W. MacKenzie.* Captain Randall, recognizing the name as being similar to that of Roger's lost son, sends the ornament to Brian Fraser, who then gives it to Roger—who recognizes it as Jerry MacKenzie's RAF dog tags. [*MOBY*]

x McLeod, Colonel Donald—(ca. 1720–1776) One of the leaders of the Scottish Highlander division of British Loyalists mustered to fight the Patriots at the Battle of Moore's Creek Bridge. McLeod died by Patriot gunfire during the last Highland charge. [*Ashes*]

McLeod, Rabbie—One of Jem's close friends on Fraser's Ridge, he becomes infested with head lice. These promptly migrate to young Jemmy's head, causing Jem's head to be shorn—revealing an important birthmark. [*Ashes*]

McLeod, Rufe—Rabbie's uncle. Jem claims that Rufe was also infested with head lice, indicating that all the men in the McLeod household were to be shaved bald by Rabbie's mother. [*Ashes*]

McManus, Jonathan—A resident of Boone, whose name appears on a list General Donald MacDonald gives to Governor Martin as someone able to supply possibly three supporters to the British cause. Claire, who removed a gangerous toe from McManus, knows him as a drunkard and a thief, with the only likely pledges he could bring being other family members—also poor recruits. [*Ashes*]

McMillan, Jay, Reverend—The Presbyterian minister in Edenton who hosts Roger and several other colleagues prior to Roger's ordination. [*Ashes*]

McMillan, Mrs. Reverend—Wife of Reverend Jay McMillan and mother of three daughters, all with a penchant for cleaning. [*Ashes*]

McTaggart, Tom; Taggie—Brian Fraser's hired hand at Lallybroch in 1739. [*MOBY*]

Meadows—A soldier in Hector's regiment; a Scotsman ambushs him with a rock to the head, but Hector kills the Scotsman. [*PM*]

Meleager, Thomas—Head of a Pennsylvania militia company at the Battle of Monmouth. [*MOBY*]

Mélisande—"Madame Mélisande Robicheaux" was Geillis Duncan's alias while living in Paris following her escape from Cranesmuir and the witch trial. [*SB*]

Menzies—Family name of a group of Scottish settlers who are also at the Gathering and whose leader proclaims them in attendance at the bonfire on the final night. [*Fiery Cross*]

Menzies, Lionel—The kind headmaster at Jem's school, who is forced to punish Jem for swearing at his teacher after she assaults him for speaking Gaelic. He is understanding, though, and encourages Roger to hold classes in Gaelic for students and their families so the "old ways" aren't lost. He is also a Freemason (who attends lodge with Roger) and a cousin of Rob Cameron (who belongs to the same lodge). When Cameron launches his attack on the MacKenzies, Menzies comes to Brianna's aid, rescuing her and the children. Brianna, in desperation, confides in him. Despite his skepticism, he helps her to reach the stone circle, and at the last moment he supplies the necessary gemstones (from his Masonic ring) for the children to make it safely through. [*Echo, MOBY*]

Merbling, Captain Randolph—Young British officer who shares a tent with William before the Battle of Monmouth. [*MOBY*]

Mercer, Captain—The other young British officer who shares a tent with William prior to the Battle of Monmouth. [*MOBY*]

Merilee—One of Governor Martin's kitchen slaves at the Governor's Palace in New Bern. [*Ashes*]

Meyer—The name Sergeant O'Connell gives at the Lavender House when trying to sell off the stolen reports; unfortunately, the name is not known to anyone at the molly-house. [*PM*]

Mickelgrass, Harvey—A justice of the peace in Hillsborough, he refuses to take custody of Claire Fraser, the accused murderess, from Richard Brown and his gang or to try any other cases, due to the hostile political sentiments of the times. [*Ashes*]

Millard—The cousin of one of the men wounded at Alamance, under Claire's care in the hospital tent. [*Fiery Cross*]

Miller, Abigail—The young, pretty wife of an officer in the Continental army, who flirts with Ian, much to the consternation of her much older husband. [*Echo*]

Miller, Colonel—Abigail Miller's jealous husband, who is nearly twenty years older than his comely wife; while walking with

Jamie, he catches his wife attempting to seduce Ian. [*Echo*]

Millikin, Patrick, Sergeant—An Irishman in William's regiment who, at William's request, inspires the regiment on the night march through Long Island with some bawdy songs to keep the men awake. [*Echo*]

Milly and Blossom—Brianna's milk cows at Lallybroch. [*Echo*]

Mirabeau—A temperamental cow inhabiting the stables at le Couvent des Anges. A swift-thinking Joan gets the cow to cooperate for an uneventful milking—before they are disturbed by the Comte St. Germain. [*SB*]

Mirabel—A nanny goat belonging to Marsali and Fergus. Germain is sent to milk her, shortly before a band of brigands and thieves arrives at the malting shed. [*Ashes*]

Miranda—The mild-mannered, wide-backed bay mare William purchases before heading toward Middlebrook Encampment. [*MOBY*]

Mitchell, Betty—Lady's maid to Geneva Dunsany prior to her death, Betty took the same position with Geneva's sister, Isobel. Possibly a close confidante of Geneva, she may know the true paternity of William—making her a danger to Jamie. [*SP*]

Molly—Irish-born whore in Savannah who's interested in obtaining pox cures from Claire prior to the British occupation. [*MOBY*]

Molly—Governor Martin's cook at the Governor's Palace in New Bern. [*Ashes*]

x **Monckton, Brigadier**—(1726–1782) General James Wolfe's second in command during the Battle of Quebec; Robert Monckton later became governor of New York. [*CA*]

Monsieur Brechin—A passenger on the boat to France who notices and comments on Joan's shapely figure as being wasted on a nun. [*SB*]

Monsieur de Ruvel—A courtier at the court of French king Louis XV and acquaintance—possibly an intimate one—of Madame de la Tourelle. [*Fiery Cross*]

Monsieur/Mademoiselle L'Oeuf—"Mr./Miss Egg," the French name Fergus and Marsali give to her swollen belly during her pregnancies. [*Ashes*]

x **Montcalm, General Louis-Joseph**—(1712–1759) Leader of the French forces in North America during the Seven Years' War (aka the French and Indian Wars). He was killed during the Battle of Quebec, also known as the Battle of the Plains of Abraham. [*CA*]

Moore, Captain—Based on real-life Captain John Montresor (1736–1799), the British officer who allowed Nathan Hale the use of his tent to write letters to his family before his execution; Montresor/Moore was also present at the execution and may have heard Hale's final and famous speech moments before his death. [*Echo*]

x **Moore, Colonel**—(1737–1777) James Moore served as a captain in the militia under Governor Tryon during the Battle of Alamance; after his strong opposition of the Stamp Act, he became a Son of Liberty and directed the Patriots' victorious campaign at the Battle of Moore's Creek Bridge. Jamie and Claire meet him at River Run, during a political altercation at Flora MacDonald's barbecue. [*Ashes*]

x **Moore, Maurice**—(1735–1777) North Carolina judge who openly opposed the Stamp Act of 1765; because of his outspoken opinion, he was stripped of his judicial appointment by Governor Tryon but later regained it and continued to serve as a justice until his death. [*Fiery Cross*]

Moray, Stephen—Wilmington, N.C., silversmith who creates Claire's surgical scissors after her medical kit is lost in the fire on Fraser's Ridge. [*Echo*]

x **Morgan, Abigail**—(unknown) Daniel's common-law wife. When Dan quotes the Bible to Jamie, who looks surprised, Morgan laughs and says that his wife Abigail is "a reading woman" and has been reading the Bible to him in hopes that something will rub off. [*MOBY*]

x **Morgan, Daniel**—(1736–1802) Leader of "Morgan's Riflemen," a regiment of handpicked sharpshooters who figured prominently in the Battle of Bemis Heights, where one of Morgan's snipers killed British General Simon Fraser and drove Burgoyne's forces into retreat. During the Saratoga campaign, Jamie is an officer under Morgan in the newly formed Rifle Corps, and the men remain good friends. When Morgan comes across Jamie by chance outside Philadelphia, he insists that Jamie accompany him. They meet George Washington, and Morgan suggests to the general that he appoint Jamie to take the place of a general of militia who has recently died. [*Echo, MOBY*]

Morgan, Sam—An under footman at Helwater. [*SP*]

Morris—Tom Byrd's uncle, an able-bodied sailor who contracts a mysterious illness that causes severe vomiting, the results of which prove fatal. [*SP*]

Morrison, Davey—A farmer from Hunter's Point, a man of some substance and worth, as well as an athlete in the "heavy" games at the Gathering. His large extended family, all upstanding members of North Carolina society, is rather judgmental, but he is also the fiancé of Hilda McGillivray, whose family is in danger of scandal when her brother, Manfred, is nearly arrested. [*Fiery Cross*]

Mortlake—One of Captain Craddock's men. When Craddock is killed by a cannonball, leaving his two teenaged sons shocked and the rest of his men in turmoil, Jamie deputes Mortlake to take over as captain temporarily. [*MOBY*]

Morton, Isaiah—A militiaman from Granite Falls, who fought with Jamie in the War of the Regulation and who is a bigamist; he marries Alicia Brown of Brownsville while already in possession of a wife, the notorious Jezebel Hatfield Morton. [*Fiery Cross, Ashes*]

Moses—One of the sailors on the fishing boat used to troll up and down Ocracoke Island looking for Brianna when she's being held at Stephen Bonnet's secret location. [*Ashes*]

Mother Hildegarde—The Mother Superior of le Couvent des Anges, in Paris. [*SB*]

Moxley, Captain—One of the captains under Jamie's command at Monmouth. [*MOBY*]

Mr. A.—An unknown man who was Percy's regular lover; Percy breaks off the relationship with him upon meeting and desiring a relationship with John Grey. [*BL*]

Mr. Stevens—The steward at Boodle's, where Harry Quarry is a regular for supper on Thursdays. [*BL*]

Mr. X, the Soup-Spitter—A crude, mysterious man who appears at the Fraser campsite, claiming to have heard Willie Coulter's last words, which reveal who really killed Dougal MacKenzie the night before the Battle of Culloden. After the threatening man insults Claire, Ian, and

Jamie, Ian murders him—but the murder is witnessed by Colonel Martin and several others. [*Echo*]

Mueller, Ewald—One of Gerhard Mueller's sons. [*Fiery Cross*]

Mueller, Frederick—Gerhard Mueller's son whose wife and infant child die in a measles epidemic. [*Fiery Cross*]

Mueller, Gerhard—Patriarch of a large German Lutheran family near Salem. After the deaths of his daughter-in-law and grandchild in a measles outbreak, in his grief he becomes convinced that the Indians have hexed his family; in retribution, he kills three Indian women he meets in the forest, including Nayawenne, a Tuscarora shaman who is Claire's friend. [*Fiery Cross, Echo*]

Mueller, Paul—One of Gerhard Mueller's sons. [*Fiery Cross*]

Mueller, Petronella—Daughter-in-law of old Gerhard Mueller and wife to Frederick, she and her first child die in a measles epidemic on the Ridge. [*Fiery Cross*]

Mueller, Tommy—Another of Gerhard Mueller's many sons. [*Fiery Cross*]

Mulengro—The last name of the gypsy witch and of Private Koenig's wife, Hanna, and one of the women recruited by the Austrians to spread rumors of the succubus among the Hanovarian and English troops. [*SU*]

Mulroney, Dominic—An Irishman Mrs. Bug knew in Edinburgh, he walked face-first into a church door, causing terrible bruising; Mrs. Bug is comparing Mulroney's facial injuries to those suffered by Claire. [*Ashes*]

Mumford, Lady—Hector Dalrymple's mother. Still grieving many years after her son's death at Culloden, she dotes on Lord John as if he were her own son, never realizing the type of relationship John and Hector really shared. [*PM*]

Mumford, Lord—The late Wally Dalrymple, Hector's father. [*PM*]

Munns, Mrs.—The MacKenzies' neighbor, she pounds on the wall when the young couple make too much noise, but Jerry retaliates by pounding back, making the wall quiver and boom like a drum. [*LW*]

Murchison, Sergeant William; Billy—An old and unfriendly acquaintance from Jamie's days in Ardsmuir Prison; one of a pair of sadistic twins. His brother, Robert, met a mysterious death at Ardsmuir, while the sergeant met his own end after becoming involved in a smuggling scheme with Stephen Bonnet and died in a warehouse fire. [*Fiery Cross, Ashes*]

Murphy, Mr.—Claire's first toothache patient in Savannah, who gratefully offers his vacant shop as a place for Claire to practice her craft. [*MOBY*]

x **Murphy, Tim**—(1751–1818) One of the most famous marksmen of the Revolution and one of Daniel Morgan's handpicked riflemen. He was credited with mortally wounding British General Simon Fraser and his aide, Sir Francis Clerke, at the Battle of Bemis Heights. [*Echo*]

Murray, Caitlin Maisri—Jenny and Ian Murray's sixth child, who died after only a day or so; she was Jenny's last child until Young Ian was born. Her gravestone at Lallybroch is recognizable as only a small square lichen-covered stone. [*Fiery Cross, Echo, MOBY*]

x **Murray, George, Lord**—(1694–1760) Scottish general and leader of the Scottish forces at the Battle of Prestonpans; he was one of Charles Stuart's key military leaders, although he was frequently at odds with Stuart's poor military strategy. [*SP*]

Murray, Ian James FitzGibbons Fraser Murray; Young Ian—Jamie Fraser's youngest nephew, Ian's destiny seems entwined with his beloved uncle's. Ian's family expect never to see him again and are shocked and delighted when he returns to Fraser's Ridge, where he saves Jemmy and Roger from being savaged by a wild boar. It's not until much later that Ian tells his cousin Brianna the circumstances of his return: that he and Emily, his Mohawk wife, had a stillborn daughter (named Iseabàil), followed by a number of miscarriages. The Mohawk believe that pregnancy results when the man's spirit fights with and overcomes the woman's; Ian's wife and the rest of the community therefore believe that the failure of her pregnancies is Ian's fault, and his wife divorces him in the Mohawk way. Ian is heartsick and has no idea what his life may now become, but fate takes a hand when he finds a young man in the Dismal Swamp, wounded and out of his mind with fever: his cousin William. Ian bundles Willie up and takes him to the nearest doctor, a Quaker physician named Denzell Hunter. An attraction springs up between Ian and Hunter's sister, Rachel, but both of them try to ignore it, given the deep cultural divide between them: how could a devout Quaker wed a man who has always lived a violent life and likely always will? Their difficult courtship is further complicated by Arch Bug's vendetta against Ian for the accidental death of Arch's wife; the old man declares he will take what Ian most loves—and comes close to succeeding, but William saves both Rachel and Ian, killing the murderous old man. When Ian and Rachel finally admit their love to each other and become betrothed, Ian confesses to Rachel that he may not be able to give her a child and tells her about his marriage to Emily; Rachel is shocked but accepts the possibility. Ian goes with Jamie and Claire when they join the Continental army at the Monmouth campaign, and Rachel accompanies her brother to help with medical attention for the troops. In the course of the battle, Ian is nearly killed by a couple of Abenaki scouts and almost dies as a result of the subsequent fever. Rachel saves his life, and she tells Ian that she can't bear for him to be alone with his painful memories and such further evil as the war may bring and that they need to be married, no matter what the difficulties may be. They're married at the same time as Denzell and Dorothea and later have a son (nicknamed "Oggy"), born on Fraser's Ridge, where they have come with Jamie and Claire following the turmoil of battle. [*All*]

Murray, Ian Alastair Robert MacLeod; Old Ian—Jamie's best friend and brother-in-law; Jenny's husband; father to Young Ian and his siblings. Factor of Lallybroch. [*All*]

Murray, James Alexander Gordon; Young Jamie—Oldest son of Ian and Jenny; Jamie Fraser's nephew and namesake; father of Matthew, Henry, Caroline, and Benjamin. Inherits Lallybroch as a result of a deed of sasine written by his uncle prior to the Battle of Culloden. [*All*]

Murray, Janet Ellen—Daughter of Jenny and Ian, twin sister to Michael, elder sister to Young Ian. [*Fiery Cross, Echo*]

Murray, Janet Flora Arabella Fraser; Jenny—Jamie Fraser's sister; wife to Ian Murray, mother of Young Jamie, Maggie, Kitty, Michael, Janet, and Young Ian (also Caitlin, stillborn). Her joy at being reunited with her prodigal son, Ian, is much tempered by the impending death of her husband, Ian the Elder. Ian Mhor is dying slowly of consumption, and the family is desolated, though comforted somewhat by Ian's very matter-of-fact attitude regarding his impending demise and the fact that he has time to talk privately with all his children and his brother-in-law, Jamie. Jenny is not comforted, though, and blows up at Claire when the latter confesses that her healing skills can do nothing for Ian's condition. Following Ian's death, Jenny surprisingly tells her brother that she means to come back with him to America; the estate is safely in the hands of her elder son, and there's not room for two mistresses at Lallybroch. More than that—she wants to meet Rachel, the young Quaker woman whom Ian loves, and to spend time with her youngest son, taken from her when he was barely a teenager. She comes home with Jamie, and—past the trauma and stress of Ian's death—reconciles with Claire. A good thing, too, as this means she's present to help when Jamie disappears with Lord John and when Harold, Duke of Pardloe, shows up looking for his brother. She's also present to lend a hand with Marsali and Fergus's brood and to help hold their family together after the death of Henri-Christian. She returns to Fraser's Ridge with Jamie and Claire and is at hand to offer support and advice when Claire unexpectedly sees the man who raped her when Hodgepile's men abducted her. Jenny—who understands Jamie in this regard much better than Claire does—also tells her brother, who proceeds to do what he thinks is necessary. [*All*]

Murray, John; Auld John—Ian Sr.'s father and one of Jamie's foster fathers. He taught Jamie a good many of the old ways, including the prayer to the four airts that Jamie performs on the way back to Fraser's Ridge after the Gathering on Mount Helicon. Roger meets him briefly when Brian takes him to make inquiries about Jem. [*Fiery Cross, MOBY*]

Murray, Joseph Boswell (aka Joey)—Laoghaire's lover at Balriggan; although they love each other, they have been living in sin, as Laoghaire doesn't want to lose Balriggan or the alimony Jamie has been paying her since Claire's return. [*Echo*]

Murray, Katherine Mary; Kitty—The third child of Ian and Jenny Murray; sister to Young Jamie, Maggie, Janet, Michael, and Young Ian. [*Fiery Cross, Echo*]

Murray, Lillie; Lilliane—Michael Murray's beloved wife, who died along with their unborn child during an influenza epidemic in Paris. [*Echo, SB*]

Murray, Margaret Ellen; Maggie—Jenny and Ian's oldest daughter. She is raped by her brother-in-law but keeps silent and raises the child as her husband's, to avoid bloodshed between the brothers and strife within the families. [*Echo, MOBY*]

Murray, Michael—Second son to Ian and Jenny Murray; twin to Janet Murray and older brother to Ian the Younger. Sent to France to be apprenticed to Jared Fraser, Michael becomes a junior partner in the wine business, Fraser et Cie, and returns briefly to Lallybroch a widower, his French-born wife, Lillie, dead of influenza. When he returns to France after his father's death, he takes with him Joan MacKimmie, bound for a convent. Looking out for the young woman helps to distract him slightly from his intense grief for his dead wife—little does he know just how distracting things can get in the vicinity of a novice who hears voices. [*Fiery Cross, Echo, SB*]

Myers, John Quincy—A hunter and mountain guide. At the Mount Helicon Gathering, he summons Jamie to help deal with the issue of a thief-taker trying to arrest Robin McGillvray's son, Manfred. [*Fiery Cross*]

Myra—The Hillsborough prostitute who infects young Manfred McGillivray with syphilis (aka "the pox") and then dies. [*Ashes*]

N

Nan—A former prostitute at Magda's, she was apparently a favorite of Harry Quarry when he utilized the facility. [*PM*]

Nanny Elspeth—William's dour, stoic nanny when he was a child at Helwater, who frightened him by saying that the dead came down with the fog. [*Echo, SP*]

x **Nawab of Bengal**—(1729–1757) Siraj ud-Daulah, the last independent provincial ruler, or "nawab," of Bengal before his military defeat in 1757 by Robert Clive and the British East India Company. [*PM*]

Nayawenne—Tuscarora shaman who tells Claire of a prophetic dream regarding Claire's healing power and gives her guidance finding and using herbs on the Ridge. When she is mistakenly killed, she leaves her amulet for Claire. [*Fiery Cross, Ashes, Echo*]

Neary, Patrick—A settler on Fraser's Ridge, one of whose sons, Jamie warns Roger, may be a thief. [*Fiery Cross*]

Ned—Bodyguard/bouncer at Magda's brothel, where William first meets Jane. [*MOBY*]

x **Newcastle, Duke of**—(1720–1794) While mentioned fictitiously as brother to the Duke of Cumberland, he was in fact Cumberland's uncle. It was reported by Horace Walpole that Newcastle nearly fainted at the funeral of George II and that he was standing on the train of Cumberland's cloak to avoid the chilly floor. [*SP*]

Nicholls, Edwin—One of the attendees at Miss Woodford's party, he was a drunk, unsociable bore whose lascivious behavior toward his host caused Lord John to punch him, leading to a duel. [*CA, SP*]

Nordman—One of the footmen at Argus House, the London home of Lord John's mother. [*BL*]

Norrington, Arthur—An old acquaintance of Lord John and the current head of England's Black Chamber; an aficionado of ivory miniatures from Japan. [*Echo*]

x **North, Frederick, Lord**—(1732–1792) Second Earl of Guilford, prime minister of Great Britain under George III. He deferred strategy of the war to his subordinates Lord Germain and the Earl of Sandwich. Despite victories at New York and Ticonderoga, Lord North was forced to resign, due to a "lack of confidence" by members of Parliament, after Burgoyne's surrender at Saratoga and the British defeat at Yorktown. [*PZ, Ashes, Echo, MOBY*]

Northrup, Thorogood—A Wilmington merchant and warehouse owner and possible smuggler. [*Echo*]

Nortman—The Duke of Pardloe's butler. [*BL*]

Nuckelavee—Hybrid fairy sea creature of Northern Scottish folklore, it often left the sea to feast on human flesh. While it could take on human shape, in its natural form it had a head ten times the size of its body, a single fiery eye, a huge jutting mouth, and arms reaching to the ground that doubled as flesh-and-bone swords. In addition, it had no skin, so its muscles and blood vessels could be seen, giving it the appearance of raw living flesh. Roger is therefore startled when his son, Jem, in some distress, tells him that there is a nuckelavee living in the broch at Lallybroch. Going to investigate, Roger finds evidence that *someone* has been staying in the broch, but he doubts that it's a nuckelavee. The mysterious stranger shortly reveals himself to Roger: he's William Buccleigh MacKenzie, Roger's four-times great-grandfather, who has accidentally time-traveled through the stones at Craigh na Dun and, having gone to Inverness in search of some familiar place or thing, has seen Roger—whom he last saw being hanged at Alamance. He's therefore come to see who and what Roger now is, and when he meets the children unexpectedly, tells them he's a nuckelavee in order to frighten them off. [*Echo*]

O

Oakes—The man Richard Brown leaves in command after the arrest of Jamie and Claire for the murder of Malva Christie. [*Ashes*]

O'Brian, Tige—An Irish settler and Regulator near Fraser's Ridge who, along with his family, is killed when their cabin is burned by unknown persons; Roger and Jamie follow the smell of smoke and arrive to bury the dead family. [*Ashes*]

O'Connell, Francine, Mrs. (aka Mrs. Francine Scanlon)—Widow of the late Sergeant Timothy O'Connell, who severely beat her. After the sergeant mysteriously turns up dead in an alley, Francine marries the apothecary, Scanlon. [*PM*]

O'Connell, Sergeant—One of the soldiers in Pardloe's regiment during the Jacobite uprising of 1745, who instructed a very young Lord John and others in the art of sneaking up on a foe from behind and dispatching him with a dagger. [*BL*]

O'Connell, Timothy, Sergeant—A middle-aged Irishman and lifelong soldier, he rose through the ranks not only by his competence but by his ability to intimidate subordinates with his surly attitude. He is murdered by an unknown assailant. [*PM*]

O'Donnell, Kitty—A recently deceased woman in London's Irish slum, the Rookery. She was so popular that her mother refuses to let her body be buried, and the party-like atmosphere of the Irish wake lasts for the better part of two weeks, much to the dismay of the neighbors. [*BL*]

O'Donnell, Ma—Kitty O'Donnell's greedy mother. So much money is donated during Kitty's wake that her mother continues it for the better part of two weeks, forcing the inhabitants of the Rookery to live with the smell of decay—until the O'Higgins brothers intervene. [*BL*]

Oggy—Short for "Oglethorpe," Rachel and Ian's nickname for their baby. [*MOBY*]

Ogilvie, Andrew—A young Scottish private under Lieutenant Archie Hayes. He informs the Frasers that Hayes's Sixty-seventh Highland Regiment is the last of the Crown's regular troops to withdraw from the colonies, since the French and Indian Wars are over and the French have withdrawn. He saves Germain from drowning at the Mount Helicon Gathering. [*Fiery Cross*]

Ogilvie, Miss—A young woman, one of the fisher-folk, who is invited to attend a luncheon with Jocasta Cameron, Mrs. Forbes, and several other ladies living near River Run. [*Ashes*]

Ogilvie, Mr. (the older)—Family patriarch and grandfather to Rogerina, the young child Roger baptizes upon his return from the ministry; Mr. Ogilvie compliments Roger on his sermon but confides to his wife that Roger can't carry a tune. [*Ashes*]

Ogilvie, Mrs.—A very young Presbyterian wife, she and her teenage husband believe that their infant daughter is dying, so they call Roger, who performs his first baptism. Brianna diagnoses wee Rogerina with a vicious case of colic. [*Ashes*]

Ogilvie, Rogerina; Rory—The first child of the young Ogilvies, who honor Roger by naming her after him, in thanks for his christening the infant. [*Ashes*]

Ogilvy, Mrs.—Staunch member of the Ladies' Altar and Tea Society at the Free North Church in Inverness, who is concerned about Brianna's mortal soul since she is a Papist and doesn't attend services with Roger. [*Echo*]

x **Oglethorpe, James**—(1696–1785) Founder and first royal governor of the colony of Georgia. [*MOBY*]

O'Hanlon, Peter—The fictitious name a quick-thinking Jamie gives to Siverly when asked which instructor he knew at Trinity University in Dublin. [*SP*]

O'Higgins, Michael; Mick—One of a pair of Irish brothers, possibly deserters from the Irish Brigade but enlisted soldiers in Lord John's regiment. Prone to a variety of "free enterprise," lawlessness, and trouble, they often turn up when most unexpected. [*BL, SP*]

O'Higgins, Raphael; Rafe—One of a pair of Irish brothers, possibly deserters from the Irish Brigade but enlisted soldiers in Lord John's regiment. Prone to a variety of "free enterprise," lawlessness, and trouble, they often turn up when most unexpected. [*BL, SP*]

O'Keefe, Judge—Virginia neighbor of William and Lord John, a justice and one whom William trusts to leave letters for his father if necessary. [*Echo*]

Okwaho'kenha—See "Wolf's Brother."

Old Cotterill—An elderly, near-deaf patron of Lord John's favorite London club, the Beefsteak. [*HF*]

Oliver, Gideon—A resident of Fraser's Ridge who has outlived three wives, the implication being that they've all died during childbirth. [*Fiery Cross*]

Olson—A corporal leading one of the companies in William's regiment at the Battle of Long Island. [*Echo*]

O'Neill, Bob—One of the residents of Fraser's Ridge who helps build various businesses, including Ronnie Sinclair's cooperage, a smithy, and general store. [*Fiery Cross*]

O'Neill, Father—Of St. George's Church in Philadelphia; he oversees Henri-Christian's funeral service. [*MOBY*]

Orden—One of Stephen Bonnet's crewmen; he is told to find other female companionship for Bonnet since Brianna is with child—a condition that Bonnet finds discomfiting and repugnant. [*Ashes*]

Orden, Lewis, Lieutenant—One of the lieutenants under Jamie's command. [*MOBY*]

O'Reilly, Mr.—The Irish cellist with the music ensemble hired to play at Jocasta and Duncan's wedding. He insults the inebriated naval officer Lieutenant Wolff and is warned by fellow musicians to beware of Wolff, who may not be as drunk as he appears and is known for a vengeful temper. [*Fiery Cross*]

Ormiston, Joe—An injured crewman of the British ship *Pitt* and staunch Loyalist to the Crown. He recognizes "John Smith" as the deserter Bill "Jonah" Marsden. [*Echo*]

Osborn, Colin—A second lieutenant from William's regiment in Wilmington. [*Echo*]

x **Osborne, Adlai**—(1744–1814) A well-to-do North Carolina merchantman attending Jocasta and Duncan's wedding; he inadvertently distracts Phillip Wylie, taking him from his amorous pursuit of Claire. In 1775 he was appointed a colonel of Minute Men for Rowan County by the Continental Congress. [*Fiery Cross*]

Oscar—A slave at River Run, he blows a kiss to Phaedre when he's returning to the summer kitchen with an empty fish platter. [*Ashes*]

x **O'Sullivan, John, Sir**—(1700–1746) Irish Jacobite and quartermaster for Charles Stuart during the Rising of 1745–1746. [*SP, Fiery Cross*]

Oswald, Mortimer, the Honorable—One of the three members of the military tribunal investigating Lord John's part in the explosion of a cannon during the Battle of Crefeld; he was elected to Parliament by nefarious means—i.e., bribery. [*HS*]

Oswald, Mortimer Montmorency III—Late father of the Honorable Mortimer Oswald, the corrupt politician from Sussex. He receives a medal for good conduct from the army, which later proves to be a damning bit of evidence in a case of political corruption uncovered by Lord John. [*HS*]

Otter-Tooth (aka "Robert Springer")—Ta'wineonawira is the Indian name taken by the leader of the Montauk Five, a group of twentieth-century Native American purists who disappeared in 1968. Members of the national group AIM, the smaller, outspoken group had protested against the treatment of the first Americans by the European whites. Upon arriving in the past, Otter-Tooth is labeled a troublemaker and is killed by the Mohawk. The skull—with silver fillings—that Claire finds buried under the roots of a red cedar is apparently his; buried with him was an opal, which Claire is told he called his "ticket back." [*Fiery Cross, Ashes, MOBY*]

Otway, Harrison, Private—The middleman for the passage of information between Captain Bates and the solicitor Ffoulkes, brother-in-law to a French army colonel. [*BL*]

Owen—An elderly widower whose name is mentioned by a group of young unmarried girls playing a marriage prediction game during Hogmanay at the Big House. [*Fiery Cross*]

Owen, Colonel—Commander of an artillery company at Monmouth. [*MOBY*]

P

x **Paine, Thomas**—(1737–1809) Revolutionary writer (the author of "Common Sense," the inflammatory pamphlet that was the first American bestseller and a major incitement to the rebellion) whom Lord John meets briefly. Lord John is not impressed, describing Paine (accurately) as "a malnourished, ill-dressed wretch." [*Echo*]

x **Palmer, General J.**—(1716–1788) General of the militia and a member of the Committee of Safety, Joseph Palmer penned the "Lexington Alarm," a document bearing witness to the slaughter on Lexington Common; it was sent by express riders throughout the countryside to notify other militias that the war had begun. Frank Randall had a copy of the Lexington Alarm, and Claire is startled and horrified when she realizes that a copy of this document has been sent to Jamie for his own signature. [*Ashes*]

x **Palmer, Robert**—(1724–1790) A lieutenant general in the North Carolina colonial militia and close friend of Governor Tryon, he was also a member of the council of war prior to the Battle of Alamance. [*Fiery Cross*]

Parker, Jack—One of the residents of Fraser's Ridge and a member of Jamie's militia unit. [*Fiery Cross*]

x **Parker, Peter, Sir**—(1721–1811) British admiral of the fleet that arrived at the mouth of the Cape Fear River on April 18, 1776, at the bequest of Governor Martin, to help calm fears and protect the Loyalists in North Carolina. He fought bravely and was knighted for his participation in the Charleston campaign and eventually succeeded Howe as admiral of the fleet. [*Ashes*]

Paul—A footman employed by Michael Murray. [*SB*]

Paulie—The elderly brother of Ma O'Donnell, he is drafted to retrieve his drunken sister from her daughter's wake and proceeds to drag her home by her heels. [*BL*]

Peabody, Lulu, Mrs.—A very drunk and very pregnant woman at Coryell's Ferry. Claire takes care of her and, while waiting to see whether the comatose Mrs. Peabody will either awaken or go into labor, has a long discussion with Dorothea and Rachel about wedding nights, sex, and how to make a man say, "Oh, God." [*MOBY*]

Peabody, Simon—The husband of Lulu Peabody. [*MOBY*]

Pearsall, Olivia—See "Olivia Stubbs."

Pearsall, Papa—Olivia's deceased father. [*PM*]

Peg—A prostitute from Devonshire employed at Magda's; as she is a large-breasted blonde, she's in line to become Harry Quarry's new favorite. [*PM*]

Peggy—A prostitute at Mrs. McNab's establishment who helps William overcome his temporarily broken heart when he realizes that his previous paramour, Margery, is entertaining another gentleman. [*Echo*]

Peggy, Mrs.—Baby William's under-nursemaid at Helwater. [*SP*]

x **Pellew, Edward**—(1757–1833) The midshipman (a cadet or lowest-ranking officer) who valiantly took command of the *Carleton* during the heated naval battle of Valcour Island on Lake Champlain in October 1776, after his commanding officers were mortally wounded in the fighting. For his bravery and quick thinking, he was immediately given command of the *Carleton*—quite an accomplishment for a nineteen-year-old. [*Echo*]

Pendragon, Elizabeth—A dark-haired Welsh heiress whom the Dunsanys mistake as Lord John's secret admirer when a lock of dark hair falls from an unsigned note John receives upon arriving at Helwater. [*BL*]

Penstemon—Wife of Cherokee chief Tsisqua (Bird-who-sings-in-the-morning). [*Ashes*]

Pépin, Charles—Married with children, he has an affair with Léonie, the sister of Michael Murray's wife, Lillie. Lèonie becomes pregnant, and Charles, overcome by debt and the messiness of his affairs, kills himself. [*SB*]

Pépin, Eulalie—Wife of Charles Pépin. [*SB*]

Perkins, Private—A private who furnishes William with a horse at the Long Island landing, he is eager in his duties but not altogether bright, as his lack of better direction causes William to lose his bearings in the dense Long Island fog. [*Echo*]

Perriman, Captain—One of two previous superintendents appointed by the Crown to oversee the maroons on Jamaica and act as their emissary with the British settlers. [*PZ*]

Peter—A hired oarsman and Duff's partner for the day, ferrying Cape Fear residents from Wilmington to Smith Island to see the grounded whale. [*Fiery Cross*]

Peters, Samuel, Judge—The local magistrate in King's Town who sentences two maroons to whipping for theft based on circumstantial evidence; Peters travels to the Bahaman island of Eleuthera before Lord John is able to question him regarding the sentence. [*PZ*]

Peterson, Reverend—A minister for the New Light Church in Wilmington, he helps Tom Christie make peace with his feelings for Claire and her "demise" in the house fire. [*Echo*]

Phaedre (aka Faydree)—Jocasta Cameron's former body-servant and Hector Cameron's illegitmate daughter, after leaving River Run she begins a new life as a barmaid in an ordinary in Wilmington. [*Fiery Cross, Ashes, Echo*]

Philemon; Phil—A lovely bay horse belonging to Lord Dunsany. Two-year old William fearlessly hugs the horse despite its enormous size, which reminds Jamie of his own early introduction to horses by his father, Brian, when Jamie was about the same age as William. [*SP*]

Phillip—Wounded Loyalist suffering from heatstroke, brother of Sally-Sarah. [*MOBY*]

Phillips, Jonas—Fergus and Marsali's Jewish neighbor, whose children often played with Henri-Christian. [*MOBY*]

Phillips, Sam—The son of Jonas Phillips and neighbor of Fergus and Marsali; he unknowingly finds the Fraser stash of gold, disguised as lead type for the press. [*MOBY*]

Phillipson, Mr.—A militiaman and tailor from Morristown. [*MOBY*]

Pickering, Captain—General Howe's aide-de-camp at the Long Island sea landing. [*Echo*]

Pickering, Colonel—A military officer in charge of a regiment stationed in London during 1758. [*BL*]

Pilcock—A footman at Argus House, the London residence of the Duke and Duchess of Pardloe. [*SP*]

x **Pitcher, Molly**—(1754–1832) Nickname for Mary Ludwig Hays; said to have been at the Battle of Monmouth, supplying water to the Continental troops and helping with cannon duty when needed. [*MOBY*]

x **Pitt, Mr. William**—(1708–1778) Prime minister of England during the Seven Years' War and a member of Lord John Grey's favorite gentlemen's club, the Society for Appreciation of the English Beefsteak. [*PM*]

Platt, Aunt—Mrs. Endicott's sister living in New York. [*MOBY*]

Plonplon—Lillie's pug dog. [*SB*]

Pocock, Frances; Fanny—Arabella-Jane's tongue-tied younger sister. Intelligent and watchful, she's fiercely protective of her elder sister, the only family she has. She also harbors feelings of great guilt, as it was Captain Harkness's threat to her virginity that caused Jane to kill the man—and then to be arrested and condemned for the murder. Jane commits suicide rather than be hanged, leaving her young sister alone and helpless. Fanny's only succor is William, who takes what care he can of her, confiding her to the care of Jamie and Claire, who embrace her as part of their own family and take her with them to Fraser's Ridge. [*MOBY*]

Pocock, Jane Eleanora (aka Arabella)—The legal name of the whore known as Arabella. A "fancy piece," Arabella-Jane meets William in the course of his rampage following the revelation that Jamie Fraser is his father. Distraught and angry, William goes with her for distraction, but things don't go as either party intended and the encounter ends in embarrassment and disaster. The next evening, William encounters her by accident while very drunk and, moved both by chivalry and a desire to make amends, saves her from the advances of a depraved and cruel captain of dragoons named Harkness, by hiring her for the night at the cost of his silver officer's gorget. This encounter goes somewhat better, but it isn't, as William expects, a one-night stand. The Pocock girls' fate seems entwined with his, and when Jane and Fanny flee the brothel and Philadelphia, he takes them under his protection, intending to help them reach safety in New York. He doesn't know at this point that they've fled because Jane has killed the nasty Captain Harkness and is wanted for his murder. Eventually she's caught and arrested, and while William and Jamie try urgently to save her, they are too late; overcome by despair and unable to face the thought of hanging, Jane cuts her wrists with a broken bottle, leaving Fanny alone in the world—except for William. [*MOBY*]

x **Poor, General Enoch**—(1736–1780) Commander of an eight-hundred-man brigade at Saratoga, his forces combined with those of General Learned to break through the Hessian forces. Poor was also the president of the court-martial that ordered the arrest of Benedict Arnold, although Arnold managed to escape before his arrest. [*Echo*]

x **Pope, the (Clement XIII)**—(1693–1769) The head of the Catholic Church, his papacy began in 1758 upon the death of Pope Benedict XIV. A notable meddler in politics, as noted by Hal. [*BL*]

Potts, Dr.—A physician and associate of Lord John Grey; he examines Bobby Higgins after the injury to one eye during the Boston riots but deems Bobby's vision loss to be permanent. [*Ashes*]

Poundstone, Ezekial—The official hangman for Newgate Prison and witness for Captain Bates's signed confession. [*BL*]

Poutoude, La Comtesse—A Paris salon attendee who swoons upon hearing Jamie's somewhat fabricated tales of the bloodthirsty Indians of the colonies. [*Echo*]

x **Prescott, William, Colonel**—(1726–1795) Commander of Rebel forces at the Battle of Bunker Hill, he is one of the officers credited with coining the phrase, "Do not fire until you see the whites of their eyes," although there is no proof that this was ever shouted. [*Ashes, MOBY*]

x **Prevost, Mark, Major**—(1736–1781) Commander of a British company from Florida, marching north to join forces with Colonel Campbell to take Savannah. [*MOBY*]

Priestly, Ronald—Priestly and Phillip Wylie own a warehouse in Portsmouth, Virginia, and are rumored to store goods smuggled by Stephen Bonnet. [*Fiery Cross*]

Priestly, Walter—A wealthy Cape Fear merchant, he also owns warehouses in the coastal cities of Charleston, Savannah, Wilmington, and Edenton, and has business interests in Boston, as well; to complicate things more, he is a friend to the governor. [*Fiery Cross*]

x **Prince Tearlach**—See "Charles Stuart."

Private _____—An unnamed enlisted man who is part of the gun crew when Lord John takes over its command during the Battle of Crefeld; he is brought to London to testify before the tribunal regarding the explosion of the cannon during the heated battle. [*HS*]

Protheroe, Dr.—One of the surgeons assigned to Hal's regiment in Prussia; Lord John has Tom Byrd locate him, in order that he might bleed John. [*BL*]

Puddin'—The mule belonging to one of Amy McCallum's sisters, who have traveled to Fraser's Ridge for Amy and Bobby's wedding. [*Echo*]

x **Putnam, Daniel**—(1755–1819) Massachusetts resident whose letter (later known as the Lexington Alarm) circulated throughout the colonies, noting the rise of militia companies and requesting arms and powder for those companies. [*Ashes*]

x **Putnam, Israel, General**—(1718–1790) Connecticut farmer turned soldier and veteran of the French and Indian Wars, "Old Put" had the reputation early on of a staunch patriot, was a brigadier general of militia at Bunker Hill, and during the Boston Siege commanded the American center under his new rank of major general. Possibly due to his stubbornness, Putnam was never a very adept field commander and failed to inspire young soldiers with his outdated warfare tactics. [*Ashes, Echo*]

Q

Quarry, Harry, Colonel; Handsome Harry—Career British military man and Lord John's longtime friend, he was John's predecessor as governor of Ardsmuir Prison and has continued to assist Lord John with various intelligence tasks when needed. [*HF, PM, BL, HS, CA, SP, Echo, MOBY*]

Quarton, Mr. and Mrs.—Farmers where Jerry was caught stealing food. They imprison Jerry in their cow byre, from which he's rescued by Roger and Buck. [*MOBY*]

x **Queen, the**—(1900–2002) The Queen Consort, Lady Elizabeth (Bowes-Lyon), Duchess of York, and wife to King George VI (Bertie). During the London bombings of WWII, she stayed in London with her family; Claire tells Roger that she saw her, visiting injured troops with the King. [*Echo*]

Quiet Air—The sachem (a sort of underchief) in one of the Cherokee villages; he sees potential in Jamie's temperamental stallion, Gideon, and offers three deerskins for the chance to breed his spotted mare to him. [*Ashes*]

x **Quincy, Josiah**—(1744–1775) American Patriot and Boston lawyer. While he was outspoken against the British suppression and injustices to the American people, he, along with John Adams, defended Captain Preston and the British soldiers after the Boston Massacre, securing an acquittal for the men by proving they fired upon the Boston mob in self-defense. Not all the accused were acquitted, though; Bobby Higgins was one of the soldiers convicted of murder and consequently branded in the face with the letter "M." Later, Lord John writes to Jamie that he suspects Quincy of being the man who gave Jamie's name to the Committees of Correspondence. [*Ashes*]

Quinn, Tobias (Tobias Mac Gréagair Quinn)—A mysterious Irishman and Jacobite, he knew Jamie during the time before the Rising of 1745 but escaped the tragedy of Culloden. He and others have kept alive the dream of Charles Stuart as the ruler of England, and he tries to draw Jamie back into plotting for another Jacobite uprising, an invitation Jamie wisely refuses to accept. His caution is for naught, though, when Hal (Duke of Pardloe) forces Lord John and Jamie to go together to Ireland to arrest Gerald Siverly. Tobias, delighted by this development, meets them in Ireland, where he tries repeatedly to lure Jamie into pursuing his schemes. [*SP*]

Quinton, Lady—One of London's society matrons and hostess of a party that Olivia, Lord John's young cousin, attends. [*PM*]

R

Racket, Granny—Local (Northumbrian) healer and herb woman. [*MOBY*]

Rains Hard—One of the Montauk Five, a group of twentieth-century Native American purists who disappeared in 1968. [*Fiery Cross*]

Raintree, Mr.—A resident of Cross Creek, he purchases the apothecary's wagon horse, Jack, the particular pet of Miranda Bogues, daughter of the apothecary. [*Ashes*]

Rakoczy, Paul—An RAF pilot who has trained with Jerry; he is surprised by an aerial move and exchanges Polish curses with Jerry over the maneuver. [*LW*]

Rakoczy, Paul—The name used by the mysterious Comte St. Germain while in Paris during 1778; the family name appears again during the 1940s, but we don't know whether these are two different men with the same name or perhaps the time-traveling Comte in a new adventure. [*LW*]

Ramsay, Captain—One of General Howe's senior staff. He is to debrief William regarding his intelligencing expedition after William reveals key information regarding the Continental forces on Long Island in a staff meeting. [*Echo*]

Randall, Alexander—Younger brother of Black Jack Randall. Lover of Mary Hawkins; he dies of consumption before their son, Denys, is born. [*Outlander, Dragonfly in Amber*]

Randall, "Black Jack"—See "Jonathan Wolverton Randall."

Randall, Denys—See "Denys Randall-Isaacs."

Randall, Franklin Wolverton; Frank—Claire's first husband; former WWII agent of Britain's MI6 and a professional historian with a deep interest in the eighteenth century; stepfather to Claire's (and Jamie's) daughter, Brianna. Originally disbelieving Claire's story after her return from the past, he later has Claire swear not to tell Brianna anything of her life in the past or of Brianna's biological father—at least not until after his own death. He leaves Brianna a clue to her real father's identity and also writes her letters that tell the truth—about a lot of things. [*All*]

Randall, Jonathan Wolverton, Captain (aka Black Jack)—Frank Randall's five-times great-grandfather, a captain in the English army, and a man of violence and perverse desires, with a special place in his black heart for Jamie Fraser. He marries Mary Hawkins, the pregnant lover of his dying brother, Alex, in Paris, with Jamie and Claire as witnesses. Black Jack dies at Culloden Moor on April 16, 1746. [*All*]

Randall-Isaacs, Denys, Captain (aka Denys Randall)—A young British officer William is assigned to accompany to Canada but who has his own agenda. He is the child of Mary Hawkins and Alex Randall, though Jonathan (Black Jack) Randall marries the pregnant Mary while Alex is dying of consumption and so becomes Denys's stepfather. After Black Jack is killed at Culloden, Mary marries a Jewish merchant named Robert Isaacs. Denys adopts his stepfather's name as a mark of respect but drops it after his stepfather's death, as a Jewish name is a handicap to an up-and-coming young officer. [*Echo, MOBY*]

Ransom, William Clarence Henry George; Ninth Earl of Ellesmere; Viscount Ashness; Baron Derwent—The heir of Lords Ellesmere and Dunsany; illegitimate son of James Fraser and Geneva Dunsany. William was raised by his stepmother/aunt Isobel Dunsany and stepfather Lord John Grey. He harbors fond memories of the Scottish groom, "Mac," who was his friend and mentor through early childhood. These memories are substantially impaired when William meets Jamie face-to-face in Philadelphia and is struck—as everyone who sees them together is—by the startling resemblance. All Is Made Clear—or so William thinks, and he's both shocked, humiliated, and enraged when he realizes that not only is he not carrying the noble blood of the Ellesmere line—rather, that of a Scottish criminal and traitor—but that everyone he's ever trusted has been lying to him his entire life. His efforts to get a grip on his temper and his perspective and decide what the bloody hell to *do* about the situation are further disturbed by conflict with his newfound cousin Ian, who is betrothed to Rachel Hunter, a Quaker girl that William is strongly attracted to. One distraction from his troubles, though, comes in the form of a young whore named Jane Pocock and her younger sister, Frances (Fanny). William's attempts to protect the girls and see them to safety come to naught when Jane is arrested for the murder of Captain Harkness (a sadistic brothel customer who threatened Fanny). Desperate, William appeals to the last resource he has—his father. Jamie instantly joins William in an attempt to rescue Jane, but they arrive too late; despairing and unable to face the prospect of hanging, Jane has cut her wrists. Grimly desolate, William entrusts Fanny to the care of Jamie and Claire, and he leaves, presumably to pick up the pieces of his life. [*All, SP*]

Rastus—One of Farquard Cambell's slaves. Claire treats the hand he burns badly while removing grilled fowl from a skewer during Jocasta and Duncan's wedding feast. [*Fiery Cross*]

Raven, Mrs.—The childless wife of a New Hampshire militia officer, she becomes Claire's "assistant" while the Continental army is at Ticonderoga; she has a ghoulish fascination with the morbid side of Claire's medical duties but is competent enough not to faint or become sick while Claire is operating. She takes her own life out of morbid fear when she thinks Indians are attacking. [*Echo*]

Rawlings, Daniel, Dr.—Original owner of the medicine chest Jamie gives to Claire. He disappears under mysterious circumstances; it is later discovered that he was murdered and placed in Hector Cameron's tomb after finding the stash of gold Jocasta Cameron had kept hidden for thirty years. [*Fiery Cross, Ashes, Echo*]

Rawlings, David, Dr.—Twin brother to Daniel Rawlings. Claire meets him after the Battle of Bemis Heights, where he was a British doctor in attendance at the death of General Simon Fraser. [*Echo*]

Raymond—A great shaman reputed to have the ability to transform himself into birds or animals, and one who could walk through time; he taught the Montauk Five about traveling through time, warning them that some sort of gemstone would aid as protection during their passage; Claire suspects he could be Master Raymond (Maître Raymond), whom she met in Paris prior to Culloden. [*Fiery Cross, Ashes, MOBY*]

Rendill, Lieutenant—Soldier helping William on the quay during the evacuation of Philadelphia. [*MOBY*]

Rennie, Andrew—See "Raphael Wattiswade." [*SP*]

Rennie, Mina—Minnie Grey's alias during the Rising, when she was a Jacobite spy. [*SP*]

Ricasoli, Signor—One of the slave buyers expected to attend the special sale, which included Brianna, at Stephen Bonnet's coastal hideout on Ocracoke Island. [*Ashes*]

Richards, Johanna—A young mother on the Ridge who has lost two children to croup; Brianna is very concerned when Jem comes down with croup at River Run during Jocasta's wedding celebration. [*Fiery Cross*]

Richardson, Ezekiel, Captain—A British spy, Richardson asks William if he would like to be a special messenger to carry special dispatches to General Howe, dangling a chance for inclusion on Howe's staff upon his arrival in Halifax. William sees the mission as one filled with adventure, but in a letter, Hal warns William that he really shouldn't be involved with Richardson. He shouldn't: Richardson sends him on a mission to Dismal Town (in the center of the Dismal Swamp) that nearly gets him killed—and would indeed have gotten him killed, had he actually got there. He later tries to inveigle William into further intelligence work, but William wisely resists. Richardson reappears unexpectedly in Savannah, wearing a Continental uniform, and tries to suborn Claire with various threats, among these the revelation that he knows what Lord John is—i.e., a homosexual. Claire rejects his overtures emphatically but is obliged to tell John of the threat. [*Echo, MOBY*]

Richardson, Governor—A fictional character based on a factual incident; during the uproar regarding the Stamp Acts of 1765, an effigy of Boston's Stamp Commissioner Andrew Oliver was hung from the Liberty Tree near Boston Common and burned. [*Fiery Cross*]

x **Richelieu, Duc de**—(1696–1788) Armand de Vignerot du Plessis, diplomat, statesman, and soldier. Richelieu rose in his military career to become marshal of France; after taking command of the French forces during the Seven Years' War, he failed to conquer Hanover, retreating instead, and was relieved of his command. [*BL*]

Richie and Jed—Two of Wendigo Donner's henchmen, they are helping him ransack the Big House, looking for a cache of jewels, when fire breaks out and destroys the house on Fraser's Ridge. [*Ashes*]

x Richmond, Private Billy—(1763–1829) A former slave assigned the duty of securing the hangman's rope for Nathan Hale's execution. At only thirteen years of age, Richmond may not have realized that the new rope would stretch, preventing a hard drop and clean break of the neck. Instead, Hale suffered death by suffocation while the crowd watched. [*Echo*]

Ridley—Young man who shows Roger and Buck the location of the standing stones that they suspect Jerry MacKenzie came through when his Spitfire crashed during a training exercise in WWII. [*MOBY*]

Rigby, Captain Gilbert—One of Benedicta's suitors after the apparent suicide of Lord John's father, Gerard Grey, the Duke of Pardloe, and now the supervisor of a foundlings home. Lord John meets him in the course of investigating Gerard Grey's death. [*BL*]

Roarke, Captain—The skipper of the fishing boat Jamie hires to look for Bonnet's hideout on Ocracoke Island; while sharing a beer with Claire, he imparts some important information regarding the tides in the inlet and how the various channels will be affected as the tide goes out. [*Ashes*]

Robert—Michael Murray's valet in Paris. [*SB*]

Roberts, George—Senior footman at Helwater and ardent admirer of Betty, Isobel's lady's maid. [*SP*]

Roberts, Melisande; Melly—One of Lady Joffrey's unmarried relations, whom she attempts to pair with Lord John's new stepbrother, Percival Wainwright. [*BL*]

Roberts, Trustworthy, Captain—Captain of the *Tranquil Teal,* the small American ship that is to take Jamie, Claire, Ian, and Rollo back to Scotland. [*Echo*]

Robertson, Jimmy—One of the men in Jamie's militia unit, who prepares a warm stew on the cold winter march to meet the Regulators. [*Fiery Cross*]

Robinson, Mr. Jno.—Former proprietor of the *New Bern Intelligencer;* due to the kidnapping and transporting of Mr. Robinson at the hands of the local Committee of Safety, Fergus is able to purchase and take over as sole proprietor and editor in chief of *L'Oignon–Intelligencer.* [*Ashes*]

Rodham, Lieutenant—The British soldier in New York who brutally beats a whore, then sets her on fire when he discovers that she is infected with the pox (syphilis). [*Echo*]

Rodrigo—One of the footmen at the governor's home in Jamaica, he is young and handsome, but due to bad decisions of a personal nature, island justice has rendered him zombie-like. [*PZ*]

Rogers—A member of White's who lays a two-guinea wager that the person lying in the gutter outside is dead. [*BL*]

x Rogers, Robert, Major—(1731–1795) Veteran of the French and Indian War and one of the originators of "irregular" or guerrilla-type warfare, Rogers was brilliant at recruiting and leading men in "ranging" parties; those units earned the title "Roberts Rangers." Rogers uses William—who saw Nathan Hale at a checkpoint he was supervising and could therefore identify him—to find and capture the inept American spy. [*Echo*]

Rollo—Young Ian's gigantic part-wolf dog, acquired as a gambling prize in Charleston shortly after arriving in the colonies. Rollo is large, fierce, and devoted to his master; he thrives in the wilderness and accompanies Ian everywhere. A good thing for Ian that he does: among other things, he saves Ian's (and Rachel's) lives when Arch Bug attacks them with an ax and defends his master from threats ranging from sea pirates to his own cousin William. Rollo is so much a part of Ian's life that when Ian marries Rachel, Rollo follows Ian up to the front of the church, causing Lord John to remark to his brother (in Claire's hearing), "And here, of course, is the best man." Despite his very adventurous life, Rollo lives to a ripe old age and dies peacefully next to his master's bed. [*All*]

Ronson, Captain—One of the officers at the Continental encampment at Middlebrook, the American settlement where William goes in hopes of gaining information regarding his cousin Benjamin, who was reported to have died there as a prisoner of war. [*MOBY*]

Roscoe—Lord John's dachshund. [*MOBY*]

Rosenwald—A Jewish goldsmith in Paris, he is contracted to engrave a chalice to be donated to the chapel at le Couvent des Anges by the family of Jared Fraser and Michael Murray. [*SB*]

Roswell, Lady—An apparently prudish friend of Benedicta Grey. [*PM*]

Roswell, Lieutenant—Young British army officer sent by General Clinton to Lord John's house in search of him. Failing to find his lordship, he escorts Claire to Clinton's office. [*MOBY*]

Rowbotham, Honorable Helene—A lesser member of the peerage and a beautiful London socialite in attendance at Lady Joffrey's salon, where Lord John recognizes both her beauty and her ability to use it to her advantage. [*BL*]

Royce—Trevelyan's chief man of business for his shipping firm. [*PM*]

Running Fox—Second-in-command to Tsisqua (Bird-who-sings-in-the-morning), leader of one of the Snowbird Cherokee villages. On a raid, Fox captures a young Tuscaroran woman, wife to Light on Water, a young Tuscaroran brave who is determined to retrieve his wife or die trying. [*Ashes*]

x **Rush, Dr. Benjamin**—(1746–1813) Prominent physician in Philadelphia whom Lord John seeks to treat Henry's severe stomach wounds. A Patriot and Founding Father, Rush was elected to the Continental Congress and served briefly as the surgeon general of the middle department. He promoted bloodletting—often several times a day—to cure disease, to the extreme that his contemporaries objected, stating that he had killed more patients with this method than he had cured. He studied mental illness and campaigned for more-humane housing conditions for the mentally ill, as well as occupational therapy for those institutionalized. [*Echo, MOBY*]

x **Rutherford, Captain Griffith Loch**—(1721–1805) A captain of the North Carolina militia, a resident of the Salisbury area, and head of a unit that fought the Regulators at the Battle of Alamance. [*Fiery Cross*]

x **Rutherford, John, the Honorable**—(1724–1782) Receiver general of the quit rents and member of the Royal Council of North Carolina, under Governor Tryon. [*Fiery Cross*]

Ruysdale, Colonel—Commander of the combined forces of England's Thirty-fifth and Fifty-second Foot regiments stationed in Gundwitz, Prussia, during the Seven Years' War. [*SU*]

S

Sally-Sarah—Phillip's Patriot sister, requiring amputation of the arm after a grenade blast. [*MOBY*]

Sampson—The printer's helper, or "devil," working for Amos Crupp, owner of the *Gazette*, the Wilmington newspaper that prints the notice of a deadly fire on Fraser's Ridge. [*Ashes*]

Samson—A young Prussian artilleryman who has a romantic liaison with Franz, another young soldier, but is experienced enough to hide his emotions—and the truth—when taunted by his peers. [*SU*]

Samson and Delilah—Samson—a small noisy dog with long brown hair—and Delilah—a large, white mixed-breed hound with a languid temperament—were presented to Jocasta by her husband, Duncan, for protection and to keep her company. [*Ashes*]

Sanders, Mr.—A friend of Lord John and William's, who resides in Philadelphia and is a point of contact for them. [*Echo*]

Sanderson, Mr.—While dealing with arguing factions in Brownsville, Roger draws upon on the image of Mr. Sanderson, one of his schoolmasters—an especially fearsome man, who often lifted quaking students off their feet for infractions—in order to calm the Browns and keep them from shooting his men. [*Fiery Cross*]

x **Sandwich, Fourth Earl of; John Montagu**—(1718–1792) A British statesman who held several high military offices. He was notoriously associated with Sir Francis Dashwood's Hellfire Club, where he panicked when he mistook a baboon—dressed as the devil by another member—for the real devil. [*HF*]

Sansom, Corporal—Lord John's aide on the trail to the Twelvetrees and Rose Hall plantations. [*PZ*]

Sapp, Sergeant-Major—One of General Ruysdale's men who was to show Lord John where to deliver the body of Private Bodger, but Sapp was not in camp. [*SU*]

Sassenach—While typically a Gaelic word for an "English person," this is the name Jamie has affectionately called Claire since they met. [*All*]

Scanlon, Finbar—An Irish apothecary who marries the widow O'Connell; he also tries to help Trevelyan and his lover with an innovative medical treatment—using the high fevers of malaria to burn out syphilis. [*PM*]

Scanlon, Francine, Mrs.—See "Mrs. Francine O'Connell."

Schnell, Jacob—One of Lizzie Wemyss's suitors, son of a German cobbler and a friend of the Muellers; as Jacob is a Lutheran and lives near Salem, Jamie doesn't think he'll be a suitable match for Lizzie. [*Fiery Cross*]

Schnell, Lieutenant—Jamie's aide-de-camp at Monmouth. [*MOBY*]

x **Schuyler, Philip John, General**—(1733–1804) Commander of the Northern Department of the Continental army. After losing Fort Ticonderoga to the British army in 1777, Schuyler was reprimanded and relieved of command by General Horatio Gates. More than a year later, a court-martial acquitted Schuyler of charges of incompetence, and he resigned his commission in 1779. [*Echo*]

Scotchee—See "Alexander Cameron."

x **Seaforth, Earl of**—A patron of the Brahan Seer, and responsible for some of the Seer's prophecies being written down to edify future ages. [*MOBY*]

Seaumais Ruaidh—See "Jacob MacKenzie" and "Jamie Fraser." (Jacobus is the Latin name equivalent of James, so both Jacob and James are treated the same in terms of translation.)

Seona—A Scottish woman with a lazy eye from Surry County, and cousin to Archie, Hilda McGillivray's husband; her name is mentioned as a possible bride for Ronnie Sinclair. [*Ashes*]

Seppings—The butler at Lavender House, a meeting place for homosexual men. [*PM*]

Sequoyah—A Cherokee who brought the bones of a dead settler to Jamie to prove the Cherokee were not killing settlers. [*Ashes*]

Shaffstall, Abe—A militiaman who kindly shares food and drink with Lord John, after he is discovered by the Reverend Woodsworth's militia company. [*MOBY*]

Shelby—A parlor maid employed at Fanshawe's manor, she relayed information to Barbara regarding the severity of Marcus Fanshawe's injuries. [*HS*]

Sheridan, Lady—A woman attending the wedding of Benedicta Grey and General Sir George Stanley. She gives Lord John a flirtatious smile over her fan while he's attempting to alert a woman—any woman—to Olivia's distress due to her advanced pregnancy. [*BL*]

Sheriff of Orange County; David Anstruther—He carries a letter from Governor Tryon to the Regulators, telling them to disassemble and go home or else prepare to fight. [*Fiery Cross*]

Sherston, Hubert—An acquaintance of Jocasta Cameron. After Roger's terrible ordeal at Alamance, he is carried to the Sherstons' home in Hillsborough, to recuperate. [*Fiery Cross*]

Sherston, Phoebe (identified as Penelope in early editions)—The impulsive wife of Hubert Sherston, she appears after the Battle of Alamance with food, then offers her Hillsborough home to Roger and Brianna while Roger recuperates from his near-death experience; Brianna has been commissioned to paint the portrait of Mrs. Sherston, so she and Roger stay until he's able to be moved. [*Fiery Cross*]

x **Shippen, Edward**—(1729–1806) Philadelphia Loyalist and father of Peggy Shippen. [*MOBY*]

x **Shippen, Peggy**—(1760–1804) Born into a prominent Philadelphia family, she helped Peggy Chew and John André with the decorations for the mischianza; she later became the second wife of Benedict Arnold, shortly before he switched sides and became a traitor to the Continental army. In our story, we see her briefly when Claire is summoned (by Benedict Arnold, then a friend of the Shippen family) to attend Peggy's cousin, Tench Bledsoe, who has been attacked and badly injured by the Sons of Liberty in Philadelphia. Claire observes the young Miss Shippen's eyeing of General Arnold, like that of "a fisherman who has just seen a fat trout swim right under the lure." [*Echo, MOBY*]

Sholto, Mr.—Owner of one of the largest apothecaries in Philadelphia, he supplies Lord John—and thereby Claire—with the vitriol (sulfuric acid) for the creation of the ether to be used on both Henri-Christian and Henry Grey. [*Echo*]

Shoreditch, Jebediah, Corporal—A Continental soldier wounded after bravely charging the Great Redoubt at Saratoga; he is recuperating but, due to his injuries, needs help attending to the call of nature. [*Echo*]

Sibelius, Dr.—The doctor who was caring for Governor Martin's wife in New Bern prior to Claire's arrest, he is a proponent of bloodletting and dosing his pregnant patient with laudanum, practices that Claire frowns upon. [*Ashes*]

Simmonds—One of the surgeons assigned to Hal's regiment in Prussia. [*BL*]

Simms, Fogarty—Proprietor of the *Chronicle,* the local newspaper for Cross Creek.

When a riotious crowd tries to tar-and-feather him for publishing unpopular opinions, Jamie Fraser comes to his aid, distracting the crowd. His efforts are aided by Fergus, who slashes a feather mattress and rains feathers over the astonished crowd, enabling Jamie to snatch Simms away to safety. [*Ashes*]

Simon and Peter—Germain Fraser's pet frogs—one green and one yellow—which he tosses in Percy Wainwright's path on the Wilmington docks. [*Echo*]

Simpson, Mr.—An official employed at the Arsenal at Woolwich, where Lord John has been summoned for a royal inquiry. [*HS*]

Simpson, Mrs. (Zachary)—Wife of the farmer storing Jamie's printing press, and breeder of the short-legged chicken known as the Scots Dumpy. [*MOBY*]

Simpson, Zachary—A farmer outside Savannah, Georgia, hired by Richard Bell to store Jamie's printing press in his barn. [*MOBY*]

Sinclair, Ronnie—A bachelor and one of the ex-prisoners from Ardsmuir who make Fraser's Ridge their home; a cooper by trade, his skill in making whisky casks earns him land and a shop—which is a focus for gossip and news from the surrounding countryside. [*Fiery Cross, Ashes*]

Sister Amos—The head nurse when Claire was a nurse during WWII. [*MOBY*]

Sister Anne-Joseph—One of the nuns who work in the stable. She warns Sister Gregory (Joan), who is helping with the milking, that Mirabeau the cow has a bad temper and has kicked three nuns and spilled the milk twice in less than a week. [*SB*]

Sister Eudoxia—An elderly Anglican nun and distant relative of Lady Dunsany's, Jamie met her when she stayed at Helwater for a time; she explained to Jamie about "fridstools" as a solitary place of meditation and reflection. [*SP*]

Sister Eustacia—The senior nun in charge of the postulants at the Convent of Angels. [*SB*]

Sister George—The stout nun from the Convent of Angels who carries the household fund to the market, zealously protecting it—and the food it purchases—against pickpockets and thieves. [*SB*]

Sister Gregory—See "Joan MacKimmie."

Sister Jeanne-Marie—One of the nuns who is upset after Mirabeau kicks not only the nuns but the milk pail, as well. [*SB*]

Sister Marie Romaine—A nun at Brianna's parochial school, who cautioned that Catholics were not allowed to do divination of any kind because it was a seduction of the devil; the nun's warning worked well for Bree, preventing her from having her college friend read her tarot cards. [*Fiery Cross*]

Sister Marie-Amadeus—One of the supervisory nuns at L' Hôpital des Anges, she directs the postulants on their duties. [*SB*]

Sister Mathilde—A nun from le Couvent des Anges. [*SB*]

Sister Miséricorde de Dieu; Mercy—One of the postulants at le Couvent des Anges. [*SB*]

Sister Philomène—A timid young nun who blushes easily. [*SB*]

Siverly, Gerald, Major—Charlie Carruthers's commanding officer in Canada, he is cruel and corrupt, raiding and plundering the villages. Instead of sharing the bounty with his men, as is the army's custom, he withholds it to sell in the private market, then begins to withhold the soldiers' pay, causing his men to mutiny and physically protest his practices. Carruthers, knowing he hasn't long to live, has compiled a damning dossier of Siverly's crimes, which he confides to his good friend (and onetime lover) John Grey, saying that he trusts Lord John to see justice done. John is determined to do just that, despite the slightly awkward fact that Siverly saved his life during the Battle of Quebec, and he shows the dossier to his brother, Hal, who—a career soldier and the colonel of his own regiment—is shocked and infuriated, then determines to convict Siverly of his crimes. To this end, he dragoons Jamie Fraser, a prisoner of war, to accompany John to Ireland and bring Siverly back to face court-martial. Their attempt is foiled by Siverly's murder. There are several suspects (Lord John himself is arrested on suspicion, he having found the body), but the crime is ultimately proved to have been committed by Jamie's erstwhile Irish Jacobite friend Tobias Quinn. [*CA, SP*]

Siverly, Marcus—Gerald Siverly's father. One of the Wild Geese—the Irish brigades that fought for the Stuarts during the Williamite wars of the late-seventeenth century. [*SP*]

Siverly, Mrs.—The estranged wife of Gerald Siverly. She moved back to live with her parents when her husband was sent to Canada, and she stayed with them after her husband's return. [*SP*]

Siward—One of the characters in Shakespeare's "Scottish play," *Macbeth,* and possibly the secret name given to Victor Arbuthnot by other conspirators involved in the Jacobite plot to kill King George and sit James Stuart in his place. [*BL*]

Six Turtles—One of the Montauk Five, a group of twentieth-century Native American purists who disappeared in 1968. [*Fiery Cross*]

Sleeps with Snakes—One of Ian's Mohawk comrades and a renowned storyteller for the tribe. [*Ashes*]

Smith, John—See "Bill Marsden."

Smith, Watson, Colonel—Smith is a turncoat, a British officer who has taken service with the Continental army. Lord John meets him when the militiamen who took him from Jamie Fraser bring him to their commanding officer—Smith, whom Lord John last met over cucumber sandwiches in his sister-in-law's drawing room. The slight social awkwardness of this meeting is quickly submerged by the real possibility that John may be hanged as a spy once Smith sends him to General Wayne—and by the interesting fact that John feels a considerable physical attraction to Smith. Neither hanging nor seduction lies in the cards, though, as John's niece, Dorothea, helps him to escape before either possibility can eventuate. [*MOBY*]

Soeur Immaculata—Mother Superior at the Ursuline convent where William spends his winter while in Quebec with Captain Randall-Isaacs; she claims to know Lord John, who possibly met her when he was part of the invading force during the Battle of Quebec in September of 1759. [*Echo*]

Sophronia—Young slave belonging to Mr. Bradshaw; she suffers from an embarrassing fistula that occurred while she attempted to give birth to her owner's child. [*MOBY*]

Sorrel, Mr.—A Philadelphia neighbor of Fergus's family, and also an annoying and ardent admirer of Fergus's wife, Marsali. [*MOBY*]

x **Spencer, Joseph, Colonel**—(1714–1789) An obstinate old soldier and veteran of two previous colonial wars. He's a friend of Hal's, who warns William not to play cards with the wily old colonel. [*Echo*]

Springer, Robert—See "Otter-Tooth."

Sprocket, Mrs.—Wife of William Sprocket. [*MOBY*]

Sprocket, William—Fellow Quaker; he and his wife were forced from meeting, but they support Denzell and Dottie (and Rachel and Ian) in their desire to marry. [*MOBY*]

x **St. Clair, Arthur, General**—(1737–1818) Head of the New Jersey militia, who attained the rank of general in the Continental army; after the humiliation of abandoning Fort Ticonderoga to British General Burgoyne's forces, he was court-martialed for the loss but was exonorated during the trial. Jamie Fraser, present during the lead-up to the attack on Ticonderoga, had frequent arguments with St. Clair over his incompetent preparation. [*Echo*]

x **St. Germain, Robert François Quesnay de** (aka Comte St. Germain)[1]—A very mysterious man, once a member of Louis's French court; a noble with a reputation for dabbling in the occult and Prince Charles Stuart's business partner; he is also suspected of being the secret biological father of Fergus "Claudel" Fraser. Different accounts also give the family name as Rakoczy, and the Comte is reported on (vaguely) from a number of different locations in Europe over a surprising span of time—not all that surprising, given his capacity for time travel. [*Echo*]

x **St. Leger, Barry, Colonel**—(1733–1789) Officer selected by General Burgoyne to lead combined forces of two thousand men in the western offensive for the Saratoga campaign, a large number of Joseph Brant's Mohawks being part of this contingency. After several difficulties, St. Leger attempted to rejoin Burgoyne's main army at Saratoga but only got as far as Fort Ticonderoga before Burgoyne surrendered his army in September 1777. [*Echo*]

Stactoe, Lieutenant—A surgeon with the Continental army at Fort Ticonderoga, he is more concerned with keeping Claire away from the patients and his instruments than with the cleanliness of his instruments and welfare of his patients. [*Echo*]

Stan—The builder hired by Brianna to renovate and update Lallybroch after the MacKenzies return to the twentieth century. [*Ashes*]

Standing Bear—One of the Cherokee elders from Bird's tribe; he receives the honor of possessing one of the rifles that Jamie has promised Bird. [*Ashes*]

Stanhope, Lloyd—One of Phillip Wylie's friends and cohorts at Jocasta and Duncan's wedding. While also quite prosperous, Stanhope is more subdued than Wylie in his dress; he's amused by Wylie's attraction to the much older Claire—and by her disdainful reaction. [*Fiery Cross*]

Stanley, George, General, Sir—Third husband to Benedicta Grey and stepfather to Lord John, Hal; he's also stepfather to Percy Wainwright, son of Stanley's deceased first wife. [*BL, HS, SP, Echo*]

Stapleton, Neil; Neil the Cunt (aka Goldie-Locks)—A secretary for Hubert Bowles; he keeps a secret life as a homosexual man employed by a government official. [*PM, BL, HS*]

[1] *The Comte St. Germain was indeed a real historical person, but his origins, reputation, and activities are sufficiently mysterious as to admit of a good deal of novelistic license.*

x **Stark, John, Colonel**—(1728–1822) Later promoted to brigadier general, Stark gained fame due to his cry before the attack on Baum's Hessian dragoons at the Battle of Bennington, proclaiming victory or his wife would become a widow. He is also one of several officers present at Bunker Hill credited with giving the instruction, "Don't fire until you see the whites of their eyes!" [*Ashes, Echo*]

x **Stark, Molly**—(1737–1814) The wife of Colonel John Stark, she gained fame due to her husband's cry before the Bennington attack on Baum's Hessian dragoons, proclaiming victory or his wife would become a widow. [*Echo*]

Stebbings, Worth, Captain—Captain of the British naval cutter *Pitt,* he boards the *Teal* with the intention to press its men—including Ian and Jamie—into His Majesty's navy. [*Echo*]

Steffens, Kaptain—An officer in von Namtzen's regiment. [*SU*]

Stern, Laurence—A German Jewish naturalist who meets Claire in a mangrove swamp on Hispaniola, when she flees the *Porpoise* in search of Jamie. Jamie has heard of the philosopher during his conversations with Lord John during his own captivity. [*Fiery Cross, Echo, SP*]

Still Water—Brother to Cherokee chief Tsisqua (Bird-who-sings-in-the-morning) and war chief for the village. [*Echo*]

Stoelers, Herman—The lean, pleasant manager of Beardsley's trading post in the backcountry of the Carolina mountains. (Also, coincidentally, the name of the husband of my good friend, Elva Stoelers.) [*MOBY*]

Stokes, Iphigenia—Timothy O'Connell's London mistress. She is a woman of Greek descent, a seamstress, and one of a family of petty smugglers of contraband goods but not smuggled secrets, though she is known to Hubert Bowles and his Black Chamber. [*PM*]

Stornaway, Mr.—A resident of Fraser's Ridge who passes a stone; the stone is later shown to Jem and Germain. [*Ashes*]

Stoughton, Howard—Master founder of the Royal Armory, he has been at the heart of a plot to steal copper from army artillery to sell to the British navy at a profit. [*HS*]

Strasse, Heinrich—A suitor for Senga McGillivray's hand. He is dashing and handsome but also a poor Lutheran; still, strong-willed Senga chooses him as her husband over her mother's favored suitor, Ronnie Sinclair. [*Ashes*]

Strong Walker—One of the Montauk Five, a group of twentieth-century Native American purists who disappeared in 1968. [*Fiery Cross*]

x **Stuart, Charles Edward** (aka Prince Tearlach)—(1720–1788) The Young Pretender; Bonnie Prince Charlie; son of James (III of England, VII of Scotland). Heir to the exiled Catholic royal dynasty, in 1745 he attempted to invade and overthrow British rule in Scotland. Despite leading over six thousand loyal Scottish troops to battle, he suffered the worst defeat on native soil, at Culloden Moor on April 16, 1746, when the Duke of Cumberland crushed the Scots using superior artillery firepower across an open battlefield. When it became clear his cause was defeated, Charles abandoned his troops and fled for the coast, where he escaped to Italy and lived out his days in exile. [*SP, All*]

x **Stuart, John**—(1718–1779) A former militia captain, Stuart gained valuable knowledge working with the Native Americans and was appointed by the British government as superintendent in the Indian Department to oversee relations with all the southern tribes; he was so successful that when the Revolutionary War broke out, most of the tribes in the area supported the British. [*Ashes*]

Stubbs—Owner of a Fleet Street printing shop where copies of Harry Quarry's book of erotic poetry could be purchased (no apparent relation to Malcolm Stubbs). [*SP*]

Stubbs, Bryce—Malcolm's brother with the Forty-sixth Foot (soldiers), stationed in Calcutta as part of Robert Clive's assault against the Nawab of Bengal. [*PM*]

Stubbs, Cromwell Percival John Malcolm—The name given to Olivia Stubbs's baby, in honor of the two men who helped deliver him—John and Percy—as well as in reference to Oliver Cromwell, whom John jokingly told his cousin Olivia her newborn son resembled. [*BL, CA*]

Stubbs, Malcolm, Captain—An officer in Lord John's regiment, he later marries John's cousin, Olivia, but is assigned to duty in Canada before their first child is born. He also has an illegitimate child with an Indian mistress in Canada, but he abandons the boy when he is seriously wounded during the Battle of Quebec and is subsequently sent back to England. (Lord John takes the boy after the death of his mother from smallpox and confides him to the care of a Catholic orphanage, giving him the name John Cinnamon, for the color of his hair.) [*PM, BL, CA*]

Stubbs, Melissa—Malcolm's twin sister, whom Malcolm is eager to introduce to Lord John as a possible match. [*PM*]

Stubbs, Olivia (aka Olivia Pearsall)—Lord John's cousin, formerly Olivia Pearsall. Orphaned as a child, she is Hal's ward and lives with John and Hal's mother, Benedicta Grey. She was betrothed to Joseph Trevelyan when she was sixteen, but the contract was canceled; she later marries Malcolm Stubbs, a lieutenant in Lord John's regiment, who is assigned duty in Canada. She gives birth to their first child under the organ loft during the wedding ceremony for Benedicta and Sir George Stanley. [*PM, BL, HS, CA*]

Stummle—The mute doorkeep at Magda's brothel; *stumm* is the German word for "dumb" (mute), so the name is appropriate and a key to the doorman's discretion. [*PM*]

Sub-Genius—Harry Quarry's secret pen name, used when composing erotic poetry. [*BL*]

Suddfield, Horace—The owner of the South American electric eel and the one who encourages Lord John to participate and grab the tail of the eel—which thereby sends an electric current through more than forty people at Lady Joffrey's party. [*CA*]

Sukie—One of Governor Martin's servants at the Governor's Palace in New Bern, she agrees to sneak Claire's messages out of the palace to Fergus's printshop. [*Ashes*]

Sun Elk (aka Ahkote'ohskennonton)—A jealous Mohawk warrior who covets Emily and marries her sister, Looking at the Sky, just to be near Emily; his wife is later abducted by an enemy tribe, leaving him a single man again. After Ian is forced to leave the tribe, Sun Elk quickly marries Emily and establishes a family with her. Although Emily may still love Ian, the ease with which Sun Elk fathers

Emily's children is a blow to Ian's self-esteem and something that Sun Elk uses to gloat, causing further friction between Ian and the Mohawk. [*Ashes, Echo*]

Sungi—One of Tsatsa'wi's sisters at the Cherokee village. [*Fiery Cross*]

Susan—A prostitute employed at the MacNabs' London brothel. [*BL*]

Sutherland, Geordie—A young male resident of Fraser's Ridge, mentioned by a group of young unmarried girls playing a marriage prediction game during Hogmanay at the Big House. [*Fiery Cross*]

Sutherland, Lord—A friend of William's, an officer with the British troops withdrawing from Philadelphia. William asks Sutherland's groom to tend his horses so that his own groom, Zeb, can go to the surgeon to have a horse bite dressed. [*MOBY*]

Swiftest of Lizards (aka Digger)—The Mohawk name given to Emily's son by Ian, after he declares that he will bless all of her children but the boy is his to name. The Mohawk believe that the boy is the son of Ian's spirit, though he may or may not be Ian's biological child. [*Echo*]

Sydell, Bernard, Colonel—An elderly commander of Hal's regiment during his absence, he is strict and crotchety, knows little about his troops, and shows little interest in the men under his command. [*PM*]

Sylvie, Mrs.—The madam of a Cross Creek brothel and well acquainted with Ian, she allows Claire to treat her "girls" with penicillin after exposure to someone known to be infected with syphilis. Ian brings the orphans Hermione and Trudy to her to tame and teach them to be maids. [*Ashes, Echo, MOBY*]

Symington, Ewart, Colonel—The second regimental colonel, he ranks just below Harry Quarry, who is the first regimental colonel of the Forty-sixth. [*BL*]

T

Talks with Spirits—One of the Montauk Five, a group of twentieth-century Native American purists who disappeared in 1968. [*Fiery Cross*]

Talltree, Robert—Cherokee village elder in Tsisqua's village, he appears astonished by a dazed Jamie's tale of killing fourteen men on Culloden Moor. Talltree blows smoke from the sacred pipe over Jamie, to cleanse the darkness from his soul and to show respect to the Scottish warrior. [*Ashes*]

x **Tarleton, Banastre, Lieutenant Colonel**—(1754–1833) An ambitious British soldier, his outstanding abilities as a cavalryman and leader allowed him to work his way up through the ranks. Considered ruthless and somewhat cruel to both man and animal, historians gave him the title of "Bloody Ban" and "The Butcher," due to his actions at the Battle of Waxhaws, where he and his men mercilessly killed the retreating Patriot forces. Prior to this, he has a notable run-in with William over a girl. Having caught sight of Jane and made overtures to her, Tarleton is told that she's under William's protection. When William admits that this is the case, Tarleton offers to fight him for the girl—and does. The fight is interrupted by the appearance of Continental soldiers, and the young men part, but no bad blood is in evidence when Tarleton comes to William's tent the next morning—looking rather the worse for wear—to tell the wounded William that Tarleton has recovered William's stolen horse. Despite his violent reputation, Tarleton doesn't hold grudges. [*Echo, MOBY*]

Tarleton, Berkeley, Major—The father of Richard Tarleton, Lord John's ensign during his campaign in Prussia. [*SP*]

Tarleton, Richard, Lieutenant—Cousin of Banastre Tarleton, Richard was previously Lord John's ensign at Crefeld during the Seven Years' War. [*BL, CA, SP, Echo*]

Taylor, Captain—Captain of a lobster fishing boat with a flair for Gaelic cursing, for whom Roger worked when he was a young man in Inverness. [*Echo*]

Taylor, Henry, General—A field general of militia, who inconveniently dies just as the British prepare to withdraw from Philadelphia. Knowing a battle is imminent and desperately needing an experienced officer to take charge of Taylor's miscellaneous militia companies, George Washington gratefully seizes Daniel Morgan's suggestion that Jamie Fraser succeed Taylor—a suggestion that Jamie is unable to reject, much as he'd like to. [*MOBY*]

x **Teague, Joshua**—(ca. 1732–1804) One of the Regulators identified by Waightstill Avery in his deposition before Justice William Harris; he was recognized and excluded from Governor Tryon's pardon following the Battle of Alamance. [*Fiery Cross*]

Tearlach, Prince—See "Charles Stuart."

Tebbe—One of Claire's captors and a member of Hodgepile's gang of bandits, he believes that Claire holds some sort of spiritual power and tries to protect her from the other members of the group, asking her to remember his kindness so her spirits won't harm him. [*Ashes*]

Teresa—One of Jocasta Cameron's house slaves. She was caring for Betty, the slave found drunk and doped with laudanum on the evening of Jocasta and Duncan's wedding, but eventually she has another slave seek out Claire's assistance. [*Fiery Cross*]

Tess—Last legal wife of Toby Quinn, she left him after Culloden, without a divorce. [*SP*]

Tewaktenyonh—Sister of war chief and sachem in the Mohawk village where Roger is held captive, she is an elderly woman who befriends Claire and tells her the story of Otter-Tooth. She is also Emily's grandmother and the one who tells Ian to leave the village after so many failed pregnancies with Emily. [*Fiery Cross, Ashes, Echo*]

Tewkes, Peter—A friend of Lord John's who dies of syphilis while using the mercury treatment for the disease. [*PM*]

x **Thacher, James, Major**—(1754–1844) Prominent surgeon in the Continental army, he wrote several books regarding his experiences treating the wounded during the Revolutionary War. Claire becomes familiar with his work during the Monmouth campaign. [*Echo*]

Thackeray, Anne—After her father, a Sussex minister, breaks off her attachment with Philip Lister, she elopes with him instead. The scandal causes her family to disown her; she is left pregnant, alone, and destitute when Lister is killed during war in Prussia. [*HS*]

Thackeray, Barbara—Daughter of a Sussex minister, she wishes to help her disowned sister, Anne, and gives Lord John some limited information to help his investigation into Anne's whereabouts. [*HS*]

Thackeray, Reverend Mr.—Father of Barbara and Anne, the girl who eloped with Philip Lister; he disowns his daughter and, rather than taking her and her child in upon Philip's death, sanctimoniously refuses all contact with her. [*HS*]

x **Thayendanegea**—See "Joseph Brant."

Thomas—One of Dougal MacKenzie's men in 1739, when Dougal is summoned by Angus MacLaren to come and have a look at the two suspicious strangers: Roger and Buck. [*MOBY*]

Thomas—A footman at the Jermyn Street home of Benedicta Grey, Lord John's mother. [*PM*]

Thomas—One of Princess von Lowenstein's footmen. [SU]

x **Thomson, Robert**—One of the Regulators identified by Waightstill Avery in his deposition before Justice William Harris. [*Fiery Cross*]

x **Thynne, Thomas**—(1734–1796) Viscount Weymouth, secretary of state (of England) for the Southern Department, responsible for foreign relations with the American colonies as well as with all the Catholic and Muslim countries of Europe—at least until 1768, when relations with the American colonies shifted to the Northern Department. [*Echo*]

Tinsdale—The cook on Governor Martin's ship, the *Cruizer*. He is a free black man who treats Claire kindly when the governor brings her aboard after fleeing New Bern. [*Ashes*]

Tolliver, Doc—One of the physicians working with Claire and Denzell Hunter to treat the wounded Patriots after the battles of Saratoga. [*Echo*]

Tolliver, Maisie, Mrs.—The wife of New Bern's sheriff, she sees to the care of the female prisoners but is also a drunkard and will do almost anything for a price; she summons Claire to be midwife when a prisoner accused of killing her children is giving birth to her latest child. [*Ashes*]

Tolliver, Sheriff—The sheriff of New Bern, not very popular but one of the last law-enforcement officers in the area during the state of rebellion, all of the others having fled or been taken by mobs. [*Ashes*]

Tomlinson, Mr.—A wealthy member of Parliament. He is married to Susannah, who is unfaithful to him, involved in a love affair with Captain Michael Bates. [*BL*]

Tomlinson, Susannah, Mrs.—A married woman and mistress to Captain Bates, who is sentenced to hang for sodomy and treason. [*BL*]

x **Tomlinson, Turner**—(unknown) One of the Regulators in North Carolina. When detained and questioned by Governor Tryon, he admitted nothing except his inclusion as one of the Regulators. [*Fiery Cross*]

Tommy—A young slave boy at River Run, Jocasta Cameron's plantation. [*Fiery Cross*]

Townsend, Mr.—A resident of Cross Creek and a visitor at River Run who is robbed by Wendigo Donner, a time traveler; Townsend wants the culprit tried as soon as possible and requests magistrate Farquard Campbell to sit as justice on his behalf. [*Ashes*]

x **Tracy, Andrew Hodges, Lieutenant**—(unknown) An Irish officer from Major Ebenezer Stevens's artillery battalion. Disguised and purported to be a British spy, Tracy was placed in a cell with a captured British regular to obtain any information on British movements. During a night of jovial conversation, Tracy discovered the location and strength of Burgoyne's forces, which was then provided to General St. Clair. [*Echo*]

Tranter, Will—A locksmith near Lallybroch. Brianna calls him to come and change the locks at the estate, following Rob Cameron's intrusion, but Tranter leaves a note saying that he's been delayed on another job. This causes Bree to take the children to Fiona for safekeeping. [*MOBY*]

Travers, Howard—Local sheriff of Drunkard's Creek, who has let the power of his office go to his head, turning a blind eye to crime and instead greedily evicting residents for inability to pay their taxes; once the property is vacant, Travers distributes it as he sees fit—namely, to his family members. [*Fiery Cross*]

Trevelyan, Joseph, the Honorable—A Cornish nobleman possessing a large fortune from tin mines, with family connections in Parliament; heavily invested in the East India Company and possibly infected with syphilis. He is also engaged to marry Lord John's young orphaned cousin, Olivia Pearsall. [*PM, BL*]

Trevorson, Squire—Owner of Mayapple Farm and a neighbor to Edgar DeVane. Trevorson's gunpowder mill comprises one-third of the Sussex consortium headed by Edgar, Lord John's older stepbrother. [*HS*]

Trowbridge, Mr.—Lord Dunsany's solicitor living in Bowness-on-Windermere, he was chosen to handle the matter of Lord John's guardianship of William, the Ninth Earl of Ellesmere, due to a conflict of interest with the Dunsanys' local solicitor. [*SP*]

x **Tryon, William, Governor**—(1729–1788) Royal governor of the colony of North Carolina and an important ally—or dangerous foe—to Jamie and Claire Fraser; he charges Jamie with the task of forming a militia to support the British during the War of the Regulation. [*Fiery Cross, Ashes*]

Tsatsa'wi—Peter Bewlie's Cherokee brother-in-law, who indicates that Jamie, "Bear-Killer," and Claire, "White Raven," will have the power to kill the mystical white bear terrorizing his village and people. [*Fiery Cross*]

Tsisqua—See "Bird-who-sings-in-the-morning."

x **Tullibardine, Earl of**—(1689–1746) William Murray, second son of the Duke of Atholl, was a Jacobite supporter of Charles Stuart and the Rising but was later executed and excluded from succession for his participation. [*SP*]

Tweedledum & Tweedledee—Claire's nicknames for the chairmen (apparently brothers) who carry Hal's sedan chair in Philadelphia. [*MOBY*]

Twelvetrees, Edward—One of three brothers who have had entanglements with the Grey brothers several times in the past; Edward is killed in a London duel by Lord John. [*SP, PZ*]

Twelvetrees, Nancy; Nan—Sister to Philip Twelvetrees, she had been courted in London by Derwent Warren, who set her aside for an heiress. She went to Jamaica with her brother to get over the upset, only to find that Warren was the new governor for the island. [*PZ*]

Twelvetrees, Nathaniel—A former captain of the Thirty-second Foot. He backed a wager at White's indicating that Gerard Grey, the Duke of Pardloe, was indeed a traitor. Twelvetrees later died in a duel with the duke's son, Hal, after Hal discovered that Twelvetrees had seduced his wife, Esmé. [*BL, CA, SP, PZ*]

Twelvetrees, Philip—The new owner of a Jamaican plantation, previously owned by his recently deceased cousin, Edward Twelvetrees. [*PZ*]

Twelvetrees, Reginald, Colonel—Assigned to the Royal Artillery regiment with very influential friends, he was one of the three members of the military tribunal investigating Lord John's part in the explosion of a cannon during the Battle of Crefeld; there are extenuating hostilities between the Grey family and the Twelvetrees family—namely that Hal, Lord John's older brother, killed the colonel's younger brother Nathaniel in a duel several years prior. [*BL, HS, CA, SP*]

Two Spears—The Mohawk war chief of the village where Roger was held captive and the one who ordered Father Alexandre to be burned at the stake. [*Echo*]

U

Ulysses (aka Joseph)—Jocasta Cameron's butler and her secret lover for over twenty years. He was born a freeman, enslaved as a child, and renamed "Ulysses" by the schoolmaster who purchased him. An educated man, fluent in French and English and able to read both Greek and Latin, he becomes the eyes and keeper of secrets for his mistress when she loses her sight. Although she has never seen his face, Jocasta says that he smells like light. [*Fiery Cross, Ashes*]

Uncle Joe—See "Dr. Joseph Abernathy."

Uncle Lamb—See "Quentin Lambert Beauchamp."

Unwin, the Misses—The Quaker daughters of Mr. Unwin; William met them once, at a musicale, although neither religion nor philosophical differences were discussed. [*Echo*]

Unwin, Mr.—A wealthy merchant and head of a Quaker family in Virginia, with whom William is acquainted because they are friends of Lord John. [*Echo*]

Unwin, Priscilla—A London acquaintance of both Lady Dorothea and Dr. Denzell Hunter. [*Echo*]

x **Urmstone, the Reverend Mr.**—(ca. 1685–1772) John Urmstone was one of the earliest Anglican ministers in North Carolina, arriving prior to 1710; he was originally a missionary in the Ablemarle area and preached on the sins of man, often targeting specific members of the congregation as examples of sinful behavior. [*Fiery Cross*]

V

van Humperdinck, Henryk, Dr.—A London doctor specializing in mental issues, especially depression. He is found near death in the street outside White's, where patrons are busy taking bets regarding the victim's prognosis rather than seeking help. After John is wounded in Prussia, Lord and Lady Stanley urge him to consult with Humperdinck regarding his lingering depression, but they tell John that the doctor is a chest specialist. [*BL*]

Venus—An ill-tempered pony used by the Dunsanys to pull the pony trap, a small two-wheeled carriage. [*SP*]

x **Vergennes, Monsieur**—(1717–1787) French foreign minister during the American Revolution and a silent partner in the Hortalez et Cie company, which was really a front for supplying the Americans with arms and ammunition. [*Echo*]

Vermin/Trudy; Ermintrude Kuykendall—One of two young ragamuffin boys who attempt to rob the Frasers on their way to New Bern; Ian is nominated to try to locate their relatives near Bailey Camp. During the journey, it's discovered that the "boys" are actually girls in disguise; when Ian can't find any relations of the children, he takes them to Mrs. Sylvie's brothel in Cross Creek and pays her to "tame" the girls and make them housemaids. He later encounters Ermintrude and her sister, Hermione, as the Wurm brothers, at Beardsley's trading post. (See also "Herman/Hermione Kuykendall.") [*Echo*]

Vickers, Mr.—A pink-cheeked young man about eighteen years old, one of Governor Tryon's aides-de-camp at Alamance. The governor directs him to assist Claire in carrying buckets of water; he's later dispatched to fetch the governor's horse after Jamie's Highland screech causes it to rear, unseating the governor. [*Fiery Cross*]

Visigoth; Goth—One of William's horses. A massive gelding, Goth carries William to battle at Monmouth. When William is thumped over the head and thrown off a bridge by Hessian mercenaries, Goth goes missing but is retrieved by Banastre Tarleton, who returns him to William. [*MOBY*]

x **Voltaire**—(1694–1778) Born François-Marie Arouet, he was a French philosopher, writer, and frequent guest of intellectual salons in France during the Enlightenment period of the eighteenth century; he was also in attendance at the salon Jamie attends in Paris with Mr. Lyles. [*Echo*]

x **von Knyphausen, Wilhelm, General**—(1716–1800) Commander of a body of Hessian troops under the overall command of Sir Henry Clinton. Von Knyphausen's troops were to help protect refugees and provide additional support to Clinton's troops during the British withdrawal from Philadelphia and thus took part in the subsequent Battle of Monmouth, when Washington's troops pursued and attacked the retreating British army. [*MOBY*]

von Lowenstein, Gertrude, Dowager Princess—Princess Louisa's mother and Stephan's mother-in-law; she is an elderly but feisty woman, very protective of her family and susceptible to local superstitions. [*SU, BL*]

von Lowenstein, Louisa, Princess (aka Gräfin von Erdberg)—A wealthy widow and single mother hungry for a husband, at one time she had her eyes on both Lord John and von Namtzen. She eventually marries the widower Stephan von Namtzen, gaining the title Gräfin von Erdberg. [*SU, BL, SP*]

von Lowenstein, Siegfried; Siggy—The young son of Princess von Lowenstein; he is almost abducted by a supposed "witch." [*SU, SP*]

x **von Munchausen, Captain**—(1720–1797) Von Munchausen was actually one of Sir Henry Clinton's aides-de-camp at the time of the Battle of Monmouth. He's better known as a teller of extravagant tales and has given his name to an interesting psychological disorder in consequence. [*MOBY*]

von Namtzen, Stephan, Graf (aka Graf von Erdberg)—A Hanovarian baron and captain in command of a regiment assisting England in the Seven Years' War. He and Lord John form a close friendship during the Seven Years' War, where they both sustain severe battle wounds, von Namtzen losing an arm and Lord John suffering shrapnel wounds; John recuperates at von Namtzen's lodge in Hanover. [*PM, SU, BL, HS, SP*]

x **von Riedesel, Frederika, Baroness**—(1746–1808) Wife of Hessian commander General Friedrich von Riedesel, the baroness showed her bravery and devotion to her husband when she traveled from England to Canada with her three children, all under the age of five. Her home at Saratoga was used as an infirmary, where General Simon Fraser was taken after being mortally wounded by an American rifleman. [*Echo*]

x **von Riedesel, Friedrich, Baron**—(1738–1800) German general in command of the Hessian troops assisting British General Burgoyne at Fort Ticonderoga in September 1777. When British General Simon Fraser was mortally wounded at Saratoga, von Riedesel volunteered his home to treat the general, who died shortly after being deposited on the baron's dining table. [*Echo*]

x **von Steuben, Friedrich Wilhelm**—(1730–1794) Prussian-born officer in the Continental army, he became inspector general; he trained the Continental army in military drills, tactics, and disciplines, and wrote a manual about military drills, which was used by the Americans until the War of 1812. [*Echo*]

W

x **Wade, General**—Referenced by Roger Wakefield during his search for Jem, as he trudges the Highlands of Scotland and recalls the poem, "If you had seen this road before it was made, you would throw up your hands and bless General Wade." The Irish general had been charged with building roads through the Highlands earlier in the eighteenth century. [*MOBY*]

x **Waddell, Hugh, General**—(1734–1773) The foremost British soldier in North Carolina, he led the militia—including Jamie's provincial forces—during the War of the Regulation. [*Fiery Cross*]

Wainwright, Jethro—An itinerant peddler who traveled the North Carolina wilderness, transporting packages and trade goods from the cities into the backcountry. [*Fiery Cross*]

Wainwright, Mrs.—Mother to Percy; she was briefly married to General Sir George Stanley before she stepped into the path of a coach and was run down, although Lord John's mother and third wife of General Stanley—Benedicta—believes the woman died of consumption. [*BL*]

Wainwright, Perseverance (commonly known as Percy; aka Percival Beauchamp)—He shares the secret of his birth name—Perseverance—only with Lord John Grey, his stepbrother by marriage, who becomes his lover and introduces him to a career as a soldier. Their relationship comes to an abrupt and sordid end when Percy is discovered *in flagrante* with a Hanoverian soldier in Prussia. Convicted of sodomy, he begs Lord John to save him. Percy's death in prison is faked with Lord John's help to avoid a scandal and dishonor to the family—and also because John can't see a man he loves die for a crime of which he is guilty himself. Percy escapes to Ireland and then to Rome, and we hear no more until John encounters him suddenly in North Carolina nearly twenty years later. At this point, we learn that Percy has married into a French noble family, adopted his wife's name, and has been working for some time for France's Black Chamber spy network. He has other ties to influential French "interests" and has come on their behalf to make an offer to the English government, using John as go-between. [*PM, BL, SP, Echo, MOBY*]

Wakefield, Mrs.; Gran—Marjorie's mother and wee Roger's grandmother; her brother is the Reverend Reginald Wakefield, who will one day become Roger's adoptive father. [*LW*]

Wakefield, Reginald, Reverend—A Presbyterian minister, historian, and friend of

Frank Randall, as well as Roger MacKenzie's adoptive father. His historical preference was for the eighteenth century, and since his pack-rat instincts caused him to store everything in the manse garage, there could be some very interesting information waiting for Roger and Brianna regarding her parents. [*All, LW*]

Wakyo'teyeshsnonhsa—see "Emily."

Waldemar, Herr—Reinhardt Mayrhofer's personal valet, who was in charge of procuring large quantities of shaving soap for his employer. [*PM*]

Walking Elk—See "Glutton."

Wallace, Grannie—Mother of Mrs. MacLaren. [*MOBY*]

x **Walpole, Horace; "Horey"**—(1717–1797) The son of Prime Minister Robert Walpole, he was a famous writer, friend, and lover to poet Thomas Gray and member of the House of Commons until he retired from his seat in 1768. He was also an inveterate gossip and a writer of witty, observant letters. Lord John overhears some of his unexpurgated opinions while John and Hal are suffering through George II's funeral obsequies. [*BL, SP*]

Walpole, Robert—(1676–1745) First prime minister of England and undisputed leader of the Hanoverian cabinet; godfather to Hal, the Duke of Pardloe. [*BL*]

Walsing, Colonel—An officer under Wolfe's command, he mentions to Lord John that Wolfe gave him a pendant to return to his fiancée's family in case Wolfe should fall in battle the following day. [*CA*]

Wardlaw, Mr.—A London shopkeeper and acquaintance of Jerry MacKenzie, he assures a devastated Jerry that Dolly and their son were not killed in the blast that demolished their home but were at Dolly's mother's home. [*LW*]

Warren, Derwent, Governor—Governor of Jamaica, corrupt in his professional life and an abuser of women, both gentlewomen and slaves; he is mysteriously killed and his body maimed by "zombies." [*PZ*]

Washington, Cartwright, Harrington, Carver—Mysterious Loyalists (possibly real-life characters) whom William is to rendezvous with in Dismal Town, on the edge of the Great Dismal Swamp. Unfortunately, William runs into troubles of his own and the meeting never takes place. [*Echo*]

x **Washington, George, General**—(1732–1799) A veteran of the French and Indian Wars and one of the Founding Fathers; when the Second Continental Congress convened in Philadelphia in 1775, he was appointed commander in chief of the Continental army, and in 1787 was elected as first U.S. president. Jamie meets him unexpectedly while trying to return to Claire in Philadelphia and is obliged to accept appointment as a field general in the Continental army. While Jamie is impressed by Washington, both as a man and a soldier, neither sentiment stops his resigning his commission—in blood—when Claire is shot at Monmouth. [*MOBY*]

Washington, Henry—William is given this name as a contact for his intelligence-gathering mission to Dismal Town and is staggered to be told by Ian Murray that the man is not a Loyalist, as he'd been informed, but almost certainly is a Rebel. [*Echo*]

Wattiswade, Raphael (aka Andrew Rennie)—A rare-book collector who uses this as a front for his duties as a spymaster; also father to Minnie Grey, the Duchess of Pardloe. [*SP*] x **Wayne, Anthony, General**—(1745–1796) General of the Continental forces, his fierce battle tactics and exploits—such as a bayonet-only night attack at the Battle of Stony Point—not only earned him respect from his men but also earned him the nickname of "Mad Anthony." [*Echo*]

Weatherspoon, Dr.—The rector at the Old High Church of St. Stephen's in Inverness, who gives says he'll pray for Roger to find his way back to his faith (or whatever he is lacking since his return to the twentieth century). [*Echo*]

Webb, George—Secretary to the last royal governor of North Carolina, Josiah Martin. [*Ashes*]

Weber, Ober-Lieutenant Michael (pronounced "Mee-chay-el")—A young Hanoverian officer from von Namtzen's regiment, he tells Lord John of von Namtzen's hunting accident and subsequent loss of his arm due to blood poisoning. More notably, he's caught having sex with Percy Wainwright and is executed for the crime of sodomy by his commanding officer, Stephan von Namtzen. [*BL*]

Wee Gilbert—See "La Fayette."

Weems, Sergeant-Major—One of the soldiers in Pardloe's regiment, who confiscates a large automated fortune-telling machine from the Irish O'Higgins brothers. [*BL*]

Weisenheimer, Mrs.—A German patient in Savannah whom Claire diagnosed as suffering from gallstones. [*MOBY*]

Welch, Private—A private under William's command on Long Island; he is placed under arrest by William for attempting to bargain for contraband brandy at a checkpoint the men were supposed to be guarding. [*Echo*]

Wellman, Mrs.—Widow of a Continental soldier after the evacuation of Fort Ticonderoga; her son—a patient of Claire's—may have the mumps. [*Echo*]

Wemyss, Becky—Rob Cameron's cousin and one of the dancers at the stones at Craigh na Dun. [*MOBY*]

Wemyss, Joseph—Lizzie's father, also a former bond servant and loyal friend of the Frasers; he is most displeased by his daughter's pregnancy and current bigamist marriage but has found happiness with his bride, Fraulein Monika Berrisch, and as "Opa" to Lizzie's children.[*All*]

Wemyss, Lizzie (aka Lizzie Wemyss Beardsley)—Brianna's former bond servant and current bigamist resident of Fraser's Ridge, she is married to both Josiah *and* Keziah Beardsley, identical twins with whom she fell in love and then became impregnated by; she doesn't know—or care—by which one. [*All*]

Wemyss, Monika—See "Monika Berrisch."

Wemyss, Rodney Joseph—The first child of Lizzie Wemyss Beardsley and either Josiah or Keziah Beardsley, her twin husbands. [*Ashes, Echo, MOBY*]

Weston, Mordecai, Captain—A member of the Third Regiment of Foot (infantry), commonly called "the Buffs" due to the buff-colored facings on their uniform coats. [*SP*]

Weston, Mrs.—Hal's housekeeper at Argus House. [*SP*]

Whelan, Mr.—A volunteer under Jamie's command at Monmouth. [*MOBY*]

x **Wherry, Kitman**—A Quaker and former Regulator from Salisbury. Jamie meets him and several other men on their way to a Committee of Correspondence meeting in Halifax, where Jamie knows delegates for the Continental Congress are to be chosen. [*Ashes*]

Whewell, Captain—One of the captains under Jamie's command at Monmouth. [*MOBY*]

Whibley, Mr.—Young Benjamin Grey's tutor, who was hired to teach him the basics of Latin but has perhaps been enlightening him in more-base studies. [*SP*]

x **Whitcomb, Benjamin**—(1737–1828) Captain and leader of Whitcomb's Rangers, who functioned primarily as scouts and spies under the direction of General Gates; one of a breed of men called "Long Hunters," known for their ability to live off the land for weeks at a time without human contact. [*Echo*]

Whitbread—A member of White's wagering that the person lying in the gutter outside White's was dead. [*BL*]

x **Whitehead, Paul**—(unknown–1774) A minor poet, he was the secretary and steward of Sir Francis Dashwood's Hellfire Club. Upon his death, his heart was left to Dashwood, who kept it in a special urn; his ghost is said to haunt the Hellfire Caves of West Wycombe Park. [*HF*]

White Raven—The name given to Claire as the result of a dream by the Tuscarora medicine woman Nayawenne. [*Fiery Cross*]

Whitey and Mike—Two mules in the stables of Lord Dunsany. Jamie uses Whitey in an emergency "rescue" of the disillusioned Lady Isobel from a possible scandal and a real rape at the hands of her wicked suitor, the bigamous and greedy Mr. Wilberforce. [*SP*]

Wiedman, General—A British field general present at the Battle of Crefeld, he gives Lord John Grey a field promotion to lieutenant-colonel, but the official confirmation is held up by Colonel Twelvetrees's investigation into a cannon explosion while under Lord John's command during the battle. [*CA*]

Wilberforce, Mr.—Lord Dunsany's local attorney, who is attracted to Isobel Dunsany; he runs away with her to marry her in Scotland and nearly succeeds in raping her (which would assure the marriage, even before the ceremony could be performed) but is prevented by Jamie's timely arrival and forceful interference. [*SP*]

Wilbraham, Arthur—One of the men who support the accusations of treason and Jacobitism directed at Lord John's father, Gerard Grey, the Duke of Pardloe; he is also a member of Lord John's club, the Beefsteak. [*BL, HS*]

Wilbur, Colonel—The officer for whom Ian will be scouting at the Battle of Monmouth. [*MOBY*]

Wilbur, Mr. and Mrs.—A Hillsborough couple and friends of the Sherstons, they are eager to gossip about the compensation set by Governor Tryon for Roger's injuries suffered after the Battle of Alamance. [*Fiery Cross*]

Wilhelm—Stephan von Namtzen's butler, he assists in Lord John's recovery from poisoning while in London with von Namtzen and requests the same assistance from Lord John regarding von Namtzen's reckless behavior following the amputation of the graf's arm. [*PM, BL*]

x **Wilkes, John**—(1725–1797) An affluent English politician with radical ideas and a known member of the notorious Hellfire Club. He is rumored to have presented a baboon dressed as the devil to a meeting of the club, where the Earl of Sandwich mistook the monkey for the real devil. [*HF*]

Wilkins, Mrs.—Philadelphia neighbor of

Mrs. Hempstead and mother of Tommy Wilkins, who relays a message from Mr. Jessop to his playmate, Mary Hempstead, regarding a tall Scottish man who is looking for Fergus. [*Echo*]

Wilkins, Mrs.—Mother with a teething son. Claire has a major difference of opinion with Captain Leckie, a Continental army surgeon, regarding what ails the boy. [*MOBY*]

Wilkins, Peter—Teething baby who also has an ear infection, according to Claire. [*MOBY*]

Wilkins, Tommy—The young boy who delivers a message for Fergus, saying that a tall Scottish man is looking for him. [*Echo*]

Wilkinson, Horatio—A young Continental soldier who brings a wounded friend to Claire for treatment during the Battle of Monmouth. [*MOBY*]

Williamson, Melchior, Sir—Justiciar of Athlone, whom Lord John and Jamie meet with upon their arrival in Ireland on the trail of Gerald Siverly. [*SP*]

Willie B.—One of Young Grannie Abernathy's grandsons, ordered to locate a bag of turnips to pay Claire for treating Old Grannie Abernathy. [*Ashes*]

Willoughby, Mr.—Jamie's Chinese former associate in Edinburgh, a poet and acupuncturist with a marked foot fetish. "Yi Tien Cho," as he was known in China, was a political refugee who preferred his freedom rather than live as a eunuch in the emperor's palace. His acupuncture treatment, which he teaches to Claire, helps relieve Jamie's severe seasickness. Jamie and Claire reminisce about him briefly while at Fort Ticonderoga, wondering whether he escaped Jamaica and, if so, what he's been doing all these years. We may possibly find out. . . . [*Echo*]

Wilmot, Captain—One of the officers in Lord John's Forty-sixth Regiment of Foot. [*PM, BL*]

Wilson, Annie—Young Tammas's mother. [*MOBY*]

Wilson, Ephraim—Hiram Crombie's great-uncle, and possibly the Scottish wanderer who helped beget a branch of Wilsons among the Cherokee population. Malva Christie uses some of his bones to make a charm called "the Venom o' the North Wind." [*Ashes*]

Wilson, Mouse—A jovial Cherokee woman whom Claire treats for a broken tooth; she causes a stir when a horrified Hiram Crombie reveals that his wife's family shares the same last name. [*Ashes*]

Wilson, Mr.—Annie's husband and Tammas's father. [*MOBY*]

Wilson, Mrs.; Grannie Wilson—Late mother of Mairi Crombie and mother-in-law of the Presbyterian settler Hiram Crombie. She astounds everyone present at her wake by sitting upright and admonishing Hiram for the poor offering; Claire quickly determines that she is suffering from an aortic aneurysm, which bursts, causing the old woman to die peacefully—again. [*Ashes*]

Wilson, Red Clay—A Cherokee who accompanies his sister, Mouse, to see Claire for treatment of a broken tooth. [*Ashes*]

Wilson, Tammas—A two-year-old child on Fraser's Ridge who is suffering from pinworms and has spread it to his entire family. [*MOBY*]

Windom, Corporal—Leader of the so-called mercy detail to which a young Lord John is assigned after the Battle of Culloden; under the Duke of Cumberland's orders, the detail's job is to execute any wounded Scots located on the battlefield, giving them mercy from their wounds. [*PM*]

Wingate, David—A militia casualty of Alamance. Claire operates on his shattered elbow, damaged after a musket ball strikes him. [*Fiery Cross*]

x **Wolfe, James, General**—(1727–1759) During the Seven Years' War in Canada, he devised the attack on the French fort at Quebec, ordering British troops to secretly land below the fort at night and scale the unprotected cliffs to the open plain above. Lord John, who had come to pay his respects to Wolfe before commencing an investigation into Gerald Siverly, one of Wolfe's officers suspected of corruption, is not impressed by the man personally. Still, Wolfe's plan works, allowing his forces to defeat the French. General Wolfe was mortally wounded at the beginning of the battle but was reported by his aide to have said (upon being apprised that the French were fleeing—it was a very short battle), "Now, God be praised, I die contented." Lord John, who had seen many men die, rather doubted the coherence of Wolfe's utterance, but tactfully forbore to take issue with the statement, which consequently went down in history. [*CA, SP, Echo*]

Wolff, Lieutenant—A representative of the British navy charged with negotiating lucrative naval-stores contracts with the timber owners along Cape Fear; he is an unfortunate choice for the position, given his dislike of Scotsmen. At one point he proposes marriage to Jocasta Cameron, not out of love or even affection but simply to get his greedy hands on her land and wealth. His drunken appearance at her wedding to Duncan Innes is not especially welcomed but is noted as having dire consequences. [*Fiery Cross, Ashes*]

Wolf's Brother (aka Okwaho'kenha)—The Mohawk name given to Ian Murray when he was adopted into the Mohawk tribe; he washed himself free of his white blood to become one of the Kahnyen'kehaka, the Guardians of the Western Gate. [*Fiery Cross, Ashes, Echo*]

Wolverhampton, Mr.—A settler near Fraser's Ridge, he lives alone, but when a self-amputation of toes damaged in a woodcutting incident fails, he walks seven miles to his nearest neighbor, who then bundles him onto a mule to transport to Claire for further treatment. [*Ashes*]

Woodbine, Jethro, Corporal—With Dunning's Rangers. Corporal Woodbine and his men take custody of Lord John Grey following his fight with Jamie Fraser outside Philadelphia and turn him over to Colonel Watson Smith. [*MOBY*]

Woodcock, Mrs. Mercy—A free black woman whose home in Philadelphia has been commandeered by the British and where wounded Henry Grey lies waiting for either medical assistance or death from his wounds. Claire provides the assistance, performing a dangerous but successful intestinal resection and saving Henry's life. Mercy, whose husband, Walter, is off fighting in the Continental army, nurses Henry devotedly and they fall in love. When last seen (by Claire), Walter Woodcock appeared to be on the point of death, but his fate is unknown, preventing Henry Grey and Mercy Woodcock from following their hearts. [*Echo, MOBY*]

Woodcock, Walter—A prisoner from the Ticonderoga evacuation and one of the few free black men who fought there, Walter is also a recent amputee, whom Claire tries to help. He is married to

Mercy Woodcock, the Philadelphia free woman in whose house the British soldier Henry Grey lies, gravely wounded. [*Echo, MOBY*]

Woodford, Alfred; Lord Enderby—Caroline Woodford's irate brother, who believes that Lord John has disgraced his sister by fighting a duel over her honor and basically demands that Hal do something about it—namely, have Lord John marry Caroline. [*CA*]

Woodford, Captain—A British officer, unrelated to Caroline or Lord Enderby, encamped on the island in the St. Lawrence River where Lord John is deposited. [*CA*]

Woodford, Caroline—A female acquaintance of Lord John's family and a good friend, she is bright, pretty, capable of writing witty and clever poetry, and given to mad escapades, such as being shocked by an electric eel—the event that results in Lord John fighting a duel for her honor. To avoid a forced marriage over the scandal of the duel, Lord John is assigned to duty in Canada until the Woodford matter calms. [*CA, SP*]

Woodford, Simon—Caroline Woodford's uncle, he shares her interests in natural history and is the one who escorts her to the Joffreys' electric-eel party. [*CA*]

x **Woodmason, Charles, Mr.**—(ca. 1720–1776) A South Carolina planter turned Anglican itinerant minister and fierce supporter of the Regulator movement, he preached against the evangelical movement throughout the colonies and the "infestations" of the backcountry religions, such as the New Lights, Baptists, Moravians, and Methodists. [*Fiery Cross*]

Woodsworth, Peleg, Reverend—Captain of the Sixteenth Pennsylvania militia. His men discover Lord John following his escape from Captain Smith and, taking him for an escaped prisoner from the British army, free him from his fetters and induct him into the American militia. [*MOBY*]

Woolam, Charlotte—An attractive and very devout young Quaker woman and sister to Richard Woolam of Woolam's Mill; when Jem hears the term "harlot" from Jamie, he mistakes it for the young woman's name. [*Ashes*]

Woolam, Richard—A Quaker resident of Woolam's Mill, and brother to Charlotte. [*Ashes*]

Worplesdon, Lord—A literary reference to the Earl of Worpledon, from the popular "Jeeves" stories by British author P. G. Wodehouse (one of my five literary role models). [*PM*]

Wright, Hosea—A Cape Fear merchant, banker, and business associate of the smuggler Stephen Bonnet. Wright also owns warehouses in Edenton and Plymouth, as well as a plantation called Four Chimneys, located near Phillip Wylie's plantation; to complicate things further, he is a friend to the governor. [*Fiery Cross*]

Wulfie—A soldier in the Prussian artillery who jokingly accuses Samson and another young soldier of having a romantic meeting near the river. [*SU*]

Wurm, Herman—Formerly Hermione Kuykendall, now bodyguard/bouncer for Mrs. Sylvie and her brothel. [*MOBY*]

Wurm, Trask—Formerly Ermintrude Kuykendall, now bodyguard/bouncer for Mrs. Sylvie and her brothel. [*MOBY*]

Wylie, Phillip—Co-owner of a Portsmouth, Virginia, warehouse rumored to store goods smuggled by Stephen Bonnet. Wylie, an accomplished flirt, emboldened pursuer of older women (mainly Claire), and horseman of some esteem, is the owner of Lucas, a beautiful Friesian stallion that he loses to Jamie in a card game; Jamie's participation in the game is due to his fierce jealousy of the attention paid by young Wylie to Claire. [*Fiery Cross, Ashes*]

X

Xenokratides, Aristopolous—Patriarch of the Stokes family, he was a Greek sailor who jumped ship in London, married a local girl, and took his wife's last name to blend into the English citizenship. [*PM*]

Y

Yarnell, Corporal—An enlisted man in William's regiment on Long Island when William becomes lost in the fog. [*Echo*]

Yeksa'a—Mohawk for "little girl," she was Ian's daughter with Emily; although unnamed by the Mohawk because she was stillborn, Ian calls her Iseabaìl. When Ian finally returns to Lallybroch for his father's death, he finds that his parents have placed a memorial stone for his daughter, bearing only the word "Yeksa'a," as his parents didn't know at the time what the child's name was. Brianna finds the stone in the twentieth century, with only a faded name beginning with "Y." [*Ashes, Echo*]

Z

Zenn, Abram—The ship's boy on board the American privateer the *Asp*. He helps Claire and Jamie when they are taken aboard the *Asp* after their second ship attack in twenty-four hours. [*Echo*]

x zu Egkh und Hungerbach, Joseph—(unknown) A wealthy Austrian baron and head of the family residing near Graz, famous for its red Schilcher wine; his heir (fictitious), Reinhardt Mayrhofer, resides in London. [*PM*]

Part Four

SEX AND VIOLENCE

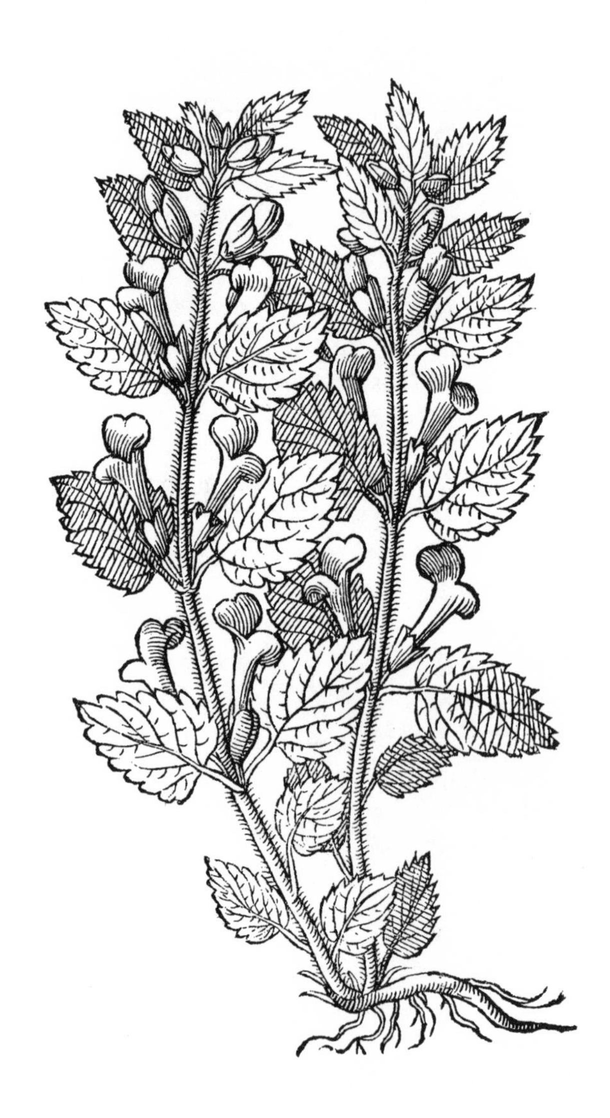

Spanking, Beating, Flogging, and Other Interesting Topics Involving Physical Interactions of a Non-Consensual Sort

As I've said, everyone responds to a book (or film) in a different way, depending on a *lot* of different factors. I've had any number of people write to tell me that at first reading they thought "X" about some element of one or more of my books, but upon reading it again five years later they saw things in quite a different way—or saw things that they hadn't noticed at all the first time.

Expanding that idea from individuals to a larger society, I think the same thing happens.

With regard to the spanking scene in *Outlander,* I've had very distinct *waves* of outrage/sensitivity/protest from readers. Right after the book came out, there were two or three years where any mention of it would start a huge fight on certain online sites (especially the romance sites on GEnie. These particular fights normally escalated into whether *Outlander* was or wasn't a romance, with people being bent out of shape on both sides). Then, for about five years . . . almost nothing.

The book went on selling—I knew that much from the royalty statements—but protest about the spanking scene was limited to the very occasional single letter from a reader, mostly someone who obviously had either completely misread the passage (I had one very distraught and outraged young man who was *convinced* that Claire had been beaten raw and bloody over her entire body, he having evidently not noticed her tendency to hyperbole and having interpreted her *beaten within an inch of my life* in a way rather at odds with her subsequent behavior and descriptions) or who very plainly had personal issues with the subject that had nothing to do with the story as such. Virtually no public controversy at all.

Then we had another little blip of messages that would incite public discussions: "But he's the *hero*. A hero would *never* do that!" Calm for several years, back again with a wave of accusations that my writing such a scene was immoral and irresponsible, as it would obviously <cough> cause women suffering from domestic abuse to conclude that it was perfectly all right for their husbands or boyfriends to knock their teeth down their throats.

(My impolitic response to that was to

note that any woman capable of reaching such a conclusion on the basis of a historical novel was plainly too dumb to read one of my books. And for what it's worth, I've never once heard from or about any woman who *did* think that. On the contrary: I've often had a woman step briefly into such a discussion to say that she was a survivor of domestic abuse and that this particular scene was clearly *not* that. Also usually adding that she had enjoyed the scene itself.)

Calm for a number of years . . . and so on. I don't know what's caused the present blip—perhaps it's just that the notion of seeing this scene played out onscreen in the Starz TV series has incited the imagination of people who *did* have a sensitivity to it, or perhaps it's an extension of the not-quite-current media hysteria over domestic violence among professional athletes.

Mind, I'm by no means saying the latter issue doesn't exist—plainly it does. But a) it existed for a long time before the media decided to take notice, and b) I mention that because of the accompanying word-choice phenomenon. To wit, the athlete who (and I quote) "beat his four-year old son with *a tree branch*!" Same verbiage used by every single newscaster and media host. Because, of course, the word "switch" sounds so much less like something everyone should be Horrified about.

Now, frankly, I don't think that people who *see* the episode in which this scene occurs have a negative reaction to it. Quite the opposite: the writer, director, and actors succeeded brilliantly in capturing the exact spirit of the original—it's slightly menacing, very funny, and mildly erotic (the dialogue is all straight out of the book); he's plainly not "beating" her, and the completely contradictory (and completely understandable) positions of both Jamie and Claire are crystal clear.

The TV version has a considerable advantage in this respect, in that it can easily accommodate both viewpoints, whereas the book was limited only to Claire's perceptions. On the other hand, I do figure that any number of people who merely *hear* about it will be jumping up and down without bothering to ask questions or (heaven forbid) actually read or watch it.

This is kind of tedious but probably okay in the long run. I certainly didn't write the scene with the intent of making something controversial—but it's perfectly true that controversy sells.

Anent the types of controversy, one that's cropped up only in the most recent round of Concern is the notion that Jamie was trying to "break" Claire (whether in body or spirit) by taking a strap to her bottom.

Well, the bottom line, and the reason *why* the scene is able to play out as it does, is that he didn't try to "break" her. He wasn't trying to damage her, nor was he in a fury himself. Certainly he *could* have, but he was entirely in control and doing exactly what he meant to do: punish her, in exactly the same way he'd been punished himself, as a child and obnoxious pre-teen—and to precisely the same ends.

Jamie's father wasn't trying to break his spirit, let alone his body, by thrashing him; he was trying to compel the kid's attention and suggest (strongly) that he start complying with the social order, for the benefit of everybody, not least Jamie himself.

To Jamie—and everyone else around him—that's the point of punishing someone. It's not revenge and it's not anger; it's not meant to crush someone, either physically or spiritually. It's to preserve order and keep the offender within the safety of the group.

People (from North America and Western Europe) in the early twenty-first century do not, by and large, value order. (Turn on the TV and watch for fifteen minutes. . . .) People in earlier times—including the earlier part of the twentieth century, which is where Claire comes from—did, from necessity. The only hope of survival in a harsh environment, with recurrent threats from other groups, was to stick together. People could NOT go off and do their own thing without endangering themselves and (possibly) the group they belonged to.

This idea just doesn't penetrate for someone born after 1965, say—because they've never seen necessity of that sort.

I'm reminded here of one of my book-tour stops, in Traverse City, Michigan. After the very long evening, I was invited to have supper with some of the organizers, and we went to a casual restaurant downtown, where we were joined by a couple of other people, including a very interesting gentleman, also an author, but principally a speaker. I forget the details of his profession, but he was a fascinating man—had been a Marine in his earlier life, lived all over the world—and we had a lot of good talk about wars, history, etc. He was somewhat older than I am, probably in his late sixties or early seventies, but in good shape.

It was late, as I say—the restaurant had kept their kitchen open specifically for us, and we'd eaten hasty hamburgers and salads—and when we set out to walk back to the hotel, the only people on the streets were ones hanging around in front of bars. As we approached one such group, we could see them looking at us with interest, glancing away and shoving one another, talking loudly and generally behaving in a way that, had I been alone, would have made me turn around and go around the block to avoid them.

The ex-Marine—business suit, tie, and all—instantly stepped to the front of our little group and said calmly, "Let me go first. Keep behind me and stay close." Which, I assure you, we all did. (The group included two other men, who instantly did as he said, too—but they flanked the three women, without a thought.) Our little gang arrowed through the larger group, who gave way with no more than the odd vulgar shout, and we made it to the end of the block and turned for our hotel without incident.

Vide, a group with good social order, approaching a random assemblage with the potential for unpleasantness, if not violence, and thus emerging with no harm done to anyone.

Jamie wouldn't have articulated it to himself (let alone Claire) in that way, but that's exactly what he's doing and why.

And going on from there to a further note on group dynamics: As Jamie tells Claire, very carefully and explicitly, her crime was not that she didn't follow his orders (though she should have, by the custom of the day) but that she put "all the men" in danger by not doing so. And she *did.* Many of them might have been killed or taken prisoner, to say nothing of what would have happened to Jamie himself (and he says nothing about that during his explanations in the televised version; he mentions it very briefly in the book version).

He does tell her what would have happened to a man who'd done what she'd done—severe physical punishment, if not death. The Highlanders are a tight-knit group, who depend *on* the group for safety. To that end, they have customs and traditions that enforce and preserve the order and cohesion of the group.

Claire is, by virtue of her marriage to Jamie, a member of that group, and—so far as they're concerned—needs very badly to be informed of How Things Work. It's Jamie's duty to do this—and had he declined to do it, very likely Dougal or one of the other men would have, probably publicly.

Now, a subsidiary concern that's sometimes raised is that Jamie admits to having enjoyed punishing her. One person in an online forum raised this issue, to which I replied as follows:

He enjoyed it (in part) because she'd just put him through HELL for the previous twenty-four hours.

Aside from being (he thought—and with complete justice, as she didn't/couldn't tell him why she'd wandered off) irresponsible, disobedient (and not just willful—she deliberately did what he'd told her not to do, and it wasn't an unreasonable order under the circumstances), and featherheaded (why would anyone think it was a good idea to wander around alone, with redcoats and deserters in the vicinity? And Jamie and Claire have just *had* their deadly encounter with British army deserters), she doesn't realize that she nearly got a large number of men killed in rescuing her and doesn't express any remorse over what she's done.

She also scared the crap out of him; he *knew* what Randall might/would do to her and that there was every likelihood that he, Jamie, would never see her again.[1]

In addition to this, she's put him in the position of being responsible for administering justice and bringing her back into social acceptability within the group. He's a brand-new husband, and suddenly he has to do this semi-public and somewhat embarrassing thing, because it's his duty to bring his wife back in line

Add in his personal history with Black Jack Randall (whom he's just come face-to-face with and alerted to his presence, causing ongoing danger to him and everyone with him) and the fact that he had to take her out of Fort William, with its memories of his own imprisonment, grief, pain, and rage, and . . .

You *wonder* that he enjoys smacking her bottom? The man's forbearing, but he's not a saint.

"DON'T YOU THINK THAT'S A LITTLE RAPEY?"

During the press blitz surrounding release of the first season of the *Outlander* TV show, I traveled for a week with Ron Moore and several of the principal cast members, doing two premieres and a solid week of interviews. Some of these were panel-type appearances, where everyone was involved, some were solo interviews, and quite a few

[1] *Ever seen a parent whose kid has narrowly avoided being run over by running out in the street? They generally don't scoop the little fiend up and hug the dickens out of him—they normally grab the miscreant, whack him on the bottom, and bellow, "What's* wrong *with you?!?"*

were paired interviews—Ron and I handling a video interview together, while Sam Heughan (Jamie) and Caitriona Balfe (Claire) did the same at a roundtable filled with journalists, and vice versa.

One of the odder interview types was what they call a "satellite" interview—because it's handled via satellite, as sequential international interviewers call in to ask questions. On one occasion, Ron and I were doing one of these, seated together on either side of the satellite speakerphone and busily occupied in signing piles of Starz *Outlander* posters while we talked with people from Venezuela, Sweden, Germany, etc. I believe it was a male interviewer from Germany who kicked off the interview by asking, didn't we think the story was "a little rapey"?

Ron and I stopped signing our names, looked at each other in astonishment, and mouthed—silently and simultaneously—"Is that even a *word*?"

Frankly, I think it's not, but I have encountered—many, many times over the course of the last twenty-five years—both direct and indirect opinions to the effect that the commenter feels there's a fairly high incidence of rape in the book(s), along with the corollary implication that This Is a Bad Thing.

These commenters and interviewers presumably realize that if I *did* think that, I wouldn't have written the book(s) that way and are therefore either 1) trying to ask what I intended by the inclusion of such incidents, 2) seeking to further a conversation regarding sex and violence in the arts . . . and/or 3) trying to get me to say something quotably irascible that they can use to attract an audience.[2]

Regardless, conversations #1 and #2 are worth having. So let's talk. . . .

The question of rape in literature—and in the *Outlander* novels in particular—is pretty complex, so let's begin by separating out a few of the relevant aspects of the topic.

FACTUALITY

Is there an unusual or striking incidence of rape in either the book or TV show? Plainly that's a subjective question to start with, and it's one that's strongly affected by current cultural concerns.

As I note later in this book (see "Romance and the Written Word"), thirty years ago rape was a regular staple of many romance novels and was usually depicted in ways that would cause screams of outrage and mass book burning in 2015. At the time, books with such incidents were merely considered entertainment or, at worst, dismissed as "housewife porn."

I'm not sure how one would reasonably estimate incidence of any given event in a book, as the numerical occurrence must clearly be balanced by the impact of any single occurrence. For example, in the earlier romance novels I mentioned, usually there was a single occurrence of rape, generally used as a plot device.[3] There were not usually lingering physical effects, and such psychological effects as there were were, um, transitory. In other novels, rape was used repeatedly, but again without any apparent

[2] *I'd bet pretty heavily on Door #3 being the correct one, but I'm a natural-born gambler.*

[3] *There are some romance authors who used it openly and repeatedly—within a single book—for the clear purpose of sexual titillation. I don't wish to seem to cast aspersions—styles in literature change, but I believe I can reasonably cite Bertrice Small's work as an example of this style.*

trauma that couldn't be cleared up by having subsequent sex with the hero.

But getting down to cases . . . let's see . . . in *Outlander*, there is a definite sexual threat by Captain Jonathan Randall toward Claire when he first encounters her. It's not clear that this would have become attempted rape, but it might have, if the captain had not been interrupted by the appearance of Murtagh.

Later, at Castle Leoch, during the Gathering, Claire is accosted by several drunken clansmen, who demand a kiss and paw her. She definitely perceives them to have more than a kiss in mind, but in fact they don't sexually assault her, being driven off by Dougal MacKenzie—who then makes a heavy pass at her but doesn't evince any intent of committing rape.

Jamie, telling Claire his own history with Black Jack Randall, tells her that Randall raped his sister, Jenny. He believes this to be true, but in fact it isn't. Still, Randall definitely *intended* rape and indeed attempted it, being foiled in the attempt by Jenny's laughing at him and failing to show the fear he was looking for.

Okay, score so far: two sexual threats, one attempted rape.

In the course of later events, Jamie tells Claire that the small Bible he carries once belonged to a prisoner named Alex MacGregor, who killed himself after involvement with Captain Randall. The clear implication is that MacGregor was raped (and quite possibly tortured) by Randall, but we don't hear this from either of the principals involved, and we see nothing of any interaction between them.

Two sexual threats, one attempted rape, one implied offscreen actual rape. Three hundred pages down, three hundred to go . . .

After their hasty marriage, Claire and Jamie repair to a deserted (they think) glade to enjoy a bit of marital felicity. Here they are surprised by a pair of English deserters, one of whom definitely attempts to rape Claire; she kills him by stabbing him in the kidney.

Later, Claire is captured by Captain Randall, who attempts to rape her but fails when she refuses to act afraid of him, giving Jamie time to rescue her.

Two sexual threats, three attempted rapes, and a partriiidge in a—no, wait . . .

In the course of events, Jamie reveals to Claire that at one point in his colorful history with Randall, the captain had offered Jamie clemency in the matter of being flogged for a second time, if Jamie would *"make free of my body."* Not sure this could be considered a rape attempt, but it's certainly a sexual threat.

Three threats, three attempts, one implied offscreen rape.

And then, in the fullness of time, Randall succeeds in capturing Claire again, and in order to save her life, Jamie offers to submit to Randall, who does indeed rape him. (Again, not onscreen, but we certainly hear enough of the details afterward to be sure it took place.)

Sum total: three sexual threats, three attempted rapes, one implied-but-likely rape, and one undeniable (and very brutal) actual rape.

That's over the course of 629 pages (hardcover edition). So . . . one definite rape in six-hundred-plus pages. Adding in attempted rapes, that's four, or one negative sexual incident per hundred fifty pages. Is this excessive, average, below average?

I'm rather hoping that most of you reading this will perceive the tongue-in-cheek nature of this statistical analysis. Obviously, frequency of occurrence is Not Really the Point. The use of sexual incidents (whether positive or negative) by a writer pretty much has to be one thing or another: titillation of the audience, or . . . done for a specific and serious purpose.

You'll notice that I didn't say "gratuitous titillation of the audience." Some books' actual purpose is indeed the arousal of sexual feeling, whether as the primary literary purpose of the book (i.e., erotica) or as an important auxiliary support to the main emotional narrative. Such books are normally bought with the specific intent of enjoying such arousal, and it's therefore not gratuitous in the least.

I use sexual encounters between married couples in *Outlander,* for example, to demonstrate and support the emerging emotional closeness of the main characters, growing from the marriage of strangers to the point where a woman can save a man's soul.

But rape?

The correct question to be asking about any element of concern in a book is, "What's the author trying to do with this?" I.e., is there an apparent purpose—whether achieved or not—to the use of this element? (After that, you can legitimately ask whether the author *did* achieve his or her purpose—but you need to know what it was first.)

So. What was my purpose in employing rape as I did?

Not to start over with the statistical analysis, but look at when and how these negative sexual encounters occur. To wit: there's one sexual threat from drunken clansmen at the Gathering (I think we include Dougal's pass in that incident), and there's one attempted rape by English deserters.

All the other negative sexual activity is being carried out by Captain Jack Randall. Might my purpose possibly have been character development? As in, perhaps I wanted to introduce him as a person with, shall we say, poor impulse control, escalate through indications that he might just possibly be taking undue advantage of his social position to oppress women, adding delicately that he apparently enjoys the infliction of pain of a general nature, and, moving right along, complete our portrait of a Sexual Sadist?

If that was your guess . . . you're correct!

The man is a sexual sadist—naturally he's going to be shown doing or attempting to do what such a person does. He's also the chief antagonist of the story.

Is it therefore appropriate—in a purely artistic sense—to include such incidents as would make Captain Randall a) clearly drawn, b) clearly labeled as an antagonistic threat, c) plainly dangerous?[4]

Now, there are other ramifications to the use of rape as a noticeable element in the story, and these have to do both with the nature of rape and with the thematic narrative of this particular story. We'll look at both those aspects a little farther on.

For the moment, let's broaden the discussion a bit. The adverse commentary regarding rape takes note that it occurs elsewhere in the series, not just in *Outlander,* and such comments often imply (when not coming out and stating it as a generally

[4] *That's not a rhetorical question. The answer is yes.*

accepted fact) that the author is either using the element gratuitously, as a means of shocking the audience and thus keeping their interest (which would presumably otherwise be waning after half a million or so words . . .), or is unhealthily obsessed with the notion.[5]

HISTORICITY

There is no reliable data on historical incidence of rape, though any number of vivid historical accounts (*vide Boadicea*, the rape of the Sabine women,[6] etc.) make it clear that the act has been around as long as people have.

However, we do know quite a bit about the social structures of some times and places. In the Scottish Highlands, well up into the early-twentieth century, most of the population lived in small, tight-knit communities, where everyone knew everyone else (and most of them were related in one degree or another). Owing to the harshness of life and the customs of the times, women normally went from the protection of their father's hearth to that of their husband.[7]

There were no career paths for unmarried women, unless they wanted to undertake a long and arduous journey to the nearest city, where they *might* find employment or (more likely) be obliged to resort to prostitution—or undertake a longer and more arduous journey to a convent. But the point here is that women did *not* wander around the countryside by themselves, unprotected.[8] They lived with their families and were protected by the men of those families.

You note that when Dougal MacKenzie is faced with the prospect of handing Claire over to a man he knows to be a dangerous sadist, the first and best idea he has is to instantly marry her to someone. And you note what Jamie Fraser promises her on their wedding night: *"You have my name and my family, my clan, and if necessary, the protection of my body as well."* He meant it, and as Claire later realizes: *It was no romantic pledge he had made me, but the blunt promise to guard my safety at the cost of his own.*

And the point here is that such protection was needed. A woman wandering about by herself was in fact fair game. You see this concept embodied in Scottish songs and folklore. A maiden on her way to visit a relative strays into the province of a bold forester, who accosts her and tells her that the price of passage across his land is her

---

[5] *I'm having a T-shirt printed with the slogan:* Life is too short to waste on people who think I'm mentally ill.

[6] *N.B.: Bear in mind that with regard to the Sabines, the "rape" actually meant abduction, from the Latin word* "raptio." *However, the women were abducted and carried away into forced marriage, so there is an overlap of meaning.*

[7] *Interestingly enough, marriage didn't happen at a particularly early age in the Highlands. Average age at marriage for a woman in the eighteenth century was about twenty-two, and about twenty-six for a man. The reason given by the author of the research paper that I read on this subject was that the difficult economic conditions of the Highlands made it very hard for a young man to come by enough money, land, or livestock with which to support a wife and family. In fact, most young men eventually managed it by a process known as "ligging," which essentially meant begging tools, stock, furnishings, etc., from friends and relatives.*

[8] *In some Highland areas, women did go out with the grazing flocks in summer, to the shielings—the high meadows—where they remained for some weeks, leaving the men to tend the croft. However, this was also a very social activity, and the women went in groups, not alone.*

maidenhead—which he promptly takes. A young woman goes alone to the mill and demands that the miller grind her corn for her—whereupon he tosses her down on a sack of grain and quite graphically does so.

Now, there are two things to note here: Firstly, the fact that Claire encounters sexual menace (from Captain Randall, from the drunken Highlanders, and from the English deserters) is not the result of the author's lack of imagination in devising conflict; it's a reasonable depiction of the cultural context of that time and place and the perception of and danger to an unaccompanied woman—particularly an attractive one who seems to be running around in her undergarment. And secondly, the fact that Captain Randall appears to prefer male victims is likely the result of opportunity rather than inborn sexual orientation; he simply doesn't often encounter women in a situation where he can assault them with impunity—he *does* have a pretty free hand with male prisoners under his control. Back to this in a moment . . .

The context of female safety—or lack of it—and the necessary protection by men is the basis of Claire's forced marriage to Jamie. There needs to be a credible and exigent threat to her safety, and no other reasonable recourse, for this to be believable. Therefore, we (and Claire) need to see the situation she's in—an Englishwoman alone, in a place where no Englishwoman should be in the first place, and where no woman should be alone, because to *be* a woman alone makes you fair game.

Returning to the effects of this social structure on Jack Randall's character and situation: we see or are told of four sexual assaults committed by Jack Randall—two on women and two on men. All four take place when the victim is isolated from his or her social support and is in the physical power of the captain.

He finds Jenny Murray apparently alone at Lallybroch (she isn't, but when he discovers that her brother is there, he deals with *that* nuisance in short order), and he doesn't succeed in raping her only because she refuses to be terrified and instead laughs at him.

We hear that a young prisoner named Alexander MacGregor apparently killed himself while in the captain's custody, and the clear inference is that he did so as a result of mental damage caused by sexual assault.

Captain Randall comes across Claire quite unexpectedly—alone, disheveled, and apparently undressed—and reacts like a dog finding an unexpected bone. He's stopped from committing serious assault only by the fortuitous arrival of Murtagh. Which is worth noting: a beneficial concomitant of the Highland social structure is the male code obliging a decent man to protect any woman, not merely his own. You see Murtagh, Dougal, Colum, Dougal's men, and finally Jamie all step up to acknowledge this responsibility with regard to Claire.

(This isn't the time or place to go into a detailed discussion of the evolution of sexual attitudes—and I do mean "evolution" in a biological sense, not a social one—but, essentially, in our species women are less mobile, because they're attached to children, who are helpless for a long time. The necessity of preserving his DNA causes a man to risk his own life to save those of his mate and children. The upshot of this is that women are much less sensitive to the dangers of their wider environment, while men instinctively know what it is to be alone, and helpless.)

MALE RAPE

This leads us to the final climax of *Outlander,* wherein Jamie sacrifices himself to save Claire's life, ending up alone, helpless—and at the mercy of Jack Randall.

There's been (as one might expect) a lot of comment about this over the years, ranging from accusations that I am obviously mentally ill even to have thought of such a thing, to congratulations on my socially enlightened and egalitarian attitude toward rape.

All I'll say about that is that there are . . . you'd have to call them styles, I think, in perception of and social attitude toward just about every human experience, from child raising to law enforcement to personal violence. At the moment I'm writing this, we're in a very rape-conscious period; there's a lot of interest and a terrible lot of talk about it. (If there wasn't, this particular article would be a lot shorter, I can tell you that much. . . .)

In all honesty, the story plays out this way because (bear in mind that I wrote it for practice and never intended to show it to anyone, let alone try to publish it) I'd read several romance novels in which the heroine was threatened by rape or actually raped—and having already decided in a moment of whimsy that Jamie should be the virgin bridegroom . . . I sort of shrugged and said, "Hey, turnabout's fair play. . . ."

As with many artistic decisions, once made, that one had unexpected and very interesting consequences. I may have decided on the whim of a moment that Claire was a time traveler and that Jamie was raped—but having made those decisions, I took them seriously and explored the physical and emotional ramifications thereof.

At this point, I think I need to acknowledge the Starz production of *Outlander* and the very truthful adaptation produced by Ron D. Moore. Ron, bless him, didn't shy away from any of the more sensitive or difficult material in the book and thus from Jamie's experience in Wentworth. Everyone involved, from writers and director to cast and crew, did the most tremendous job (and I mean that in all senses of the word) in bringing those scenes to life—a life true to the original story.

I talked at length, and separately, with Ron Moore, Tobias Menzies (Black Jack), and Sam Heughan (Jamie) about these scenes, supplying them with as much insight and background as I could. And what I said to each of them at the end of all the talking was, "I'm fine with whatever you can make work between you. I trust you."

I mention the show in the context of this discussion because I'm writing this article the day before the final episode airs: Episode 16, "To Ransom a Man's Soul." This is the episode that shows Jamie's rape and its effects on him, and if there's anything in life I'm sure of, it's that there's going to be a Lot of Talk about it—both the episode on its own merits and (with luck) a much wider discussion of male rape.

Which leads us to . . .

IDEOLIZATION OF RAPE AND INDIVIDUALITY OF EXPERIENCE

Okay, look carefully at that word. It's not "idealization." Ideolization means conversion of a cultural phenomenon to an ideology.[9]

I get enormous amounts of mail and email. About everything under the sun, including a few things I didn't even know existed. But I've never had a letter or email from a person who's told me that he or she suffered sexual assault and then was traumatized or negatively affected by something they read in my books. Really. Not once, in twenty-five years.

On the other hand, I've had a lot of mail from people in this position who have said things about the books like "cathartic," "validating," "healing," and "hope."

While I never have or ever will write from a political position or with a sense of mission or agenda—I think that results in books that are mediocre at best and bad at worst—I do think there's an important point in this with regard *to* current political attitudes.

I call it the ideolization of rape (though it happens with other social phenomena, as well). People focus on an issue that merits serious concern, which is admirable, but the effect is often to codify the issue rather than deal with it. Thus we get "rape isn't about sex, it's about power," repeated as if it's Holy Writ. An ideology becomes established as to how the phenomenon is perceived, described, and handled—and God forbid you disagree with an iota of its scripture.

The intent is commendable, but a side effect of the process is to depersonalize this most personal of incidents, to treat it as a universal and undifferentiated event, and—often—to pass unjust laws or take steps that lead to unintended consequences, because something is done in response to the ideology that then impacts individuals.

The point to be made here is that when rape occurs in one of my books, it's a specific, individual, unique event, and so is the person to whom it happens, the person who perpetrates it, and the way(s) in which the—geez, I dislike the term "survivor," but I dislike "victim" even more[10]—person who has suffered the event is, we hope, able to deal with it and perhaps regain their sense of self.

The novels following *Outlander* aren't dealing with a central theme that involves rape, but there are two major incidents—one in *Drums of Autumn* and one in *A Breath of Snow and Ashes*—in which a major character is raped,[11] and the effects of the crime reverberate through the book—and sometimes further. (Presumably this is one of the factors that make some people describe the series as a whole as "rapey.")

The point is that rape is a unique occurrence. Every time. How it happens, when,

[9] *Certainly it's a word.*

[10] *Why? Because both words are labels that carry a lot of emotional baggage, that's why. I don't think it's right to lumber people with assumptions and preconceptions when they're already suffering the effects of traumatic assault.*

[11] *Going on the statistical model, this amounts to one rape approximately every 1.3 million words, which hardly seems excessive, but, as noted above, pure math may not be an appropriate yardstick to employ.*

to whom and by whom, and what happens next. What damage may be done, and—most important—what people do *next.* How do they retake possession of themselves? Because people *do.*

The current ideology may term people who weren't murdered during the attack as "survivors," but the cultural expectation seems to be that this is something that can't be healed, that the person who's suffered rape will in some way always be dramatically marked by it. Maybe so, and maybe no, as Jamie puts it.

I have fortunately never been raped,[12] but I've talked to—and, more important, *listened* to—a great many people who have. Some of them have suffered terribly and have long-lasting, debilitating effects. For some, it was a brief experience that they wish hadn't happened, much as they wish the stranger who turned left into their passenger door at an intersection hadn't done so, but they were able to accept it merely as something that happened, rather than as a defining moment of either their life or their subsequent persona.

If you look at the three rapes in the series that are described in what might be called a personal, long-term way, you see how different they are. All very bad experiences for those involved, but very different in what happened and in how the people involved dealt with what happened.

To take just one small example, when Brianna is raped (by a man who in fact didn't consider what he'd done to *be* rape, since he paid for it), she—like many women in such circumstances—was upset by the continuing thought that she should have fought to resist the attack.

Her father had, at roughly the same age, suffered a vicious rape in which he was prevented from fighting back and had ultimately found healing when his wife (as Jamie himself puts it in a later book) "drugged me and fornicated me back to life," thus giving him an opportunity to fight, psychologically. Above all people, Jamie *knows* what his daughter feels like—and he knows what to do about it.

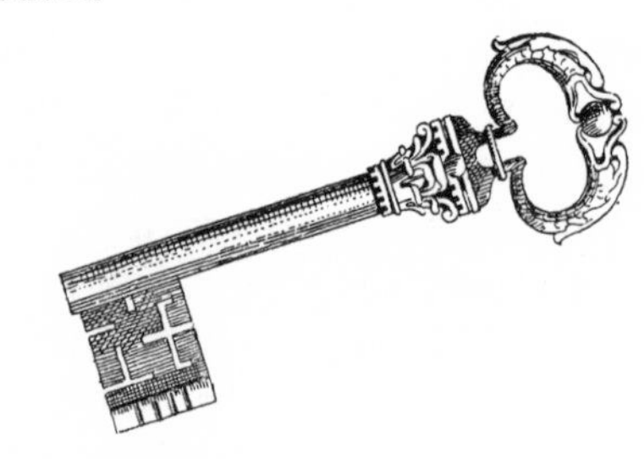

The point is that rape is not one-size-fits-all. I think that's why my correspondents so often say they feel validated, heard, that someone gets it, etc. And I appreciate that more than I can say.

---

[12] *In case you were wondering, and you probably were, human nature being what it is.*

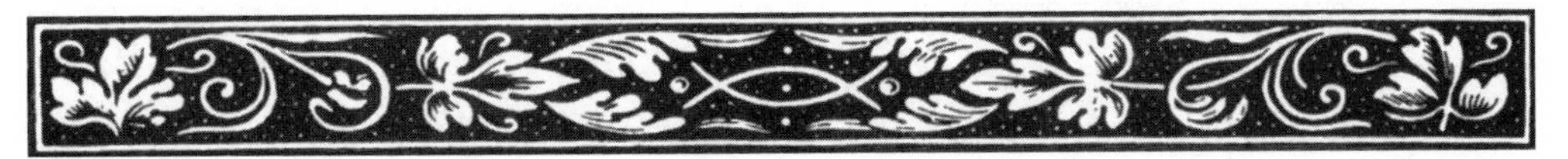

Excerpt from *Drums of Autumn*

She jerked her head up, to find him watching her over his undrunk cider. He didn't look upset, and the jelly in her backbone stiffened a little. She clenched her fists on her knees to steady herself, and met his eyes, straight on.

"I need to know whether it will help. I want to kill . . . him. The man who—" She made a vague gesture at her belly, and swallowed hard. "But if I do, and it doesn't help—" She couldn't go on.

He didn't seem shocked; abstracted, rather. He raised the cup to his mouth and took a sip, slowly.

"Mmphm. And will ye have killed a man before?" He phrased it as a question, but she knew it wasn't. The muscle quivered near his mouth again—with amusement, she thought, not shock—and she felt a quick spurt of anger.

"You think I can't, don't you? I can. You'd better believe me, I can!" Her hands spread out, gripping her knees, broad and capable. She thought she could do it; though her image of how it might happen wavered. In cold blood, shooting seemed the best, perhaps the only certain way. But trying to imagine this, she had realized vividly the truth of the old saying "Shooting's too good for him."

It might be too good for Bonnet; it wouldn't be nearly good enough for *her*. In the night when she flung off her blankets, unable to bear even this slight weight and its reminder of restraint, she didn't just want him dead—she wanted to *kill* him, purely and passionately—kill him with her hands, taking back by the flesh what had been taken from her by that means.

And yet . . . what good would it be to murder him, if he would still haunt her? There was no way to know—unless her father could tell her.

"Will you tell me?" she blurted. "Did you kill him, finally—and did it help?"

He seemed to be thinking it over, his eyes traveling slowly over her, narrowed in assessment.

"And what would be helped by your doing murder?" he asked. "It willna take the child from your belly—or give ye back your maidenheid."

"I know that!" She felt her face flush hot, and turned away, irritated both with him and herself. They spoke of rape and murder, and she was embarrassed to have him mention her lost virginity? She forced herself to look back at him.

"Mama said you tried to kill Jack

Randall in Paris, in a duel. What did *you* think you'd get back?"

He rubbed his chin hard, then drew in his breath through his nose and let it out slowly, eyes fixed on the stained rock of the ceiling.

"I meant to take back my manhood," he said softly. "My honor."

"You think my honor isn't worth taking back? Or do you figure it's the same thing as my *maidenheid*?" She mocked his accent nastily.

Sharp blue eyes swung back to hers. "Is it the same thing to *you*?"

"No, it is not," she said, through clenched teeth.

"Good," he said, shortly.

"Then answer me, damn it!" She struck a fist on the straw, finding no satisfaction in the soundless blow. "Did killing him give you back your honor? Did it help? Tell me the truth!"

She stopped, breathing heavily. She glared at him, and he met her eyes with a cold stare. Then he raised the cup abruptly to his mouth, swallowed the cider in one gulp, and set the cup down on the hay beside him.

"The truth? The truth is that I dinna ken whether I killed him or no."

Her mouth dropped open in surprise.

"You don't *know* whether you killed him?"

"I said so." A slight jerk of the shoulders betrayed his impatience. He stood up abruptly, as if unable to sit any longer.

"He died at Culloden, and I was there. I woke on the moor after the battle, with Randall's corpse on top of me. I ken that much—and not much more." He paused as though thinking, then, mind made up, he thrust one knee forward, pulled up his kilt and nodded downward. "Look."

It was an old scar, but no less impressive for its age. It ran up the inner side of his thigh, nearly a foot in length, its lower end starred and knotted like the head of a mace, the rest of it a cleaner line, though thick and twisted.

"A bayonet, I expect," he said, looking at it dispassionately. He dropped the kilt, hiding the scar once more.

"I remember the feel of the blade strikin' bone, and no more. Not what came after—or before."

He took a deep, audible breath, and for the first time she realized that his apparent calmness was taking a good deal of effort to maintain.

"I thought it a blessing—that I couldna remember," he said at last. He wasn't looking at her, but into the shadows at the end of the stable. "There were gallant men who died there; men I

loved well. If I didna know their deaths; if I couldna recall them or see them in my mind—then I didna have to think of them as dead. Maybe that was cowardice, maybe not. Perhaps I chose not to remember that day; perhaps I cannot if I would." He looked down at her, his eyes gone softer, but then turned away, plaid swinging, not waiting for an answer.

"Afterward—aye, well. Vengeance didna seem important, then. There were a thousand dead men on that field, and I thought I should be one of them in hours. Jack Randall . . ." He made an odd, impatient gesture, brushing aside the thought of Jack Randall as he might a biting deerfly. "He *was* one of them. I thought I could leave him to God. Then."

She took a deep breath, trying to keep her feelings under control. Curiosity and sympathy struggled with an overwhelming feeling of frustration.

"You're . . . all right, though. I mean—in spite of what he—did to you?"

He gave her a look of exasperation, understanding mingled with half-angry amusement.

"Not many die of it, lass. Not me. And not you."

"Not *yet*." Involuntarily, she put a hand over her belly. She stared up at him. "I guess we'll see in six months if I die of it."

That rattled him; she could see it. He blew out his breath and scowled at her.

"Ye'll do fine," he said curtly. "Ye're wider through the hip than yon wee heifer."

"Like your mother? Everybody says how much I'm like her. I guess she was wide through the hip, too, but it didn't save *her,* did it?"

He flinched. Quick and sharp as though she'd slapped him across the face with a stinging nettle. Perversely, seeing it filled her with panic, rather than the satisfaction she'd expected.

She understood then that his promise of protection was in good part illusion. He would kill for her, yes. Or willingly die himself, she had no doubt. He would—if she let him—avenge her honor, destroy her enemies. But he could not defend her from her own child; he was as powerless to save her from that threat as if she had never found him.

"I'll die," she said, cold certainty filling her belly like frozen mercury. "I know I will."

"Ye won't!" He rounded on her fiercely, and she felt his hands bite into her upper arms. "I will not let you!"

She would have given anything to be-

lieve him. Her lips were numb and stiff, rage giving way to a cold despair.

"You can't help," she said. "You can't do anything!"

"Your mother can," he said, but sounded only half convinced. His grip slackened, and she wrenched herself free.

"No, she can't—not without a hospital, without drugs and things. If it—if it goes wrong, all she can do is try to save the b-baby." Despite herself, her gaze flickered to his dirk, blade gleaming cold against the straw where he had left it.

Her knees felt watery, and she sat down suddenly. He snatched up the jug and slopped cider into a cup, pushing it under her nose.

"Drink it," he said. "Drink up, lass, you're pale as my sark." His hand was on the back of her head, urging her. She took a sip, but choked and drew back, waving him off. She drew a sleeve across her wet chin, wiping off the spilled cider.

"You know what's the worst? You said it wasn't my fault, but it is."

"It is not!"

She flapped a hand at him, bidding him be quiet.

"You talked about cowardice; you know what it is. Well, I was a coward. I should have fought, I shouldn't have let him . . . but I was scared of him. If I'd been brave enough, this wouldn't have happened, but I wasn't, I was scared! And now I'm even more scared," she said, voice breaking. She took a deep breath to steady herself, bracing her hands on the straw.

"You can't help, and neither can Mama, and I can't do anything either. And Roger—" Her voice did crack then, and she bit her lip hard, forcing back tears.

"Brianna—*a leannan* . . ." He made a move to comfort her, but she drew back, arms folded tight across her stomach.

"I keep thinking—if I kill him, that's something I can do. It's the *only* thing I can do. If I—if I have to die, at least I'll take him with me, and if I don't—then maybe I can forget, if he's dead."

"Ye willna forget." The words were blunt and uncompromising as a blow to the stomach. He was still holding the cup of cider. Now he tilted back his head and drank, quite deliberately.

"It doesna matter, though," he said, setting down the cup with an air of businesslike finality. "We shall find you a husband, and once the babe's born, ye willna have much time to fret."

"What?" She gaped at him. "What do you mean, find me a husband?"

"You'll need one, aye?" he said, in

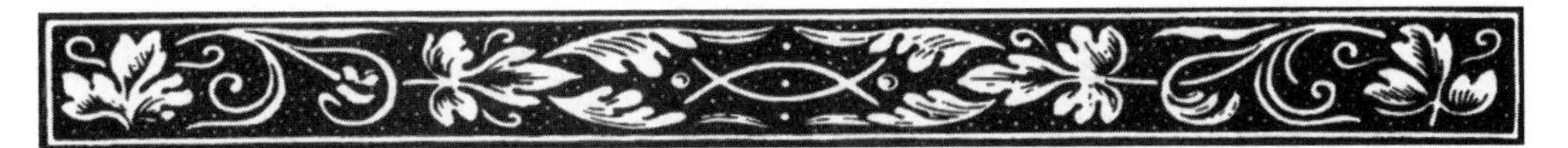

tones of mild surprise. "The bairn must have a father. And if ye willna tell me the name of the man who's given ye a swollen belly, so that I might make him do his duty by ye—"

"You think I'd *marry* the man who did this?" Her voice cracked again, this time with astonishment.

His voice sharpened slightly.

"Well, I'm thinkin'—are ye maybe playin' wi' the truth a bit, lass? Perhaps it wasna rape at all; perhaps it was that ye took a mislike to the man, and ran—and made up the story later. Ye were not marked, after all. Hard to think a man could force a lass of your size, if ye were unwilling altogether."

"You think I'm *lying*?"

He raised one brow in cynicism. Furious, she swung a hand at him, but he caught her by the wrist.

"Ah, now," he said, reprovingly. "Ye're no the first lass to make a slip and try to hide it, but—" He caught the other wrist as she struck at him, and pulled them both up sharply.

"Ye dinna need to make such a fuss," he said. "Or is it that ye wanted the man and he threw ye over? Is that it?"

She swiveled in his grip, used her weight to swing aside, brought her knee up hard. He turned only slightly, and her knee collided with his thigh, not the vulnerable flesh between his legs she had been aiming for.

The blow must have bruised him, but didn't lessen his grip on her wrists in the least. She twisted, kicking, cursing her skirts. She hit his shin dead-on at least twice, but he only chuckled, as though finding her struggles funny.

"Is that all ye can do, lassie?" He broke his grip then, but only to shift both her wrists to one hand. The other prodded her playfully in the ribs.

"There was a man
In Muir of Skene,
He had dirks
And I had none;
But I fell on him
With my thumbs,
And wot you how,
I dirkit him,
Dirkit him
Dirkit him?"

With each repetition, he dug a thumb hard between her ribs.

"You fucking *bastard*!" she screamed. She braced her feet and yanked down on his arm as hard as she could, bringing it into biting range. She lunged at his wrist, but before she could sink her teeth in his flesh, she found herself jerked off her feet and whirled through the air.

She ended hard on her knees, one

arm twisted up behind her back so tightly that her shoulder joint cracked. The strain on her elbow hurt; she writhed, trying to turn into the hold, but couldn't budge. An arm like an iron bar clamped across her shoulders, forcing her head down. And farther down.

Her chin drove into her chest; she couldn't breathe. And still he forced her head down. Her knees slid apart, her thighs forced wide by the downward pressure.

"Stop!" she grunted. It hurt to force sound through her constricted windpipe. "Gd's sk, stp!"

The relentless pressure paused, but did not ease. She could feel him there behind her, an inexorable, inexplicable force. She reached back with her free hand, groping for something to claw, something to hit or bend, but there was nothing.

"I could break your neck," he said, very quietly. The weight of his arm left her shoulders, though the twisted arm still held her bent forward, hair loose and tumbled, nearly touching the floor. A hand settled on her neck. She could feel thumb and index fingers on either side, pressing lightly on her arteries. He squeezed, and black spots danced before her eyes.

"I could kill you, so."

The hand left her neck, and touched her, deliberately, knee and shoulder, cheek and chin, emphasizing her helplessness. She jerked her head away, not letting him touch the wetness, not wanting him to feel her tears of rage. Then the hand pressed sudden and brutal on the small of her back. She made a small, choked sound and arched her back to keep her arm from breaking, thrusting out her hips backward, legs spread to keep her balance.

"I could use ye as I would," he said, and there was a coldness in his voice. "Could you stop me, Brianna?"

She felt as though she would suffocate with rage and shame.

"Answer me." The hand took her by the neck again, and squeezed.

"No!"

She was free. So suddenly released, she pitched forward onto her face, barely getting one hand down in time to save herself.

She lay on the straw, panting and sobbing. There was a loud whuffle near her head—Magdalen, roused by the noise, leaning out of her stall to investigate. Slowly, painfully, she raised herself to a sitting position.

He was standing over her, arms folded.

"Damn you!" she gasped. She

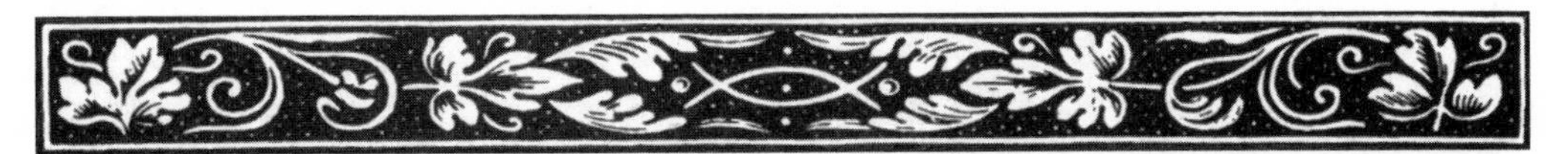

slammed a hand down in the hay. "God, I want to kill you!"

He stood quite still, looking down at her.

"Aye," he said quietly. "But ye can't, can you?"

She stared up at him, not understanding. His eyes were intent on hers, not angry, not mocking. Waiting.

"You *can't,*" he repeated, with emphasis.

And then realization came, flooding down her aching arms to her bruised fists.

"Oh, God," she said. "No. I can't. I couldn't. Even if I'd fought him . . . I *couldn't.*"

Quite suddenly she began to cry, the knots inside her slipping loose, the weights shifting, lifting, as a blessed relief spread through her body. It hadn't been her fault. If she had fought with all her strength—as she had fought just now—

"Couldn't," she said, and swallowed hard, gasping for air. "I couldn't have stopped him. I kept thinking, if only I'd fought harder . . . but it wouldn't have mattered. I couldn't have stopped him."

A hand touched her face, big and gentle.

"You're a fine, braw lassie," he whispered. "But a lassie, nonetheless. Would ye fret your heart out and think yourself a coward because ye couldna fight off a lion wi' your bare hands? It's the same. Dinna be daft, now."

She wiped the back of her hand under her nose, and sniffed deeply.

He put a hand under her elbow and helped her up, his strength no longer either threat or mockery, but unutterable comfort. Her knees stung, where she had scraped them on the ground. Her legs wobbled, but she made it to the haypile, where he let her sit down.

"You could have just *told* me, you know," she said. "That it wasn't my fault."

He smiled faintly.

"I did. Ye couldna believe me, though, unless ye knew for yourself."

"No. I guess not." A profound but peaceful weariness had settled on her like a blanket. This time she had no urge to tear it off.

Comments by Readers

If I may address this from experience . . . intellectually knowing there was nothing you could do, being told by a therapist there was nothing you could do, does not change that nasty voice in your head, nor the subtle message from society, that if you really didn't want to you could have stopped him.

Speaking as a survivor, the scene between Bree and Jamie in the barn thunders. It is a glory of text. If the woman had written nothing else, contributed nothing else to literature or science, that one scene would have been contribution enough.

It should be ripped from the pages and slapped into the pile of clinically detached paperwork they hand you.

On top.

*I'm of the opinion this book (*Drums of Autumn*) should be handed to any woman seeking help after an assault; it is the only piece I have ever seen which hits at the helplessness of the victim accurately, viscerally, and in a manner making it possible for the victim to truly accept they weren't at fault for not fighting "hard enough." The scene is truth: bright as a diamond, hard as granite.*

T. Burke

As a survivor of violence and sexual abuse, I appreciate that you do not look away when you write. Looking away tends to keep the abused victims, while looking straight on allows the abused to do more than react, allows them to go on and grow and develop and deal. And that gives hope . . . expands the possibilities of what it means to live to the fullest.

Cat Finch

BLACK JACK RANDALL—A STUDY IN SADISM

Author's Note: I wrote this following piece specifically for Tobias Menzies (the actor who plays Black Jack Randall—and Frank Randall—on the Starz television series), who'd asked me about the captain's family background, social class, and general SOP. In the process of discussing Jack Randall's background, psyche, and motives, though, I combed back through several years of discussions from the CompuServe Books and Writers Forum and compiled—with the invaluable help of Kristin Matherly, a born archivist—a number of bits and pieces regarding Jack Randall that I thought might be useful to both Tobias and Sam Heughan, who was going to have to deal with Jack Randall at close range during the filming of Outlander. *I sent both the biography and the compiled discussion (in the form of a Q&A with additional commentary) to the show's writers and production team, as well as to the two actors.*

The Randalls of Sussex are very minor aristocracy; the eldest brother, William,[13] has a hereditary knighthood. They're not a wealthy family, though they are landed gentry: enough money for the sons to be privately educated (Jack mentions his tutors to Claire, with regard to his civilized accent) and to purchase a captain's commission for Jack.

The sons took the traditional path: eldest inherits the estate, second son enters the military, and the third goes to the Church—Alex, the youngest brother, is a Church of England curate.

There is a long-standing estrangement between William and his two younger brothers but not specified what caused it. It's resulted in William refusing to help Alex financially and refusing to bring Jack's body home to England when he's killed at Culloden (not that this would have been very unusual; soldiers most often *were* buried where they were killed, or somewhere nearby).

Alex is the one person in the world whom Jack cares for. (And if you want to go for an acting trifecta in the second season, Tobias, Alex looks enough like Jack that both Claire and Jamie think he *is* Jack when they encounter him unexpectedly in Paris.[14])

Don't know if it's in the script, but at one point in their prolonged (book) encounter, Jack says to Jamie, *"Tell me that you love me, Alex."* People have been trying for years to figure out whether a) Jack knows that one of Jamie's middle names is Alexander (he probably does, army paperwork being what it is), b) he means his brother (and what does that imply about his relationship with his brother, if so?), or c) he means a young Scottish prisoner named Alex MacGregor, who hanged himself a few months previously while in Randall's custody (and following a few personal encounters with the captain).[15]

Jack is, as Claire notes, a sadist with a sense of humor—and thus particularly dangerous. He's witty and fairly refined in manner, though not posh as such.

Mm, the duke [the Duke of Sandringham]. I rather think he met Jack a few years before, when Jack was with a regiment quar-

[13] *Also referred to as Edward.*

[14] *Alas, the production team didn't see it my way and cast a separate actor to play Alex.*

[15] *I rather doubt they'll ever find that out, for sure. . . .*

tered in London. We don't know whether he's presently commanding a garrison in the remote Highlands because he did something (or some things) in London that made his superiors nervous, or whether he chose to go there voluntarily, either because of his relationship with the duke (i.e., if the duke is indeed a secret Jacobite—and I kind of think he is[16]—he may have arranged for Randall to be transferred to a regiment in the Highlands (as distinct from a Highland regiment) for the purpose of keeping an eye on political developments there) . . . or because it was a better hunting ground for someone with his tastes.

There are fewer opportunities in terms of women—though there are always a few prostitutes, these would be well known to whichever village they live in, and the virtuous women are almost all under the protection of men, or in groups of women. When he finds one unprotected—like Jenny Fraser—or alone—like Claire—he's more than ready to take advantage, but that doesn't happen often.

But the opportunities offered to a man who's more or less in sole charge of male prisoners, with no one to answer to, and mostly no one with the power to make real inquiries . . . that's another thing.

Anyway, he probably met the duke in London. The duke is straightforwardly homosexual (so to speak) in his personal tastes (Randall isn't gay; he's an equal-opportunity sadist), but very astute psychologically. He recognizes what Jack is and exploits that knowledge to use and control him. (We don't know what little jobs Jack may have done for the duke over the years, but pretty sure there was some wet work, as they say these days.)

The interesting thing is that the duke is cheerfully and coldly amoral. Jack's not. He *knows* what he is, knows it's despicable—but doesn't struggle against it. He's addicted to what he does and has grown a thick callus over what sensitivity he might once have had, in order to survive mentally.

BLACK JACK RANDALL— Q&A, WITH ADDITIONAL COMMENTARY[17]

Author's note: These answers and comments are drawn from stuff I've posted on the CompuServe Books and Writers Forum over the course of the last fifteen or twenty years, in response to the recurring discussions there about the character of Black Jack Randall.

Q: Do you think Captain Randall is a sociopath—by which I mean somebody totally fixated just on his own needs/desires? Or does he know that he's a villain?

A: Interesting question, though one that I've never doubted the answer to.

He *does* know what he is, and the knowledge accounts for a good deal of the depth of his character. Stephen Bonnet, by contrast, doesn't know—and wouldn't care. Jack Randall does know, and does care. Not that he wants to reform, but the fact that he does know gives him an existential despair that lies at the root of the damage he does.

---

[16] *Though he's much more likely an opportunist, much like the Old Fox, Simon Fraser—willing to play both sides against the middle and join whichever side looks like winning.*

[17] *With great thanks to Kristin Matherly, who kindly compiled all of these questions and comments for me.*

Now, *why* he is what he is is another question, and I'm not yet sure whether we'll know the answer to that.

Q: I hear some people wonder why Jamie held Jack Randall when he cried during the torture, but I wonder what effect Jamie's humane response had on Jack. I think what Jamie did—even though he told Claire he didn't know WHY he did it—might be connected with the whole thing about forgiveness. It certainly says a lot about Jamie's character that he should be capable of compassion, even in those circumstances! I wonder about Jack's, though.

A: Well, we might reasonably assume that Jack Randall had probably never encountered that kind of humanity in that kind of situation before. See the next question and its answer for further thoughts on this. . . .

Q: Do you think Jack Randall's assaulting Fergus was done randomly, or was it intentionally to hurt Jamie?

A: Sociopaths and psychopaths view other people simply as objects, for the most part. "Evil" as a concept does not exist to them, no more than "good" does. I think it's important to note, though, that both these terms are just useful constructs in the work of understanding how people at the extremes of human behavior operate; neither one is a blueprint for what an individual might think, feel, or do. I.e., I don't think you can say absolutely, "Oh, this person is a sociopath; therefore, he's completely incapable of feeling anything for anyone else, ever." IF such a person did form a connection with another person, such as to establish actual communication and give him a glimpse of empathy, I imagine that connection and that person would be very important indeed. I imagine Jack Randall had such a connection with his brother, who is therefore immensely important to him. Jamie and Claire (and Fergus; and of course it's random—how would Captain Randall know of Fergus's association with Jamie? He isn't tracking him around the city, hoping for an opportunity to do something mean to him, for heaven's sake. Lust driven by sadism is one thing, and it has nothing in common with that sort of pettiness) are pretty much just objects to him.

I say "pretty much" because it's possible that he *did* feel a brief (and doubtless deeply unsettling) connection with Jamie at one point.

Q: Is it the fact that men are usually less helpless/vulnerable that makes dominating another male more of a challenge for Jack Randall than terrorizing or raping a woman might be?

A: And that much more gratifying when accomplished. Yes, I think that's so, as a general rule. On the other hand, the captain had plainly never run into women like Jenny Fraser and Claire Fraser before.

Q: Do you think Jamie had negative associations with oral sex after Wentworth?

A: Well, according to what he told Claire, Jack didn't *hurt* him while giving him oral sex—which unnerved him a lot more than if he had but thus probably didn't give him immediate revulsive associations with the act, either.

There was then quite a bit of back and forth on sadism, homosexuality, and bisexuality with a lot of short responses. The relevant bits of my response are below:

Jack Randall's a sadist. He's not wanting to rape Jamie because he's hot stuff—the man isn't basically a homosexual at all (*vide* his attacks on Jenny and Claire and the reports Frank found of "interference" with women of the countryside)—he wants to do it because it will cause Jamie great pain and emotional distress; that's what Jack feeds on. Sex is just the weapon that he uses—an end to his own means.

Still, I didn't say he didn't want Jamie particularly. I said a) Jack Randall isn't a homosexual, and b) he didn't want to have sex with Jamie as a matter of normal sexual attraction. He *wants* him, all right, though.

I've seen Jack Randall described as a bisexual sadist—and have used that description myself on occasion, if only because it's factually correct, and you need a bit of shorthand when doing interviews; you can't really delve into character very deeply under those circumstances. Still, he's not really bisexual, either, save by default. He's a genuine sadist. The gender of the person he's working on is not all that relevant to him, save as a matter of technique.

(I would point out, though, that the "Alex" Jack refers to while assaulting Jamie may not be his brother but rather Alex MacGregor, the Scottish prisoner who hanged himself following a similar assault.)

In response to an observation that a reader thought Jack preferred men and his attacks on women were to divert suspicion:

No, it's just that his position as an officer gives him access to men (in prison) who are helpless and at his mercy, whereas it's harder for him to find women who are totally unprotected and available to him.

I often get questions as to just *how* I go about "creating" characters like Jack Randall. This is not specifically related to Jack, but just in general:

I'm not sure how to go about explaining, but I *think* that what a writer does is very much like what an actor does (insofar as I understand that process). You kind of reach . . . *out* . . . for whatever is out there, in terms of the material, the script, the plot, the background, the story, what you know intellectually about the character(s) involved. And then you reach . . . *down* . . . into yourself, for whatever you find there. Then you try to deal as honestly as you can with what you're holding in your hands.

In response to speculations about why Jack wanted Jamie (or the unidentified Alex) to tell him he loved him:

Possibly, forcing a victim to admit "love" for him is the final indication of his mastery over them; he's broken the victim completely. So he's victorious—but then it isn't fun anymore, either: hence, Jamie's conviction that Randall would kill him if he said it. Game over.

Just a suggestion.

(Though with ref to Jack Randall suffering from rosy visions of himself as a sadistic Romeo . . . well, we will refrain from speculation as to what various of the readers may have been smoking while reading <cough> and merely indicate that I've seldom met *anyone* more self-aware than the aforesaid Jack Randall. Vicious, yes; self-deluded, no.)

In response to a question about the healing scene in the abbey:

Claire correctly perceives, both from what Jamie tells her and from her knowledge of him, that the heart of his depression stems from the fact that he was not able to fight Jack Randall. Had he fought and been overcome, then beaten and violated, that would have been bad, but his sense of himself as a man would likely have remained intact, if bruised. But he gave his word to save her life and thus surrendered himself. Which is a very self-sacrificing, thoroughly Christ-like thing to do. But he's *not* Christ, he's a man, a young man, and a man from a warrior culture, trained from boyhood to be willing to lay down his life to protect his own—but only at the point of a sword, and taking as many enemies with him as possible. The giving up of his body has mortgaged his soul, as well.

As I say, Claire sees this, though she doesn't say it explicitly. She rouses the ghost, so to speak, and gives her *own* body in turn in order to incarnate it, so that Jamie *can* fight Randall and thus reclaim himself. At the same time, she still is herself, with her woman's body—and Jamie's rage can thus seek a sexual outlet, mingling violence with sex (you will have noticed that sex and violence are always fairly close, with them; this is one reason why Randall was able to do so much damage, since he fully recognizes and uses that link) and reclaiming his soul by the same means by which it was taken.

Q: Do Randall's tearful confessions of love to Jamie during Wentworth mean something regarding his character? There seems to be an implication in *Dragonfly in Amber* that Randall's relationship with the Duke of Sandringham involves "punishment." Could that be a sort of penance?

A: Well, just to be completely accurate—Jack Randall really doesn't make "tearful confessions of love" to Jamie at Wentworth (this being clear in my mind because I had a long discussion on that point with one of the executive producers not ten hours ago). He says to Jamie (and I don't *think* I said anything about his demeanor while saying it, but I don't swear to that. We're hearing about it *from* Jamie, who was in no condition, really, to notice the fine points), *"Tell me that you love me, Alex."* And Jamie says to Claire that *his* conviction was that if he'd said it, Randall would have killed him on the spot.

What we don't know, of course, is who he was speaking *to*. Did he *know* that one of Jamie's middle names was Alexander? Was he referring to his brother Alex and having some fevered expression of frustrated incestuous longing (or, more sinisterly, a flashback to some such incident?), or was he referring to the young Scottish prisoner Alex MacGregor, who hanged himself after being tortured and raped by the captain? And those are just the possibilities we know about; it could have been someone else entirely.

Neither do we know his intent in issuing that command/plea. My personal impression—with which the executive producer agreed—was that a) he's a sadist, b) he derives sexual pleasure from hurting people, both physically and emotionally, and c) he thus tries to break them, in one or both senses. But what would happen if he *did* break a victim and make them surrender unconditionally? Presumably it would be a great thrill—but a momentary one. He wouldn't be able to get anything further out of a victim who has no further to go. Which would explain why Jamie thought Randall would have killed him if he'd given in to that final demand—he likely would have.

Q (from Mandy Tidwell): How personal do you think Randall's encounter with Jamie at Wentworth really was? He doesn't use Jamie's name prior to that—just derogatory nicknames—and I thought perhaps Jamie was just a substitute for whoever "Alex" was. But reading *Dragaonfly* again, I really noticed how shocked Randall is at seeing Jamie in Paris. Maybe it becomes personal after you torture someone and don't get that total surrender.

A: Well, you know, you'd probably feel rather intimately connected to someone with whom you'd shared the experience (and believe me, they did share it; that's why Jamie is shattered beyond the merely physical—Randall forced him into emotional engagement) of torture and repeated rape over a period of ten or twelve hours.

Someone then requested elaboration on this answer—and got it:

Hate and fear are emotions, and really destructive ones, too. Especially if they go so deep that you can't let go.

Imagine some fairly harmless situation—being in a boring business meeting, for instance. Normally, your body would be sitting there in durance vile, but your mind would be off roaming, thinking about dinner, remembering a conversation from earlier in the day, looking forward to watching the last episode of *Breaking Bad* after dinner, making mental lists of errands, etc.

But what if you weren't allowed that mental escape? What if someone who could read your mind was sitting right next to you and poked you sharply every time your attention wandered even slightly from what was going on? You *can't* escape mentally, any more than you can physically. Think about that for a bit . . . forced to pay close attention to what's going on, every single minute, no matter how much you dislike what's going on. How long would it take for you to go mildly nuts? Majorly nuts, if it didn't end? Majorly nuts if someone was deliberately *hurting* you and making you pay attention, asking you questions about what they were doing and how *that* felt . . . and so on? Majorly nuts if the person hurting you insists not only on hurting you and making you attend to the details of your own humiliation and agony, but engages your mind by making you think about something you Really Don't Want to Think About—e.g., the nature of your sexual relations with your beloved?

That kind of emotional engagement.

And further discussion:

Someone who's abused over a long period of time *does* become accustomed to it and eventually grows to feel that this is "normal" (as in, they don't see any other way for things to be). I won't go into the possibilities for a victim actually to believe they enjoy the interaction—and I *really* won't go into consensual BDSM (other than to note that it's something completely different; in a real relationship of that kind, it's really the submissive partner who holds the power), as that's a bit outside the scope of the discussion.

That wasn't the case for Jamie; what he suffered was not habituation but an abrupt dislocation, an assault on his sense of self as well as on his body. He *did* still know what "normal" was, though, which gave him a way back, once Claire had rescued him from the immediacy of despair and helped him to heal his worst physical wounds, so that he had the strength for the struggle to survive spiritually as well as physically.

Speaking of *Dragonfly,* I've had a good many people ask, over the years, why on earth Jamie didn't immediately kill Jack Randall when encountering him at his brother Alex's deathbed.

Well, a) a deathbed—and remember, Jamie *likes* Mary Hawkins—and the scene of a tragic wedding is no place for personal violence, no matter how justified. And b) Jamie at this point suddenly perceives the commonality of humanity—regardless of personalities—and is moved to a compassion that embraces not only Mary and Alex but also recognizes the suffering in Jack. And in that recognition, he realizes (probably with some surprise, though he doesn't discuss the occasion with Claire) that his own burden of rage has eased a little. This *is* where he begins to realize that his only way of recovering himself entirely is to forgive Randall; he already realizes that simply killing the man probably wouldn't amend his feelings of violation and hate.

That is, of course, a big thing to realize, let alone to accomplish—and it takes him a good long time (and constant practice) to accomplish it. But he does begin to realize it here, and that's why he quietly escorts Randall back through Edinburgh afterward, both men alone with their thoughts.

[Edited to add that I not infrequently hear this question, which seems to be based on a rather simple "Hey, this SOB *raped* me; *I'd* jump him on the spot, no matter what!" reflex assumption of what's proper. The thing is . . . Jamie isn't a simple man. Beyond that—he's *already* done vengeful violence to Randall and both achieved whatever relief can be gained from that (what additional good might be done from attacking him here, for goodness' sake?) and seen just what kind of collateral damage can result. He's not stupid, and he has great self-control.]

Additional comment from a reader (Tess Jones) participating in the discussion:

You know, in my initial reading of *DIA,* I wasn't surprised with Jamie's behavior during the Alex/Mary/Jack deathbed/wedding scene. For one reason, Jamie had *already* acted once on the killer urge toward Jack Randall . . . with some pretty disastrous consequences! And for another, he sees Jack in a way he's never seen him before, and I think he's immobilized by the shock of his own empathy for Black Jack just then. But there it is. Jack was not a monster in front of him but a man grieving over the dying brother that he loved. Jamie had once had a brother whom he loved and lost to illness. Now, Teacher can come hit me with a ruler if I am wrong, but I think it is *because* Jamie was able to identify with Jack in this way (having lost & grieved a brother himself) that began his process toward forgiveness. It's sort of ironic to note Jamie's earlier statement: that it was his identification with Jack in terms of those baser instincts he saw within himself (thanks to Jack's thorough education of him at Wentworth) which he gave as the reason he could *not* forgive Randall. Two different connections, both profoundly affecting Jamie's ability to forgive Randall.

I wasn't surprised that, rather than going for his sword, Jamie was rooted to the floorboards, stunned by the scene before him and his own epiphany. I think (as another participant said) that it *does* become more clear once we read his lesson to Bree in *Drums of Autumn* and see what he's learned about forgiveness in the twenty years since. I think also, if we bounce forward a bit, it's drawn even sharper for us in reading Jamie's attempt (in *The Fiery Cross*) to help Roger see Stephen Bonnet as *not* a monster, just a man; no more, no less. Jamie had Black Jack Randall thoroughly built up into a monster in his mind until the moment he saw him with dying Alex.

To which I responded:

Dear Tess—
Yep. You got it.

Reacting to a reader struggling to forgive and accept Jamie's attempts at forgiveness:

It's good that you find it difficult, I think. One of the things I wanted to get across—not in that scene, but in the entirety of that theme through several books—is just how hard it *is* to practice forgiveness. Even when you think you've accomplished it, rage and hurt and nasty things come sneaking back, and there it all is to be done over again. Except that it becomes a little easier, maybe, because you know it *can* be done.

I'm kind of wondering what might come sneaking back in Jamie's fitfully recovered memories of Culloden, myself. (That's not a tease; I really *am* wondering. . . .)

And some more thoughts along those lines:

Well, he certainly didn't forgive him on the spot during the deathbed scene, no. Nor, probably, even consider "moving on." He just experienced a jarring moment of empathy, suddenly seeing Jack's love and grief for his brother. That wouldn't have been anything he'd ever have expected to feel, and it must have rocked him. But he is a thoughtful man, and always has been, even in his younger years; he'd have thought about that unsettling moment of compassion and, with luck, realized that it offered him a way out, difficult as that way might be.

As another participant in the discussion points out, he'd already taken physical revenge on Jack Randall and not found it to be either satisfaction or catharsis. And it *did* cost him substantially. (He must at some point have thought that if he'd done as Claire asked and left Jack Randall alone, their child would have lived. This probably isn't true, as Claire's miscarriage was almost certainly due to physical factors and would have happened even without her rushing off to prevent the duel—but under the circumstances, I imagine almost any man would blame himself.) But he wouldn't be inclined just to leap blindly on Jack Randall and start throttling him on impulse, even if the more bloodthirsty readers would have liked him to.

[Edited to add that on looking back at Tess's message, I see that it also refers to the events in later books. Yes, I see the point—but I do think that learning to let go is an important step in forgiveness, even if it isn't everything. And he does remind himself that Jack Randall is only a man—which is both a reminder that Randall doesn't possess any supernatural power over him *and* a reminder of that common humanity he saw in Randall. And I think that acceptance is another step on the road to forgiveness.]

In response to a discussion of why Jamie didn't fight back after Claire was released in Wentworth:

Well, it wasn't *entirely* a matter of honor. There are two additional factors operating there: 1) Claire's escape—if Jamie fights back but fails to kill or disable Randall, Randall presumably would and could send soldiers after her. He (Jamie) *has* to keep Randall occupied long enough for her to get away. And 2) the man's been imprisoned for weeks, starved, maltreated, and has just had his hand smashed with a hammer and nailed to a table. You have any idea how painful that would be and how much physical shock it would cause? (Claire does.) Randall did it (broke Jamie's hand) not merely to be mean but with the specific intent of incapacitating him.

Anyway, that would have anyone with less strength of mind and body writhing on the floor, incapable of thought or movement. Besides which, Jamie has just used whatever remaining resources he had in fighting Marley. He simply doesn't *have* the strength to kill Randall and knows it—and he dare not try and fail, for reason #1.

I mean—he's not Superman.[18]

In response to someone complaining about Jenny laughing at BJR:

Well, I would note that had she *not* laughed at Jack Randall, he would undoubtedly have raped her. And it's not as though she had any idea at the time what he'd proceed to do to her brother.

For that matter, she *expected* to be raped and was willing to sacrifice herself to keep Randall from cutting Jamie's throat in the dooryard. I really don't see much room to find fault with her through that exchange, myself.

[18] *Irresistible editorial note from Kristin:* More like Batman.

Comment:

Diana, doesn't Claire realize the same thing about Randall (that Jenny did)? Maybe not to the point of laughing and taunting him, but realizing that he wouldn't manage to succeed if she wasn't hurt or afraid.

Yes, exactly. When he urges her to scream, she realizes that "*he wasn't going to enjoy it* unless *I screamed*"—and therefore doesn't.

In response to a discussion about the graphic nature of the Wentworth descriptions, including a protest by one reader that this part of the book made her feel "gross and filthy" and that I had, in effect, raped her:

It was indeed the writer's intent to make the reader feel assaulted and filthy, in re the Wentworth exposition. I call it that, rather than "scenes"—because (and this is what's interesting to me. My reply to the original poster is all I have to say on the subject of pornography, etc. It's Form Letter #13; very useful in these situations[19]) in fact . . . you never *do* see what happened between Jamie and Jack Randall after Claire left the building, so to speak.

What you *do* see is a) Jack Randall driving a nail through Jamie's hand, which is certainly explicit but not sexual save in the metaphorical sense (and I doubt most readers noticed the metaphor, or if they did, they assumed it to be a Christian metaphor—and it is, of course, that, *too*), and b) Jack Randall kissing Jamie, very simply (i.e., nothing explicit whatever in terms of physical description of the kiss).

This is undeniably shocking and creepy—but it's shocking and creepy largely because the explicitness lies on the side of violence, and the sexual context is revealed rather than shown.

That's why—in the purely "craft" sense—we never do see exactly what happened. We don't live through it in real time with Jamie. We imagine things, based on the nail scene, and later we see the state of Jamie's body from Claire's point of view—both as physician and as outraged wife—and still later Claire hears an account of what happened—but we don't. What we get are tiny, vivid details (very few of them explicit), embedded in the emotional matrix, which itself is rendered in poetic terms (and I don't mean the Wordsworth/daffodil sort of poetry, either. Think *Beowulf* or Chaucer). We don't live through it with Jamie; we live through it with Claire.

I.e., this particular part of the book is probably the least "explicit" of any of the scenes involving sex—but it's by far the most shocking, and it *is* so shocking precisely because we never look straight at it. Things seen from the corner of the eye are much more frightening than a monster in full view (something that escapes all but the most skillful horror-film directors), and by giving the reader only those small, horrid glimpses, you take hold of the most powerful tool any writer has—the reader's imagination.

Now, I have no idea whether the person complaining about grossness and filth was speaking only of the Wentworth expositions or whether the depictions of married sex truly struck her as gross and filthy . . . but if she meant Wentworth,

[19] *Form Letter #13: Not all books are for all readers. I hope you enjoy whatever you read next.*

she's dead on. I *did* rape her. And I meant to. Because the power of Jamie and Claire's relationship (and of their whole story) depends in large part on us identifying with everything felt by the two of them through this situation and its (long-reaching) ramifications. The best (possibly the only) way of doing this, as the writer, is to pull the reader into that same situation and make them experience—as opposed to merely read—it.

A blow-by-blow description of what went on in Wentworth, seen in print in real time, probably *would* be pornographic, insofar as its value would chiefly lie in arousing (one way or another) the reader.

The commenter is, however, wrong in saying that it's the explicit or graphic nature of the text that offended her. It was quite the opposite.

[N.B.: I'll add a note here with respect to the TV show's treatment of the Wentworth material. You can do things in a visual medium that you can't do so effectively in print—and vice versa. Also, while the entirety of the book is told from Claire's point of view—and therefore we can't see anything that she doesn't—the show can and does deal in multiple points of view and take in things happening in different places at the same time. Therefore, it derives a lot of its suspense and narrative force from the audience seeing what's happening to Jamie at the same time that we see Claire's increasing desperation as she tries to find and save him.

It's a different narrative structure, and very effective. But because television *is* a visual medium, you're telling the story in terms of pictures, much more than in words. I can use people's thoughts in a way that the show can't; but they can use the stunning beauty of images to rouse and direct emotions in a very economical way, which I really can't do in words. I think that Ron Moore and the production team (to say nothing of the very talented actors) did an amazing job in conveying the same sense of events and thus remaining very true to the essential story, while telling it in a necessarily more graphic way.]

Part of a response to a conversation about changes during the editing process:

Then there was the scene I've heard described (often) as "master mmphm" <cough>—the sex scene after Jamie gives Claire the wedding ring. The editor was concerned that it was too violent and suggested I take it out. I said I thought it was a necessary step in the relationship, as well as a necessary thematic element in the (linkage of) sex-and-violence thread that runs through the book—i.e., Claire succeeds in saving Jamie's soul at the abbey *because* she understands how close sex and violence may be, has a relationship with Jamie in which those elements are often closely linked, and isn't afraid to use them both to oppose the encounter he had in Wentworth (which was exactly the same thing, but not consensual—and a trifle more violent). She couldn't believably do what she did *unless* we'd shown that element of edgy violence happening between them earlier. I could, though (I said), perhaps rebalance that scene a little.

So I did. Essentially, all I did was alter some of the verbs and rearrange one or two sentences. The editor looked at it afterward and said, "I can't even tell what you *did,* but it worked!" I'm sure there were other small things, but really, no big fights about anything—and no decent editor would buy a manuscript and then try to change the author's intrinsic style, surely?

Part of a discussion on how to write villains:

Oh, he (Jack Randall) doesn't/couldn't exist in a vacuum—but neither did he need a story to walk into. He evolved along with the story. The first scene I wrote involving him was the one in which Claire meets him, right after emerging from the stones. In that scene, all I knew about him was that he was Frank Randall's ancestor and looked like him. I had a vague thought that perhaps he'd turn out to be a strong love interest for Claire, and thus the conflict might be whether she was in love with her twentieth-century husband or with his ancestor. . . . That seemed mildly cliched, but who knows? As it was, though, the minute he saw her and they began talking, I knew he wasn't *that*. And by the time Murtagh rescued her (thus making the link between the cottage scene where she meets Dougal and Jamie, which I'd already written quite a bit earlier, and the coming-through-the-stones part), it was clear to me that Captain Randall was rather dangerous.

I still didn't know what his part in the story was, though; he might just have been a superficial antagonist—something for Jamie to escape from, a generic British officer after a Highland criminal. Every time he turned up, though, I got a stronger sense of his personality and the nature of his feelings toward Jamie—not by any means just duty-to-catch-a-criminal or even personal vengeance—much more of a personal interest/obsession. Why was that? I wondered. So then Jamie explained (to me, as much as to Claire) his past history with the captain.

Well, plainly a villain: here he is raping Jamie's sister (Jamie thinks he did, at this point in the story), as well as stealing chickens, etc. (At this point, I wrote the scene that occurs early in the book where Frank and Claire visit the Reverend and Frank talks to him about his notorious ancestor.)

But then Randall catches Claire while she's fleeing from Jamie, hoping to get back to the stones. And I realized that he was a *lot* more interesting than I'd thought. As Claire remarks to herself in the scene in his office, a sadist with a sense of humor is *very* dangerous. And then, of course, he proved to be impotent with her, when she wouldn't act fearful. I hadn't previously realized that he was, in fact, a sadist, not just your average everyday rapist. So that added another dimension to his relationship with Jamie, didn't it?

At this point, the notion of what happened at Wentworth began to stir in the back of my mind: not in any detail, and I had *no* idea how we'd ever end up there—or where "there" was, for that matter—but the idea of Jack being in the position he wanted, with physical mastery over Jamie. What on earth might happen *then*? (The classic, of course, would be Jamie overpowering and killing him, but somehow I didn't think that was what happened. . . .)

Anyway, I didn't have the courage to try writing something like whatever was going to happen at Wentworth just then, but with the vague notion of it, that was enough for Jamie to confess to Claire (after he spanks her, on their long walk together) that the captain wants his body. But, see, I *knew* that about Captain Randall, long before I wrote that piece of the story; hence that part (and a number of others) exist as they do only because I knew who this guy was—though I wouldn't have learned who he was, had I not been writing scenes involving him. I normally do discover characters as I work with them; I rarely, if ever, try to psych them out ahead of time.

In response to a post questioning why Jamie kept his word to Jack, while in a (much) later book concluding that he's not bound by the oath of loyalty he was forced to swear as a condemned prisoner:

Jamie comes to his conclusion about the validity of his oath to the crown over a long period of time, following considerable thought, and as a matter of reasoned principle. He didn't have time or capacity for thought regarding his word to Jack Randall, and it isn't a matter of principle; it's a clear and urgent matter of saving Claire's life.

I didn't mention it elsewhere—because surely to God there's sufficient other reason without that, and because the sort of reader who thinks Jamie *is* Superman just won't see it—but bear in mind also that Black Jack Randall is an experienced sadist, and he's plainly already been working to soften Jamie up (helllooo? Kept in chains? Breaking hand with mallet?), both physically and psychologically, with the intent of raping him. By the time he nails Jamie's hand to the table, he's achieved a major degree of psychological dominance; Jamie's giving him his word cements that.

Jamie's bargain is just about the last bastion of his rationality; once Claire's gone (and presumably on her way to safety), he surrenders to despair (he says so; you see him do it). There's no point in fighting anymore—and the thought of fighting doesn't enter his mind. He's achieved what he had to, and he's ready to die. You don't suddenly turn around from that point without some remarkable stimulus—and he doesn't have one. Randall comes back into that cell with total power—both physical and psychological—over him.

It's the necessity of coming back from *that*—rather than recovering from abuse and degradation—that nearly costs him his life again at the abbey. As I said, you don't come back from a position of such abjection without some remarkable stimulus—and Claire is able to give him that stimulus *at* the abbey.

From a discussion on Stephen Bonnet vs. Jack Randall:

Black Jack Randall, on the other hand, is capable of love and self-awareness—he knows he's a pervert; he hates himself and turns that hate outward when he can—but still can act selflessly on his brother's behalf.

I never considered Jack Randall to be a gay character. He's a bisexual sadist—a pervert. Not gay. I mean, look at what's actually in the book: he attacks two women, two men. He doesn't succeed very well in the attacks on women that we see (Jenny and Claire), because of who he's dealing with and the fact that he's interrupted. But we know he does molest women on other occasions, because of what Frank tells Claire about the letters of complaint about his ancestor.

His attacks on Jamie and Alexander MacGregor have more impact on us because these are successful, as it were. But it's hurting people that he likes, not having sex with men, per se.

As to his line to Jamie, *"Tell me that you love me"*—maybe he feels that compelling a declaration of "love" while the person is being abused is the symbol of his complete victory over this person; the indication that he's succeeded in mastering and destroying his victim, mentally as well as physically.

EPILOGUE

Let me conclude by noting that I probably come to this material from a different perspective than most people. I'm a biologist by training, with a specialty in animal behavior. I see human beings in the same evolutionary context as other animals, and I see behavioral patterns in terms of purpose and effect, not morality.

Violence is a necessary part of life for all organisms. Even plants conduct chemical and mechanical warfare, against each other and as defense against animals that eat them. Whether we perceive violence in a given situation, and what we make of it, depends much more on our own frame of reference than it does on objective reality. And that frame of reference tends to be both idiosyncratic and extremely malleable.

Sex is also a necessary part of life for all organisms. And given the physical logistics that attend both sex and the further aspects of reproduction, it shouldn't be in any way surprising that sex and violence are deeply entwined in the human psyche. (Any woman who's given birth knows just how violent reproduction is.)

Looking at other animals and their sexual behavior, you very often see an explicit linkage, wherein the mate of the dominant gender (and it isn't always the male) will physically subdue their mate before completing the sexual act (these can be pretty various, too . . .). The evolutionary argument for this is that by exhibiting physical force, the dominant mate is proving his (or her) genetic quality—i.e., you don't want a ninety-eight-pound weakling fathering your children. And thus—by extension of the argument—human evolution has produced a tendency for females to find exhibitions of strength by males sexually arousing and to be attracted both to physically imposing men and to men whose obvious character is powerful, violent, or both. Political correctness, of course, would have none of this, but evolution has been around a lot longer and has more to say about it.

Anyway, the point is that I see sex as not only a matter of reproduction in humans but as a form of very effective communication (these two purposes are plainly not exclusive). And like all channels of communication, sex can carry a multiplicity of messages. Therefore, as a novelist, you can use scenes involving sexual material to communicate a tremendous range of emotions and information—and the fact that the frame of reference you provide is a sexual one means that the viewer's attention and response will be enhanced. Sex is so important to humans that they'll watch *anything* have sex. And their attention will be instantly drawn to *anything* with a sexual context, whether the specifics of the situation are personally attractive to the individual viewer or not.

The downside, of course, is that it's easy to abuse that innate interest—and almost any advertiser will do it, sooner or later. So do a lot of artists—writers, filmmakers, painters, you name it. My personal feeling is that one shouldn't do this; that it's appropriate to use both sex and violence in art if there is a clear and specific reason for doing so—but not just to draw in eyeballs. I hope I've done it right.

PART FIVE

HISTORY AND HISTORICAL FICTION: ORGANIZING THE PAST

History, Historical Fiction, and the Three Levels of Lies

I. The Facts— or: What Really (Sort of) Happened

Beyond the most basic of physical events—this battle occurred on this date, this person was born/died/married/ascended a throne/made a proclamation—there are very few unequivocal "facts."

Almost any recorded event affects more than one person. That being so, both the effects of an event and the immediate perceptions of it will be as varied and numerous as the people who participate in it and are affected by it.

Even the most objective of accounts (and virtually none of them are) will be substantially altered by the author's choice of subject and focus.

Example: Henry VIII's desire for a son had a major personal impact on (to name only a few) Catherine of Aragon, Anne Boleyn, Mary Tudor, Elizabeth Tudor, and Thomas More. While all of these people were affected more or less negatively (fatally in two cases), the impact on each of them would have been quite individual.

On a larger scale, Henry's schism with Rome—which was part and parcel of his difficulty—had enormous and long-ranging effects on his subjects—who all experienced events individually, as well as collectively. And at the base of things was the (retroactively deduced) fact that Henry appears to have suffered from syphilis and died of scurvy—both conditions that might have rendered him poor father material. Meaning that ultimately, one individual's bad health habits resulted in an upheaval that affected hundreds of thousands of individuals over a period of eighty-odd years.

In other words, there are a number of "facts" involved in any historical event, most of which probably have some objective basis in reality. However, "what really happened" depends not only on facts but on the frame of reference in which those facts occur. This being so, we pass on to the next level of "history."

II. The Documentary Record—or: The First Level of Lies

Speaking personally, and just as a quick illustration of the theoretical accuracy of historical accounts:

I've been interviewed repeatedly (as in

hundreds—literally, hundreds, if not thousands—of times) about my books, my background, and other common topics. Interviewers tend to ask the same questions[1] about these things. E.g.:

"How did you get the idea to write these books?"

"Are you Scottish? Why did you pick Scotland?"

"How did you get published?"

"What's your daily writing routine?"

"How did you get from being a scientist to being a novelist?"

"Do you *use* your scientific background in your writing?"

Etc., etc., etc., *ad infinitum* . . .

(One interviewer, to whom I'd sent copies of previously published interviews as background material, called to thank me, adding, "But I'm chagrined to find that I asked all the same questions everybody else does!"[2])

After the first fifty or so times, I found that I had evolved a shtick: the same (reasonably interesting and/or witty) lines used over and over in answer to these questions.[3] That means that every single interviewer who's asked me these questions for the last twenty years has got the same answers, usually word for word.

I naturally don't see *every* interview, but I have seen a lot of them. If I'm telling all the interviewers the same things, presumably most of the interviews should be reasonably accurate, give or take human error like the recording device failing in the middle or trouble in note-taking, that sort of thing. So . . . are they accurate?

Not on your tintype. I paused to calculate this once: out of roughly eight hundred interviews (that I'd seen), *two* of them were entirely accurate. Just two.

Now, I am not a controversial person (in the political sense, and the questions asked are not normally controversial). I.e., I think we can dismiss the possibility of deliberate misrepresentation in interviews (reviews are another matter . . . but reviews aren't meant to be factual, and interviews *are*).

And, in fact, almost all the mistakes made in interviews are apparently due to one of two basic causes: inattention on the part of the reporter, or space constraints that resulted in a misleading omission or juxtaposition.

One very common example—my association with universities is as follows:

B.S. in Zoology from Northern Arizona University

M.S. in Marine Biology from Scripps Institution of Oceanography, UCSD

Ph.D. in Quantitative Behavioral Ecology from Northern Arizona University

Followed by:

Post-doctoral appointment, University of Pennyslvania

[1] *One who doesn't is rare and refreshing fruit indeed.*

[2] *Oddly enough, she was the only journalist who's ever expressed the slightest sense of embarrassment about this.*

[3] *It saves wear and tear on my molars.*

Post-doctoral appointment, UCLA

Assistant Research Professor, Arizona State University

In all justice, there are three universities in Arizona, all of which include the words "University" and "Arizona" in their names:

Arizona State University (Tempe)

Northern Arizona University (Flagstaff)

University of Arizona (Tucson)

It's therefore not unusual for me to read an interview that states that I was either educated at or worked at the U of A (University of Arizona)—though this is in fact the only state university with which I've never had an association.

Okay, that's not accurate, but neither is it a particularly big deal. I mean, who cares? Nobody—now.

But what IF we move down the ages fifty years or so, and some bright soul gets the notion to write a biography of me?[4]

As my potential biographer sits down to go through Google's collection of guff about me, they may well find several pieces purporting to be interviews with me, stating that I went to the University of Arizona.

In search of someone who may have known me there, or of evidence of my student life, my biographer goes to the U of A alumni association, or perhaps the records office, and requests information—only to be told that I was never there.

What does our biographer conclude? That I was one of those people who aggrandize themselves by claiming degrees and awards and medals to which they're not entitled? They might, were they a superficial researcher, particularly if they came across several interviews with this same (very common) mistake.

I'll tell you something else from personal experience: once something has been put in print, a) it never goes away, and b) people will repeat it endlessly, rather than pause to check something or write something in a fresh way.

This is why I insist on writing my own flap copy (when possible) and on seeing press releases before they're sent out. Had I but world enough and time, I'd comb my Wikipedia page weekly in order to weed out mistakes, but I don't.[5]

As one example of misleading information—years ago, I wrote an essay for the local newspaper in Flagstaff, telling the story of my parents' very dramatic courtship and marriage.[6] This essay was picked up and either inserted into my Wikipedia page or quoted from in that venue. The result of this was a widespread misapprehension that I'm Mexican, or "Mexican-American."[7,8]

---

[4] *A couple of people have suggested doing such a thing* now. *I think I'd rather wait 'til I'm dead, frankly. . . .*

[5] *The last time I looked at it, I discovered that someone had added my middle name—but they'd got it wrong and put it down as "Jane" (it's "Jean")—and someone else had removed my mother's name and replaced it with my stepmother's name.*

[6] *"Myths and Mountain Birthdays."*

[7] *And a lot of tiresome suggestions by people who think one should be doomed to write only about one's own ethnic heritage, that I should write something with a Mexican setting.*

[8] *I hate this sort of stupid ethnic hyphenation. What's the point? You're an American or you're not, and* everybody *comes from somewhere, or multiple somewheres, none of which make the slightest difference to anyone's real life. My mother's people come from Yorkshire, for heaven's sake—with one German*

I'm Hispanic, but not Mexican. None of my family members are Mexican. None of them have ever *been* Mexicans, save for a brief period of some thirty years between the War of Mexican Independence and the Treaty of Guadalupe Hidalgo.[9,10]

But owing to the nature of local idiom in rural Arizona in the 1940s, anyone of Hispanic origin was referred to as a "Mexican." Virtually none of them *were* Mexican—that was just what the local populace called them. And I quoted this idiom in the essay I wrote about my parents, because it was the term used, and it had a specific relevance to the underlying cultural conflict that was a large part of their story.

Because of this, though, I'm constantly being introduced (if I'm not quick enough to ask to see the introduction beforehand) as a "Mexican-American" and have such experiences as the Turkish hair-and-makeup stylist who came to work me over in Munich, and who—having conscientiously looked up my Wikipedia page in order to have some subjects of conversation—was charmed at the notion that I was "a Mexican girl!" and did her best to make me look like Jennifer Lopez (whose parents are Puerto Rican).[11]

None of these small things are a big deal—but they are, for better or worse, part of the historical record. And the point is—if errors are as common as they are in contemporary accounts of someone for whom there is no reason to suspect bias . . . how accurate do you think the records you're reading from two hundred years ago are?

And as a brief example of the "limited space" problem: I always tell people the exact same story, as to how I happened to be online, how and why I began posting pieces of my work, how I was encouraged to look for a publisher, how I was advised to seek an agent, how I did so, and what happened

branch (though the family name there was "Schweitzer," which means "the guy from Switzerland," and his father was apparently born in Ireland, so your guess is as good as mine). Should I be "British-American"? Nobody's British-American, because it's a pointless distinction. The hyphenation is generally used either to discriminate (in the meaning of "point out how this person is different") or to brag ("Kiss me, I'm Irish!"), and I'm having none of either.

[9] *Los Gabaldones—my father's side of the family—come originally from a small village in Spain, called (reasonably enough) "Gabaldon" (I've read something that says it derives from a local—extinct—Celtic tribe called the Gabaldi, but I haven't the slightest scrap of evidence that this is the case). The first Gabaldon of my branch in the New World settled in Santa Fe in about 1591 (there* is *documentary evidence of that, at least). Not huge adventurers (though see the next footnote), they stayed there for the next five hundred years. With perhaps the odd Apache, Comanche, or Pueblo Indian inserted into the genetic mix, they remained citizens of Spain until 1810 and the War of Mexican Independence. At which point, they became Mexicans, until 1848 and the Treaty of Guadalupe Hidalgo made them Americans—all without moving a step.*

[10] *There is, however, a family legend that we were at some point* conversos*—Jews, forced to convert to Catholicism by the Inquisition. If true, that would probably explain how people as apparently allergic to travel as the Gabaldons ended up in Santa Fe in the first place.*

[11] *I have the strangest-looking publicity photos from Germany—in part because the airlines invariably lose my baggage (so far, British Airways has lost it four times, and Lufthansa only twice. I will say Lufthansa gives you a nice amenities bag that includes a T-shirt to sleep in) and I'm being photographed in whatever I could grab out of the nearest airport store in fifteen minutes. (Should you ever find yourself in this position, buy black or navy blue, and include a loose-fitting top and a patterned or colored scarf or wrap, which you can drape around your neck for distraction from the rest of your clothes.)*

when I found one. (The whole story, if you're interested, is in the "Prologue" of *The Outlandish Companion, Volume One.*) I've told this story so many times that I invariably tell it with identical vocal inflections and hand gestures, no less. The journalistic version then normally emerges something like this: *Diana Gabaldon wrote her first novel online. In no time, she was snapped up by a New York publisher, and the rest is history!*

Um, yes. "History"—as in "written version of events"—is *just* what it is. It's also wildly inaccurate and misleading and causes people to turn up periodically in inappropriate places online with the statement that they have just written a novel and are there any agents here who would like to sign them up?

Now, the interviewers who publish these lopsided versions of events are not trying to distort reality at all—quite the opposite. However, they usually have major constraints of space and time—they can't faithfully repeat everything I said, verbatim, because it wouldn't fit into the column inches allotted. They have to compress the story substantially, and how well they do that depends on a good many factors beyond my control—how much room they have, how well they listened, what parts of my remarks were interesting to them personally, what sort of notes they took, and how well they understood what I was talking about.

It isn't just me, either. I've talked to a good many other people who have had events "covered" in the popular press, and on several occasions I have read journalistic accounts of events that I've personally experienced or know about (my dad was a state senator and held various other public offices. The resemblance of the account to any public event is seldom more than 50 percent or so).

Okay. Given that modern news reports will eventually become the "history" of the future—how much distortion do you figure there is in your average "historical" document? The fact that something was written a long time ago doesn't make it any more trustworthy (rather the contrary, since there are fewer contemporaneous accounts by which to check it).

Historical documents are influenced by just as many distorting factors as are modern reports: lack of time, lack of space (if you had to scrape a sheep's skin clean in order to have a writing surface, you probably wouldn't be all that verbose), lack of understanding. And these are the *unconscious* distortions! Which leads us in turn to . . .

III. INTERPRETATION AND SELECTIVITY—OR: THE SECOND LEVEL OF LIES

Interpretation and perspective are drawn from—and imposed onto—the primary record. It's necessary to achieve a certain level of historical perspective—or simple distance—because the complexities as viewed at ground level would quickly overwhelm any story.[12] If history is the backdrop, rather than the focus, of a story, a higher ground of perspective will have to be chosen—a more inclusive, less tightly focused one. This is necessary, even if the change of perspective involves the sacrifice of detail and subtlety.

Even the writing of historical narrative, or historical nonfiction, requires this sort of

[12] Vide *the mass of trivia I quoted above regarding my own personal record.*

perspective; the choice of what to include, what to leave out, what weight of importance to allocate to an incident, a person, a time period—all of these will alter the shape of the account and will result in a different impression of "the facts" (such as they are) being communicated to a reader.

How does a writer (or would-be historian) choose what to include and what to leave out? Human beings being what they are, I imagine the usual process is to spend more time on what the individual writer considers interesting or important, adding other information via footnote and appendixes for the sake of an appearance of completeness and objectivity.[13]

This being the case, anyone wanting to form a reasonable impression of a time period, person, or complex event would be well advised to read a variety of sources. Historians, of course, prefer primary sources—documents generated by persons who were alive at the time recorded and preferably witness to the events mentioned. These documents include letters, diaries, newspapers (to some extent), recorded oral histories, etc. Photographs (such as Mathew Brady's well-known Civil War photos) are probably among the most valuable resources—but I tell you what, the camera can indeed lie, even without the benefit of Photoshop. (Some Civil War photos—not necessarily Brady's—were recently analyzed and found to have been deliberately staged, with bodies having been moved postmortem and repositioned to give the impression of a massacre having occurred that actually hadn't.)

So how is a responsible writer of historical fiction to make sure that he or she is being accurate in depiction of an earlier time? Well . . . you aren't. Even if you were writing about something that happened yesterday, to you personally, your account would be shaped by the details you recall (whether right or wrong), by your emotions at the time, and by your *ex post facto* responses and analysis.

You try to avoid making obvious errors of fact, and to make an honest effort to keep faith with the dead. Beyond that, you just have to accept that history, for everyone, will always be seen through a glass, darkly.

Though since we mention honesty. . . .

IV: INTRODUCTION OF DELIBERATE FICTIONS—OR: THE THIRD LEVEL OF LIES

In terms of historical fiction, there can be no such concept as "the truth"—at least not so far as facts are concerned (there is of course an artistic truth that is not only possible but highly desirable—but that's not the question we're dealing with here). The impression you (as the reader) come away with will depend not only on What Really Happened, and on the skill of the writer in depicting that, but on the myriad choices—selectivity/accidental distortion/active suppression/deliberate misrepresentation—made by all those writers who lie (and I do mean lie) between Now and Then.

---

[13] *No, I'm not cynical; I just read a lot.*

Because writers do tell deliberate lies, for an assortment of reasons, ranging from self-interest or self-protection, to the promotion of a political agenda,[14] to a desire to aggrandize or destroy, or simply to make a better story.

This is why historical fiction matters, really. It's the blending of what can be approximately known of events and circumstance with what can certainly be known of people—for the emotional truth that we share by reason of our common humanity is the same from age to age. By this means, we gain insight and perspective not only of the past but of our here and now.

[14] *You know why the majority of accounts of the American Revolution deal with battles and incidents in the northern colonies, with relatively little attention paid to the Southern Campaign? It's because the North won the Civil War, and most of the overview/perspective accounts of the Revolution were thus written by writers with a distinct northern bias. (Or at least that's* my *notion. . . .)*

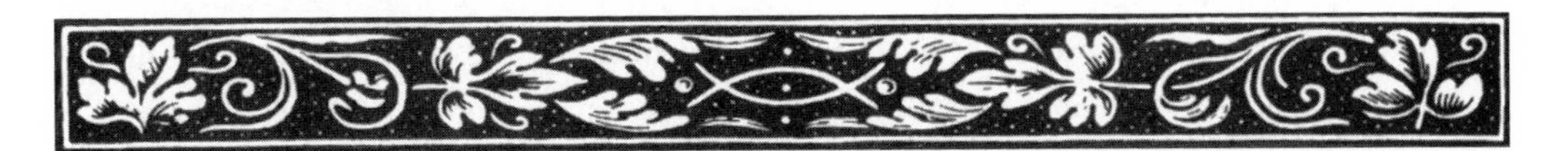

Myth and Mountain Birthdays

Author's Note: I wrote this in 1999, at the request of the Flagstaff newspaper, the Daily Sun, *for one of their features on the history of the town.*

My birthday was always the coldest day of the year. If not literally true, it was family legend, and everyone knows that myth is much stronger than meteorology, even in the north country, where the snow lies deep on the mountaintops, and houses are built to keep the heat in, not out.

This particular legend had its origin—reasonably enough—on the date of my birth, January 11, 1952. My family lived in Flagstaff, but the family doctor had been having a difference of opinion with the hospital board, and had moved his practice to the Williams Hospital. So, when my mother went into labor early in the morning, my twenty-one-year-old parents were obliged to drive thirty miles over a two-lane ice-slick road, through the teeth of a driving blizzard, in order to get to the doctor.

When I was finally born, just at dark, my father was so unnerved by the entire experience that he went out to a nearby restaurant and ordered ham and eggs for dinner—forgetting that it was Friday. (Way back when, Catholics didn't eat meat on Fridays.) Driving the thirty miles home through snow and black ice, he ran off the road twice, got stuck in the drifts, and—as he later recounted—managed to free himself only because he couldn't stand the thought of freezing to death and leaving my mother with a one-day-old child.

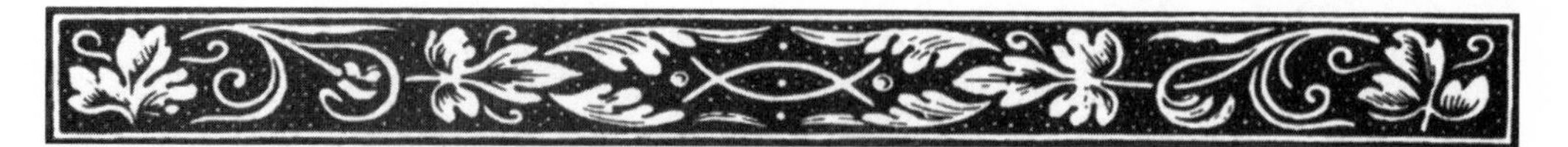

At the age of two days, I too made the perilous trip through the dark pines of the frozen landscape, to become a third-generation native of Flagstaff. There aren't a lot of us, if only because Flagstaff isn't that old.

Among the early founders of the town were my great-grandparents. Stanley Sykes was born in Yorkshire, England, but at the age of fifteen was diagnosed with consumption. The only chance, his doctor told him, was to leave England; go to Arizona, where the warm, dry air was good for the lungs (well, it was 1868, after all; the midwesterners hadn't got here with their damn mulberries and Bermuda grass yet). Stanley heeded this advice, and with his elder brother Godfrey, set sail for the New World and the healing balm of the desert air.

Like many another outlander—my husband, for example—who thought Arizona was a desert, Stanley was startled to find that the northern third

of the state sits atop the Colorado Plateau, and that the San Francisco Peaks are covered with the largest forest of ponderosa pine in the world. In search of desert, Godfrey went south . . . but Stanley stayed, seduced by the rush of wind through the pines and the clear dark skies of the mountain nights, thick with stars.

Great-grandmother Beatrice Belle Switzer came from Kentucky, along with her seven brothers and sisters, when the family farm was flooded out. It must have been a flood of biblical proportions, because once the Switzers started moving, they didn't stop until they came to Flagstaff, which—at 7,000 feet—they evidently considered high enough ground to be safe.

The air in Flagstaff may not have been hot, but apparently it was dry enough, since Stanley lived to be 92, finally dying on a vacation to San Diego (the winter fog will get you every time). I was four when he died, and still have a vivid memory of him in his armchair, the smoke from his pipe drifting in the lamplight, as he taught me the delicate art of building houses out of cards—a skill that's stood me in good stead since.

His son, Harold—my grandfather—became the mayor of Flagstaff—and thereby hangs another family tale.

It was a scandal, in fact—or so everyone said—when my mother, Jacqueline Sykes, the mayor's daughter, descen-

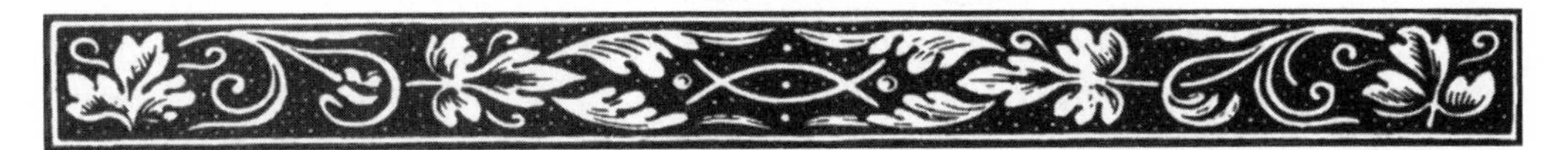

dant of one of the First Families of Flagstaff, fell in love with Antonio Gabaldon. Tony was smart, handsome, athletic, hardworking—and a Mexican American, born in Belen, New Mexico. In 1949, in a small Arizona town, this was miscegenation—or so everyone said.

My mother's friends said so. Mrs. X, her English teacher, said so, telling her firmly that she couldn't possibly marry a Mexican; her children would be idiots. The parish priest who refused to marry them said so; such a marriage would never last. The "interested parties" who took out a public petition against the match said so; it was a scandal. Her parents said so—and at last she was persuaded, and reluctantly broke the engagement.

My mother's parents sent her south, to the University of Arizona in Tucson, to leave the scandal behind; to forget. But she didn't forget, and six months later, on a dark December night, she called Tony and said, "I still want you. If you still want me—come and get me."

He drove down from the snow-covered mountain to the desert and brought her back the same night—and they were married at 6:30 the next morning, by a priest from another parish.

It was a long and happy marriage—dissolved only by death—and thirteen months after the wedding, I arrived, the third generation born on the mountain.

We (and the fourth generation) live in Scottsdale, but I still keep the family house in Flagstaff, and escape there regularly to write; to me, the ideal weather for writing involves a gleaming portcullis of icicles to keep out all intruders, soft white drifts on the pines and the sidewalks, and the muffled grind of cars in the distance, crushing cinders into the slippery packed snow as they labor uphill. No salt on these roads; the San Francisco Peaks are in fact one mountain, the remains of an extinct volcano—or least we hope it is extinct; the U.S. Geological Survey is not so sure.

It's 72 on this Christmas Day, and the dogs are swimming in the pool. My husband gives me warm slippers, though, knowing I'll need them soon. My birthday, after all, is always the coldest day of the year.

(Oh . . . Mrs. X? You were wrong.)

WHAT IS THIS WORD . . . *ORGANIZATION*?

"How do you organize all your research?" people ask me. And "How do you keep *track* of everything that's going on in one of your books?"

"What makes you think I *do*?" is my usual reply.

People often ask me what my writing space looks like and then immediately tell me what they *think* it must look like—obviously, they've spent some time trying to imagine it. The most frequent guess is (as one person recently put it) "a huge wall covered with charts and dozens of Post-it notes in different colors, with colored thumbtacks everywhere and a spiderweb of colored strings running from one point to another!"[15,16]

If I did that, I think I really *would* have trouble keeping track of things. I'd also probably be so busy trying to build and maintain such a monument to organization that I'd never write a word. Of all the ways there are to avoid writing, the impulse to "organize the material" is probably near the top of the list. (See "Mind Games," Part 7.) Making lists is lots easier than writing.

Personally, I love lists. They're very soothing. You usually write them slowly, so they're tidy-looking even if you don't have good handwriting. They also give you a sense of reassurance that you really do know what you're doing, and they incite the pleasant delusion that Things Are Under Control. Unfortunately, once I've written a list, I find that I don't want to do anything on it.[17,18]

I do in fact like to use color to keep track of things, but that—like everything else—is just a function of the way my brain works (i.e., messily) and hasn't much to do with

---

[15] *There are probably a lot of writers who do work this way, given the number of people who find Scrivener the bee's knees. I've tried to use it two or three times, because I hate and despise Beastly Word, but I find that I just don't think the same way it does.*

[16] *People always ask what "special writing software" I use. Alas, there is no such thing. Your brain is the special writing software—what the computer is using is just a word processor, and any of them will work just as well as another for the basics. Which one you get along with personally is purely a matter of individual preference.*

That said, some are more amenable than others. I used WordPerfect 5.1 for years and loved it. It did everything a word processor should do: let me use two documents at once, and let me change the colors for text and background; other than that—it kept the heck out of my way. Then they "improved" it to make it look and work like Microsoft Word. Blech. If you're going to have a program that junks up your screen with ten billion bells and whistles you don't need, does incomprehensible things, and jerks your cursor off the spot where you're typing every time it refreshes the page . . . you might as well use Word, since it's the de facto *standard for business, and if you're lucky, you'll one day need to exchange files with agents, editors, and copy editors, and having a common software program helps.*

Yes, there are alternatives; I've looked at several of them. Unfortunately, Word is the only one that lets me use different background colors for pages. This has nothing to do with organization per se, *but I normally keep a dozen or so documents open at once, and making them different colors helps a lot when flicking to and fro among them. Besides, I like colors.*

[17] *I do write grocery lists. Sometimes. I have to, if I want someone else to do the shopping, or if I'm doing the shopping for something like Easter lunch or a dinner party for sixteen people. More often than not, I write such a list and then forget to take it with me, or I shove it into my pocket as I'm going out to the car and then forget I have it when I reach the store.*

[18] *I often have enthusiastic readers tell me that they'd happily read my grocery lists. One Christmas season, the husband of one such reader wrote to me*

organization, as such. I'm happiest working on multiple projects—or parts of projects—at once.

I've recently come to the conclusion that I have some benign form of ADD. I deduced this on the basis of a newspaper quiz purporting to pinpoint symptoms of this condition. Idly answering the questions while conducting a phone interview[19], I noticed that the questions seemed to fall into two groups: some questions had to do with anger management/irritability/frustration issues, while others dealt with distraction—"Do you often feel like you're watching a television set with all the channels going at once?" (Of course . . . doesn't everyone?), or "Do you commonly feel as though things are rushing past your ears?" (Yes, it kind of tickles), and so on.

I answered all of the anger questions "no" and most of the distraction (if you want to call it that) questions "yes."

This actually explained a lot. I normally *do* think on about eight levels at once, and there are only a few things that are sufficiently intense or absorbing as to give my concentration a single focus.[20]

The way people write—or write most effectively—has everything to do with the way their brains are wired up, and learning to write effectively means learning how you personally *are* wired up.

I discovered my own wiring arrangement more or less by accident (all the important things in my life have happened more or less by accident—with the exception of having children. *That*, I planned[21]). I was working as a university professor—writing grant proposals, textbooks, quizzes and exams, scholarly articles, popular science articles, etc.—and freelancing almost full time for the computer press, doing software reviews, articles, and opinion pieces for *Byte*, *InfoWorld*, and other such publications. I also had three children under the age of six, and it's all Mozart's fault that I decided that *now* was the ideal time to begin writing a novel.[22]

This meant I was doing a lot of writing, of diverse sorts. And I quickly noticed that whatever I was writing, it stuck roughly two-thirds of the way down the page. Fiction, nonfiction, it didn't matter. I could get two-

---

to ask if I would send him one of my grocery lists, signed, as a present for his wife. I did, and apparently she enjoyed it.

[19] *I hasten to add that I don't normally do this, but it was one of the interviews in which the journalist, having conducted no research at all (if they start out calling me "Diane," it's a bad sign), asked every single clichéd question possible. To be honest, when someone says, "So . . . how did you get the idea to write these books?" it's like pulling the string on a Chatty Cathy. (Chatty Cathy is a doll from the 1960s. I never had one—my parents being much too smart to let something like that in the house—but I saw the commercials. I think she said sappy things like, "Do you want to be my friend?" and "I like to have my hair brushed," but I don't swear to that. It wasn't absorbing conversation, though.) You'll get an intelligent, coherent, somewhat amusing answer—it'll just be the same answer (word for word) that's been printed in (literally) hundreds of blogs and articles over the years.*

P.S. If you actually want the answer to that question, it's in The Outlandish Companion, Volume One, Revised and Updated Edition*)*.

[20] *Reading a truly absorbing book, writing, and sex being the main ones. . . .*

[21] *The university where I worked at the time had a more-or-less generous maternity-leave policy, which amounted to, "You can take off as much time as you want, but we aren't going to pay you for any of it." "Fine," I said. "I'm on a nine-month academic-year contract; you don't pay me in the summers anyway." Which is why all the kids were born in May.*

[22] *Mozart died at the age of 36 and I was 35. I thought I'd best get started, just in case.*

thirds of a page with relatively little trouble and then . . . nothing.

Now, this happens to everybody. It may be two pages instead of two-thirds of a page, but at some point . . . you stick. The normal thing to do at this point is get up, go to the bathroom, get a snack, stroll down the street to Starbucks, take the dog for a walk . . . Often the writer doesn't come back, and that's why so many people never finish their books.

I couldn't afford to do this. My husband had just started his own business, I was temporarily our sole support—and I *had* to keep writing in order to get paid. So as soon as a grant proposal stuck, I'd just reach for the next software package on my review pile, and when *that* stuck, I'd switch immediately to the novel scene I was working on—and by the time that one stuck, one of the others would have come loose and I could go back to that one. This round-robin method kept me sitting there and kept me productive.

I still do this, often shuffling two or more scenes from the same book or a novel scene and a piece of a separate novella with some nonfiction bit like a blog or Facebook post—or with some of the omnipresent email.[23]

Readers who don't know any writers personally and therefore don't understand How It Works often tell me (online) to "Stop posting X and get back to writing the next book!"[24]

The other result of this scattershot mentality is that I don't work with an outline, and I can't work in a straight line. I write in bits and pieces, wherever I can see things happening. Little by little, I get more pieces, and gradually these begin to stick together and make larger shapes. It's kind of like playing Tetris in my head but really slowly.

If you read How-to-Write books, you'll find all kinds of advice on How to Write (reasonably enough). The important thing to bear in mind is that whatever method is being presented is Not Necessarily True—for you. It's true for the person who wrote the book, because that's how his or her mind works. If your mind is wired up in a similar way, then the advice is likely to be helpful, but if it's not . . . it's not. This does not mean you're doing something wrong. It just means you haven't yet figured out how your own mind works best. Keep working; you'll get there.

Now, what were we talking about? Oh, yes . . . organization.

All of the above notwithstanding—one really does need to be able to find things when you want them. What I do is simple and squalid, but it works:

I write in bits and pieces, and when I begin a piece—which will normally turn into a more-or-less coherent scene eventually—I give the file a name. Now, I began

[23] *I call it the daily rash. Nearly every day, I get about half a dozen emails from people who have some legitimate claim on my time and effort: publishers, editors, publicists, marketing people from Starz or Sony, interviewers, audiobook producers, etc. All these emails contain demands (couched politely as requests, to be sure . . .) for me to write something. An introduction for a DVD booklet, a dozen hi-res photos of myself with captions, an opinion (with possible revisions) of the latest cover copy for a new book, an outline of my whereabouts for the next three months, and so on.*

[24] *Yes, actually, I* do *think that's rude. I charitably assume they don't intend it that way, since if I point out (politely) that how or when I write what is none of their business, I'm accused of being "harsh," and there's a lot of entitled huffing about what an author "owes" his or her readers. My opinion is that I owe them the best story I can write, and that's it. They get honesty as a bonus.*

writing *Outlander* (for practice) in 1988. Is anybody out there old enough to know what DOS stands for?[25]

Well, the DOS naming conventions say that you can give a file a name up to eight characters long, with a three-character extension (if you want one). Like this: xxxyyyzz.abc.

So I give all my file names for a given book one word that stands for that book—all the main books in the *Outlander* series are JAMIE, for instance, with a number: JAMIE, JAMIE2, JAMIE3, JAMIE4, etc. (*The Scottish Prisoner* was PRISON, and *The Brotherhood of the Blade* BROTHER, and so on.)

This one-word designation is followed by a single symbol that stands for the current year, because I usually require more than one year to write a book (it doesn't always take more than a year, but I'm usually working on more than one project). I use the symbols on the top line of the keyboard for this—!@#$%^&, etc.—followed by a period.[26]

And then I give it a two- or three-character extension standing for the date on which I began writing the file.

So, if I were to begin writing a new scene today, for instance, for the ninth book in the *Outlander* series, the file name would be JAMIE9!.42. This stands for "the ninth book in the main *Outlander* series, file begun April 2, 2015."

Now, this is just my own idiosyncratic method of file-naming; the only real requirement is that a file name be unique, and if you're one of the people who really does get along with a Mac, you no doubt have file names like, "File I Started Writing on April 2, 2015, about why Joanne called her mother a fish-eating cow."[27]

The other part of this system—if you can dignify it as such a thing—is the Master File. This is just a document (always called MFILE and stored in the same directory/folder as the other files for a given book) that lists all the file names, with a few keywords next to each one that describe roughly what or who is in that file and sometimes its connection to some other file or files.

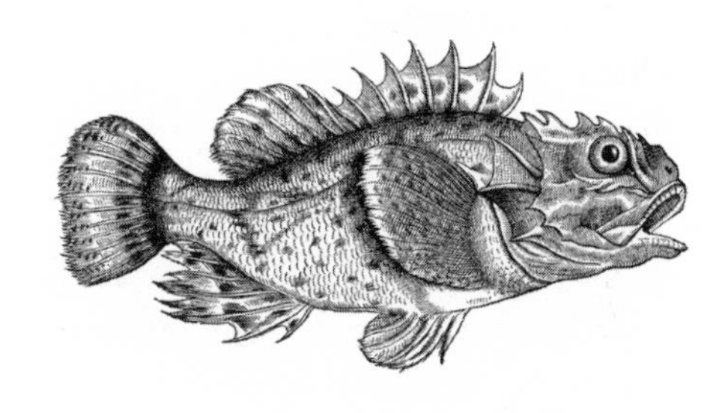

---

[25] *Disk Operating System. It's an internal software application that a computer uses to handle and locate information. Other such systems include Apple's iOS, Linux, CP/M, and others. But DOS is what PC computers used (and still do).*

[26] *If, as sometimes—though rarely—happens, I have an alternate version of some scene, I add an* A, B, *or* X *to the main part of the name. This usually happens because the file has been corrupted by the bloody Mac and the current version won't transfer to the PC, or because the bloody Mac won't find a file I know perfectly well is* there, *and I have to start working from where I know I left off and then glue the pieces together when I get back to the PC and can find the first part again.*

[27] *I don't get on with the Mac mentality, possibly because I am an autocrat and so is a Mac. It thinks it's in charge, and I think* I *am. You know how theoretically "Finder" will locate anything you're looking for on a Mac? It won't. The PC version of this function does not have a cute icon or even a name—but it actually* will *find things, most of the time.*

If I'm having a lot *of trouble with a Mac not finding something I want, I generally end up calling the file—when I finally pry it from the machine's reluctant clutches—something obscene, in capitals (like* USE THIS ONE YOU EFFING BASTARD!!!*) Oddly enough, when I do this, the Mac, evidently cowed by my fury, will obediently find it again, no problem.*

The MFILE for *Written in My Own Heart's Blood* looks something like this:

JAMIE8`.528—fragment "blood of my blood"—(add to .516)

JAMIE8`.530—Willie and the Whore—follows .521

JAMIE8`.723—Jamie and William—"Are you sorry?"

JAMIE8`.830—Roger and Buck—"Do you know who your father was?"

JAMIE8`.915—Claire and Jamie—"And what did he give you?" (goes w/ .37, .424)

JAMIE8`.O13—Ian/Rachel/William—"Bloody Men"

JAMIE8`.N9—Lord John and Jenny—"How?"

JAMIE8`.N17—Jamie and Claire—goes w/ .424, .516, .525)

JAMIE8`.D26—pulling the Christmas lights from the tree—imagery

JAMIE8!.110—Hal and Willie discuss the title

JAMIE8!.123—fragmentary, good Rachel/William stuff—betray my principles

JAMIE8!.221—Jem in the turbine chamber

I update the MFILE once a week (see "Basic Housekeeping"). And in the fullness of time, as the bits and pieces begin to stick together, I'll write something that I know goes with something already extant. To find the other piece, I just open the mfile and search for whatever I recall about the piece I'm looking for, like *Are you sorry?* or *blood of my blood*—and, bingo, there's JAMIE8`.723 or JAMIE8`.528.

So that's it for organization of the writing: file names and a list.

Now, organizing research . . . a discussion of research really deserves its own separate essay. I have actually taught a weeklong seminar on the art and science of research, but here I'll just explain briefly how I manage to find the information I've already collected, rather than how to go about finding it in the first place. (I warn you, it isn't going to be very useful.)

Research material is usually either stored on my computer or it's in a book on my shelves. Bear in mind that the Internet in its present state didn't exist when I began writing novels. There *were* no websites, blogs, YouTube videos, etc. There was such a thing as "online," but aside from government sites like DARPA, what was available to the public lay mostly in the "information services": GEnie, Delphi, and CompuServe.

I also used America Online, when that became available, but pretty much reverted to CompuServe as being the most useful and enjoyable. I hung around with a CompuServe group called the Literary Forum (Go

LitForum, for those old enough to recall[28]), and after people there found out that I was writing a novel, they would kindly offer me bits and pieces of information that they thought I might find interesting or useful (like the Scottish word "mool,"—meaning grave dirt—or *loa-loa* worms and the means of removing one from someone's eye—all good, ripe stuff).

These bits I would store in a directory/folder called JRESRCH (for "Jamie—Research"), and when I needed to know what someone had told me about Quaker Plain Speech, I could just do a quick search through the file names in the folder for Quaker, and there it was.

This is still pretty much what I do, though with the increasing sophistication of computers over the last twenty-five years, I do now also bookmark useful websites and skim through the bookmarks for a site I know I've visited.

But overall, the bulk of my research material has always been books. I have perhaps 1,500 books in my core research collection at home (there are currently more than 2,200, including smaller collections here and there), and about half of these are in the huge built-in bookshelves that my husband gave me as a birthday present some years ago.

These books aren't filed by author name, color, or size (See "A Brief Footnote on Tidiness"); they're filed by general subject—*my* idea of a general subject, that is. From top to bottom of the first bay, for instance, the top three shelves are filled with herbals: books on herbal medicine, the herbology of different cultures and geographical areas, the chemistry of phytoactive substances, with the occasional volume of plant-related folklore or books on growing and using herbs, both historically and presently. Within that category, I make no attempt to organize the books; there are five or six that I find most useful, and those are in the middle of the top shelf. But knowing that *anything* I want to know about herbs is probably in the upper left corner of the shelves is enough for me to find the book I want.

Other general categories include war and weapons, society and social behavior of England, Scotland, France, or whatever, general stuff on Scotland, stuff about the American Revolution (with the books on specific battles kind of grouped, ditto the books about slavery and the ones with descriptions of army life, but that's about as far as it goes), and so on.

As I work my way into a book, I'll find perhaps half a dozen references that are really useful, and these books I'll actually read all the way through (the others I use for looking things up). As I read (I used to do this while walking on a treadmill, but now I walk outside with dogs, so I mostly do this kind of research reading while my husband is watching true-crime shows on TV), I mark anything that's sufficiently detailed that I might want to look it up again with a Page Point. These are little metal thingies that slip over the edge of a page, to mark a line or paragraph. They're neater than stickies, and as I seldom take notes, there's no need for a writable surface.

---

[28] *This group still exists, though it's now called the CompuServe Books and Writers Community. It isn't a writers' group* per se *but rather is a group of people who like books and like to talk about books and writing. That said, there are writer-oriented sections on it. Personally, I've never "done" writers' groups as such—the last thing I'd ever do would be to join a critique group (that's a matter of my personality, rather than an opinion of critique groups; evidently they're very helpful to some people, and if they are, more power to you).*

Beyond grouping my books, listing my files, and marking a few passages with Page Points, though . . . I don't really do anything of an external nature. I don't take notes, because once I write something down, it's *gone.* Not only will I never find the note again, I won't remember either that it exists or what was in it.

What I'm doing as I read research material is fitting it into the shape(s) of the story. Some of this is very direct—on-the-spot research, as it were—where I'm writing a scene, think that I need to know something, like what kinds of insects live in the Dismal Swamp, and either look it up online or go pull the appropriate book out. I then return to the scene and put in whatever details I just learned.

The background stuff—the order of battle for a particular fight, for instance—I just fit as an approximate mental note into the shape of the book, and later, when I'm actually writing about that battle, will be able to go to the file or book and pull out the necessary information. Though what I do with that information isn't necessarily straightforward. . . .

For example, I used the *Osprey Men-at-Arms* book on the Battle of Monmouth as my chief reference for the technical background of that battle (for *Written in My Own Heart's Blood*). Having read through the book once, I knew that there was a list of the various divisions and their commanding officers, plus the staff officers present at the battle, in the back of the book, and that there was a series of maps in the body of the book, showing where every division and company was at different points of the daylong fight.

I wouldn't have known those lists and maps were there had I not read the book, but as I had read it and did know—there was no point in my writing down lists of names, especially as I had no idea where, when, or if I'd use them.

So when I was writing about William's decision to ignore his orders from General Clinton and go off on his own, I handled the logistics by having an officer bring him a note to take to someone, so that he could pretend that he'd received that note and left before seeing General Clinton's. Fine. So someone brings him a note—who? A staff officer, but not a high-ranking one; an aide-de-camp, probably. Check list of officers present and pick one of Clinton's aides-de-camp (he had six at that battle); pick another officer to whom the note should be delivered; check map to be sure that man's company would be in a useful direction, and if not, go back and pick another one. *Voilà!*

Or it would have been *voilà*! if I'd actually done that. As it was, while I was looking at the list of aides-de-camp, it occurred to me to wonder whether Major John André had been at Monmouth. I knew I was going to eventually deal with Benedict Arnold's betrayal later on—not in this book, but eventually—and it was probably a good idea to mention John André once in a while to keep him in the reader's mind now and then. (That's why Claire met him at the Mischianza in Philadelphia toward the end of *An Echo in the Bone*. I'd read an account of the party and learned that Major André had been not only present but deeply involved in organizing the affair—and that's why Claire went to the Mischianza in the first place—so I could mention John André.)

As it was, Major André wasn't on the *Osprey* book's list of officers—but I knew he'd been an aide to General Clinton (having read a couple of brief biographies of him) . . . when did that happen? I checked, and he became Clinton's aide just after Monmouth—but he was at the time of

Monmouth an aide to one of the lesser generals under Clinton and therefore might reasonably have been there, even though he wasn't listed.[29] (Checked quickly through Google, Wikipedia—which has its limits in terms of historical research but is reasonably good for fast date-checking and occasionally turns up interesting bits of trivia—plus several shelf references, found an intriguing account of the establishment of the British Legion—Tarleton's unit[30]—and couldn't find any solid evidence that he'd been somewhere *else*, so . . .)

And since my mind was now dealing with the notion of mentioning people who might be useful later on, I thought of Banastre Tarleton; I'd always intended to use him somewhere in the later books, during the Southern Campaign; he was an immensely colorful and somewhat well-known character,[31] and he was involved in a small but memorable massacre at Waxhaws, which I might want to use later (if only because no one's ever heard of it). So . . . where was *he* during Monmouth?

He wasn't on the lists, either—but he might easily have been at the battle. A bit of quick Wikipedia work, plus a flip through *The Green Dragoon* (a biography of Tarleton; it's one of the books I'll eventually read all the way through but haven't yet), and it was apparent that I *could* plausibly have him there—and nobody could prove he wasn't. So . . . Major André came and asked William to carry a note for him to Colonel Tarleton (with whom William then has a fight over a whore[32]), and there are Major André and Colonel Tarleton in the story. Neither of them was *on* the *Osprey* list of officers—but it was the fact of those lists that made me think of them.

(See, I told you this part wouldn't be useful.)

---

29 *Having read the* Osprey *book through completely, I was aware that the Battle of Monmouth was such a huge mess that it was by no means thoroughly documented; a number of militia companies from New Jersey and Pennsylvania were known to have taken part in the battle but weren't mentioned by name, for instance. It wasn't a traditional eighteenth-century battle but rather a series of pitched battles, fought on the run by three different bodies of the British army and innumerable units of Continental regulars and militia, often under a command that shifted repeatedly. Plenty of room for a novelist to operate comfortably, in other words.*

30 *General Clinton himself raised the British Legion, in New York, in June of 1778, and it didn't go into commission until a month after Monmouth. However . . . the legion consisted of two separate units, artillery and cavalry. Now, plainly a cavalry company takes much less time and trouble to get into operation than does an artillery company. Why, if General Clinton expected trouble while leaving Philadelphia (and we know he did), would he not send a messenger to his protégé Tarleton, asking him to bring the new cavalry unit (which Tarleton commanded) down at once to help out with the hazardous removal of troops and civilians? Were I General Clinton, that's what* I *would have done—and I scarcely think Sir Henry Clinton was less perspicacious.*

31 *Mostly thanks to that execrable movie,* The Patriot, *starring Mel Gibson, for giving us the hideous caricature of Tarleton in the form of the character played by Jason Isaacs, which led readers insisting to me for years that Black Jack Randall must be played by Isaacs—a good actor whose only crime is having strikingly light eyes; he looks totally normal when wearing brown contacts.*

32 *Banastre Tarleton was twenty-four at the time of the Battle of Monmouth; he would have been about twenty-one at the time* The Patriot *theoretically depicted. He also never burned down a church full of rebels. Not that facts actually mean anything to filmmakers in general, but they often do to historical novelists.*

My overall attitude to research is that I just collect stuff that may be useful, read the stuff that seems likely to be *most* useful, and memorize where to find specific information when wanted. Beyond that . . . I just keep an eye out for the interesting and unexpected. It's all over the place; you just have to be looking.

Research methods, like writing methods, are very individual. Some writers feel that they have to do a great deal of research before they even think of writing something.[33] Other writers (naming no names . . .) just start writing and do the research on the run, as it were.

When I began writing *Outlander,* my only intent was to learn how to write a novel—and I chose historical fiction because it seemed the easiest thing to try; I was a research professor (albeit in the sciences) and I knew my way around a library. However (I said to myself), the point was to learn how to write a novel, not to learn everything there was to know about Scotland in the eighteenth century. Therefore (I concluded), I'd go to the university library and start looking at once—but I'd also start writing at once.

After all (I thought), if I wrote something that was later contradicted by the research . . . I'd just change it. It is, after all, only words on the page—nothing easier.

So that's what I did and have pretty much continued to do. For me, the research and the writing feed off each other in a useful sort of way: I begin a scene, realize that I need to know X, go and look up X, and in the process discover something fascinating about Y (which I would never have thought to look for in the first place), which triggers a completely different scene, which in turn requires information about Z . . . and so on.

This approach makes perfect sense to some writers and makes others foam at the mouth even to contemplate it. Your mileage may vary.

Now, there *are* patterns for doing research, and reasonable suggestions (for instance, if you're doing a quick preliminary overview of a setting or a time period, check the children's section of the library or Amazon. Children's books *have* to be short, clear, and entertaining; thus, they normally have a good, brisk overview, sprinkled with a lot of the kind of picturesque facts that novelists like), but what you find is going to depend a lot on what you're looking for—and what period you're working with.

The eighteenth century is a great period to write about, because so much original material from the 1700s still exists. Primary sources abound: diaries, letters, speeches—anything written down by an eyewitness (with a cautionary note about newspapers: eighteenth-century journalists weren't any more careful, scrupulous, or free of bias than twenty-first-century ones—frequently much less so), and secondary sources (things written after the fact, which are often valuable for their perspective or the collection of facts and opinions) are everywhere. A great many artifacts of the period still exist, too, including buildings, rooms, furniture, clothing, tools, art, etc.

Beyond the accessibility of sources, it's a

[33] *The trouble with this philosophy is that there's no conceivable way of knowing when you've done* enough *research, since there's always more that could be found out. A corollary difficulty with this method is that it offers such a temptation to feel that you can't possibly write anything until you've done* more *research—and thus never write anything. (I do know people who have been "writing" historical novels for the last ten years, but who have in fact never written a word. They never will, either—but they'll know a heck of a lot about third-century Byzantium. . . .)*

great benefit that the original sources are mostly in documents that are still readable by a modern person without special training in ancient languages. There are differences, of course—but the Declaration of Independence, say, or Tom Paine's "Common Sense,"[34] is perfectly comprehensible to a modern person, and so are George Washington's letters or the writings of Voltaire and Diderot (if one reads French).[35]

Third-century Byzantium? Not so much, and you may need to find someone knowledgeable in ancient Greek to assist you. On the one hand, having few research sources from your period means less work on the upside—but a lot more on the downside, as you'll need to use a lot more imagination in creating immersive settings and interesting psychological studies of your characters.

For obscure periods, therefore, your research might be somewhat more abstract and esoteric. You might read first-person accounts of displaced persons, for instance, in order to work your way into the mindset of St. Patrick, a young Roman who was kidnapped and enslaved by Irish raiders.[36] You might stumble across (or find in the course of your painstaking researches) the Museum of London—which has an excellent section on Roman settlements and villas of Britain, with scale models of estates and towns.

You might be working with Appalachian settlers in the eighteenth or nineteenth century and find the *Foxfire* books useful. These are an invaluable set (twelve books, I think) of traditional mountain techniques and folklore, compiled by a teacher named Eliot Wigginton and his students. The first volume includes "Hog Dressing, Log Cabin Building, Mountain Crafts and Foods, Planting by the Signs, Snake Lore . . ." and a number of other fascinating (and useful) topics.

Or you might have a friend send you—out of the blue—the three-volume set of the Encyclopedia Britannica—published in 1771. Just in case you want to know what people believed and how they did things in general, I mean. . . .

Essentially, doing research is like winding a tangle of string up into a tidy ball: you find a loose end and pull. But as a general rule, if you're working diligently in a particular direction—and it's the direction you *should* be following—the universe usually comes out to meet you.

A Brief Footnote on Tidiness

In the interests of entertainment and communication, I do now and then post snapshots of my office (on Twitter, Facebook, and/or my website[37]). In particular, I put up photos of my bookshelves (see page 432). People who like books are always curious as to what someone is reading—and people who read historical novels like to know what some of the sources are that go into said novels.

---

[34] *Which I had the privilege of writing an introduction for, when it was reprinted as a Modern Library Edition in 2004. Great writing! (Tom Paine's, I mean, not mine.)*

[35] *I can't* speak *French, but I do read it, having been obliged to learn both French and German for graduate school, since when I got a Ph.D. in science (back in the Dark Ages), English was not yet the* lingua franca *(so to speak) of the scientific world, and you had to be able to read in one or two foreign languages in order to keep up with the literature of your field.*

[36] *I do a fair amount of psychological research, too, searching out accounts by soldiers, officers, people who have been assaulted (physically and/or sexually), people abandoned or orphaned, and so on. Research isn't all just facts.*

[37] *Writer_DG on Twitter; Facebook.com/AuthorDianaGabaldon; dianagabaldon.com.*

I'm as fascinated by the audience's responses to my bookshelves as the audience is by the books and other impedimenta. It seems to be about 20:1 in terms of "OMG, this looks just like my shelves!/I love it!" vs. "What a mess!/How can you FIND anything!/Let me come and organize that for you!"

I appreciate both schools of thought—and my sincere thanks to the kind souls who think I would do better (in some undefined way) if my books were alphabetized, sorted by color, arranged by height, or generally tidied into a visually pleasing (to them) formation that has nothing to do with what's actually *in* the books.

Now, putting aside any of my private opinions regarding the psychology that causes people to value Tidiness *Über Alles* (I think y'all do it out of a sense of pervasive anxiety that makes you want to control your environment, but that's just an opinion based on observations of close family members and friends)—tidiness *qua* tidiness has two possible aspects that recommend it as a virtue: aesthetics and/or function.

As to aesthetics, I'll just note that there are people who like Gustav Klimt and there are people who like Mondrian, and leave it at that. Aesthetics rests on the perception of pattern, and there are patterns in total chaos (this is the basis of chaos theory). Some people like simpler patterns, some like more complex ones, and that's fine.

Now function. That's the "How can you FIND anything in there?" response, which assumes that, in fact, I can't find anything *unless* the books are filed according to an arbitrary pattern that they personally find aesthetically appealing. Okay, this is conflating the two virtues of tidiness, which do not in fact operate in correlation with each other.

For an alphabetized system to be useful, the user has to know that the book he or she wants is written by a specific author. This in turn means that the user has to have read every word in all of the books to hand (so as to know what's in them) and be sufficiently familiar with them as to recognize almost any author's content. If I had twenty books, I could do that, though there wouldn't be much point to it.

As it is . . . let me illustrate, briefly, how I work and how I use reference books. (This is, by the way, my core reference collection. The books I read for pleasure—mostly fiction—are mostly alphabetized by author, because in that case I'm usually *looking* for a specific author, and not for specific content.)

As I work my way into the writing of a new book, I begin to pick up certain research books—from either the extant collection or new acquisitions—that I think *might* be useful as background or specific references to the novel I'm working on. I'll put these on a shelf by themselves and add occasionally to this mini-core collection, as new thoughts occur to me or as I come across new relevant reference books. One book that's been on the mini-core shelf for the last several *Outlander* novels is *The World Almanac of the American Revolution.* This lists and briefly describes a huge variety of the events—large and small—that occurred during the Revolution, organized by date.

I use the *Almanac* not only to check dates but to choose historical events that a) have intrinsic interest or importance historically, b) have or can have *fictional* or dramatic significance to the people in my story, and c) are plausible to use in a geographical or chronological sense.

Now, I left everyone in the eighteenth-century part of the story in Philadelphia at the end of *An Echo in the Bone,* in mid-June of 1778. Ergo, even though many interesting historical events occurred in 1778, a lot of them were much later in the year and/or weren't anywhere near Philadelphia. (In some cases, I could begin a new book substantially later than where the last one stopped, but owing to the spectacular triple cliff-hanger at the end of *Echo,* I pretty much had to resolve those cliff-hangers in *Written in My Own Heart's Blood,* and therefore *MOBY* (*My Own Heart's Blood* = *MOHB* = *MOH-B* = *MOBY.* Geddit?) pretty much had to start where *Echo* ended.)

So what happened in or near Philadelphia in the middle of June 1778? Three very interesting things: 1) Benedict Arnold became the military governor of Philadelphia for the Continental army on June 18, 2) the British troops withdrew from their occupation of Philadelphia on June 19, and 3) the Battle of Monmouth took place near Philadelphia on June 28.

These events can all serve my purposes. So I need to know a few things as I work. I need to know who the commander-in-chief of the British forces in Philadelphia was, what his personality and background were, and (insofar as possible) what he looked like. I need to know where Benedict Arnold was in terms of his personal political arc at that time. And I need to know what the location, order of battle, chief historical personalities present, and outcome of the Battle of Monmouth were.

Let's start with the battle. If you look at the original photo of my bookshelves, just above and behind Otis's[38] right ear you'll see a book on which the word BATTLES is clearly visible. I have no idea who wrote this book; it isn't important. What *is* important is that it's an encyclopedia of historical battles throughout the ages. What's also important is that it's standing with five other encyclopedias of battle. And it's standing on *that* shelf because that's where the general-purpose military books—encyclopedias of battle, treatises on weapons and artillery techniques, *Osprey Men-at-Arms* books dealing with the history and equipment of relevant regiments, a novel on the siege of Havana, two books on dueling, and *The Military Experience in the Age of Reason* (an excellent survey of the military structures and operations in effect across Europe in the eighteenth century)—are.

Now, I have much-more-specific references that deal with the American Revolution, and there are a couple of detailed books that will give me maps and exhaustive descriptions of the Battle of Monmouth (those are in the smaller bookshelf, which you haven't seen, and which contains most of the American Revolution–specific references)—but there's no point reading through all that until/unless I decide that I really want to use that battle. So I start with the general reference, which tells me—among other things—that General Washington commanded the American and allied troops at that battle. Cool. Jamie/Claire et al haven't yet met George Washington, but this might be a good opportunity.

So . . . if, say, Jamie is going to meet George Washington, what do I (as his amanuensis) need to know about GW? I need to

[38] *Otis the pug is my son's dog, not mine. I have two big, fat standard dachshunds named Homer and JJ.*

know what he looks like, what his overall impression (as in personality) was, and how he talked. Where will I find that sort of information? In fact, I found what color his eyes were by Googling that question, but other specific information is on my mini-core shelf, in the form of *Angel in the Whirlwind,* an excellent biography of GW by an author whose name I don't know and don't need to know, because I know exactly where that book is.[39]

And here's where that little research foray ended up:

Excerpt from Written in My Own Heart's Blood

Jamie ducked under the lintel after Dan and found himself in a dark, shabby room that smelled of cabbage water, grime, and the sharp reek of urine. There was one window, its shutters left open for air, and the sunlight coming in silhouetted the long-skulled head of a large man sitting at the table, who raised his head at the opening of the door.

"Colonel Morgan," he said, in a soft voice touched with the drawl of Virginia. "Have you brought me good news?"

"That's just what I brought you, General," auld Dan said, and shoved Jamie ahead of him toward the table. "I found this rascal on the road and bade him come along. This'll be Colonel Fraser, who I've told you of before. Just come back from Scotland, and the very man to take command of Taylor's troops."

The big man had risen from the table and put out a hand, smiling—though he smiled with his lips pressed tight together, as though afraid something might escape. The man was as tall as Jamie himself, and he found himself looking straight into sharp gray-blue eyes that took his measure in the instant it took to shake hands.

"George Washington," the man said. "Your servant, sir."

"James Fraser," Jamie said, feeling mildly stunned. "Your . . . most obedient. Sir."

"Sit with me, Colonel Fraser." The big Virginian gestured toward one of the rough benches at the table. "My horse pulled up lame, and my slave's gone to find another. No notion how long it may take him, as I require a good sturdy beast to bear my weight, and those are thin on the ground these days." He looked Jamie up and down with frank appraisal; they were much of a size. "I don't suppose you have a decent horse with you, sir?"

Okay. Going back to the original set of questions, plainly I need to know the particulars of Benedict Arnold's actions, context, and state of mind when he took over as military governor of Philadelphia. Fine. In the mini-core collection is *George Washington and Benedict Arnold: A Tale of Two Patriots,* a very detailed and excellent biography whose author I could check by looking at the spine, but I don't care who wrote it, only that I can find it when I need it.[40]

Excerpt from MOBY

I thought I could manage the three blocks to the livery stable without incident, but at the corner of Walnut[41] *I was hailed by a familiar voice from a carriage window.*

---

[39] *A sense of fairness and a residuum of academic responsibility made me go look at the author's name. It's Benson Bobrick.*

[40] *Oh, all* right, *then. A conscience is a terrible thing, I tell you . . . Dave Richard Palmer.*

[41] *I found a good, simple, interactive map of downtown Philadelphia in the eighteenth century at http://teachingamericanhistory.org/convention/map/.*

"Mrs. Fraser? I say, Mrs. Fraser!"

I looked up, startled, to see the hawk-nosed face of Benedict Arnold smiling down at me. His normally fleshy features were gaunt and lined, and his usually ruddy complexion had faded to an indoor pallor, but there was no mistaking him.

"Oh!" I said, and made a quick bob. "How nice to see you, General!"

My heart had sped up. I'd heard from Denny Hunter that Arnold had been appointed military governor of Philadelphia but hadn't expected to see him so soon—if at all.

I should have left it there but couldn't help asking, "How's the leg?" I knew he'd been badly injured at Saratoga—shot in the same leg that had been wounded a short time before, and then crushed by his horse falling with him in the storming of Breymann Redoubt—but I hadn't seen him then. The regular army surgeons had attended him, and from what I knew of their work, I was rather surprised that he was not only alive but still had two legs.

His face clouded a bit at that, but he continued to smile.

"Still present, Mrs. Fraser. If two inches shorter than the other. Where are you going this morning?" He glanced automatically behind me, registering my lack of a maid or companion, but didn't seem disturbed by it. He'd met me on the battlefield and knew me—and appreciated me—for what I was.

I knew what he was, too—and what he would become.

The hell of it was that I liked *the man.*

And, not by serendipity but by the fact that historical events form a logical nexus when people are writing about them *ex post facto*, the *Almanac, Angel in the Whirlwind*, and *George Washington and Benedict Arnold* all mention that General Clinton had taken command of the British troops in Philadelphia at the time of the withdrawal, and our friend Wikipedia supplies me with a painting of the general and his birth date (so I know how old he is in 1778).

Portrait painted by Andrea Soldi, presumably sometime between 1762–65. The general was born in 1730 so would be in his mid-thirties in this portrait, in his mid-forties when Claire meets him.

Now, if Claire—it has to be Claire, for logistical reasons—is going to talk to General Clinton, I need to know a few other things, like what she'd be wearing and how she would travel. The bottom shelf of the second bay of my shelves has the large pictorial books on historical costume, while Aileen Ribeiro's *Dress in Eighteenth-Century Europe* is among the books on social/cultural English/European background—these being just to the right of the encyclopedias of battle.

Vide: *Excerpt from* MOBY

By the time we'd got my hair done up in something resembling order, corralled in a snood and pinned respectably under a broad-brimmed woven straw hat, I'd come up with at least a rough notion of what to tell General Clinton. Stick to the truth as far as possible. *That was the first principle of successful lying, though it had been some time since I'd been last obliged to employ it.*

Well, then. A messenger had come for Lord John—one had—bringing a note—he did. I had no idea what was in the note—totally true. Lord John had then left with the messenger but without telling me where they were going. Also technically true, the only variance being that it had been a different messenger. No, I hadn't seen in which direction they had gone; no, I didn't know whether they had walked or ridden—Lord John's saddle horse was kept at Davison's livery on Fifth Street, two blocks away.

That sounded good. If General Clinton chose to make inquiries, I was reasonably sure he'd discover the horse still in its stall and thus conclude that John was somewhere in the city. He would also presumably lose interest in me as a source of information and send soldiers round to whatever haunts a man such as Lord John Grey might be supposed to be visiting.

And with any luck at all, by the time the general had exhausted such possibilities as Philadelphia offered, John would be back and could answer his own damned questions.

Beginning to see how this works? For me, that is. I imagine some of the tidier-minded writers of historical fiction actually spend years poring through their references, tidily transferring bits of information to index cards (or their electronic equivalent) so that they can instantly look up *women's clothing, Revolutionary War battles, George Washington, physical appearance,* and the like.

If that suits the way they work, great. Anything that helps you get words on the page is the right thing to do. This is just how *I* do it.

Basic Housekeeping

By "housekeeping," I mean the drudgery that ensures you don't lose your work and you stand a reasonable chance of being able to find it when you need it.

BACK THINGS UP

I'm continually appalled by people who don't back things up, but there are a horrifying number of them. Personally, I hate losing even a paragraph of my work and go to some trouble to prevent it. My procedures may seem excessive—and perhaps they are, depending on circumstances. But for heaven's sake, do at least do the first two steps on this list.

Step 1: Turn on the automatic backup feature on your word processor. (Use the Help feature, if you don't know where it is.)

This feature normally allows you to choose how often to back things up automatically; what interval you choose may depend on your system and whether the automatic backup causes a noticeable slowdown in other functions. (Personally, I use a huge Alienware laptop with The Max in memory and RAM. I could probably back up the Bible every thirty seconds and not notice a thing, but your mileage may vary. . . .)

Step 2: Copy your work periodically to a "cloud" service and/or an outside device. I use Dropbox myself, but there are many offsite services that allow you to store stuff in the cloud. Being paranoid, I also usually save my work to a thumb drive (what if Chinese hackers figure out how to appropriate the entire cloud?)—and I save it every time I leave my computer, even to go to the bathroom (an important consideration if you have pets, small children, or husbands who want to check their email and don't realize that this can be done without closing everything else on the laptop . . .). I also save very large files—the interim pieces I call "chunks," as well as complete sections of a book—by emailing them to myself. Gmail isn't a foolproof archive, but it *is* quickly searchable.

Step 3: It's partly a function of how I work and partly the ability of a writer to envision far-fetched disasters, but I print off my work. (What about solar flares? What about hostile forces blasting every electronic circuit in the United States with an EMP?[42]) Not every day, but when I've completed a scene, I'll print it off for my husband to read. (He's the only person who gets to see what I'm working on while I'm working on it. Anything I post online is pretty much as good as I can

[42] *Electromagnetic pulse.*

make it and certified fit for human consumption.) He normally returns these pieces with marginal comments (like *Nipples, again?* or *No guy would do that* . . . but sometimes *WOW!*, which is Very Gratifying), and after reading these, I file the annotated scenes (well, I throw them into a banker's box, but leave us not be picky here . . .).

I used to print off all new work once a week, however incomplete, but have sort of lapsed on that, what with all the travel—I'm not invariably (or even often) home on the same day every week, and you really need to do this as a matter of weekly routine, if you're going to go that far.

Step 4: Put copies in different places. By which I mean, it will do you no good to have copies on two laptops, a thumb drive, an external drive, and a hard-copy dump, if your house burns down. Backing up work to a cloud service or emailing it to yourself is a safeguard against such a contingency—but I do have friends who put a copy of important work at a friend's house (I have one friend who put her last book's manuscript in her freezer, just in case of fire, flood, or burglary), or mail a hard copy to a relative.

Really, you don't need to do *all* these things. But for pity's sake—do *one* of them.

ROMANCE AND THE WRITTEN WORD

Back in the day—say, around the sixteenth century—a work of entertainment called "a romance" meant essentially that it was a work of fiction. Comedy, tragedy, love story, adventure—if it wasn't a factual account, it was a romance. And people were accused of being "romantical" when you thought they were lying or embellishing their accounts.

This concept of "romance" continued past Shakespeare and all the way through the seventeenth and eighteenth centuries (*Robinson Crusoe* is a romance—in spite of the fact that there are neither women nor love affairs in it); in the nineteenth, "romance" began to drift more in the direction of relationship stories—particularly those written by women, *vide* Jane Austen and the Brontë sisters.

In fact, the German word for a work of fiction—regardless of genre—is still "Roman."

But come the mid-twentieth century, and the word became solidified as meaning a very specific type of fiction: a courtship story, usually between a young man and an even younger woman, with a happy ending in which the couple are united in marriage and/or bed (hopefully in that order).

"Romance," in terms of story, no longer meant "excitement, adventure, fantastic experiences beyond the bounds of normal daily life." It meant Love, in the sense of a pair bond.

Now, as I've noted elsewhere,[43] I wrote *Outlander* for practice and chose the broad general category of "historical fiction" on grounds that I was a research professor and knew my way around a library. As I wrote, though, I used any element, literary device, or classical trope that struck my fancy—and I read a lot, I like all kinds of things . . . and I used 'em all. After all, it didn't matter what "kind" of book this was—no one was ever going to see it!

Well, the best-laid plans of mice and men, and all that . . . Stuff happened, and I put a small bit of the book in the library of the CompuServe Literary Forum[44] in order to win an argument with a man about what it feels like to be pregnant. Everyone who'd been following the argument went to read the piece and came back asking for more. So I'd put up bits and pieces now and then . . . and people began asking, "What sort of book *is* this?"

"Beats me," I'd reply, and go on working.

But the forum folk, bless them, remained interested and helpful and after a time began suggesting things that my book *might* be. These suggestions varied wildly, depending on what bit I'd just posted, and ranged from mystery to fantasy to thriller to . . . romance.

I'd read quite a lot of the earlier fiction that was called romance but somehow had never encountered a modern romance novel. "Really?" I said. "Well, who knows—maybe it *is* a romance." So I went to the grocery store and picked three romance novels whose covers said they were *New York Times* bestsellers, figuring this should be a representative sample.

By what I later realized was coincidence, all three of these novels featured an eighteen-year-old heroine who was raped. In two instances, she fell in love with the man who'd raped her (he being driven mad by her desirability and/or having married her by arrangement and then taken advantage of his marital rights). In the other, she was comforted and shown the true delights of sex by a nicer guy, whom she then married.

While I found these books entirely entertaining—in one of them, the heroine is thrown across a table and taken by the hero, who courteously paused "to allow her to adjust to his size" (causing me to say out loud, "Yeah? So . . . how small *is* he?")—I was pretty much convinced that whatever it was I was writing, it wasn't a romance novel.

Well, other Stuff happened, and in the fullness of time I acquired a literary agent, finished the book (in that order), and then got a publisher and an editor. Now, the book was acquired for Delacorte Press (a Random House imprint) by Jackie Cantor, a general-fiction editor who bought the book because she loved it.

The publication process is a long and torturous one (ask any production person), but it begins with the editor who buys a book going to an editorial meeting, at which all the editors present their "list" of projects, reporting new acquisitions and progress on existing manuscripts, and where preliminary plans are laid for marketing, cover designs,

[43] The Outlandish Companion, Volume One, *"Prologue."*

[44] *Now the Books and Writers Community.*

and advertising budgets. Clearly an important occasion for a new book.

So Jackie, bless her heart, took *Cross Stitch*[45] to the editorial meeting, where she waxed enthusiastic about how wonderful this book was, how much she adored it, it was the best book she'd ever read, and they must do something Really Special for it.

"Great!" said the assembled meeting. "What kind of book is it?"

"Ahhh . . ." said Jackie.

Without going into the gory details—it took them eighteen *months* to decide how the heck to sell a book that nobody could describe.[46] Having no idea of the speed of publishing processes, I'd just been working along on the second—similarly genre-less—book,[47] without the slightest idea that anything might be amiss.

So one day my agent called and said, "Well, they've finally decided what to do with your book. The hardcover is no problem—it will just go up front with all the other hardcover fiction.[48,49] But they think they'd like to sell the paperback as romance."

"As what?" I said. By this time I'd read quite a lot of romance novels, and while a number of them were well written and a larger number enjoyable, I was pretty sure that wasn't what I'd written. "I have two objections to that: one, I will never be reviewed by *The New York Times*.[50] I can live with that, but, two, that will cut off the entire male half of my readership. Men see different things in the book than women do, and I don't want to lose that."

"Yes, I know," said my (male) agent. "And we could insist that they publish it as science fiction or fantasy, because of the weird elements. But bear in mind that a bestseller in fantasy is fifty thousand in paperback—a bestseller in romance is five hundred thousand."

"You have a point," I said, after a moment's pause. "Sell it as romance."

Because, you see, my beloved editor had told me, "These *have* to be word-of-mouth books, because they're too weird to describe to anybody."

That being so, I reasoned, obviously it was better to expose the book to half a million readers who would all go out and tell their friends—who would, presumably, be able to draw their own conclusions as to what the book was or wasn't—than to start with a tenth that number.

And so we agreed to allow *Outlander*'s paperback to be published as romance, but with the proviso that I would get dignified covers—no mad bosoms or writhing hair—and that, if the book(s) should become "vis-

---

[45] *My original working title.*

[46] *My favorite attempt is by* Salon*'s reviewer Gavin McNett: "the smartest historical sci-fi adventure-romance story ever written by a science Ph.D. with a background in scripting Scrooge McDuck comics."*

[47] *They'd been reckless enough to give me a three-book contract.*

[48] *The book was published in 1991, when there were still a lot of bookstores and Amazon.com did not exist.*

[49] *For later reference—at this point in time, romance novels were not published in hardcover, only as paperback originals.*

[50] *Dead right; I never have been. Having read a lot of book reviews by this time (and having written quite a few myself—I used to write reviews for* The Washington Post*'s "Book World")—I think that's probably just as well. . . .*

ible" (publisher-ese for "hit the *NYT* Bestseller List"), they would at that point "reposition" the books as fiction.[51]

So the hardcover was published. Now, at this point, there were two big bookstore chains: Waldenbooks and B. Dalton, which both had stores in every mall in America[52] and whose buyers held the power of life and death over all published books. The Waldenbooks buyer bought ten thousand copies for the chain, a very respectable number for a debut novel. The B. Dalton buyer bought three hundred copies. For the whole chain. This amounted to roughly one-quarter of a book per store, I estimated at the time.

However . . . those three hundred copies sold out. Reordered. Sold out and reordered again. At this point, the fiction buyer for B. Dalton said, "What's this weird book that keeps popping up at the bottom of the list every month?" The buyer read it—and ordered ten thousand copies.

In spite of the difficulties, the publisher manfully (and womanfully) set to and, as part of their support for the book, arranged to give away 1,200 hardcover copies at that year's Romance Writers of America convention. This is a common thing for publishers to do at writers' conventions of all kinds, in order to publicize new books or authors to a hard-core niche audience. What was unusual in this instance was that the book was a hardcover—and a big, fat, impressive-looking one, too—and at that point in time, romance novels were never published as anything but paperback originals.

I went to the convention, having no idea what to expect, but was rather pleased to see big stacks of *Outlander* piled up behind the volunteers running the registration table. The volunteers were handing out goody bags filled with bookmarks, key chains, postcards, and other marketing tchotchkes, along with four or five paperback books. The hardcover wouldn't fit conveniently in one of these bags, so they were handing it over to each attendee separately.

So . . . I walked up to the registrar in charge of "F–N" and said "Gabaldon."[53] To which the volunteer responded, "How do you spell that?"[54] I pointed at the gleaming pile of *Outlanders* behind her and said, "Like that." Whereupon she rose to her feet, grabbed my hand, and clasped it to her bosom, exclaiming, "It's *you*!"

The book made quite an impression at that conference, though not always a favorable one. Quite a number of people paused in elevators and in hallways to tell me that they just couldn't read "a book that *big*!" Other people told me they'd stayed up all night reading it—and before the three-day conference was over, the question of whether the book was or wasn't a romance was already being hotly debated.

---

[51] *Which, in fact, they very honorably did.* Voyager, *the third book, did hit Da List, and they immediately put foil bars across the flowers on the covers and put* FICTION *on the spines. This had no effect whatsoever on Barnes & Noble, but that's a story for a little farther down the page. . . .*

[52] *This was even before the concept of "big box" stores.*

[53] *As one does . . .*

[54] *As everyone does . . .*

Frankly, it is. It's the only one of my novels that has the structure of a romance—which is to say, it is a courtship story, if hardly an orthodox one. It also has a happy ending. However, it has rather a lot of things that normal romance novels don't usually have—and certainly didn't have in 1991, I'll tell you. . . .

Scarcely before the ink had dried on the pages, the question as to what the heck this was was being hotly debated in chat rooms and forums all over what wasn't quite yet the Internet. Most "real" writers of romance were very firm in their insistence that it wasn't a romance. It was Way Too Long, it had "all that boring *history,*" and the H/H[55] didn't even *meet* for fifty pages, and she had a husband, for heaven's sake, and she was still in *love* with him, and . . . (horror of horrors), "The Hero *beats* the Heroine!" A good many readers—I'm told—gave up reading the book at this point, frequently throwing it against the wall (they told me) to emphasize their outrage.[56] Allowing the Hero to be tortured and anally raped wasn't nearly as bad as letting him smack the Heroine's bottom, but that wasn't anything you ought to find in a "normal" romance, either![57]

And . . . crime to end all crimes . . . I had written the book *in the First Person*!!! Honest. For years and years, I'd have total strangers come up to me at conferences (or in bookstores) and ask, lowering their voices in deference to implied scandal, "How did you *dare* to write in the first person?"[58]

Any number of kindly romance writers assured me earnestly that you couldn't do that. Readers didn't like it. Editors didn't like it.[59] Romance readers don't want to *be* the Heroine (I was told); they want to be her best friend and enjoy her adventure vicariously.

To be perfectly honest, I wrote the book in the first person because it was the easiest thing to do. (Though if you care to make a brief survey of Great English Literature, you'll find that about half the enduring books are in fact written in the first person, from *Fanny Hill* and *Moby-Dick* to *David Copperfield* and the lamentations of Jeremiah.)

On the other hand . . . somebody seemed to be reading the book. The RWA has (as do other genre organizations) a prestigious award, called the Rita Award, given in a number of categories, and in 1991 *Outlander* was nominated in four of them.[60]

At this point, I no longer recall what all four were, but I do recall telling my husband (who accompanied me to the awards banquet, bless him) that I wasn't going to win any of them. All but one of the Rita awards were juried awards; a panel of six judges read all the nominated books in each category, and the total of their numbered scores determined the ranking of the books in that category.

The judges—I served as a judge myself several times in later years—were given a set of scoring guidelines. You could give a book

---

[55] *There's a lot of inside jargon associated with most genres, I imagine. The "H/H" of romance are the Hero and Heroine, and there are other Required Elements, like "the black moment," and so on.*

[56] *See Part 4, "Sex and Violence."*

[57] *Darn tootin', Petunia. . . .*

[58] *To which I would politely reply, "Easy. I just sat down and typed, 'I.'"*

[59] *I didn't usually say so, but having written the first novel without the slightest concern whether* anybody *would like it, I wasn't about to start worrying about such things later.*

[60] *Writing a book with no genre has its drawbacks as far as marketing is concerned, but it's not without other advantages.*

any number between 0 and 6, with 1 being "Really bad" and 6 being "I wish I'd written this myself!" Zero, though, meant, "This may be a great book, but it isn't a romance."

I don't know whether nominees are still given their scores afterward or not, but they were then. And, sure enough, my scores in all three judged categories were evenly divided between 0's and 6's.

The fourth category, though, was different. For one thing, this was the sole award that was voted on by the membership at large, not by a panel of judges. For another, it didn't depend on genre; any book could be nominated. It was called the "Best Book of the Year" award. Best *Book,* not Best Romance. I believe they revised that guideline after I won it and now require nominees to be romances—but win it I did.

Needless to say, my editor, Jackie Cantor, was right about the book being word-of-mouth, and *Outlander* and I were notorious in the romance-writing community pretty much from the start. I got more so with the release of *Dragonfly in Amber,* which *really* wasn't a romance, was still written mostly in the first person, didn't even have a happy ending . . . and ended on a major-league cliff-hanger, to boot.[61,62]

Still and all, I enjoyed—and still do enjoy—both romance novels and the people who write them. What I didn't like was the popular misconception that all romances are illiterate bodice rippers, and that that being so . . . plainly that's what I'd written.

Now, that's a double whammy of a misconception there: first, all romances *aren't* That Sort of Book, but second—I don't write romances to begin with, so why ought I to suffer a discrimination that doesn't even belong to me?

I was therefore left with the choice either of trying to defend the entire genre and raise it to an image of literary respectability—or find a way to separate my novels from the genre, insofar as was possible. I concluded pretty quickly that I had neither the stamina nor the desire to try to change the image of romance novels overall (there were a great many people already working on that, most of them with a lot more talent for such things than I have), so I'd best do the other thing.

In this regard, I was hampered primarily by the behavior of Barnes & Noble. The big-box store had arisen, displacing the smaller mall stores, and B&N was the biggest of the boxes. It also has a top-down corporate model of marketing, wherein the powers at the top of the company construct a monthly "model" of which books are to be sold where, in what number, and where these are to be placed in B&N stores. And (I was

---

[61] *All other aspects notwithstanding, my novels can't be romances, because a romance novel is by its nature a one-off. Romance novels do not have sequels; once the happy couple are united, the story is Over.*

[62] Romantic Times, *a magazine that hosted its own convention and awards (they still do, though they now refer to it as the "*RT *Booklovers Convention"), doubtless stunned at my temerity, gave me and* Dragonfly *a foot-high award in purple aluminum, for "Lifetime Achievement in Contemporary Fantasy."*

told), since my first novel was a romance, therefore everything else I wrote for the rest of my life was a romance, too, as far as Barnes & Noble was concerned.

Now, the publisher was as good as their word, and when *Voyager* hit the *New York Times* list in 1994, Bantam Doubleday Dell obligingly put foil strips over the flowers on my paperback covers and changed the stamp on the spine from *Romance* to *Fiction.* B&N went right on shoving the books into the romance section. And I got increasingly tired of people saying to me, "Oh, I don't read *that* kind of book . . ." or (my husband's oldest friend, in sympathetic tones), "It must get really tedious, writing those bodice busters."[63]

In the course of business and book tours, I went into a lot of bookstores, and in any independent store—or a mall store where the manager had discretion over where things were placed—I could pretty much get them to move my novels to fiction in the course of a fifteen-minute visit. But not B&N, the eight-hundred-pound gorilla. . . .

So this went on for years. And then I accidentally wrote a novel about Lord John Grey.[64] Now, Lord John is a thoroughly admirable man: honorable, witty, brave, a minor nobleman and career soldier, clever, adventurous . . . and homosexual, in a time when that particular proclivity was a capital offense. Thus, his stories always have an underlying thread of innate conflict and lurking danger, no matter what else is happening. What they *don't* have is a heroine, or—at least in the first book—a love affair, or even any hetero sex. And yet B&N was shoving *Private Matter* in the romance section.

I went into a dozen B&N stores in the course of a week of California book touring and got angrier and angrier. Finally, I decided that I wasn't going to take this anymore, called my editor, and told her I wasn't setting foot in another B&N store as long as they were putting Lord John in the romance section. Thus freed of the afternoon's commitments, I left my hotel and went to walk up and down the sands of Half Moon Bay, fuming. And I made up my mind that I had nothing to lose.[65]

So I went home and composed a rude letter to Steve Riggio, then the CEO of Barnes & Noble. It said (more or less):

Dear Mr. Riggio,

I assume that you might be familiar with my name, as it pops up at the top of bestseller lists whenever a new book of mine comes out.

I also assume that you may be familiar with my novels, as they occupy quite a bit of shelf space in Barnes & Noble bookstores.

I likewise assume that you're familiar with a bookstore chain called Hastings.

---

[63] *No, I didn't choke him—but only because I couldn't reach him across the table.*

[64] Lord John and the Private Matter. *I thought it was a short story when I wrote it but was otherwise informed by my two agents, who said (as one), "That's the size* normal *books are."*

[65] *Which, as any revolutionary can tell you, is when Things Begin to Happen.*

They may not be B&N, but they aren't chopped liver, either.

Now, I assume that you don't *know that Hastings sells 40 percent more of all my titles than you do.*

I do assume that you'd like to know why that is?

Well, I tell you, Steve—they're not putting them in the effing romance section.

* * *

Cordially yours,

So I sent this missive off by registered mail and it was received, by someone with an illegible signature, but I heard nothing and had dismissed it as a failed effort. Six weeks later, though, I got a call out of the blue from Mr. Riggio himself. We had a reasonably civil ten-minute conversation, at the conclusion of which he said he would "have somebody look into it."

I figured that was that and returned to work. But sure enough, twenty-four hours later, I got a call from the B&N VP of marketing, who said briefly, "We checked into it, and you're right. We're moving the books." And they did. God bless you, Steve.[66,67]

[66] *Borders, curse them, promised to move the books out of romance but never did. And you see what happened to* them. . . .

[67] *And my grateful thanks to the staff and leadership of Barnes & Noble for their years of enthusiastic and imaginative support!*

Part Six

A COMPREHENSIVE SCOTTISH LANGUAGE GLOSSARY AND PRONUNCIATION GUIDE— BY ÀDHAMH Ó BROIN

eo a-nis, a chàirdean! Here we go, friends!

The Scottish-language section of this veritable smorgasbord of a book is complete. What a pleasure it is to be sitting here mulling over both the content of this glossary and once again the significance of Diana Gabaldon's unprecedented contribution to the "Scottish cultural situation."

Us Scots have all made more than the occasional gripe about American portrayals of our indigenous cultural themes over the years. In the case of certain pieces of literature and cinematography, this has quite often been perfectly justified. In coming to Diana's work, however, I wish strongly to suggest that my fellow Scots revise this now-ingrained knee-jerk reaction. The very first time I met Diana, she was above anything else absolutely preoccupied with making sure I didn't think she'd made a pig's ear of the Gaelic. I told her what I've said many times since—that if people are concentrating on a couple of erroneous spellings and contextual misuses, then they are obviously habitual wrong-tree-barkers. My take is this: Diana could save on a whole load of hassle and leave Scottish language out altogether, or she could employ the same tenacious pursuit of detail that pervades every page of these remarkable novels and give it its place in what has turned out to be a multimillion-selling, wildly successful Scottish fantasy franchise. *Taing dhut,* I'll take the latter.

Perhaps Diana also did what most people from outside Scotland who aren't intimately aware of our cultural situation would do—she assumed that when speaking after the Germanic fashion, eighteenth-century Gaels would speak Lowland Scots. She assumed that Scottish people of the time would be proud of both their living native languages, and what's more, most all the Gaelic-speaking characters in *Outlander* are fluent in Mercian (standard) English, too, meaning that the portrait Diana has painted of us Scots is of a trilingual, culturally vigorous, but very much outward-looking people. To be perfectly honest, Ms. Gabaldon has cast us in the best possible light linguistically speaking, and I am very grateful for this. In our modern, culturally whitewashed age, a proudly trilingual people would seem like something to be marvelled at indeed, because we often forget that there are actually people all over the world for whom this situation is entirely natural and normal. While history has all but deprived us Scots of what multilingualism we had, two of our indigenous languages survive, and we now have an even better chance to stop the rot, backed as we are by a whole world of fresh interest and respect for our native culture. More than ever, this world is watching to see what we'll do next.

What will determine the outcome of this will not be government legislation, community funding, or Gaelic-medium education—despite these seemingly being the preoccupation of the majority—but individual drive, passion, and commitment to making our native languages the absolute center point of our cultural existence as Scots. As denizens of the Western World, we have become used to giving up our sense of agency over much of our lives and have plugged into the mainframe, often relinquishing the ability to affect real change in the spheres of our existence which truly matter. One of those spheres is that of language, and I sincerely believe that the content of Diana Gabaldon's books has gifted us the opportunity for new focus, which may not have appeared through anything other than the magnifying glass now applied to our endeavors from the outside. The fact that the story has also appeared in such terrific fashion as *Outlander* the TV series means that the platform on which we operate in promoting what is precious about our culture is a wider and altogether more effective one. I for one am relishing the chance to act on this most fortuitous circumstance.

In returning to the current work, I had a few thoughts when first approaching this language glossary. I reckoned I could discuss directly the content of the books, giving a commentary on the situations which gave rise to the language employed. Alternatively, I could use the space instead to expand the reader's experience of how the Scottish Gaelic and Lowland Scots languages are used, backing this with anecdotes, random facts, etymology, lessons on pronunciation, and a dip into the mostly very regular realm of Gaelic orthography. And as you'll soon find out, I went with the second option. I figured that there are plenty of blogs, reviews, and commentaries out there on the content of the books and so the most useful thing to bring to the table would be those extra perspectives that come from being both a fluent Gael and fluent Scots speaker, something which those of you from both across the Loch and elsewhere might be surprised to hear is extraordinarily rare. I can count on one hand the people I know in this situation.

Whatever the approach, the style is a personal one, as the content is personal to me—many of the words and phrases being those I use in my everyday life, both in Gaelic and Scots. It was not difficult to write about material I consider precious; in fact, it was often difficult to know when to stop! I must emphasize that my grasp of rural Scots forms is not complete, and therefore my perspective is mostly one of an urban Scots speaker—and a speaker of the Glasgow dialect, at that.

My approach to Gaelic orthography—how the language is spelt—is also a personal one. As a successful Gaelic learner and now tutor of many years' experience, I look at the teaching of the language from a very practical perspective. Our orthography is a versatile and regular one, like that of Spanish or Finnish, and I prefer to make use of that to its fullest extent.

Northern and southern dialectical varieties are given full rein to stretch their wings with use of *ia* or *eu* vowel combinations, depending on how a word is most often pronounced rather than on an arbitrary spelling convention in modern Gaelic. Examples are given in the text. This allows the language the versatility of catering to all dialects.

Likewise, I have retained the full verbal root *bith,* "to be," in all circumstances, as I have found this to be a most confusing issue for learners who have to deal with both *bi* and *bith* and wonder what the difference is when in truth there is none!

I have also removed the *th* from *thu* to leave the unambiguous *u* (as it is universally pronounced not /hoo/ but /oo/) for the informal "you," more about which will also be explained in the text.

Modern spelling convention changed the spelling of all words containing final *u* to *a*—e.g., *àluinn* to *àlainn* and *maduinn* to *madainn*—but for some inexplicable reason left one word unreformed, namely *agus*. Unsuprisingly and for reasons of consistency, I present it here as *agas*. All other words present in the text with final *u* have also been reformed in my suggestions under the main quotes themselves.

A most peculiar thing that befell us rather recently was the removal of the acute accent in Gaelic spelling, which appears to have done no good whatsoever except to confuse and disable. I have therefore reinstated this most useful feature of Gaelic spelling, which now allows learners to ascertain immediately whether they should be saying *è* /e/ or *é* /eh/ or *ò* /aw/ or *ó* /oh/. I hope to see use of the acute accent spread once again in the ensuing years!

Where I have made suggestions or corrections to the text in the books, I have done so either because there was a slight spelling error, because the orthography was irregular or could be confusing to learners who will make up a large section of the readership, or because usage was too modern. In this glossary, as with *Outlander* the TV show, I have always erred on the old-fashioned side. It would have been a little over the top to insist on the language of the period—eighteenth-century Ross-shire Gaelic, in other words—which would have been somewhat incomprehensible even to most native speakers! However, I believe it is very important to be conservative idiomatically as a concession to the fact that the story is set at times as far back as two hundred seventy years ago. Standards of spoken Gaelic have fallen perilously over the last fifty years especially, and I therefore consider it a matter of principle to join others so disposed in retaining a corner of the Scottish Gaelic world as the preserve of strong, idiomatic speech!

If I have differed in my take on the spelling of words or on idiomatic usage from Diana's other sources for the Gaelic language, this does not necessarily mean that I consider what they have provided to be wrong—in the majority of cases most definitely not; it simply means that I have presented my own take at all times for the sake of consistency. In repackaging material from the first glossary, I have not always rewritten the accompanying notes, although at all times the phonetic system has been tidied up in line with how I have presented the rest of the work.

My phonetic system is pronounced for the most part exactly as it appears.

If you see something that looks exactly like an English word—e.g., /SHAME/—then you can assume it is pronounced just as it would be in English.

/ch/ sounds like either the German *ich* or the Gaelic and Scots *loch,* while the sound at the beginning of the English word "chair" is represented using /tch/ as at the end of "catch."

The sound at the end of English words like "carry" or the surname "Rennie" will be represented with /i/ at the end of the phonetics—e.g., *àrsaidh* /ARsi/ (ancient).

Where capital letters are used, this is to denote emphasis. So where you see capitals, go right ahead and stress that syllable—e.g., *madainn mhath dhuibh* /MA'din VA yooiy/ "good morning to you."

As you can see just here, I have also employed an apostrophe occasionally. This denotes a point at which a *d* or *t* falls in the middle of a word. This sound must "dance" across the tongue rather than being voiced deliberately, as it does in the likes of the British English pronunciation of the word "butter." The less-dentalised pronunciation in American or Canadian English is in fact much closer to what I'd be looking to hear from learners attempting this sound in Gaelic! Not often you hear that!

There are more than a couple of Gaelic sounds with which we are not familiar in English. I have chosen to represent two of these using characters from the International Phonetic Alphabet, as they are nigh on impossible to render using English-language phonetics.

The first is /ɣ/ which is made by repeating the sound /g/ very quickly at the back of the throat until the throat itself has gone somewhat "slack." It's a sound that you spend your entire life attempting not to make, and here I am encouraging you to do it! Whenever you see /ɣ/ you know to give this sound a try.

The second is /ə/ which is a neutral sound best spoken of as identical to the *e* at the end of the English definite article "the." Say "the" a few times over and you will hear that the final vowel sound is a sort of dead, neutral one. That's the one you want! So whenever you see this symbol /ə/ you know to make this sound.

I have also made use of the umlaut /ö/ for the sound in the French *ouef* or the German *möchte*. This is another sound that we do not have in English, and yet it appears fairly often in Scottish Gaelic, especially in my own dialect of Dalriada, where it is almost impossible to predict from the spelling! If you're not familiar with either French or German, perhaps you can compare this sound to something between an /oo/ and an /ee/. Imagine your reaction to the most putrid smell—"ewww!"—and you're close!

In general, my orthography and phonetic representations of the language are very much the product of my own take on its teaching and my experience of learner uptake during that. Therefore, my usages in this volume are simply for the ease of understanding and pleasure of the reader. I am not making suggestions for the improvement of the language in general unless stated as such! More often than not, I would seek to avoid phonetic guides altogether, but for the purposes of the written word in a volume such as this, they are verging on the essential. If there are irregularities, I can only apologise in advance and hope you will forgive this on account of my not being used to representing Gaelic sound in this way!

I LEAVE YOU now to peruse the following pages; to enjoy, to learn, and hopefully to laugh, and I myself take leave of this work with a sense of great satisfaction at having been involved in such a pleasurable and hopefully useful pursuit.

My thanks go to all my own teachers past and present. Perhaps you didn't fully realise I was scrutinising your every syllable and pilfering your every word! My further thanks must be extended to Ruairidh MacCoinnich of Gairloch, who put up with my pestering phone calls at all times of morning and evening to ask him about the Gaelic of the MacKenzie during my research for the TV show. Much of what I learned infuses these pages, also. To all the lovely men and women of a certain vintage in the Highlands who have received me with such hospitality and patience as I attempted to keep alive your wisdom and grace by aping your very ways, *gu robh móran math agaibh!*

To my wife and kids for backing my every venture and keeping me grounded when I was ready to take off into the clouds.

And of course to Herself . . . or "Mrs. Wumman," as she is affectionately known in "the Patter" of Glasgow. I called the cavalry and you arrived. *Mo bheannachd ort.* It takes a particular kind of person both to write and also to read eight 1,200-page novels . . . several times! Outlanders have redefined what I have come to expect from the "fan," with their intelligence, discernment, and cultural awareness, and I hope to meet many more of you in person in the years to come. Thank you all for your continuing support of Scottish languages and culture. Its importance is something that is impossible to measure in words, whatever the language.

Slàn leibh air an àm
(health be with you for now),
Àdhamh Ó Broin
Glasgow, Scotland
01/05/15

Phrase *(as printed)*	Phrase *(if revised)*	Phonetic transcription	Book
a bann-sielbheadair	**a bhan shealbhadair**	/ə van HELLəvadər/	OLC Vol. I
a bhalaich		/ə VALich/	FC
a bana-mhaighistear		/ə VANAvaiyshtchər/	ABOSA
a bhean		/ə VEN/	FC
a bheanachd	**a bheannachd**	/ə VYANəchk/	OLC Vol. I
a bhràthair		/ə VRAhər/	FC
a bhràthair-mathàr	**a bhràthair mo mhàthair**	/ə VRAhər mo VAhər/	MOBY
a boireannach	**a bhoireannaich**	/ə VAWrənich/	ABOSA
a ceann-cinnidh	**a chinn-chinnidh**	/ə cheen-CHEENyi/	ABOSA
a chait		/ə CHATCH/	FC

Key: OLC Vol. 1—*The Outlandish Companion* FC—*The Fiery Cross* ABOSA—*A Breath of Snow and Ashes*

pb	hc	Language	Translation
	253	Gaelic (Gàidhlig)	"Mistress": more literally "owner of a bond of indenture."
86	59	Gaelic (Gàidhlig)	"Oh, laddie": this is still an extremely common form of address, even among those in the Isles who have let go their Gaelic, along the lines of "all right, *a bhalaich*—how's it going?" Personally—as you might have imagined—I would prefer a wee *ciamar a tha u?* But we don't always get what we want, especially in the case of Gaelic's modern history!
349	240	Gaelic (Gàidhlig)	"Mistress."
806	543	Gaelic (Gàidhlig)	"Oh, woman/wife": *a bhean* (vocative case) can be used in this sense, as Duncan addresses Jocasta, but is also the correct although now old-fashioned way to address one's mother. My children—although they seldom speak Gaelic to my wife—will sometimes attract her attention by use of *a bhean.*
	253	Gaelic (Gàidhlig)	"My blessing": in the vocative case when speaking *to the blessing itself.*
138	93	Gaelic (Gàidhlig)	"Oh, brother."
566	411	Gaelic (Gàidhlig)	"Oh, brother of my mother."
428	294	Gaelic (Gàidhlig)	"Oh, woman": amusingly, this is one of a small number of Gaelic nouns which does not belong to the obvious gender. The Gaelic word for "woman" is—you guessed it—masculine! Likewise, the Gaelic word for a laborer or farm servant, *sgalag*, is feminine. So, is the suggestion that women wear the pants and do the real hard work? There is a lovely Gaelic version of "wearing the pants" which translates as "that hen certainly sports the cockerel's comb": *'S ann air a' chirc ud tha cìr a' choilich* /saown aira CHEERK oot ha KEER ə chölich/.
434	298	Gaelic (Gàidhlig)	"Clan chief": you can hear Colum say *faodaidh tu brath a ghabhail corr' uair 's tu mac a' chinn-chinnidh* /fö̆di tu BRA ə ɣal caw-roor stu MACHk ə cheen-CHEENyi/ "you can take advantage now and again when you're the son of the chief" to Hamish in the *Outlander* TV show, episode 3, "The Way Out."
251	170	Gaelic (Gàidhlig)	"Oh, cat."

EITB—*An Echo in the Bone* MOBY—*Written in My Own Heart's Blood*

Phrase *(as printed)*	Phrase *(if revised)*	Phonetic transcription	Book
a charaid		/ə CHAridge/	FC
a charaid, bith sàmhach		/ə CHAridge, bee SAAvəch/	OLC Vol. I
a chliamhuinn	**a chliamhainn**	/ə CHLEEavin/	FC
a choin		/ə chon/	EITB
a chompanaich		/ə CHOMpanich/	MOBY
a chuisle			ABOSA
a Dhia!		/ə YEEa/	FC
a Dhia, cuidich mi		/ə YEEa, kootchich me/	EITB
a Dhia, tha e 'tionndadh dubh!	**a Dhia, tha e (a') fàs dubh**	/ə YEEa, HAiy-FASS doo/	FC
a dhiobhail	**a dhìobhail**	/ə YEEal/	OLC Vol. I
a dhuine		/ə ɣOOnyə/	FC
a dhuine dhubh	**a dhuine dhuibh**	/ə ɣOONyə ɣooiy/	MOBY
a draigha			FC
a fang Sassunaich	**fhaing Shasannaich**	/ang HASSanich/	MOBY
a ghille ruaidh, a charaid! Ciamar a tha thu?	**a ghille ruaidh, a charaid! Ciamar a tha u?**	/ə yEELə rooaiy ə CHAridge, KIMerə HAOW/	FC

pb	hc	Language	Translation
19	14	Gaelic (Gàidhlig)	"Oh, friend": very common expression in the vocative case, used when addressing someone in a friendly manner.
	245	Gaelic (Gàidhlig)	"Oh, friend, be quiet."
131	88	Gaelic (Gàidhlig)	"Oh, son-in-law."
32	23	Gaelic (Gàidhlig)	"Oh, dog": this is one of those funny instances when a word in a different grammatical case—this time the vocative—looks vastly different from the original, *cù*/koo/.
261	188	Gaelic (Gàidhlig)	"Oh, companion."
288	200	Gaelic (Gàidhlig)	"Oh, vein."
113	77	Gaelic (Gàidhlig)	"Oh, God!"
134	95	Gaelic (Gàidhlig)	"Oh, God, help me."
113	77	Gaelic (Gàidhlig)	"Oh, God, he's turning black!": I would tend to say *tha e (a') fàs dubh*/ha fass doo/"he is growing black" as that's the way Gaelic expresses to "turn" or "become," but either way—powerful stuff, that gunpowder, or *fùdar* /FOOdər/ as we call it.
	252	Gaelic (Gàidhlig)	"Oh, ruin."
771	520	Gaelic (Gàidhlig)	"Oh, man": can also be used in the English-language sense of "How are you, man?"/*Ciamar a tha u, a dhuine?*/
277	200	Gaelic (Gàidhlig)	"Oh, black(-haired) man."
887	600	Gaelic (Gàidhlig)	I confess I didn't get right to the bottom of this one and despite having consulted a number of friends, must admit defeat!
698	505	Gaelic (Gàidhlig)	"Oh, English vulture."
1124	762	Gaelic (Gàidhlig)	"Oh, red laddie; oh, friend! How are you?"

Phrase *(as printed)*	Phrase *(if revised)*	Phonetic transcription	Book
a ghoistidh		/ə ɣOSHtchi/	MOBY
a ghraidh	**a ghràidh**	/ə ɣraiy/	MOBY
a leannan	**a leannain**	/ə LYAnain/	FC
a luaidh		/ə LOOaiy/	ABOSA
a madadh	**a mhadaidh**	/ə VAdi/	ABOSA
a màthair, a màthair	**a mhàthair, a mhàthair**	/ə VAhər ə VAhər/	ABOSA
a mhic a pheathar		/ə veechk ə FE'hər/	FC
a mhic an dhiobhail	**a mhic an diobhail**	/ə VEECHKən JEEal/	FC
a mhic mo peather		/ə VEECHk mo FEhər/	ABOSA
a mhic mo pheathar		/ə veechk mo FE'hər/	FC
a Mhicheal bheanaichte	**a Mhìcheil bheannaichte**	/ə VEEchəl VYENICHtchə/	FC

pb	hc	Language	Translation
322	233	Gaelic (Gàidhlig)	"Oh, godfather": this is an interesting word and one I sometimes use among friends when wishing to offer respect to someone I consider worthy of a little extra, especially if the person is a little older than me. Used by Jamie to Murtagh in *Outlander* the TV series, episode 16, "To Ransom a Man's Soul": *Is anmoch an uair, a ghoistidh*/"late is the hour, oh, godfather".
230	166	Gaelic (Gàidhlig)	"Oh, dear": in the sense of bestowing a term of affection rather than that of bemoaning a calamitous circumstance!
128	86	Gaelic (Gàidhlig)	"Oh, sweetheart/beloved."
206		Gaelic (Gàidhlig)	"Oh, dearest": heard beautifully in a version of the song "o Luaidh" by *Caitlin NicAonghais* (Kathleen MacInnes).
884	604	Gaelic (Gàidhlig)	"Oh, dog": *cù* is what you hear most often for "dog," although the names for several other animals contain the word *madadh*, too, like *madadh-donn*/madəɣ down/"otter", *madadh-allaidh*/madəɣ AHli/ "wolf", and *madadh-ruadh*/madəɣ rooaɣ/ "fox".
514	352	Gaelic (Gàidhlig)	"Mother, Mother."
1410	956	Gaelic (Gàidhlig)	"Oh, son of his sister."
247	167	Gaelic (Gàidhlig)	"Son of the devil": for many people, insults are a somewhat intriguing area of a language, and the common perception that Gaels do not swear in Gaelic is for the most part true. We don't have an "F" or "C" word as such, and those words we do have for anatomical regions or functions we don't often make a habit of using to insult people. In fact, that particular practice is really quite odd when you think about it. It surely makes much more sense if one intends to hurt a person's feelings to liken them to the son of the root of all evil than to the female sexual organs, which in truth have many vital and often celebrated functions!
944	644	Gaelic (Gàidhlig)	"Oh, son of my sister."
767	518	Gaelic (Gàidhlig)	"Oh, son of my sister."
259	175	Gaelic (Gàidhlig)	"Oh, blessed Michael."

Phrase *(as printed)*	Phrase *(if revised)*	Phonetic transcription	Book
A Mhìcheal bheannaichte, dìon sinn bho dheamhainnean	A Mhìcheal bheannaichte, dìon sinn bho dheamhain	/ə VEEchəl VYENICHtchə, JEEN sheen vo YOWain/	OLC Vol. I
a muirninn	a mhúirnín	/ə vurNYEEN/	FC
a nighean		/ə NYEEin/	FC
a nighean donn		/ə NYEEin down/	FC
a nighean na galladh	a nighean na galla	/ə NYEEin nə GALə/	FC
a nighean ruaidh		/ə NYEEin rooaiy/	MOBY
a òranaiche	òranaiche	/AWRANichə/	FC
a piuthar	a phiuthar	/ə fewer/	ABOSA
a piuthar-chèile	a phiuthair-chéile	/ə fewer CHAYlə/	MOBY
a righ! a righ!	an rìgh! an rìgh!	/ən REE, ən REE/	ABOSA
a Shasunnaich na galladh, 's olc a thig e ghuibh fanaid air bas gasgaich Gun toireach an diabhul fhein leis anns a bhas sibh, direach do Ifrinn!!	A Shasannaich na galladh, 's olc a thig e dhut fanaid air bàs gaisgich Gun toireadh an diabhal fhéin leis anns a' bhàs sibh, dìreach do dh'Ifrinn!!	/ə HASSənich nə galəɣ, solk ə heeka ɣuht fanitch air BAAss gashgich. Goon tawrəɣ ən JEEal hain laish auwns ə VAAss sheev, JEErəch do yeefarən/	OLC Vol. I
a Sheaumais	a Sheumais	/ə HAYmish/	ABOSA

pb	hc	Language	Translation
	249	Gaelic (Gàidhlig)	"Oh, blessed Michael, defend us from demons."
322	217	Gaelic (Gàidhlig)	"My darling."
110	75	Gaelic (Gàidhlig)	"Oh, lassie": we can see here the use of the vocative case when addressing someone, the *a* /ə/ meaning something like "oh"—i.e. "oh, lassie."
163	109	Gaelic (Gàidhlig)	"Oh, brown(-haired) girl/daughter."
427	289	Gaelic (Gàidhlig)	"Oh, bitch's daughter."
277	201	Gaelic (Gàidhlig)	"Oh, red(-haired) lass."
109	74	Gaelic (Gàidhlig)	"Oh, songsmith": someone who is adept at "making songs," as we say in the Gaelic, *a' dèanamh* or *a' dianamh òrain*/ə JEniv *or* JEEaniv AWrain/ (the *a* is actually not required here before a noun beginning with a vowel in the vocative case).
446	307	Gaelic (Gàidhlig)	"Oh, sister."
59	42	Gaelic (Gàidhlig)	"Oh, sister-in-law."
1345		Gaelic (Gàidhlig)	"The king! The king!"
	249	Gaelic (Gàidhlig)	"Wicked Sassenach dogs, eaters of dead flesh! Ill does it become you to laugh and rejoice at the death of a gallant man! May the devil himself seize upon you in the hour of your death and take you straight to hell!" Good point, well made.
231	160	Gaelic (Gàidhlig)	"Oh, James."

Phrase *(as printed)*	Phrase *(if revised)*	Phonetic transcription	Book
a Sheumais ruaidh		/ə HAMISH ROOaiy/	FC
a shionnach	**a shionnaich**	/ə hyunich/	OLC Vol. I
a smeòraich		/ə SMYAWRich/	FC
a Sorcha	**a Shorcha**	/ə hawrəchə/	ABOSA
a thaibse	**a thaibhse**	/ə HIGHshə/	MOBY
abigail			OLC Vol. I
air mo mhionnan . . .		/air mo VYOOnain/	FC
alagruous			OLC Vol. I
amadain		/AMAdain/	FC
an amaidan	**amadain**	/AMAdain/	MOBY
an athair	**athair**	/ən Ahər/	MOBY
an e'n fhirinn a th'aqad m'annsachd?	**an e'n fhìrinn a th' agad m' annsachd?**	/ə nyayn EERin ə hakəd MANsəchk/	OLC Vol. I

pb	hc	Language	Translation
116	79	Gaelic (Gàidhlig)	"Oh, red James": vocative form of *Seumas Ruadh*/ SHAIMəss ROOaɣ/, which can be heard in *Outlander* the TV show, episode 2, "Castle Leoch." Colum says to the expectant crowd: *"Faodaidh Seumas Ruadh seo a ghiùlan"*/fö'di SHAIMəss rooaɣ shaw ə YOOlan/"Red James may take this (punishment for Laoghaire)". It was an extremely common thing for Gaels to distinguish one another by hair color, as there were often several men named James in the one township and things could get rather confusing—or possibly even controversial if a report of the wrong James was given on a matter of some urgency!
	249	Gaelic (Gàidhlig)	"Oh, fox."
78	53	Gaelic (Gàidhlig)	"Oh, thrush": *smeòrach* /SMYAWrəch/ was often utilized as a term of affection to women because of the beautiful call, the inference being that said woman's throat was capable of emitting similar sounds. It has also been used in reference to songsmithery: *is smeòrach le Clann Dòmhaill mi*/iss SMYAWrəch le claown DAWL mee/"I am the mavis (i.e., mouthpiece) of Clan Donald". Here we have the word in the vocative case, as used when addressing a person.
510	349	Gaelic (Gàidhlig)	"Oh, Claire": the Gaelic for Claire appears to be entirely etymologically unrelated to its English equivalent.
314	227	Gaelic (Gàidhlig)	"Oh, ghost."
	246	Lowland Scots	A female servant.
230	155	Gaelic (Gàidhlig)	"On my swearing" (I swear).
	250	Lowland Scots	Grim or woebegone.
898	607	Gaelic (Gàidhlig)	"Oh, fool."
822	595	Gaelic (Gàidhlig)	"Oh, fool": *amadan* slenderizes in the vocative case—i.e., takes an extra *i* in the final syllable. Neither requires *a* before it or the article.
354	256	Gaelic (Gàidhlig)	"Oh, Father": *athair* remains as is in the vocative case, requiring neither the *a* before it nor the article.
	253	Gaelic (Gàidhlig)	"Is it the truth you have, my love?" In other words, "Are you telling me the truth?"

Phrase *(as printed)*	Phrase *(if revised)*	Phonetic transcription	Book
an fhearr mac Dubh	**an fheàrr mhic dhuibh**	/ən YAAr veechk ɣui/	OLC Vol. I
an gealtaire salach Atailteach!	**An gealtaire salach Eatailteach!**	/ən GYALtarə saləch AYTaltchəch/	OLC Vol. I
an gille ruaidh		/ən GEELə ROOaɣ/	FC
Archibald mac Donagh			ABOSA
arisaid	**earasaid**	/yerasatch/	OLC Vol. I
athair-céile		/Ahər-KAYlə/	EITB
auld besom		/auld bizm/	ABOSA
avbhar, coire	**aobhar, coire**	/Övər, CAWrə/	FC
bainisq	**bainisg**	/banishk/	EITB
bairns			FC
balach biodheach	**balach bòidheach**	/BALəch BOYəch/	OLC Vol. I
balach math		/BALəch ma/	OLC Vol. I
ballag buachair	**balgan-buachrach**	/BALagan BOOACHrach/	OLC Vol. I
ban-druidh	**ban-draoidh**	/ban DRÖI/	OLC Vol. I

pb	hc	Language	Translation
	254	Gaelic (Gàidhlig)	"Best of the offspring of the Black One": I'm not altogether sure about this one, but I give you here the translation from the first *Companion* and what I think it maybe should be in Gaelic.
	247	Gaelic (Gàidhlig)	"The filthy Italian coward."
33	24	Gaelic (Gàidhlig)	"The rusty(-haired) lad": this in fact is a nickname of a very good friend of mine who has worked with me for years on Gaelic projects in and around Glasgow and Argyll!
1429	974	Gaelic (Gàidhlig)	Curiously, the name Archibald—most often shortened to Archie—comes out in Gaelic as *Gilleasbaig*/ gilESPik/, from which derives the surname Gillespie.
	244	Gaelic (Gàidhlig)	Scots word from the Gaelic (earasaid). Square of cloth, usually tartan, worn over the shoulders of females and fastened with a brooch; female robe.
395	280	Gaelic (Gàidhlig)	"Father-in-law."
590	405	Lowland Scots	Old pest. *Besom* is an oft-used word in Scots, although it mostly comes out something like /bizm/.
1410	956	Gaelic (Gàidhlig)	"Reason," "corrie": a corrie is like a little depression in among hills. The Gaelic words for this and "kettle, cauldron" are spelled identically and are barely distinguishable from one another in terms of pronunciation; they most probably came originally from the one concept. Compare /kawrə/ with /kohrə/.
923	655	Gaelic (Gàidhlig)	"Little old woman."
62	42	Lowland Scots	Children: rural and Eastern dialects. Not used in Glasgow (see "wean"), this word entered Scottish speech via Scandinavian language, where it is still current in the form *barn*. Swedish: *Har du barn?*/"Have you child(ren)?"
	249	Gaelic (Gàidhlig)	"Beautiful boy."
	252	Gaelic (Gàidhlig)	"Good boy."
	239	Gaelic (Gàidhlig)	"Mushroom": literally "manure bubble." I am convinced that the concept of a "ball" or "bubble" in this sense has brought about the English slang word "bollock" for the male testicle!
	245	Gaelic (Gàidhlig)	"Female druid": female sorcerer or worker of magic.

Phrase *(as printed)*	Phrase *(if revised)*	Phonetic transcription	Book
ban-lichtne	**ban-lighiche**	/ban-LEEichə/	ABOSA
ban-sidhe	**ban-sìth**	/banSHEE/	FC
baragh mhor	**baradh mór**	/BArəɣ MORE/	OLC Vol. I
bas mallaichte!	**bàs mallaichte!**	/BAASS MALichtchə/	OLC Vol. I
bawbee			OLC Vol. I
beannachd leat, a charaid		/BYAnachk lecht ə CHAridge/	MOBY
bein-treim	**banntrach**	/BANtrəch/	ABOSA
besom		/bizm/	OLC Vol. I
bi samnach, tha mi seo	**bith sàmhach, tha mi 'n seo**	/bee SAvəch, hami'n SHAW/	FC
bi socair, mo chridhe	**bith socair mo chridhe**	/bee SOCHkər mo CHREEə/	FC
bioran		/BEEran/	FC
Bliadha Tearlach	**Bliana Theàrlaich**	/BLEEanə HYARlich/	ABOSA
bodhran		/BOHran/	OLC Vol. I
bothy	**bothie**		OLC Vol. I

pb	hc	Language	Translation
227	157	Gaelic (Gàidhlig)	"Female doctor": *lighiche* comes from the practice of applying leeches to a patient's body in order to heal all sorts of ills, real and assumed. Doctors in the early days, then, were literally spoken of as "leechers"!
1205	817	Gaelic (Gàidhlig)	"Female fairy": where we have taken the word "banshee" from, as in to "scream like a banshee," since banshees were thought to wail before the impending death of a clan member, often a chief.
	238	Gaelic (Gàidhlig)	"A large Baragh": I'm not altogether sure what this one is! The only thing I can find that resembles it is *baradh*, which means a "hindrance" or "obstacle."
	243	Gaelic (Gàidhlig)	"Accursed death."
910	253	Lowland Scots	A Scottish halfpenny.
	661	Gaelic (Gàidhlig)	"Blessings with you, oh, friend."
502	344	Gaelic (Gàidhlig)	"Widow": I'm not familiar with *ban-treim*. The word *banntrach* originally comes from *bean deurach*/ben-JERach/"tearful woman" and we still use this in Argyll today, although it's now pronounced /BENjerrach/.
	245	Lowland Scots	Ill-tempered woman.
925	625	Gaelic (Gàidhlig)	"Be quiet (calm); I am here."
925	625	Gaelic (Gàidhlig)	"Be at ease, my heart."
1403	951	Gaelic (Gàidhlig)	"Little pointed stick": literally, "little jagged."
669	459	Gaelic (Gàidhlig)	"Charlie's Year": this refers to the period 1745–46, which culminated in Prince Charles Edward Stewart leading many Gaels to their demise at Culloden. *Teàrlach* follows another name or noun and so therefore takes the genitive case *Theàrlaich*. As *bliana* is nowhere pronounced /BLEEəɣna/, I have removed the *dh* for ease of learning.
	250	Gaelic (Gàidhlig)	A flat, circular drum with a stretched-skin head over a wooden frame, beaten with a short double-headed stick.
	241	Lowland Scots	Mountain shack. From Gaelic *bothan* /BOHhan/.

Phrase *(as printed)*	Phrase *(if revised)*	Phonetic transcription	Book
braw			FC
bree			OLC Vol. I
breugaire		/BRAYgərə/	ABOSA
broch		/broch/	OLC Vol. I
Broch Tuarach		/broch TOOArəch/	MOBY
brose			OLC Vol. I
buidheachas dhut, a Sheumais mac Brian	**buidheachas dhut, a Sheumais 'ic Bhriain**	/BOOyachəs ɣoocht, ə HAMISH ichk VREEain/	FC
buidheachas, mo charaid		/BOOyachəs mo CHAridge/	OLC Vol. I
burras		/BOOrass/	OLC Vol. I

pb	hc	Language	Translation
33	23	Lowland Scots	Good. Comes originally from Norse language *bra* and is still heard daily in Scandinavia today. I have recently been picking up a bit of Swedish, as I have friends from the area, and it's really remarkable how much the Lowland Scots language and her Scandinavian neighbors have in common, from word order to vocabulary. I can also hear elements of both the Lewis and, believe it or not, Newcastle accents in Scandinavian speech, something which may or may not thrill the denizens of those two rather distinct places!
	253	Lowland Scots	A great disturbance; also a soup. "Partan bree" is a crab soup.
1104	753	Gaelic (Gàidhlig)	"Liar": another example of the north/south Gaelic dialect divide, we in the middle of Argyll would pronounce this as shown, while to the north and in MacKenzie country it would be *briagaire*/BREEAgərə/.
	240	Gaelic (Gàidhlig)	"Iron Age tower": the predecessor of the Highland castle.
284	206	Fictional placename	"North-facing tower": now, technically the word *tuarach* doesn't exist—it would be *tuathach*/TOOach/"northerly"/—but I happen to think as made-up names go, it seems exactly what a fictional Gaelic word would look and sound like!
	245	Lowland Scots	Broth, a certain type, often made of barley or kale. Iain Mac an Tàilleir (language advisor for *The Outlandish Companion Volume One*) notes: "This is not Gaelic, but the brose I and my fellow islanders knew was a stiff mix of the local grain meal—oats or barley, etc.—cooked with water, butter, and salt. Same ingredients as porridge, but much stiffer consistency. Supposed to be 'good for you.' Never liked it myself."
119	81	Gaelic (Gàidhlig)	"Gratitude to you, James, son (of) Brian": *Brian*, a Gaelic name, would be pronounced /BREEan/; *mac*/machk/ and *Brian* would also be declined in the vocative case to *mhic*/veechk/ or *'ic Bhriain*/eechk VREEaiyn/. You sometimes see *buidheachas*/BOOIYəchəs/ used on album sleeves or books where you might use "acknowledgments" or "thanks to" in English.
	240	Gaelic (Gàidhlig)	"Gratitude, my friend."
	244	Gaelic (Gàidhlig)	"Caterpillar."

Phrase *(as printed)*	Phrase *(if revised)*	Phonetic transcription	Book
cá bhfuil tú?		/ka fwail too/	ABOSA
cack-handed			OLC Vol. I
caithris		/KArish/	FC
calman geal	**calman geal**	/KALəmən gyal/	OLC Vol. I
Campbell	**Caimbeul**	/KAIYMbəl/	FC
camstairy	**camstairie**		OLC Vol. I
canty	**cantie**		OLC Vol. I
casteal an duin	**caisteal an dùin**	/KASHtchəl ən DOON/	FC
Casteal Dhuni	**Caisteal Dhùnaidh**	/KASHtchəl ɣOOni/	OLC Vol. I
cat a mhinister	**cat a' mhinisteir**	/cat ə veeneeshtchər/	EITB

pb	hc	Language	Translation
187	131	Gaelic (Gaeilge)	"Where are you?": our Scottish equivalent to this is practically identical: *cà' bheil u?* There really is very little difference between Scottish and Irish. In fact, on either side of the Straits of Moyle, the Gaelic was far more similar than that of the northeast and southwest of Scotland—or than the northeast and southwest of Ireland, for that matter—were to each other. It is only politics that has caused any kind of divide. I blether very freely with Irish language speakers, using my own dialect of Scottish and them Irish and worrying none about the little bits we don't understand. A sublime pleasure, in fact, to share a pint of Guinness and a good Scottish dram and let the conversation flow free!
	252	Lowland Scots	Left-handed. This can also mean awkward or maladroit.
1383	938	Gaelic (Gàidhlig)	"Lament": I know this word as meaning "watch." *Caithris na h-oidhche*/karish nə HÖichə/"the night watch" took place over the corpse of a deceased person. One night when two old Islay men were watching the body of a deceased friend, they fell asleep by the fire, only to wake suddenly to the table on which the corpse was lying bouncing violently up and down. Little did they know that a huge pig had been rooting around the village during the night, looking for food, and had decided to settle down for a rest under the table, whereupon it began to scratch itself vigorously!
	240	Gaelic (Gàidhlig)	"White dove": *geal* also carries the meaning "bright."
26	19	Surname	"Crooked mouth": and the Campbells did their chances of avoiding the "crooked by name, crooked by nature" aspersion no good by playing whatever side in whichever conflict they could to further their grip on power in Gaelic Scotland.
	250	Lowland Scots	"Obstinate, riotous, unmanageable."
	240	Lowland Scots	"Lively, pleasant, cheerful": implying also "something small and neat" or "a person in good health."
887	600	Gaelic (Gàidhlig)	"Castle of the mound!": a battle cry.
	250	Gaelic (Gàidhlig)	"War cry of Clan Fraser": I have offered an alternative spelling here as I believe the one used is representative of an era when an older, less-regular orthography was in use. Pronunciation would be much the same.
325	230	Gaelic (Gàidhlig)	"The minister's cat."

Phrase *(as printed)*	Phrase *(if revised)*	Phonetic transcription	Book
caurry-fisted	**caurie-fistit**	/KORi-FIStet/	OLC Vol. I
cèilidh	**céilidh**	/KAYli/	MOBY
ceo gheasacach	**ceò geasach**	/KYAW GUESSəch/	OLC Vol. I
cèolas	**ceòlas**	/KYAWlas/ or /KEolas/	EITB

pb	hc	Language	Translation
	244	Lowland Scots	"Left-handed": either from the Gaelic *ceàrr* ("wrong") or from the tradition of the Kerr family, who taught their sons to fight left-handed up a turnpike stair when attacking an enemy's tower-house residence (style of diminutive Scottish castle built during the late 15th, 16th, and 17th centuries), as these were designed to favor the defender, who simply by the law of averages would most likely be right-handed. So this could be either *ceàrrie* or *Kerrie*-fistit, which over time became *caurie*.
827	599	Gaelic (Gàidhlig)	"Dance, party": originally derives from the concept of *dol a chéilidh air daoine*/dollə CHAYli air döinyə/"going to visit (on) people", which resulted in what were called *taighean-céilidh*/taiyen-KAYli/"*céilidh* houses." We could equate this today with that house we all remember from when we were children: perhaps it was a friend of your parents or one of your grandparents—who knows, maybe it was your house? But either way, it was somewhere people knew they could knock on the door at almost any time of day or night and there would be a cup of coffee or a dram to be had and all the news of the local area. Many of us have lovely hazy memories of these kinds of houses and of the feeling of warmth and friendship which existed there, as large numbers of people descended once the word of a gathering had got out. The *taighean-céilidh* were just that. They also had dancing and singing and storytelling of the highest order. Although houses just like the ones described above still remain all across Scotland, the traditional Gaelic *taigh-céilidh* atmosphere is all but lost, and the Fingalian legends, which took days to recite from start to finish, are a thing of the past, this specific style of storytelling now a lost art.
	247	Gaelic (Gàidhlig)	"Magical mist."
652	462	Gaelic (Gàidhlig)	A terrific annual festival of Gaelic music and culture that takes place in *Uibhist*/OOishtch/"Uist"/ in July. Well worth a week off to attend—so I've heard! I reckon I had better try it out myself sometime. Let's hope *Gillebrìde*/geeləBREEjə/ hasn't seen this or I'll be for it. Interestingly, the spelling in the book rather reflects what happens to words spelled *eo* in the Gaelic of *Uibhist, Barraigh*/BAraiy/"Barra"/ and *Arra-Ghàidheal a Tuath*/araɣaiyl ə TOOa/"North Argyll"/: the emphasis shifts from the *o* to the *e*, so instead of *ceòl*/kyawl/, you get *cèol*/ke'ol/.

Phrase *(as printed)*	Phrase *(if revised)*	Phonetic transcription	Book
ceud mile fàilte	**ciad mìle fàilte**	/keeәd MEElә FALtchә/	ABOSA
cha chluinn thu an còrr a chuireas eagal ort	**cha chluinn u'n còrr a chuireas eagal ort**	/cha CHLUIYN-yoon KAWRә choorәss aykәl orst/	EITB
Cha ghabh mi'n còrr, tapa leibh		/cha ɣav meen KAWR, tachpә löiv/	OLC Vol. I
cha mhór		/cha VORE/	EITB
chan eil e ag iarraidh math dhut idir		/chanALE a GEEari ma ɣoocht EEJәr/	EITB
chaneil facal agam dhuibh ach taing	**chan eil facal agam dhuibh ach taing**	/chanALE FACHkil AKum ɣooiy ach TANG/	FC

Key: OLC Vol. 1—*The Outlandish Companion* FC—*The Fiery Cross* ABOSA—*A Breath of Snow and Ashes*

pb	hc	Language	Translation
682	467	Gaelic (Gàidhlig)	"100,000 welcomes": the overarching hospitality of the Gael. We're not content just to say "welcome"—there have to be 100,000 of them, although we are happy to do all 100,000 in the one phrase rather than individually! Much as in old Arabian culture, hospitality was a very seriously taken thing, and in welcoming a band of MacDonalds, as the major is doing here, it would have to be done right! In days gone by the word *ceud* was pronounced almost like the first name /KATE/ but has since morphed into /KEEət/. I believe that the spelling should move too to reflect this, as it has in other words such as *sgian*/SKEEan/"knife", which was once *sgeun*.
807	571	Gaelic (Gàidhlig)	"You shall hear no more that puts fear on you" (that scares you).
	251	Gaelic (Gàidhlig)	"I'll take no more, thank you": *tapa* is more often written *tapadh,* although the former spelling is perhaps more representative of how it is pronounced.
637	451	Gaelic (Gàidhlig)	"Almost, just about": literally "not great" in the sense of "not great was the margin by which that was not the most beautiful thing I ever saw!" The answer to the question about the lovely silver fish would normally be more fully rendered *cha mhór nach e*/cha VORE nach AY/.
854	604	Gaelic (Gàidhlig)	"He wants no good for you at all."
110	75	Gaelic (Gàidhlig)	"I have no word for you but thanks": this is the correct way to say "I have only." Often today, the word *dìreach*/JEErəch/ is misused to mean "only" when in fact it means "exactly, directly"—e.g., *'S e dìreach taing a th' agam dhuibh*/shay JEErəch taing ə HAKum ɣooiy/. It's useful to remember that Gaelic is still naturally "old-fashioned" in many ways that English has ceased to be. The title of one of my favorite songs that I grew up listening to, "*'S Fliuch an Oidhche*"/sflyooch ən ÖIYchə/ (covered among others by the superb Gaelic singer and friend of Diana, *Catrìona-Anna Nic a' Phì*/kəTREEənə anə neechkəFEE/), means literally "wet is the night." Now, wouldn't it be cool if we all still spoke like that? In Gaelic you can yet, and with impunity!

EITB—*An Echo in the Bone* MOBY—*Written in My Own Heart's Blood*

Phrase *(as printed)*	Phrase *(if revised)*	Phonetic transcription	Book
Chisholm	Siosalach	/SHEESSaləch/	FC
ciamar a tha thu?	ciamar a tha u?	/KIMerə HAOW/	ABOSA
ciamar a tha thu, a charaid?	ciamar a tha u, a charaid?	/KIMerə HAOW, ə CHAridge/	EITB
ciamar a tha thu, a choin?	ciamar a tha u, a choin?	/KIMerə HAOW, ə choñ/	MOBY
ciamar a tha thu, an gille ruaidh?	ciamar a tha u, a ghille ruaidh?	/KIMerə HAOW, ə YEElə rooaiy/	FC
ciamar a tha thu, mo athair?	ciamar a tha u, m' athair?	/KIMerə HAOW, MAhər/	EITB
ciamar a tha tu, mo chridhe?	ciamar a tha u, mo chridhe?	/KIMerə HAOW, mo CHREEə/	OLC Vol. I
ciomach		/keeməch/	ABOSA
cirein croin	cirein-cròin	/KEErən-CROin/	OLC Vol. I
clarty	clartie		OLC Vol. I
clattie imp			OLC Vol. I
clot-heid		/klot-heed/	OLC Vol. I
co a th'ann?	có a th' ann?	/KOə HAOWN/	FC

pb	hc	Language	Translation
35	25	Surname	There is a very poignant lament that I sing both to the children and elsewhere, entitled "*Cumha do dh'Uilleam Siosal*"/KOOa do ɣoolyəm SHEESSəl/"Lament for William Chisholm"; also sometimes called "*Mo Rùn Geal Òg*"/mo ROON gyal AWg/"My Young Pale Love", by a woman about her husband who met his end at Culloden, leaving her destitute, with nothing but his shirt for company. Grim stuff, but lovely listening.
230	159	Gaelic (Gàidhlig)	"How are you?": the classic greeting, which I spell with the *th* removed from *thu,* as I finally realized—when teaching none other than the *Outlander* TV show cast—that it causes entirely unnecessary problems. The word is pronounced /oo/, while the beginning of all other words beginning with *thu* are pronounced /hoo/: for instance, *thuirt, thug, thugam* ("said," "gave," "to me"). There is no reason whatsoever to retain this *th,* which causes learners to pronounce the phrase /kimmer a ha hoo/ when it should be /kimmer ə ha-oo/ or /KIMerə HAOW/, as it sounds in colloquial speech. And so I take great pleasure in simplifying your lives by including it here as it was learned by our beloved clansmen!
814	576	Gaelic (Gàidhlig)	"How are you, oh, friend?"
177	128	Gaelic (Gàidhlig)	"How are you, oh, dog?"
342	230	Gaelic (Gàidhlig)	"How are you, oh, red-haired boy?" Interestingly, we can discover the origins of the surname Gilroy here, *(mac) g(h)ille ruaidh*/GEELərooiy/.
960	682	Gaelic (Gàidhlig)	"How are you, my father?"
	253	Gaelic (Gàidhlig)	"How are you, my heart?"
386	266	Gaelic (Gàidhlig)	"Captive."
	253	Gaelic (Gàidhlig)	"Sea monster; sea serpent."
	253	Lowland Scots	Dirty, filthy.
	245	Lowland Scots	Filthy imp.
	245	Lowland Scots	Cloth-head; idiot or imbecile.
1370	929	Gaelic (Gàidhlig)	"Who's there?"

Phrase *(as printed)*	Phrase *(if revised)*	Phonetic transcription	Book
có tha faighneachd?		/KOha FAIYnyəchk/	EITB
có thu?	**có u?**	/ko-oo/	EITB
cobhar		/KOar/	OLC Vol. I
cockernonny	**cockernonnie**		OLC Vol. I
coil			OLC Vol. I
coimhead air sin!	**seall air sin!**	/COYit air SHEEN/ or / SHAOwl air SHEEN/	EITB
collieshangie			OLC Vol. I
come ben		/kum ben/	MOBY
coof			OLC Vol. I
coronach		/korənəch/	ABOSA
craicklin'	**craicklin**		OLC Vol. I
cranachan	**crannachan**	/KRAnachən/	MOBY
croich gorn	**cròich-gòrn**	/KROIch GAWRN	OLC Vol. I
cuidich mi, a Dhia!		/KOOtchich mi ə YEEa	MOBY
cuimhnich		/KOOIYnyich/	EITB
cuir stad		/koor STAT/	OLC Vol. I
cullen skink			OLC Vol. I

pb	hc	Language	Translation
790	560	Gaelic (Gàidhlig)	"Who's asking?"
790	560	Gaelic (Gàidhlig)	"Who (are) you?"
	240	Gaelic (Gàidhlig)	"Foam."
	241	Lowland Scots	"A gathering of hair into a neat bundle."
	243	Lowland Scots	A difficulty or troublesome circumstance.
637	451	Gaelic (Gàidhlig)	"Look at that!": literally, "watch on that." I would tend to say *seall air sin* here: "look at that."
	246	Lowland Scots	An uproar or squabble.
245	177	Lowland Scots	Come in. Lowland Scots shares many words with other Germanic languages, not least Dutch. You can see the similarity between the languages in the Dutch *kom binnen*, which also means "come in."
	252	Lowland Scots	Silly person, idiot.
503	345	Gaelic (Gàidhlig)	"Coronal; of or belonging to a crown or chaplet."
	250	Lowland Scots	Hoarse croaking or snoring sound.
251	181	Gaelic, Lowland Scots	"Beaten milk": a treat served at Halloween, which differs in spelling between Gaelic and Scots only in the dropping of one of the middle *n*'s in the latter language.
	240	Gaelic (Gàidhlig)	Diana says: "Your guess is as good as mine—probably better." My guess isn't much better, I'm afraid. *Croich* appears to be either "a gallows, a gibbet," or *cròich*, "difficulty breathing." Certainly after hanging from the gallows, the latter circumstance may well come into play! *Gòrn* is noted in Dwelly's great Gaelic dictionary as either an "ember," "firebrand," "the force of poison," or a "murdering dart." So with these fine definitions at your disposal, have at it!
596	433	Gaelic (Gàidhlig)	"Help me, oh God!"
852	603	Gaelic (Gàidhlig)	"Remember."
	244	Gaelic (Gàidhlig)	"Put a stop to": imperative command for gerund *cur*.
	240	Lowland Scots	Diana: "As one of my cookbooks remarks, 'This is not an offensive small animal, but a traditional recipe for soup from the Moray Firth area.' It consists of haddock and mashed potatoes, simmered in milk and cream with onion, butter, mace, parsley, and salt and pepper."

Phrase *(as printed)*	Phrase *(if revised)*	Phonetic transcription	Book
dags			OLC Vol. I
deamhan		/JEwan/	OLC Vol. I
dèan caithris		/jen KArish/	ABOSA
Death Dirge	**An Tuiream Bàis**	/ən TOOrəm BAASH/	MOBY
Declaration of Arbroath			ABOSA
deed of Sasine			OLC Vol. I
Dia eadarainn 's an t-olc		/JEEa aidereen san TOLCHK/	MOBY
diabhol	**diabhal**	/JEEal/	FC
dittay			OLC Vol. I
do mi! do mi!	**thugam! thugam!**	/HOOKəm! HOOKəm!/	OLC Vol. I
doiters			OLC Vol. I

pb	hc	Language	Translation
	241	Lowland Scots	"Pistols"(obsolete).
	253	Gaelic (Gàidhlig)	"Demon, devil."
509	349	Gaelic (Gàidhlig)	"Make watch": *dian caithris*/jeean KArish/ in Northern and Western Isles dialects.
1050	764	Gaelic (Gàidhlig)	This piece can be found in the four volumes by *Alasdair MacIlleMhìcheil*/ALASdər machgeeləVEEchəl/Alexander Carmichael entitled *Carmina Gadelica*, a veritable treasure trove of old prayers, charms, and verses in the Gaelic, to which Diana referred during the creation of these novels.
667	457	historical document	*"Cho fad 's a mhaireas ciadnar againn beò, cha chrùb sinn fo smachd na Beurla"*: these are lines from an Anna Frater poem to which I put music and are of a most encouraging nature as regards the language. She paraphrases the declaration, whereby the lairds of Scotland gathered in 1320 to make known to the pope in Rome their intention to prevent Scotland becoming beholden to England. Anna instead states that "as long as a hundred of us [Gaels] remain alive, we will not yield to the control of the English [language]." A most admirable statement and one to which—shock, horror—I fully subscribe!
	244	Lowland Scots	Deed transferring property under Scottish law.
280	202	Gaelic (Gàidhlig)	"God between us and the evil."
208	140	Gaelic (Gàidhlig)	"Devil": this made me think of something which will no doubt amuse. There is a sharp natural rock feature in the Cairngorms which is known as *Bod an Diabhail*. Now, when Queen Victoria discovered it on vacation in Scotland, she was so offended that there was a rock by the name of the "Devil's Penis" that she requested forthwith that it be referred to as the "Devil's Peak." I rather think something was lost that day, and if one really had to imagine what shape the Dark Prince's johnson might take, then this nasty-looking crag would be it!
	240	Lowland Scots	A court document, an indictment.
	254	Gaelic (Gàidhlig)	"To me! To me!"
	245	Lowland Scots	Blundering fools.

Phrase *(as printed)*	Phrase *(if revised)*	Phonetic transcription	Book
doits			OLC Vol. I
donas		/DOnass/	OLC Vol. I
drammach	**dramach**		OLC Vol. I
dreich		/dreech/	MOBY
droch aite	**droch àite**	/droch AAtchə/	OLC Vol. I
duine		/DOONyə/	OLC Vol. I
duine uasal	**duin' uasal**	/doon-OOasəl/	OLC Vol. I
Duncan Innes	**Donnchadh Aonghais**	/donachəɣ ÖNish/	FC
dunt			OLC Vol. I
each uisge			OLC Vol. I
earbsachd		/eribSUCHK/	FC
eirich 'illean! Suas am bearrach is teich!	**éirichibh 'illean! Suas am bearrach 's teichibh!**		OLC Vol. I

pb	hc	Language	Translation
	245	Lowland Scots	Small copper coins.
	240	Gaelic (Gàidhlig)	"Devil, demon."
	239	Gaelic (Gàidhlig)	"A mixture of oats and water, uncooked": said to have been partaken of and thoroughly enjoyed by the Bonnie Prince!
299	217	Lowland Scots	Inclement. It is thought that originally this word may have come from the old Gothic for "slow" or "tedious"—*drig*—rather than anything to do with an inclement environment. These days, though, it is very much linked to the concept of nasty weather: cold, blustery, pishing with rain . . . you get the idea. You might imagine we use this word a lot—you would be right!
	251	Gaelic (Gàidhlig)	"A bad place."
	240	Gaelic (Gàidhlig)	"A man; an individual."
	251	Gaelic (Gàidhlig)	"A gentleman; a man of integrity."
25	18	Surname	This name derives from the practice of referring to someone in terms of their father. To differentiate between *Donnchadh 1* and *Donnchadh 2*, you could use their hair color or size, but if both were brown-haired and tall, you could revert to use of a patronymic, which often may actually have been first choice, anyway, especially if the father was famous—e.g., the greatest Gaelic warrior of all time, *Alasdair mac Cholla chiotaich* (Alexander, son of ambidextrous Coll). The Duncan currently in question would become *Donnchadh Aonghais*, which, when written in a census or other official document for lack of an actual surname (common until relatively recently), would be Anglicized as "Duncan Innes."
	244	Lowland Scots	A blow.
	251	Gaelic (Gàidhlig)	"Water horse": known as a "kelpie" in Scots, these mythical beings were used as bogeymen by parents wishing to keep their kids in line. I have heard of old men telling of their genuine terror as children at the mere mention of water horses.
231	155	Gaelic (Gàidhlig)	"Trust."
	246	Gaelic (Gàidhlig)	"Up, lads! Over the cliff and flee!": I'm not familiar with the word *bearrach* for cliff.

Phrase *(as printed)*	Phrase *(if revised)*	Phonetic transcription	Book
eìsd ris	**éist ris**	/AISHtch reesh/	ABOSA
fash			OLC Vol. I
fear- siûrsachd	**fear-siùrsachd**	/fair-SHOORsəchk/	ABOSA
feasgar math	**feasgar math dhuibh**	/FACEkər ma ɣooiy/	EITB
Fèileadh beag	**féilidh-beag**	/FAYli bake/	MOBY
feumaidh gun do dh'ìth mi rudegin nach robh dol leam	**feumaidh gun do dh'ìth mi rudaigin nach robh dol leam**	/faymi goon d'yeech mi rootigen nach ro dawl-löm/	EITB
fiddle-ma-fyke			OLC Vol. I
Fionnaghal		/FYOONagəl/	ABOSA
fois shìorruidh thoir dha	**fois shìorraidh dha**	/fosh HEEori ɣa/	EITB
fricht		/fricht/	OLC Vol. I
fuirich agus chi thu	**fuirich agas chì u**	/FOOrich AGəss CHEEoo/	EITB
fuirich, a choin		/FOOrich ə choñ/	MOBY

pb	hc	Language	Translation
173	121	Gaelic (Gàidhlig)	"Listen to him!" bellowed Kenny Lindsay: by coincidence, Kenny Lindsay was our lovely actor who gave us such a good rendition of Laoghaire's father on the *Outlander* TV show, episode 2, "Castle Leoch." Kenny, a good friend of mine, learned his Gaelic from scratch, and a fine grasp of it he has, too!
	245	Lowland Scots	Bother, stress, worry: *dinna fash* (don't stress) is the archetypal use of this phrase, now regarded as very Aberdeenshire in its flavor and belonging to the Scots dialect known as Doric, still thankfully very much alive in the northeast.
1104	753	Gaelic (Gàidhlig)	"Lecher": this actually sounds to me like about the closest we could manage in Gaelic to "pimp"!
644	456	Gaelic (Gàidhlig)	"Good evening (to you)."
733	531	Gaelic (Gàidhlig)	"Small kilt," literally "the small fold": as opposed to the "big fold" the *féilidh-mór* /MORE/ worn by Sam Heughan and co. in the *Outlander* TV show. The small kilt as it is known today was popularized by the British military during the late-18th and early-19th centuries but was not unknown before this time. It is thought that similar garments may have been worn as far back as the 1690s and the concept itself is most certainly an ancient one.
814	576	Gaelic (Gàidhlig)	"I must have eaten something that didn't go with me" (didn't agree with me).
	245	Lowland Scots	A silly, overfastidious person.
675	462	Gaelic (Gàidhlig)	"Fiona": it is from *Fionnaghal* that we derive the modern first name.
403	286	Gaelic (Gàidhlig)	"Everlasting peace to him": or, put another way, "God rest his soul." It is interesting to note that the word *sìorraidh* comes from the two words *sìor*/sheer (or sometimes /sheeor/"ever", in the sense of "constantly, consistently") and *ruith*/rooi/"run, running", so in other words "ever-running" or "everlasting."
	244	Lowland Scots	Fright.
1120	794	Gaelic (Gàidhlig)	"Wait and you'll see."
477	346	Gaelic (Gàidhlig)	"Wait, oh, dog."

Phrase *(as printed)*	Phrase *(if revised)*	Phonetic transcription	Book
gaberlunzie		/GABBERlunzi/	OLC Vol. I
Gabhainn! A charaid!	**a Ghabhainn! A charaid!**	/ə ɣAVain ə CHAridge/	OLC Vol. I
Gaelic cursing			EITB
Gaelic discouraged			EITB

pb	hc	Language	Translation
	241	Lowland Scots	Small lead badge given to beggars as a license to beg within the borders of a parish.
	249	Gaelic (Gàidhlig)	"Oh, Gavin! oh friend!"
644	459	historical note	Such a familiar feeling, the one Roger has here as he addresses his class! And a topic often raised by people dabbling in any language—cursing. "*We haven't got bad words in the* Gàidhlig . . . *Which is not to say ye can't give a good, strong opinion of someone,*" as Roger says. How right he is, although you need just consult the Naughty Little Book of Gaelic to get a sense of what is yet possible!
399	283	historical note	This passage in *Echo in the Bone* is reminiscent of the life of so many Highland children who were savagely beaten by those loyal to the British education system for speaking the only language they knew, and in their own country, often by those with Gaelic themselves, like Mr. Menzies! I am very happy that we have moved past such times but also very grateful to Diana for including this kind of material in her books, highlighting the true history of cultural oppression in Scotland. I know of people who had the meter stick broken across their backs, were belted until their hands broke out in welts; one monolingual boy in Perthshire received such a beating about the head for speaking his native language that he went deaf in one ear, and some children in Lewis in the 1950s were forced to wear a human skull hung round their neck if they were caught speaking the only tongue they knew. This kind of thing left Gaels with a terrible sense of betrayal and anger, which often became directed at the language itself rather than at the establishment which had encouraged this repulsive violence and psychological abuse toward children. And so, among the ashes of Gaelic pride, myself and others work. The respect and appreciation shown by *Outlander* fans for our tongue and culture promises to be a precious and motivating force in the years to come.

Phrase *(as printed)*	Phrase *(if revised)*	Phonetic transcription	Book
Gàidhlig		/GAAleek/	EITB
garbel			OLC Vol. I
German			FC
gille			OLC Vol. I
girdle			OLC Vol. I

pb	hc	Language	Translation
382	271		Scottish Gaelic: this is the most common pronunciation of the language moniker and the reason why many people pronounce the English equivalent /gahlick/. In fact, the English word refers to something more akin to a language family and does not hold any kind of national significance apart from when coupled with either the words "Scottish," "Irish," or "Manx." To be a Gael was indeed once to be part of a "nation," in a sense, but bound by linguistic and cultural ties rather than the arbitrary drawing of lines across a map. *Clanna nan Gàidheal ri guailibh a chéile*/klana nən GAIYL ree GOOailəv ə CHAYlə/"children of the Gael at each other's shoulder" attests beautifully to this. And so there is no great sin whatsoever in calling our language "Gaelic" in English, just as the word looks, because, after all . . . not all Gaels are Gals!
	245	Lowland Scots	To rumble, as an empty stomach.
			I grew up bilingually, but not as you might expect, with Gaelic and Scots—no, not that lucky. Along with the standard English I spoke as a first language, however, I picked up passable colloquial German from my father, a reluctant WWII veteran who stayed in Germany for three years after the fighting had ceased, for the love of a woman whose husband returned most unexpectedly from the Eastern Front to find my father wearing his slippers. As our teenagers take great pride in saying these days: "Whoa . . . awkward!"
	241	Gaelic (Gàidhlig)	"A boy, a servant": sometimes corrupted in English usage to *gillie*, you can also find it in Glasgow parlance as *keilie*.
	245	Lowland Scots	A flat iron plate set over the fire and used for cooking. Small girdles were often carried by Scottish mercenaries, swung on their belts, enabling them to make oatcakes in the field. Similar in meaning and derivation to the English "griddle."

Phrase *(as printed)*	Phrase *(if revised)*	Phonetic transcription	Book
Glasgow kiss			FC
gomeral		/GOMerəl/	OLC Vol. I
gowk			OLC Vol. I
gralloch			OLC Vol. I

pb	hc	Language	Translation
898	607	Lowland Scots	A head butt—more correctly "Glesga kiss" or often "stickin the nut in sumdie," meaning to strike someone with the use of one's head. I have witnessed one of these bad boys delivered on several occasions and am thankful never to have been the recipient. It is seen as something of a martial art form in Glasgow and if administered correctly will generate terrific force, despite no use of the arms for further thrust. On a Saturday night in Glasgow town center, I once saw a huge bald man in a brightly-colored shirt "stick the nut" in an opponent with such gusto that it sent the man *up* five steps at the front of a department store. This may well be a good place to add a note about the name "Glasgow" itself, often said—and I believe erroneously—to mean "dear green place." There is nothing to suggest that any word for "dear" is part of the name, and the assumption that *gow* is derived from Old Welsh I also believe to be a false one. *Glas* is clearly the Gaelic word for "green" or "gray," but when you discover how the word is pronounced in my home area of Dalriada, you hear old men from Lochfyneside (John MacVicar, School of Scottish Studies Archives) saying /GLASSachəv/. Now, what this sounds distinctly like is *glas-achamh* (*glas-achadh* elsewhere), or "green field." In the eastern part of Dalriada—in Cowal, and also east of there in Stirlingshire by all accounts, the areas that border Glasgow itself—it sounds like /GLASSəchoo/, which would give very obvious rise to the modern Gaelic *Glaschu* (pronounced exactly like that). I am of the firm belief that I'm onto something here and that the place name Glasgow is derived exclusively from Scottish Gaelic and means "green field."
	245	Lowland Scots	Fool, idiot.
	253	Lowland Scots	Awkward, silly person; also cuckoo. You can see the similarity between the Gaelic *cuthag*/KOOak and Scots "gowk." The question is which gave rise to which! Although most often Scots has borrowed from Gaelic, the opposite is also quite often the case.
	245	Lowland Scots	Slaughter, specifically the knife stroke that disembowels a killed animal. I have the feeling that this may indeed be a Scots' borrowing from Gaelic, but reference to the original Gaelic I cannot find.

Phrase *(as printed)*	Phrase *(if revised)*	Phonetic transcription	Book
greetin'	**greetin**		FC
Griogal Cridhe		/greegəl KREEə/	EITB
griss			OLC Vol. I
gu leoir!	**gu leòr!**	/g'LYAWr/	OLC Vol. I
gum biodh iad sabhailte, a Dhìa	**gum biodh iad sàbhailte, a Dhia**	/goom beeɣ ad SAvəltchə, ə YEEa/	EITB
gun robh math agaibh, a nighean	**gu robh math agad, a nighean**	/g'ro MA-akəd ə NYEEin/	ABOSA
harled			OLC Vol. I
hauld your wheesht!	**haud yer wheesht!**	/hod yer wheesht/	MOBY
havers		/HAYvərs/	OLC Vol. I
hiddie-pyke			OLC Vol. I

pb	hc	Language	Translation
62	43	Lowland Scots	"Crying." Both Swedish and Danish contain words very similar to this, which mean to mourn or lament. It's an everyday expression in Lowland Scotland, where you will hear people saying to their children the likes of, "Och, pack yer greetin in" ("Stop your crying") and "She's a richt greetin-faced wee besom!" ("She's a rather sullen little broom!") "Besom," meaning initially a "household broom," has happily transferred into Scots as this super fun rebuke! Don't you just love the way we Scots think?
124	88	Gaelic (Gàidhlig)	"Darling Gregor," literally "Gregor (of the) Heart": This is a very old song and a lovely one, performed by many great artists over the years.
	239	Lowland Scots	Nail.
	244	Gaelic (Gàidhlig)	"Plenty, enough!"
838	593	Gaelic (Gàidhlig)	"Let them be safe, oh, God."
435	299	Gaelic (Gàidhlig)	"Let you have good": this is the form of "thank you" that we use in Dalriada—where I'm from, in Argyll—as well as throughout Ireland. In this case, in talking familiarly to someone, you'd be more likely to use the informal *agad* than *agaibh*. The phrase itself is a sort of fossilized form, and I am unsure as to its exact origin.
	240	Lowland Scots	Plastered. Harling is a specific technique for coating the outside of a building: small stones would be mixed with the plaster, and the mixture would then be hurled at the wall. There are many lovely castles of the 16th and 17th century in Scotland which are spoken of as having been harled, some of them in a weak sort of rosie pink, which, believe it or not, looks very attractive!
245	177	Lowland Scots	"Hold your quiet." The word "wheesht" in fact comes originally from the Gaelic *ist*/eeshtch/"shush" which is derived from the word *éist*/aishtch/"listen". It is still preferred in some dialects of Lewis Gaelic to the contracted *ist*. *Wheesht* is one of hundreds of Gaelic words borrowed into Lowland Scots, a fact rarely ackowledged by its speakers, often out of genuine ignorance. There is work to be done there, for sure!
	243	Lowland Scots	To speak incoherently, inaccurately or without obvious purpose. "A hink ye'r haverin pal!" ("I believe you to be talking complete nonsense!")
	246	Lowland Scots	A miser, a niggard.

Phrase *(as printed)*	Phrase *(if revised)*	Phonetic transcription	Book
hough			OLC Vol. I
hurley			OLC Vol. I
hurly-burly	**hurlie-burlie**		OLC Vol. I
Ian Mòr	**Iain mór**	/EEaiyn MORE/	MOBY
ifrinn an Diabhuil! A Dhia, thoir cob-hair!	**ifrinn an Diabhail! A Dhia, thoir cobhair!**	/EEfarin ən JEEal ə YEEa hor KOhər/	OLC Vol. I
ifrinn!		/EEfarin/	MOBY
is e Dia fèin a's buachaill dhomh	**is e Dia féin as buachaille dhomh**	/shay jeea FAIN əs booachil ɣaw/	EITB
is fhearr an giomach na 'bhi gun fear tighe	**is fheàrr an giomach na bhith gun fhear-taighe**	/SHAAR ən GEEmach nəree goon AIR TIEə/	OLC Vol. I

Key: OLC Vol. 1—*The Outlandish Companion* FC—*The Fiery Cross* ABOSA—*A Breath of Snow and Ashes*

pb	hc	Language	Translation
	245	Lowland Scots	A shin of beef.
	239	Lowland Scots	A noise or tumult, or a wheel or handcart. "Hurley, hurley, round the table" indicates the passing of food round a table, with concomitant noise and conversation, a "hurl" being a short, impromptu journey. A hurley in more modern usage is a child's makeshift vehicle, constructed of pram wheels and the like; also known as a "bogie," and a matter of great pride and showing off if one can be built to a decent standard.
	243	Lowland Scots	A tempest; a tumult.
685	497	Gaelic (Gàidhlig)	"Big John": used to denote the difference between Ian junior and senior, the name Ian would normally be spelled *Iain* in Gaelic and is the most direct equivalent of John in English. *Eóghann*/YOan/ is another example.
	250	Gaelic (Gàidhlig)	"Devil's hell! God help us!"
57	41	Gaelic (Gàidhlig)	"Hell!"
60	43	Gaelic (Gàidhlig)	" 'Tis God himself who is my cowherd": given that the Highlands were near enough devoid of sheep until the people were thrown from the land and replaced by these white menaces, it is perhaps nice to consider this very Gaelic version of the sentiment "the Lord is my shepherd." Here, God is the Gael, and the Gael his cattle! The word "shepherd" comes, of course, from "sheep-herd." Interesting that the word "cowherd" then came to give us "coward."
	250	Gaelic (Gàidhlig)	"Better a lobster than no husband": Scottish Gaelic proverb. I reckon many a modern woman would happily differ—no begging required!

EITB—*An Echo in the Bone* MOBY—*Written in My Own Heart's Blood*

Phrase *(as printed)*	Phrase *(if revised)*	Phonetic transcription	Book
is mise Seaumais Mac Choinnich à Boisdale	**is mise Seumas MacCoinnich á Baghasdail**	/əs meeshə SHAYməss machKUNyich e bözdal/	EITB
kebbie-lebbie			OLC Vol. I
ked			OLC Vol. I
kine			OLC Vol. I
kirk			FC
kittle-hoosie	**kittle-housie**	/kittle-hoossi/	OLC Vol. I
kittock! mislearnit pilsh!			FC
kivvers			OLC Vol. I
knivvle			OLC Vol. I
lang-nebbit			OLC Vol. I

pb	hc	Language	Translation
790	560	Gaelic (Gàidhlig)	"I am James MacKenzie of Boisdale": I remember cycling through Uist with friends, getting to Loch Boisdale, setting the bikes down, and getting comfy with a cup of tea and a toasted sandwich, only to see a tiny boy astride my huge mountain bike—his legs too short for him to sit any higher than the bar below the saddle—whizzing past the café window at breakneck speed and as cool as you like. Having got up sharply and no little umbrage taken, three lads—two of whom had grown up exclusively in Glasgow—were told by the lady who ran the café: "Don't stress yourselves, boys, he'll be back." And he was, about five minutes later, wearing a huge, cheeky grin, having tried out the bike for size. That's the island attitude for you in a nutshell: "Calm down; you'll live longer!"
	251	Lowland Scots	An altercation where a number of people talk at once. A "to-do."
	246	Lowland Scots	A sheep louse.
	245	Lowland Scots	Cattle.
79	54	Lowland Scots	Church. This word can be found in a similar form in several other Germanic languages: Icelandic, *kirkja;* Swedish, *kyrka;* Dutch, *kerk;* German, *kirche.*
	246	Lowland Scots	Whorehouse, brothel. A double *o* is in fact not correct Scots spelling. It is in actuality the *ou* which makes the /oo/ sound in Scots, meaning that words like "house" and "mouse" are correctly spelled just as they are in English.
330	222	Gaelic (Gàidhlig)	"Trollop! Uneducated, low-born!": normally *pilshoch.*
	246	Lowland Scots	Covers, bedding.
	246	Lowland Scots	To beat or thrash.
	252	Lowland Scots	Long-nosed. An interfering, nosy person would be referred to as being lang-nebbit.

Phrase *(as printed)*	Phrase *(if revised)*	Phonetic transcription	Book
lassie			EITB
let them awa' and bile their heids	**let them awa an bile their heids**		ABOSA
lug			OLC Vol. I
m' athair-cèile	**m' athair-chéile**	/MA'her-CHAYLə	FC
m'annsachd	**m' annsachd**	/MAOWNsachk/	OLC Vol. I

pb	hc	Language	Translation
221	157	Lowland Scots	A young girl. This is a classic Scots word but also features strongly in northern English dialects. You can still hear it in everyday speech in Northumberland, Cumbria, Yorkshire, and Lancashire, to name but some, albeit mostly in its non-diminutive form, "lass." It appears to come originally from Old Norse, although the etymology is somewhat shrouded by time. The term "lassie" can be applied very earnestly here in Glasgow in a few different ways, but two of these might be: "Och, she's a crackin lassie" ("Oh, she's a really decent girl"), said when beaming at the mention of the name of a friend or acquaintance, and also in the more pejorative sense of "She's jist a pure daft wee lassie" ("She's nothing but a silly little girl"), which is very often applied to young women attempting to act beyond their years and failing to convince!
106	74	Lowland Scots	Let them go away and boil their heads (i.e., let them take their stress somewhere else). One of the superior Scots idioms, this still sees very regular use! We have one, in fact, that is even less tame. What Gaelic lacks in swearing and general nastiness, Scots makes up a hundredfold! Sitting at the back of the famous 62 bus after a night out in Glasgow's feral city center, I have had the dubious but no less appreciated pleasure of overhearing the following conversation: Man, middle class, sixties: "Could you please put out that cigarette?" Lassie, straight off the housing scheme, thirties: "Ye gaunae geez an ashtray, then?" ("Would you please be so kind as to furnish me with an ashtray, then?") Man: "Well, as you can imagine, I don't happen to have one with me. Could you please find a way of extinguishing your cigarette?" Lassie: "Och, away an take yer face fur a shite, ya tumshie!" ("Oh, be off with you and facilitate the passing of feces through your mouth, you halfwit!") In other words, your face might as well be your backside for all I'm willing to listen to you! Charming. On a completely unrelated note, I sometimes wonder whether "tumshie"/TUMshi/ is derived from *tom-sìth*/tom-shee/ "fairy mound." It might be worth another look!
	239	Lowland Scots	Ear.
1439	975	Gaelic (Gàidhlig)	"My father-in-law."
	253	Gaelic (Gàidhlig)	"My best-beloved."

Phrase *(as printed)*	Phrase *(if revised)*	Phonetic transcription	Book
Mac Dubh			FC
mac na galladh	**mac na galla**	/machk nə GAlə/	MOBY
MacIfrinn		/machkEEFArin/	EITB
MacLennan	**MacIllFhìnein**	/machkeeLEEnən/	FC
MacNair	**Mac an Uibhir**	/machkən-YOOar/	FC
MacNeill	**MacNéill**	/machkNYAIL/	FC
MacRae	**MacRàth**	/machKRAA/	FC
madain mhath	**madainn mhath dhut/ dhuibh**	/MA'din VA ɣoocht/ ɣooiy/	FC
maduinn mhath, maighistear	**madainn mhath dhuibh, a mhaighstir**	/MA'din VA ɣui ə VAIYSHtchər/	ABOSA
maighistear àrsaidh	**maighstir àrsaidh**	/maiyshtchər ARsi/	ABOSA
mar shionnach		/mar HYIUnəch/	OLC Vol. I

pb	hc	Language	Translation
28	20	Gaelic (Gàidhlig)	Jamie's nickname. Use of "black" in this manner most often appeared in nomenclature as the Anglicized Highland surname "Black," common in Argyll, and it looked like this: *MacGhilleDhuibh*. Or it was slightly shortened to *MacIlleDhuibh*, literally "son of the black-haired servant." The full form of a name given to Jamie in light of his father's appearance would be something like this: *Seumas, mac Bhriain dhuibh* (James, son [of] black[-haired] Brian).
189	137	Gaelic (Gàidhlig)	"Son of the bitch."
952	677	Gaelic (Gàidhlig)	"Son of hell."
16	12		"Son of the servant of St. Finan": a common surname yet in the Western Isles, especially Lewis.
26	19		"Son of the sallow": there were plenty of MacNairs in Cowal, Argyll, where I'm from, and one of them, Jimmy, just celebrated his 102nd birthday!
27	19		"Son of Neil": although the MacNeills had lands in Argyll, they are best known as the Barra clan par excellence, retaining the castle of Kisimul in Castlebay, an island well worth a visit if you happen to venture up to the Western Isles. I am happy to say that the *Barraich* are still proud of their language and culture and many will still speak Gaelic as a matter of preference!
71	48		"Son of the fortunate": the MacRaes are a real Ross-shire family, like the MacKenzies, and are still a numerous bunch around their traditional seat of *Eilean Dònain*, the most photographed castle in Scotland.
1208	818	Gaelic (Gàidhlig)	"Good morning (to you)": Gaels used greetings like this very sparingly until recent times, when the influence of English began to take a hold on our perception of how the language should be spoken. It was very natural to "praise the day," as we called it, but this would more often than not be a genuinely intended observation on weather or times, rather than a flippant pleasantry.
503	345	Gaelic (Gàidhlig)	"Good morning, master": I tend to always employ the old-fashioned *dhut* or *dhuibh* (to you) here, especially in this more formal occurrence.
1219	832	Gaelic (Gàidhlig)	"Ancient master."
	249	Gaelic (Gàidhlig)	"Like a fox."

Phrase *(as printed)*	Phrase *(if revised)*	Phonetic transcription	Book
Marsali	**Màrsaili**	/MARsali/	FC
McGillivray	**MacGhilleBhraith**	/machGEELəvraiy/	FC
mo airgeadach	**m' airgeadach**	/MERRAg'dəch/	OLC Vol. I
mo brathair	**mo bhràthair**	/mo VRAhər/	EITB
mo buidheag	**mo bhuidheag**	/mo VOOyək/	OLC Vol. I
mo charadean	**mo chàirdean**	/mo CHAARSHjin/	FC
mo charaid		/mo CHAridge/	OLC Vol. I
mo cheann		/mo CHYAOWN/	FC
mo chridhe		/mə CHREEə/	ABOSA

pb	hc	Language	Translation
20	15	Gaelic (Gàidhlig)	"Marjorie": my mother's given name!
35	25		"Son of the servant of judgment": an old Argyll family from Mull and Morvern, who eventually came under the wing of the Clan Chattan federation. This surname has emerged from antiquity sounding rather melodramatic!
	240	Gaelic (Gàidhlig)	"My silvery": Jamie is likely referring to Claire's skin here, as opposed to her hair, and while perhaps not common usage, there is nothing to say that he isn't just improvising in his native tongue. There's many a usage never caught on!
983	698	Gaelic (Gàidhlig)	"My brother."
	240	Gaelic (Gàidhlig)	"Goldfinch": this can be used for any small yellow bird, as it means literally "little yellow."
1361	923	Gaelic (Gàidhlig)	"My friends/relatives": Gaelic makes no distinction between friends and relatives, as people were so close-knit as communities until relatively recently in Gaelic-speaking Scotland that if a neighbor wasn't your direct relative, you could bet your bottom dollar they'd be related to you somewhere back down the line. It was not unknown right into the 1970s for people to have rarely moved outside their home village. When interviewing one of our lovely old people from Argyll in 1975, my good friend David Clement got an unexpected answer to his question *"An robh sibh riamh anns an Óban?"* ("Were you ever in Oban?" which is Argyll's main town.) *"Cha robh! Cha d' fhàg mi Loch Obha."* ("I was not! I never left Loch Awe.") Oban is but ten miles from Loch Awe!
	244	Gaelic (Gàidhlig)	"My friend."
764	516	Gaelic (Gàidhlig)	"my head": *ceann* often appears in Scottish placenames, Anglicised as Kin, referring to the extremity of a loch or other geographical feature, e.g. *Ceann Loch Bearbhaigh* / kyaown loch BERavi/ "the Head of loch Bervie" which has come out in Scots as Kinlochbervie.
209	145	Gaelic (Gàidhlig)	"My heart."

Phrase *(as printed)*	Phrase *(if revised)*	Phonetic transcription	Book
mo chuilean		/mo chooløn/	MOBY
mo chù		/mo CHOO/	MOBY
mo duinne			OLC Vol. I
mo fuil	**m' fhuil**	/mool/	FC
mo gaolach	**mo ghaolach**	/mə ɣÖLəch/	ABOSA
mo ghille		/mo ɣEELə/	OLC Vol. I
mo ghràidh		/mo ɣrAAiy/	MOBY
mo gràdh ort, athair	**mo ghràdh oirbh, athair**	/mo ɣRAA awriv Ahər/	OLC Vol. I
mo luaidh		/mo LOOaiy/	OLC Vol. I
mo maise	**mo mhaise**	/mo VASHə/	OLC Vol. I
mo mhaorine	**mo mhúirnín**	/mo voorNYEEN/	FC
mo muirninn	**mo mhúirnín**	/mo voorNYEEN/	OLC Vol. I
mo nighean		/mo NYEEin/	OLC Vol. I
mo nighean donn		/mo NYEEin doo/	ABOSA
mo nighean donn bhoideach	**mo nighean donn bhòidheach**	/mo NYEEin down VOYəch/	EITB
mo nighean dubh		/mo NYEEin doo/	OLC Vol. I

pb	hc	Language	Translation
910	660	Gaelic (Gàidhlig)	"My puppy": you can find this term of endearment in the song "*Dèan Cadalan Sàmhach*" /JEn CATalən SAAvəch/ (pronounced *Dian*/JEEan/ in the north), about an immigrant to the huge forested wastes of Canada during the 19th century. It is sung by, among others, the fantastic Karen Matheson and Capercaillie, on whom I practically raised myself. No one else in my home was interested in Gaelic or music! I am very pleased that my own children's experience of cultural life is a vastly different one.
910	660	Gaelic (Gàidhlig)	"My dog."
	242	Gaelic (Gàidhlig)	An incorrect Gaelic form, perhaps deriving from *mo dhuine* (my man)?
976	661	Gaelic (Gàidhlig)	"My blood."
229	158	Gaelic (Gàidhlig)	"My beloved."
	252	Gaelic (Gàidhlig)	"My boy, my lad."
911	661	Gaelic (Gàidhlig)	"My dear."
	253	Gaelic (Gàidhlig)	"I love you, Father": literally "My love on you, oh, Father."
	244	Gaelic (Gàidhlig)	"My beloved."
	241	Gaelic (Gàidhlig)	"My beauty": *maise* means "ornament, great beauty, elegance." Iain Mac an Tàilleir notes that common usage is more likely *mo nighean mhaiseach*/mo NYEEən VASHəch/"my beautiful girl"/.
208	140	Gaelic (Gaeilge)	"My darling."
	244	Gaelic (Gaeilge)	"My darling."
	245	Gaelic (Gàidhlig)	"My daughter, girl."
348	240	Gaelic (Gàidhlig)	"My black(-haired) girl": another classic Jamie-to-Claire nickname, now heard so often delivered between Sam Heughan and Caitriona Balfe in *Outlander* the TV show.
790	559	Gaelic (Gàidhlig)	"My beautiful brown-haired maiden": it is almost impossible to count the number of songs which have *mo nighean donn* in them, and this phrase must constitute part of the chorus of at least two of the most famous ones!
	246	Gaelic (Gàidhlig)	"My black-haired lass."

Phrase *(as printed)*	Phrase *(if revised)*	Phonetic transcription	Book
moil			OLC Vol. I
moran taing	**móran taing dhut**	/MOrən tang ɣoocht/	EITB
mozie auld poutworm			OLC Vol. I
mumper			OLC Vol. I
my jo	**ma jo**		OLC Vol. I
na tuit		/na tootch/	ABOSA
nach e sin an rud as brèagha a chunnaic thu riamh	**nach e sin an rud as briagh a chunnaig u riamh**	/nachAY SHEEN ən root əs BREEa ə choonik oo REEəv/	EITB
nàmhaid		/NAvitch/	EITB
nay bother	**nae bother**		FC
neb			OLC Vol. I
neffit qurd	**neffit quird**		OLC Vol. I
nettercap			OLC Vol. I

pb	hc	Language	Translation
	245	Lowland Scots	"Difficulty, trouble."
166	119	Gaelic (Gàidhlig)	"Many thanks": I would always include use of *dhut* here, as it was in days gone by. An interesting point of note is that God is addressed using the likes of *u, dhut,* and *leat,* rather than *sibh, dhuibh,* or *leibh;* in other words, in the informal, something that surprised me when I first learned of it. I had thought that since Christians regard God as the Father, formal use might apply to Gaels, as it would when speaking with their own fathers. Instead, there is a sense of intimacy conveyed by use of the informal, which is not unknown in other languages and is seen in English in the King James Version of the Bible, with "thou" as in most Latin languages as well some others. Diana has her characters discussing just this on page 801 of MOBY!
	244	Lowland Scots	Overripe old grub.
	244	Lowland Scots	One who chews without teeth; one who gums his food.
	244	Lowland Scots	My close friend; my dear companion. As evidenced in Burns's famous verse "John Anderson, my jo, John."
287	199	Gaelic (Gàidhlig)	"Don't fall."
637	451	Gaelic (Gàidhlig)	"Isn't that the loveliest thing you ever saw?": I spell *briagh* the way I do because it has ceased to be pronounced /BREa/ anywhere and is now universally pronounced /BREEa/, just as *ceud*/kate/"one hundred"/ is now *ciad*/keeət/. With a language that is more and more reliant with every passing day on its learner community, every effort must be made to put Gaelic's very regular spelling system to use and, where there is no conceivable reason not to, to spell the words accordingly. If the sound is /EEa/, let's spell it *ia*. You can look up *briagh* in Dwelly's great Gaelic dictionary!
437	309	Gaelic (Gàidhlig)	"Enemy."
46	32	Lowland Scots	No problem. This is a cracker to know if you ever visit my current hometown of Glasgow. Prepare to ingratiate yourself with the locals if you inform them that something is "nae bother." Do it, they'll love it!
	246	Lowland Scots	Nose.
	245	Lowland Scots	Little shit.
	244	Lowland Scots	Spider.

Phrase *(as printed)*	Phrase *(if revised)*	Phonetic transcription	Book
nighean na galladh	**nighean na galla**	/NYEE in nə GAlə	ABOSA
nighean nan geug		/NEEin nən GAYg/	MOBY
o thoir a-nall am Botul	**o thoir a-nall am botal**	/oh hawr ə-naowl um BOTəl/	EITB
oidhche mhath	**oidhche mhath leat/ leibh**	/öichə va lecht/löi/	MOBY
parritch			FC
pibroch			OLC Vol. I
piobreachd	**pìobaireachd**	/PEEbərəchk/	ABOSA
pog mo thon!	**pog mo thòn!**	/poke mo HONN/	OLC Vol. I
pooch nane	**pouch nane**		OLC Vol. I
poolie	**poulie**	/pooli/	OLC Vol. I
proddle			OLC Vol. I
rach a h-Irt	**rach a Hiort**	/rach ə heersht/	MOBY
ratten			OLC Vol. I

pb	hc	Language	Translation
588	403	Gaelic (Gàidhlig)	"Daughter of the bitch."
102	74	Gaelic (Gàidhlig)	Gaelic lullaby; pronounced *Nighean nan Giag*/geeəg/ in the north.
53	39	Gaelic (Gàidhlig)	"Oh, pass over the bottle": this reminds me of a nice Hogmanay (New Year's Eve) verse from my homeland of Cowal: *a bhean an taighe, a chuibhheil an fhòrtain, aiseig a-nuas am botal ud. Gabhaidh sinn deoch dheth 's cuiridh sinn a' bhochdainn ás nar cuimhne* (lady of the house, wheel of fortune, ferry down that bottle there. We shall take a drink of it so as to kill off the memory of poverty from our minds). It leaves you in no uncertain knowledge of how difficult life was back in those days.
457	332	Gaelic (Gàidhlig)	"Good night (with you)": *leat/leibh* (singular/plural, polite) are normally employed when departing someone's company.
19	14	Lowland Scots	Porridge. In Gaelic, we call porridge *brochan*/brawchən/ or in some places *lite*/LEEtchə/. The staple breakfast this side of the Loch! My father used to ask me of a morning, "Huv ye hud yer parritches yit?" ("Have you had your porridge yet?")
	244	Gaelic (Gàidhlig)	"Pipe music": see *piobreachd*.
685	469	Gaelic (Gàidhlig)	"Piping": *pìobaireachd* is rather different from the jigs and reels heard at ceilidhs, even those played on the *uileann*/oolən/"elbow or Highland pipes". It is a slow, sonorous style of playing. They say that it takes seven years to learn the pipes to a decent degree and another seven to learn *pìobaireachd*!
	249	Gaelic (Gàidhlig)	"Kiss my ass!"
	239	Lowland Scots	Pouch none. Put nothing in one's sporran; don't take anything away from the table. I have here erred on original Scots orthography, with use of *ou*/oo/ rather than the modern English language phonetic *oo*.
	245	Lowland Scots	A louse.
	244	Lowland Scots	To prick, goad, stab.
1099	801	Gaelic (Gàidhlig)	"Go to St. Kilda": in other words, "Sod off!"
	245	Lowland Scots	A rat; also a small person or animal, and a term of endearment.

Phrase *(as printed)*	Phrase *(if revised)*	Phonetic transcription	Book
ravens	**fithich**	/FEEeech/	FC
ruaidh	**ruadh**	/ROOa/	OLC Vol. I
Rugadh e do Sheumas Immanuel Hayes agus Louisa N'ic a Liallainn an am baile Chill-Mhartainn, ann an sgire Dhun Domhnuill, anns a bhliadhna seachd ceud deug agus a haon!	**Rugadh e do Sheumas Immanuel Hayes agas Louisa NicIllFhaolain ann am Baile Chille-Mhàrtainn, ann an sgìre Dhùin Dhòmhaill, anns a' bhliana seachd ciad diag agas a h-aon!**	(see translation)	OLC Vol. I
ruith		/rui/	EITB

pb	hc	Language	Translation
37	26		*"Live with Highlanders long enough and every damn rock and tree meant something!"*—Claire Fraser. This is not at all far off the truth. If you imagine a land without Internet and phone, where even newspapers would have been few and far between, then what had you to predict your fortune in any given year but the direction of the wind, the portent of rain in far-off clouds, or the movements of birds. Ravens, as in this case, were thought to come in threes for the souls of the wicked, to carry them off to the bad place. In a story from my own home county of Argyll, three dark strangers passed a night traveler on the road close to Loch Awe in silence; having then been seen taking themselves off up the road to a local man's house, they were never encountered again. The man was found dead the next day, and the men were generally accepted by Loch Awe folks to have been ravens in human form. In fact, there is a standing stone—rather conveniently named *Clach an t-Seasaidh*/ clachən TCHASEY/"the Standing Stone"—near Muir of Ord, west of Inverness, where it is reputed that three ravens will soon gather to "drink their three fulls, for three successive days, of the blood of the MacKenzies!" Descendants of Dougal beware!
	241	Gaelic (Gàidhlig)	"Rusty colored" : as autumn leaves or ginger hair.
	249	Gaelic (Gàidhlig)	"He was born of James Emmanuel Hayes and of Louisa MacLellan, in the village of Kilmartin in the parish of Dundonnel, in the year of Our Lord seventeen hundred and one!" I have chosen not to include a pronunciation guide here, as it's just too long and many people will get to the end having forgotten how in the heck to pronounce the beginning! Interestingly, Killmartin is a village within my home dialect area, and although I have not heard of a parish called Dundonnel, it is close to Kilmartin in Argyll, where Queen Scota is said to have arrived from Egypt in our national origin myth and named the land she found after herself! It is said that the marks where her horse's hooves met the rock are still to be seen. Unsurprisingly perhaps, I am yet to track them down!
857	607	Gaelic (Gàidhlig)	"Run."

Phrase *(as printed)*	Phrase *(if revised)*	Phonetic transcription	Book
's beag 'tha fhios aig fear a bhaile mar 'tha fear na mara bèo	**s beag a tha fios aig fear a' bhaile mar a tha fear na mara beò**	/SPAKE ha FEESS ek fair ə VALə mərə ha fair nə marə BYAW/	FC
saft			OLC Vol. I
Samhain	**Samhainn**	/SAwain/	OLC Vol. I
saorsa		/SÖRsə/	OLC Vol. I
sark			FC
Sassenach		/SASSənəch/	FC

pb	hc	Language	Translation
1410	956	Gaelic (Gàidhlig)	"Little does the landsman know how the seaman lives": and this is too true. When she and her family were cleared from their land in the early 19th century, my four-times-great-grandmother Janet Gunn left her croft in Braemore, Caithness, in a herring creel atop her father's shoulders. He carried her twenty miles like this to the coast, but the creel would have been about all he knew of fishing. These people were left to fend for themselves in Latheron, a coastal village where life was dominated by the mood of the sea and your living depended on braving it—without any prior knowledge of fishing, boats, or nets. They survived, of course, and my grandmother spoke often of their Gaelic language and old ways, which had unfortunately become lost to us by that time. I am happy to say that I have righted that particular wrong!
	240	Gaelic (Gàidhlig)	"Soft": figuratively, a light drizzle, as in "*saft* weather," or foolishness/mental deficiency, as in "*saft* in the *heid*."
	245	Gaelic (Gàidhlig)	"Halloween": the ancient Scottish equivalent to the Feast of All Hallows, October 31. There are many variant pronunciations for this, but I have stuck to the one we used in *Outlander* the TV show, for consistency's sake!
	251	Gaelic (Gàidhlig)	"Freedom": my youngest daughter's name. When she was born, we realized very quickly that we had chosen the correct name. She was free by name and free by nature and continues to be a force to be reckoned with! Her twin brother is Lachann (in Argyll, there is no second L), while her older sisters are Caoimhe (hospitable one) and Eilidh (Helen). All speak our local Gaelic dialect with great pride!
21	16	Lowland Scots	Shirt.
7	7	Lowland Scots	English person. The classic Jamie-to-Claire nickname. Interestingly, what we have here is actually the Scots spelling of the Gaelic word *Sasannach*, but this is perfectly appropriate given that he is addressing her not in Gaelic but in Scots/English. Were he speaking Gaelic, it would actually be quite different, as use of the feminine prefix *ban* would be necessary, and the vocative (when addressing people) case would come into play: *a bhan-Shasannaich*/ə van-HASSəneech/.

Phrase *(as printed)*	Phrase *(if revised)*	Phonetic transcription	Book
Scots			
sealg		/SHELLak/	OLC Vol. I
seas!		/shace/	FC
seas ri mo lâmh, a mhic mo thaighe	**seas ri mo làmh, a mhic mo thaighe**	/SHACE ree-mo-LAAV, ə VEECHk mo haiyə/	FC

Key: OLC Vol. 1—*The Outlandish Companion* FC—*The Fiery Cross* ABOSA—*A Breath of Snow and Ashes*

pb	hc	Language	Translation
			Lowland Anglic. Gaelic once held the national moniker in Scotland, known simply as "Scottish" in English. When the English border was settled in 1237, there existed in Scotland a large minority of Anglic (English) speakers who had long been "caught on the wrong side," for want of a better phrase. They spoke a northern dialect of Old English and, over time, began to exert greater influence on politics in Scotland. They managed to wrestle control from the Gaels through various means but mostly by way of association with southern English ways and culture, in comparison with which Gaelic manners and customs were seen as crude, barbaric, and at the very least old-fashioned. And so Gaelic ceased to be referred to as Scottish and became known as "Erse," because it was seen by Anglic-speaking Scots as an Irish—i.e., foreign—language. The Old English of the Lowlands then took on the national moniker of "Scots" to distinguish itself from "Inglis"—the name with which it had previously self-referred but which now came to mean exclusively that particular brand of Anglic speech south of the Scottish border. But to cut this rather long and confusing story short . . . Scottish Gaelic was once spoken throughout Scotland, having given birth to most everything we now associate with Scottishness, from kilt to pipes, whereas Scots—as much as I love it—has in truth only ever been a regional language of Scotland and so falls a little short in my opinion of being deserving of the national moniker, which is why I note it here as "Lowland Scots." Either way, however, it is never a bad thing to have both one of the most beautiful, musical tongues in the world and the language of the world's most famous poet as your two native speech forms, a situation of some linguistic luxury if only we Scots could actually bring ourselves to speak the darn things! In terms of language families, Gaelic is Celtic, related distantly to Welsh, Cornish, and Breton, while Scots is Germanic and related quite closely to Norwegian, Dutch, and, most closely, English.
	239	Gaelic (Gàidhlig)	"Hunting."
247	167	Gaelic (Gàidhlig)	"Stand!"
1440	976	Gaelic (Gàidhlig)	"Stand at my side (hand), son of my house."

EITB—*An Echo in the Bone* MOBY—*Written in My Own Heart's Blood*

Phrase *(as printed)*	Phrase *(if revised)*	Phonetic transcription	Book
seas ri mo lâmh, Roger an t'oranaiche, mac Jeremiah mac Choinneich	seas ri mo làmh, a Ròideir an t-òranaiche, mhic Iaraimìa MhicChoinnich	/SHACE ri mo laav, ə Roger ən TAWranichə, veechk yarraMEEa veech CONyich/	FC
seas . . . ciamar a tha thu, a ghille mhoir?	seas . . . ciamar a tha u, a ghille mhóir?	/shace... KIMerə HAOW, ə YEELə VORE/	FC
Seaumais mac Brian	Seumas mac Bhriain	/SHAMEuss machk VREEaiyn/	ABOSA
Seaumais Ruaidh	Seumas ruadh	/SHAMEuss rooaɣ/	EITB
Senga		/SENGga/	ABOSA
seo mac na muice a thàinig na bu thràithe gad shiubhal		/shaw machk nə mooichkə ə HAHnik nəboo RAIYə gad hyool/	EITB
sgaogan		/SKÖgan/	FC

pb	hc	Language	Translation
1440	976	Gaelic (Gàidhlig)	"Stand at my side (hand), oh, Roger the songsmith, son of Jeremiah MacKenzie."
730	493	Gaelic (Gàidhlig)	"Stand . . . how are you, oh, great laddie?"
235	163	Gaelic (Gàidhlig)	"James, son of Brian."
791	560	Gaelic (Gàidhlig)	"Red James."
27	20	Lowland Scots	A girl's name, playfully spoken of as being "Agnes" spelled backward. As to the truth of this, I can neither confirm nor deny, but the name has always been associated—in Glasgow, certainly—with that singular breed of person we call the *ned,* young lads and lassies who hang around bus stops in groups and go out of their way to cause trouble for anyone passing by. A *senga* is the female variety of the aforementioned demographic, and during my youth they were known for their scraped-back ponytails, tight red jeans, ten-packs of "Club" cigarettes, and wickedly sharp tongues as you walked by minding your own business: "Here you! Whit ye gawkin at? A'll boot your baws!" ("I say! What is it you're looking at? I shall kick you in the testicles!") Those were definitely not "the days."
854	604	Gaelic (Gàidhlig)	"This is the son of a pig who came earlier looking for you": it is interesting that I have never heard *siubhal* used in this context. In Dalriada we would say *gad rùrachamh*/gad ROOrəchəv/. Dialects are fascinating!
489	330	Gaelic (Gàidhlig)	"Giddy youth": here meant in the sense of a "changeling." The babies who had allegedly been left by the fairies in place of the genuine article were known by their discontented nature, constant crying, and distorted-looking person. If certain experiences with my four were anything to go by, a rather more simple explanation could be the key—namely, colic!

Phrase *(as printed)*	Phrase *(if revised)*	Phonetic transcription	Book
sgian dhu	**sgian dubh**	/SKEEan doo/	ABOSA
sguir		/skoor/	OLC Vol. I
sheas!	**seas!**	/shace/	ABOSA
sheas, a nighean	**seas, a nighean**	/SHACE ə NYEEin/	EITB
sìdheanach	**sìtheanach**	/SHEEanəch/	FC
silkie	**selkie**		OLC Vol. I
sionnach		/SHOOnəch/	OLC Vol. I
skelloch			OLC Vol. I
skirlie			FC
skrae-shankit skoot	**skrae-shankit skout**		OLC Vol. I
slàinte		/SLAANtchə/	FC
slan leat, a charaid choir	**slàn leat, a charaid chòir**	/SLAAN leht ə CHAridge chaur/	OLC Vol. I
sluire	**sluit**		OLC Vol. I
small cairn			ABOSA
smoor	**smour**	/smoor/	OLC Vol. I

pb	hc	Language	Translation
1143	780	Gaelic (Gàidhlig)	"Black knife": like the one Claire receives for training with Angus in episode 8, "Both Sides Now," of the *Outlander* TV show. This knife was secreted about the person in whichever place made sense in order to keep it hidden. It later came to be associated with modern Highland dress due to the practice of wearing it in the sock, a thing the Highlander of days gone by rarely had! The /oo/ in *dubh* is pronounced very short, almost like the word "do" in "do it!"
	239	Gaelic (Gàidhlig)	"Desist": remember to roll that *r* at the end—or at least try! Go on, it's fun!
513	352	Gaelic (Gàidhlig)	"Stand!"
807	571	Gaelic (Gàidhlig)	"Stand, oh lass."
1431	817	Gaelic (Gàidhlig)	"Fairy."
	240	Lowland Scots	Seal. Also the name by which the mythical "seal people" are known.
	249	Gaelic (Gàidhlig)	"Fox": in Dalriada, we say *seannach*/SHAnach/.
	242	Lowland Scots	A shout, scream, or cry of alarm.
1410	956	Lowland Scots	Fried oatmeal.
	246	Lowland Scots	"A spindle-legged braggart" : a term of contempt. Perhaps the braggart comes originally from "brag-hard" somewhat similar to "blow-hard."
228	153	Gaelic (Gàidhlig)	"Health": the quick version of *slàinte mhath*/SLANtchə va/"good health"/ or, where I come from in East Argyll, *slàinte mhór*/SLANtchə VORE/"great health"!
	252	Gaelic (Gàidhlig)	"Farewell, kind friend."
	245	Lowland Scots	A sloven or slut.
16	12		This practice still remains in the phrase *cuiridh mi clach air a chàrn*/koorie-mi CLACH aira CHARN/ "I shall place a stone on his cairn"/, said in condolence to the bereaved on the passing of a loved one. I can only imagine it worked just as well the other way—*clach air do chàrn!*/"a stone on your cairn!"—to someone on whom misfortune was wished!
	244	Lowland Scots	To smother, specifically to bank a fire.

Phrase *(as printed)*	Phrase *(if revised)*	Phonetic transcription	Book
snark			OLC Vol. I
snuff mull			OLC Vol. I
soghan	**sòghainn**	/SAWain/	FC
spalpeen	**spailpín**	/spaLPEEN/	OLC Vol. I
spiorad		/SPEErət/	FC
sporran			FC
St. Kilda	**Hiort**	/hyoorst/	FC
stad, mo dhu	**stad, mo charaid dhubh**	/stat mo CHAridge ɣu/	OLC Vol. I
stramash		/straMASH/	FC

pb	hc	Language	Translation
	241	Lowland Scots	To snore, to fret, or to find fault.
	241	Lowland Scots	A container for snuff, often made from a sheep's horn.
18	13	Gaelic (Gàidhlig)	"Pleasant, agreeable, cheerful."
	246	Gaelic (Gaeilge)	"A low fellow, a scamp or rascal."
391	265	Gaelic (Gàidhlig)	"Spirit" : *an ainm an Athair, a Mhic 's an Spiorad Naoimh* /ən enyəm ən Ahər, ə VEEchk, sən SPEErət NÖiyv/ (in the name of the father, the son and the Holy Ghost).
54	37	Lowland Scots	Purse. Although the Scots word *sporran* has come to refer to the reworked hanging pouch for modern Highland dress, its meaning in the original Gaelic *sporan* covers the "dewlap" of a cow, the English sense of a "purse" or "wallet," and also the sense of the "public purse": *an sporan poblach*/ən spawran POPElәch/. Whichever way, infinitely cooler than the fanny pack!
103	70		The name in its current form was given by the Vikings, and Hiort is identifiable as such by the initial *H*, which is not found in native Gaelic language but seen throughout the area of former Norse influence. The group of tiny islands collectively known in English as St. Kilda is the farthest-flung archipelago in the Hebrides and was inhabited until the 1930s. So remote was it from the everyday lives of even most Gaels that a dismissive phrase arose for use when wishing rid of irritating company. You hear it from Jamie to the MacDonald boys in *Outlander* the TV show, episode 10, "By the Pricking of my Thumbs": *thalla gu Hiort!*/HULLə g'HYOORST/"away to St. Kilda (with you)!"/. Even worse is the phrase *b' fheàrr gum bithinn ann an Hiort am broinn mairt*/BYARlәm gәm BEEin aownin HYOORST әm broin MARSHt/"I'd rather be in St. Kilda in the belly of a cow than (insert intolerably disagreeable alternative)!"/.
	239	Gaelic (Gàidhlig)	"Stay, my black one": I have offered here the possibility, given Jamie is talking to his horse, that he might well say something along the lines of *stad, mo charaid dhubh*/"stop, my black friend"/, as the usage in the book is not quite grammatically correct.
25	18	Gaelic (Gàidhlig)	"Uproar, chaos, conflict": the etymology is uncertain, but this is a fantastically onomatopoeic word meaning "a situation caused by unchecked Scottish aggression"!

Phrase *(as printed)*	Phrase *(if revised)*	Phonetic transcription	Book
taing	**taing dhut/dhuibh**	/tang ɣOOCHT/ ɣOOIY/	FC
taing do Dhia		/tang do YEEa/	MOBY
tannasg		/TANask/	OLC Vol. I
tannasgeach	**tannasgach**	/TANəsgəch/	FC
tapadh leat Iain. Cha robh fios air a bhith agam		/TACHpə LECHt EEaiyn. Cha ro feess air ə vee akəm/	EITB
Tearlach mac Seamus	**Teàrlach, mac Sheumais**	/TCHAARləch machk HAMISH/	OLC Vol. I
teuchter		/TCHOOCHtər/	OLC Vol. I
tha ana-cnàmhadh an Diabhail orm		/ha ANəKRAAvəɣ ən JEEal ORəm/	EITB

pb	hc	Language	Translation
59	40	Gaelic (Gàidhlig)	"Thanks": not normally used (until relatively recently) by itself, this has become a common way of saying a brief "thank you." In the TV show, we used *taing dhut/dhuibh*/"thanks to you"/, the form current in much of northern mainland Scotland and correct for the Ross-shire Gaelic of the MacKenzie clan. I have my suspicions that its use comes originally from contact with Vikings, as the Swedes and Norwegians today still use the similar word *tack/takk*, which is clearly cognate with "thank." However, southern dialects of Gaelic, including my own, use the same form as in Irish, which I believe to be closer to early Gaelic usage: *gu robh math agad/agaibh*.
385	280	Gaelic (Gàidhlig)	"Thanks to God": you can hear Jamie say this in the *Outlander* TV series, episode 1, "Sassenach," when Claire puts his shoulder back into place.
	239	Gaelic (Gàidhlig)	"Spirit, ghost": this is our word in my part of Argyll, although I have also heard *taibhse*/TYEshə/, *bocan* /BOCHgən/, and *tamhasg*/TAvask/, among other things, to describe a denizen of the lonely space between worlds.
745	503	Gaelic (Gàidhlig)	"Abounding in specters."
854	604	Gaelic (Gàidhlig)	"Thanks with you, John. I hadn't known": it is interesting that *tapadh leat* has taken hold as the standard form of "thank you" in the Western Isles, because it is quite likely that originally it was more of a parting gesture than a show of gratitude while someone was still in your company, more of a "thanks (be) with you," like *latha math leat*/LAa ma leht/"a good day (be) with you", or *oidhche mhath leat*/"a good night (be) with you". "Thank you and goodbye," in other words.
	241	Gaelic (Gàidhlig)	"Charles, son of James": Charles Edward Stewart, the "Bonnie Prince."
	253	Lowland Scots	A Gaelic speaker. A rather derogatory term used by Lowlanders for Highlanders. Roughly equivalent to "hick" or "hillbilly."
814	576	Gaelic (Gàidhlig)	"The Devil's ingestion is on me": I've got terrible indigestion.

Phrase *(as printed)*	Phrase *(if revised)*	Phonetic transcription	Book
tha ball-ratha sìnte riut		/ha baowl-raa SHEENtchə root/	MOBY
tha gaol agam oirbh, a mhàthair		/ha GÖL AKəm AWriv ə VAhər/	MOBY
Tha mi gle mhath, athair	**tha mi glé mhath, athar**	/hami gLAY va Ahər/	OLC Vol. I
tha mi gu math, mo athair	**tha mi gu math, m' athair**	/hami gMA Mahər/	ABOSA
tha nighean na galladh torrach!	**tha nighean na galla torrach!**	/ha NYEEin na GALə TAWrəch/	FC
Tha sinn cruinn a chaoidh ar caraid, Gabhainn Hayes	**Tha sinn cruinn còmhla gus ar caraid Gabhann Hayes a chaoidh**	/ha sheen krooin KAWLə goose ar CAridge GAvan Hayes ə CHÖIY/	OLC Vol. I
thalla le Dia		/HULLə lə JEEa/	MOBY
theirig dhachaigh		/HAIRik ɣACHi/	ABOSA

pb	hc	Language	Translation
1103	804	Gaelic (Gàidhlig)	"A lucky, erect penis is against you": I had the singular pleasure of reciting this poem in Gaelic to the lovely Ginger and Summer of the *Outlander* podcast! *Abair plòigh!*/Abər PLOY/"what fun!". This demonstrates the former lack of shame shown by the Gael in discussing the kind of thing that came to be thought of as rude by "polite British society." The long-faced Presbyterian outlook did not always hold such sway in the Highlands!
5	5	Gaelic (Gàidhlig)	"I love you, Mother"—literally, "I have love on you": the interesting point in Gaelic language about many things that we don't necessarily have innately—like particular emotions, feelings, diseases, and states of being and circumstance—is that they "come onto" and "go from" us rather than us "having" or "doing" them, as in English. Although we do "have" love in Gaelic, the recipient of the love has it put "upon" them by their counterpart, rather than them "being loved." There is no verb "to love" as there is in English. Likewise, even a cold "comes on you," and you would say *tha cnatan orm*/ha KRAtan orəm/"(a) cold is on me" when you have the common cold.
	253	Gaelic (Gàidhlig)	"I am very well, oh, Father."
541	371	Gaelic (Gàidhlig)	"I am well, my father": when two vowels come together, one generally loses the fight and disappears, hence *mo athair* becoming *m' athair* in colloquial speech and also now in writing.
282	190	Gaelic (Gàidhlig)	"The daughter of the bitch is fertile": I don't recognize the form *galladh*/GALəɣ/. I don't think we use this in mid and south Argyll. Something you still hear commonly enough is *taigh na galla leat!*/tie nə GALə lecht/"to the bitch (whore) house with you!"
	249	Gaelic (Gàidhlig)	"We are come together to lament the loss of our friend, Gavin Hayes."
479	348	Gaelic (Gàidhlig)	"Go with God."
44	31	Gaelic (Gàidhlig)	"Go home!": we have lots of ways to say "go!" from different areas of Scotland: *falbh, thalla, rach, reach, theirig*. The Gaelic is nothing if not rich and, in fact, where I'm from, *thalla*—rather confusingly—means "come"!

Phrase *(as printed)*	Phrase *(if revised)*	Phonetic transcription	Book
thig a seo, a bhean uasa	**thig an seo, a bhean uasal**	/heek ə shaw, ə ven OOAsal/	FC
thig a seo, a chuisle	**thig an seo, a chuisle**	/heek ə shaw, ə CHOOSHlə/	FC
thig a seo, a Shorcha, nighean Eanruig, neart mo chridhe	**thig a' seo, a Shorcha, nighean Eanraig, neart mo chridhe**	/heek ə shaw, ə HAWrəchə, NYEEin EUNrik, NYARst mo chreeə/	FC
thig air ais a seo!	**thig air ais a' seo!**	/HEEK a RASH ə shaw/	FC
thig a mach!	**thig a mach!**	/HEEKə mach/	FC
thig crioch air an t-saoghal ach mairidh ceol agus gaol	**thig crìoch air an t-saoghal, ach mairidh ceòl 's gaol**	/heek KREECH airən TÖL ach marry KYAWLis GÖL/	MOBY
thole			OLC Vol. I
thugham! thugham!	**thugam! thugam!**	/HOOKəm! HOOKəm!/	FC
tiugainn!		/TCHOOkeen/	MOBY
trusdair		/trooster/	EITB
tulach ard!	**tulach àrd!**	/toolaCHAARST/	FC
tynchal		/TINshal/	OLC Vol. I

pb	hc	Language	Translation
227	152	Gaelic (Gàidhlig)	"Come here, oh, noble woman": you will hear our very own Sam as Jamie using these words to Colum in episode 2, "Castle Leoch," of the *Outlander* TV show: *m' uasail chòir* /"my dear laird"/, as it works as both the noun and adjective "noble."
976	661	Gaelic (Gàidhlig)	"Come here, oh, vein": *chuisle* may well be used colloquially in some places as "blood," as in the sense it is here, but I know it only as "a vein" or "an artery."
229	154	Gaelic (Gàidhlig)	"Come here, oh, Claire, daughter of Henry, strength of my heart."
208	140	Gaelic (Gàidhlig)	"Come back here!"
416	281	Gaelic (Gàidhlig)	"Come out!"
1061	773	Gaelic (Gàidhlig)	"An end shall come on the world, but love and music shall endure": a particularly pleasant sentiment!
	251	Lowland Scots	To put up with, to endure. *"A canna thole any mare o yer snash."* ("I can't endure any more of your cheek.")
887	600	Gaelic (Gàidhlig)	"To(ward) me!": we use this prepositional pronoun—don't you just love grammatical terminology?—when talking about phoning one another. In Gaelic you still talk about "placing a call": *nach cuir u fón thugam?*/nach KOOroo phone HOOKəm/"Won't you place a phone (call) to(ward) me?"/.
575	417	Gaelic (Gàidhlig)	"Let's go!": our equivalent of "Let's roll!" Most often spoken very quickly, like the sound of clicking the fingers of each hand in quick succession.
1019	723	Gaelic (Gàidhlig)	"Scoundrel."
352	237	Gaelic (Gàidhlig)	"High mound": battle cry of the MacKenzies, now made famous by "Speak *Outlander*," featuring Graham McTavish, Gary Lewis, and yours truly!
	239	Lowland Scots	A ceremonial hunt. Neither *Iain Mac an Tàilleir* nor myself has found a direct Gaelic equivalent for this. Answers on a postcard! The assumption is that it is Lowland usage, but it sounds more French to me, truth be told.

Phrase *(as printed)*	Phrase *(if revised)*	Phonetic transcription	Book
uillean pipes		/OOLən/	OLC Vol. I
uisge		/OOSHkə/	OLC Vol. I
uisgebaugh	**uisge-beatha**	/ooshkə-BAYhə/	ABOSA
urisge	**ùraisg**	/OORishk/	EITB

pb	hc	Language	Translation
	238	Gaelic (Gàidhlig)	"Elbow pipes": air is supplied by an elbow-pressed bellows rather than by a mouthpiece. *Uillean* pipes are generally used for musical entertainments, as opposed to the Great Northern Pipes—the traditional "bagpipe" most often seen in films—which were used almost exclusively outdoors and were considered by the British to be a weapon of war.
	253	Gaelic (Gàidhlig)	"Water."
285	198	Gaelic (Gàidhlig)	"Life-water" (whisky): illicit stills were as common a thing in Scotland as in North America, and the practice extended down through the years until relatively recently. There are endless stories about how the excisemen—or the "gadgers," as they were called—were waylaid by any means necessary to prevent them from reaching the still in question. This normally consisted of them being "kindly" taken in, fed up to the hilt, and plied with as much booze as possible, until they chose bed over continuing their exertions on the trail of the bootlegger. The best of it was that it was often the very illicit whisky they sought upon which they had supped themselves into this condition!
769	545	Gaelic (Gàidhlig)	"Water spirit": *known to frequent lonely and sequestered places,* says Dwelly's dictionary on the *ùraisgean*/OOrishkən/. My guess is that the word originally derives from *ur* /"child, person" and *uisge*/ OOSHkə/"water", becoming *ur-uisge* and finally *ùruisg* before the spelling was reformed, as with all final unstressed instances of *u,* to an *a*—like *àluinn,* now *àlainn,* and *maduinn,* now *madainn.* These water spirits seemed to be quite friendly fellows as long as they were treated with respect and would only grow mischievous if dealt with unkindly. There is a terrific cartoon by West Highland Animation which features them. Great fun for the kids! Incidentally, I tend to spell *agus* as *agas,* with a final *a.* It was the only one of the above type of word left unreformed and so stuck out like a sore thumb! If you're doin one, do 'em all!

Phrase *(as printed)*	Phrase *(if revised)*	Phonetic transcription	Book
verra			FC
wame			OLC Vol. I
wean		/wane/	FC
weirrit		/WEErit/	OLC Vol. I
yeuk		/yook/	OLC Vol. I
yows			OLC Vol. I

pb	hc	Language	Translation
9	7	Lowland Scots	Very. This is an interesting one, due to its rocketing use among fans and media alike, and something that derives from the word "very" being spoken quickly. We Scots would never actually spell the word this way, but it's useful in the novels to illustrate the fact that the *y* at the end of the word is unstressed in rapid speech and often sounds like an *a*. We have other words to mean the same thing, like *gey*/giy/"very". Similarly, there's *fair* (fair[ly]), *awfie* (awful[ly]), and, peculiar to Glasgow, *pure* and *dead* (extremely), as in the famous phrase *pure dead brilliant,* meaning "exceedingly good." Now, if only all my kinsmen were as diligent with their Scots and Gaelic as Ian!
	246	Lowland Scots	Belly.
33	23	Lowland Scots	Child. In Glaswegian dialect, this compound noun comes literally from the Scots words "wee" (small) and "yin" or perhaps "ane" (one), over time melding into one. Heard extremely often in such phrases as: "Wantae you git they weans tellt?" ("Would you be so kind as to reprimand those infants?")
	247	Lowland Scots	Strangled. Often an addition to the sentence of burning—a criminal might be allowed the mercy of being strangled before being consigned to the flames.
	244	Lowland Scots	The itch. Colloquial expression for any sort of rash or skin inflammation.
	244	Lowland Scots	Ewes; female sheep.

Part Seven

WRITING, AND OTHER GAMES YOU PLAY BY YOURSELF

MIND GAMES

The greatest thing about writing is that it's just you and the page. The most horrifying thing about writing is that it's just you and the page. Contemplation of that dichotomy is enough to stop most people dead in their tracks.

Success in writing—and by that I mean getting the contents of your head out onto the page in a form that other people can relate to—is largely a matter of playing mind games with yourself. In order to get anywhere, you need to figure out how your own mind works—and believe me, people are not all wired up the same way.

Casual observation (i.e., talking to other writers for thirty years or so) suggests that about half of us are linear thinkers. These people really *profit* from outlines and wall charts and index cards filled out neatly in blue pen with each character's shoe size and sexual history (footnoted if these are directly correlated). The rest of us couldn't write that way if you paid us to.

The non-linear thinkers are described in all kinds of ways, most of them not euphonious: chunk writers, pantsters (I *really* dislike that one, as it suggests one's literary output is not from the upper end of the torso), piecers, etc. All these terms carry a whiff of dismissal, if not outright disdain or illegitimacy, and there's a reason for that.

(This is the insidious principle that underlies Politically Correct speech, by the way—the undeniable recognition that names have power, coupled with the invidious notion that by insisting on a specific term, the person assigning the name thus controls the person named, by controlling the perception of the named party. Hence the tiresome attempts to rename political parties as "haters," "tax-and-spend liberals," etc.

Stupidly annoying as this may be—it works. Frankly, it's a lot older than the notion of PC; it's one of the baseline techniques of exorcism and voodoo. As a character in one of my books observes [paraphrasing], "Ye don't call something by name unless ye want it to come.")

Anyone educated in the art of composition in the Western Hemisphere at any time in the last hundred years was firmly taught that there is One Correct Way to write, and it involves strictly linear planning, thought, and execution. You Must Have a Topic Sentence. You Must Have a Topic Paragraph. YOU MUST HAVE AN OUTLINE. And so forth and so tediously on . . .

Got news for you: you don't have to do it that way. *Anything* that gets words on the page is the Right Thing to Do.

As a non-linear thinker myself, I prefer less-pejorative terms. I like "network thinker." Consider thinking and writing as a process that lights up your synapses (which it does): a linear thinker is like a string of holiday lights. Red-blue-green-yellow-orange-red-blue-green-yellow-orange-red! And it lights up and then you can wind it around your Christmas tree or your Kwanzaa flagpole and it's all pretty.

Well. You know those nets of lights that you throw over your front wall or your cactus or anything else that it would be inconvenient to staple strings of lights to? Those look like this:

```
Red - Yellow - Blue - Green - Red
 |       |       |       |       |
Blue - Orange - Red - Yellow- Green
 |       |       |       |       |
Yellow - Green - Blue - Red - Orange
```

The logical connections (the electricity, if you will) between any two lights in that network are *there*. It isn't random, and in the end, it's logical. It's even linear. It just . . . isn't necessarily a *straight* line.

Now, the reason that the educational establishment insists on the linear model of writing is that you can force a non-linear writer to work linearly (or at least pretend to). You can*not* make a linear writer work non-linearly. (In fact, every time I describe the way I write to a linear-thinking person, they get annoyed. "You can't *possibly* do it that way!" they say. By which they mean that *they* can't possibly do it that way—and they can't.)

But you can make any fifth-grader cough up a reasonably coherent essay using the linear model—and no one ever mentions that this *isn't* the only way to do it. (Every time I go talk to an elementary-school class for Career Day, I pause midway and ask the teacher to turn his or her back. Then I tell the kids, "Okay, the teacher can't see you, so tell me the truth. When you get one of those essay assignments and you have to turn in an outline and a rough draft and a polished draft and a final copy—how many of you just write the final copy and then fake up the rest?" About a third of the class will raise their hands. I think it would be more, but some of them are scared to admit it.)

Beyond the fascinating process of figuring out how your brain works, though, are the more mundane but nonetheless important mind games: the ones you play with yourself (or others) in order to write—or not write—in the first place.

THE "I'LL START MY BOOK AS SOON AS . . ." GAME

This is the one where you avoid even beginning to think about writing, by making the assumption that you can't possibly write anything worthwhile unless you have several hours every day to be dedicated to writing, the full approval and support of family and friends, and a Room of One's Own, equipped with ergonomic chair, footstool, and keyboard.

I had a friend like this, at the university where I used to work. After I published *Outlander,* all my friends and colleagues in the department[1] were agog, and several of them began to consider the possibilities of writing

[1] *No, not the English department, nor yet the history department. I was a biologist in my previous academic incarnation (though I'd sort of slid sideways and become an "expert" in scientific computation—it's easy to be an expert if only six other people in the world do what you do . . .) and worked at the Center for Environmental Studies at Arizona State University.*

a novel themselves. Whenever I saw this one friend, he would tell me all about his novel: he had a wonderful premise (it really *was* a wonderful premise), and as soon as he finished the seminar he was teaching and got this pesky report out of the way, "I'll have a big chunk of time and can sit down and get started!"

After several repetitions of this, I drew a deep breath and sadly told him the truth. "Bill,[2] you're never going to write that book." And sure enough, he never did, alas.

It's a simple but harsh truth: nobody ever *finds* the time to do something; you *make* time, or you haven't got any.

Where a lot of people go wrong, I think, is in the assumption that you can't write unless you do have large blocks of time that you can dedicate to the activity. This actually isn't true. (In fact, some people *can't* write for long stretches. I'm one of them. . . .) What *is* essential is that you actually do write—no matter how much time you have available.

If you have no more than ten minutes a day in which you can write (while your spouse is showering, perhaps), then write for ten minutes. Eventually you'll have a book. If you say, "Oh, I can't write unless I have three uninterrupted hours" . . . you won't have a book.

If you'll pardon a bit of personal testimony here: when I made up my mind to write a novel, I had two full-time jobs[3] and three children under the age of six. Both my jobs required constant writing, and I wrote in the middle of the night, because that's when you work if you have small children and work out of your home.

I couldn't do what people normally do when they encounter a block in the writing—i.e., get up, wander away, and never come back—because I had to keep producing words in order to get paid. So what I did instead was sort of tag-team writing: when the grant proposal I was working on stuck, I'd shift immediately to the top software package waiting on my review pile and start a piece for *Byte* or *InfoWorld.* When that stuck, I'd either go back to the proposal—which might have unstuck itself while I was gone—or start in on a handout for one of my seminars.

When I decided to write a novel,[4] I just added it to the rotation: grant proposal, software review, textbook chapter, scene from novel. This method kept me sitting at my keyboard, being productive. So during the three or four hours I'd normally work at night,[5] I was probably hitting the novel scene three or four times and ending the night with five hundred to a thousand words . . . to say nothing of half a software review, two pages of textbook, and two or three paragraphs of a grant proposal.[6]

---

[2] *Not his name.*

[3] *In addition to being an assistant research professor, I also wrote virtually full time (freelance) for the computer press and eventually started my own journal on scientific computation, as well as teaching international seminars on laboratory automation, data acquisition and analysis, and all the hot technology of the early eighties. Wrote tons of documentation, tutorials, and assorted guff.*

[4] *In retrospect, this was clearly insane. But you can't let considerations of that sort stop you.*

[5] *I still do the bulk of my writing at night, usually between midnight and 4:00 a.m.*

[6] *Hate writing grant proposals.*

Not saying this approach will work for you, mind, but you won't know what *does* work unless you try things.

Moving right along, we come to the sort of games that rely on other people to stop you.

THE "I FEEL TOO GUILTY TO WRITE" GAME

This one is gender-specific; only women play it. "How can I possibly be so selfish as to take time away from my *family* to do something that I probably can't do, and even if I could do it, it wouldn't make any money, and . . . and . . . and . . ."

Ahem. Do you by chance watch television? Oh, you do. Do you feel guilty about it? Do you have a hobby? Do you have friends? Do you feel guilty about those things?

While you ponder that one, I'll admit that often it isn't entirely misplaced guilt; your family really *will* try to stop you from writing, because they feel threatened by anything you want to do that doesn't involve them. Their instincts tell them that if they wanted you, you would instantly stop watching television or doing Pinterest and attend to their needs, whereas if you were *writing* something . . . maybe you wouldn't.

Also, in all justice, they understand things like scrapbooking, gardening, and having coffee with your next-door neighbor. They *don't* understand writing, because they don't know anyone who does it, and everyone feels threatened by things they don't understand.

This suspicion is particularly acute in husbands, who fear not only the loss of your attention but harbor the suspicion that the book will seduce you away from them. (Fortunately, this type of interference is fairly easy to deal with: take him to bed and wear him out—thus simultaneously reassuring him of your affections and putting him to sleep—then get up and go write.)

A refinement of this game is "the dreaded silence," as someone of my acquaintance described her family's and friends' response to her writing. This is where you brave the disapproval (real or imagined) of your family and write *anyway*, but when you attempt to share the fruits of your labors with them, they meet your overtures with indifference, refusing to comment at all.

I've often heard stories from writers about family members being dismissive or hostile about their work. Which, you know, should kind of tell you something. Like . . . don't show your stuff to your family and friends.

I never did; I didn't even tell them what I was doing. On the one hand, it puts people in a really difficult position: almost no one (other than another—experienced—writer, and often not *then*) is equipped to give genuinely constructive feedback. Your family? Almost certainly the only thing they *could* say would be either a feeble "Oh, I like it" or "Oh, God, this makes me squirm to read it." More often than not, they'll just avoid the discomfort of trying to find *something* to say by ignoring it.

On the other hand . . . having a writer in your immediate vicinity is genuinely disturbing—not to say threatening—to a lot of people. On the most basic level, they—your family, and particularly your spouse—feel that you're taking time and attention away from *them* to do this weird thing that isn't likely to result in any positive outcome. And, you know . . . you are. Which is why a lot of women who write feel terribly guilty about it and often give up. (Men, oddly enough, seldom feel at all guilty about taking time and attention away from their families to build kit cars or play golf. . . .)

On a higher level, family and friends may feel disturbed because they don't understand how writing actually works (nobody *does*, except the people who do it) and think that you are literally transcribing incidents from your life (they having dimly apprehended some aphorism about "write what you know") and are "putting *me* in your book."

(Frankly, I'm not sure silence isn't better than the other possible reactions, like people constantly asking when you're going to finish "that book" and sell it to the movies for a million dollars, or asking if you're writing smut, because they understand that's really profitable, or suggesting that you write children's books—instead of historical fiction, say, or mysteries—"because that's really easy and you'd be done sooner.")

So you really have two choices about this:[7] brass it out, announce to your family what you're doing, grit your teeth, and resist all their efforts to sabotage you, or . . . hide what you're doing until it's too late to stop you.

Me, I hid. Not entirely on my family's account—but because I didn't want anyone trying to tell me how to do it or pressuring me to do this or that (or not do this or that); I needed to figure it out for myself.

Everybody does.

All right. So you defy family, friends, and the clock and actually write something. The mind games aren't over. . . .

THE "I KEEP DELETING" GAME (AKA "THE EDITOR ON MY SHOULDER WON'T SHUT UP . . .")

This is the one where you write a sentence, decide it's no good, and delete it. You write another one, decide *that's* no good, and delete it. And so forth and so on. I can't count how many times I've seen someone post a lamenting message saying something like, "I worked all day and have *nothing* to show for it! I deleted all three thousand words I wrote and I feel like crap."

Yeah, who wouldn't?

Fortunately, the answer to this one is simple: Don't Do That.

I mean, really—why assume that pressing the DELETE key is progress? It isn't.

Part of this is purely psychological, and another part is totally pragmatic:

One) If you end the day with a blank page, you will naturally feel as though you aren't getting anywhere, because you have nothing to show for your work. You deserve credit for your work! (Whether it's good work at the moment or not, it cost you a chunk of your life. It counts.)

Two) As one well-known author often says, "You can't fix a blank page." Look. Perfect sentences do not "just flow" from a writer's fingertips. It doesn't work that way. Still less do elegant and intricate stories pour unfettered from a writer's brain—*any* writer's brain.

Now, I've never read How-to-Write books

[7] *We don't accept the notion that giving up before you start is a valid choice. Dismiss it from your mind.*

(I was born with a strong "says who?" gene that tends to inhibit my taking on faith anything that's authoritatively stated), but I have read writers' biographies and stories about How They Did It. *That's* very valuable, because it shows you a little bit about how writers actually work—as opposed to "Step 1: get a large sheet of whiteboard and pin it to your wall . . ." or "Never write in the first person . . ."

P. G. Wodehouse, for example (a very famous—and very good—British writer of comic novels), worked regularly, six hours a day (and produced something like ninety-five novels as a result). He wrote for three hours in the morning, had lunch and a nap, then spent three hours fixing what he'd written in the morning.

He described his office, with the pages of the novel he was working on pinned all along the walls; the pages that worked and that he thought were good were pinned up straight, while the ones he didn't like were pinned crookedly, so he could see at once what needed work.

This guy didn't delete stuff he thought was imperfect; he fixed it.

Ross Macdonald (pseudonym of award-winning crime writer Kenneth Millar) described how, when he was starting out, he decided that he must take writing seriously, as though it was a real job. He couldn't afford to rent an office but talked the superintendent of his building into letting him work in the boiler room. So every morning he would dress carefully in his only suit, with a clean, ironed shirt and tie, pick up his briefcase, and go downstairs to work.

As it *was* his only suit, when he reached the boiler room, he took it off, hung it on a hanger, and sat down to work all day in his underwear. Pretty sure he wasn't deleting stuff, either—he took his job seriously.

I should probably admit that I've never understood the "editor on your shoulder" concept, because I don't have one. Not (I hasten to clarify) that I don't view what I write with a critical eye nor yet that I don't take infinite trouble over my work—just that I've never seen the point of deliberately getting in your own way.

I see a *lot* of writers—mostly women, though some guys do it, too—who go on and on about how they can't get anything done because they keep throwing away their work, and they're obviously bad at this, and why did they think they could write in the first place, and it's so depressing, etc. I mean . . . why add the component of self-blame to what's already a noticeably difficult profession? You don't *have* to do that.

I suppose it doesn't behoove a nice Roman Catholic girl descended (perhaps) from *converso* Jews to admit to not possessing a sense of guilt, but I really don't see the point. I mean, maybe you should feel guilty about spreading gossip or not giving the bum on the corner a dollar when you have one in your pocket, but about your own *work*? C'mon . . .

What you do when you write is a noble thing, no matter what the outcome. Give it—and yourself—a little respect.

Words have power; use them carefully. And now . . . watch this:

"A CODA IN THREE-TWO TIME" (ANNOTATED)

Last year, I was a presenter at the Surrey International Writers' Conference. This is my very favorite conference—the only one I go to every year. That being so, though, I've given the same (more or less; I kind of ad-lib them) workshops several times: Details, Character, Dialogue, etc. So when the organizers asked me what I'd like to teach that year, I decided on the spur of the moment to Do Something Different.

This requires a little backstory: a few months prior to this, I'd been asked to write a foreword for a Writer's Digest Annotated Classics edition of *Jane Eyre.* Now, "annotated" here means something different than it usually does: this was to be a special edition for writers, and the annotations were meant to point out to aspiring writers exactly what Charlotte Brontë was actually *doing* at various points of the novel, in terms of technique.

I thought that was a great idea. Because a lot of aspiring writers are always looking for "the secrets of great writing" (or however the latest how-to book chooses to put it), and that always struck me as misleading—because the simple (and appalling) truth is that writers don't *have* secrets. Anything a writer knows how to do is Right There on the page. And if you're looking with an analytical eye (or maybe just read a lot), you'll see what it *is* that Writer X knows how to do.

Apparently a lot of people don't read with an analytical eye, though (shocking, I know . . .). But with this interesting new *Jane Eyre* project fresh in mind, I said to the conference organizers, "How about a workshop called How to Read Like a Writer?"

Either they loved the idea or were anxious to send their program to the printer, but one way or the other, that's what I taught. As it was my first time doing that, it was even more off the cuff than usual, but it went well and a number of people told me afterward that they'd found it both interesting and helpful. So I thought I might show y'all a bit of what I was doing there—possibly for the instruction of aspiring writers, and more likely just for the entertainment of people who like to know the hows and whys of writing, as well as the story.

Now, when I taught this, I used extracts from half a dozen different authors, reading the extract aloud and then going back through it, making observations about the techniques characteristic of Charles Dickens, Jim Butcher, James Lee Burke, and a few others. And then I finished up with the "Coda" section from *MOBY.* I don't like to overuse my own work, but a) it saves worrying about copyright infringement, if I need to do handouts, b) I don't have to work very hard at finding suitable excerpts, since I know where everything is, and c) I know for sure what *I* was thinking or intending when I wrote something.

As those of you who've read *MOBY* know, the "Coda" is a section of three wedding-night interactions: Denzell and Dorothea, Ian and Rachel, and Jamie and Claire (that's why the section is called "A Coda in Three-Two Time"—three couples, geddit?). I'm not going to do the whole thing here, because it would take days, but here's 1) the first short scene from Denzell and Dottie's wedding night, and 2) the annotated version of that scene, with my observations on the craft involved. Hope you find it interesting!

*

Excerpted from Written in My Own Heart's Blood

Denzell and Dorothea

It was the best party that Dorothea Jacqueline Benedicta Grey had ever attended. She had danced with earls and viscounts in the most beautiful ballrooms in London, eaten everything from gilded peacock to trout stuffed with shrimp and riding on an artful sea of aspic with a Triton carved of ice brandishing his spear over all. And she'd done these things in gowns so splendid that men blinked when she hove into view.

Her new husband didn't blink. He stared at her so intently through his steel-rimmed spectacles that she thought she could feel his gaze on her skin, from across the room and right through her dove-gray dress, and she thought she might burst with happiness, exploding in bits all over the taproom of the White Camel tavern. Not that anyone would notice if she did; there were so many people crammed into the room, drinking, talking, drinking, singing, and drinking, that a spare gallbladder or kidney underfoot would pass without notice.

Just possibly, she thought, one or two whole people might pass without notice, too—right out of this lovely party.

She reached Denzell with some difficulty, there being a great many well-wishers between them, but as she approached him, he stretched out a hand and seized hers, and an instant later they were outside in the night air, laughing like loons and kissing each other in the shadows of the Anabaptist Meeting House that stood next door to the tavern.

"Will thee come home now, Dorothea?" Denny said, pausing for a momentary breath. "Is thee . . . ready?"

She didn't let go of him but moved closer, dislodging his glasses and enjoying the scent of his shaving soap and the starch in his linen—and the scent of him underneath.

"Are we truly married now?" she whispered. "I am thy wife?"

"We are. Thee is," he said, his voice slightly husky. "And I am thy husband."

She thought he'd meant to speak solemnly, but such an uncontainable smile of joy spread across his face at the speaking that she laughed out loud.

"We didn't say 'one flesh' in our vows," she said, stepping back but keeping hold of his hand. "But does thee think that principle obtains? Generally speaking?"

He settled his glasses more firmly on his nose and looked at her with intense concentration and shining eyes. And, with one finger of his free hand, touched her breast.

"I'm counting on it, Dorothea."

[And now . . . the Annotated Version. . . .]

Denzell and Dorothea

It was the best party that Dorothea Jacqueline Benedicta Grey had ever attended. She had danced with earls and viscounts in the most beautiful ballrooms in London, eaten everything from gilded peacock to trout stuffed with shrimp and riding on an artful sea of aspic with a Triton carved of ice brandishing his spear over all. And she'd done these things in gowns so splendid that men blinked when she hove into view.

What's the first line doing? It's setting the viewpoint character—Dorothea—in a particular but unspecific place, at a party. (Always a good idea to give the reader a way to fix themselves in reality immediately.) But what else? Why did I use all four of her names? Because this is the first note in a riff on her social position (which you see explicated in the rest of the paragraph), and also because it's an echo of her marriage vows (where people normally recite all their names). And I said only "a party," because that's enough for the moment—we'll get more specific as we move into the scene.

The rest of this paragraph enlarges on Dottie's social position and experience. To this end, I used a lot of very specific details—in a brief space—to give a visual picture of what her life in London had been like. The thing about using a lot of details, though, is that you a) want to do it gracefully, so the readers don't feel that they're having a bucket of chum flung in their faces, and b) want to keep the list kind of contained, not sprawling all over the place. So let's have a quick look at the internals of that second sentence: *She had danced with earls and viscounts in the most beautiful ballrooms in London, eaten everything from gilded peacock to trout stuffed with shrimp and riding on an artful sea of aspic with a Triton carved of ice brandishing his spear over all.*

She had danced—anchoring our frame of reference in the past; *with earls and viscounts*—she's either a member of the aristocracy or at least was accustomed to move in such social circles; *in the most beautiful ballrooms in London*—specifying the place, giving a vague picture of elegance (and note the alliteration: *beautiful ballrooms*; overt and internal alliteration is one of the things you use—carefully—to make a long sentence flow). *Vide, eaten everything and then stuffed with shrimp and riding on an artful sea of aspic* (say that last bit over to yourself; do you hear the rhythm of it? *STUFFED with SHRIMP and RIDing on an ARTful SEA of ASpic.* That rhythm carries on through a *TRIton CARVED of ICE*). The imagery of the sentence overall goes from a gilded peacock—easily envisioned but generic—to the shrimp-stuffed trout riding on a sea of aspic, and then we see the icy Triton brandishing his spear—that's unique, and while we need a moment to build the image, it's one worth having, as it impresses us with the style of party to which Lady Dorothea has been accustomed. This is a lot of work for one sentence to do, and it was a lot of work to construct it elegantly so it would do that—but worth it.

The final sentence then brings us back to Dorothea herself (thus closing the paragraph artfully, as we began with her), and we see her in gorgeous dresses, admired by all these earls and viscounts who are already in our mind's eye.

But *then* . . .

Her new husband didn't blink. He stared at her so intently through his steel-rimmed spectacles that she thought she could feel his gaze on her skin, from across the room and right through her dove-gray dress, and she thought she might burst with happiness, exploding in bits all over the taproom of the White Camel tavern. Not that anyone would notice if she did; there were so many people crammed into the room, drinking, talking, drinking, singing, and drinking, that a spare gallbladder or kidney underfoot would pass without notice.

Her new husband didn't blink. Okay, now we know what kind of party this is; it's a wedding reception of some kind. (Observe the rhyme/repetition of *blink* and *drinking/drinking/drinking*—that's rhythmic, as well as funny, as well as being descriptive of the party.) And the fact that her husband doesn't blink carries us from the last sentence of the preceding paragraph *and* tells us something about how he feels about his new wife. But what does he feel? *Why* is he not blinking? (That's one of the little subliminal questions that one wants to keep raising throughout a scene, making the reader want to know the answer even without realizing that you've given them a question. Along those lines, note that we mentioned only a *party* in the first line of this scene and then told you what kind of party she's used to—but we should be wondering idly just what kind of party *this* is, since there are sufficient grounds for thinking it probably isn't the sort she's used to.)

He stared at her so intently through his steel-rimmed spectacles that she thought she could feel his gaze on her skin, from across the room and right through her dove-gray dress, and she thought she might burst with happiness, exploding in bits all over the taproom of the White Camel tavern.

Okay, let's look at that. He's not blinking, because he's staring at her intently—we may still be wondering what his intent is—but by the time we get to the end of this sentence, we know he's staring intently because he's enraptured by her; we know this because the effect of his stare is to make Dorothea think she might burst with happiness. So that's the cause/effect of this sentence: he's staring at her and it makes her happy. That's the main thing we want to get across. But we can do more with that. We'd like to know a little about what these people look like (even though we've met them before in this book, we want to know what they look like now, at this party), and naturally we are not crass enough to just start off with a police Identi-Kit description of them. No-no-no . . . we use carefully chosen single details: the steel-rimmed spectacles and the dove-gray dress (I ought really to have said *gown* there, for the alliteration—but I chose dress as sounding modest in contrast to the gorgeous gowns she's used to wearing, because that's what I want to get across here—the contrast between her former life and the one she's chosen now). Likewise, Denny's spectacles aren't anything a London beau would be wearing, but they add to our mental image of the intensity of his gaze (and we've used his spectacles before as a useful prop for his character—since, like anyone who habitually wears glasses, he's constantly wiping them, taking them off, putting them on, peering through them, etc. So we're using them here also as repetition, to recap and strengthen our mental notion of Denny).

Okay, *she thought she might burst with happiness* is a perfectly reasonable description of her feelings, but it's also a cliché. You can *use* clichés, but when you do, you want to subvert, deconstruct, or enhance them. In this instance, I subverted it in this sentence and in the next enhanced it and, in the process, got across the subtext of Denny's being a doctor (and Dorothea having assisted him in his

profession—thus her casual familiarity with gallbladders and kidneys). AND this last bit gives us our first sense of who Dottie really is and what her "voice" is like.

We also now pin down the place where the party's taking place (part of the answer to the question raised by the word "party" in the beginning): the taproom of the White Camel tavern. This was a real tavern in eighteenth-century Philadelphia, but that's just to give me a quiet feeling of gratification at the excellency of my research—I don't really expect the reader to recognize it. Even if it had been a made-up name, though, it's important to give the tavern a specific name. This is how details work in a story: you don't want to overwhelm the reader by having tons of them; you want to pick specific, vivid ones that will give the reader mental landmarks to use in visualizing things.

Just possibly, she thought, one or two whole people might pass without notice, too—right out of this lovely party.

The first two paragraphs were essentially "backstory"—establishing who, what, where, when—and the need to know the answers to those things got the reader this far. But now we need to be getting on with the action. This one-sentence paragraph is our transition. (See the internal alliteration again? *Possibly/people/pass/party.* And there's a rhythmic couplet in the middle: *one or two whole people/ might pass without notice, too.* Rhythmic structure is one of the tools you use to hold up a long or complex sentence (punctuation is another—important—one). And now . . . on with the action!

She reached Denzell with some difficulty, there being a great many well-wishers between them, but as she approached him, he stretched out a hand and seized hers, and an instant later they were outside in the night air, laughing like loons and kissing each other in the shadows of the Anabaptist Meeting House that stood next door to the tavern.

What a character—or characters—*want* is what drives a story. Your protagonist needs to want something in the beginning of the story, and the story then is about what he or she will do to get it—and about whether he or she *does* get it, gets it but then wants something else, doesn't get it but is better off without it, or changes his or her mind about what he or she wants. You can also use what a character wants in a much lesser context, though, to drive a scene. What Dorothea and Denny *both* want here is to get the heck out of the party and be alone with each other. They do it with considerable dispatch, but the doing of it raises yet another (small) question for the reader: what's going to happen next?

The art of making people turn the page is the art of raising a cascade of such small questions; the desire to have those questions answered will draw the reader's eye right down the page and on to the next one. So we answered the first question—what does Dorothea want—and Denny immediately asks another:

"Will thee come home now, Dorothea?" Denny said, pausing for a momentary breath. "Is thee . . . ready?"

She didn't let go of him but moved closer, dislodging his glasses and enjoying the scent of his shaving soap and the starch in his linen—and the scent of him underneath.

Watch those "s"s. Watch also the sudden invocation of the sense of smell. Most of our details so far have been purely visual or audible. Using *scent* this way—and, again, being *specific* about scent; not just "he smelled good"—not only brings Denny into sharper focus, it gives us a sense of intimacy.

"Are we truly married now?" she whispered. "I am thy wife?"

"We are. Thee is," he said, his voice slightly husky. "And I am thy husband."

These people are Quakers: he's a lifelong Quaker; she's converted in order to marry him. So they use plain speech ("thee/thy"). Otherwise, note the basic rules of dialogue: keep it short/make it individual. Short sentences, short paragraphs; the things they say are specific to these particular people and their situation.

She thought he'd meant to speak solemnly, but such an uncontainable smile of joy spread across his face at the speaking that she laughed out loud.

"We didn't say 'one flesh' in our vows," she said, stepping back but keeping hold of his hand. "But does thee think that principle obtains? Generally speaking?"

He settled his glasses more firmly on his nose and looked at her with intense concentration and shining eyes. And, with one finger of his free hand, touched her breast.

Besides the simple physical actions—smiling, keeping hold of his hand, touching her breast—we're using small visual cues to intensify the sense of connection between them: *uncontainable smile of joy; intense concentration and shining eyes.*

Note also that we're firmly in Dorothea's point of view through this passage; we see what she sees. None of this "she pushed her fingers through the honey-blond tangle of her curls" nonsense. Nobody runs their hands through their hair and thinks anything conscious about it, unless they suddenly encounter the sticky lollipop that their kid left on his parents' pillow that morning. What we

know about Dorothea's appearance is indirect and given in a way that provides an excuse for the detail other than the obvious desire on the author's part to describe the person: i.e., we know that gentlemen used to blink when she hove into view (and the fact that she'd use an expression like *hove into view* tells us that she's maybe not your usual young lady of quality), and then when her husband *doesn't* blink, she imagines his gaze passing through her *dove-gray dress.* We don't feel that *dove-gray* as an authorial intrusion, because we're seeing Dorothea thinking of the contrasts between parties of the past and this one, so it's natural for her to observe in passing the contrast of her modest dress (specific, because it's vivid to her) with the earlier (nonspecific) beautiful ball gowns (which are vaguely referred to, while the food is described in great detail—telling us something else about Dottie's personality and proclivities). But we come away from this passage (I hope) with the impression that Dottie is young, pretty, and has a noticeable sense of humor.

"I'm counting on it, Dorothea."

And Denny has a sense of humor to match, though his is quieter.

Okay, that's as far as I'm going with the annotation here, not to bore anyone. But I will provide the rest of Dorothea and Denzell's initial encounter, since it seems rather mean to stop there. . . . Having seen how it's done, you might want to try to pick out the various techniques on display yourself.

She'd been in his rooms before. But first as a guest, and then as an assistant, coming up to pack a basket with bandages and ointments before accompanying him to some professional call. It was quite different now.

He'd opened all the windows earlier and left them so, careless of flying insects and the butcher's shop down the street. The second floor of the building would have been suffocating after the day's heat—but with the gentle night breeze coming through, the air was like warm milk, soft and liquid on the skin, and the meaty smells of the butcher's shop were now overborne by the night perfume of the gardens at Bingham House, two streets over.

All trace of his profession had been cleared away, and the light of the candle he lit shone serenely on a plainly furnished but comfortable room. Two small wing chairs sat beside the hearth, a single book on the table between them. And, through the open door, a bed fresh-made with a smooth counterpane and plump white pillows beckoned enticingly.

The blood still thrummed through her body like wine, though she'd had very little to drink. Still, she felt unaccountably shy and stood for a moment just inside the door, as though waiting to be invited in. Denny lit two more candles and, turning, saw her standing there.

"Come," he said softly, stretching out a hand to her, and she did. They kissed lingeringly, hands roaming slowly, clothes beginning to loosen. Her hand drifted casually down and touched him through his breeches. He drew breath and would have said something, but wasn't quick enough.

"One flesh," she reminded him, smiling, and cupped her hand. "I want to see thy half of it."

* * *

"Thee has *seen such things before," Denny said. "I know thee has. Thee has brothers, for one thing. And—and in the course of . . . of treating wounded men . . ." He was lying naked on the bed, and so was she, fondling the object in question, which seemed to be enjoying the attention immensely. His fingers were sliding through her hair, playing with her earlobes.*

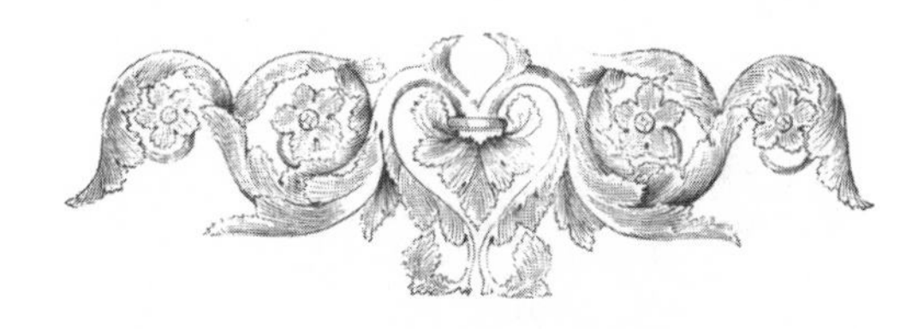

"I hope thee doesn't think I ever did this to any of my brothers," she said, sniffing him with pleasure. "And those of wounded men aren't generally in a condition to be appreciated at all."

Denny cleared his throat and stretched himself a little, not quite squirming.

"I think thee should allow me to appreciate thy own flesh for a bit," he said. "If thee expects me to be able to make thee a wife tonight."

"Oh." She looked down at his cock and then at herself, surprised. "What do—does thee—mean? Why wouldn't thee be able to?"

"Ah." He looked pleased and eager—he was so young without his glasses—and bounced off the bed, going into the outer room, his bottom pale and tidy in the candlelight. To Dottie's astonishment, he came back with the book she'd noticed on the table and handed it to her. It was bristling with bookmarks, and as she took it, it fell open in her hands, displaying several drawings of a naked man in cross section, his private parts in various stages of operation.

She looked up at Denny in disbelief.

"I thought—I know thee is a virgin; I didn't want thee to be frightened, or unprepared." He was blushing like a rose, and instead of collapsing in howls of laughter, which she badly wanted to do, she shut the book gently and took his face between her hands.

"Is thee a virgin, too, Denny?" she said softly. His blush grew fierce, but he kept her gaze.

"Yes. But—I do know how. *I'm a physician."*

That was too much, and she did laugh, but in small, half-stifled blurts of giggling, which infected him, and in seconds they were in each other's arms on the bed, shaking silently, with occasional snorts and repetitions of "I'm a physician," which sent them into fresh paroxysms.

At last she found herself on her back, breathing heavily, Denny lying on top of her, and a slick of perspiration oiling them. She lifted a hand and touched his chest, and gooseflesh rippled over him, the dark hairs of his body curly and bristling. She was trembling, but not with either fear or laughter.

"Is thee ready?" he whispered.

"One flesh," she whispered back. And they were.

* * *

The candles had burned down nearly to their sockets, and the naked shadows on the wall moved slowly.

"Dorothea!"

"Thee should probably be quiet," she advised him, briefly removing her mouth in order to talk. "I've never done this before. Thee wouldn't want to distract me, now, would thee?" Before he could summon a single word, she had resumed her alarming actions. He groaned—he couldn't help it—and laid his hands gently, helplessly, on her head.

"It's called fellatio, did thee know that?" she inquired, pausing momentarily for breath.

"I did. How . . . I mean . . . Oh. Oh, God."

"What did thee say?" Her face was beautiful, so flushed that the color showed even by candlelight, her lips deep rose and wet . . .

"I said—oh, God."

A smile lit her shadowed face with happiness, and her already firm grip on him tightened. His shadow jerked.

"Oh, good*," she said, and with a small, triumphant crow of laughter, bent to slay him with her sharp white teeth.*

ONE WORD SPEAKS VOLUMES (THEMES OF THE NOVELS)

Books don't write themselves, as anyone who's ever tried to write one can tell you. And if there is a secret to writing anything—fiction, nonfiction, TV scripts, greeting cards, poetry, or epitaphs—it's this: the only way to write is one word at a time. This is either reassuring or Absolutely Horrifying, depending on how you look at it, but it's the truth.

But, as anyone who writes books can also tell you, books do have a mind and a voice of their own. And a successful book is one that talks to the reader.

The interesting thing is that they talk to the writer, too. (Some writers suffer from the notion that *they* are in charge. Maybe they know something I don't.[8])

If you've ever been exposed to high school English classes, you've doubtless been forced to discern and explicate the theme of a novel. This is ungodly boring but possibly helpful to those who've never heard of a theme before. (Frankly, my opinion is that if you read a lot, you absorb this notion by observation, and if you don't like to read in the first place, being forced to look for themes in books you don't care about to start with is not likely to change your aversion to the practice.)

Still, the general notion of a theme is sometimes useful to a writer, in that it influences both the content and the organization of your story. Not always—or even often—in a deliberately conscious way, but it's *there*. And once you've assembled most of a book, you really ought to be able to tell someone who asks what the theme is.

I didn't really think about the themes of my books for some years, but some intelligent NPR interviewer[9] asked me one day whether I could sum up the book we were talking about in a single sentence—and I realized that, in fact, I could summarize the theme of each book in a single word.

These are as follows:

Outlander—Love

While my books are often referred to (by people at a loss as to *what* to call them) as romance novels, they aren't. However, *Outlander* is in fact the only one that has the necessary structure to even pass as a romance novel. I.e., it *is* a courtship story; its central mechanism concerns the coming together of two people in a (theoretically) permanent pair bond. Beyond that, though, it explores the nature of love on a number of levels and in a variety of contexts.

We have Claire's conflict over (truly) loving two men. We have Jamie's love for his father, his sister, and his home, and Murtagh's love for his godson. We have the deeply conflicted love between the brothers MacKenzie. We have the love of the clansmen for one another, their laird, and their home. We have the very complicated emotions of Captain Jack Randall—though whether any of these constitutes love, or merely obsession, is a matter for the reader to decide. And we have Divine Love, which Claire more or less stumbles into as an act of desperation. But almost every relationship in the book rests on love, and the entire story is a testament to the power of love.

---

[8] *Then again, maybe they don't . . .*

[9] *NPR always has the* best *interviewers. A real pleasure to talk books and writing with any one of them.*

Dragonfly in Amber—Marriage

This book deals primarily with the development of a specific marriage—Jamie's and Claire's—but along the way looks at quite a few other relationships and arrangements that explore the concept. We have the arranged marriage of Mary Hawkins and the elderly, warty Vicomte Marigny. We have the loveless but pragmatic marriages of class and convenience seen in the French court and the casual, selfish affairs that contrast so strongly with the sense of commitment and self-sacrifice at the heart of a good marriage. Later we see the doomed love between Mary and Alex Randall—and the pragmatic marriage between her and Jack Randall (based on Jack's love for his brother, rather than for Mary). We see the guilt of a broken-and-patched marriage in Claire's resumption of her relations with Frank, and the peace of a long-term, deeply committed marriage between Jenny and Ian at Lallybroch—and appreciate the various threats there are to these social bonds and how people sustain a marriage—or don't.

Voyager—Identity

Voyager has a lot of adventure, changing of times and places, seeking of destiny, and so on—but the underlying theme is that of a person's search for identity and how they define themselves, in their own eyes, or those of another, or those of society at large. By marriage, by career, by calling—or by recognition of one's own essential being. You see this worked out most noticeably (of course) in Claire's and Jamie's story, first as she seeks the husband she's lost and longed for, and then as they look for safe landing and a place in which they can survive together.

The continuing metaphor lies in their names: Jamie has five to choose from, plus a title, plus various nicknames, and he lives under an assortment of *noms de guerre* (often quite literally *de guerre*) throughout the book, in response to his changing roles and who's after him at the moment. Claire, of course, has gone from Beauchamp to Randall to Fraser to Randall, and is now once again about to be Claire Fraser—or is it Mrs. Malcolm? Or perhaps Madame Etienne Marcel de Provac Alexandre? (Symbolizing the linking of her fate with Jamie's, aye?) As Jamie tells Claire mid-book,

> *"For so many years," he said, "for so long, I have been so many things, so many different men." I felt him swallow, and he shifted slightly, the linen of his nightshirt rustling with starch.*
>
> *"I was Uncle to Jenny's children, and Brother to her and Ian. 'Milord' to Fergus, and 'Sir' to my tenants. 'Mac Dubh' to the men of Ardsmuir and 'MacKenzie' to the other servants at Helwater. 'Malcolm the printer,' then, and 'Jamie Roy' at the docks." The hand stroked my hair, slowly, with a whispering sound like the wind outside. "But here," he said, so softly I could barely hear him, "here in the dark, with you . . . I have no name."*

The two of them adopt, discard, and adapt roles as they go from an Edinburgh brothel to Lallybroch to the Caribbean and at last, cast ashore by a hurricane,[10] to America. There—stripped of everything except each other—Jamie finally reclaims and restates his identity, when he introduces himself to a rescuer: *"My name is Jamie Fraser. . . . And this is Claire . . . My wife."*

Drums of Autumn—Family

If *Dragonfly in Amber* deals with the establishment and growth of a marriage, *Drums* does the same with the concept of family and its importance in a person's life. One of the major notions—developed throughout the books—is that a family doesn't consist only of people who share DNA, nor does a family cease to be important if the members of it are separated—or dead. Jamie and Claire's family as they settle in North Carolina consists of Fergus and Marsali, their son, Germain, and Jamie's nephew Ian—as well as Brianna, the daughter Jamie has never seen.

As for that daughter, her shock at learning the truth of her parentage leads her to find her family and risk everything to save them, while Roger MacKenzie Wakefield (born a MacKenzie but adopted by his great-uncle) risks everything for *her* sake—and becomes her family, as well, along with her child, Jeremiah (who may or may not be Roger's but whom Roger claims firmly as his own).[11]

As Brianna writes in her note to Roger, enclosed with her family silver, photos, and memorabilia: *"Everyone needs a history. . . . This is mine. . . ."*

The Fiery Cross—Community

The Fiery Cross[12] continues the "building" sense of the books, from courtship to established marriage to family and now to the formation of a community, as Jamie reclaims his original destiny as laird and leader, supporter and protector of a community. We saw him do this (briefly) at Lallybroch and

---

[10] *Yes, there* are *hurricanes off the coast of Georgia in the spring. The U.S. government, for reasons best known to itself, collects and publishes all sorts of factual arcana, and among these is a sprightly volume that lists every hurricane recorded as having touched the coasts of the States since 1795 or so. Check out the U.S. Government Printing Office sometime; the results are either horrifying (if you're a taxpayer) or fascinating (if you're a researcher of any sort).*

[11] *Some astute readers have noticed the large number of orphans in the books: Claire, Roger, Fergus, Jane, and Fanny . . . In part, this is just a matter of emotional and logistic simplification. If you have people being moved around in time and/or space and subjected to physical and emotional upheaval,* and *they have parents, siblings, grandparents, cousins, etc., all over the place,* and *you wish them to be normal people with feelings of empathy and attachment—then everything's going to be much harder if you jerk them out of their setting, and they're constantly having to worry about the effect of their disappearance on a parent or sibling or wonder what on earth Great-Aunt Maude will think when they don't turn up for their usual once-a-month visit at the nursing home. . . .*

[12] *It's pronounced "FY-er-ee." (As in "Fire.") I was quite surprised, when this book was published, to find how many people had evidently never encountered the word, as readers constantly asked me if it was* "The FEE-ry Cross . . . ?"

then during the years after Culloden, when he led the prisoners at Ardsmuir and kept them (mostly) sane and alive by forging them into a community. Jamie has always been defined (to himself, as well as to the reader) by his strong sense of responsibility, and here we see it in full play, as he gathers tenants to his land at Fraser's Ridge, with the help (and occasional hair-raising hindrance) of the time travelers in his family.

As with any worthwhile story, the self-definition of a protagonist (whether that's a single person or a group) is a process both of discovery and of conflict. Stumbling blocks, opposition, and danger are the tools that nature uses to carve a striking personality from the native rock. And thus we see not only the formation of the community of Fraser's Ridge (a parallel and microcosm of the emerging America) but the individual struggles of Jamie, Claire, Brianna, Roger, and others, to fit into their changing environment and preserve their own identities and discover their callings in the process.

A Breath of Snow and Ashes—Loyalty

I'm tempted to say that the one-word theme of this book is "survival," but the means by which so many people survive the vicissitudes of a world spinning rapidly out of control is really a better theme, I think. In this instance, we explore the fierce loyalty of Claire and Jamie to each other and to their family. But beyond loyalty to people, loyalty to ideals and ideas is a huge thing at this time in the history of America, and the conflict of those loyalties is paradoxically both the cause of social fracture and the means of survival when the world is coming apart at the seams.

We see other forms of loyalty at work—the loyalty of greed and self-protection, among the Brown gang and Hodgepile's band of marauders; the loyalty to tradition and leaders among the Cherokee; the loyalty to King, country, and regiment shown by John Grey—and the loyalty of friendship, as we see between Lord John and Jamie.

And ultimately we see the loyalty and love of parents, who will make any sacrifice for the sake of their children and the future.

An Echo in the Bone—Nexus

The icon on the cover of the U.S. edition of this book is a caltrop—a military weapon dating back to Roman times.[13] The icon on the U.K. edition of the book is a very beautiful skeletal leaf—showing the superiority of the Orion art department to my own artistic instincts but embodying the same underlying concept: the complex and fragile linkages between people, times, and circumstance.

The book follows four major story lines, which connect in major and minor ways and—depending on which cover image you prefer—display the importance and resilience of such connections in time of wars and personal conflicts or show the underlying veins of nurture and sustenance between people that keep them whole in spite of the stresses of passing time.

As with *A Breath of Snow and Ashes*, I considered an alternate one-word theme—in this case "mortality." Not death, as such, but a realization of the finite nature of life and what this does to people. That was a much harder concept to put on a cover, though.

[13] *The Romans used large economy-sized caltrops to disable charging elephants, while modern day highway-patrol units use smaller ones to stop fleeing cars. It's a versatile weapon.*

Written in My Own Heart's Blood—Forgiveness

If *Echo*'s word was "nexus," most acute readers are probably expecting *MOBY*'s to be "spaghetti"—or, possibly, "octopus."[14] It isn't, though; it's "forgiveness"—both the giving of that balm, and the refusal to forgive, and what giving or refusal does to both giver and recipient in either case.

We see this concept in operation among the major characters—particularly with regard to William's response to discovering his true paternity, and with regard to Claire's efforts to deal with meeting the man who raped her *and* her response to what Jamie does about it. But we also see it in the lesser passages dealing with incidental characters: Mrs. Bradshaw and the slave Sophronia, for example. Mrs. Bradshaw shows a courageous determination to help the girl (thus forgiving her for what might have been seen by a lesser woman as complicity in her husband's infidelity), despite her inability (and who could wonder at it?) to forgive her husband and the apparent internal struggle the situation costs her.

Rachel forgives Ian instantly upon his confession that he was married before and his admitting the fear that he might not give her children.

Jamie forgives Claire and, reluctantly, Lord John, for having slept with each other while thinking him dead—but can't bring himself to forgive Lord John for baldly acknowledging his own desire for Jamie.

Claire instantly forgives Jenny, the sister-in-law she once loved deeply. Jenny emphatically doesn't forgive Hal, the commander of the men who hurt her family and contributed to her husband's death—but she counsels and supports Claire, who must deal with her realization that the man who raped her is alive, by sharing her daughter's experience.

Buck MacKenzie can't forgive himself for the ways in which he failed his wife. Roger explicitly forgives Buck for his role in getting Roger hanged—but demonstrates the boomerang effect of forgiveness, in which the sense of injury returns and must be dealt with afresh.

Fanny forgives William and Jamie for not being able to save Jane—but you can plainly see that they don't forgive themselves and will live with the effects of their failure for some time.

"Spaghetti" is probably the right term, really. . . .

---

[14] *I told my various editors for a year before publication that I wanted an octopus on the cover of the book (I'm fond of octopuses, and there* are *eight major viewpoint characters—with attached story lines—in the book). The usual response to my cover suggestions is a polite silence, obviously in hopes that I will come to my senses before anything actually has to be done. As it was, I found a very beautiful octothorpe—and after frustrating several attempts on the parts of various art departments to hide it in a brooch or other piece of jewelry (as I pointed out to a new U.K. editor, "Male historical novelists get castles and swords; the female ones always get jewelry. You might as well stamp* WOMEN ONLY *on the cover, and I don't write women's fiction. We're not doing that." And to their credit, we didn't. I got a castle, a sword, and a number of other interesting icons, only two of which look like brooches, but at least they look like they could be the sort you clasp a military cloak with. I just don't do girly), we compromised on the wax seal with embedded octothorpe. It's a less striking design than the simple black octothorpe-on-white-background I'd originally envisioned, but it has more story value.*

Recipes

"You know," my husband observed over dinner the other night, "nobody's going to have to write a biography of you, or do scholarly analysis of your books, or theorize about what you were like after you're dead. You already wrote it all down for them."

He's, um, not exactly *wrong* there. My favorite review (so far) of *The Outlandish Companion, Volume One (Revised and Updated),* describes my style as "endearingly garrulous. . . ."

Actually, it's just what I call the "teacher gene." I feel a great compulsion to explain things accurately—and as completely as possible. (Or, as my husband puts it, "You're congenitally incapable of losing an argument.") I can't say that this book is a complete picture, either of the *Outlander* books or of me—but it does probably add to the corpus. And two of the questions that people often ask me—which aren't specifically addressed in this book—are 1) what's your daily routine like? and 2) what do you like to do when you're not writing?

The first question there will have to wait, because my daily routine is changing pretty much . . . well, daily, at this point, given that I've added "show consultant" and "scriptwriter" to my résumé, that I'm constantly invited to go do weird but interesting things (in March of this year, I was invited to speak at the Oxford Literary Festival—a great honor!—and the very next day, I was invited to come be "godmother" to a river cruise ship, christen it in France, and sail down the Seine for four days. Neither of which were things I'd ever thought of doing, but both great fun), and that I do have a lovely husband with whom I like to spend my time, and we often go places and do things that have nothing whatever to do with my work, thank God. . . .

But as to the second . . . Well, when I'm not writing, I read. Lots. All the time. (See "*The Methadone List.*") I knit, as time and the necessity to sign billions of books, tip-in sheets, and book plates allows. I watch old science fiction/fantasy movies, *Perry Mason* and *Twilight Zone* reruns, and Alice in Wonderland on TV with my husband. I watch the daily footage from the *Outlander* show by myself. I dig in my garden (I grow salad vegetables, herbs, and flowers. I grow grapes, too, but mostly by accident. And the ants eat them). And I cook.

Enchiladas

My father was always one to recognize both merit and shortcomings. Consequently, while he was often generous with praise, all his compliments came with a "BUT . . ." attached. "This is wonderful, BUT . . ."

In fact, I remember only three unqualified compliments from him. Thirty years ago, he told me that my swimming stroke was perfect. Twenty years ago, he told me that my children were beautiful. And on Christmas Day, two weeks before he died, he told me that my enchiladas were as good as his. (I have witnesses!)

Christmas Day was the last time I saw him. But he'll always be with me, in the pull of water past my arms, in the faces of my children—and in the smell of garlic and chili, floating gently through the air of my kitchen.

For them as don't know, an enchilada is an item of traditional Mexican food, composed of a tortilla (mostly corn tortillas) rolled into a cylinder around some type of filling (traditionally cheese but can be anything from chicken or beef to spinach, mushrooms, and seafood, particularly in nouveau Southwest or *turista* restaurants), covered with spicy sauce, and baked.

The traditional (cheese) form requires:

garlic
olive oil
flour (a few tablespoons)
tomato sauce
red chili (in any usable form: puree, frozen, powdered, or already mixed with the tomato sauce, which is my preferred variety; I use El Pato–brand tomato sauce, which has the chili already in it)
canola oil (or other light cooking oil)
cheddar cheese
white or yellow onion
corn tortillas

I'm not giving quantities as such, because you can make enchiladas in any quantity—but if you're going to the trouble, you might as well make a lot of them. (They freeze well, though the tortillas will degrade when frozen and give you enchilada casserole rather than discrete enchiladas.)

As a rule of thumb, a pound of cheese will make about a dozen enchiladas; sauce takes about one to one-and-a-half cans of El Pato and about three to four tablespoons of olive oil. I almost always use three cans of El Pato and end up with two and a half to three dozen enchiladas.

Procedure:

All right. For starters, mince four or five cloves of garlic finely. Cover the bottom of a heavy saucepan with olive oil (about ⅛-inch deep) and sauté the garlic in the oil (the bits of garlic should just about cover the bottom of the pan). *Cook until the garlic turns BROWN, but be careful not to burn it.*

Turn heat down to low (or pull the pan off the burner temporarily) and add flour, a little at a time, to make a *roux* (about the consistency of library paste). Add the El Pato (or plain tomato sauce) and stir into the *roux*. Add water, in an amount equal to the tomato sauce (I just fill up the El Pato cans with water and dump them in). Stir over low heat to mix, squishing out any lumps that may occur. If you used plain tomato sauce, add chili to taste (or if you use El Pato and want it hotter, add extra chili).

Leave on very low heat, stirring occasionally, WHILE:

1) Heating oil (I use canola oil, but you can use any vegetable oil, including olive) in a small, heavy frying pan over medium heat, and watching it as it gets hot; if it starts to smoke, it's too hot—turn it down.

2) Grating cheese.

3) Chopping onion coarsely.

At this point, the sauce should have thickened slightly and will cling to a spoon, dripping slowly off. Turn off the heat under the sauce. (If at any time the sauce seems too thick, stir in a little more water.)

Now put out a clean dinner plate for assembling the enchiladas and a baking dish to put the completed ones in.

With a pair of tongs, dip a fresh corn tortilla *briefly* (just long enough for the oil to sputter—two to three seconds) into the hot oil. Let excess oil run off into the pan, then dip the now-flexible tortilla into the sauce, sort of laying it back and forth with the tongs to coat both sides.

Lay the coated tortilla on the dinner plate (and put down the tongs). Take a good handful of cheese and spread a thick line of it across the center of the tortilla (you're aiming for a cylinder about two fingers thick). If you like onions in your enchiladas (I don't, but Doug does, so I make half and half), sprinkle chopped onions lightly over the cheese. Roll the tortilla into a cylinder—fold one side over the cheese, then roll up the rest of the way—and put the enchilada in the baking dish. (They won't have a lot of sauce on them at this point.)

When the baking dish is full, ladle additional sauce to cover the enchiladas thoroughly, and sprinkle additional cheese on top for decoration (I also sprinkle a few onions at one end of the baking dish, so I know which end is onion). Bake at 300 degrees for ten to fifteen minutes—until cheese is thoroughly melted—you can see clear liquid from the melted cheese bubbling at the edge of the dish, and the enchiladas will look as though they've "fallen in" slightly, rather than being firmly rounded. Serve (with a spatula).

The method is the same for other kinds of enchiladas; you'd just make the filling (meat, seafood, etc.) as a separate step ahead of time, and use as you do cheese. For chicken enchiladas, brown diced chicken slowly in a little oil with minced garlic, onion, and cilantro (coriander leaf)—red and green bell pepper optional, and in very small quantity.

It usually takes me a little more than an hour to do three dozen enchiladas, start to finish. Once the sauce is made, cheese grated, etc., though, the assembly is pretty fast.

Hope y'all enjoy them!

—Diana

Drunk Chicken Pasta Salad

Warning: This is kind of addictive, so if you want leftovers, make a lot of it.

Ingredients:

garlic (lots)
1 medium red onion
extra-virgin olive oil
3–4 large chicken breasts (1 breast per person, but you can't usually fit more than 4 in a large sauté pan)
tequila (any kind)
bottled margarita mix
1 lb. asparagus
2–4 T. butter
rosemary
basil
marjoram
oregano
6–7 large mushrooms (just the usual white or brown cèpe type, though if you really like other kinds, you can certainly substitute or use them in addition. Just be

careful if you use portobello, as the gills will shed dark stuff all over the pasta)

1 lb. farfalle (bow tie) pasta (I like Barilla, myself)

artichoke hearts—2 small jars or 1 large one

about 1 cup of olives (pitted, preferably, and strong-flavored, but any kind you like. Spanish queen olives are good; so are kalamata and the big green Greek olives. I don't recommend the little Sicilian ones, just because they're such a pain to cut up)

1 pkg. Good Seasons Zesty Italian salad-dressing mix

a good balsamic vinegar

fresh Romano or Parmesan cheese, grated or shredded

1 very large bowl

Procedure:

Okay. To start, you mince up four or five (or six or seven, depending on size and how much you like garlic) cloves of garlic, plus about a third of the red onion. Sauté two-thirds of the minced garlic and all the chopped onion in a deep frying pan with enough olive oil to cover, and add some rosemary.

Trim the chicken breasts, then gash each one deeply several times on both sides. Put chicken in the sauté pan to brown, and pour a tablespoon or so of tequila over each breast. As the chicken cooks, alternate additional applications of tequila with equal applications of margarita mix. As the chicken browns, the liquid in the pan will cook slowly down into a thick blackish glaze; make sure the breasts are well coated on both sides with this. Continue until chicken is completely cooked through, then set aside on chopping board.

While the chicken is browning, sauté the remaining third of the minced garlic and red onion in a couple of tablespoons of melted butter. Break cleaned asparagus into small pieces (one or two inches long) and add to sauté pan. Add herbs, finely minced. Add sliced mushrooms, stirring frequently. When asparagus is tender and mushrooms have absorbed all the butter, set aside.

Cook the pasta in a large quantity of boiling water. While it's cooking, quarter the olives, halve the artichoke hearts, and slice the remaining red onion into thin rings.

Mix the Good Seasons salad-dressing package with balsamic vinegar and extra-virgin olive oil.

Dice the cooked chicken breasts.

In a very large bowl, combine a) the sliced olives, artichokes, and onions, b) the sautéed asparagus and mushrooms, c) the diced "drunk" chicken, and d) the cooked bow-tie pasta. Slosh about three-quarters of the salad dressing over the mixture and toss thoroughly.

Serve warm, with fresh Romano or Parmesan cheese grated or shredded on top and additional dressing as desired. (If you do manage to have leftovers, it's very good cold, though you can of course reheat it.)

It's not at all difficult, but it *is* time-consuming; it normally takes me about an hour and a half to do. Worth it, though!

—*Diana*

New Year's Green Chili

What do you want to eat on New Year's Day? Well, if you ask a Scot what the ideal breakfast is to follow a proper Hogmanay piss-up, it's a sausage square or bacon butty,[1] washed down with a can of Irn-Bru.[2]

If you ask a New Mexican, though . . . it's green chili, with eggs, beans, tortillas, or all three.

This is my father's green chili, which I watched him make hundreds of times. He never wrote down the recipe, but it's a fairly easy dish—and it's one that gets better with standing, so good to make it the day or night before.

Ingredients:

oil—I use olive oil, but my dad used corn oil (the only "vegetable oil" commonly available at that time), and canola, safflower, or any other oil you like will work fine

6 or 7 cloves garlic, minced

an equivalent amount of onion, minced

1–2 lbs. diced/sliced lean beef—any kind will do, but try to get some without a lot of gristle or fat. The sort you'd use for stir-fry is good

2 cans Ro-Tel tomatoes. I use the kind spiced with lime and cilantro, but there are several types; any that you like will work. This recipe specifically requires Ro-Tel canned tomatoes, though; I take no responsibility for how it turns out if you use something else

a few spoonfuls of flour—regular wheat flour (unless you're gluten free, in which case use quinoa or whatever works for you)

2 cans hot green chilis (diced)

2 cans mild green chilis (diced)

You can adjust the proportions of hot and mild to suit your own palate. Using an equal amount of each produces a dish that's spicy but not hot enough to burn your mouth.

Procedure:

Use a large cooking pot—four quarts or so. Put in enough oil to cover the bottom of the pot. Add the minced garlic and onions and sauté over medium heat, stirring now and then, until the alliums (the garlic and onions) just begin to brown.

Add meat and brown, stirring frequently. When meat is completely browned, sprinkle it with flour. You want to coat the meat but not have big lumps of flour, so just stir it in a little at a time.

Dump in the tomatoes and green chilis and stir.

This is basically it. The rest is just cooking: you need to simmer this for at least an hour (more is better), stirring every ten minutes or so to prevent sticking or scorching, and adding a little water every so often as it cooks down (you're aiming for a consistency rather like freshly cooked oatmeal, though tastes differ—some people prefer a thinner, more watery consistency, which is

[1] *The sausage isn't bad. Bacon butties are, on the whole, vile. "Bacon" in the U.K. is not what you in the United States are used to; it's limp, stringy, ultra-salty, thin-sliced fatty ham. Serve in a squidgy white bun with ketchup, and you've really got something. Mind you, contemplating this probably* would *take your mind off the hangover. . . .*

[2] *Imagine a combination of Karo corn syrup and club soda, dyed a brilliant orange. Then think what your intestines will look like after drinking it.*

fine. Just add water to achieve the texture you like).

Once the chili is made, you can turn off the heat, cover the pot, and let it stand overnight, heating it up to eat the next day. You can eat it fresh, but it's really better if it stands; the acids from the tomatoes and chilis tenderize the meat and mingle to give the dish a deeper flavor.

Serving:

Green chili can be eaten alone, in a bowl with a spoon—or you can make burritos of it (my own personal favorite), spooning a line of green chili down the middle of a flour tortilla (any size), with or without beans added, then folding over one side of the tortilla, folding up the bottom, and folding over the other side. (Pinto beans are traditional, and the kind I always use for this. I don't usually bother cooking the beans myself, though; Ranch Style pinto beans in a can work fine.)

But it's a versatile dish; it works well served over fried eggs or mixed with scrambled eggs, over grilled steak or hamburger, or just mixed with beans and eaten with a spoon.

As to what you wash it down with, beer is traditional, but I generally have Diet Coke. Champagne is fine, though, if you happen to have some left over.

Happy New Year!

Part Eight

THE INVISIBLE TALENT

Author's Note: "Talent" is what publicists, producers, and agents call the people who provide the visible face of entertainment—actors, for the most part. But anyone who is even temporarily appearing in his or her own persona is "talent"—even me. But what about the people who give so much to the TV show and the world of Outlander, *who normally* don't *show their faces and talk about what they do?*

I asked a few of the many, many talented people who create the world of the TV show (and other aspects of the ever-increasing world of Outlander*) to give us a brief glimpse of what they do and how they do it.*

TERRY DRESBACH

Costume Designer

Author's Note: Terry kindly allowed me to reprint here three of her excellent blog entries, dealing with the work she and her brilliant costume department do on the Starz Outlander *TV show. The blog itself—titled* An 18th Century Life*—is at terrydresbach.com and well worth reading in its entirety. Not only for the entries but for the glorious pictures, which we are, alas, not able to reproduce for you here, owing to legal constraints and to the limitations of black-and-white printing.*

WHAT WE DO

Let's see, what are we currently doing?

Well, we have found the 24,000 buttons, give or take a few thousand. It seems I underestimated how many we needed.

We have dyed and decorated about three–four thousand shoes. We've made about a thousand costumes in the last six months. That means frock coats, waistcoats, breeches, shirts, cuffs, stocks, coats, gowns, skirts, stomachers, caraco jackets, capes, petticoats, chemises, corsets, fichus, cuffs, shawls, reticules. We have accumulated gloves and jewelry, made and decorated hats, dyed and printed thousands of meters/yards of fabric.

Last weekend Ron and I did our first appearance together at a fan convention organized by UK *Outlander* fans. It was an amazing experience. I had the opportunity to give a talk about what I do, what we do in the costume department, and it inspired me to reach out to the broader audience and share a bit more of the process of costume design.

It is the same basic process that all Costume Designers and Costume Departments work to, with variations on the theme depending on if you are working on a Space Odyssey or a Western. But there are always particulars to any creative project.

As I have referenced before, no two snowflakes are alike.

I wasn't so sure I wanted to do *Outlander* three years ago. Yes, it was a book series I loved and read many, many times since they were first released, but I knew how huge it was, and one of the reasons I got out of the business over a decade ago was the dwindling amount of time given to prep these massive shows. Prep, as we call it, is the period of time before a show begins where each department pulls everything together needed to do a show. The Art Department builds the sets, Costume Department makes the costumes, Props make all the props, Writers write, and so on. You live and die over the course of a season depending on how much prep time you get. That amount of time decreases every year in our business, so you rarely get the time needed. I knew there wasn't going to be enough time to do a massive show like *Outlander,* without it being completely crazy. But Ron wore me down, and I finally agreed.

So this process begins with reading the scripts. That's when you get a feeling for the tone and direction of a piece, where you begin to get to know the characters and the story. But at this point there were no scripts yet, but there was a book and I figured that would be a tremendous help as I knew the story and characters so well. Sometimes scripts are really bad, but sometimes you get an opportunity to work with a gifted writer like Ron Moore, and that makes everything better, on every level.

So, that was a plus.

The second plus was that I was married to the Executive Producer of *Outlander,* and figured that would put me ahead in the information department. Information in the film and television business is like some sort of secret buried treasure. Those of us who make the costumes and build the sets spend weeks trying to glean any information we can. What are we doing? When are we doing it? Where will it be, and WHO is doing it?? All of those answers are locked in some secret vault, and we are safecrackers doing everything we can to get in. Usually we end up just hurling our crowbars at the damned thing after all else has failed. Living with the vault keeper seemed like it might help.

So based on those two "pluses," I threw my brain and every bit of sense I possessed out of the window and signed on. In retrospect, I cannot help but laugh, that cynical me, who knows exactly what this is like, was still so idealistic and optimistic, still believing that this one would be different from all the others. This is a woman who once went temporarily blind in one eye on a show, due to stress. Believe me, I am no lightweight, I am a tough broad, but the closest thing I can think of to being in the film business would probably be the military, albeit with no REAL weaponry.

We needed about twenty weeks minimum to prep a show of this size. When all was said and done, we had eight.

Eight weeks out, we had a raw space, no tables, no sewing machines, no phones, no racks, no crew, no cast, no costumes. We had also discovered that we were not going to be able to rent any costumes except the barest minimum. Every TV show and movie in Hollywood was shooting in the UK, and the vast majority of costumes were not available.

To top it all off, I had personal challenges. My family was unprepared for me to get back in the business, we had two teenagers still in school, and had just moved into a new house. I had been out of the business for ten years and all of my crew had scattered, not that I could take any of them anyway. I knew NO ONE in the UK in the costume game. No contacts, no one who knew anyone, no one at any of the rental houses, no dyers, no equipment hires, no suppliers, not even fabric stores. Like any business, you spend years building contacts you can call on when you need them, and I had nothing. But yeah, let's walk away from life as we know it, kids, pets, unpacked boxes, and do this!!

So, back to prep. The first thing you need to do is to find is a really good Costume Supervisor.

A Costume Supervisor is your right hand on all things of a practical matter. They are the Project Manager. While you deal with everything creative, and even though you are responsible for the budget and oversee the running of the department, you need someone who will deal with all the nuts and bolts. So the supervisor hires the crew and has ALL the contacts and connections for everything else. In this case, as I had none, this position was the key to happiness and fulfillment. Will any crew member be good or bad? In our business, we try to get a crew together that we can keep for years and years, so starting from scratch is scary. As I had none, I hired a costume supervisor recommended by our UK producer. It is a leap of faith. The wrong choice can be disastrous.

Once the supervisor was in place, we could get started. But it wasn't quite so easy. Just as there were no costumes available, there was almost no crew available either. Every studio is currently filming in the UK right now, taking advantage of tax breaks, like Canada in the 90s. Almost everyone is employed. Crew is at an absolute premium, so finding anyone to work in such circumstances was problematic at best. The few people who were available were highly sought after in a highly competitive market.

Another challenge.

So we searched for crew, and while we were climbing that little mountain, we turned our attention to building a costume house. When you do a show you need access to resources, supplies, and vendors. Very few of those exist in Scotland. If you want to rent a costume, it has to come from a costume house in London. If you're in the States, it comes from a costume house in Los Angeles. But that means that someone has to fly to London to find that costume, that fabric, the buttons, everything, every time we need something. We didn't have time for that. So we had to build our own Costume House, filled with everything we need.

Our Costume Supervisor had found an Assistant Designer, and the beginnings of a crew of 12. We needed sewing machines and the tables to put them on, lighting, phones, desks, shelving, office supplies, hangers, irons, steamers, racks, dyeing vats and dyes, aging supplies, sewing supplies, hooks, tapes, linings, interfacing; an endless list of items. And understand that it is not a home sewing kit, it is an industrial sewing kit. Hundreds and hundreds of spools of thread, a couple of thousand hangers, thousands of yards of fabric. It is big, really big.

Where do you hang all the clothes, and store all the shoes, and accessories? Racks and shelves, enough to hold hundreds and hundreds of costumes. You have to install a racking system that goes from floor to ceiling in the warehouse. Floor to ceiling shelving systems also have to be built, and hundreds of boxes purchased to store everything in. The aging and dyeing department has to be set up. They are seriously an industrial endeavor. They need to dye and age hundreds and hundreds of items. Chemicals, machinery, these women actually blow torch costumes to age them.

Setting all that up takes months that we didn't have. But you have no choice but to go forward and hope for divine intervention.

The Assistant Designer is absolutely essential. They have to live in your head. The

Assistant Designer is the one that you download everything to. They are the one who see it through, taking your sketch to the cutters, who make the patterns and cut the fabric. They make sure the fabric is dyed exactly that right shade you want, and make sure it all happens on schedule. They gather all the bits and pieces, help with research and sourcing materials, schedule the fittings, and interface with our set crew.

While the Assistant Designer is buying bolts and bolts of woolens and linens in London, the equipment begins to arrive, and the fabric is shipped in from London, the cutters and makers are starting to show up. But we still have no actors, so we start them making extras clothing, while we wait.

When I am not figuring out how much rack space we need, I am designing, thankfully for characters I know so well. In the beginning of a show, everyone wants to see sketches, the studio, the network, directors and producers. The first part of my job is to put what is in my head onto paper. So, you do a million sketches. It is harder than one would anticipate. Not only do you have to do a lot of them, because you need to convey a real overview of the entire season and all the characters, but those drawings need to be good. So you draw, and redraw, then redraw again. A lot of designers hire illustrators, but I can't do that. Drawing is what I do, and it is where the design is formed. I wouldn't be able to do it any other way.

On *Outlander* it became very clear not long after arrival that everything I thought the costumes would be was completely irrelevant, due to the climate. I had to throw out everything I had designed before coming to Scotland. If the characters of *Outlander* had pranced around in the fine silks associated with the 18th century, they would have all died. Scotland is so very cold and damp, and it was clear that people would have had to wear fabrics much heavier and warmer. I had to figure out how to redo the 18th century silhouette in heavy woolens, something a lot easier to do with paper and pencil than actual fabric. But eventually it began to take a shape of some sort, though it felt very vague and theoretical. Nothing to really grasp a firm hold onto. No solid research, paintings that can be anything the painter or subject wants them to be. Surrounded by chaos and stress, you just have to hold on and have faith in your own experience and talent. It was a shaky hold after being out of the business for ten years.

Sam Heughan was cast first as Jamie Fraser. He was the easiest actually, because I never saw him as having more than a couple of costumes, and because I had such a clear image of him in my mind. Plus he is a delightful and lovely human being. We have been very blessed with our cast. All lovely and accommodating people. We took care of Jamie Fraser and waited for the rest of the cast.

I am not sure how to describe how absolutely mad things are at this point in production. Building the studio, writing scripts, a million meetings, building sets, finding crew, all at once, everything down to the wire. Waiting for cast, waiting for Claire. All in one breathless, gasping rush. It's a pretty stressful place.

Finally Caitriona Balfe was cast as Claire, two weeks before we began shooting. Then the rush really began! I wish I could tell you how we pulled it off, but I can't really remember. It was pretty tough going, there were a lot of tears, people falling apart, and sleepless nights. Maybe it is a good thing that we really can't remember how we did it, otherwise we might have all run screaming, as we approached Season Two. I think it was just cobbled together out of a mad combination of faith, panic and experience. Things come back to you from years and years ago, like riding that proverbial bicycle, just as everything is about to burst into flames.

But it seems to have all worked out. The response from the fans and the press to the costumes has been wonderful and extremely gratifying for the entire Costume Department.

We are now a department of fifty, instead of fourteen. My Costume Supervisor stuck with me, I have two wonderful Assistant Designers. We've added an embroidery department with four embroiderers and five super embroidery machines. My Alchemy lab (aging and dyeing) are still in their room grinding up frogs and bats' blood, or whatever the hell they do in there. An amazing textile artist has joined our staff, as we continue to discover that we may as well just make everything, since it is what we do. The walls are all in place, the machines hum, the crew is solid, and there are fewer and fewer tears. Things still get really crazy sometimes, but a rhythm and flow is beginning to take place, and a system is taking hold, that keeps us afloat when the going gets rough.

And here we are just beginning Season Two, sewing on about 30,000 buttons.

I often rage against the machine. The pace, the stress, the lack of humanity. My "justice issues," as Ron calls them, run rampant. I am the child of union organizers, after all, and this business needs all the "justice issues" one can possibly throw at it. But Ron gave me a lecture the other night about who I am and what I do. That I need to accept it and make peace with it. I am considering the possibility.

Maybe, just maybe, this is what I do. But don't quote me on that!

THE DEVIL'S MARK

I've been thinking about this episode and what to write. There are no new costumes, unless you count Ned Gowan's lace stock, and maybe Jamie's trews, though we did see those once before.

But our job is so much more than designing really great-looking costumes for the stars of the show. It is about creating a world that YOU the audience can believe. It is about what we do TO those costumes to make you feel that world, to make it feel real. It is about the costumes for all the rest of the people you see on camera, some of whom never say a word. Some have a few lines, but they are as essential as the lead actors.

There are hundreds and hundreds of them, way more of them than our leading cast. They all have to be costumed. We make all those costumes, we age and breakdown all of them, and then we fit hundreds of them over the course of many days, continually through the show. It is a staggering amount of work. My team on this show is truly brilliant, and there is no one whose costume is not as important as Claire's or Jamie's. In a way the costumes on the day players and extras (supporting artists) can sometimes be MORE important, because they don't have to look good, they just have to look real. They are the ones who sell the authenticity, the ones who make you believe what you see on your screens.

Many of you now look at the details on

our lead actors, but when you watch an episode for the 5th time, look at all those other people. Look at the crowd surrounding Claire and Geillis through the streets of Cranesmuir, or in the courtroom. Some of those clothes are made out of old bedspreads and vintage sweaters that have been completely repurposed into 18th-century villagers' costumes. It is extraordinary work, full of absolutely beautiful details and textures. My team seriously rocks.

Then there is what we actually DO to the costumes. If Claire and Geillis are thrown into a filthy, vermin infested pit, you have got to believe it when you see them.

We have a zillion meetings about what is in that pit.

"How wet is it, really?"

"What do you mean, there will be water pouring down the walls?"

"How much water?"

"What are they sitting on?"

"Dry leaves and filth, or wet leaves and filth?"

"As long as everyone knows we only have two of their costumes, and one has to stay clean."

"Are you shooting in sequence, or out?"

"As long as you understand that we are going to have to predict how filthy and torn they are, if you shoot the end before the beginning."

"It might not match in continuity if we do it that way."

"Just want everyone to be absolutely clear!"

Once all of that is done, we set our aging and dyeing on the task of destroying the costumes, slowly, stage by stage, to match what we are shooting. Except Claire's skirt, because we are going to need that for a few more eps, so you can get it sort of dirty, but you may not tear it!

They paint them, dye them, scrape them, burn them in their magical alchemy lab. . . .

It all goes back to Storytelling. The visuals are as much a part of things as the actors, the words, the music. It is all a part of the same piece. Again, that symphony. If the music is wrong, or the costumes too clean or modern, the sets jarring, the hair and makeup too contemporary, then the whole piece is not working in tandem.

Everyone watches television episodes many times now. One of those times, just look at all the sets, then look at how they work with the costumes. Gary Steele, our production designer, and I are lucky, we inhabit each other's creative brains, after 25 years of being best friends. I suppose we became friends because we saw through the same eyes. You should be able to see that when you watch the show. In truth, you can see Ron and I when you watch. We are always in synch creatively, it is how we came together.

It is that old buzzword, synchronicity.

THE COATS

The coats. There has been quite a response to these two coats. What I find fascinating is the focus and interest Claire's coat is receiving. We have seen it before, in a couple of episodes now. But the renewed interest is a great example of how costume design is so much more than "picking out cute clothes." Costume designers create visual ensemble pieces, the same way you have an ensemble of actors, or musicians. The costumes must work together, harmonize, and bring out the best in each other.

We knew this was a very dramatic and key scene between these two characters. It keeps setting up their relationship. How they work together visually, how their costumes reflect and provide contrast to each other, and yet harmonize, is like creating music. Each instrument has its own part to play, but together, you have a symphony.

And it is not just the costumes, it is the environment. What are the surroundings, the colors, whether it is outside or on a set, it all has to come together as one. The real beauty is when it comes together without a lot of effort. I think what a lot of people are reacting to in this episode is our orchestra all finally finding harmony. We are playing now from the same sheet of music, we all know each other and have found a kind of perfect symmetry. Gary Steele and I have worked together forever, and share a kind of visual intimacy that is the closest thing I have ever experienced to a marriage, other than my actual marriage. I don't have to see anything he does ahead of time, and neither does he need to see what I am doing. Whatever we do separately will work perfectly together. Ron is the conductor, the maestro. He brings together all of us and guides us to the harmony. It is hard to sing his praises enough as an artist, I always fear that what I say will be discounted because I am his wife. But he really is a gifted and singular artist.

It can be a beautiful thing when it works.

Claire's coat. Well, we have seen it before. I will put it on a mannequin this week so I can show the details. But for now, here it is.

This coat is dramatic. It served a couple of purposes, the first being that it kept our actress warm. We were sending her out into freezing temps every day, on horseback. This is the hardest-working actress in Hollywood, and we treasure her.

I wanted her to be cozy and comfortable. And beautiful.

I wanted drama. This is the part in the story where we begin to really understand just how courageous this woman really is. She is about to head out into the Scottish Highlands with a bunch of pretty intimidating and fierce men. One woman alone. She had better be pretty fierce herself, and yet very much a woman. A strong woman able to hold her own. This coat supports that. And in this instance, does it really matter if we have a sign that loudly points to its history, and where it came from? We don't have time for that in an hourlong show, we have a story to tell. Suffice it to say that Mrs. Fitz has a prodigious number of trunks stored away, just for times like this.

Enter Geillis.

Who the hell is this strange woman; there is something about her that is clearly different, but what is it? I don't want you to know the answer to that, I want you to not be able to place your finger on who or what she is. I want it to bother you a bit.

This little jacket is based on a real garment, as are all our costumes.

I am so obsessed with this coat. I need to just re-create it at some point. But you are seeing the basic design for the first time in this ep.

The best part of the story is that we were planning an entirely different coat. We had chosen this amazing fabric, and were literally waiting for it to arrive. It was nail biting time, and it was clear the day before shooting that the fabric was not going to arrive in time. One of those moments. You'd better

Claire
Castle Leoch
T. Dresbach 1/13
Claire
through the
Stones
Outlander
- Cream Wool Crepe
- self fabric bow
at neck
- Brown leather belt
- add wool wrap
pre-stones
- Brown leather
brogues
Claire
Wedding Dress
- silver linen
gown
- sheer silk smocked sleeves
- silk stomacher
and underskirt
- metal embroidery
acorn branches
falling leaves
Terry Dresbach
2014

Jamie Fraser

Outlander

- Féileadh-mòr (Great Kilt)
- Brown & Grey Outlander Tartan
- Brown linen waistcoat
- linen shirt & stock
+ Highland Jacket in dark wool
- French Military Boots (18c.)

Terry Dresbach 5/13

figure it out, and fast. So we found this gold fabric on a shelf, but it was kind of dull. So we added the decorative stitching. But it still said nothing much. This was Geillis: In the woods with a Faery babe and Claire!! It had to be special, and by this time it is the night before shooting. I look over on Liz's (our embroiderer) wall, and she has something pinned up there that looks like some sort of disease on the bark of a tree.

"What the hell is that?" I ask our mad scientist. "Oh, just a wee experiment I did with scraps off the floor," she says.

Cut to the chase, we are all digging scraps out of the garbage and off the floor. No, I am not exaggerating. Before you know it, Liz is doing some weird felting technique on the machine. We are patchworking the bark growth onto this coat, and it finally starts to look like something. But it still hadn't completely harmonized. It needed some pop. I pulled out this yellowish/chartreuse thread, and had Liz work that into the mossy growth. Finally we dyed cording to match for a closure, and there it was. When we put it on Lotte, it was absolute magic. That little point! It was gleeful, audacious, once again, Geillis challenges you! A perfect costume moment, created out of thin air, and some stuff from the trash.

I am frequently asked what my favorite garments are. These two coats are at the top of the list. . . .

For all of the historians who will freak about Geillis, again. TRUST US. Trust that we know what we are doing, and that sometimes, you have to just let the story go about its business, and see what happens. I am just not one of those people who reads the last chapter of a book first.

It's Super Rupert, displaying his prowess with skateboard and laser-sword, ready to take on the British army and anybody else who gets between him and his next cup of ale! This delightful cartoon was drawn by Grant O'Rourke, the lovely actor who plays Rupert in the Outlander TV *show, for his son. I saw it, though, was enchanted, and asked his permission to share it with you.*

BEAR MCCREARY

Composer

Author's Note: Bear, like Terry, keeps a wonderful blog, in which he discusses—among many other things—the scoring of each episode, with historical notes, descriptions of the instruments and musical sources, and the emotional necessities of the score. See more at bearmccreary.com.

I have visited Scotland more than once, when I was very young. Little remains in my immediate memory, but the country left an unmistakable imprint on my heart. Scottish music and culture became my passion. Growing up in Bellingham, Washington, my friends and I faithfully attended the Highland Games every year. The games were every summer's highlight, and by the end of each day, the rolling B♭ flat drone of the pipe bands had buried itself so deep in my brain that it would reside there for days, a residual echo. In high school, I blasted bagpipes from my car speakers, and I began researching the folk songs of the Jacobite uprising. I was awestruck by their ability to communicate tales of tragedy and triumph through lyrics with double meaning, woven along deceptively simple melodic lines and evocative harmonic progressions. I fell in love with the writings of Robert Burns and Robert Louis Stevenson. Shortly after high school, I picked up an accordion and began playing folk tunes, transcribing my own arrangements, and composing new harmonic progressions for classic melodies. One of my first was "The Skye Boat Song."

I carried this Scottish passion with me into my professional life. My first job as composer was scoring *Battlestar Galactica*, where I met series creator and executive producer Ronald D. Moore. *Battlestar* offered me the opportunity to write Celtic-influenced themes for uilleann bagpipes and fiddle. After *Battlestar*, I wanted to incorporate bagpipes into all my scores! I quickly found that producers' eyebrows raised when they heard bagpipes, and I realized that if I wanted a career, I would need to write for other instruments instead. Then Ron called me again, to work on his new Starz series, *Outlander*.

I was familiar with Diana Gabaldon's famous series of time-travel novels and delighted that the story centered on the doomed Jacobite uprising of the 1740s. The series has all the sweeping adventure, romance, fully realized characters, and driving tension a composer could ever hope for. Knowing my background, Ron announced my involvement as composer to a crowded hall of fans six months before the series premiered and quipped, "It turns out by happenstance that Bear is a Jacobite . . . so he's the perfect guy to do this."

From the beginning, I wanted to draw predominantly from Scottish instrumentation and folk music. Instruments such as the fiddle, bagpipes, accordion, penny whistle, and bodhrán (a type of frame drum) form the backbone of the score, supported by orchestral strings, haunting vocals, and larger percussion.

The first task to tackle was the series' Main Title, and Ron and I decided it would be my arrangement of "The Skye Boat Song." The melody was perfect, but the lyrics by Sir H. Boulton did not capture the essence of the show. Thankfully, vocalist Raya Yarbrough recalled another set of lyrics by Robert Louis Stevenson. The Stevenson lyrics are better suited to Claire's story, and we altered two words to make them even more so. "Sing me a song of the lad that is gone," a direct reference to Bonnie Prince Charlie, was changed to "Sing me a song of a lass that is gone." This simple alteration connects the lyric more directly to Claire. Raya Yarbrough's intimate and poignant vocal performance solidifies the song's connection to Claire.

Later in the first episode, the score introduces another important new theme, "The Stones Theme," when Claire and her husband, Frank, witness the dance of the Druids at Craigh na Dun. For this important moment, I called in my resident music historian, Adam Knight Gilbert, who confirmed my suspicion that no music from the Druids survives today. With no truly authentic piece to draw upon, I decided instead to adapt the oldest lyrics we could uncover. Adam found several candidates, and from those I chose a poem called "Duan Na Muthairn," or "Rune of the Muthairn." These were drawn from a collection by Alexander Carmichael called *Carmina Gadelica,* published in 1900, which was at the forefront of the Gaelic revival movement of the time period. The song is performed in Gaelic by Raya Yarbrough. In English, the text means:

Thou King of the moon,
Thou King of the sun,
Thou King of the planets,
Thou King of the stars,
Thou King of the globe,
Thou King of the sky,
Oh! lovely Thy countenance,
Thou beauteous Beam.

I set this text to an original theme, composed in Dorian Mode, a scale I employ frequently on *Outlander* for its "old world" flavor and elegant implied harmonies.

Once Claire gets to 1743, I introduce the "Claire and Jamie Theme," the most important musical melody in the series.

I was careful in the early episodes not to overstate this theme. I let their relationship unfold realistically, always allowing their intimacy to happen first and commenting on it with music afterward. The audience needed to wait for their romantic story to unfold, so the music needed to wait as well. Their theme is never heard in its entirety until "The Wedding"—I saved the fullest expression of their melody for their wedding night!

As Claire adjusts to life in the eighteenth century, I explored more historically accurate instrumentation. On her first morning at Castle Leoch, Claire is awoken by Mrs. Fitz, bringing her breakfast and dressing her. Mrs. Fitz's theme sounds like a traditional folk song but is actually an original theme I composed for her. Her tune is jaunty and lyrical, personal and slightly intimidating all at once, like Mrs. Fitz herself. This piece features the viola da gamba, a string instrument popular in the late Baroque period, and a Scottish fiddle. I frequently used the viola da gamba to represent other aspects of Highland life, as well, most notably for Colum MacKenzie's signature theme.

In the first season, I composed over a dozen original themes for specific purposes. However, I also stayed true to my original inspiration and incorporated traditional Scottish folk music wherever possible. I used "Comin' Thro' the Rye" for a lively montage of Claire practicing medicine, "Clean Pease Strae" for an aggressive game of shinty, and underscored the doomed Jacobite cause with heartbreaking renditions of "The Skye Boat Song," "The Highland Widow's Lament," "Ye Jacobites by Name," "MacPherson's Farewell," and several others. I frequently select songs based on their lyrical relevance to a scene. Though they are purely instrumental arrangements when used in the score, anyone who knows the songs will have an augmented experience when they realize the song choices comment on the drama.

Outlander also gave me the opportunity to invent new folk music. The third episode features several musical performances by Gwyllyn the Bard, played by Scottish musician Gillebrìde MacMillan. His final song, "The Woman of Balnain," references a woman who journeys through standing stones, giving Claire hope that she can escape back to her own time. I composed an original song based on Diana Gabaldon's text and collaborated with Gillebrìde so he could perform it on set. I then incorporated his performance into my score to form a single piece of music that seamlessly transitions from on-camera performance to narrative score.

The richly layered characters in *Outlander* make every episode more creatively challenging. Rarely do I write music solely for the obvious events onscreen. Instead, I strive to comment on the subtext beneath the surface. A fantastic example of this kind of scoring is the sixth episode, "The Garrison Commander."

The episode opens as Claire and Dougal travel with redcoats to their garrison. The travel-montage cue I composed is a mixture of English military sounds and Scottish folk instrumentation. Military field drums provide a tense, ominous rhythm, perfectly suited to the rigid British soldiers. Above them, small Scottish pipes, bodhrán, and acoustic guitars offer Highland colors, while the orchestral strings provide an energetic cinematic backbone. The music, I believe, perfectly captures the feeling of clashing cultures as British and Scottish sounds spar against one another.

Once the characters arrived at the garrison, I asked my historian Adam Gilbert about the kind of music an eighteenth-century British officer might be familiar with. We discussed the music of George Frideric Handel and Johann Christoph Pepusch as potential candidates, but their music didn't fit the scene for me. Adam then introduced me to the works of Thomas Arne. Arne was a British composer of the time period, best known to modern-day audiences for his patriotic songs "Rule, Britannia!" and "God Save the King," which would eventually become the British national anthem. Obviously, any of those melodies would have been cliché choices for this scene. However, Arne also composed a short piece for harpsichord and viola da gamba, "Blow, Blow Thou Winter Wind," which worked elegantly. The tune features a harpsichord and viola da gamba that evoke upper-class parlor music. Music-history fans will chuckle knowing that the tune was by the composer most inextricably connected to the British Empire.

Enter Black Jack Randall. Alone, face-to-face with Claire, Randall tells the story of Jamie's lashing. Scoring this scene was a tremendous challenge. My job was to make the scene as excruciating as possible. With a lugubrious bed of heartbreaking strings to constantly heighten the emotional tension, the music poured salt, so to speak, on the audience's wounds, forcing them to watch the horror unfold.

In the lashing scene, the physical tension is obvious: one man ruthlessly whips another. Yet we know that Jamie will survive. So why are we on the edge of our seats as we watch it? The tension comes from trying to anticipate why Randall is telling the story. We are waiting to see what effect the telling of this story will have on his emotional state. While there is always a physical threat to Claire when in Randall's presence (the music has moments of dissonance to reflect them), the scene is told through Randall's perspective, not Claire's. He believes this bloodshed to be beautiful, describing the creation of a "masterpiece." I strove to write a score that would comment on the depths of his psyche that are revealed in his story: his stages of rage, exhaustion, pride, and awe. The music is, in a horrifying way, strangely beautiful.

The joy of scoring *Outlander* is that nearly every scene is constructed with this level of dramatic nuance. As the composer, my job is to help guide the audience through the narrative, and the path is rarely obvious. This is the kind of project I love to score the most, and somehow, I feel that *Outlander* is the score I was born to write. The series allowed me to write the kind of music I had dreamed about since I was a boy, hanging out at the Highland Games, listening to bagpipes and arranging folk songs. In these scoring sessions, hearing the orchestra reach its highest soaring notes while watching the drama unfold, I am frequently overwhelmed with emotion, gratitude, and exhilaration.

The onscreen journey of *Outlander* is just beginning. More drama and music await in the second season and beyond!

Dr. Claire MacKay

Herbalist

Author's Note: I made the acquaintance of Claire MacKay when she was employed as an herbal consultant to the television show, and I asked her whether she might be interested in contributing some of her very extensive expertise in historical Scottish herbology to this book. In addition to her other activities, she's been instrumental in putting together a fascinating exhibition on historical herbs, to be mounted at the Inverness Museum and Art Gallery.

From Highland Heathens to Healthcare Innovation

Gaelic-speaking peoples in the Highlands of Scotland had a simple outlook and way of life that was preserved in proverbs still found in use today. Examples of such proverbs are:

Health is an inheritance to be bequeathed to one's children, or *Man by nature is healthy.*

However, it's the proverb *There is no disease without a remedy, and there is no turning back of death* that really gives an insight into the determination and optimism of the Highlanders in the healing arts as well as their realism in the acceptance of death. In the noble mindset of the early Highlanders, when your time was up, your time was up—no arguments!

Gaelic traditional medicine has a strong association with the official healing physicians of the Middle Ages (namely the Beaton clan) as well as distinctly Celtic influences.

The Celts were lovers of riddles and puzzles, and this is mirrored in many of the incantations and chants (known as *eolas,* meaning "charms") that accompanied the early healing methods of the Gaelic tradition. Also, the many Gaelic proverbs still in use today are a reflection of this entertaining oral tradition of passing on healing and wisdom.

As in many other cultures, in the Gaelic language the names given to medicinal plants are often a window into the world of the ancient people. Plant names often refer to the medicinal use at the time: for instance, *rein an ruisg,* "water for the eye," is the Gaelic name for eye-bright, which has been used traditionally to heal conditions of the eye and improve sight. Additionally, Gaelic plant names may refer to the typical habitat of the plant, and a plant may have several names. *Lus-nan-leac* is an alternative name for eye-bright, meaning "hilltop plant."

Gaelic plant names may also be a way of plant identification, referring to the plant form or shape, such as *Copan-an-druichd,* or "dew cup," commonly known as lady's mantle, which famously collects the morning dew as glittering pearls in the center of its leaves. Names may also point to the folklore associated with the plant: St. John's wort was known as *achlasan Chaluimchille,* "Columba's armpit package," referring to a Celtic fable that reminds us of how St. Columba cured a boy of melancholy by placing the herb under his right armpit. Interestingly, St. John's wort is now scientifically confirmed and in use as an antidepressant. The folklore and stories attached to an herb often remind us of their healing virtues, which the early folk in the Highlands often believed were attributed to divine entities or deities.

During the Great Witch Hunt, the Highlanders in many regions retained their earlier customs. In Catholic areas especially, the Church accepted and tolerated the traditional pre-Christian customs alongside the practices of the Church. There were reasons for this:

1. It was too costly and time consuming to go through the bother of translating Gaelic kirk sessions (of accused witches) into English;

2. Prosecution would have involved relocating the accused from remote Highland places to the cities of Inverness or Edinburgh, to be sentenced—and those were less commutable times.

With few exceptions, the Highlands escaped the persecution of the witch trials that other places in Scotland and Europe encountered and thus preserved the early pagan customs and traditions for much longer than many other places. The Presbyterian Church was less tolerant, and although not many cases were brought to sentencing in the Highlands, the Free Church was known to bully the practice of local customs into hiding.

The survival of the early tradition included the knowledge of medicinal plants, since many cases elsewhere in Scotland involved women sentenced as "witches" merely for such knowledge. For this reason, the physicians of the Scottish Highlands were able to face the eighteenth century and Scottish Enlightenment period armed with an arsenal of in-depth knowledge of native plant medicines. Thus, the Beaton lineage of physicians was to become refined in the advanced knowledge of plant cures and was to go on to influence the first Scottish medical school in Edinburgh and the Holyrood Phy-

sicians' Garden, also in Edinburgh. The teachings of this globally esteemed school of medicine were to inspire the opening of the first American hospital in Pennsylvania, which based its education curriculum on that of the Edinburgh medical school. This came as a direct result of the Scottish settlers bringing with them their knowledge of cures and their medical training.

By this route, it is possible to see how the humble herbal folk medicine of the Highlands has influenced medicine on a global level and helped produce some of the most highly educated physicians in history.

THE BEATON PHYSICKS—CONTEMPORARIES TO THE DRUID PRIESTS?

The Highland hereditary physicians, who went by the family name of Beaton, gained support not only from clan chiefs, who offered them land and funded their education (often abroad): they were also highly esteemed in the eyes of the Scottish court and received prestigious patronages.

Their origin is said to come from an Irish woman named Agnes, who married Angus Og, the Lord of the Isles in the early thirteenth century. She was awarded a dowry of "seven score" of men, among whom were those of the name *MacMeic-bethad*. Among these men were a medical kindred with long-standing medical knowledge in Ireland. In Scotland they would be known from then on as the MacBeths and from the sixteenth century onward as the Beatons.

The Beatons were well versed in Irish medicine and were also Gaelic-speaking. They didn't arrive in Scotland as outsiders but were welcomed with open arms: they both absorbed and were accepted by the local culture. They were well respected, and it wasn't long before they were sitting in high positions within the Scottish courts. In fact, between the reigns of Robert I and Charles II, the Beaton doctors were employed by every Scottish monarch.

Their esteemed position allowed them to amass a wealth that enabled them to travel and bring back copies of medical manuscripts, transcribed into Gaelic, from all over the world. The Beatons' manuscripts that survive today show that their knowledge came from the influence of Greek and Arabic countries as well as from the Latin world. In fact, from the only Gaelic medical manuscript that has been fully translated into English to date (*Regimen Sanitatis, "Rule of Health,"* translated and contributed to by John Beaton of Islay, 1563), we can see that the knowledge the Highland physicians had at the time was far superior to that of their counterparts in lower Britain or other parts of Europe.

Many of the Beaton references cite Hippocrates, and it is interesting that the Hippocratic oath promises:

> *. . . I will hand on precepts, lectures and all other learning to my sons, to those of my master and to those pupils duly apprenticed and sworn, and to no other.*

This is entirely fitting with the hereditary practice of the Highland physicians and indeed of the Gaels as a whole. Over centuries, the Beatons gathered and collated medical knowledge from their travels and from many esteemed medical schools, often translating texts into Gaelic and adding to the teachings their own knowledge of the Highland native plants. These manuscripts remained in the family lineage throughout history, until they were submitted to the national libraries for safekeeping.

Although it is thought that no women were Beaton physicians to the monarchs and that Highland women were not generally educated in the official medicine of the time, the Gaelic medical works are permeated with the teachings of the advanced medical school of Salerno. The school was famed for its attitude of encouraging women as students and teachers of medicine and for disregarding the restrictions of color, creed, and class. It is known that by the nineteenth century there were Beaton women healers in the islands of Scotland, and oral accounts say that there existed female Beaton healers in history before this.

Peggy Beaton is one such healer. She died only a few years ago, in 2013, was a resident on Kyle of Rona, and was known by the locals for her knowledge of herbal cures. She claimed to be a descendant of the famed Beaton healers.

In many ways, this esteemed lineage of wisdom and healing resembled the legendary traveling Druid priests of the pre-Christian Highlands (there is a legend of a lineage of Irish Druids influencing the medicine of Scotland under the reign of Josina, Ninth King of Scotland, second century B.C.: he was said to be educated in Ireland and to have brought back a book of healing cures, learned from Irish Druids). The Beaton physicians in a similar style were healers who absorbed the local customs but also held secret knowledge gained from exotic places, and who were in many ways put on a pedestal by those who encountered them. So, it's not surprising then that life wasn't *always* a bed of roses for the Beaton healers.

PERSECUTED FOR A DIFFERENT KIND OF KNOWLEDGE

In the seventeenth century, on Husabost on the Isle of Skye, a physician by the name of Neil Beaton was accused of witchcraft. It was said during a kirk session that his cures came from a *compact with the Devil* and that he pretended to *judge the qualities of plants and roots by their tastes* and likewise *has ways of Observation of the Colours of their flowers, from which he learns their astringent and loosening qualities.* Unfortunately, the fate of Neil Beaton has not been recorded.

The "doctrine of signatures" was a method of observing traits in plant forms and colors that could reveal their healing virtues, the most humorous being the observation of *Ranunculus ficaria* (commonly known as pilewort), said to have roots that resemble hemorrhoids: traditionally (and in modern times), this plant has been used as a salve to treat piles/hemorrhoids. There is now clinical evidence to show that it is an effective way of treating this condition, and so *perhaps* Neil Beaton was ahead of his time with his observations.

It's also worth noting that we can indeed glimpse certain chemical knowledge of a plant by color alone. We know, for instance, that the green pigment in plants is caused by the presence of chlorophyll, and that berries and fruits that are red, blue, or purplish in color contain antioxidant anthocyanins or carotenoids, and that orange colors in plants are a result of carotenoids or beta-carotenoids. Interestingly, this brings to mind an old wives' tale that eating carrots improves the eyesight: beta-carotene is the precursor to vitamin A, which is now known to be important to eye health.

Taste is also an important way of learning about the qualities of plants. Think of a time when you have tasted something that had "gone off"—your taste buds are a signal to let your body know whether something is good for you or not. There's a reason hemlock doesn't taste good. You don't want to eat a lot of that. Poisons are generally not pleasing to the taste buds.

It may have seemed like the work of the devil in the seventeenth century, but with the advent of modern science we have been able to confirm the presence of certain chemical constituents in plants and we now know the taste of many of them:

Alkaloids—a metallic bitter taste that lingers on the tongue, often at the tip or sides.

Resins—a mildly bitter taste that leaves a waxy coating at the back of the tongue.

Iridoids—an intensely bitter taste over the whole tongue that causes salivation and dissipates quickly.

Coumarins—often smell like freshly cut grass or hay in herbal teas or tinctures.

Acids (such as citric acid, ascorbic acid, and tartaric acid)—are sour and often taste like lemons/vinegar.

Tannins—have a drying and astringent effect in the mouth, drawing in the sides of the cheeks.

Saponins—taste like soap.

Terpenoids and Steroidal Saponins—taste sweet like "artificial sweeteners."

We now know that each of these chemical groups has a general type of action in the body: bitters produce saliva and stimulate secretions, tannins are drying and toning, etc. It is possible that while our predecessors, like Neil Beaton, could not identify the names or isolate the constituents they knew by taste, they were able to identify their action in the body, therefore knowing or approximating the virtues of the plants by taste or smell.

BEATONS: A BRIDGE BETWEEN FUTURE AND PAST

Having arrived from the twentieth century with her advanced medical knowledge, it is perfectly appropriate that Claire should be first appointed as the castle physician in the surgery of Davie Beaton, the previous castle physician. The Beaton physicians of the eighteenth century really represented the future of medicine in the modern world, and while Claire consulted with the likes of many other influential characters in medicine of the time (wise women, folk healers, monks, and native medicine people), as the Beatons did, her role as physician in a lineage of Beatons is representative of her medical knowledge of the future.

MEDICINE OR MAGIC?

Looking at medieval folk remedies in the Highlands, it is impossible to separate the medicine from the magic, because illness and healing were viewed as highly complex processes at the time. Healing was considered in a much more holistic way at that point in history, and although many of the "cures" may appear bizarre to us now, they survived through centuries because they had *some* basis in the experience of these early peoples. It is also important to note that many healing powers attributed to the medicinal plants of the time have been validated by chemical analysis. Perhaps some of the folklore surrounding illness and healing was there to fill in gaps in the early people's understanding of diagnosis or pathophysiology.

Sometimes what was superstitious back then is just logical in modern times. For instance, around Inverness there were sacred wells (*tobar-slainte,* "healing wells") believed to have healing properties. It was believed that no animal should be allowed to drink from the wells, lest an *evil spirit* enter the well and pollute it forevermore. Well, I don't know about superstitious, but I certainly understand the reasoning behind protecting your water supply from pathogen-carrying animals. Fresh and clean water has been a saving grace to the health of many communities throughout time in the Scottish Highlands.

In some cases, it's hard to argue that "cures" are anything but magic. A story from 1901 recounts a Highland woman with a *wen* (boil, cyst, or growth, normally a swelling of a sebaceous gland) on her head. Doctors were not interested in treating *wens* at this time, and her friend known as a "skilly woman" (Scots: "wise woman") offered to remove it for her, if she would follow the treatment accordingly. In agreement, she walked two miles across the countryside every morning before breakfast to the healer's home. When she arrived, she sat quietly in a seat while her friend held a needle over the wen, as if to hold it in place, and mimicked cutting around it with a knife, while making a chant in Gaelic:

> *"The big mountain, the little mountain; the black dog, the spotted dog, the brindled dog."*

It is said that after a week of this treatment the *wen* disappeared permanently.

Of course, we can never know what the *wen* was in the first place. Did it even exist, or was the "healer" a trickster and the only one to see it? Would it have "cured" itself in a week without any treatment? Did the morning walk stimulate the immune system? Or was there an element of the placebo effect at work?

What is interesting is that this type of sympathetic magic is similar to shamanic practices, which can be found in indigenous cultures all over the world. Modern science has proven on many occasions that the mere intention to heal can have powerful effects on the ability to heal. The placebo effect exists, and we don't quite know how it works.

CHARMS, CLOUTIE TREES, AND CLAY PEOPLE

I knew the sort of person she meant; some Highland charmers dealt not only in remedies—the "graiths" she'd mentioned—but also in minor magic, selling lovephilters, fertility potions . . . ill wishes.

—THE FIERY CROSS

The use of charms or effigies was something that existed both for healing and harm in the early Highland culture. Remember Laoghaire's ill wish to Claire? That could easily have been a protective posy of white heather (soaked in urine). A popular lucky amulet, still found to this day. It might not sound appealing, but it's the thought that counts, right? The image of a person was crudely formed in clay, known as a *corp-creadh;* depending on the intent, it was then either cleansed in a stream, for healing, or held over fire and some say destroyed, to cause harm. Another possibility is that it was destroyed to get rid of an illness or negativity. Mrs. Bug's fertility figure of a pregnant woman carved in stone is based on the concept of the *corp-creadh.* The importance of these potent beliefs is that they reflect the strongly held idea that all things have their origin in a higher being. Illness was believed to come from a higher level of consciousness, which was why it was thought that a person's health could be affected on a supernatural level—for better or worse!

I said a brief prayer to St. Bride and slipped it round my neck and down inside the bodice of my dress. I was so much in the habit of wearing the amulet when I set out to practice medicine that I had almost ceased to feel ridiculous about this small ritual—almost.

—THE FIERY CROSS

The belief that everything had a spirit was perhaps a legacy of the *Daoine Sidhe,* "the Shining Ones" or "the People of Peace." These are believed to be an early race of vanquished Celtic pagan gods, who were banished to live underground. It was very difficult for the early Christian Church to persuade the Celts to shun their own deities. They ended up living in coexistence with the Christian saints for a long time, and then these beings became the nature spirits and fairies, dwelling in wild places, so common in the Gaelic folk stories.

In fact, when you visit the Highlands today, you will still find in many places the remnants of the superstitions of the past. Trees beside sacred wells are adorned with cloth rags, blowing in the wind like Tibetan prayer flags, for that is exactly what they are, prayers for healing, originally offered to the deities of the sacred wells. At other sites you will see silver coins studding a fallen tree in a sacred place, such as the "wishing tree" at the Fairy Glen, on the Black Isle. Silver was traditionally offered to the lunar goddesses, a tradition dating to the pre-patriarchal times in Scotland.

Grannie Bacon's Women's Plant

. . . dauco seeds wrapped in a small bag.

As it turns out, Grannie Bacon learned of these seeds from the Indians, and they are used for birth control. Claire remembers Nayawenne and that she referred to this plant as the "women's plant."

In the Highlands, plants with abortive properties were used. In those times, when women were often taken against their will, not to mention the unwanted extra mouths to feed in times of famine, the use of these plants was deemed by some women a necessary skill. In the luxury of our modern society this may seem callous, but in fact "back-street abortion" is still practiced in many developing countries, where female rights are the equivalent of those of these eighteenth-century Highland women. In the eighteenth century, without contraception, it really was a matter of survival. The gift of knowing which herbs could prevent and dispel pregnancy was an empowering one to women healers of the time—and equally one that caused many women healers to perish at the stake during the Burning Times.

The *dauco* seeds offered to Claire by Grannie Bacon (*The Fiery Cross*), along with the crude drawing that Claire recognized as distinctive to the *Umbelliferae* family (think fennel and cumin seeds), is most likely to be the wild carrot, or a relative. The Latin name *Daucus carota* is an intriguing link to the name the Indians give for the plant, suggesting cross-cultural influence. There are several plants in this family, including parsley seed, that were perhaps used as abortifacients (and, if taken regularly, as contraceptives). However, interestingly, carrot has been used as a female plant in many early traditions.

Women's Plant—Phallic Interpretations

The Sunday before St. Michael's Day (Michaelmas) was known in the Highlands as *Domhnach Curran,* or "Carrot Sunday." This whole day was dedicated to customs and rituals relating to the symbolic harvesting and offering of carrots as fertility and love emblems. Young girls would spend the day collecting wild carrots and tying them into small bunches with red ribbons, to offer to the menfolk they were besotted with. Even the digging was done ceremoniously; a triangle was made around the plant, and a three-pointed mattock (symbolic of St. Michael's trident and of the Trinity, most likely referring to an earlier association with the triple aspects of the goddess) was used to dig out the root. Once the carrots were gathered in bunches, women would place them in sacks around a dance hall, where the St. Michael's Day celebrations would be held, with their personal symbol visible to others. Throughout the

night, men would take carrots from a sack and the women would replenish them. When a woman entered to refill her sack, she would say (in Gaelic):

"It is myself that have the carrots, whoever he be that would win them from me. It is myself that have the treasure, whoso the hero could take them from me."

Basically, this was a flirtatious challenge and announcement that she was on the lookout for a suitor.

Fascinating that the carrot was a symbol of love and fertility for young women, as well as being used to procure a woman's courses (bring on menstruation) or as an herbal remedy efficient in terminating a pregnancy. Therefore the carrot was very much an herb of women throughout all stages of womanhood to the early Highlanders, as it was to indigenous women of many other cultures.

Caution! While it is known that carrot seed acts as an abortifacient and was historically used as a contraceptive, it is not known at what dose. Carrot seed is a poison at a relatively low dosage, and women experimenting with it in this context have actually lost their life. Many remedies of the past went out of fashion for a reason. It is also a reminder that a single plant can be a food, a medicine, and a poison all at once.

AMERICA'S CAULDRON OF CULTURES

When the Scots arrived in the colonies of America, they brought with them their physicians, their knowledge of Scottish native medicinal plants, their medical knowledge and skill.

Those that were able to survive the long voyage to reach the coastal regions stepped ashore and unpacked their cultural cargo at all levels of society.

Medics, military men, plantation owners, ministers, and manual workers made themselves at home in the New World.

The First World people—the black African slaves and the Europeans—all congregated in the colonies, and although the advance of the knowledge from the natural world appeared publicly to come from the white Western, predominantly male society, there was inevitably an exchange of knowledge among all cultures.

A GARDEN OF THE FUTURE

Alexander Garden (who named the gardenia flower), a famous Scottish physician, botanist, and zoologist, born in Aberdeen and from the Edinburgh medical school, held a reverence for the knowledge of the indigenous people. He believed that the black slaves of the plantation owners knew more of the natural world and the local medicines than they did. He also developed a successful vaccine during the 1760 smallpox outbreak in Charleston, South Carolina, and inoculated over two thousand people. He later wrote an essay on the medicinal properties of a native plant he discovered in South Carolina, pinkroot. He was a perfect example of the melting-pot effect of the colonies: a Scottish physician, head of the Edinburgh physic garden, familiar with native Scottish cures, who in the colonies learned from the black slaves and the local plants and was also a pioneer of modern medicine, during the advent of inoculations.

O TEMPORA! O MORES!

A lesser-known Scottish physician of this time is William Murray, of Dumfries, an acquaintance of Alexander Garden who traveled to Charleston in the 1750s. His brother, John Murray, later followed and was an esteemed military man who built forts with the Cherokee Indians (whom he described as *savage inhabitants*).

William Murray, the doctor, very much *feels* as if he could have been a real-life Murray MacLeod, the apothecary of *The Fiery Cross.* He is a blend of the contemporary medicine of the time with simple herbal cures, mentioned in his letters, and although the innovation of inoculations was imminent, he, like many, continued to use leeches in his clinical practice:

> *If the loch leeches are lent, all the nursing they require is to keep them in a viol glass with fresh water which must be changed now and then.*
>
> —LETTER (1765) FROM A FRIEND ADVISING HOW TO KEEP LEECHES

Through correspondence between the Murray brothers, their mother, cousins, and their friends, we get a sense of how the world "opened up" during this time and the impact that it had on modern medicine.

Europeans were importing (and exporting) seeds and plant specimens and exchanging cures among themselves:

> *I came here too late in the season to make a proper collection of seeds and plants for him but will in the fall send him a compiled one of all our curious trees and plants.*
>
> —A MILITARY FRIEND SENDS A MESSAGE FOR DR. MURRAY, FROM SPAIN

Remember Claire's joy at finding the contents of Hannah Arnold's medical chests in *An Echo in the Bone*?

> *The herbs were interesting and useful in themselves, being plainly imported: cinchona bark—I must try to send that back to North Carolina for Lizzie, if we ever got off this horrible tub—mandrake, and ginger, things that never grew in the colonies. Having them to hand made me feel suddenly rich.*
>
> —AN ECHO IN THE BONE

African black slaves, away from home, were discovering remedies of their own, and later these would also be included in the modern American Pharmacopoeia. Alcohol was being imported from abroad to make medicines, and news was being sent home of new cures and exotic plants:

> *Would you inform Doctor Murray I have imported from Madeira a piper of the best pale wine which I shall keep during the summer and send home to Carolina in the fall according to his directions.*
>
> —A FRIEND IN THE MILITARY COLLECTS MADEIRA WINE FOR THE DOCTOR TO MAKE MEDICINES WITH

Inoculation was advancing as a new way of tackling smallpox epidemics, which allowed Western physicians to rapidly gain wealth and critical acclaim:

> *... he would now have had an opportunity of enlarging his fortune as the smallpox rages in toun and the doctors are getting money very fast.*
>
> —WILLIAM'S BROTHER, JOHN, WRITES FROM CHARLESTON (1760) TO ADVISE HIM TO RETURN TO HIS MEDICAL PRACTICE

Of course, physicians, botanists, and naturalists wrote home with their latest cures and curious finds:

> *I am pretty positive your lungs are quite sound and that your cough is occasioned only by a weakness of the glands about your throat and in such cases I would advice you to gargle your throat with plum water in the morning and when your cough is troublesome, this I am hopeful will strengthen the laxed parts and in some measure prevent your cough. If it should not answer it can do no harm—only do not swallow it if you can help it. You'll please let me know its success ... I pray for your health and happiness and am, my dear mother, your most affectionate son and humble servant.*
>
> —WILLIAM MURRAY, CHARLES TOWN, MAY 22, 1756

It was the influence of doctors like William Murray and Alexander Garden of the Edinburgh medical school that helped the expansion of healthcare in the United States, beginning with the opening of the first hospital in Pennsylvania (1752).

From the opening of the first hospital in America, the world of medicine organized itself, formed societies, invented the stethoscope, isolated chemicals, and developed anesthetics; then finally, in 1849, Elizabeth Blackwell became the first woman M.D. in America and the first recognized woman on the U.K. register of physicians.

For a while it seemed like the wise women of the past were being honored.

[The correspondence and memoirs of the Murray brothers, John and William, can be found in the Murray of Murraythwaite Estate, Dumfries archives, at the Scottish National Archive (NAS) Centre, Edinburgh.]

WORLD WAR CONFLICTS

Even with the advancement of pharmaceutical science, by the time the Second World War hit in Europe, plants continued to be relied upon as the primary source of medicine. However, there was a problem. Although penicillin had already been discovered, chemists hadn't found a way of producing enough quantity to meet the demand of the battlefield. By this time, 96 percent of the plants needed for medicines in the U.K. came from abroad. There was also malnutrition creeping in from the wartime rationing. With the war in full fury, in 1941, the British government sent out a plea to women's organizations all over the country to forage the countryside for medicinal herbs. Nettles were collected for iron, rose hips to make rose-hip syrup for vitamin C, sphagnum moss for dressings on the battlefield, and many other known native medicinal plants.

Interestingly enough, in this same year the government passed a law in the U.K. that would effectively ban the practice of herbal medicine (with the exception of doctors) until the year 1968.

While women with knowledge of herbs were out collecting them in the countryside for their men at war and children, they were also banned from using them therapeutically for the following twenty-seven years.

With herbs now on the back burner, it was a good thing that antibiotics were swiftly made available to the world. From this point on, physicians (and patients) gave a sigh of relief—for a while—as previously life-threatening conditions became manageable.

ANCIENT BIOTICS

Some way or another, however, history repeats itself, and in this rapidly evolving modern world we live in, we are now confronted with the "megabug" bacteria crisis that threatens a world once protected by antibiotics. MRSA and other antibiotic-resistant strains of bacteria have become a prime topic for researchers. Ironically, in a search for new cures, the world of science is looking once more to the ancient world of traditional cures for ideas. At Nottingham University, an Anglo-Saxon literature researcher discovered an ancient antibiotic cure in an eye-ointment recipe from the tenth-century Anglo-Saxon herbal, *Bald's Leechbook.* This book also lists native Highland remedies, and scientists were intrigued by a remedy that used garlic and another native allium, mixed with ox bile, as a remedy for the eyes.

To their surprise, when the scientists reconstructed this remedy in a laboratory, they found it to be 96 percent effective against MRSA—better than any other agent they had tested.

In an eighteenth-century handwritten herbal notebook recently found gathering dust on a shelf in the library of the Royal College of Physicians and Surgeons, in Glasgow, Scotland, a very similar remedy using the bile from a hare is listed as a salve for *wab of the eye.* This looks to suggest that these tenth-century remedies in *Bald's Leechbook* remained in use, with variations, for a further eight centuries.

REVISITING THE PAST

It is refreshing to think that the healing potential of plants, which were once discarded as heretical and superstitious, can be rediscovered in a beneficial way through the new eyes of modern science.

Accounts of history have been sitting on a shelf for centuries, silently untranslated, waiting to be picked up and rediscovered through a fresh awareness of the world.

Many of the medical manuscripts of the Beaton lineage of healers in the Gaelic medical tradition await translation to this day. Will the medical researchers of the modern world, at some point, travel back in time like Claire, taking with them their modern drugs and knowledge of medicine to develop their own cures and become our "Druid priests" of the future?

AN OUTLANDISH MATERIA MEDICA

Nine herbs from Claire's medicine kit:

Willow Bark

Salix alba (Latin); Saileach or *Saille (Gaelic).*
Parts used: Bark.

> *Boil the leaves of willow trees in watter till thy be thick as a poltice: and Aply them to the Roines of the back as hot as yow can indure it: and if it be at the time when the willows have no lives take the iner Rins of the bark of the tree and in 4 or 5 times dressing it yow will be heall.*
>
> —*An herbal application for a sore back, using willow, from the eighteenth-century handwritten herbal notebook, Royal College of Physicians and Surgeons, Glasgow*

By the eighteenth century, the medicinal use of willow bark for pain relief and treatment of fever was widespread in the Western world as well as in the Orient. Its famed analgesic properties caught the attention of chemists in the early nineteenth century, and by the 1820s a yellow, bitter-tasting compound had been isolated and identified as the "active principle" in willow bark.

Traditional use: Fevers, headaches, pain relief, menstrual cramps.

Modern use: Salicylic acid, an active constituent in willow, is the origin of aspirin.

The name is a derivative of *Salix* (the Latin name for "willow"). It is a modern painkiller, known to reduce fevers.

Outlander: Used as a tea for pain relief in *Outlander,* and later Claire suggests Jamie drink it with sow fennel as a hangover cure in *Drums of Autumn.*

Pine

Pinus sylvestris scotica (L); Guithas (G)—meaning "juicy," in reference to the abundance of sap.

Parts used: Leaves, resin, and bark (traditional use only).

> *There is no tree that looks nobler than it does towering amongst our bens and glens.*
>
> —*Charles Fergusson, 1878 (Gaelic Society)*

The Scots have such a strong identity with pine trees that in 2014 the government officially made it their national tree.

Traditional use: Used topically (antiseptic) and also for "agues" (fevers and shivering, possibly viruses). Respiratory infections. Pine tea was probably used to ward off scurvy.

Modern use: Known as a powerful antiseptic and expectorant, mainly used as a respiratory herb and in antiseptic products. The needles are a good source of vitamin C.

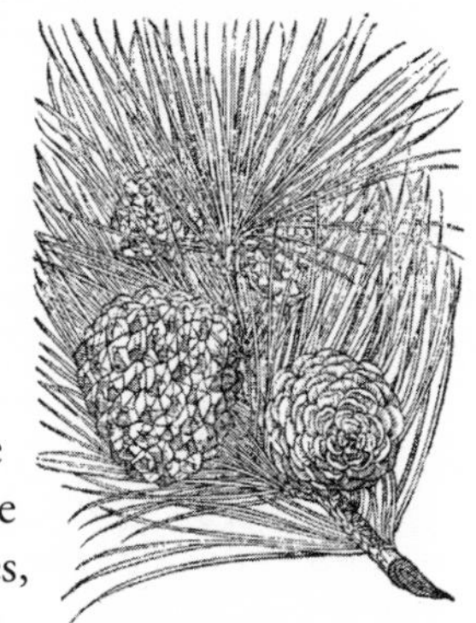

Outlander: Although no reference is made to the use of it medicinally, the fragrant tones of pine permeate the series, from the banks of Lallybroch to Fraser's Ridge and the plantations. Without a doubt its medicinal properties would have been known to Claire and others, and it most certainly would have been used as a beverage or medicine.

Comfrey (Boneset)

Symphytum officinale (L); *Meacan dubh* (G)—meaning "many black roots," referring to the abundance of "dirty" knobbly roots.

Parts used: Leaves and roots.

Traditional use: Comfrey as a *plaister* was applied to broken bones. The roots are highly mucilaginous; however, when applied on thin muslin to the affected part, the pulverized root would set—restricting movement and acting like a modern plaster cast. We now know that comfrey contains a special kind of alkaloid that is absorbed through the skin and promotes the production of osteoclasts, which aid in bone healing. The mucilage was also said to heal ulcers internally.

Modern use: Comfrey is used with caution now, because we know that the alkaloids it contains can be stored in the liver and can accumulate, causing harmful effects. However, the leaf, which contains less alkaloids, is still used by herbalists in treating connective-tissue complaints. The young leaves are a source of B12 and were once part of the staple diet. (The young leaves contain less alkaloids.)

Outlander: From the very beginning, comfrey makes an appearance, as Claire and Mrs. Fitz tend to Jamie's shoulder in the early chapters of *Outlander.* A definite "must have" for the castle clinic.

Foxglove (Poison)

Digitalis purpurea (L); *Lus-nam-bansith* (G)—fairy woman's plant (pronounced ban-SHEE).

Parts used: Leaves and roots.

The common name foxglove is said to derive from a corruption of "folk's glove"—as in "fairy folk."

There are many associations with this plant and the fairies in the Highlands and farther afield.

When the settlers arrived in America from Scotland, this is one of the plants they introduced.

Traditional use: For "dropsy," a condition we now understand as edema resulting from cardiac failure. As a "drawing ointment" on boils or swellings. For the skin complaint we now know as "rosacea."

Modern use: In 1785, one of the most important breakthroughs in medical history was made when glycosides were extracted from foxgloves, which enabled the treatment of heart failure by allowing the heart muscles to work more efficiently. This reduces the workload on the heart and also on the kidneys. It is now only available in drug form, as the plant is very poisonous.

Outlander: Claire makes an extract of dried leaves for Alex Randall for his cough and heart palpitations in *Drums of Autumn.*

St. John's Wort

Hypericum perforatum (L); *achlasan Chaluim-chille* (G)—the "armpit package" of Columba.

An important plant of the Highlands in both folklore and medicine. Carried to ward away the evil eye. St. Columba is said to have cured a boy with melancholy by placing it under his armpit.

Parts used: Herb tops, flowers.

Traditional use: For wounds, as a sedative, and for shock.

Modern use: The chemical composition of *Hypericum perforatum* has been well studied. The documented pharmacological effects include antidepressant, anxiolytic (against anxiety), antiviral, and antibacterial. Used in treatment of depression, anxiety, and sleep disorders; modern clinical studies have shown it to be as effective as antidepressants in treating mild to moderate depression.

Caution! Since St. John's wort can interact with some medications and antidepressant drugs, it's best to consult with a physician or herbalist.

Outlander: Mrs. Fitz adds it to the mix to stop the bleeding effect of willow tea. She comments on the best time to harvest it, at the full moon. Claire also later suggests it for headaches.

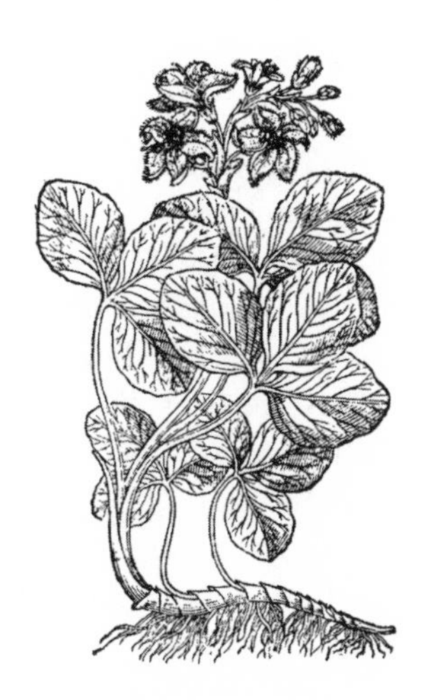

Bogbean

Menyanthes trifoliata (L); *Lui'-nan-tri-beann* (G)—"three-leaved plant," also *milsean monaidh* ("sweet plant of the hill").

Parts used: Leaves, stem, and roots.

Traditional use: A potent tonic, drunk in springtime for that reason; sometimes pulped for the juice and stored in stone jars for winter. Teaspoon doses of the mix were used for coughs, and the leaves were applied to wounds and boils to "draw pus." The roots were eaten in convalescence and also used in place of hops to make beer. Also taken for "weak stomachs" and for pain after jaundice, and was said to "open the tubes" in asthmatic conditions.

Modern use: Today there are still places in the western isles that use bogbean as a tonic in spring, and it is now used by practitioners in treating arthritic and rheumatic conditions, perhaps due to its cleansing action, which helps clear the joints of problematic "waste products."

Outlander: Bogbean was used as a febrifuge at the abbey of Ste. Anne de Beaupre.

Garlic (Wild)

Allium ursinum (L); *Creamh* (G).

Parts used: Aerial parts and bulbs.

Traditional use: On the Isle of Skye, it is recorded that wild garlic was not only used in cooking as a "pot herb" but as a "blood strengthener" and to treat kidney stones all over the Highlands, as well as being used topically in poultices, to draw pus. There is a Gaelic saying that "a cure for everyone is garlic in May butter and a drink with that the milk of white goats," indicating the prolific use of garlic in Highland medicine.

Modern use: Science has now extensively researched the properties of garlic and found it to be highly antibiotic, as are many of the alliums. On top of this, it lowers cholesterol, blood pressure, and also blood sugar levels, making it beneficial in treating some heart conditions, high blood pressure, diabetes, and also infections. A remedy from the tenth century containing wild garlic, or a relative, is currently showing promising signs of a breakthrough in antibiotic solutions against new superbugs such as MRSA.

Outlander: Garlic is mentioned many times, for wound-cleaning mixes and in culinary ways. It is also worn in a silver pomander locket to ward off illness. This is indeed something that was done in many places at the time of the Plague!

Marsh Mallow

Althea officinalis (L); *fochas* or *leamhad* (G)—meaning "itch" or "insipid."

Parts used: Roots.

Traditional use: It's recorded as being used as an herb for lung complaints in the eighteenth century, although it wasn't a common wild plant in Scotland and was most likely cultivated. The abundance of mucilage the plant bestows made it useful in treating inflammation and irritation internally and as an emollient externally. The Gaelic names probably refer to its use for itching.

Modern use: The mucilage content is still used in similar ways today, as a soothing remedy for coughs and catarrh and also for the digestive tract, as well as an emollient topical application for skin complaints and irritation.

Outlander: Grannie MacNab tells Claire it is good for a cough, and it is mentioned as one of the herbs Geillis used to treat her husband's persistent flatulence.

Yarrow

Achillea millefolium (L); *Lus chosgadh na fola* (G)—meaning "the plant that stops the bleeding."

Parts used: Aerial parts.

Traditional use: As the name suggests, yarrow was used both internally and externally to stop bleeding. An ointment was used to heal and dry wounds, and the juice applied to the nose can stop a nosebleed, although the way of administering this treatment was previously to place a rolled-up leaf inside the nostril. Yarrow flowers were also drunk in a tea to calm a fever. It was one of the plants used on the battlefields of World War II and most likely in many battles before then. In fact, its spear-like leaf led it to be considered a "warrior's plant" in many early cultures, in the same way as pine. Yarrow, likes so many wildflowers, was believed by young girls to hold the power of divination of a future lover. They placed it under their pillows to dream of the "one they would marry."

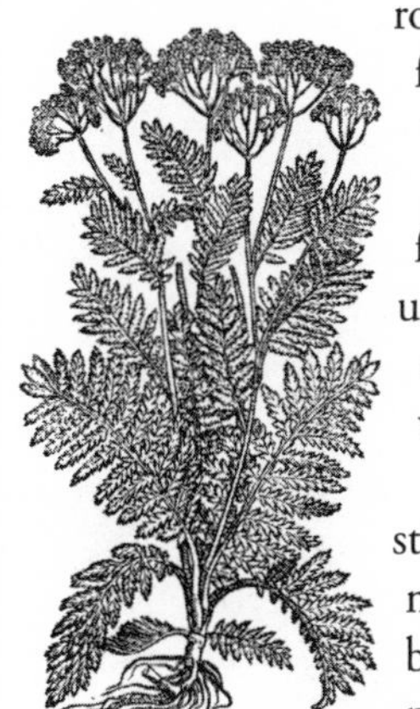

Modern use: Yarrow is still used today in the treatment of fevers, often combined with elderflower and peppermint, and is also used as a strengthening tonic and for circulatory issues such as varicose veins.

Outlander: Claire uses yarrow as a disinfectant and febrifuge in *Outlander,* and Mrs. Fitz uses it in the garden as a companion plant to "keep the bugs away."

ANCIENT BIOTICS

Probably one of the most important remedies that would have been necessary in the eighteenth century, anywhere in the world, was a topical antibiotic. In times before antiseptic was widely available, the slightest injury or wound could become infected easily. Simple wounds that would seem insignificant in today's medically advanced times could have proved fatal back then.

A Gaelic favorite (on top of bathing with wild garlic) was an ointment of St. John's wort (*Hypericum perforatum*), goldenrod (*Solidago virgaurea*), and germander speedwell (*Veronica chamaedrys*). The herbs were finely chopped and added to salted butter. The salt was to act as a preservative, but, inevitably in those days, products like this would degrade quickly, and so small batches were made when necessary. Animal fat lasted longer, so *hogsgreese* (pig fat) was often used as a base for ointments, sometimes with powdered resin added for medicinal properties and also as a preservative.

With the refinement of modern chemistry, ointments were found that had a longer-lasting shelf life, using a combination of oils and wax. Beeswax was used traditionally; however, emulsifying oil was often substituted.

Of course, these days, with the access we have to ingredients from all over the world, it isn't really necessary to go around smeared in and smelling of pig fat. It is also possible to make an ointment that doesn't require beeswax, and with the bees increasingly threatened, perhaps it is advisable to put as little demand as possible on current populations.

Here's a recipe from traditional Highland medicine, which I've adapted for modern use:

Daisy Salve

The daisy (day's eye) got its name because its flowers open with the sunrise.

The common small daisy, Bellis perennis, *was widely used in the Highlands for bumps, bruises, and sprains, much as arnica ointment is used in warmer climes. Of course, arnica is also known as the "mountain daisy" and is in the same family as the humble daisy, so it's not surprising they have similar uses, as is often the case with herbs in the same plant family.*

Daisy ointment was applied to wounds, injuries, and aching or swollen joints. It is safe to use unless you have an allergy to the daisy family. You should also avoid contact with broken skin.

You will need:

60 g coconut oil

30 g shea butter (or cocoa butter)

Around 100–200 g fresh daisies (about a good dessert bowl's worth)

12 drops essential oil (optional; try lavender or chamomile)

2 x 60 g ointment jars with lids (make sure they are sterilized)

Bain-marie (or double boiler)

Labels

Here's how to do it:

Boil water in a deep pan. Place a Pyrex or glass bowl above it—without touching the water and so that the steam can't escape. We're making our own bain-marie here.

Now add the coconut oil, and stir until it melts. Add the cocoa butter or shea butter, until it has completely melted. Next, fill the bowl with enough flowers that the oil completely covers them. It doesn't matter how much—you can add more if it isn't strong enough, and it is unlikely to be *too* strong. So start with a good few handfuls. They will begin to reduce down in size and you can add more if necessary.

Cover the bowl with a large pot lid, and leave on heat until the flowers begin to crisp. This can be 1–2 hours.

(If the flowers seem to shrink, you can add more.)

Pay attention! Check back to see if your oil needs more flowers, and give it a stir frequently to get an even exposure to heat. You also don't want to "cook" the petals—so look closely for them becoming crisp and remove from heat when this happens. Otherwise, you get a "greasy fries" smell to your ointment—not so good.

Remove from heat. Strain, add drops of essential oil, stir, and store in sterile jars. Let it cool and then place in the refrigerator; this will help the salve set.

If you feel it is not strong enough in color (green) or smell, you can allow it to cool and repeat the process again—using more flowers and the first infusion. If the salve has not set enough, you can melt it again and add a little more cocoa butter or shea.

Label the jars with date and the name DAISY SALVE.

Slàinte leat!

Theresa Carle-Sanders

Author's Note: While Theresa Carle-Sanders isn't associated with the TV show, she's one of the Very Interesting People who have taken inspiration from Outlander *and brought their own special skills to an interesting ancillary project—in this case, Theresa's new cookbook,* Outlander Kitchen, *with recipes inspired by and/or based on descriptions of the cookery and food in the books. I therefore took advantage of her knowledge of historical cookery and asked her to write this entertaining and informative essay—hope you'll enjoy it as much as I did!*

The Diet and Cookery of Eighteenth-Century Highlanders

"The food was either terribly bad or terribly good," Claire had said, describing her adventures in the past. "That's because there's no way of keeping things; anything you eat has either been salted or preserved in lard, if it isn't half rancid—or else it's fresh off the hoof or out of the garden, in which case it can be bloody marvelous."

—*Drums of Autumn*

Prior to the Clearances that forced tens of thousands from the land and left it as one of the least densely populated areas in all of Europe, the Scottish Highlands were home to a much larger population, mostly tenant farmers living in small collective groups of crofts called townships. These townships typically housed a hundred people, often extended family, who grew, raised, foraged, and, if near the water, fished to survive amongst the north's unforgiving landscape with its short growing season, harsh climate, and poor soil.

The typical diet of a Highland Scot through the first half of the eighteenth century varied widely, according to their place in the economic and social structure. The tables of the great halls in castles such as Leoch and the dining rooms of manor houses like Lallybroch were laden with venison and wild boar, beef and lamb, fowl and songbirds.

They had imported delicacies in their storerooms: dried fruit, citrus peel, expensive spices like pepper, cloves, and cinnamon. Sugar, still a very expensive commodity in the early eighteenth century, was used to make sumptuous desserts and puddings. They drank beer brewed on their estates, as well as whisky—*uisge beatha*, or the water of life, malted and distilled onsite—and enjoyed fine wines from Europe's best grape-producing regions.

The cook in a wealthy kitchen turned a bountiful combination of locally grown produce and ingredients from afar into a tasty and nourishing assortment of dishes distinct from those in the rest of the British Isles. Scotland's near-four-hundred-year Auld Alliance with France against the English left a lasting influence on Scottish culture, including her cuisine. Terms such as the French *escalope* became the Scot's *collop,* for a slice of meat, and a boiling fowl, *Hetoudeau*, became *Howtowdie,* a dish of boiled chicken with spinach and poached eggs.

The diet of the poorer classes, including the crofter, was a much leaner, plain, and monotonous one. Bannocks, oatcakes, porridge, and vegetable pottages, very occasionally enriched with a small piece of meat or a bone, made up the bulk of a farmer's diet. Meat was expensive and eaten rarely. Farmers grew crops of oats, barley, and pease (peas) at a subsistence level and raised animals, especially cattle, primarily for their by-products, such as milk, butter, and cheese. Wheat for leavened bread wouldn't grow on the poor, unimproved soil, and there was no oven in a farmer's croft in which to bake it.

Kitchen gardens, or kailyards, supplemented farmers' families' diets with year-round crops of kale, leeks, and other vegetables hardy enough to survive the ruthless winters. Kale's historical popularity as a mainstay of Scottish cooking owes much to the simple fact that it can survive a Highland winter. So ubiquitous was kale that its name became metonymically associated with everything food, from the family vegetable plot to the dinner bell:

> *But hark! The kail-bell rings, and I*
> *Maun gae link aff the pot;*
> *Come see, ye hash, how sair I sweat*
> *To stegh your guts, ye sot.*
>
> (Watty and Madge, *David Herd's Collection of Scottish Songs, Volume ii, p. 199)*[1]

Mustard, spinach, carrots, and cabbage from the garden provided welcome variety in a crofter's diet from summer through early winter. The hardest time of year was undoubtedly after the failing of the previous winter's kale crop in early spring, through until the first harvests in early summer, when food stores were near bare and the last of the kale had gone to seed. Foraged wild vegetables such as nettles, sorrel, and garlic filled in the food gap and provided much-needed nourishment to fuel the plowing and planting activities of spring. Wild berries in summer were a rare sweet treat.

The first recorded example of potatoes being grown in Scotland is 1701, but it wasn't until the last quarter of the century that they found their way into the average family's vegetable plot. Turnips were introduced at about the same time, adding diversity and substance to the Highland diet. Both vegetables also stored well, improving food security.

Near the shores, most men split their time between the fields and the sea. These

---

[1] *Jamieson, John.* Scottish Dictionary and Supplement: In Four Volumes. *Supplemental Kab-Zic, Volume 4, 1841, http://bit.ly/1aPCLCc.*

fishermen–farmers had the most varied, nutrient-rich diet of the Highland's working poor, thanks to plentiful fish and seafood. They used seaweed to fertilize their gardens and made salt to season and preserve their food, as well as to barter with it with the inland population.

Across the Highlands, food for the workingman was required to be easily transportable and resistant to spoilage. Men would commonly carry a small bag of oatmeal in their sporran, which could quickly be made into a basic porridge or oatcake while in the fields or away from home. This type of food-to-go is thought to account for the origins of haggis, but it's important to note that the first printed reference to that eminently Scottish dish is in an English cookbook, although it most likely extends back much further, to the Viking occupation of Britain.

Crofts were sturdy, small, windowless homes built to shelter their inhabitants from the ruthless conditions in the Highlands. Just inside the single door used by both humans and animals was a sunken room with a cobbled floor, where the animals, mostly cattle and chickens, were kept, along with the farmer's *cas-chrom*, or foot plow, and his wife's milk churn.

Up a step from the byre was the croft's center section, which served as the family's living room, dining room, kitchen, and bedroom. The floor was packed dirt, and the walls were made of thickly cut turf or clay and wattle. The roof was thatched in whatever was available—heather, broom, bracken, straw, or rushes.

The peat fire in the center of the living area burned day and night to provide light and warmth. The family sat around the fire on low wooden stools, where the smoke was not as thick, and if there was fish, they were hung above the fire to smoke. An opening in

the roof was offset from the fire to allow smoke to escape, but the walls and roof were covered with black ash from the fire. The walls were scraped of ash, which was collected along with the blackened thatching to use as fertilizer in the fields; this may explain why their oat crops grew so well on the substandard soil.

Cooking equipment and utensils were very basic, and cooking was a necessary chore that held none of the creative appeal seen in today's ergonomic and sanitary kitchens. The woman of the house prepared and cooked her family's meals from her perch on the edge of her stool, with only the dim fire to light her efforts, unless the family could afford an oil-burning rush lamp for additional lighting.

The cast-iron girdle (griddle) was nestled into the ashes of the fire and used to bake bannocks and oatcakes. The kettle for cooking the family's porridge and pottage was either balanced on top of the fire or hung just above it, from a chain attached to the ceiling. The pot was perpetually filled morning to night with the family's next meal, bubbling away unobserved while the woman of the house completed the rest of her exhaustive list of chores, including the back-breaking work of fetching water for cooking and cleaning, as well as hauling back and stacking the peat cut by the men in the fields to ensure a constant supply of fuel for the fire.

In stark contrast to the dim picture painted of the crofter's living space and cooking area were the large—sometimes vast—kitchens in clan castles and large homes, which were generally housed on the building's lowest level and equipped with at least one major hearth and chimney. The inventory of large equipment would have included a brick oven beside the hearth for baking, as well as a stew hole in the wealthiest and most up-to-date of kitchens.

The stew hole was a raised freestanding structure that allowed the cook to stand instead of sitting or crouching at the hearth and was a precursor to the cast-iron stove. A fire was built in the base, and pots were set on grates over the fire to cook or warm, depending on their distance from the heat.

In addition to iron kettles and girdles, the list of small equipment would likely have included spits to turn the meat and fowl, copper and clay pots, a variety of knives, tongs, ladles, mallets, sifters, and molds, all designed to make the preparation of modern, more refined foods faster and easier.

Meal times were also dependent on class and status. While breakfast in a croft was an almost nonexistent pre-dawn sup of milk and a bowl of hastily consumed porridge or brose, praise was sung from as far as London regarding the wide variety of fish and meat available at the laird or clan chief's morning feast, taken later in the morning. Supper was a light evening meal for all classes, with the exception of celebratory feasts, and was usually leftovers from that day's most substantial meal, dinner, which was eaten at or around midday.

Defeat at Culloden saw the systematic destruction of the clan system and a need for cash to satisfy the demands of the court in London. These changes were at least partially responsible for the switch in the Highlands from a barter economy to a cash-based one. Tenant farmers who had paid their rent with labor and goods in kind for generations now found themselves unable to come up with the coin their landlords demanded.

Over subsequent decades, the majority of the land was enclosed for grazing and, often, entire townships evicted to make room for more-profitable sheep. The more fortunate evictees were relocated to the cities of Edinburgh and Glasgow, while the less fortunate were transported to faraway colonies such as Australia and North America, most never to see their homeland again. Many of the poor that arrived on America's Atlantic shores moved into the backcountry, including wilderness areas of North Carolina like the fictional Fraser's Ridge.

To begin, their diet remained based primarily on boiled grains and vegetable stews, although they quickly adapted to incorporate a number of locally grown ingredients such as corn (maize), beans, squash, and collards, a close cousin to kale. Potatoes, which were still new to the first emigrants forced from the Highlands, became an important staple. The lush natural larder of their new home also regularly provided animal protein, in the form of small game and birds, resulting in a much more varied and nutritionally complete diet for all.

Because they were released into the woods as young shoats to run wild until they matured, hogs were relatively simple and low cost to raise. Eventually, much of the North Carolina and surrounding colonies' diets were based on pork and corn, with the average person consuming five pounds of pork for every pound of beef.[2] This "hog and hominy" diet, as it came to be called, stretched across all levels of society, with the wealthiest consuming the choicest cuts of the animal and leaving their workers and slaves with what remained. All parts of the animal were consumed or repurposed, and the diet was supplemented with a bevy of collard greens or cabbage.

As they had been at home in the Highlands, smoking and salting were the primary means used to preserve meats and fish. Potted meat, the process of sealing cooked meat in fat, was another common technique. Salted meat was perpetually on the menu in most homes and taverns. Hogs were never slaughtered in summer, and their meat was seldom eaten fresh, except after a large slaughter, when giant smoking pits would be dug and people were invited for miles around to join the feast. The great tradition of Southern barbecue originates from these early gatherings.

In their new home, fruits and vegetables were dried and pickled, then packed in fresh straw to sit alongside cheese and barrels of salted meat, as well as cider and beer, in the cool air of small underground house cellars. In cold seasons, fresh meat was also stored for short periods of time. Those without such spaces stored food for a short time in springs or wells, in containers set into the cold water. Only the very wealthy, as well as large dairies, possessed separate icehouses.

In the homes of plantation owners, large farmers, and wealthy merchants, traditional foods were being transformed at the hands of their African cooks. Spices were used heavily to enhance flavors as well as to disguise spoiled meat in the warm climate. Vitamin-rich "pot likker," the previously discarded cooking water in which vegetables had been slow-cooked, was now kept and savored. Slave cooks produced fried chicken and fritters, adding the African method of deep-fat frying to the growing list of new cooking techniques.

Access to cheap sugar, for centuries so costly as to be out of the reach of all but the very rich, meant that everyone could now afford to make puddings, custards, and other sweet treats regularly. The imposition of heavy taxes on staple foodstuffs also resulted in dietary changes. Examples include the replacement of the popular molasses-based rum with liquor made from locally grown corn and the rise in popularity of coffee as the supply of tea dried up leading up to the American Revolution.

The settlers' wooden backcountry cabins were small; however, they included a fireplace with hearth and chimney, an important improvement over a croft's centrally located fire on the floor. As it had been back home, cooking of any meal was a major undertaking and equipment was basic. Activity was centered on the fireplace, with the cast-iron pot hanging from a chain or rod over the wood fire and the baking kettle and/or girdle nestled into the ashes of the fire.

In larger households, the kitchen was often separated from the house to keep the

[2] *Taylor, Joe Gray.* Eating, Drinking and Visiting in the Old South: An Informal History. *Baton Rouge: Louisiana State University Press, 1982.*

heat, smells, and staff far from living quarters and guests. These kitchens contained the same basic equipment and tools as found in backcountry cabins but better made and from higher-quality materials. In addition, more-expensive inventory, such as mechanized spit jacks and stew holes, made the cook's job faster and easier, while allowing more control over the final taste and appearance of the dish.

The other large feature of wealthier kitchens—including those of the burgeoning middle class, such as merchants and tradesmen—was the presence of a bread oven, either beside the hearth or outside the house. Baking was an all-day affair undertaken once per week and involved the baker rising early to prepare her dough and light the fire within the oven. Once the fire had reduced to ashes, the oven floor was swept clean and the loaves and pies placed inside, with the help of a long wooden or cast-iron peel. The oven door was then closed and the contents left to bake. It was often well after dark when a day's baking was finally done, and meals on these days were generally leftovers or simple stews that could be left to cook unattended.

Much like it had been in the Highlands, breakfast was taken early if you were poor and later for those of greater means. For most, it began with home-brewed cider or beer and a bowl of porridge cooked overnight in the embers of the fire. It was among the Southern planters that breakfast became a leisurely and delightful meal, more like our modern brunch, featuring large spreads of breads, cold meats, and cheese.

Dinner was the main meal of the day, served in early afternoon. A typical wealthier family in the late 1700s served two courses for dinner. The first included soups, meats, savory pies, pancakes and fritters, and a variety of sauces, pickles, and catsups. Desserts appeared with the second course, which included an assortment of fresh, cooked, or dried fruits, custards, tarts, and sweetmeats. "Sallats," or salads, were more popular for supper, a light meal served just before bed, but were sometimes served at dinner to provide decoration for the center of the table.

The life of an eighteenth-century Highland crofter was one of constant toil and strife. The workday was long, food scarce. And while their relocation to the Americas resulted in death for some and a cruel loss of country and family for thousands more, eventually those who survived in the New World adopted a life of continuing hard work but greater food and nutritional reward. The increase in protein and variety of diet undoubtedly fueled many Highlanders' rise from crushing poverty and their contribution to the fight for their new nation's independence.

Part Nine

MAPS AND FLOOR PLANS

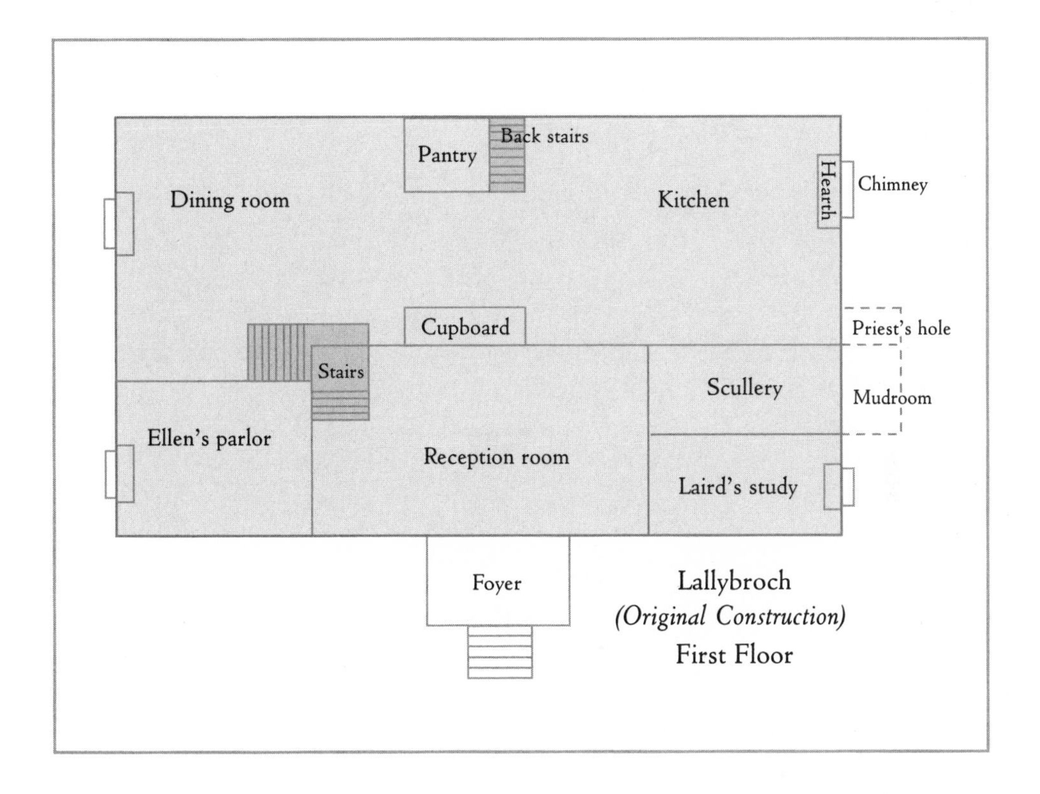

LALLYBROCH—FIRST FLOOR

What you're looking at here is the original house, as built by Brian Fraser for his bride, Ellen MacKenzie. The house would have been added to over the years, as was common, and so the house that Roger and Brianna acquire in the 1980s would have a couple of additional wings and, of course, would have had interior renovations, particularly in the kitchen.

I have, however, indicated the location of the priest's hole (and the mudroom that disguises it), which was installed by Jenny at Claire's behest, prior to the '45 Rising.

I've never bothered thinking out a floor plan for the house before, so when sitting down to do it this time, I made some effort to reconcile what I know of the house with what viewers have seen of the televised version. So the floor plan you see here matches the rooms you've seen in the show—with one minor exception: given where the reception room is, in the center of the house . . . there's no conceivable way (given the normal construction methods of the eighteenth-century Scottish Highlands) that there would be an open hearth in that room.

Chimneys were always at the ends of the house; I've never seen a building of that vintage with a central chimney stack (and, in fact, you don't normally see a chimney in the middle of *any* house; they're always located on an outer wall, for both structural and operational reasons).

Naturally, the very excellent set designers for the show wanted the hearth there for visual reasons, and, television being what it is, they can have anything they want.

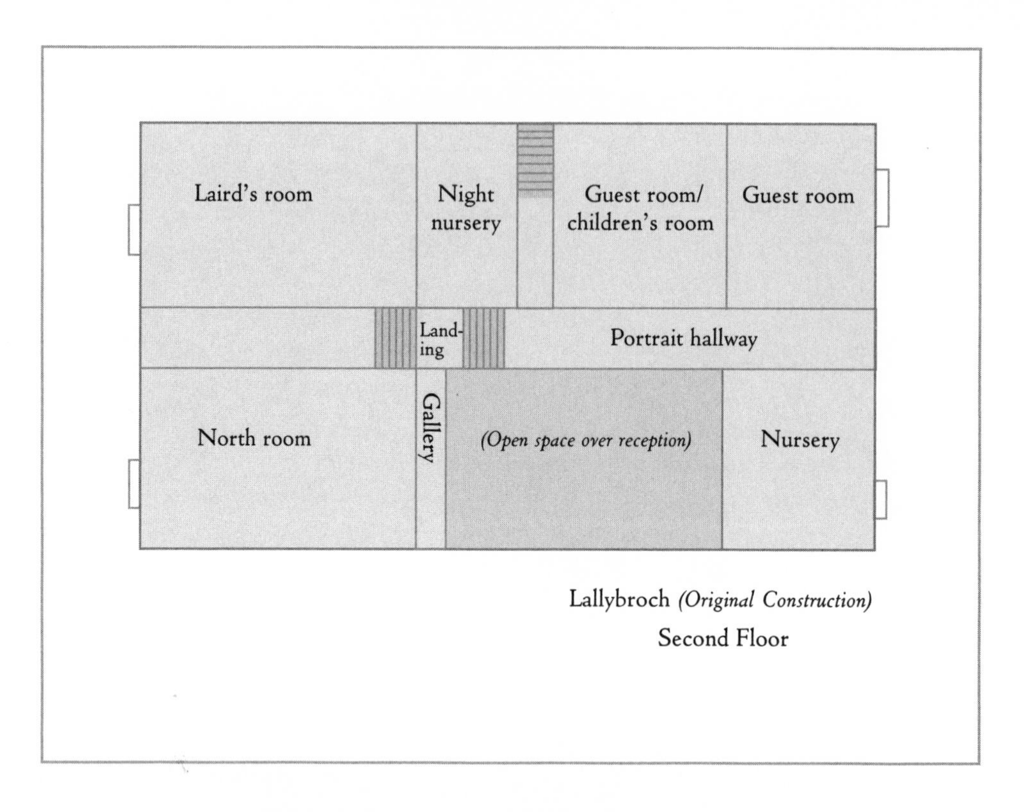

Lallybroch *(Original Construction)*
Second Floor

LALLYBROCH—SECOND FLOOR

Again, I made an attempt to reconcile a reasonably traditional floor plan with the purely visual version produced by the TV show. It's reasonable for there to be a gallery running outside the Laird's Room (from which Claire can observe MacQuarrie holding a gun to Jamie's head), but as the Laird's Room also has a hearth (and is therefore at one end of the house, that being where the chimneys are), *and* we saw a staircase with a noticeable turn, I was obliged to do some fancy internal engineering of the stairs when we reached the second and third floors.

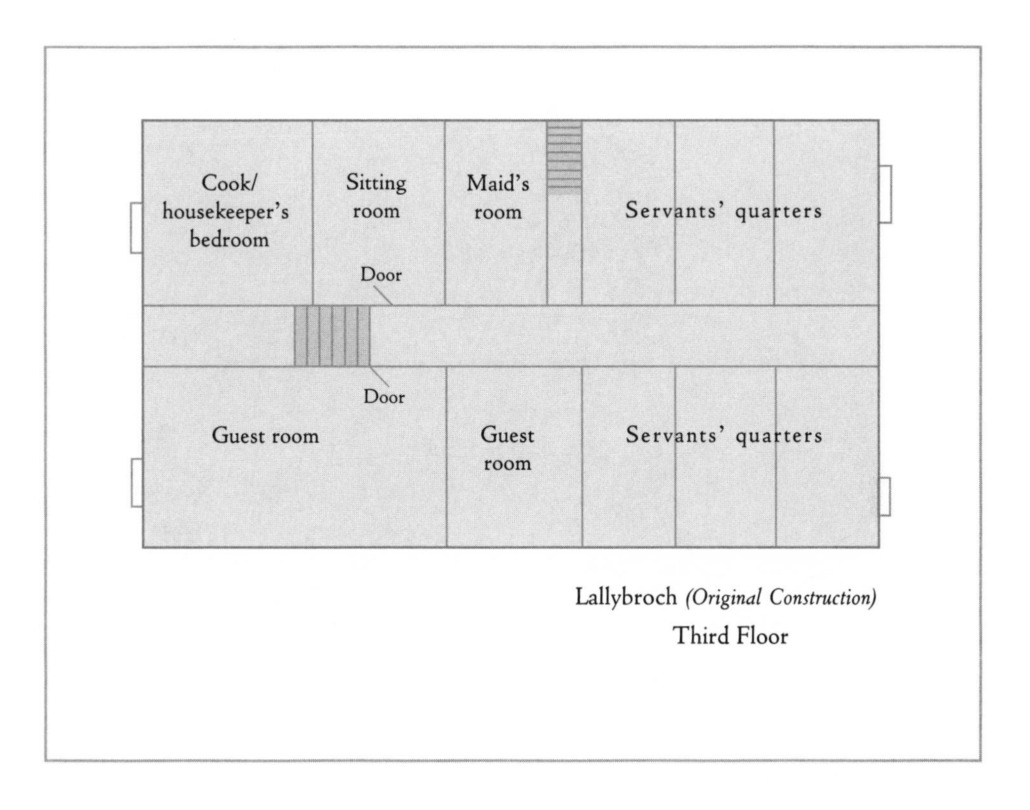

Lallybroch *(Original Construction)*
Third Floor

LALLYBROCH—THIRD FLOOR

As those of you who have been watching *Downton Abbey* (or *Upstairs, Downstairs,* in an earlier age) know, the servants' quarters of a big house tended to be small, spartan, and on the top floor. Lallybroch is no exception in this regard. In later years of the house's existence, some of these small rooms may have been knocked into larger ones or serve as attics rather than living space.

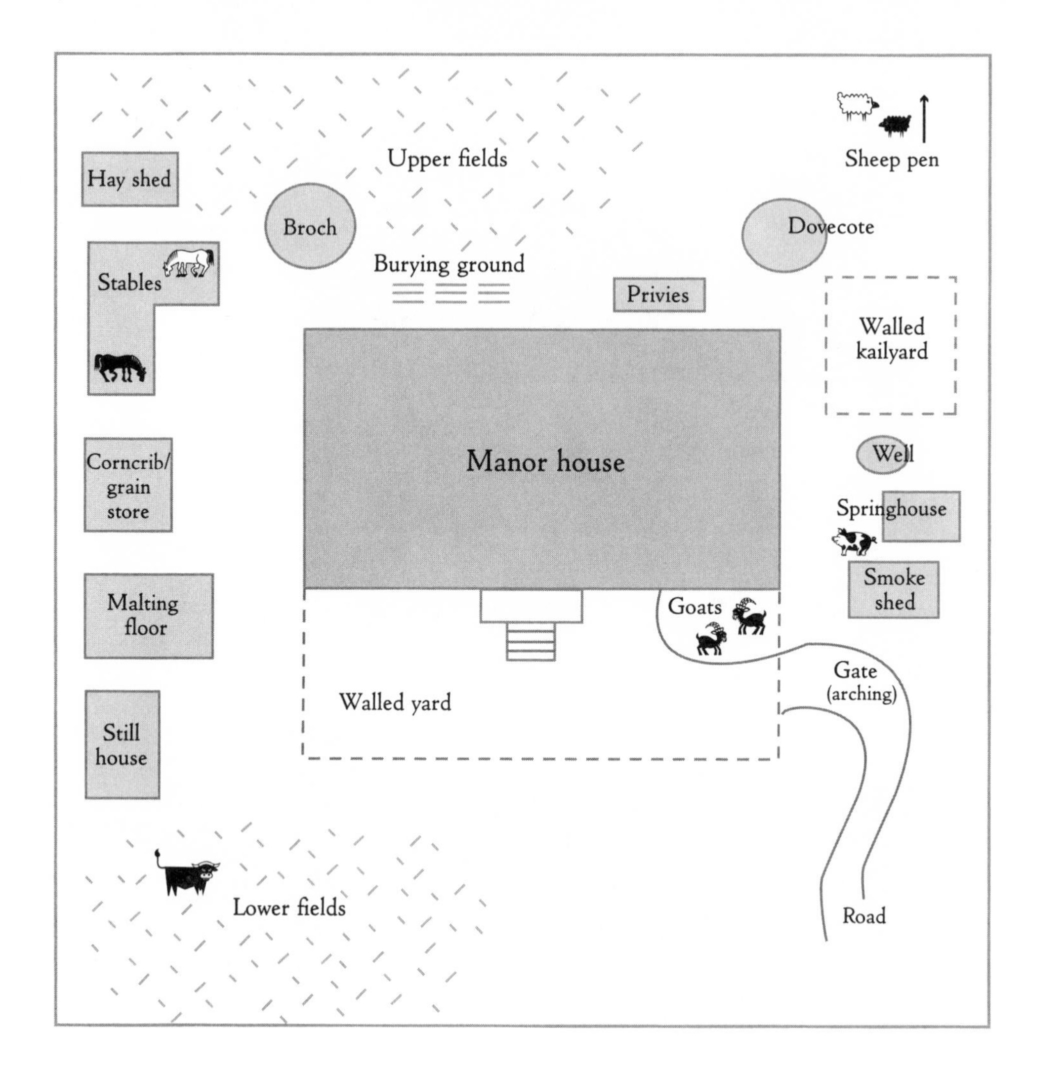

LALLYBROCH ESTATE

You can see from this map some of the complex operations that having an estate entailed and why people who had estates had a lot of servants and employees. *Somebody* had to be tending the dovecote, the kailyard, the goats, and the horses. *Somebody* had to be excavating a new pit for the necessary house every year or so. *Somebody* had to be harvesting grain, malting it, then fermenting and distilling. All of this outside the normal household operations of food preparation, clothing manufacture and mending, and just keeping the general chaos of life under control.

One thing I like about the television staging of Lallybroch is that they show things breaking down (the mill) and people constantly repairing things in the background. Lallybroch is a working farm, and the word "working" is apt.

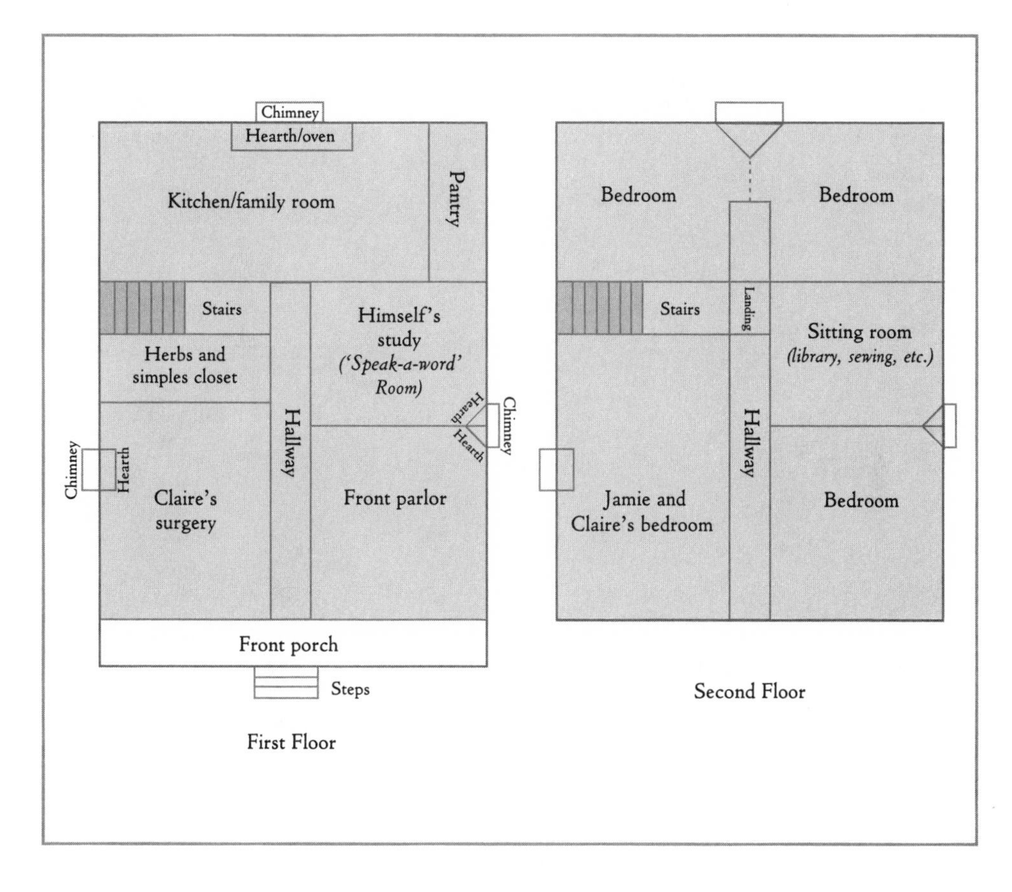

FRASER'S RIDGE—BIG HOUSE (ORIGINAL)

As Jamie hasn't yet finished building the New Big House, we don't know quite what it will look like. But this is the general layout of the original house that he built for Claire. (Obviously the Fraser men are given to ambitious constructions. . . .)

The usual construction of this period and place would likely have been slightly more simplified, with a four-up, four-down sort of layout. However, Scottish manor houses have much more complex layouts (owing in part to their evolution over many generations), and Jamie grew up in several of these. He also needed to provide Claire with a decently large, well-lighted space in which to conduct her surgery—which means that the Big House sported more and bigger windows than were usual, as well as having a more complex downstairs floor plan.

I don't think we have ever seen any business of living being conducted in the front parlor. This is probably a reflection of the fact that people wealthy enough to have a front parlor didn't use it, save for ceremonial occasions like a wedding or funeral. And if you contemplate the realities of housekeeping (with children) in a time when a twig broom, a rag mop, and a bucket of water were your only tools, you can see why not.

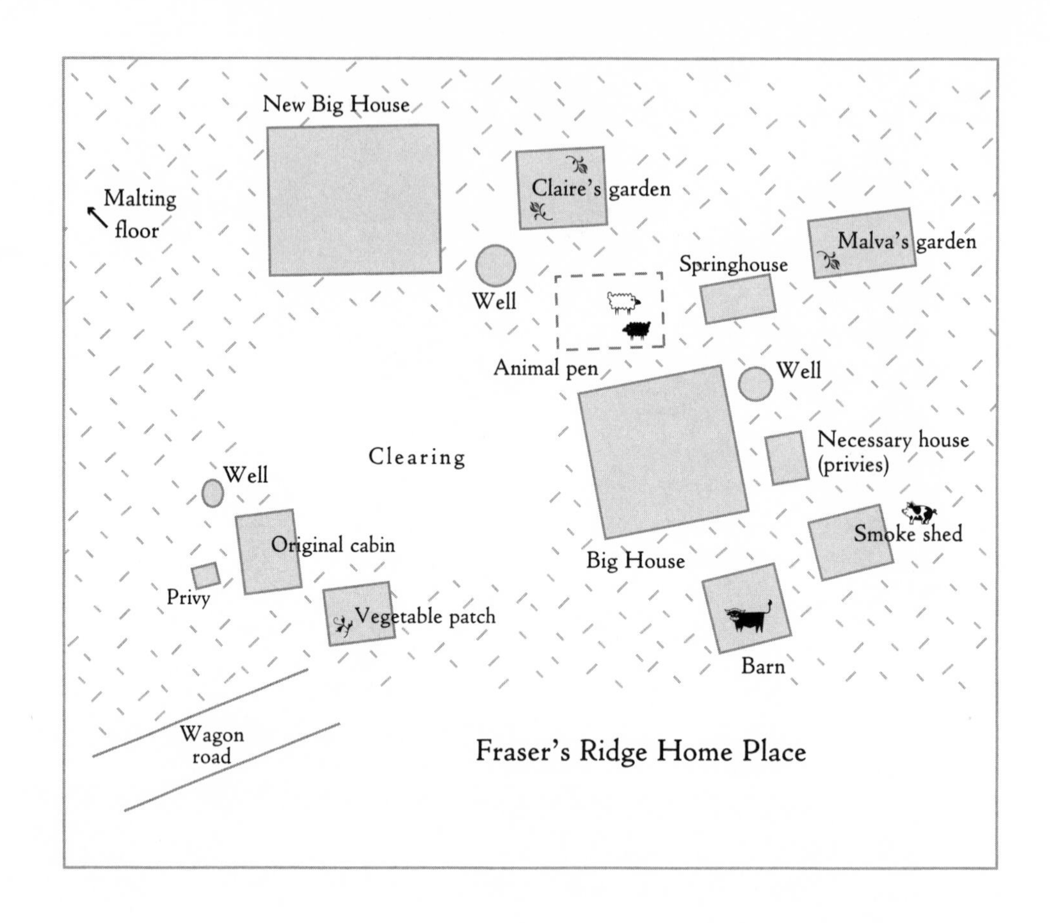
New Big House
Malting floor
Claire's garden
Malva's garden
Springhouse
Well
Animal pen
Well
Clearing
Necessary house (privies)
Well
Original cabin
Smoke shed
Big House
Privy
Vegetable patch
Barn
Wagon road
Fraser's Ridge Home Place

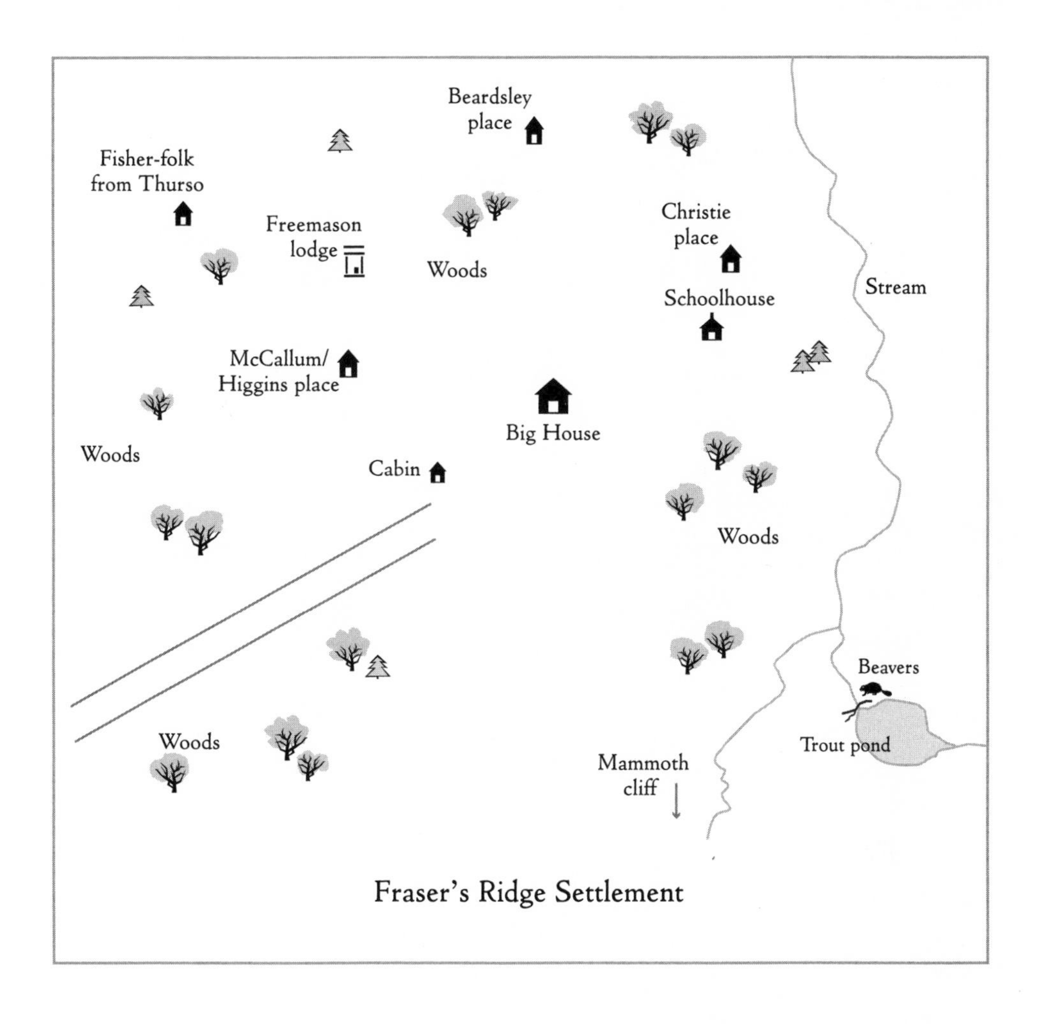
Beardsley
place
Fisher-folk
from Thurso
Freemason
lodge
Woods
Christie
place
Stream
Schoolhouse
McCallum/
Higgins place
Big House
Woods
Cabin
Woods
Beavers
Woods
Trout pond
Mammoth
cliff
Fraser's Ridge Settlement

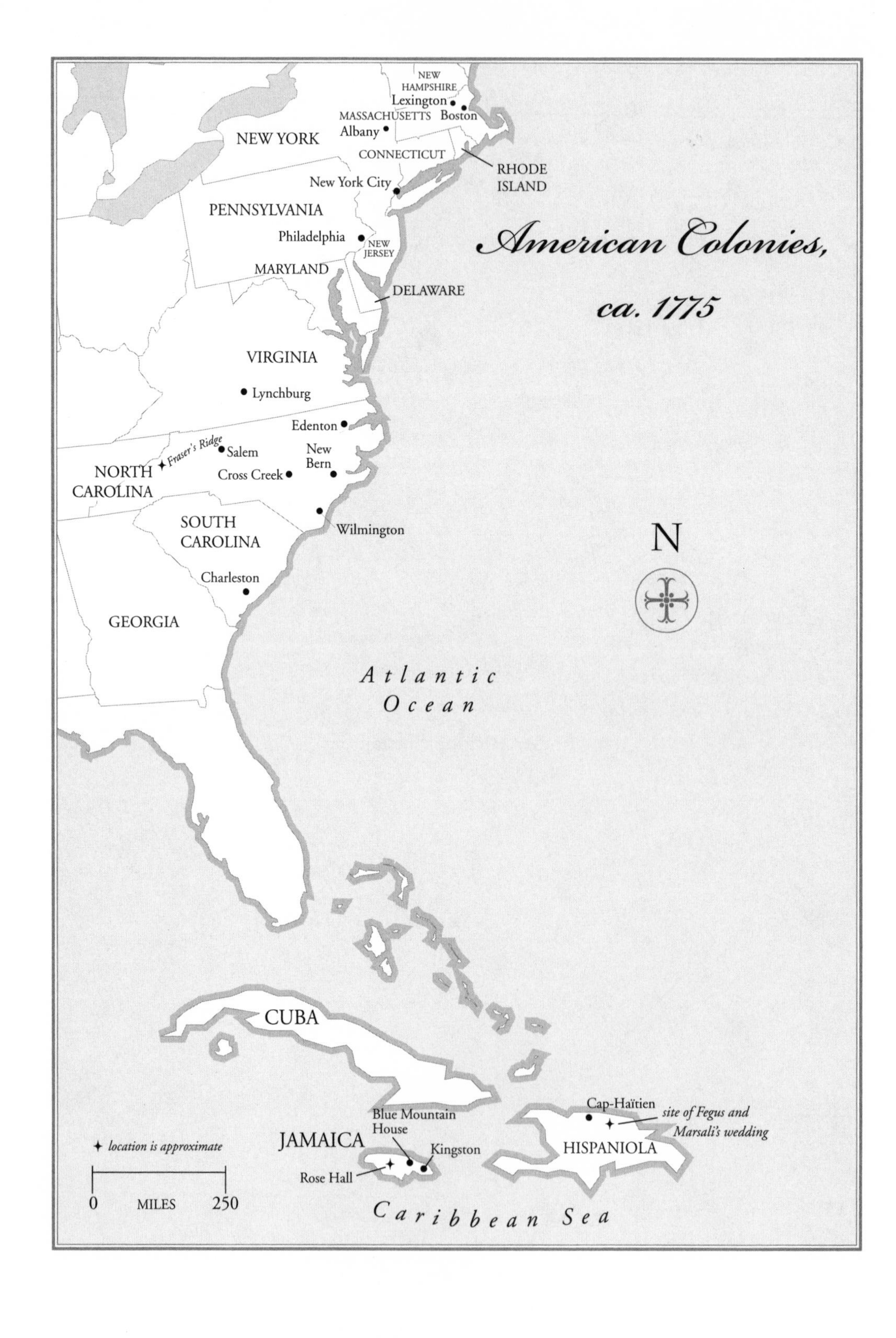
American Colonies, ca. 1775
NEW HAMPSHIRE
Lexington
MASSACHUSETTS
Boston
Albany
NEW YORK
CONNECTICUT
RHODE ISLAND
New York City
PENNSYLVANIA
Philadelphia
NEW JERSEY
MARYLAND
DELAWARE
VIRGINIA
Lynchburg
Edenton
Fraser's Ridge
Salem
New Bern
NORTH CAROLINA
Cross Creek
SOUTH CAROLINA
Wilmington
Charleston
GEORGIA
N
Atlantic Ocean
CUBA
Blue Mountain House
JAMAICA
Kingston
Rose Hall
Cap-Haïtien
site of Fegus and Marsali's wedding
HISPANIOLA
✦ location is approximate
0 MILES 250
Caribbean Sea

The British Isles
HIGHLANDS
Ardsmuir
Castle Leoch
Moray Firth
Beauly
St. Kilda
Inverness
Culloden
Lallybroch
Atlantic Ocean
Fort William
Craigh na Dun
SCOTLAND
Stirling
Prestonpans
Glasgow
Falkirk
Edinburgh
Wentworth Prison
Carlisle
York
Irish Sea
IRELAND
ENGLAND
Derby
Ludlow
London
Celtic Sea
English Channel
Abbey of Ste. Anne de Beaupré
N
Le Havre
Rouen
Amiens
Compiègne
Versailles
Paris
Fontainebleau
FRANCE
location is approximate
0
MILES
200

City of Philadelphia

1 *Benjamin Rush House**
2 *Bingham Mansion*○*
3 *Christ Church**
4 *Christ Church Burial Ground**
5 *City Tavern**
6 *Debtors' Prison**
7 *John Dunlap's Print Shop**
8 *Free Quaker Meeting House**
9 *Old City Hall**
10 *Mrs. Dailey's Boarding House**
11 *Mrs. Marshall's Boarding House**
12 *Old St. Paul's Church**
13 *Old St. Mary's Church**
14 *Old St. Joseph's Church**
15 *Society Hill Synagogue**
16 *Walnut Street Prison**
17 *No. 17 Chestnut Street□*
18 *Fraser's Printshop*
19 *Anabaptist Meeting House*
20 *White Camel Tavern*
21 *2nd Reformed Methodist Church△*

* *a real historical site*
○ *General Clinton's headquarters*
□ *Lord John Grey's House*
△ *Rev. Mortimer Figg presiding*

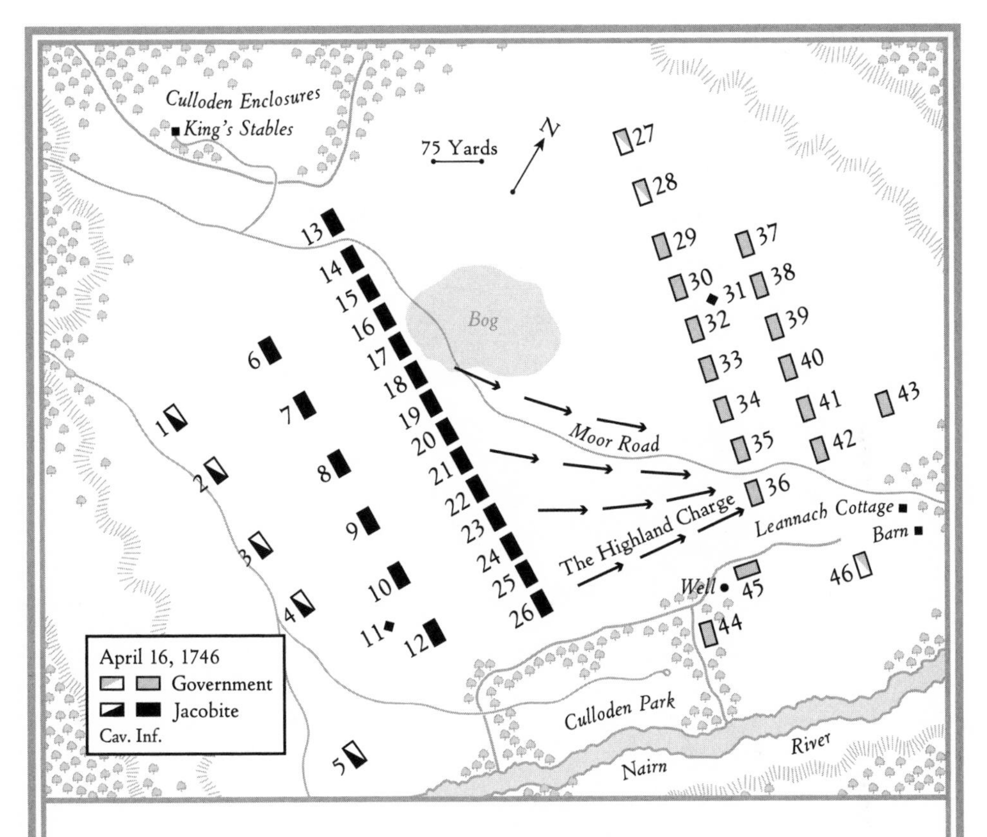

The Battle of Culloden

1 Kilmarnock
2 Strathallan
3 Pitsligo
4 Balmerino & Elcho
5 Fitzjames
6 Irish Picquets
7 Royal Écossais
8 Duke of Perth
9 Glenbucket
10 Gordon
11 Prince Charles
12 Ogilvy
13 Glengarry
14 Keppoch
15 Clanranald
16 Chisholm
17 MacLeans & MacLachlans
18 John Roy Stewart
19 Farquharsons
20 Clan Chattan
21 Lovat's Frasers
22 Stewarts of Appin
23 Lochiel's Camerons
24 Atholl
25 Atholl
26 Atholl

27 Cobham's 10th Dragoons
28 Kingston's Light Horse
29 Pultaney's 13th
30 Royal Scots 1st
31 Duke of Cumberland
32 Cholmondeley's 34th
33 Price's 14th
34 Campbell's R. S. H.
35 Munro's 37th
36 Barrell's 4th
37 Battereau's 62nd
38 Howard's 3rd
39 Fleming's 36th
40 Conway's 59th
41 Bligh's 20th
42 Sempill's 25th
43 Blakeney's 27th
44 Campbell's
45 Wolfe's 8th
46 Kerr's 11th Dragoons

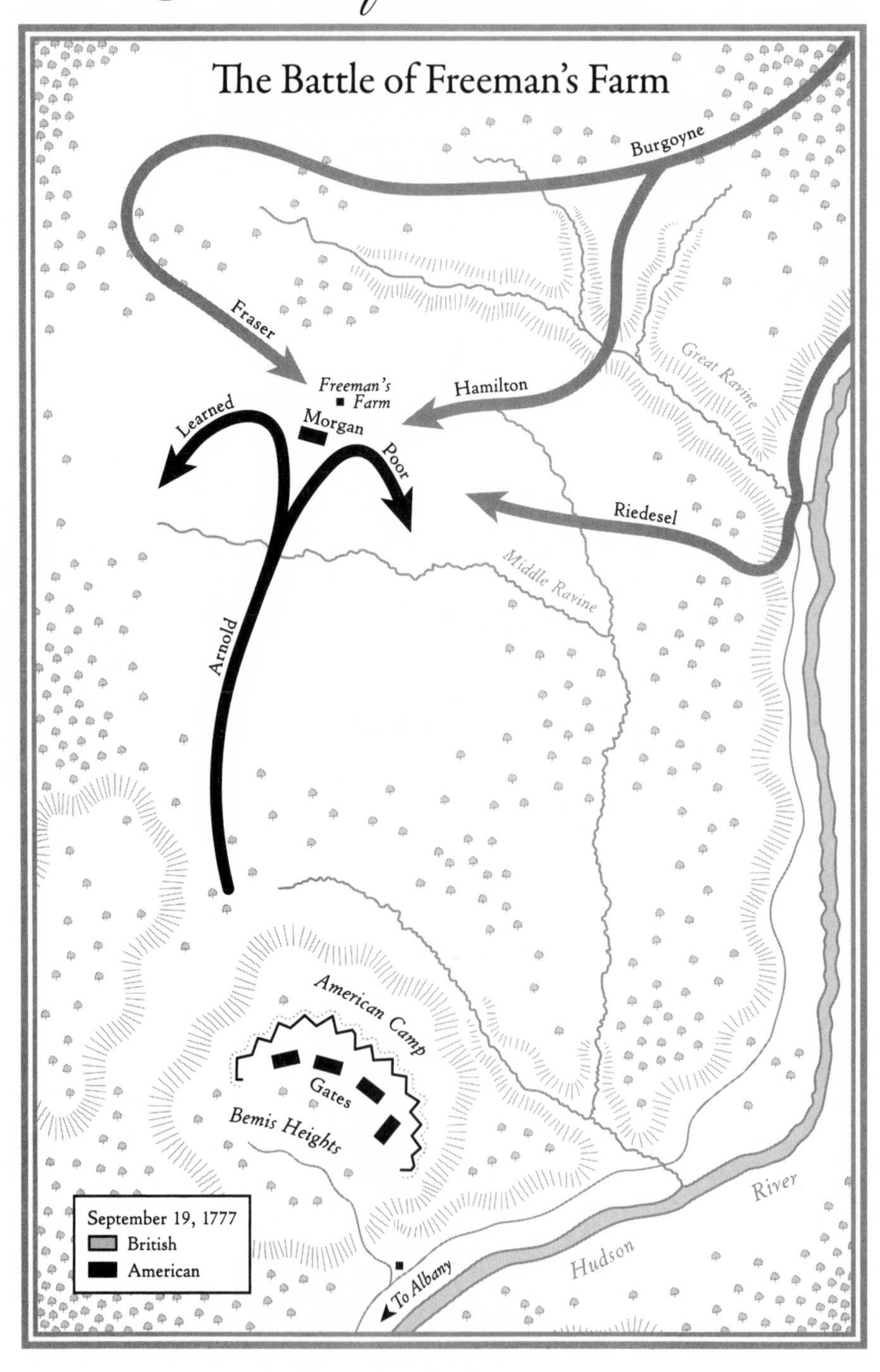
The Battle of Freeman's Farm
Burgoyne
Fraser
Freeman's Farm
Hamilton
Learned
Morgan
Poor
Great Ravine
Riedesel
Middle Ravine
Arnold
American Camp
Gates
Bemis Heights
River
Hudson
To Albany
September 19, 1777
British
American

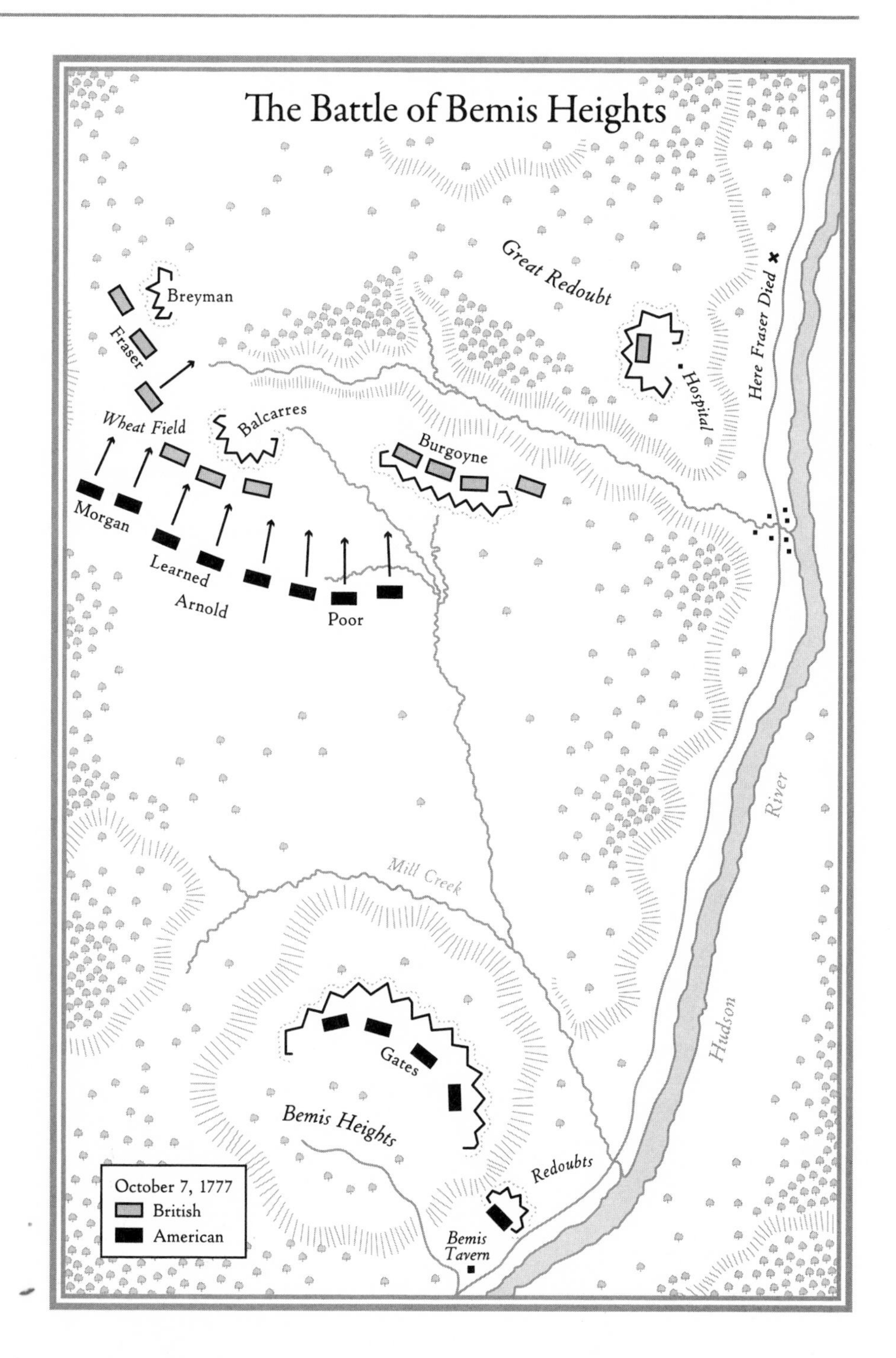
The Battle of Bemis Heights
Great Redoubt
Breyman
Fraser
Here Fraser Died
Hospital
Wheat Field
Balcarres
Burgoyne
Morgan
Learned
Arnold
Poor
Mill Creek
River
Hudson
Gates
Bemis Heights
Redoubts
Bemis Tavern
October 7, 1777
British
American

PART TEN

THE METHADONE LIST

o . . . you've re-watched the first season of *Outlander,* the TV series, twenty or thirty times and your family is becoming restive about not being able to watch football or play video games, and you've gone through all the Big Books (again) *and* all of the Lord John novels *and* all the novellas . . .

And thus find yourself facing the Universal Question:

WHAT THE HECK AM I GOING TO READ NOW?!?

Oddly enough, people ask me that pretty often. So, some years ago, I started "the Methadone List." This is a brief descriptive list of books that I personally can recommend for quality. I'm a very eclectic reader, and thus the Methadone List has a wide variety of titles, everything from the easily recognizable genres to the frankly odd and indescribable.

Now, everyone's tastes are different, and I don't expect y'all to like all the same things I do—but you may find something here that appeals. I *can* guarantee that everything on the list is well written, has Deeply Interesting Characters, Excellent Plots, and good grammar.

The first installment of the Methadone List was published in the revised and updated *Outlandish Companion, Volume One,* but I've updated it at intervals on my website (www.DianaGabaldon.com)—and will continue to add to it whenever I encounter (or remember) another excellent book or series.

* *The City Stained Red,* by Sam Sykes.

* *God-Thing: And Other Weird & Worrisome Tales,* by Amy Dupire.

* *The Long Way Home,* by Louise Penny, the latest and tenth book in her Armand Gamache series.

* Good crime fiction by a couple of Roberts that I know: Rob Byrnes and Robert Dugoni.

* *The Secrets of Pain,* by Phil Rickman (Merrily Watkins Mysteries).

* Thumbnail reviews of three of my favorite books: *The Knife Man,* by Wendy Moore; *Love in the Time of Cholera,* by Gabriel García Márquez; and *Haunting Bombay,* by Shilpa Agarwal.

* *The Children's Book,* by A. S. Byatt.

* The Kate Shugak series, by Dana Stabenow.

* *Pandaemonium,* and other books by Christopher Brookmyre.

I thought that when recommending books, when possible, I might include a small bit of text so as to give a taste of an author's style. (N.B.: An author's works are naturally copyrighted, but quoting a short passage for review purposes is considered "fair use.")

The City Stained Red, by Sam Sykes

Sykes's books are described most often as "epic fantasy"—which apparently means that they're composed of serpentine plots executed by entertaining characters, and the humor is as high as the body count. While the setting is definitely of Another Place and Time, the people—and other things—you'll meet there are so real that you'd like to hang out with them, if it wasn't so dangerous to be in their vicinity.

(In the Interests of Full Disclosure, Sam Sykes is my son, and while he's never read any of my books—none of my children has; as my Eldest Daughter says, "I don't want to read sex scenes written by my *mother*!"—he rather eerily seems to have inherited my pacing, my sense of dialogue, and my penchant for Extreme Vocabulary. I had no idea that sort of thing was coded for in DNA.)

Here's a brief excerpt from *A City Stained Red.* (Another excerpt is available on Sam's website: www.samsykes.com.)[1]

Right. Deep breaths. Try not to look crazy.

Lenk pulled himself out of line and began to walk past people toward the gate. Head down, eyes forward, wearing a face he hoped looked at least a little intimidating. The only way this was going to work was if this no-necked guard believed Lenk was mean enough to not be worth stopping.

"Ah." A gloved hand went up before Lenk's face. "Stop right there."

Of course, *he sighed inwardly.*

"I didn't specifically say *'no mercs,' I know." The surly-looking guard angled his voice down condescendingly. "But I did say no unstable types, didn't I?"*

Lenk's hand was up before either of them knew it, slapping the captain's hand away.

"Marshal your words with greater care, friend," he whispered threateningly, voice low and sharp like a knife in the dark. "Or I shall hasten to incite you to greater discipline."

What the hell was that?

The guardsman blinked. Once. Slowly. "What?"

Well, don't change now. He'll know something's up.

"Was I too soft in my verbiage?" Lenk asked. "Did you not feel the chill of death in my words?"

"Look," the guard captain sighed, rubbing his eyes. "I'll tell you what I told the tulwar: no oids, no adventurers, no . . . whatever the hell you are."

The captain looked him over with a glare that Lenk recognized. Usually, he saw it only a moment before swords were drawn. But the captain's stare was slow, methodical. He was sizing Lenk up, wondering just how much trouble this was going to be worth.

Lenk decided to give him a hint. He slid into a tense stance, making sure to roll his shoulders enough to send the mail under his shirt clinking and show just how easily he wore the sword on his back.

"I don't see any colors on your shirt," the captain muttered. "I don't see any badge at your breast. I don't see coin at your belt. Which means you're not someone I want in my city."

"You're wise to be wary," Lenk said. "And I advise you to listen to that wariness and cut a path for me, lest I show you why my name in the old tongues means 'bane of death.'"

---

[1] *Quoted by permission of the publisher: Orbit/Gollancz*

The captain stared and repeated flatly, "Bane of death."

"That's right."

He blinked. "You're serious."

Lenk cleared his throat. "I am."

"No." The captain clutched his head as if in pain. "Just . . . just no. Back to the harbor, bane of death. No room for your kind here."

"What kind?" Lenk's face screwed up in offense. "A person of my . . . uh . . . distinct verbotanage must not be denied righteous passage into—"

"Boy, I wouldn't be impressed by this routine even if you weren't *only as tall as my youngest."*

"Look, I don't see what the problem is." The bravado slipped from Lenk's voice in a weary sigh as he rubbed his eyes. "I've got business in the city. In fact, my employer got in shortly before I got here. His name is Miron Evenhands. We both came off the ship Riptide. *If you'll just let me find him, he'll—"*

"Here's the problem," the guard interrupted. "You've got no colors and no affiliation, but you've got a sword. So you've got the means to kill people, but not the means to be held responsible." He sniffed. "Parents?"

"What?"

"Any parents?"

"Both dead."

"Hometown?"

"Burned to the ground."

"Allies? Compatriots? Friends?"

"Just the ones I find on the road. And in a tavern. And, this one time, hunched over a human corpse, but—"

"And that's *the problem. You're an* adventurer.*" He spat the word. "Too cowardly to be a mercenary, too greedy to be a soldier, too dense to be a thief. Your profession is wedged neatly between whores and grave robbers in terms of respectability, your trade is death and carnage, and your main asset is that you're completely expendable."*

He leaned down to the young man and forced the next words through his teeth.

"I keep this city clean. And you, boy, are garbage."

The young man didn't flinch. His eyes never wavered, not to the captain's guards reaching for their swords, not to the captain's gauntlets clenched into fists. That blue didn't so much as blink as he looked the captain straight in the eye, smiled through a split lip, and spoke.

"Human *garbage."*

For more information on *The City Stained Red:*

http://www.samsykes.com/books/the-city-stained-red.

God-Thing: And Other Weird & Worrisome Tales, by Amy Dupire

As the title suggests, Amy Dupire's *God-Thing: And Other Weird & Worrisome Tales* is a collection of short stories, ranging from the evocatively sinister to the outright creepy. Not *exactly* horror . . . but you can feel a cool breeze blowing on the back of your neck as you read.

I am Deeply Impressed by anybody who can tell a decent story in fewer than 300,000 words, as that's a skill I don't personally possess. I first encountered Amy Dupire's work some years ago, in the course of judging entries for the Surrey International Writers' Conference Storyteller's Award.

I support the storyteller's prize along with my good friend (and wonderful historical novelist) Jack Whyte. All the entries are screened by the conference organizers, and Jack and I judge the dozen or so finalists, which are all sent to us as blind manuscripts—i.e., no author's name attached. So it isn't until the banquet at which all the writing awards are announced that we find out who actually wrote the winning story.

. . . and the winner is . . . !

Well, for several years, Amy's stories were either the winner or the runner-up, and I got used to hearing her name read out during the banquet.

Which in turn led to an interest in what *else* she might be writing . . . and ultimately to the welcome publication of *God-Thing,* her first collection (her first novel, *All Kinds of Hell,* is likewise available on Amazon .com).

The stories here are written with delicacy, humor, and a healthy dose of uneasiness. And they are . . . well, you know . . . *short.* Whether you're in need of a literary appetizer or dessert, immersion or distraction—you might just find what you're looking for in this collection of *Weird & Worrisome Tales.*

The Long Way Home, by Louise Penny

The September 8, 2014, edition of *People* magazine[2] outraged me by referring to Louise Penny's new book (*The Long Way Home*) as "a cozy, croissant-filled mystery." Granted, the blurblets *People* uses allow no room for subtlety, but using such a dismissive phrase for Penny's books is like calling the Bible "a random collection of Jewish history."

You can indeed smell the croissants in Penny's books. You can smell the snow and feel the touch of wind and water on your face, the sun-warmed firmness of the wooden bench you're sitting on. You can stand on a precipice over the great St. Lawrence River and feel the awe of the first person ever to see it. Her books will suck you in effortlessly, and you'll wake up from their trance blinking and wondering where you've been for the last several hours.

Her books have a living pulse, but her talent for immersive description is the least of it. Most of the books are set in the remote, mysterious, and somewhat magical (in a non-gimmicky way; no werewolves roam the woods) village of Three Pines. Founded by United Empire settlers (the American colonists who fought on the side of King George III and then fled the war to a safer refuge in Canada), Three Pines continues to be a place of refuge.

One of the people drawn to it is Chief Inspector Armand Gamache, former head of Quebec Sûreté's homicide unit. It is, of course, murder that draws him—for even a peaceful place like Three Pines has human beings whose personalities or histories drive them to violence. Three Pines also has one of the most charming assemblages of complex, engaging characters I've ever encountered.

Not all warm fuzzies, by any means—but all so deeply human that you feel the conflict in the heart of even the most (apparently) wicked.

And it's that sense of deep humanity—perceptive but always compassionate—that makes Penny's books so remarkable. The plotting is good, the setting magnetic, the characters engaging (and frequently hilarious)—but what Penny does is different from any other author I've met. She addresses the deep emotions of the human

---

2 "People *Picks: A Dozen Cool Things to See, Hear, Read and Download This Week," edited by Tom Gliatto, Steven J. Snyder, and Kim Hubbard.* The Long Way Home *is listed under "Number 2: Best New Books." Volume 82, Number 10.*

heart with amazing directness and simplicity. You not only feel for the characters; after closing one of her books, you feel that you've touched truth.

Now, it is a long-running series: *The Long Way Home* is the tenth book, and the series evolves beautifully from the first, the slightly offbeat *Still Life,* to the truly stunning latest.

I had the pleasure of meeting Louise for the first time recently; she was in town to do a signing for *The Long Way Home* at the Poisoned Pen. So should any of you be wanting to check out a new author/series—I can tell you where to get autographed books.

(In fact, you can get autographed books by many of the authors listed here—certainly almost all of the crime writers, as well as my books and those of Sam Sykes. The Poisoned Pen is my local independent bookstore, and I go by every other week or so to sign their waiting orders. They'll ship anywhere in the world.)

You can also check out Louise Penny's official home page at:

http://www.louisepenny.com.

Good Crime Fiction by a Couple of Roberts that I Know: Rob Byrnes and Robert Dugoni

I was amused, but pleased, to have my novella "Lord John and the Plague of Zombies" nominated for an Edgar Award by the Mystery Writers of America, for "Best Short Mystery Story" of 2011. Given that that particular story is not exactly a mystery, and certainly isn't short, I didn't really expect to win (which was a good thing, since I didn't) but certainly was flattered to be nominated.

And I did have a tax-deductible reason to go to New York (for the awards dinner), where I had the double pleasure of seeing my husband in his tux (he wears it about once every three years) and of meeting a number of mystery-writing friends that I see too rarely. Among these was the talented Rob Byrnes, who writes gay crime caper novels (there's a niche market for you . . .). I've known Rob for years and have read and enjoyed several of his books (I'm not sure, but I think I appear as a mention in one of the early ones—I was in the first draft, at least . . .). Think Donald Westlake with good dress sense. His latest is *Holy Rollers,* in which the Gang That Can't Do Anything Straight sets out to steal seven million dollars from the Virginia Cathedral of Love.

AND there's my good friend Robert Dugoni, whose bestselling *Murder One* joins his other bestselling thrillers. Bob writes prose as taut as a trampoline and has plots like an octopus running an obstacle course. If thrillers are your thing, I strongly recommend him.

The Secrets of Pain, by Phil Rickman

I wallowed in this book for several days when I got it. Rickman is one of my favorites; he has the sort of characters you know and treasure, who have reality and depth and get deeper as they go along. To say nothing of flat-out wonderful, evocative writing, terrific plots, and a marvelously creepy strand of the supernatural twining like smoke through the story.

The Secrets of Pain is the latest in his Merrily Watkins mysteries series. The Reverend Watkins is an Anglican priest, widowed, with an unpredictable teenaged daughter—and is the official exorcist (though the Church now prefers to refer to her discreetly as a "deliverance consultant") for the Diocese of Hereford. Merrily smokes like a chimney, is having an affair with the emotionally damaged rock musician across the road, and wrestles constantly with the knowledge that most of the world thinks what she does is irrelevant at best and at worst insane.

The Secrets of Pain involves—as one might expect—secrets of various kinds. The official kind—Hereford is the home base for the SAS, one of the most elite and secretive regiments in Her Majesty's armed forces—the political kind, wherein the forces of commercialism and modernity threaten the increasingly fragile tradition and history of a very old part of the country; and the supernatural kind, where "men with birds' heads walk out of the river mist" and a *very* old and bloody religion proves not to be quite gone.

Besides the wonderful characters and storytelling, what I like best about Phil's work is the ongoing conversation throughout the series between religion and secular society, the subtle questions about the nature (and power) of belief. These are beautifully layered books that can be reread periodically—and the release of a new one is always a great excuse to go back and start all over with the first volume, *The Wine of Angels.*

Three Favorite Books

***The Knife Man,* by Wendy Moore**
This immensely entertaining and well-researched biography is the story of John Hunter, one of the founders of modern medicine and a first-class nut. Renowned as a genius and reviled as a body-snatcher, Doctor Hunter was one of the most colorful characters of the eighteenth century—a time not lacking in such people.

***Love in the Time of Cholera,* by Gabriel García Márquez**
Magic realism, long river voyages, prose you can sink into like an inner tube and drift downstream. One of the less likely but most appealing romances you're likely to encounter.

***Haunting Bombay,* by Shilpa Agarwal**
A book that exists on multiple levels, inviting you into death and mystery, into the heart of a family, and into the tantalizing, aromatic swirl of another culture. Beautiful, lyrical, and genuinely haunting.

The Children's Book, by A. S. Byatt

I love A. S. Byatt's work. She writes "literary fiction"—this being on one hand a catchall phrase for any book that doesn't fit conveniently into a genre designation, and on the other a term that generally implies particularly good writing, often accompanied by unique insight and acute perception. Byatt's got all of this, in spades. Some of you might remember her earlier book, *Possession: A Romance.* (One British friend told me he'd picked up a copy of this in the library, to find that an earlier reader had penciled a helpful message on the title page: *They finally do it on page 572.* I mention this in case you, too, might find it helpful.)

She also writes books in which terrifically interesting things happen—not always a hallmark of literary fiction. *The Children's Book* is a wonderful creation, set during the transition between the late nineteenth century and the early twentieth, which encompasses the flowering romanticism of the Arts

and Crafts movement in England (I found this part particularly fascinating, as my great-great-grandfather was an artist who was part of this movement), the political upheavals of suffragism, socialism, and anarchy, and the onrush of the First World War.

Now, whatever the theme, setting, and plot of a book, the really important thing is the character or characters who carry it out. And I tell you what: few people do better characters than Byatt does. Her people are remarkably multifaceted, complex, interesting, and *real*. She knows what artists are like and captures a range of them—the central egotism and ruthlessness of character that makes a good one, the helplessness of a failed artist, the mutual jealousy between the commercially successful and the unsuccessful but "pure" artist.

The story—or stories; there are many of them—centers on an unorthodox family and its friends. Olive Wellwood is a writer—a very successful writer, whose huge family provides her with both impetus and material. The "children's book" of the title refers not to a single book but to the private stories—one for each child—that she maintains in notebooks, adding to each one as inspiration comes. The way in which love works—supportive, exploitative, pragmatic, idealistic, romantic, familial, jealous, selfless, in free love or marriage—is at the core of the novel (as it is at the core of most great books).

At the same time, it's a wonderful exploration and dissection of a society—the British middle class—in a time of intellectual ferment and unprecedented political change. AND written with an exquisite eye for detail and tremendous lyrical energy. Here's a brief excerpt of the text:

> *Hedda lay in the long grass, with her skirt rucked up above her knickers, and her lengthening brown legs stretched out. She was fortunate not to have hay fever, as Phyllis did. She was not exactly reading* The Golden Age. *I am a snake in the grass, she thought, a secret snake. Violet was sitting on the roughly mown grass in the orchard, at some distance, in a low wicker armchair, sewing. Hedda spent a lot of time spying on Violet, as a revenge for the fact that Violet spied on her, going through her private drawers and notebooks. Hedda, like Phyllis, was perpetually agitated by being left out of the group of older children, Tom and Dorothy, Charles and Griselda, and now Geraint. But whereas Phyllis was plaintive, Hedda was enraged. She was the traitor in all tales of chivalry and in myths. She was Vivien, she was Morgan Le Fay, she was Loki. She despised the cow-eyed and the gentle, Elaine the lily maid, faithful Psyche, Baldur's weeping wife, Nanna. She was a detective, who saw through appearances. No one was as nice as they seemed, was her rule of judging characters.*

Much as I love series, with the possibilities of ever-evolving characters and the charm of renewed acquaintance, I love one-of-a-kind treasures like this just as much. Highly engrossing, highly recommended!

The Kate Shugak Series, by Dana Stabenow

For those who like series, mysteries, books with rich, idiosyncratic settings, engaging characters, Strong Women (which, frankly, I think is getting to be something of a cliché—not the women themselves, of course, but the mention of them as a talking point for a book. I mean, who recommends a book by saying, "The heroine is a weak, whiny, wilted piece of toast—but it's a great book!"), and reasonably hot sex on occasion . . . let me recommend Dana Stabenow.

Dana is one of those amazing people who actually produce a book a year (I gasp in envy), and she develops her characters and plots beautifully as the series progresses, though each book is a complete standalone mystery. The personal lives of the characters—particularly the main character, Kate Shugak—definitely would repay the effort of starting from the beginning, with *A Cold Day for Murder.*

Dana's Wikipedia entry gives the following description of the series, and since they do it a lot more succinctly than I can, I'll let them:

> *Kate Shugak is a Native Alaskan, an Aleut, living in a fictional national park in Alaska, based loosely on the Wrangell-St. Elias National Park & Preserve. Formerly an investigator for the Anchorage District Attorney's office, an incident during which she is badly injured on the job causes her to quit and return home to live on her own. Regular characters in the Shugak series include:*
>
> - *Mutt, Kate's part-wolf dog*
> - *Jack Morgan, Anchorage District Attorney, and Kate's lover for the first nine books*
> - *Ekatarina Shugak, Kate's grandmother*
> - *Bobby Clark, Vietnam vet and ham operator*
> - *Dan O'Brien, Ranger assigned to the Park*
> - *Sgt. Jim Chopin, a State Trooper assigned to the Park*
>
> Shugak stories:
>
> * *A Cold Day for Murder* (1992) (the first in the Kate Shugak series)—A park ranger is missing, and so is the investigator the Anchorage police sent in to look for him. Kate's ex-boss and ex-lover, Jack Morgan, convinces her to investigate their disappearances on her own terms, beginning her new career as a private investigator. This book introduces us to main characters that will remain constants in the books to come and sets the tone for the coming books. The storyline establishes the relationship between Kate and Jack and gives some background information and insight into their relationship.
>
> * *A Fatal Thaw* (1992)—A killer claims eight victims but nine bodies were found lying in the snow.
>
> * *Dead in the Water* (1993)—Kate hires on as a deckhand on a crabber where two former deckhands mysteriously disappeared. This novel talks about life on a crab fishing boat and the dangers on the sea.
>
> * *A Cold-Blooded Business* (1994)—A novel that talks about life in the oil fields above the Arctic Circle has Kate looking into drug smuggling and finding other illegal situations as well.
>
> * *Play with Fire* (1995)—While picking mushrooms, Kate and her friends stumble upon the body of the son of the leader of a religious sect.
>
> * *Blood Will Tell* (1996)—Mostly set at the annual Alaska Federation of Natives convention, which Kate attends at the insistence of her grandmother, Kate looks into the death of one of the local village's board members.
>
> * *Breakup* (1997)—Breakup is the season of early Spring, when the rivers and

ground start to thaw and people can start spending more time outdoors again. Kate looks into the death of a woman by a bear that doesn't quite add up.

* *Killing Grounds* (1998)—Set in the summer fishing season of salmon, Kate investigates the death of a fellow fisherman while working as a deckhand on a tender.

* *Hunter's Moon* (1999)—Kate and Jack take on a job to escort a group of business men and woman into the park trophy hunting.

* *Midnight Come Again* (2000)—After the events in the previous novel, Kate has gone missing from her home and friends.

* *The Singing of the Dead* (2001)—Kate hires on to protect the life of a candidate for Alaskan State Senator.

* *A Fine and Bitter Snow* (2002)—A novel that talks about oil drilling in a wildlife preserve, Kate looks into an attack on two friends of her late grandmother.

* *A Grave Denied* (2003)—Some students on a field trip discover a body in the mouth of a glacier.

* *A Taint in the Blood* (2004)—A woman hires Kate to clear her mother of a thirty year old murder, but the mother doesn't want to be cleared.

* *A Deeper Sleep* (2007)—Kate tries to get a conviction on a repeat offender while her tribal elders try to get her to take a more solid role in the tribe.

* *Whisper to the Blood* (2009)—A world-class gold mine is discovered in the Park at almost the same moment Kate is whipsawed by the Aunties into a seat on the local Native association board of directors.

* *A Night Too Dark* (2010)

* *Though Not Dead* (2011)

* *Restless in the Grave* (2012)

* *Bad Blood* (2013)

I've read all of the Kate Shugak books and love them; I've seldom met a more dependable author, in term both of productivity and quality.

I like Dana's Liam Campbell series even better (the German translator who has worked on both our books, and has read all Dana's mysteries, says that Liam Campbell is the closest thing she's seen to a modern-day Jamie Fraser—and the sex is particularly good in those), but the four Campbell books are unfortunately out of print at the moment and no more under contract, which is a shame—but they *are* available in a Kindle edition, which is great news!

Dana also has a new series of historical novels based on the journeys of Marco Polo (and his descendants), which I'm sure are also terrific, but I haven't yet read them, so can't offer much in the way of description.

So here's a tiny bit of *A Night Too Dark:*

> *She heaved a martyr's sigh. "All right," she said, as they had both known she would. "I'll find him and talk to him for you. I'd like to see this Lothario for myself, anyway."*
>
> *She came around the counter and sauntered toward him. He admired her while she did so. Yeah, maybe she didn't have the figure Laurel had, but when she wanted to, Kate could telegraph her intentions in a way that was little less than incitement to riot. Jim had watched plenty of women walk in*

his lifetime, both toward him and away, and he had never appreciated the amalgamation of brain and bone, muscle and flesh the way he did when it came wrapped in this particular package.

"Beat it," she said to Mutt.

Mutt flounced over to the fireplace, scratched the aunties' quilt into a pile, turned around three times, and curled up with her back most pointedly toward them.

Kate smiled down at Jim. Just like that, Jim got hard. And she knew it, he could tell by the deepening indentations at the corners of that wide, full-lipped mouth. "Jesus, woman," he said. If he wasn't flustered, it was as close as he ever got.

"What can I say," she said. "I have special powers." He was pulled to a sitting position with a fistful of shirt and she climbed aboard.

(My husband caught sight of one of Dana's books on the kitchen table, asked me what it was, and upon being told that it was a murder mystery set in Alaska, exclaimed, "And her name is Stab-'em-now?! What a *great* name for a mystery writer!" Alas, it's really pronounced STAB-uh-no, but still great books.)

See more about Dana at http://www.stabenow.com/.

Pandaemonium, by Christopher Brookmyre

I seldom write fan letters to other authors. Not that I don't want to; there are lots of wonderful books that move me to admiration, laughter, tears, etc., and I'd love to let the authors of them know that. In some cases, the authors in question are dead, though, which kind of renders a fan letter moot, though I do Say a Word during my evening rosary—that was my Lenten devotion this year, saying the rosary every night (provided I don't fall asleep in the middle; lovely, peaceful meditation). In most cases, though, I just don't get around to it. You know, busy life, obligations, family, dogs, book tours, saying the rosary, answering the nice messages people send me, etc., etc.

Which is why I particularly appreciate the letters and emails people send me; I know just how much effort it takes to actually do something like that, rather than just think about it. So it's all the more remarkable that upon reading Christopher Brookmyre's *Pandaemonium* recently, I put down the book and actually wrote him a fan letter. Which said:

Dear Christopher–

I've just finished wallowing in Pandaemonium, *pausing occasionally to gasp with admiration at your sheer technical brilliance (we'll take the tremendous energy, amazing ear for dialogue and eye for social dynamics, and your talent for chronic hilarity (ranging from subtle to belly-laugh) as read). All of which is* nothing *to my enjoyment of the way your mind works. I couldn't have done a clearer explanation of just what science is (and how it works) myself—and I do it frequently, what with the appalling state of prevalent ignorance and the many practitioners thereof. And the sheer bloody brilliance, not only of the concept, but the ending . . . !*

I've been enjoying your books for years, and you've been getting better and better, juggling the ideas so deftly with the satire and the plot (speaking of juggling, I adore your magician from The Sacred Art of Stealing *and* Snowball in Hell, *too). This one is Just Great. Thanks so much.*

—Diana

So, anyway, still in the grip of this unaccustomed burst of energy, I thought I'd mention Chris as the latest recommendation on the Methadone List, and an excellent one he is, too—not only for the quality of his books but the quantity, as well; he produces something close to a book a year (a feat that excites my envious admiration).

Brookmyre's books are all violent, bloody, and absolutely hilarious. They're not a single series; some of the books feature a recurring main character, the journalist Jack Parlabane, two of them have a wonderful, emotionally vulnerable, light-fingered magician as the hero (I fell in love with him, and I have high standards in that department), and some are one-off stand-alones. Recently, he's begun a fascinating new series featuring one Jasmine Sharp, an accidental investigator who manages to cope with everything she meets—and will, along the way, teach you how to stick your thumb in someone's eye socket and purée their brain—and Catherine McLeod, a police officer with a complicated family life and a grim sense both of duty and of humor. ALL of them are wonderfully plotted, deeply satirical, and done with a distinctly Scottish sense of humor.

Hope you enjoy Chris as much as I have!

And here's his website, too, which has brief excerpts from some of his books: http://www.brookmyre.co.uk.

BESIDES THE WEBSITE listings, I thought I'd add a few more of my longtime favorite series books here:

John le Carré—the Smiley trilogy

Tinker, Tailor, Soldier, Spy

The Honourable Schoolboy

Smiley's People

(N.B.: There are other le Carré novels that include the character of George Smiley, but these three novels form the heart of this Cold Warrior's world.)

These books were published quite a few years ago (they're set in the 1960s and '70s), but perhaps the world has now reached the point where this particular spy trilogy can effectively be read as historical fiction. Groundbreaking in style and deeply engrossing, le Carré's early spy fiction is some of the best literature of its period. His characters are painfully human, and the milieu he draws from is claustrophobic, achingly lonely—and very dangerous.

C. C. Humphreys

C. C. Humphreys's latest historical crime novel, *Plague,* has deservedly won the 2015 Arthur Ellis Award (Best Crime Novel in Canada). A historical novelist whose subjects range from Anne Boleyn (*The French Executioner*) to Vlad the Impaler (*Vlad*), his specialty is roaring-good tales based on a research so well done as to seem nearly invisible but which invests all his stories with a sense of such immediacy that you close each book with a feeling of satisfaction in the story—and a sense of relief that you live in the twenty-first century.

I am myself particularly fond of his Jack Absolute series, which follows the adventures of Captain Jack Absolute, described as *an 18th-century 007 lifted from Richard Sheridan's play* The Rivals, *who has a "talent for trouble," a rogue's way with women and more lives than a cat,*[3] but I've found all his books to be a deep and constant pleasure.

P. F. Chisholm

Patricia Finney (writing as P. F. Chisholm) is one of my very favorite historical novelists, and her Robert Carey series is a sheer delight. Firmly based on Carey—a real-life Elizabethan courtier whose biography is as adventurous as Chisholm's novels (if less detailed)—the books are also tremendously engaging and remarkably funny, without at any time straying into comic-novel territory. The humor as well as the plots spring from Chisholm's grace with characters.

At the moment, there are seven Robert Carey novels, beginning with *A Famine of Horses.* These are, for the most part, set on the dangerous Border between England and Scotland and involve feuding surnames (the Border equivalent of clans), political treachery, murder, desire (requited and un-), and the ineffable Sergeant Henry Dodd, with whom I am deeply in love.

As Patricia Finney, she also has a wonderful trilogy (also set in Elizabethan times), longer and more detailed than the Carey books and closer to the Queen in plot and substance but equally entertaining:

Unicorn's Blood

Firedrake's Eye

Gloriana's Torch

Violent Wee Buggers

I don't know what it is about Celtic writers, but they seem to have the simultaneous gifts of poetry and majorly gruesome imagination—which is, of course, a combination I personally find irresistible. Here are some of my favorite crime writers—mostly Scots, with an Irishman thrown in, and one American who, whatever his ethnic heritage, has the gift of poetic grue, in spades.

Ian Rankin

Ian's gotten to be very well known in Scottish literary circles (and is a cover boy for the National Trust of Scotland's publications—yay, Ian!) for his series of crime novels starring Inspector John Rebus. These are police procedurals, set in Edinburgh (and invariably described as "gritty"). Like any good crime books, they deal not only with the solution of the crime but with the detective's personal life and how it's affected by his/her pursuit of evil. Rebus is a fascinatingly flawed character, whose personal life outside his career is largely nonexistent—lonely, cranky, obsessed, alcoholic—but is redeemed by his obstinacy and by the friends who stick by him despite his flaws.

For best effect, the novels should be read in (rough) order, so you can follow the evo-

[3] *Publishers Weekly.*

lution (and convolutions) of Rebus's private life. They *can* be read as stand-alones, though, since each novel is a well-structured and self-contained investigation.

Adrian McKinty
McKinty is the Irishman, who debuted with a stunning trilogy (the "Dead" trilogy—very accurate): *Dead I Well May Be, The Dead Yard,* and *The Bloomsday Dead.* All three books deal with the (grisly, hyper-violent, blood-soaked) adventures of a young Irish gangster who comes to New York, promptly runs into trouble—and stays in it. Not for the weak of stomach, but both characters and language are exquisite.

The same is true for his later Sean Duffy books, set in Ireland during the Troubles: *The Cold Cold Ground, I Hear the Sirens in the Street, In the Morning I'll Be Gone,* and *Gun Street Girl.*

Val McDermid
Val does books that could best be described as thrillers (though they do have the structure of murder mysteries, for the most part), because they move a mile a minute. Most are stand-alones, though two or three have recurrent main characters. The outstanding feature of all of them is the absolutely *horrible* psychopathic villains she writes and the ghastly things they do. She's also written a series of much milder mysteries (the Kate Brannigan series), though I prefer (naturally) the grisly ones.

Stuart MacBride
Stuart MacBride's Logan McRae series is set in Aberdeen and, besides having a wonderful sense of place, is grossly violent, blood-soaked—and hilarious. He has *the* best characters, from the massive, candy-munching DI Inch to the cadaverous, chain-smoking lesbian DI Steele, who is the bane of McRae's professional life. To say nothing of criminals given to snipping off people's fingers joint by joint and forcing them to swallow the pieces . . . I really wasn't kidding about the heading of this list. You Have Been Warned. Great stuff, though!

Don Winslow (Honorary Wee Bugger)
Don Winslow is an American, and I strongly recommend all his books, from earlier titles like *The Death and Life of Bobby Z* and the Neal Carey series (*A Cool Breeze on the Underground,* etc.), which are great but not *unduly* violent, up to the amazing *California Fire and Life* and *The Power of the Dog*—which are. Wonderful characters, plots, and writing—but not, repeat NOT, for the weak of stomach.

Part Eleven

BIBLIOGRAPHY

In the first volume of *The Outlandish Companion,* I included a fairly extensive bibliography, listing about six hundred books and references that I'd used during the writing of the first four novels. A couple of years ago, I asked my assistant (the invaluable Ms. Susan Pittman-Butler) to catalog my core reference collection (the books that normally live in my office) into the LibraryThing website, in order to make the references easily available to readers who want to go more deeply into the historical background of the novels or some of the historical personalities mentioned therein. Currently, there are about 2,200 books listed in my personal "library" on that site.

That's a lotta books. If I included all of them in a bibliography for *this* volume, I'm afraid there wouldn't have been room for anything else—and not everyone is that passionately interested in the background research.

So I decided to do two things: 1) provide you with a brief description of how to use the LibraryThing website to look at my listings—which will give you access to the entire bibliography and allow you to sort the listings in accordance with your own particular interests, and 2) print here a brief bibliography that represents the books currently on my "core" shelves.

The core shelves are two shelves of my large built-in bookcase, on which I gradually collect books that I think may be of particular use during the writing of the current novel(s). (At the time of publication of *Outlandish Two,* I'm in the early stages of work on Book Nine—so called because it's untitled; titles kind of come along in their own good time.) The books on the core shelves tend to stay there during the two to three years that I'm working on the novel for which they're supplying background. These aren't the only books I consult while working on a specific novel (not by a long shot . . .), but things like herbals, medical references, field guides, etc., all have their own locations in the larger collection and are easy to find when I need one. The core shelves are for the oddball reference that might come in handy (at the moment, I don't have any African Muslims in Book Nine; I just think I might, at some point), the biography of some real person that I expect to use (Banastre Tarleton, Peggy Shippen, Benedict Arnold, George Washington, Joseph Brant, John André, etc.—though I won't have any idea how much information I may require or find useful from these), interesting "overview" books (such as *White People, Indians, and Highlanders: Tribal People and Colonial Encounters in Scotland and America*), interesting first-person accounts (*Scottish and Irish Diaries*), eyewitness accounts and information of specific historical events, particularly battles (*The Siege of Charleston, The Road to Guilford Courthouse,* etc.), and so on.

So this particular mini-bibliography is a snapshot of the references that I think *might*

be especially useful in the writing of Book Nine. Some of them will be and some of them won't; it's just a glimpse of how my mind is working with this book at the moment (the moment being now, June 2015).

All right, LibraryThing. This is easy: go to www.librarything.com. You can use the Search box in the upper right corner of the page to look for listings. Typing Gabaldon will show you an ungodly number of books, including those I've entered in the system and those that anyone else has entered with my name mentioned in the listing. For a finer-grained search, type *https://www.librarything.com/catalog/diana.gabaldon/yourlibrary.* This will show you my own "library," or collection, and will let you scroll through the site, look at all the books that are listed, and sort the library by the top headings: title, author, date (publication date, that is), date entered in the system, etc. Using various keywords like herbal, medicine, battle, and so on should help you produce specialized listings that might be helpful in your own research or reading. Have fun!

BIBLIOGRAPHY—THE CORE SHELVES

Austin, Allan D. *African Muslims in Antebellum America: Transatlantic Stories and Spiritual Struggles.* New York and London: Routledge, 1997.

Bass, Robert D. *The Green Dragoon.* Orangeburg, S.C.: Sandlapper Publishing, 1973.

Calloway, Colin G. *White People, Indians, and Highlanders: Tribal People and Colonial Encounters in Scotland and America.* Oxford, U.K.: Oxford University Press, 2008.

Cameron, Christian. *Washington and Caesar.* New York: Bantam Dell, 2004.

Cook, Don. *The Long Fuse: How England Lost the American Colonies, 1760–1785.* New York: Atlantic Monthly Press, 1996.

Borick, Carl P. *A Gallant Defense: the Siege of Charleston, 1780.* Columbia, S.C.: University of South Carolina Press, 2003.

Buchanan, John. *The Road to Guilford Courthouse: The American Revolution in the Carolinas.* New York: Wiley, 1997.

Diouf, Sylviane A. *Servants of Allah: African Muslims Enslaved in the Americas.* New York and London: New York University Press, 1998.

Duffy, Christopher. *The Military Experience in the Age of Reason, 1715–1789.* New York: Barnes & Noble Books, 1987.

Dunkerly, Robert M. *The Battle of Kings Mountain: Eyewitness Accounts.* Charleston, S.C.: The History Press, 2007.

Endelman, Todd M. *The Jews of Georgian England, 1714–1830: Tradition and Change in a Liberal Society.* Ann Arbor: University of Michigan Press, 1999.

Garfield, Simon. *Just My Type.* New York: Gotham Books, 2011.

Gruber, Ira D. *The Howe Brothers and the American Revolution.* Chapel Hill: University of North Carolina Press, 1972.

Hamilton, Ian. *The Stone of Destiny.* Edinburgh: Birlinn Ltd., 1991.

Higginbotham, Don. *Daniel Morgan, Revolutionary Rifleman.* Chapel Hill: University of North Carolina Press, 1961.

Hinshaw, Seth. *The Carolina Quaker Experience.* Chapel Hill: North Carolina Yearly Meeting, North Carolina Friends Historical Society, 1984.

Holmes, Richard. *Redcoat: the British Soldier in the Age of Horse and Musket.* New York: W. W. Norton & Co., 2002.

Isaacson, W. *Benjamin Franklin: An American Life*. New York: Simon & Schuster, 2003.

Jacob, Mark, and Stephen H. Case. *Treacherous Beauty: Peggy Shippen, the Woman Behind Benedict Arnold's Plot to Betray America.* Guilford, Conn.: Lyons Press, 2012.

Keegan, John. *The Mask of Command.* New York: Viking Penguin, Inc., 1987.

Kelsay, Isabel Thompson. *Joseph Brant, 1743–1807, Man of Two Worlds.* Syracuse, N.Y.: Syracuse University Press, 1984.

Liss, David. *A Conspiracy of Paper.* New York: Ballantine Books, 2001.

Marder, Daniel. *The Arnold/Andre Transcripts: A Reconstruction.* Monroe, N.Y.: Library Research Association, 1993.

McCullough, David. *1776.* New York: Simon & Schuster, 2005.

Morgan, Robert. *Boone: A Biography*. Chapel Hill: Algonquin Books of Chapel Hill, 2007.

Morrill, Dan L. *Southern Campaigns of the American Revolution.* Baltimore: Nautical & Aviation Pub. Co. of America, 1993.

Parry, Edwin S. *Betsy Ross, Quaker Rebel.* Chicago: The John C. Winston Co., 1930.

Ponsonby, Arthur, M.P., ed. *Scottish and Irish Diaries from the Sixteenth to the Nineteenth Century, with an Introduction.* London: Methuen & Company, Ltd., 1927.

Randall, Willard S. *Benedict Arnold: Patriot and Traitor.* New York: William Morrow & Co., 1990.

Rankin, Hugh F. *The North Carolina Continentals.* Chapel Hill: University of North Carolina Press, 1971.

Reiss, Oscar. *The Jews in Colonial America.* Jefferson, N.C.: McFarland & Co, 2004.

Rubenhold, Hallie. *The Covent Garden Ladies.* Gloucestershire, U.K.: Tempus, 2005.

———. *Harris's List of Covent Garden Ladies.* Gloucestershire, U.K.: Tempus, 2005.

Scotti, Anthony J., Jr. *Brutal Virtue: The Myth and Reality of Banastre Tarleton.* Westminster, Md.: Heritage Books, 2007.

Stone, William L. *Life of Joseph Brant, Thayendanegea, including the Indian Wars of the American Revolution, Vols. 1–2.* New York: Alexander V. Blake, 1838.

Swisher, James K. *The Revolutionary War in the Southern Back Country.* Gretna, La.: Pelican Publishing Co., 2008.

Thayer, Theodore. *The Making of a Scapegoat: Washington and Lee at Monmouth.* Port Washington, N.Y.: Kennikat Press, 1976.

Thomas, Evan. *John Paul Jones: Sailor, Hero, Father of the American Navy.* New York: Simon & Schuster, 2003.

Thorp, Jennifer D., ed. *The Acland Journal: Lady Harriet Acland and the American War.* Winchester, U.K.: Hampshire County Council, 1993.

Tuchman, Barbara W. *The First Salute: A View of the American Revolution.* New York: Ballantine Books, 1988.

Walsh, John E. *The Execution of Major Andre.* New York: Palgrave, St. Martin's Press, 2001.

West, Jessamyn. *The Quaker Reader.* Wallingford, Pa.: Pendle Hill Publications, 1992.

Wilson, David K. *The Southern Strategy.* Columbia: University of South Carolina Press, 2005.

Wood, Gordon S. *Revolutionary Characters: What Made the Founders Different.* New York: Penguin Press, 2006.

ACKNOWLEDGMENTS

The author would like to gratefully acknowledge the immense help (to say nothing of patience, grit, and sheer endurance) of

The Contributors

. . . Terry Dresbach, who kindly lent me several of her brilliant blog entries and sketches regarding her work as head of costume on the *Outlander* TV show.

. . . Dr. Claire MacKay, herbalist and consultant to the TV show, for her excellent paper on historical Highland herbal medicine.

. . . Bear McCreary, composer for the TV show, for his delightful and insightful essay on the philosophy and passion of creating music with bagpipes.

. . . Àdhamh Ó Broin, Gaelic consultant and tutor to the show, for his witty and erudite "Gaelic Glossary," which covers all the Gaelic in all eight of the so-far-published books of the main Outlander series.

. . . Susan Pittman-Butler, who compiled the entire mind-boggling "Cast of Characters" section—a work of superhuman endurance and thoroughness.

. . . Theresa Carle-Sanders, author of the popular Outlander Kitchen website (and soon-to-be cookbook), for her entertaining essay on eighteenth-century Scottish cookery.

. . . Grant O'Rourke, for his brilliant *Super Rupert* cartoon.

... and Barbara Schnell (my invaluable German translator), who contributed a number of her beautiful photos of Scotland to the illustrations in this book.

The Readers

... Huge thanks to all of the people who, over the last fifteen years, have not only kept asking for another *Companion,* but have also suggested a lot of things they'd like to see in it, many of them going so far as to contribute such things. In particular—

... The Cadre of Genealogical Nitpickers: Sandy Parker, Vicki Pack, Mandy Tidwell, and Rita Meistrell, who are responsible for the high degree of accuracy in the beautiful family tree.

... Willemina, who not only produced the Grey Family Tree, but also provided a helpful list of errors in the Kindle editions of the books.

... Robert Wealleans, for a list of Kindle errors.

... Karen Henry, Chief of Eyeball-Numbing Nitpickery, who kindly read all of the manuscript pieces for this book, with the exception of the "Cast of Characters" (only Kathy the copy editor had the guts to deal with *that* one). Her catches and suggestions saved me innumerable hours in the later phases of copyediting and proofreading.

... Sandy the archivist, Jari Backman, and several other helpful people who keep track of things that I post, and can usually locate any message or excerpt needed.

The Production Team

... Like Abou ben Adhem, Kathy Lord's name leads all the rest. I take nothing away from the many other wonderful and hardworking people on the Penguin Random House[1] production team by praising Kathy—the copy editor on this, as on many of my previous books—for her limitless knowledge, persistence, artistry, goodwill . . . and did I mention persistence? A good copy editor is prized above rubies, and Kathy is stainless steel and iridium, diamonds and platinum.

---

[1] *Though, like every other author contracted to this publishing house, I think it should have been Random Penguin. Just the thought of random penguins lends cheer to the most ordinary of days.*

. . . Also let us celebrate the gloriousness of Virginia Norey's (aka the Book Goddess) design. While the hundreds of moving parts in a book like this are a major challenge to everybody involved, they also offer Virginia full scope for the exercise of her genius.

. . . And, of course, editors Jennifer Hershey and Anne Speyer for their endless patience, tact, and persistence (if I seem to keep mentioning persistence, it's because that's the sine qua non in getting one of my books to press).

. . . And the many, many other unsung heroes of production, art, publicity, and marketing, who have so much to do with the quality and success of my books.

My Thanks Also To . . .

. . . The several kind medical professionals who have helped me over the years with advice regarding the various medical and surgical scenes in the books. Some of these good people are nameless (having been recruited by other physician friends of mine, and having then modestly declined to be specifically acknowledged) and some I have undoubtedly forgotten. But special thanks to Dr. Gary Hoff, Dr. Amarilis Iscold, and Dr. Merih O'Donaghue, and to Sarah Meyer, midwife (aka Metpatpetet).

. . . Assorted military personnel, male and female, for their deeply felt responses to various elements of the books, and their contributions to the depictions of people in combat and those whose job it is to risk their lives in the protection of others.

. . . The personal testimony, given to me over the last twenty years, of people who have suffered assault in various forms, and their stories of heroism and healing.

. . . The kind assistance of Tamara Burke, Beth and Matthew Shope, and Jo Bourne, in explaining the beliefs and historical background of the Society of Friends.

. . . The Gaelic experts: Ian MacKinnon Taylor, Catherine MacGregor, Catherine-Ann MacPhee, Àdhamh Ó Broin , and Michael Newton, who have been of inestimable help over the years, both in providing translation and commentary on this beautiful language.

. . . Philippe Safavi, Valeria Galassi, and Barbara Schnell (respectively, my French, Italian, and German translators), for their sensitive and faithful translations. My thanks also to all the other translators that I haven't met personally.

. . . And as always: the many inhabitants of the Compuserve Books and Writers Community who have been my constant companions on this journey since I stumbled into the place in 1985. Thank you for the wonderful discussions, thought-provoking questions, bizarre suggestions, and weird bits of random information that have added so much to my books over the years!

ABOUT THE AUTHOR

Diana Gabaldon is the #1 *New York Times* bestselling author of the wildly popular Outlander novels—*Outlander, Dragonfly in Amber, Voyager, Drums of Autumn, The Fiery Cross, A Breath of Snow and Ashes* (for which she won a Quill Award and the Corine International Book Prize), *An Echo in the Bone,* and *Written in My Own Heart's Blood*—as well as the related Lord John Grey books *Lord John and the Private Matter, Lord John and the Brotherhood of the Blade, Lord John and the Hand of Devils,* and *The Scottish Prisoner;* the nonfiction *The Outlandish Companion* and *The Outlandish Companion Volume Two;* and the Outlander graphic novel *The Exile.* She lives in Scottsdale, Arizona, with her husband.

dianagabaldon.com
Facebook.com/AuthorDianaGabaldon
@Writer_DG

To inquire about booking Diana Gabaldon for a speaking engagement, please contact the Penguin Random House Speakers Bureau at speakers@penguinrandomhouse.com.

ABOUT THE TEXT

This book was set in Garamond, a typeface originally designed by the Parisian type cutter Claude Garamond (c. 1500–61). This version of Garamond was modeled on a 1592 specimen sheet from the Egenolff-Berner foundry, which was produced from types assumed to have been brought to Frankfurt by the punch cutter Jacques Sabon (c. 1520–80).

Claude Garamond's distinguished romans and italics first appeared in *Opera Ciceronis* in 1543–44. The Garamond types are clear, open, and elegant.

Castle Leod
(seat of Clan MacKenzie)
EARL OF CROMARTIE

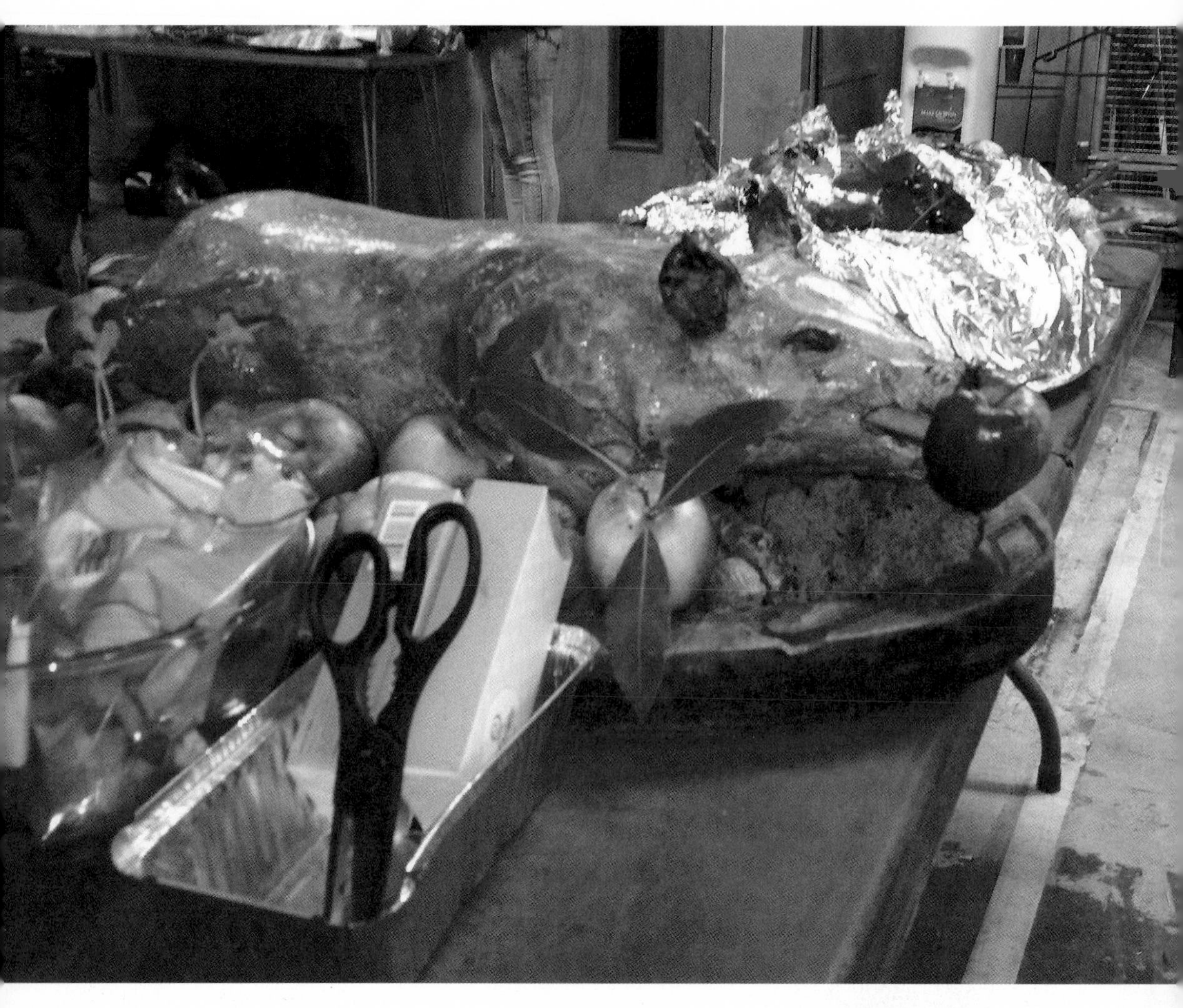

Some of the food for the Castle Leoch feast is fake . . .

DIANA GABALDON

... and some of it is fresh! Three haggises, hot out of the oven, produced by the kitchen section of the props department.

DIANA GABALDON

Me at Doune Castle

JENNIFER WATKINS

Me with standing stones on set

DOUG WATKINS

Cast dining area on set
DIANA GABALDON

Mr. and Mrs. MacTavish (me and Ron Moore)
(Yes, it's a wig.)
DOUG WATKINS

Pocket Jamie helps me sign four thousand first-edition hardcover copies of Written in My Own Heart's Blood.

DIANA GABALDON

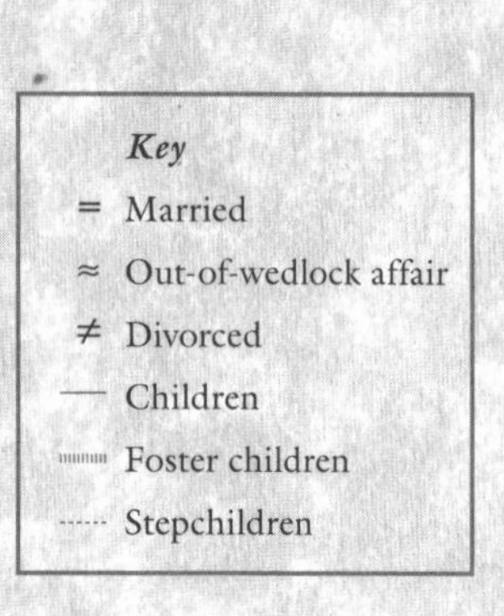

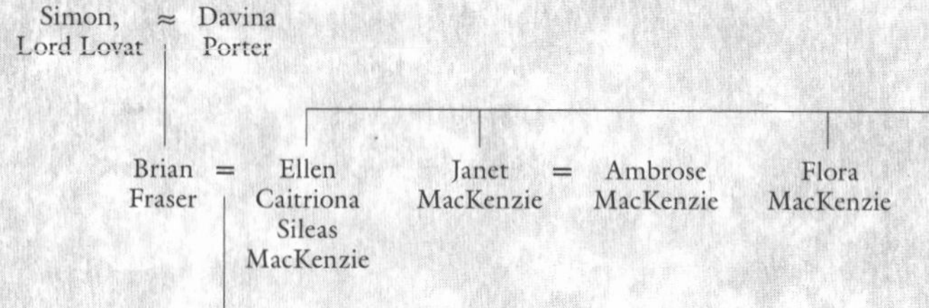

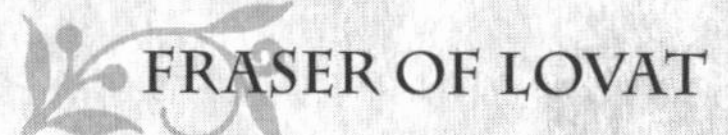

AN OUTLANDER FAMILY TREE